MAN-EATING TYPEWRITER

Also by Richard Milward

Apples
Ten Storey Love Song
Kimberly's Capital Punishment

MAN-EATING TYPEWRITER

RICHARD MILWARD

First published in Great Britain in 2023 by White Rabbit,
an imprint of The Orion Publishing Group Ltd
Carmelite House, 50 Victoria Embankment
London EC4Y 0DZ

An Hachette UK Company

1 3 5 7 9 10 8 6 4 2

A CIP catalogue record for this book is
available from the British Library.

ISBN (Hardback) 978 1 3996 0201 3
ISBN (eBook) 978 1 3996 0203 7
ISBN (Audio) 978 1 3996 0204 4

Printed and bound in Great Britain by Clays Ltd, Elcograf S.p.A.

www.whiterabbitbooks.co.uk
www.orionbooks.co.uk

Contents

FOREWORD

Raymond's reign of terror started with a paper cut to a girl in a paper dress. Later there would be wooden caskets. But first: pulp.

Here at the Glass Eye Press we're committed to publishing pocketbooks that are as stimulating for the senses as they are cheap to print and easy to secrete about one's person. In autumn 1969 we reached our two hundredth release,* capping off a decade that has seen us share tales of regal indecency (*Percy's Powdered Wig*, 1968), existential anguish (*The Lonesome Abortionist*, 1961), suburban psychosis (*Mummy's Milk*, 1959), romance (*Mouthful of Leather*, 1965), historical drama (*Kinky Tiberius*, 1964), pop and pot (*Yes Please, Mary-Jane Looseleaf!*, 1967), police brutality (*Pink Baton*, 1966), mistaken identity (*Le Fantasme Tangerine*, 1968) and that throbbing totem of the Permissive Society, free love (*Fucking by Candlelight*, 1969).

Our novels offer an invigorating escape for any jaded citizen willing to slip into a Soho bookshop or Brighton coffee-bar† with two-and-eight jangling in his mitt. We offer something new. We offer something those lily-livered Establishment publishers beyond the Tottenham Court Road refuse with stock rejection

---

* *Cannibal Cafeteria*, P. P. Flake, 2/8. A fine introduction to our heroic empire. A rollicking, riveting yarn that follows a group of disaffected, mistreated waitresses as they turn the tables on their boss and their customers – resulting in some of the most salacious and stomach-churning culinary prose ever put to paper.

† We have a number of legitimate stockists but recommend contacting us directly for a full-colour catalogue priced at just 6*d* at: The Glass Eye Press Ltd, 28 Newman Street, London W1T 3ER (MUS 2794). Discreet packaging.

letters bashed out listlessly on watermarked stationery. We aim to defibrillate the inhibited, to titillate the prudish, to slap awake this straight-and-narrow society – and yet it saddens me that many critics dismiss our entire output as filth. 'Grubby books'!

Take the average man in the street. No, better still: accost any morally flexible, free-spirited, long-haired, multisexual debaucher in the gentlemen's WC at Piccadilly Circus, and he will pretend never to have heard of our company! Is our reputation that bad? I fear it is – unless it's just a dire lack of publicity.

> *There is only one thing in life worse than being talked about, and that is not being talked about!*[*]

But still, for an outfit that sells so few books annually, we do get a hell of a lot of correspondence. In fact, we receive so much post daily, we had to change Audrey's job title from Administrative & Secretarial to Head of Complaints. When Miss Audrey Hulme appeared in London in 1964, landing jobless on our doormat fresh from the Industrial Provinces, we weren't sure if the mild-mannered dolly would crumble under the pressure of the Glass Eye's numerous (blind!) detractors. We underestimated her. It seemed no amount of hate mail, sullied *billets d'amour* or death threats could faze her – although of course none were aimed at her directly. Audrey sensitively handled the housewives' vitriol, humoured Mr Raven of Clench, Wilts.'s regular page-tearing and red-circling of supposed spelling errors,[†] and handed over to the police any threats of violence that mentioned myself or my colleagues by name and/or included detailed diagrams of weaponry and our body parts.

Bless her, Audrey reacted more strongly to the paper cut than to the human stool delivered to us in response to the giant truncheon-fingered gorilla climax of *Pink Baton*, an ending I actually rather

---

* *The Picture of Dorian Gray*, Oscar Wilde (1890).

† Incidentally, some errors in this volume are intentional.

admired. Brutal and transgressive, most certainly, but so far unparalleled in its blazing demolition of all pompous literary convention, stale moral values and supposed good taste.*

Novak drew first blood on the afternoon of Tuesday, 14th October 1969. What with the abundance of complaints following the release of *Cannibal Cafeteria* and perhaps our most controversial title to date, *Langoustine Man*, Audrey was late opening the letter that was to so transform our company. I remember she'd changed into a fresh paper dress for the afternoon: a flimsy A-line shift garnished with halved limes, lemons and oranges. As is habit, I was hunched woefully constipated in the water closet when she let out the scream. Not for the first time, I reached for the sawn-off shotgun I kept hidden under the loose laminate by the carnivorous plant. My hands were trembling but my colon hadn't twitched. I left the toilet water without so much as a ripple and scrambled through to the office with my fly undone, ready to protect my fair complaints maiden.

The cocked shotgun wasn't necessary. Audrey was sucking her thumb, sulking, while Mark 'Davy' Noon tried to console her, dressed in what appeared to be a peasant woman's blouse and patent leather jackboots. At first I thought it was a razor blade under the seal – a tiny Mae West mouth was dribbling claret at the end of Audrey's thumb. A mascara millipede slithered down her cheek. Before long, others came to gawp too. In fact, had it not been for the paper cut drawing blood – drawing our attention to the C5 manila assailant on Audrey's desk – our Head of Complaints may have simply dismissed its contents as gibberish and discarded it without a second glance.

'Dare we see what this deadly detractor was after?' Harry Howling – Head of Sales, Marketing & Finance, body of blancmange – wondered aloud, plucking the letter from its holster.

'Go on,' Audrey grumbled.

---

* And only 2/8! *Pink Baton*, Dennis Mesh (1966). Free postage. Discreet packaging.

The postmark said Mount Pleasant. The stamp was first class. Moistening a finger, Harry unfolded the typed sheet and read:

Never-Neverland, Londres W1
10th October 1969

Dear Sir/Madam,
I am an ugly man, a meese meshigena-omi, but a fashionable omi. And soon to be a molto famous omi. Lell my lapper.

Esteemed publisher of glistening livers, myself and my devotees cordially invite you to join with us in this forthcoming fame. We hereby offer you an una-in-a-lavvytime lucrative share in the high-flying, hallucinating, espresso-schlumphing, pâté-nibbling, jibbering, both-way-swinging, reprogramming, reverse-servo-lathering, Polarising, paranoid, cobblestoned, mono-bothering, line-crossing, cross-dressing, omi-jarrying, lav-hammering Raymond Novak Experience!

In duey-chenta setta-daitcha-heksa junos (276 days, for those without the lingo), myself and my devotees will commit a fantastic crime, a fantabulosa crime that will revolt the mond. My nom will be on the oyster-levers of every daffy jittery civvy as news breaks of this dazzling atrocity. My eek splattered across the cover of every inky and glossy on the newsstand. The Establishment brought to its lally-caps. The system left thoroughly smashed and charvered!

In anticipation of my untimely (and yet molto likely) demise on this date (batons, bombas, pistolets and molto sang guaranteed – or else all costs reparkered to you in full!), I am screeving my memoirs. What I propose is: if you are interested, I will send you morso-by-morso each chapter as it is tap-tap-DING!ed out upon the lav-hammer.

I am your man. But I am a meese omi, and a coddy auteur to boot. My achievements in education have not been up to dick to say the least, but do not fear: I have enlisted the help of a devoted comrade – an award-winning scholar and author – to fantomscreeve (ghostwrite, if you will) my autobiography.

I want nanti dinarli for my liver, nanti advance, nix royalties, no money for this venture. Only immortality, the lavvy-everlasting. The chance to screech my story to the masses in the event of my (ultra inevitable?) death come next summertide. And you, in turn, have this una-in-a-lavvytime opportunity to publish my truthful screeve immediately as news breaks of this mostest fantabulosa crime. It will be a real humdinger, a bona dinarli-spinner, I assure you. REVOLTING!

Esteemed publisher, if you are interested, give me a sign. Post a petite handlebar moustache in the 'Small Ads' section of the INTERNATIONAL TIMES, and in return I shall send you, chapter-upon-chapter as they are bashed out, these most specjalni sensational memoirs.

Bona lavs,

Raymond Marianne Novak (alias Lord Never-Never, alias The Guru, alias The Emperor, alias Raymond the Bastard, alias Raymond the Ponce, alias Signore Shapeshifter, alias Les Divertissements, alias The Walking Contraceptive, alias Ray le Roy, alias Ray la Purée, alias Neptunus Rex, alias Mr Sanson, alias Keith Caesar, alias Raymond le Poissonnier, alias Raymond the Poisoner, alias The Prole Dandy, alias The Scum King, alias The Carnish Mincer, alias Le Dieu-des-Indésirables, alias Le Dieu-du-Jour ...)

Yes, I have no doubts this gushing gibberish would have been banished to the wastepaper basket had Audrey been first to read it, and not Harry Howling. Some of us were more familiar with Polari – the secret homosexual lingo – than others. Howling – soon our go-to omi-palone when it came to decoding Novak's slippery slang – was a bold, thunderous queen. He had a mouth like a Billingsgate halibut and, if his cruising anecdotes were to be believed, a rectum more accommodating than a Salvation Army shelter. What he lacked in discretion Howling also, admittedly, lacked in financial nous, but the man was a favourite around the office – and now (at last!) a valuable asset to the company.

We huddled stiffly around Howling as he reread the note out loud, with gusto. Smirking, he navigated us through the linguistic assault course of 'meese meshigena-omi' (ugly madman), 'lell my lapper' (take my hand) and the verb 'to charver' (to fuck) – although there were other terms ('reverse-servo-lathering', 'molto sang') he'd never heard uttered by even the most athletic lips of Piccadilly.

'What does he mean by this "petite handlebar moustache"?' Audrey asked, still sucking the tip of her thumb.

'"Petite" is French for "small", dear heart,' Howling scoffed, fingering his own jumbo Wilhelm II tache. 'I think what the omi wants is a little handlebar mouser printed in the *International Times*, a nod and a wink as it were, if we want to read more.'

In light of the events that were to unfold over the next nine months (not to mention Novak's explicit threat of violence in this initial greeting), the law-abiding spoilsports among you may wonder why we didn't contact the police earlier. After all, we were no strangers to the constabulary, whether reporting the latest lovingly packaged turd, or watching blankly as the Dirty Squad turned over the office yet again in search of non-existent 'hard-core pornography'.

In truth, on the afternoon of the 14th October we were divided as a company. Audrey, Trefoil and McKinley felt we should ignore the note. Emily wanted to dial WHITEHALL 1212 immediately. Davy and Howling were eager to hear more from the Prole Dandy.

Ultimately, it was the accounting ledger that cemented our decision. Only Trefoil, Howling and I knew the dire state of our finances – only we knew how close the company was to folding. Did Tate/LaBianca also come into it? Most definitely. The as-yet-unsolved Manson murders were branded on everybody's brains back then. I didn't want to miss the British equivalent, the scoop of the century. Violence sells, does it not? Reported to the fuzz, the DIs might've thrown cold water on the bonfire before we had the chance to feel any benefit of its heat. My colleagues' moral compasses may have been spinning this way and that, but I saw a cool, steady stream of pound signs spewing forth from beneath that petite handlebar moustache …

We did it for the money, dear readers.

Our ad appeared alongside personal stimulators, Reichian vegetotherapy and a Cambodian masseuse in the *International Times, 67*: a six-by-six-inch presentation of our latest titles (*Cannibal Cafeteria*, *Langoustine Man*, *Jeremy's Fingers*, *Sausage Sandwich*, *The Bearded Chambermaid*) with some high-speed hyperbole from Emily (Publicity, Administrative, Secretarial & Kettle) and a miniscule but unmistakable item of facial furniture rendered by Mark 'Davy' Noon (Artwork & Design). The ad cost £3/9/1, almost twenty-six times the price of one of our humble bargain pocketbooks!

We lay in wait for five days, fourteen glassy eyes locked on the letterbox as the postman did his round. Twenty-three unconnected death threats later, a parcel appeared. We formed another stiff circle as Emily cagily picked open the seal, half expecting pink streamers, if not plastic explosives …

What we found was altogether more unusual.

And so, on to the main event. While every effort has been made to present Novak's memoirs in the state in which they were received, some insertions and omissions have been necessary for clarity, if not brevity.

Take heed of the footnotes. The constant flicking, rolling and recalibrating may irritate the eyeballs, but please do persevere. Whether knowingly or not, we all contributed to the footnotes, hence the first person plural. Sources vary: diaries were kept by myself, Trefoil and McKinley, microcassettes captured late-night ramblings, calendars fell prey to stream-of-consciousness Biros, hunches were scribbled on cigarette packets, paraphrased conversations may have been ill-remembered. As Director of the Glass Eye Press, I took the liberty of collating, editing and inserting the footnotes throughout, but by no means am I responsible for all opinions and anecdotes found therein.* Who knows? You may even find the footnotes more intriguing than Novak's inflammatory prose. After all, the joy of reading comes not only from following the fates of a gifted author's magicked-to-life mannequins, but from the sudden pyrotechnics that illuminate your brain when a certain word or phrase (unforeseen by the author) triggers a memory and calls for you.

> *Motionless we traverse countries we fancy we see, and your thought, blending with the fiction, playing with the details, follows the outline of the adventures. It mingles with the characters, and it seems as if it were yourself palpitating beneath their costumes.*†

Thumbing through Flaubert's masterpiece now, I feel perhaps the critics were right after all. Maybe our output to date has been worthless dross: grubby books barely fit even to wipe this now dysenteric director's explosive anus. But I feel this one, this heroic tome you hold today, Raymond's glistening liver, may yet make our fortunes. We have polished it so furiously we can see our own reflections in it. And probably yours too.‡

Stanley Merritt (Director), The Glass Eye Press
The lavatory of Room 220,
Hotel Continental, Tangier, Morocco
September 1970

---

* And apologies: Stanley sometimes refers to himself in the third person.

† *Madame Bovary,* Gustave Flaubert (1856).

‡ 'Probably not!' you screech.

MISTER ASTERISK*

RAYMOND M. NOVAK

* Our title. Judging by the hideous frontispiece and smeary typography supplied by Novak, he wanted to call his memoirs *Dieu-du-Jour* ('God-of-the-Day'). For fear of putting off readers of anti-Gallic persuasion (and puffing more air into Raymond's already overinflated ego), we felt *Mister Asterisk* was more appropriate.

EPILOGUE*

'Le cadavre exquis boira le vin nouveau.'

ANON.

* Parcel containing three chapters, received Tuesday, 11th November 1969 – 244 days to go until Novak's fantabulosa crime. Epigraph scrawled across the page in what appeared to be red wine: 'The exquisite corpse will drink the new wine.'

The Inkies & Glossies Screech

NOVAK WEARS NANTI SCHMUTTA EXCEPT FOR A TAG ON HIS BIG TOE. DECOMPOSITION MODEL'S OWN.

Beyond the morgue, the newsreels, inkies and glossies screech:

**MOGUES! MOGUES! MOGUES!*
GROTESQUE BLUNDERING NONENTITY RAYMOND NOVAK DEAD ON ARRIVAL AT ST BART'S**

Nix, nanti that. I wasn't going to be remembered like that.

* 'LIES! LIES! LIES!'

PROLOGUE

'Tout ce qui peut être imaginé est réel.'*

PABLO PICASSO, THE MINOTAUR IN BRETON STRIPES

---

* 'Everything you can imagine is real.' It took us some time to discover this epigraph, let alone translate it, given that Novak had scribbled it in invisible ink.

Twenty-Four-Carat Yarn

BACKSTAGE, NOVAK WEARS FULL-EEK PANCAKE, INNUMERABLE BEAUTY MORSOS, GROSS RED LIBERTY BONNET, GOLDWORKED TROPICAL TUXEDO, SHARKSKIN BELL-BOTTOMS AND GO-GO STAMPERS. HE NELLIES THE MISTRESS-OF-CEREMONIES CLEAR HER GARGLER IN THE AUDITORIUM NEX-BOR AS HE ATTACHES HIS EAR-FAKES.*

'Ladies and gentlemen, omi-palones and palone-omis, cut the cackle, please,' the bearded-donna announces, her whiskers tickling the microphone. 'It is with great pleasure I welcome you on this dolly noche to the Hotel Continental, Tangier. If you would care to lay down your claw-crackers and lift your opals from your Thermidorian lobsters una minuta. Shut your screech now. Thank you, thank you. Most gracious. Now, the molto perceptive among you may have already clocked the Gideons Bibbles in your libbages have been replaced by an altogether more powerful tome: this most glistening liver we are hereby celebrating this very noche ...'

Some splendid eeks squint back at the bearded-donna from the cabaret tables. The high society, the grand and the bona have come out in force for tonight's book launch, though many seem more interested in the complimentary bovaries and munja than the free livers. On the head table, Miss Bardo sips a bitter-gator in a gross Futurist Cleopatra headpiece, Bogey vogues up a cigarillo for King Hassan I or II, Christine Keeler jarries her last

* 'Fake ears, Harry?'
'Earrings.'

forkful of fromage de tête, meditational psych-folk duo Sage & Onion sit poised with their Hindi-strillers in the orchestra pit. Further back, other medsa-famous eeks flicker in the waxy glimmers: Melody Autruche and the Yé-Yé Dolls, the barkies of SS UNMENTIONABLE, the fantom of Madame O, a Barbary ape resplendent in a schvartz vogueing-jacket, catamites and cottagers, roamers and reamers, and the Director of the Glass Eye Press* sweating incognito under a blank bedsheet.

The tropical pomp seems better suited to a fascist dicktittler than a first-time novelist. Palm trees have been wheeled indoors, fountains spew foaming champagne and absinthe, the doormen carry pistolets. Hoisted either side of the arena, there are a dozen crimson banners shrieking bold slogans: LUBRICATE REALITY WITH DREAMS, INDIVIDUALITY FOR SALE! LONG LIVE THE SCUM KING! Et ceterarara. And the diners are all captive (if not captivated), lallies chained to the table-lallies. They began the noche cackling and reering, thinking the shackles were an amusing gimmick – but now their eeks have sunk, their ankles are smarting.

'Please, do remain seated,' the bearded-donna continues, as if there were a choice, 'and please try to refrain from screeching or vomiting, ejaculating, parnying, barnying, rioting or spontaneously glimmering as our most treasured guest takes to the stage ...'

Some of the diners vada one another with up- and down-turned oysters, uncomfortable now with the naff spectacle. Some discreetly scritch-scratch away at their lally-shackles with their cutlers.

'... and so, without any further ado, please welcome – nay, even DIP YOUR EYES IN REVERENCE as if in the presence of ten thousand glimmering suns – The Guru, The Emperor, Le Dieu-des-Indésirables, and now published screever!

---

* As it happened, Stanley wouldn't make it to Tangier until the footnotes of 'Deserters'. But we'll meet the rest of this motley crew before all that.

Our right honourable comrade, Monsieur RAYMOND MARIANNE NOVAK!'

The bearded-donna Sieg Heils the spectators with Novak's hardback liver clenched in her right lapper before gaily goose-stepping off the stage.* The lights dim, the Hindi-strillers let loose a hypnotic raga 'L'Internationale', sweet fogus-puffs seep out from under the rising curtain. Glimmer-fakements detonate. And then The Scum King appears, joshed-up to the nobbas in his gold-embroidered tux and bulbous Phrygian capella.

Raymond's trusted devotees – pockets of sycophants planted about the arena – flap their lappers together and stamp their stampers, crying out in exaggerational awe. The applause seems to reassure the other spectators – some even join in with the odd 'Yé-Yé!' or wolfy-whistle, surrendering themselves to the savagery that this omi must be important after all. He certainly looks the part. For uno momento they forget their lally-shackles, opals fixed to the stage, hoodwinked into thinking they're ogling the birth of some nova religious icon or rock-sparkle.

'Good evening, my chovis, my children. Thank you. Merci beaucoup. You're all very welcome,' Novak coos through the microphone. He pirouettes, allowing the room a 1,080-degree ogle of his outfit. 'Doppel-vented, mandarin collar, silk-lined.' He unbuttons the jacket, illustrating his point. 'The goldwork all embroidered by my fair lapper, twenty-four-carat yarn. Dry clean only.'

The schmutta would've looked ridiculous on any other pop – and in truth, it looks ridiculous on Novak. But the combination of the smoke, the glimmer-fakements, the goldwork, the

---

* To be frank, our initial reaction to this megalomaniac drivel was a collective sigh: 'O good Lord, not another pulp novel about the Third Reich,' etc. Almost a third of our output seemed to involve bloody Nazis. In fact, on the morning we received this first instalment, Davy Noon was applying the finishing touches to the enormous nipples on the cover of *The Nuremberg Nymphos* (Dennis Mesh's latest effort, a prequel of sorts to *Pink Baton*). The molested Aryan bird in the centre bore a striking resemblance to our own fair Complaints Fräulein, igniting suspicions that Audrey and Davy knew one another a tad more intimately than they let on. But more on this later.

servo-spinning raga and the lofty grandness lent by the go-go stampers and liberty bonnet shushes the spectators' ogleballs. The cult of personality! And fashion is a rapid-track route to personality, Raymond savvies this well. THE MAGICKAL CAPELLO. If The Guru were naggy, he would've been reered off the stage. Ô, if only these twonks could vada how hideous this omi is beneath the schmutta!

Hé-hé-hé-hé-hé-hé-HÉ!

Novak soaks up the last of the lapper-claps with a fist raised and opals closed, before launching into his ready-made intro: 'I'm not certain when it occurred to me I had a specjalni talent for terror. Not until I was at least eleven or twelve ...'

The Emperor's mogue handlebar mouser shimmers with sweat as his voche booms through the PA system, at once effeminate, authoritative, froggy and anglo.

'You may have gawped at the memoirs of other madmen and found hints in the petty batatats' chavvyhoods that try to explain away their future atrocities. Is it not desperately tedious, however, chewing through the stodgy mille-feuille of a self-obsessed screever's formative years? All chavvies are alike: bloody horrible – but mine was a specjalni brand of horribleness! And so, for those spectators who might've felt short-changed without it – like their handbags had been shushed from under their vonkas (cloakroom attendant has bolted, I might add) – I'll supply the obligatory resumé of my feeli years. You might well cry: was it nature or nurture that made me this way? I savvy not. Until recently I had never met my father, despite loitering in his quongs for junos prior to him ejaculating forcibly up the Madame's cunt. When I was growing up, I was told my dear papapapapapapapa was one of otta or nobba possible omis – therefore the lucky plucky spermatozoomer that tet-butted my mother's egg must've been one of a potential 1,000,000,000 or so ...

'Ô, the sweet, coddy mystery of man's multifaceted, multifaked nature!' I screamed into the grand silent auditorium.

INTERMISSION

'I want the utopian combination of security and freedom.'*

LEE MILLER, DISEMBODIED NIPPLETS TURNED SURREALIST HEROINE

* Gold ink, perfect cursive.

Womb Muzak

NOVAK WEARS NANTI SCHMUTTA EXCEPT AMNIOTIC GOO AND THE UMBILICAL CORD LIKE A LASSO ROUND HIS PALLIASS.

Flink flas tigkrr tigkrrrr
Coogoo flimizz vee flimisst ba va
Shhoolgg fvvvvvvv!
Stakadaka do stakadaka drimlll
Staka do dakadaka do daka dee stakadaka do
Ondonk doodleburgle hoooooooooooooo
Rankledankle flizz bammtankoo
Neeeeeeex!
Ponk pa dee do ponk ba dfee dfo dfo do do do do do
Hishjish caga grimmelninnel mishnish
Neeeeeeeeeeeeeeeeeex nee nix nee NEE!*

---

* Abridged. We weren't sure if this nonsense poem was supposed to represent a foetus's consciousness or the commotion outside the womb, but Novak felt it necessary to give us sixteen pages of it. As before, we were divided as a company after reading Novak's first chapters, these fanciful false starts. Some of us were seduced by the deranged language – others felt we were clearly dealing with a deluded egomaniac, a charlatan, a timewaster. Unfortunately, like the diners in 'Twenty-Four-Carat Yarn', our lallies were now shackled to the table-lallies. Once we printed that petite handlebar moustache, there was no going back, no return-to-sender, no white flag to flap to escape the onslaught of perverse prose. Stanley, not known for his optimism, nevertheless saw the upside: the ad in the *International Times* appeared to have increased sales slightly. To celebrate, he took us out to a French brasserie in homage to Novak's fantasy banquet, although it was cold, claggy *carottes râpées* we nibbled rather than Lobster Thermidor and *fromage de tête*. We were allowed one small glass of wine each. And we

scrutinised Davy and Audrey's body language but at best the lovebirds seemed hostile to each other and Audrey ended up storming out in silent seething rage, souring what was an otherwise fairly pleasant break from the office. Pressed later, Davy claimed she'd shown him some of her poetry the previous night and the closest he could get to a compliment was: 'It's wrong.' Thankfully Audrey has not attempted to share her poesies with the rest of us. The Glass Eye Press does not accept poems. Except, grudgingly, this one.

PART I

MADAME OVARY

'Nothing is serious enough to take seriously.'*

MARCEL DUCHAMP, NORMANDY RÉSPIRATEUR

* Epigraph scrawled in mustard – most likely Dijon? If it were not clear already: we are not forensic scientists.

The Hostess*

NOVAK WEARS NANTI SCHMUTTA EXCEPT WOMB-DRIBBLE AND THE CAUL LIKE A CAROON ATOP HIS BALDY TET.

I landed in Normandy, June 1944. Or was it Paris, August 1944? Or possibly Londres, May 1945? In any case, it was a heroic moment.

My Old Mare was sometimes tight-levered, sometimes brootishly frank about the multi lovers she charvered in her feeli years. Roundabout the period of my conception, she claimed she had unprotected groin-groin with eight or nine omis – some consensual, some nantwar. While it worried me I may have been spawned from the quongs of the jackbooted batatats that molested her in the ultraschvartz in Occupied Paris, my Mare screeched much more fondly of the dorcas Resistance-pop she seduced in rural Normandy, the Surrealists who pricked her during various meshigena soirées in Saint-Germain-de-Prés and Montparnasse, the rakish rosbif racketeer she gaily gobbled in exchange for vogues and army rations, the hairless trapeze artiste, the Pyrenean shepherd ...

When she wanted me to be a sophisticat, she told me I was full-froggy – when she wanted me to be more humble and tranquil, I was an Englishman. But more than anything she just wanted me to stay feeli, gay and free: free from the straitjacket of nationality, free from the rosary-garrotte of religion, free from the inferiority complexity of the class system. And, so it seemed, free from bona old-fashioned family values.

---

* Chapter received Friday, 14th November 1969 – 241 days to go.

I never knew my Mare's real nom. She called herself Madame Ovary – it might've been her joggering-nom* back in Paris, or maybe she vadared herself as a machine more than a mother: a pair of ovaries that accidentally created a monster. She was a loving palone but it was an explosive, erratic love on her own terms rather than consistent, unconditional dolly affection.

She was also somewhat partial to hatred. The duey Gross Wars had put flames in her brain. My Mare claimed she was born meshigena – a madwoman never destined to fit into norm society – but molto likely her scattiness was an allergic reaction to the absurdity of war, politicos and freedom-strangling austerity she constantly screeched and palavered about. She used the majestic plural when retelling her torments during the Occupation, which might've helped distance herself from the horrors but also made them harder to believe: 'We were forced to give gam-jobs to the geraldines ...' 'We watched them rip the fangs out of the gypsies ...' 'We were raped repeatedly ...'

Madame Ovary was a palone of contradictions: she claimed she was a Marxist despite having nanti respect for toiling proles, a penniless hag greedy for de-luxe goodies, a country crone sucked in by the city, a multi-linguist who regularly spoke gibberish.

In the 1930s she worked as a hostess at Le Spleen de Paris, a subterranean stomping-khazi in the Latin Quarter that attracted the witching hour fallout from the ajax Deux Magots, Café de Flore and Bonaparte: the breeding grounds of the Surrealists. Madame O insisted she'd charvered an eminent existentialist, kicked Kiki de Montparnasse up the corybungus, and regularly entertained the Surrealists with her mix of lingua franca, fishwife poissard slander and backslang that seemed to jetset direct from her unconscious. On Saturday noches she performed La Danse des Mannequins, her own macabre jitterbug involving several plastic lallies and the bold zelda contorting herself like

* Stage name, nom de plume, nom de guerre?

a caboosh-crash victim or an anarchist before the firing-squad – and she was semi-famous for her drogle falling off whenever she came into contact with a kamera. It was this willingness to shed her schmutta that multiplied her appeal to the Surreal-omis – and before long she was appearing in their flickers. Or rather, DISAPPEARING.*

Co-sparkling alongside a Persian longhair, Lee Miller's disembodied nipplets and duey-dozen pamplemousses in two silent shorts – LA LUNE PORTE UNE MOUSTACHE and LE CON DU CHAT† – Madame O's acting career disappeared up her bushy hortus almost as soon as it was exposed. LA LUNE PORTE UNE MOUSTACHE disgusted audiences with its extreme close-ups of feet and a climax that was tantamount to cannibalistic necrophilia – LE CON DU CHAT was even worster. The flickers were banned by the Chief of Police after a riot erupted at the Studio des Ursulines and, despite only a pogi lapperful of ogleballs witnessing her scatty performances, the lav soon got out and the Madame was branded a gross putain around Saint-Germain-de-Prés: charming for an area already rife with bonarobas, weirdies and she-wolves. Her neighbours didn't need to vada the flickers – the pictures in their tets were vile enough! The poor zelda was ostracised.

HOWEVER: rather than slithering back to Normandy or hiding away in the dungeon-like Spleen de Paris, my heroic Mare fought back, playing up to her nova demonic reputation, firing fists and mustard-gas expletives at any pop who dared criticise her lavvystyle, her acting prowess or the symmetry of her willets.‡

---

* See 'Nouvelle Vagueness'.

† *The Moon Wears a Moustache* (1938) and *The Cat's Twat* (1939).

‡ 'Breasts,' Howling exclaimed, cupping his own lopsided tits.

Though it surely couldn't endear him to the young supple queens of Piccadilly, Howling claimed he enjoyed getting fat as he got older. In fact, his weight gain seemed less a side effect of his lavish lifestyle, more the direct objective. Almost immediately after we'd hired him for our long-vacant Sales, Marketing

As the abuse escalated, Madame O took first to heavy drinking, then (after her third arrest and second miscarriage) teetotalism and what she termed la vie de folie sobre, la vie d'avant-garde, or THE LIBERATED LAVVY. Sickened by the sneers of the petty-bourgeoistards and now maxi suspicious of the mogue magickal capello of alcool, she surrendered herself entirely to an altogether more intoxicating vice: Dada and Surrealism. Just as the Surrealists rejected coddy logic in favour of living out their daffy unconscious desires, spitting in the eeks of toff hypocritters and championing the servos of criminals and the insane, so too Madame O turned her palliass to decorum and moral servitude in favour of freewheelering creativity, gaiety, absurdity, lounging, scrounging and outbursts of unprovoked troublemaking.

This was living.

BOMP!

Madame Ovary's mind blew on a Tuesday afternoon. She quit her job at the stomping-khazi, minnied aimlessly around the city in a medsa-wakey rev and alienated her so-called comrades by speaking auto-splatter full-time. She would sometimes be seen trolling the Boulevard Saint-Germain joshed-up as a papier-mâché triceratops, or perched atop the graves at Père Lachaise, tarred and feathered, squawking at the sol. She used the entrance to the Banque de France as an al-fresco pissoir.

& Finance role, Harry's appearance changed dramatically. His thinning quiff turned arctic-white, he grew an enormous imperial moustache and he began eating monumental luncheons that rapidly inflated his waistline. Whenever visitors to the office commented on his transformation, Howling seemed to enjoy concocting a new explanation each time:

'It's a disguise, dear heart. I owe quite a sizeable sum to quite a sizeable man.'

'A current lover desperately wants me to look and act like his old tyrannical sea captain.'

'I broke my psychiatrist's fingers and now wish to avoid the manipulative little turtle at all costs.'

We fear, however, the real reason may be down to occupational stress, paranoia, low self-esteem – something we are all, alas, quite familiar with by now …

She goosestepped round and round the battyfanged outline of the Bastille, babbling insurrectionary bluster. And she was arrested for a fourth time after causing a caboosh to swerve into some pedestrians in Montmartre, but evaded gaol or the asylum since she could play a straight palone just as convincingly as a meshigena palone.

With nanti dinarli coming in (and her grizzly landlord by now full-aware of her reputation around the quartier as a perverse tartlet), Madame O was evicted from her apartment, but the lattyless off-the-leash lavvy suited her fine. She found revolving accommodation all around Paris: Métro stations, waiting-chambers, sideysnickets, strange omis' chaises-longues, a hedgerow in the Jardin du Luxembourg. She would regularly walk the otta miles to Le Bourget aeroport for a free dhobi. She begged, borrowed and charvered her way into a few francs hither and thither – and, despite the mally cold and malnutrition, she convinced herself she was living this de-luxe Liberated Lavvy more purely than ever: freer and molto better off than the compliant drones she stumbled past on the strasses.

LIBERTÉ, INÉGALITÉ, INDIVIDUALITÉ!

The daydream ended in June 1940 when the trenchcoats and jackboots moved in: eagle-eeked twats preaching to some obscene supremacy caca revved up by a boiled egg in a blackshirt in Italy.

FASH BATATATATATS!

The restrictions on Parisiens before the Occupation were like fluffy handcuffs compared to the Nazis' leather-fambler stranglehold. The froggy gendarmes who barely batted an ogleriah when Madame O was caught cavorting with a kosher-omi duey months previously were now lapper-in-lapper with the Gestapo, diligently directing these same poor kosher-pops off to the Hell-camps and gas chambers.

An itinerant minny, Madame O feared she might be mistaken for a gypsy or some other subversive plop so she dollied herself up again, affected outward compliance, inwardly hated herself and prayed the Invaders wouldn't unearth her degenerate double-feature.

What with so many deserters evacuating the capital, the Madame managed to get her old job back at Le Spleen de Paris, though she was now a stomping-mono* for gerry officers rather than froggy bohemians. The City of Light suffered shortages and blackouts, and so did Madame O, smiling and shaking her corybungus with blinkers on as Paris shrivelled for the Parisiens while it bloomed for the batatats in brownshirts. If she had the kishkas, if she truly was living this subversive vie d'avant-garde, the Liberated Lady should've fought back. In her revs she dug her stilettos into the SS Officers' groins noche after noche, served up scatwurst sandwiches, pissed in der Weissbier – but in reality she blankly swallowed everything just like everybody else.

Madame O claimed she was part of the Resistance, but she was surprisingly evasive when I pressed her on her heroics. She was more forthcoming when she described the royal 'we' having to bend over for the Invaders at Le Spleen – 'We were choked with black famblers, hot blutwurst breath on our fizzers, we were raped repeatedly, oyster, flange, ripped dish ...'† – but she insisted I wasn't a Little Hitler. In any case the Nazis were more occupied elsewhere by the time one of otta or nobba omis invaded Madame Ovary's ovaries, but I savvy now I couldn't completely rule it out.

ACHTUNG!

When Madame O fell pregnant twice before, she'd fantasised about bringing up a bona fide untamed, untainted lullaby-cheet in accordance to her beloved vie surréaliste – home-schooled in scruple-proof conditions, untouched by priests, unaffected by politicos, nanti birth certificate, nix fixed citizenship, a truly free pop unchained from the Gross Machinery – but the heavy drinking mortified the dream. Now she was off the alcool

---

* Dancing monkey?

† 'Don't ask,' Howling tittered.

(healthier if not maxi well nourished), the Madame found herself with child again and yet it seemed Surrealism and Dada had perished. Many of the degenerate artistes she'd served at Le Spleen de Paris had fled or were dead: André Breton and Dalí in New York, Péret and Carrington in Mexico, Robert Desnos in striped pyjamas at Theresienstadt. And Madame O was disgusted that she'd abandoned her own daffy defiant mischief-making – disgusted that she and so many others were complicit in their city's humiliation, bending over for the Nazis, over and over and over ...

Even as the Allies piled in, my mother felt she couldn't stay much longer in Paris. When the lights came back on and the swastikas came down, la ville de l'amour looked much the same as before, but it was like carrying on living with a fortuni chiselled husband who'd stuck his colin in the most meese greaser on your strasse.

At some point during 1944, Madame O (with me on board) crossed the Channel. Apparently her grand plan was for us to find somewhere to lavvy at full leisure in the Arcadian anglo wilderness, utterly isolated from all past, present and future polluting predatory forces – and yet somehow we ended up sharing a manky frigid bed-sitter with two other solo mamas in East Londres.

The solo mamas thought she was meshigena for deserting the newly liberated City of Light. Her froggy lingo attracted maximum resentment. Whereas before she'd been criticised for her debasement, her perverted gutter-lavvy – in Londres her nova neighbours saw her as opal-wateringly decadent and toff. Twas de rigueur in those junos for Parisien palones to pomp themselves up with pompadour riah in defiance of their humiliations and in glimmering contrast to the drab austere anglos – and thusly therefore the solo mamas presumed she had barely suffered during the war, the Occupation was merely a pogi inconvenience for the frogs, the Mare had clearly been mollycoddled – if not outright pampered and fawned over – by the toppermost Nazis. The poor zelda, yet again, was ostracised.

So what to do now?

Madame O swore she only wanted the bestest for me (including my own pouffed-up chavvy bouffant), but she wasn't sure whether that meant resurrecting the Liberated Lavvy or following the Norm Lavvy like everybody else. London at that time was an ultra-Surrealistic city: battered and doodlebuggered, caught halfway between a rev and a nightmare, tugged along by l'humour noir and daffy desperate resilience. Madame Ovary still had a taste for nonconformity; she was more disillusioned than ever about the state of our coddy welt, disenfranchised, discombobulated. She felt there had to be a better lavvy than the one prescribed by the politicos – and London seemed the ideal, irregular playground. But was it not easier to just keep your tet down, grit your pearls and conform?

She wished I would give her a sign. She wanted me to choose a life for us: la vie surréaliste or la vie réaliste/la vie sécurisée/la vie enchaînée.* She couldn't savvy if it was cruel or kind to bring a bambino up amoral (not necessarily IMMORAL), unregistered, untethered, uncensored, under the radar, politically uncorrected, free to choose how I wanted schooling, free to screech, think and act how I wished.

I was a reticent chavvy until I was two. If I had any intellect at all I expressed it only in gurgles and burped raspberries, but my first lav changed everything:

'Dada.'

---

* Our *Harrap's French Dictionary* suggests: 'The surrealistic life or the realistic life, the secure life, the straitjacketed life.'

Carte Blanche*

NOVAK WEARS SOILED NAPPY, BIMPH SWADDLING, GROSS SCHVARTZ A.R.P. WARDEN'S HELMET. VOMIT STAINS MODEL'S OWN.

No matter how much I cried out 'Dada', Madame Ovary refused to believe I was pining for a father figure. I never once screeched 'Mama', and so she assumed I must've rejected restrictive family ties just as she had.

Apparently I was so desperate to live this meshigena vie d'avant-garde, I'd scream 'Dada! Dada!' almost hourly with a pink eek and parny flying out of my opals. Madame O didn't need telling twice. She was sick of being shacked up with just the one pissoir between eight families, unable to express herself without confusing, offending or inadvertently battyfanging our gloomy roommates. The solo mamas irritated her with their emphasis on Christ-worship and bona lattykeeping, not to mention their daffy suspicions that she was trying to poison them with her Continental cuisine/her profumo was giving them servo-damage/her manicured luppers had been rifling through their ration books ...

With nanti record of my birth (and Madame O accepted into the country with a mogue nom and mogue papers), we could effectively disappear. As it happened, my first lavs and second birthjuno coincided with the gloriosa Squatters' Revolt of 1946. Hacked off at cramped conditions and the jammed waiting list

---

* Chapter received Monday, 17th November 1969 – 238 days to go.

for nova housing, civvies took the law into their own lappers that summer, seizing unoccupied buildings like squadrons of disgruntled malnourished cuckoos. While the squatters tended to shush abandoned barracks at mothballed military camps or sneak into de-luxe flats under renovation, Madame O and I did our latty-sharpering around the scatty bombsites of East London. We trolled through the blitzed streets of Stepney (if you could still call them streets), duey ramblers in a morbid mountain-scape of rubble, on the lookout for a latty meese and privvy enough to live our Liberated Lavvy in peace, and not attract any other cuckoos – or the constabulary.

The Château appeared to us as if in a dream: the only two-up two-down left standing in a bombed-out cul-de-sac near the Sisters of Mercy at Shadwell. The house claimed to be Numero 14 but its nearest neighbour was a Numero 93C almost chenta yards away. Tucked in the munge of duey rubble-willets, Madame Ovary christened the house le Château Chanceux: a lucky latty in that the bombas had somehow missed it, although surely it was earmarked for demolition eventually.*

Madame O wanted me to accidentally frap a cobblestone through the fenêtre to gain entry but, as it fell out, the windows were all smashed already. The Mare scrambled in through the kitchenette, found the front door clef hanging in the hallway, then welcomed me into our nova home-sweet-home with a startled eek. The eek was down to the state of the latty: aside from

---

* Audrey, also a Stepney resident, tried to find the site of the Château but only came across blackened Peabody flats, cranes, lock-ups and grim seadog pubs on a three-hour-long traipse around Commercial Road. In many ways Audrey was our Madame Bovary: giving up her 'provincial ways' in 1964 to see for herself the spoils of the swinging city and ending up even more discontented than when she started. Audrey arrived in London aged seventeen and now, six years on, she seems utterly drained by the experience. Like many of the working-class dollies who come to the capital, the disillusionment grew as the realities of the Permissive Society failed to match the carefree pictures flowerbedded in her head. But it would take us months to realise the full scale of her problems – and by that time it was too late to help …

the shards of glaze around the carpet and a few fallen fakements, the rooms were perfectly preserved, each decorated natty with floréal wallpaper, rows of utensils and all sorts of antique livers, nova drogas and tinned munja. The libbages were in bona nick, the beds all made and laundry pressed. There was even a Singer sewing-vacaya with a fresh pair of pyjamas clenched betwixt its fangs. Was this an old kosher-tailor's bodega, perchance? The latty had the feel of a holiday cottage clinging to an asteroid. There was nanti electric and the roof leaked when it parnied, but miraculously there was running aqua in the water-pump out the back, and a coal-glimmering boiler ready to be fired up downstairs.

For the first few weeks of our occupation, Madame Ovary expected the owner or tober-omi* to reappear and exorcise us. She couldn't understand how such a dolly abode could survive the aero-raids, and why the owners hadn't returned – although there was a clue in the absence of an outside khazi. Years later I'd sometimes rev about the omi or palone from Numero 14, struggling to enjoy a relaxing lag or caca while the sirens yowled around them. I pictured a doodlebug or V-2 flushing them direct down the sewage system.

Ô, THE INGLORIOUS DEAD

Once she was satisfied we weren't going to be forcibly evicted any time soon, Madame Ovary lay down the foundations of what would be our most meshigena, mysterious nova lavvystyle. Allergic to work but ever resourceful, she provided for us by shushing coal, candles and cosmetics, swiping ration coupons, cajoling bodega-omis, flattering sailors and charvering spivs. She claimed froggy cheques were more valuable than shillings

---

* 'Tober-omi or tober-palone means a money-sucking, flesh-eating leech,' Howling stated, spinning round and round in his dilapidated swivel armchair. 'Or rather: a landlord.'

and soldis: 'Just put on ze mozzst abhhominablé Fronch acc-ent,' she would tell me once I savvied what dinarli was, 'and trrry to pay wiz ze Fronch cheque-liver for ze trolleybuz, ze taxicab, tabac, pain, ze Untergrund, et ceterarara. Zen zee what 'appen! Most often you go freee ...'

While Madame O scoured the strasses for our daily essentials, I was forbidden from leaving the Château or playing beyond the duey rubble-willets: the 'only rule'. I didn't mind much being left alone in the latty – especially after the mogues she told me about the outside mond. I savvy now it was more of an experiment than an upbringing, her playing puppeteer with my imagination, warning me of oppressive sneering toffs beyond the wasteland, forcing me to live a hermetically sealed lavvy in civvy-proof conditions. From juno uno she told me fash bats and sharpering-omis were after us, these evil eagle-eeked addle-plots who cruised the city, flushing out folk who refused to bend and grind out The Travails for the Fatherland:

'Most people's lavvies are dictated by the Big Whip,' Madame O palavered at me continually. 'What a poor, twisted mond for an infant: growing up only to be thrust into shiny lace-up booties, finding you cannot play no more, you have to work, to study, to toil, to answer to le Censeur, ze Boss Man, the supreme dicktittlers. Écoute-moi: the momento you stop ogling the mond through the eyes of a child, you start dying! Our default lavvystyles cannot be conformity, fidelity, compliance, suppression of freewheelering expression. We were all born to play, to doss, to shush, to smash, to rev, to love, to enjoy ourselves selfishly and liberally!'

'Dada! Dada Dada!'

'Exactement, Raymond.'

And yet, despite all her bluster, our nova exhilarating Liberated Lavvy was spent almost entirely horizontally, in silence, in full-blackness, in separate bedchambers. Madame O encouraged me to savour my dreams – 'Humans deplore ze alarm clock! We hate waking, Raymond! Is there any further proof needed that we're better suited to procrastinating, revving, relaxing and ruminating? We haven't evolved to race ravenous out of bed to chase the next grubby shilling or franc! Our tets demand the oriel!'* – and she screeched at me bloodthirsty if she didn't get her minimum kenza-hour beauty kip each juno.

Ogling backwards, she was probably more interested in her own freedom than mine. I fancy Madame O's ideal lavvy would be contracting a long, non-life-threatening, hallucinatory illness and being sent to convalesce at a sanatorium in the green dreamy countryside. But still, she tried her bestest to bring me up a little libertine.

DO WHAT THOU WILT was more or less the gist of the Law.

Aware that birch-wielding teachers essentially destroy creativity by enforcing conformity, Madame O home-schooled me, mumbling Rimbaud, Baudelaire and the Marquis de Sade in my nells while I slumbered, burning my ogles with Surrealist paintings when I was awake and babbling an ultra bloodlusty history of the French Revolution in a queer anglo-froggy argot that I had nix choice but to adopt myself.

As far as I can remember, twas a more-or-less merry chavvyhood. Even when Madame O was fattygayed and skitterish, she only occasionally strung me up to the banister rails and cat-o'-nine-tailed my naggy carnish. Eventually I learned to lag and caca behind the rubble-willets instead of action-painting it across the walls. I wasn't forced into any other hygiene regimes. My bod-odour was nix worster than the all-pervading drain stench. My milky pearls rapidly rotted out of my skull.

The way Madame O described it, le Château Chanceux was a bona fide haven, spoiled only by the old coco-palone's increasing paranoia. As East Londres gradually began its rehabilitation, again she feared landowners or demolition-omis might turn up with writs and wrecking-balls, and she made me hide whenever she thought she nellied a social worker or eagle-eek swooping outside.

---

* 'Our heads demand the pillow!'

As it happened, I was almost three by the time we had our first visitor. When she nellied the knock, Madame O rapidly untethered my wrists and lallies from the bedframe and stuffed me SPLATCH! BLOP! in one of the cuisine cupboards. I remember the Old She-Wolf looked set for the bungery: pompadour riah, satin gown, full-eek clownesse maquiage.

I never got to vada the visitor properly but Madame O described her as a crocodile in a black scapular and cowl. She must've been a Sister of Mercy. Apparently the nun had clocked 'alien voices' coming from the battered Château and felt obliged to offer assistance/eavesdrop/interfere.

'My good dear,' the croc crunched in clipped King's anglo, 'how do you survive in such wreckage? Please allow me to help, to offer counsel ...'

Madame Ovary warned me cloth-pops are sang-suckers, carnish-jarrying hypocritters just like all the rest. While I crouched in the munge betwixt the Bouillon Kub and broken biscuit tins, I had in my tet a terrible vision of a crashlanded avenging angel, a reptilian vamp sucking on my dear mother's neck, turning her into a petty dehydrated walnut. Curiosity got the better of me – I creaked open the cupboard door and lento peeked my eek down the hallway. For uno momento I caught the nun's opal – then secondas later there was just a black habit in a heap on the doorstep. The Sister had vadared the meese beastie staring back at her – and pronto collapsed.

Make Do & Mend*

SASHAYING UP AND DOWN THE HALLWAY, NOVAK WEARS SCRAPS, RAGS, A BROWN PAPER BAG AND PIGGYTAILS.

Though Madame Ovary always maintained I was a beautiful boy with a 'wonderfully abstract visage', she kept me from mirrors until I was eight. She might've kept me in the munge longer, only it seemed I was growing meeser and meeser with each passing year. Probably bestest to just get it over with, she ponced.

What started out as a perfectly ordinary, chubby lullaby-eek soon developed craggy shark-fangs, ratty-nells and bulbous fish-ogles that appeared to be permanently shut whether juno or noche. By the time I was eight, all my eek-features had squashed together into the middle of my tet, surrounding a flabby sniffly oink-vonka. My forehead expanded like a blank tombstone. My palliass humped. My chin retreated.

The frogs have the term 'jolie laide'† to help flatter pops with an unconventional beauty – like Humph Bogey, Jeanne Moreau, Jean-Paul Marat, Serge Gainsbourg – but this was fuckering ridiculous.

For years my Old Woman insisted it was laudanum that made the nun fade. She claimed she'd drugged the croc and buried her under the rubble in a fit of anti-clerical mania. I believe this now to be caca. But still: most importantly the fainting fit proved to Madame O I wouldn't get far on this coddy welt with such a

---

* Chapter received Wednesday, 19th November 1969 – 236 days to go.

† Literally 'pretty ugly'.

startling visage. In her own experience of lavvying fancy-free, the Madame's dolly facial symmetry enabled her to get away with more than a grotesque gutter-chavvy surely could. True enough, she'd swallowed a gross amount of abuse, condescension and scorn in her life, but she lacked the all-jarrying insecurity that comes when you're not maxi convinced by the skin your skeleton's wearing.

We couldn't afford nova schmutta nor extensive plastic surgery, but Madame O savvied I required some form of camouflage to help me in the future, should I ever need to venture out into the city (or should the rubble-willets finally clear and THE CITY COMES TO US). She collected rags, plastics and loose threads while she drifted around Stepney and, after experimenting for months on the sewing-vacaya, she conjured up a strange range of cozzies for me. Any kind of uniform disgusted Madame Ovary (in fact, uniformity was probably the crux of what she was railing against), but she savvied I needed one if I was ever going to rub up against the civvies and not wind up in a freakshow or gaol or shallow grave.

Our first fittings were a disaster. Whether she dolled me up as low-class (cloth-capella, petty-pantaloons, sabots) or Little Lord Fauntleroy (top hat, monocle, vogueing-jacket, cane),* my glaring deformities refused to fizzle away. Ogle-fakes magnified my bulbous peepy opals. Liberty bonnets exaggerated my deformed eggy tet. Brown paper bags cut off my aero supply.

'Mon Dieu, where did you get these frightful features, Raymond?' the Madame growled. 'You're a beastie! Why do you not look more like your mama? Your délicieuse mère?!'

---

* 'Look, that's like you, Davy!' Howling hooted, showing him the passage. 'Little Lord floppy-haired fop!' To be fair to our dedicated parasite of fashion, Mark 'Davy' Noon's military tunic and hobnail boots were more Lord Kitchener's Valet than Little Lord Fauntleroy. Those of us born between the wars nevertheless found his taste for militaria baffling. Stanley and Trefoil served in the Royal Navy during WWII and McKinley did his National Service – and they hoped never to put on those disgusting fucking uniforms ever again.

There was nothing else for it. After another week or so feeding and screeching at the sewing-vacaya, Madame O wrestled me into a drogle, a bonnet and a shyka of dolly blonde ringlets. She deflated my opals with ogleshadow, streamlined my eek with excessive blank pancake, goosestepped on my palliass to fix my coddy posture. I didn't mind so much being joshed-up as a filly (I considered myself genderless back then, and probably still do: genderless, albeit with a grandiose multisexual throbbering cartso) – but twas the ferocity of the joshing that frightened me.

'ACHTUNG, Raymond! Your face is a piece of degenerate art! If the eagles find you, they'll tear you to morsos! They'll crucify you!' she squeaked, schonking me repeatedly with the powder-puff. 'TOUTEFOIS! If you at least appear to be a petty mademoiselle, they might only rape you at the very worstest – like they did me! Like they did me, Raymond! And perhaps not mortify you completely!'

The palone was deranged. Deteriorating by the juno.

Once my transformation was complete, I wrongly ponced I was now free to frolic beyond our wasteland wonderland, to mingle among the general poplos, to meet and tinker with chavvies my own age.

'NON!' my Mare howled. 'This costume is but a precaution, a safeguard should the eagles sniffle us out and mistake you for a grotty troll that needs decimating pronto. You're not to mix with the civvies out thataways, Raymond. You're not to leave me! Stay put, lay lowly. Out there you'll be forced to conform – between these walls you can do whatever you please! L'incarceration vous libère! Oui? Non?'

At some point I must've suggested I'd like a brother or sister to enjoy this gay incarceration with, but her servo was full-paranoiac by now: 'Other humanoids cannot be trusted, Raymond! My womb is closed for business! BLERGGH!'

Nevertheless, the Old She-Wolf must've been at least a pogi bit concerned about my loneliness. Uno juno in 1953 or 1954 she returned from her aimless wanderings with a bijou gift: a meese ventriloquist's dummy she'd found round the back of the battyfanged Palace of Varieties.

'Hé-hé-hé-hé-hé!' she cackled as she forced the garish lump into my lappers. 'Et voilà: un petit frère pour toi! Ô, mes chéris! Happy happy family!'

The cheet was disgusting: dead opals, chattering fangs, googly gendarme goggles, periwig, petite handlebar mouser, trenchcoat, helmet, black famblers.*

'My beautiful bambinos!'

She christened the doll Le Bâtard, probably on account of him being a wholly illegitimate child – ignoring the fact that I too was a bona fide bastard. As it fell out, I would soon warm to the slack-jawed cheet as my relationship with my Mare frosted over colder and colder – but I distinctly remember parnying hysterically when I clocked the pair of us together for the first time in our pogi hallway-of-mirrors.

'My twins!' the Madame ribbitted. 'La Belle et Le Bâtard!'

Whether down to the dummy's frightening expression or my frumpy unflattering Battenberg-drogle, I was maxi inconsolable as I ogled us together in the dusty glaze – and yet my mother insisted: ajax to that gruesome petty morso, any jolie-laide freak would look truly fortuni.

---

* When finally we allowed Emily to read Novak's manuscript, she had a strange response to this passage:

'Is it me,' she murmured, her cheeks turning the colour of raw pork chops, 'or does anyone else feel like they've seen this character somewhere before?'

'The doll?' Trefoil responded. 'I thought it might be Punch and Judy, the policeman. But then I don't know – would his mother allow such a grotesque symbol of oppression into their home?'

'No, no, it's not that …' Emily squirmed in her seat, feeling like some foul trick was being played on her. 'I've seen it somewhere else, definitely … in my dreams … or … no … I don't quite know …'

Such is the incisive insight you can gain when you allow your bloody secretary in on the creative process – and yet, as we'll see, her rigorous scrutiny of the text would later turn out to be invaluable …

Salty aqua rocketed from my sockets, turning our eeks to just throbbering hexagons, swirly spirals, then nantwar.

Little did I vada I was ogling into the future, Ô comrades. Raymond 'The Brain Botherer' Novak: master of disguise, line-crosser, cross-dresser, avid collector of mannequins ...

And I would soon look fuckering fantabulosa in a miniskirt.

Kinder, Küche, Kirsche*

COWERING UNDER THE KITCHEN SINK, NOVAK WEARS AN OMI-SIZED OMO BOX, GENDARME GOGGLES AND A COLANDER ATOP HIS TET.

By the end of the 1950s, most of the action in the Château took place in the kitchen. Not only were the other chambers now practically inhospitable – leaking, crumbling, ultra-cluttered mouseholes – but the kitchen had all the vacayas to see us through our waking deeds: jarrying abstract munja, flushing away parnyaqua and dealing with unwanted lullaby-cheets ...

The frogs love to ridicule bland anglo cuisine, but Madame O rebelled against it so strongly she'd often serve up dishes that were more like inedible artwork than nourishing munja. Rather than the traditional grey rosbif, terrapoms and gravy, Madame Ovary carved Futurist sculptoids from giant concombres, kidnapped snails from soggy paves, netted crayfish and flotsam from the Grand Union Canal, foraged for wild mushrooms, and – when available – smothered, stuffed and sprinkled everything (from corned beef bourguignon to roadkill provençal) with dream-enhancing, stinking French fromage.

As puberty dug its fangs into my kishkas, I retreated back into my revs. Ultimately the 1950s for me was a boring period made just about bearable by imagining myself elsewhere. Twas around the age of twelve I developed a beastly covering of bod-riah, and

---

* Chapter received Friday, 21st November 1969 – 234 days to go.

with it came an equally beastly – but not unwelcome – stream of highly sexualised dreams. I'd not yet vadared any dollies my own age, but still my subconscious teased and tormented me with a vivid nightly runway of delicious shapeshiftering beasties with squirty milky willets, palavering flanges, dishes puckering like pink fairground goldfishies. I awoke most morns with a cartso as hard as diamond.

Ô, those feeli dreams! I miss them.

Aside from the fantastical visions, the only other skills Madame O passed down were doom-mongering and tailoring. At first she introduced me to the sewing-vacaya to distract me, to help cut my cackle in sweatshop conditions – but she unleashed a monster ...

Juno upon juno she would stagger downstairs and demand I darn her brutalised stockings, raise her hems, revolutionise her silhouette – but there was nothing I could do to help mend her ever-increasing paranoia. As the decade creepied onwards, the Mare's scatty visions only worsened. Her palavering took on an ever more fatalistic slant, injecting me with this cateva atomic fear and reckless carpe-diem claptrap I still feel to this juno ...

Pas Prêt-à-Porter

UN SKETCH

The scene is a poky kitchen at the bottom of a crumbling Victorian terrace in Stepney. The ceiling slopes down quite sharply from L to R. MADAME OVARY tips a bucket of grimy water down the plughole. It has been raining. The ceiling leaks. Mushrooms protrude from the walls like diseased nipples. Her son RAYMOND works frantically at an old sewing-machine down L. A blood-soaked umbrella stands by the sparkling hire-purchase English Electric Liberator up R.

Hanging over her grubby, but expensive skirt, Madame Ovary wears a cherry-red workshirt, but she manages somehow to look quite elegant in it.* Presently, she throws the bucket down.

MADAME OVARY. You're going so rapid you'll combust, Raymond!
RAYMOND. Does rayon burn easily, mother?
MADAME OVARY. I fathom so. Even sounds like that filth what killed the poor slopes at Hiroshima. Radium, was it not? Radon? Bof. That muck'll probably land here soon enough, if the rayon don't get you first. They say we'll burn in the heat of ten thousand suns, Raymond. We'll be drowning in a sea of fire. And if that don't do us in, well, there'll be thunderstorms of black rain. Black rain! Molten tar that is, son. Not like this stuff, grimy as it is.

She pours another bucket of rainwater down the plughole.

RAYMOND. Our house won't be hit. It dodged the geraldines' bombs, did it not?
MADAME OVARY. I dare say we'll lose this place to the H-bomb sooner than to slum clearance, put it that way. Taking their sweet time, so they are, Ministry of Housing. Priorities elsewhere, no doubt. Fix up the bourgeois estates first. Not that I'm complaining, of course.
RAYMOND. Can't we stop them dropping the bomb, mother?
MADAME OVARY. Do we have a hotline to the Kremlin?
RAYMOND. Not that I'm aware of, ma.
MADAME OVARY. All we can do is sit tight, try to enjoy ourselves while we've still got our faculties, while we've still got the feeling in our limbs, in our erogenous zones. And if they

---

* While most of us understood Novak is aping the British New Wave/kitchen-sink dramas here, Trefoil (a better reader than editor) recognised that Madame O has stolen the workshirt worn by Alison Porter in *Look Back in Anger*. Note the play on 'Porter' in the title (our doing!).

don't drop the bomb, well, it's a slow death-by-Capitalism all the same. The big-wigs, they should be pumping money not into diabolical weaponry but into new technologies to liberate us proletarians, to free us from the back-bending brain-drain of hard travails!

RAYMOND. You work, mother?

MADAME OVARY. I'm speaking more generally, Raymond. The big-wigs, these eagle-beaked Capitalists, they've got the coffers to make drudgery a thing of the past. Let the machines do all the work. Then use the profits to pay us proles to sit back. But the fash bats prefer to keep us under the cosh. They don't like to share. A utopian future? Pah. Maybe in your lifetime you'll see it happen – I fear I won't in mine. So what else can we do? Bleed the present dry. Live for today because tomorrow, well, tomorrow we'll probably all be drowning in a molten whirlpool of tar: hairless, cancerous, teeth and bones turned to sand or broken glass. Hence me asking you to politely do one upstairs tonight, if you'd be so kind. I've got a guest coming round.

RAYMOND. A guest?

MADAME OVARY. Don't play ignorant with me, son. You understand what your mother means. My period of sleeps.

RAYMOND. Why not enjoy this one in the boudoir, the chamber intended for sleeps?

MADAME OVARY. Because every time the bed shakes, we get plaster, rainwater, wallpaper, bits of bloody masonry falling on our heads. It's somewhat unromantic ...

FIN

As I grew older, I savvied the Old Woman frequently bastardised the Surrealists' ideas for her own selfish gratification. POR EXAMPLE: In the automne of 1922, the Surrealists embarked on what they called their 'époque des sommeils' or 'period of sleeps': a series of molto cerebral slumber parties that involved daffy séances in cafés or their latties as they sharpered for voches from the beyond. Experimenting with auto-screeve, trance states and psychotic jibber-jabber, the aim of these séances wasn't to communicate with the dead but to liberate the unconscious, to throttle to life all the dormant beasties and weirdy feelings lurking in the murky depths of their servos.

Madame O had her own period of sleeps in the late 1950s, but hers simply involved sleeping with as many omis as she could get her luppers on. She claimed it was free love, but I got the impression she was making dinarli with her flange-levers. I was banished upstairs whenever she came home with a nova lover, so I couldn't tell for certain whether she was charvering spivs or aristocrats, but these visits from my temporary Dadas often coincided with extra luxuries on the munjarry-table.

Along with the dinarli, toff munja and glittery groinage, the Madame's lovers also gave her some less welcome gifts: racy spermatozoomers. She fell pregnant time and time again, and I took it she wasn't molto enamoured by the success of her first-born by the way she terminated all the rest.

Madame Ovary had a Catholic's approach to contraception, and a Satanist's approach to abortion. Depending on how far gone she was, she'd fizz Coca-Cola up her hortus, schonk herself repeatedly in the kishkas, soak in a scalding mustard-biddy or jam the end of a brolly up her uterus until it rained pieces of foetus.*

Only once did I vada a broken-up lullaby-cheet. The petty pop was laid out on a vonny dishcloth, yellowish and spatchcocked with the tet on a separate platter. I didn't clock it was humanoid at first. I mewed like a kitty, salivating brootish. I was so used to my Mare's meshigena cookery, I wrongly ponced it was a marinated poussin with eels or somesuch exotic carnish. I was already chomping on its left lally when Madame O exploded. Uno

---

* Backstreet abortions were rife in the kitchen-sink dramas of the late 1950s/ early 1960s. The hot bath/sharp implement method wasn't uncommon, but Stanley's preferred technique was to induce labour with a saline shot direct to the amniotic sac and then to soothe with strong painkillers. £40. Discreet service.

bijou lupper dropped from my oyster. Her screeching caused a morso of cornice to drop from the ceiling.

BOF.

While there were nix ethics or morality taught in the Château, I rapidly savvied there were some cheets Madame O felt a chavvy shouldn't vada. Love, above all, was an alien concept to me back then. Whenever she brought a nova lover over to the latty, it sounded like the Old Mare was being strangled – and sometimes even enjoying it. Her honks and wheezy gurgles invaded my revs. Whereas before I'd enjoyed stiffening over a tranquil stream of fortuni smooth fantoms, I now pictured a butch-omi twistering the Madame's tet off while the two of them writhed about the floor like rabid abattoir beasties. What were the zots doing down there? Was this twisted love the norm? Before long, my filthy aggro-revs got so distressing I felt the only way to reset my servo was to vada for myself what goes on when an omi and palone make a baby.

Twas a midsummer noche, a gross fructish humstinker. Madame O had gone out to the bungery in her nova rayon drogle, Sophia Loren opal-shades and mandrill maquiage. More often than not she'd come home with some beery omi and make the strangling sounds, and so I decided this noche to conceal myself under the kitchen sink, ready for their return. I clambered into a grandiose Omo box, scissored a pair of ogle-holes and stuck a colander atop my tet. I snapped on Le Bâtard's gendarme goggles, in case of squirty entrails or flying quong-sirop.

I'd been boxed up quatra hours by the time the Madame finally SPLATCH!ed back into the Château with her latest conquest, cackling: 'Hé-hé-hé-hé-hé!'

She poked her eek into the kitchenette furtively, then dragged the spiv inways by his oyster-levers, kissing him furious. They were both drenched – twas parnying heavily outdoors, with the odd crackle of cloud-electric.

My boomboomer sped up as they scrabbled out of their wet schmutta. Madame O changed into a cozzy I'd never vadared before, which was mostly chains and skimpy schvartz leather. The omi was naggy now except for his stampers and almond-rocks, though he'd left his cravat on: probably some prole dandy stubbornness – or just forgetfulness.

Blinking through the steamy goggles, I learned a lot about baby-making that noche: the palone begins by whipping the omi until his corybungus turns blue, she insults him, she tries first to get pregnant down her gargler, he makes goose sounds, she shoves the tiplet of the brolly up his sphincter, opens and shuts it several times, then the palone becomes almost like a piggy, oinking on her lappers and lally-caps before the omi finally mounts her.

'Groin-groin! Groin-groin!' she exclaimed, snuffling brootish, her fizzer pressed to the grubby lino.

I watched with a twisted eek as the spiv rode my Old Woman round and round the lino, thrusting his beige bushy colin in and out of her parping flange, the pair of them grunting and 'Groin-groin'ing and knocking over utensils. There was a toilet stench coming from them both, and toilet sounds. I'd been half expecting to get a colin myself, but the manky spectacle rapidly threw aqua on my arousal. Does it need to be stated I wasn't arthuring away in that box?*

---

* The alert reader will have noticed that the story has presently taken a rather lewd turn. To help lower the temperature somewhat, now seems as good a time as any to address some Conservative legislation of the post-war years. Summer 1959 saw the passing of the Obscene Publications Act: a law that has cast a large asterisk-shaped shadow over our company ever since. Pre-1959, the three founders of the Glass Eye Press were engaged in the smuggling and distribution of outlawed 'grubby books' produced across the Channel: Dutch picturebooks mostly, or baffling yellow-jacketed novelettes written in salacious, slithery French. After the Act was passed, British publishers were now permitted to produce their own homegrown erotica, providing the work possessed that most slippery of qualities: 'literary merit'. We set up our own little publishing house at once. Many of our (blind!) detractors may argue that not an iota of literary merit exists in our entire back catalogue – however, we never print gratuitous sex and violence for gratuity's sake. What, dear reader, is your opinion of *Mister Asterisk* thus far? Do you consider the book obscene? Does it not at least reveal

'Baise-moi sur la Formica!' Madame O demanded with the filthy gamp betwixt her pearls. 'Groin-groin! Baise-moi sur la Formica!'

'You what?'

'The Formica! Do me on the kitchen unit, you silly sod.'

'Right you are.'

The parny-storm hushed on the fenêtres as Madame O clambered onto the soiled countertop on all-quatras. The spiv, a petty Napoleon-omi, had all the enthusiasm but alas none of the lally-length. He struggled to reinsert himself, grimacing, yanking at the Old Zelda's riah, desperately cocking his stubby lallies to nix avail.

'Get on the box! Hop on the box! Allez, allez!' the Mare urged, gesturing at the grandiose Omo box cowering under the sink.

Ô Jupiter. Does it need to be screeved: the spiv's arva-hunger instantly evaporated when he lunged for my Cubist cocoon and clocked duey glistening opals blinking up at him through the efinked portholes. His prick shrivelled like a poked-up turkey wattle.

'What is it?' my Mare demanded. 'Allez ... ALLEZ!'

The spiv flick-flicked a quivery lupper in my direction. As I tried to shrink backways into the munge of the box, the colander fell from my tet, clattering to the ground.

'Un espion!' Madame O screeched. 'A spy! A mole!' She leapt off the countertop and scurried back into the safety of the pantry, meanwhile urging the spiv on with demonic spittle: 'Kill him! Where's Raymond?! ACHTUNG! KILL HIM! ALLEZ!'

---

bright flashes of literary merit amidst all the shadowy writhing bodies and 'groin-groin'ing degeneracy? We, of course, must argue that it does. We insist that these rather pungent scenes of conception and abortion are integral to the plot (or will become so, in these footnotes at the very least ...), even if Emily, Audrey and McKinley (our own legal advisor, a so-called 'man of the world'!) felt uneasy reading such descriptions as 'parping flange' and the raining of 'pieces of foetus'. We can only apologise if any of you are offended thus far, but please remember: political correctness is not the default setting of any animal. Cross your legs, dear comrades, and read on.

The spiv swished on the spot, his eek like a forlorn parrot's.

'KILL HIM!' my Mare bansheed. 'This is a trespasser! The State wants to evict us! The State wants to eliminate us! YOU MUST KILL HIM! KILL HIM!'

To this juno I cannot fathom if my Mare was merely testing the spiv's heroism, or if she savvied only too clear that it was yours truly in that accursed box, or if it was just plain daffiness to blame for her scatty mistake.

As the spiv sycophantically sharpered for a suitable instrument with which to pummel me to a rustique purée, I cowered dumbstruck in my primary-coloured cube. Had the spiv clocked the butchers' efinks glimmering on the draining board, my grand lavvy-story may have been terminated right here. As it fell out, the twonk's luppers alighted on an ajax potato-masher and, savvying I could probably hold my own against this somewhat primitive torture-vacaya, I hurled the Omo box topside-turvy and made a dash for the exit. En route to the back portal I was subjected to a frantic assault, the spiv windmilling and slicing the aero with drunken abandon, seemingly unfazed by the discovery that his prey was just a pogi adolescent troll in a drogle and piggytails. VLAM! SPLATCH! AÎE! At some point Le Bâtard chivalrously came to my aid, absorbing a bona few schonks and swipes before being violently cast from my lappers, landing just shy of the back doormat. Resigning myself now to a meese systematic mortification, I dropped to my lally-caps, curling up in the foetal posture with my eek tucked into my thrumming chest. Desperately I scoured my servo-banks for some last-ditch natty emag to overcome the vicious spiv, but ultimately twas my Mare's bloodcurdly overilluminated scream from the pantry – 'RAYMOND! PEEPING-DEVIL! BEGONE! BEGONE, YOU PERVERSE PETTY BATATAT!' – that wrongfooted my naggy assailant and allowed for my escape. Like an electroshocked gibbon, I scrambled wildly for the exit, accidentally stamping on Le Bâtard's startled eek as I battyflapped my way through the back portal and hurled myself outways into the thunderous coddy noche ...

Slum Clearance*

NOVAK WEARS FULL-EEK RUBBLE DUST, BATTENBERG-DROGLE, GENDARME GOGGLES, SABOTS AND PIGGYTAILS.

It was still warm out as I hoppety-hopped round our local play area: the chenta square yards of broken bricklets and latty-skeletons surrounding the Château Chanceux. The storm was over, but the rusty stink of thundercloud still clung to everything. Somewhere ajax a grupa of factories were churnering out a fantabulosa chemical sunset.

I rarely vadared any other poplos out here, but there was change coming to Stepney. Beyond the rubble-willets I clocked smoke rising from chimneys, the odd high-rise skytickler that wasn't there last time I blinked. I nellied other chavvies' voches – feeli fillies reering in the backyards of norm happy families – but I was forbidden to vagary thataways and join them.

Pausing for uno momento at the edge of a moony crater, I plucked a petty morso of fluff from the sole of my left sabot and savvied with some twistiness that it was Le Bâtard's handlebar mouser. The cheet must've come unstuck when I inadvertently stamped upon the poor batatat's eek in the heat of the battyfanging. I pressed the bijou moustache affectionately to my top lever, then, clocking that it smelled somewhat like a dicky pilchard, tossed it into the shadowy gaping O of the crater.

Le Bâtard had become a bona companion in recent months, absorbing my teeni aggro, playful torture and parny fits with

* Chapter received Monday, 24th November 1969 – 231 days to go.

unflinching opals. What the dummy lacked in conversation, it more than made up for in tolerance and obedience – and yet I couldn't help pining for a bona fide humanoid's touch as I trolled onwards, clambering up the crooked cod-Romanoid columns: these gross perilous rotten fangs of masonry that probably used to plot out the boudoirs of beautiful proles. Every juno the bombsite seemed different: a grotesque asbestos garden maze that shapeshifted with each spell of coddy weather. Lintels collapsed, lumps of grotty home-sweet-home rolled down the slopes, tentacles of plumbing waggled in the wind. I wondered if the government was trying to save dinarli, biding their time, hoping the elements might do the slum-clearing for them.

As I scrabbled to the peak of the toppermost rubble-willet, I felt more feral beastie than civilised civvy. My piggytails were like duey cateva serpents, my wolfy luppernails encrusted with a rancid unfamiliar sludge. I nellied the distant feeli filly reering again, somewhere ajax to a cluster of rosy-roofed latties and an industrial colin piping the aero with strawberry crème. Had that bijou donna been here, I wouldn't have been able to palaver with her anyway, of course. Mine and my Old Woman's tiny totalitarian state was unsuitable for outsiders – what with its specjalni lingo, all-pervading paranoia and resistance to norms – and I probably preferred it that way (knowing no other way). The feeli filly didn't sound like a threat but, the way my Mare went on, she'd sever my tet and jarry my servo just like the rest.

I felt the rubble-willet give way a pogi bit as I clocked the spiv leaving the Château, joshed-up full-dandy again with his trilby pulled snug over his ogle-riders. He didn't look all that poked-up but I savvied my peeping out from the Omo box had mortified the romance – if you could call that brutal display romantic. As with all the Madame's lovers, I hoped never to vada this twonk's unsavoury eek again – but was this just proof her anti-civvy palavering had worked, or was it bona fide envy that the spiv (and all those pops before him) had got closer to my Mare's meshigena boomboomer than I ever could?

The sky turned from rancid Chambord to billowing purple velvet as noche dropped. Perched atop the omi-made Matterhorn, I nellied more pogi rimbumbles rising from the city: the lowly hum of humanity, ssssshssssssshhhhhssssssshing pluplubashes,* birdies cheeping off-key lullaballads, idling caboosh engines, VadaVision murmur. This tranquil blank noise might've given the impression of a community at peace, were it not for the godawful riah-prickling shrieks piercing the aero somewhere immediately underneath my perch. At first I ponced it might be a critter in distress, a flapper or purring-cheet ferricadoozed by a malnourished fox or stray lightning-bolt – but then I clocked the humanoid expletives, the anglo-froggy distress call, and my thumper ached as I savvied it was my own dear mother caterwauling hysterical in the munge of the Château.

I wondered if it was romance after all. Then again, was I capable of recognising other pops' heartbreak back then? Her screechings were not dissimilar to the twisted war-cries she let out while aborting her unwanted bambinos. I pictured her in the kitchenette, shaking a cocktail of Coca-Cola and methylated spirits up herself, lallies akimbo. But was it possible to make (and break) a baby that rapid?

As I peered down at the lonesome latty, I couldn't vada the Old She-Wolf, but I soon had an inkling what she was howling about. There was a gross gaping fissure in the roof, causing a filthy aquafall in the master boudoir that was dragging the whole ceiling down with it. Occasionally the Madame's screeches were drowned out by a VLOP! or dull PFFF! of falling plaster downstairs.

---

* It took us an age to work out what 'pluplubashes' meant, coming across it only when Novak's increasingly unsettling screeve forced us to delve more deeply into the Dada and Surrealist manifestos of the 1910s and 1920s. This ssssshssssssshhhhhssssssshing lav sprouted from Hugo Ball's 1916 Dada Manifesto: 'Why can't a tree be called Pluplusch, and Pluplubasch when it has been raining?'

By this point we were used to the odd crumble, but I near enough vomited my own tongue when I vadared what happened next.

I remember it in sickly flickers. The Old Woman's parnying was gradually replaced by the groan of Panzers or grizzlies, then a sudden clatter-shattering of bricks as the Château Chanceux's luck ran out. The aqualogged roof went first, slumping with a shrill jazz-crackle of tiles. Then the chimney pots flopped, the fenêtres sparkled, and a dizzy mushroom cloud rose as the rest of the latty went under.

The reverbs were so thunderous I lost my footing on the rubble-willet, skittering downways on my corybungus, ripping the carnish from my thews and buttocks. Once I'd righted myself, I squawked for help with an oyster full of grit but, not knowing the exact anglo lav for 'Help!', I wasn't expecting any dolly muscular hero to materialise.

When I was feelier, Madame O had warned me of a few lavvy-threatening dangers in the Château: glimmers, efinks, revving in biddyaqua. She'd never mentioned that the latty itself might collapse – nor what the contingency emag was should she be fatally ferricadoozled.

For a few minutas I was an ice-omi, regarding the mushroom cloud blankly. I don't remember parnying at first. My gargler was dry. I had a full eek of rubble dust. Twisted Buster Keaton clown maquiage.

Lento lento I felt sick as the severity of the scenario unravelled in my servo. Turning away from the wreckage, I could just about vada the chemical skyline through the haze, the factory-pops still piping strawberry to the moon. The city frightened me, but I savvied my only option now was to go beyond the Château limits, to try to gather some local eagle-eeks to help drag the Old Zelda from her grave before it was too late, before it was made permanent. I waited another minuta for her to emerge from the dust cloud, but there were only the pogi silhouettes of metal pipettes twistering in the afterwhirl and prongs of battyfanged floorboards. A vulture or pigeon circled overhead, then flopped off elsewhere.

Pointing my platters in nix particular direction, I scarpered away from our poor ruined wasteland, the terrain rapidly turning from grey quicksand to dustbowl dirt tracks to cracked Vicky cobbles to smooth asphalte. What with the geraldines' extensive doodlebuggering, twas difficult to pinpoint the nattiest route to the hallowed Land of Milk and Honeybutter. Up ahead I clocked a cluster of rosy terraces still standing, but as I drew closer I savvied the gildi palaces were just empty shells like the rest. A mogue flimsy B-movie façade.

I screeched the lav my Old Woman used whenever she needed help – 'Garçon! Garçon!' – but there was nanti garçon to be found.

The Blank City.

Still, unless the toppermost eagles had already snuffled out and jarried all East Londres proles, I savvied soon enough I would stumble upon some form of Western civilisation. Gas lamps crushed and stretched my shadow as I creepied onwards. Rimbumblings of stuttering traffic and blown whistles swelled on the sooty aero. Following the din, I ducked under the chugging-tracks and eventually emerged in the munge of a meese brick hulk emblazoned with bizarre military slogans:

THE SOUND & THE FURY
HIROSHIMA MON AMOUR
OPERATION PETTICOAT
ROCK HUDSON
NORTH BY NORTHWEST
IMITATION OF LIFE

The fortress had nix fenêtres. Duey butch-omis were guarding the back portals in black uniforms with downturned oysters. It was tempting to scream 'Garçon!' at them, but instead I steered clear, savvying it was molto likely some grandiose sharpering-khazi or gaol or gas camp.

Given my Mare's somewhat one-sided palavering about the Westernoid welt, I was in a maxi skitterish mood now as

I penetrated behind enemy lines. Any minuta I expected the city to erupt ultra-brash and monstrous from behind the naff crumbly poorhouses, an all-honking, all-glittering unfairground of inequality: feathered toffs mincing about in animal skins, voodoo priestesses pushing gildi coffins brimful with dinarli, chain-gangs of proles hanging from glimmering gallows, suicidal bonarobas joshed-up as gay arva-machines, factories jarrying humanoid carnish, neon swirlies scalding the noche with endless gruesome symbols of ze Establishment: bowler-capellas, eagle talons, imperial mousers, the scolding index lupper, the condescending ogle-rider, REGURGITATE, CONSUME, REGURGITATE, CONSUME ...

My boomboomer was clashing horrifically as I dithered, considered backtracking, then boldly turned onto a brootish boulevard with the nom: COMMERCIAL ROAD. An apt nom, I ponced, given this was to be my first ogleful of the Capitalists in their natural habitat – and yet, as I savvied rapid enough, my screeching abdabs were unnecessary.

Commercial Road was thriving compared to the sterile dustbowl I'd come from – there were bungeries and bodegas open, trolleybuses and cabooshes growling on smooth asphalte, pops minnying about in identical worsted clobber – but what struck me mostest as I sprinted onwards was how harmless and frigid it all seemed in contrast to my Mare's doomy palavering. Sharpering desperately for L'HÔPITAL or the CROIX-ROUGE, I was a pogi bit bewildered at first by the nova meshigena anglo lavs frittying in my peripheral vision –

GLASS CUT TO SIZE
NO DANCING
DOUBLE DIAMOND
FREE HOUSE
WRIGHT'S COAL TAR SOAP
RUSSIAN VAPOUR BATHS
TURF ACCOUNTANTS

NO LOITERING

QUALITY QUICK FROZEN FISH!

– but all in all the strasse was memorable not so much for its chavvy-jarrying eagles, but for the blank, twisted expressions on practically every drab pop who crept past me.

Drawn in by the latty's throbbering strip-lights, I schonked my way through a pair of glassy portals marked VV and found myself in a vast supermercado teeming with malnourished robo-civvies. The bodega had its own baffling slogan – SAVE MORE AT VICTOR VALUE – and seemingly endless Perspex shelfloads of exotic produce (Tulip Chopped Ham, Pax Peach Halves in Syrup, Peppermint Aero), nix doubt plundered from distant battyfanged colonies. Brazenly I scuttled up to a dolly feeli couple examining a packet of fishfingers and screamed: 'GARÇON!'

They regarded me like I was an overgrown maggot, eeks scrunched and lappers drawn into their chests, shielding their vital organs. Madame O had warned me the anglos cannot abide coddy manners, but I fancy twas my appearance that startled them mostest. Despite my Mare's best efforts, my askew piggytails, ripped Battenberg-drogle and demolition maquiage did not give the impression of a norm well-adjusted petty filly.

'Garçon! C'est le Château!' I yelled. 'The Madame, mortified! The Château SHRACK, CRASH, SHEBAM, SPLATCH! Oui? Nein? The Madame mortified!'

'Pardon me?' the omi polled, puffing his chest out, creating a protective barrier between his wife and me.

'It's the Madame, la femme, my mad-Madame,' I repeated, still not molto comfortable with that lav 'mama'. I splurted: 'The Château, il pleut et CRASH, SHEBAM, SHRACK! Une grande catastrophe, my Madame mortified!'

'I'm terribly sorry, squire.' The omi scritch-scratched the side of his vonka. 'I'm afraid we don't have a tuppence to spare ...'

The couple seemed less interested in fingering their fishfingers now. They scuttled off down another slick blank corridor marked EGGS as if this were a matter of gross urgency, leaving me casting quatra twisted shadows under the searing bulbs.

PHENSIC
FAST RELIEF FROM
HEADACHES

Ô MERZ. With soggy sparkles drooping in my opals, I left the frigid Capital-pops to their glittering packaging and empty slogans, and slithered back the way I came. The parny finally started flowing heavily and my piggy shyka flew off altogether as I raced back through the tunnel with the chuggers skreeeeeeeeeeeering jeeringly overhead. I felt like I'd let my mother down, unable to find a comrade on a strasse bustling with poplos, and yet I savvied there still must be a chance of saving her solo. I crushed my luppers into fists as the asphalte turned back to cracked cobbles to dirt tracks to quicksand to rubble-willets again.

In a crisis, I savvy now adrenaline can endow any animal with gildi Übermensch powers. I prayed I had the strength to shift some rocks naggy-lappered and rescue my dear Old Zelda but, when I got back to where the Château once stood, the area seemed different somehow. The dust cloud had settled, coating everything in a thick off-white snow, and I couldn't tell which pile of bricks was ours. For una minuta I was convinced I was in the wrong place – perhaps I'd re-entered the wasteland from a different sideysnicket, or the implosion had reshuffled the rubble. I recognised certain morsos of debris and the burnt Belgian waffles of old latty-fronts, but there was nix indication the Château had ever been here, and no clue as to where it had gone.

I scrabbled hopelessly through the gross wreckage, ripping the palms of my lappers open, but there was nothing humanoid to be found and before long the drooping munge made sharpering impossible. I curled up in the remains of an old khazi – a hermit crab in a bombed-out shell – and forced sleep.

Ô, THE INGLORIOUS DEAD

I declared an indefinite period of mourning. Ogling backways, it's difficult to say if I was truly twisted, truly miserable about the Madame's mortification – or just fearful for the future. I felt maxi lonesome, true enough – but would I miss any of the gay cheets we'd done together in the past? Did I ever feel real love towards the Old Mare? Or will she always be just a meshigena machine in my memory, a pair of ovaries that accidentally spat out a monster?

'Mama,' I whispered. 'Mama mama mama.'

Nothing.

Nix.

Curled up betwixt the toilet bowl and a gross creepering wisteria, I once again took refuge in my revs, which were nix less sexualised even in this black period. I rejected reality, having ogled it up close now. I sweated and shivered through the fuzzy junos and noches, entertaining myself in a fantastical dreamworld far far away from the Capitalist tundra over thataways. I comforted myself with ever more outlandish visions of winky seahorses, many-lallied mannequins, Romanoid excess, pink-levered fleurs, Mademoiselle Marianne squirting the milk of liberty from her grand naggy copper-green willets. It seemed a perfectly agreeable gutter-lavvy at first, revving in my privvy hideyhole until the civvies finally decided to build a bona utopia upon this needy wasteland ajax. I pictured myself re-emerging triumphant from hibernation, crowned boy-king of this nova gildi paradise – however, the rev was abruptly cut short when I awoke medsa-way through the third noche, kishkas full-knotted and sweating icicles. In my feeli naivety I'd ponced I might be able to remain in suspended animation like a frozen froglet for as long as I liked – however, the hunger twangs were like a satanic fambler schonking me in the gizzard every other minuta. I wailed into the frigid rubble, unable to sleep nor dream nix longer. Ô, ACHTUNG and ALACK-O-DAY, et ceterarara. It crossed my servo that, had I been able to find the Madame's corpse, I could've jarried morsos of her bod and carried on hiding and dreaming for at least another month or duey. Uno final act of true love: consuming my creator! But it wasn't to be. There was always the option of a permanent sleep, of course – SELF-OBLITERATION – but I wanted to live. I wanted to live!

I just wasn't quite ready yet for the coddy Western welt out thataways. Or was it that the mod mond wasn't ready for MOI?

I tried to force sleep once more, shush another bijou minuta or duey of sweet sickly dreams to help bolster me for whatever lay ahead – but ultimately it was the bitterfrosty aero, the cateva kishka-pains, and not least the evil stench of humanoid decay rising from some unknown morso of the wreckage that finally forced me back towards the city, back towards Commercial Road, and the mysterious mass-produced future I'd been avoiding all this time, until now ...

PART II

THE ESTABLISHMENT

'C'est vivre et cesser de vivre qui sont des solutions imaginaires. L'existence est ailleurs.'*

ANDRÉ BRETON, THE POPE OF SURREALISM

* 'It is living and ceasing to live that are imaginary solutions. Existence is elsewhere.' Epigraph scrawled in faint, quivery pencil.

A Sociable Beagle*

NOVAK WEARS HAND-ME-DOWN PYJAMAS, INCONTINENCE KNICKERS, NUMEROUS BRUISES.

They'd barely finished hosing my bod-fluids from the caretaker's brothel-creepers when I was dragged back into the Governor's bureau to face duey reptiles in juno-suits. Twas a queer office: a fogus-foggy salon stacked full of leatherbound livers and legal bimph,† with naff portraits of mortified Governors and a pair of antlers protruding from the oak cladding like duey gross petrified squirts of quong-sirop. The toff Vicky-era effect was beautifully ruined by a huge kidney-shaped avocado-green fibreglass desk, behind which the current Governor – a limp pallid fungus, like Bibendum if you sucked all the aero out of him – sat with the two lizards either side of him. One of the scaly legal-reps had riah the texture of treacle, the other the aura of having jarried only raw onion for a fortnight.

'Was ist das manky horrible odour?' I honked. I'd been at the hostel quatra months now and the concept of manners was still alien, hence the droppings in the caretaker's creepers – not to mention the startling drawings the pops were yet to find in the Sisters' privvy chapel.

---

* Chapter received Friday, 28th November 1969 – 227 days to go until Novak's fantabulosa crime.

† 'Legal toilet roll is the literal translation, so I believe,' Howling offered. 'Somewhat like your credentials, isn't that right, McKinley?'

The Hostel for Young Boys wasn't far from the Château, in the munge of the chugging-tracks on a strasse named STEPNEY CAUSEWAY. The latty had been set up in the nineteenth century by a grupa of toffee do-gooders as a sort of sanitarium or gaol for sick chavvies, feeli-delinquents and orphans – and so I fitted the bill fantabulosa.

'Raymond! What have we said about respect for one's elders?' the Governor rasped, a thatch of blank riah flapping like a trap-door atop his tet.

The Governor wasn't all cod, though it had taken some time to convince him and his comrades I existed – even in spite of me flagrantly juddering and potty-oystering the morn I appeared on their fuckering doorstep.

When finally the authorities found evidence of Madame O in the rubble, they wanted me to identify her decapitated tet before burying it again in a pauper's grave in some grim armpit of Stepney. I wasn't invited to the ceremony. The sharpering-pops parkered me off pronto to the Hostel for Feeli-Omis, but as far as the State and social services were concerned, I didn't exist. I was a fantom. The Governor wouldn't accept responsibility for me without a birth certificate, plus my anglo-froggy lingo didn't help convince them I was British made.

After some bureaucratic tugging-and-warring, the court agreed to exhume Madame O's tet and I was taken to l'hôpital for a sang-sample, which they compared against the corpse's. Fortunately I was deemed to be a close relative of this rotting monster. The State issued me with a birth certificate, this specjalni sheet to make the fantom visible at last, and from then onwards there was an almighty onslaught of drilling and grilling, medical probing, civilising-by-slipper-sole. I was registered with a quack, inoculated against a rainbow of diseases they probably imagined I already had, and then finally welcomed into the hostel with as much enthusiasm as a lattywife allowing a hippopotamus loose in her pantry.

This was existence!

'The boy speaks any English?' Spinks, the treacle-riahed omi asked as the crispy dawn lento dazzled through the fenêtres.

'Of sorts. He's learning,' explained the Governor. 'Certainly Raymond is slow for a fifteen-year-old, his brain seems tuned to a lower frequency, but remember this lad was more feral hound than upstanding gentlechild when we rescued him. These words he uses, it's almost pidgin English, peasant Gallic, but we'll shake it out of him eventually! We've been making strides – slow but purposeful strides – in teaching this little critter decorum, etiquette, his Ps and Qs. We call it the Pygmalion Effect. The lad was barely worth looking after when he came here, but we shall make a gentleman of him yet!'

I've approximated the palavering here. For months the lingo-barrier was like banging my tet against the Rosetta Rock and drawing blood. I savvied clear enough twas a specjalni privilege or punishment being dragged in before the Governor and the suits, but on this particular juno I was more interested in the cheets on the desk than the lavs spilling from their garglers.

'Look – some recognition! Christmas has come early, Raymond, yessum? Or not at all?' Gramble, the onion-omi polled, referring to that festival of Capitalism-in-Christ's-Clothing I still don't understand.

While the authorities had failed to find the rest of the Madame's broken-up bod, they'd managed to recover Le Bâtard, our sewing-vacaya and the Old Woman's French chequebook from the scatty wreckage. My dear ventriloquist's dolly looked more distressed than usual – vonka broken, trenchcoat torn, fangs missing and lallies back-to-front – but miraculously the sewing-vacaya was in perfect nick, tucked up under its grubby wooden dust cover.

'Bon bon bon BON!' I screeched, lunging for Le Bâtard.

'Don't touch, Raymond!' the Governor shrieked. 'The formalities, the formalities! There are certain procedures, administrative formalities to get through first ...'

I regarded him with gloopy opals.

'Just sign here, here and here,' ordered Mr Spinks. 'Today's date here and initial here. Countersign Form B, date at the bottom, print name here, here, here, and finally sign here, then the sewing-machine and – sign here – this handsome puppet are all yours, Raymondchild. We'll keep hold of the chequebook.'

'Was there any gent?' I asked, squirting my signature like a burst of violent squid ink across the legal bimph.

'Pardon?'

'The chequeliver. Did the Madame leave me any gent? Argent? Any silver, any monies, monsieurs, monsters, misters?'

The legal-reps squinted at my scrappy rags.

'Whatever capital we find, Raymond, we'll keep it nice and warm in a big fluffy trust fund for you,' Gramble gurgled.

'Fantastique!'

'Payable on your twenty-first birthday. Something to cling onto, eh, yessum, something to look forward to, no?'

They were humouring me, I understood that much. Back in the semi-safety of the Château, back before I had my existence signed, stamped and straitjacketed, I felt I was lavvying on a par with the gods but, since being admitted to the hostel, I savvied all too clear I was a third-rate civvy, a serf, a nonentity. I filled my incontinence knickers with warming yellow while the Governor continued: 'Come now, Raymond, we're not here just to talk money and swap gifts, lovely as they may be. There's something else the lawyers want to tell you.'

'Ô?'

'Do you like dogs, Raymond?' Spinks asked, chewing on a fangpick.

The other reptile answered for me: 'We all like dogs, but not ALL dogs. Yessum?'

'It's a modern world out there, Raymond. You're a creature of the city, a gutter child, isn't that right? You've lived here all your life?'

As the omis palavered round in circles, I became aware of a pogi humbuzzering swirling somewhere in the bureau. The Governor rasped: 'Say yes, Raymond.'

'Yes,' I polled.

'Now, you understand we've been looking for a foster family to take care of you at this, shall we say, critical stage in your upbringing,' Gramble carried on. 'But picture the scene if you will: a young, bright, well-bred, genteel family visit an abandoned dogs' home, looking for a new pet, an addition to the family. They might have in their minds a sociable beagle, a loyal Labrador, a charming terrier to match the soft furnishings. Do you follow?'

'Um. Ruff ruff rruff RUFF!' I yapped. I let my lingum hang out, still molto distracted by the swirling humbuzzing, which I clocked now was coming from a pair of bluebotties jiving through the aero. 'Ruff RUFF!'

'It's a modern world out there,' Mr Spinks repeated. 'In London, living space is at a premium. The affluent society strives for a stress-free existence. New-fangled machinery and gadgetry have relieved us of some of the monotony of housework, has it not? You wouldn't know. But, likewise, given the choice, any city-dweller wishing to bring a new pup into their home would always plump for the cheerful, sociable, bright-eyed golden retriever over the drooling, unhinged, rabid Rottweiler. Agreed?'

I sucked the hanging drool back into my gargler. 'Ruff?'

'The unruly dog, the Rottweiler, has no place in the modern urban household, Raymond,' added Mr Gramble. 'No family would allow such a beast to shake up their already well-shaken domestic life.'

'Do you understand what they're implying, what they're saying to you, old bean?' the Governor asked me.

I responded in my best toffee anglo: 'If I savvy right, I'm free to stay here at l'hôtel, the hostel forever. I'm not allowed out, nix exterior lavvying for Raymond. Stay in the dorm, in my privvy chamber, rev the junos away. Don't bite, no drool. Caca outdoors from now on. Je comprends mightily well. It suits me, monsters, mistresses. It suits me gladly.'

'No – that's not it!' Gramble squawked, flapping his lappers, moulting scaly scabs from his camisha-cuffs. 'That's not it at all!'

'Listen to us, Raymond.' Spinks again. 'Answer us this: where does a wild dog feel most at home?'

I shook my tet, poking my bottom oyster-lever out. The humbuzzering seemed to rise in pitch as I blinked dumbly at the baffling twonks. 'Destroyed, sir? Mortified? Put down?'

'No! Honestly! Out in the fields is the answer!' Mr Gramble exclaimed. 'No? Yes? Yessum! Out in the fields!'

'Out in the fields?'

'Yessum! With our – and God's – help, you'll be free to run wild in the Garden of England. To frolic, to chase butterflies and bunny rabbits, free to see the stars, to look at a cow, to experience country life to the full out of harm's way, all with one small proviso: that you abide – to the letter – by the laws of your new proud parents, the most venerable Lord and Lady Foster-Newman.'

The Governor let out a pogi girlish squeak, clapping his lappers together. 'Oh, listen to that, Raymond! Did you hear that? The countryside, Raymond! The bloody English countryside!'

I savvied it was relief on his part more than bona fide thumperthundering enthusiasm. The legal-reps' tongues zipped out of their grinning oysters and schlumphed the humbuzzing bluebotties right out of the aero.

Schlumph crunch crunch crunch.*

---

* This bureaucratic farce appealed to us immensely! In the latter half of the Sixties, with the Glass Eye Press haemorrhaging money and looking almost certain to fold, Trefoil and Merritt would often pine for the good old days before the 1959 Obscene Publications Act, when they worked underground, supplying the bookshops of Soho with all manner of contraband Continental erotica and raking in a handsome return. The smuggled books were devoid of any literary merit (in fact, many contained no words whatsoever), but never did the pair fall foul of the fuzz. The Dirty Squad ran Soho like a protection racket, accepting cash-filled handshakes in exchange for blind eyes. It was only when we set up our own (legitimate!) publishing house in 1959 (and the Dirty Squad likewise cleaned up its act) that our troubles began. We were better off working in the shadows. Under the new law, if a book is deemed to be obscene, its printers and stockists are considered as guilty as its publisher – and so many printing companies refused to ink our stinking stories, forcing us to go to less

reputable outfits, who often botched the job. For years our pocketbooks were so badly made that Merritt was forced to pretend it was an intentional design choice – 'These books are so groundbreaking, so hazardous they self-destruct after – sometimes even during – reading' – but nevertheless neither high-street nor low-brow booksellers agreed to stock our releases. The lack of pictures – or overload of startling avant-garde literary innovation – ultimately doomed our books to failure. We perfumed our filth with flowery prose only to keep on the right side of the censors but, of course, they weren't our target audience. We should've stayed underground. Our readers weren't concerned with literary merit – they just wanted abundant cocks, cunts and titties. Our delusions of literary grandeur cost us dearly. 'Come now, Stanley, we're not here just to talk money ...' one might sigh, but as Stanley's savings have shrivelled, his outlook has soured. There were many more reasons the company was almost bankrupt when Novak got in touch in October 1969, but we'll bore you with those in time. However, it might be worth noting for now that, while the Obscene Publications Act was a nuisance that plagued us throughout the Sixties, it was a different bit of legislation – the Abortion Act 1967 – that ultimately plunged our company into financial disarray ...

Pater Unfamiliar*

NOVAK WEARS A MONOCLE, BLACK FROCK COAT WITH BLANK TUX-DICKY AND GREY LALLY-COVERS. A FLEUR IN HIS BUTTONHOLE, A DAZZLING SILK HAT AND PATENT LEATHER BOOTIES COMPLETE THE EFFECT.

'And did you pass your eleven-plus, Raymond, dear?'

We were standing stiff on the snowy willet like bijou wedding-cake figurines, myself and the venereal Lord and Lady Foster-Newman, waiting for their seven sprats to return from boarding skol for Christmas. From the top of the blank slope we could vada the solo strasse in and out of the Foster Estate, and the Pile itself a few acres to the east, this chubby anachronistic choco-box with a thatched roof and omi-servants in some desolate dolly corner of the Kent countryside.

'Lux flakes mustard-salz poussin douche Electric Liberator!' I answered. The Foster-Newmans were fond of parping prayers and poesies at one another across the munjarry-table, and so I'd started screeching my own automatic verses at them whenever the questioning probed my tet too sharply.

'Tsk. That television's rotting his brain. Look, Raymond. Look!' the Lady declared, pointing a leather lupper at a distant schvartz caboosh whining down the winding road.

---

* Chapter received Monday, 1st December 1969 – 224 days to go. In the early hours that morning, news broke of the 'HIPPIE KILL CULT' arrested in California for the Tate/LaBianca murders.

'Think of the publicity, McKinley,' we cried. 'Raymond and his devotees could be the British equivalent. Think of the publicity. Think of the money!'

'It's like it's like it's like la voiture what take away the Madame. Or the mortified Madame's tet at any rate,' I commented, not yet aware that the Lord and Lady didn't appreciate me cackling about death or my past lavvy or decapitated tets or suchlike.

After a fortnight at the Pile, I hadn't enjoyed much interaction with the pair. It seemed they preferred to ignore anything mally, poky or lowly – pissoir-humour, outpourings of emotion, the omi-servants in their mufti – and for the most part they ignored me too. I wasn't sure if the toff-classes even cacked or piddled, the way they crinkled at me whenever I brought up perfectly norm bod-functions. I pondered perhaps privileged snakes like themselves excreted by shedding their skins, and twas the omi-servants' or gardener's travails to bury these cocoons in the fields at the week-ends.

Though I didn't vada it in quite so many lavs back then, the Foster-Newmans showed symptoms of chronic Conservatism from the off. Their schmutta was grave-robbed from the Edwardians, God oversaw their social lavvies and massaged their coddy uptight moral backbones, and His Lordship in particular had this meese imperialistic superiority over any pop he deemed lower or muckier-eeked than himself. The bats weren't ultra frigid-hearted, but I soon saw they treated their spawn to the same tight-levered tough love they swatted me away with. Like the staff at the Hostel for Feeli-Omis, their lavvywish was to be respected and feared – and not be touched or palavered at out of turn.

'Now, Raymond, you're ready to introduce yourself to the rest of the Foster-Newmans as a proud Foster-Newman thyself?' the Lady asked, her eek like Pascal's death mask in a Jayne Mansfield wig. 'You remember your lines?'

'Yes, Ma'am.'

The schvartz caboosh pulled up with a SHTUCK! at the bottom of the lump we were peering from. Twas a grandiose contraption, with seven doors and tinted fenêtres. The feeli

Fosters were clearly too weak to open the doors after all that gildi expensive education, and so the gangling chauffeur had to hop out and do the honours himself, tet dipped in reverence or just the cold.

As the chavvies cascaded out of the de-luxe hearse, my boomboomer quickened. For some reason I'd presumed the setta sprats would be boys, having been surrounded by only danglers in the Vicky Hostel. True enough, the first duey eeks to emerge were male, with gross Roman-vonkas and donkey pearls, and a pogi bit older than me. But then came their sisters: a fantabulosa daisy-chain of caramel-riahed, peach-eeked donnas in skol schmutta. The clobber was as detestable a uniform as I'd ogled, but the eeks! Ô, the feeli bods and dolly buttery eeks! I hadn't set opals on palones such as this before in all my petty lavvy.

Instantly I forgot about the cold. The snow now seemed to froth and bubble beneath my platters, as if the willet was suddenly brandy sauce or simmering quong-sirop, and I let myself be swept down the slope towards them. Or possibly I threw myself.

'Ruff ruff rrruff ruff RUFF!' I yapped, losing my top hat as I scamper-scarpered down the hillock. I lost more schmutta as I lost my footing, my lally-covers frittying down round my ankles, tux-dicky unravelling up to my chin and monocle yo-yoing willety-nilly.

Ogling backwards, I was probably a pogi bit overeager to meet my nova sisters. I wanted to gobble the jolly fillies up pronto, as if they were somehow a reward for all my cateva trials and troubles so far – but, like their parents, the donnas didn't want to be touched. They scuttled backways with crumply brows and clamped asterisk oysters as I collapsed eek-down at their stampers.

I was dowri tempted to sink my fangs into their ankles – or even fling my tet direct up their fusty jupes – but the unexpected garglerful of snowsparkles woke me from my wet rev. I coughed out a few icicles and glanced up at the feeli-palones, their opals wide and horrified. The snow turned yellowy around me as I pissed myself in clumsy twisted spasms. I blinked up their toffee-vonkas and spluttered my practised lines: 'How d'you do. Um. A pleasure to meet you all. Raymond Novak, Foster, Foster-Newman. Your most gracious and grateful and humble nova brother.'

'Trousers up, boy,' the Lady tsked – and that was the closest I would get to the fortuni batatats until Christmas Day.

In the weeks leading up to Jesus's specjalni juno, the feeli Foster fillies steered clear of me. As a result, I'm struggling now to remember my siblings' real noms or pinpoint solo personalities. I remember them more as a shapeshifting grupa, a misty tank of bona-vadaring gerbils, some with delicious creamy bods and some with horrific pimply cateva-carnish. For the sake of the coherence of this liver, we might as well christen them Liesl, Friedrich, Louisa, Kurt, Brigitta, Marta und Gretl.

They'd all passed their eleven-pluses, that slippery golden lappershake or servoshake granting them access to the grandest privvy skols on the island. They were molto likely destined to be legal-reps or crocuses or politicos: pops whose travails it was to look out for other pops, despite being taught to look out only for themselves all their feeli lavvies. They were tight-fisted with their toys, they used polysyllabic lavs I didn't understand, and the feeli-palones undressed in peep-proof conditions. In other lavs: stuck-up petty addle-plots.

While the Lord and Lady ignored us all equally and unconditionally, I certainly felt like the runt. The fact that I hadn't passed this daffy eleven-plus was clearly an insult to the Foster-Newmans. I savvy now the Governor must've mogued or misled them about my qualifications and temperament. The toffs pretended to be happy to have me in their latty for Christmas, but nix doubt they'd intended to parker me off to some boarding skol come spring term and catapult me all the way to Oxbridge come summer – and then just forget all about me.

When they found out I was hollow between the nells, the Lord and Lady made nanti attempt to home-school me, only grimace and tut-tut at pogi details of my teeni existence (schmutta, grammar, hygiene, posture, toilette habits, potty oyster), and let the omi-servants do the rest. I sometimes ponder if I was there only to soothe a mid-lavvy crisis, or as a zoo-omi: a low-class chavvy to be scrutinised, pitied and ponced over until they got bored of me.

Locked away in the attic, I spent most junos sewing fantastical cozzies for myself and Le Bâtard (Mao suits, mink-fur bikinis, Bonnie and Clyde, Leopold and Loeb, Henley Regatta, the Papin sisters, doppel-headed serpents and spermatozoomers ...), and my noches stitching together snatched glances of the Foster fillies into grand randy rev-tapestries. I only interacted with my nova family at the munjarry-table, recharging my kishkas with rich grub before retiring back upways for more needlework and solo-love. It wasn't a bad lavvystyle, and I wasn't ultra twisted about the lack of attention and affection. In truth I would've gladly stayed put, quietly jarrying and arthuring myself to an early grave, safe in the knowledge I'd successfully swerved skol and The Travails and all other trappings of mod Capitalist lavvying – but then the Christians and Colonics turned up ...

The choco-box erupted on Christmas Day. I was awoken by the stench of roasting flesh and cackling imperialists, the cut-glass voches so sharp they could've rolled tets. I dug my greasy eek into the pillow, trying to prolong my latest recurring rev (chasering a naggy statue of Mercury through a misty forest of erect spluttering orchids), but as the rimbumbling escalated I savvied it wasn't going to be the usual juno of tight levers and passive-aggro.

I dollied myself up in an ultraschvartz waistcoat and harem-panties fatchared from an ajax pair of curtains, then minnied debonairly downstairs, leaving Le Bâtard lazing languorously on the Chippendale dresser. Following the von of frazzled chestnuts and colonic spices, I near enough choked on my own lingum when I entered the morning chamber and clocked the army of brash dignitaries clogging the floorboards. The twonks were like overgrown toy soldiers: omis with bushy mousers and sideyboards in meese brigadier cozzies, twats in bowler-capellas and blazers with scatty Latin slogans attached, plus the odd cloth-pop trying his bestest to look meek in his flouncy cassock and bedazzling groinage.

Savvying what I savvy now, I should've greeted these nutcrackering batatats with thrown cobblestones and/or Molotov cocktails, but instead I just mumbled, 'Hullo there,' and schlumphed down my malted milk at doppel-speed like every other juno.

'Merry Christmas!' seemed to be the nova greeting as the gay eeks squinted at me.

'Who's this handsome chappy?' one of the yeomanry twats polled.

'O, Raymond. Stand up straight, dear,' the Lady said through gritted lippy. 'Not a blood Foster-Newman, naturally.'

'Not with that piggy nose!'

'We've taken him in from the orphanage for Christmas.'

'Ah! The charity continues!'

'We do our bit!'

'Intriguing dress sense! Is this what they're wearing in the East End these days, old bean?'

'Haw haw! Aw hooey!' was the general response to me standing there looking frankly fantabulosa in their own fuckering soft furnishings.

Still, I was poked-up about them ridiculing my oink-vonka – especially coming from these Roman-nose twonks. I think the Roman beak is the defining feature of the fascist eagle-eek, harking back as it does to Nero and Caligula and all the original eyetie imperialists of the Holy First Reich.* These toff-omis all

---

* Given Novak's somewhat uneven education, it's perhaps unsurprising that he muddles his ancient history here. The Holy Roman Empire (adulated by Hitler

had one, nostrils brimming with riah. In contrast, the Capitalists' wives had button-vonkas, the dolly palones joshed-up festive with sparklies and holly pinned to their Laura Ashley drogles like they'd been buried up to their necks in a flowerbed. They were immaculate zeldas, but I rapidly lost interest when the five feeli Foster fillies appeared. They entered the morn chamber in order of height, shortest to grandest, with lappers linked and dainty platters skip-skipping like ballerinas or paper dollies efinked from the pages of some high-class skin-glossy. Yet again their schmutta was deplorable – huge cherry bakewell drogles and Arctic stockings – but twas the savagery that they were naggy under that clobber, coupled with the savagery that this looked set to be a juno of meshigena unbridled excess, that made my servo glow like a radioactive green GO sign ...

Just after mid-juno we were ushered into the banqueting chamber, where a long table had been set up for this Saturnalian beanfeast or recreation of the Jesus-omi's last slurp. A prayer was belched by the omi in the cassock, then the pregnant* Queen Liz herself babbled a few lavs through the crystal set or VadaVision or whichever vacaya was popular among the toffee-classes at the time.

Given the extra corybunguses, there was no place set for me at the table. After the natty anthem I was sent to skulk in the munge of the chimney breast, where there was uno bijou doily laid out on the floor and heksa pairs of cutlers. The Foster-Newmans swapped gifts with the cloth-plops and military brass (I was thrown a gross bricklet entittled ENCYCLOPAEDIA ROSBIF, some musty old liver in a lingo I still don't fully understand), then finally a bell closhed and the omi-servants appeared with a grand lump of carnish on a silver platter.

---

as the 'First Reich') was formed in 800AD upon the crowning of Charlemagne as Emperor – a good 750 years after Nero and Caligula. But then again, fascists and fantasists alike have no qualms about rewriting history for their own ends ...

* His modern history (or at least his memory) is much better. Prince Andrew was onboard, Christmas 1959.

'Ladies and gentleman: the nine-bird roast!' the head slave screeched.

The golden lump turned out to be a quail with a saucisson stuck up its arse, stuffed inside a partridge in a woodcock in a guineafowl in a duck in a chicken in a pheasant in a turkey, all dripping with honeybutter and quack-sweat. I couldn't help reering twistily, imagining the poor holidayless cooks backstage, trying to create the dish with live flappers and nix lubrication.

'Astonishing!'

'Bravo!'

'All hail the nine-birdy roast! Haw! We thought: one bird to symbolise each member of the Foster-Newman family!' the Lady screamed somewhat unfairly – unless she was insinuating I was the saucisson stuffed up wee Gretl's aristotle.

'Breathe, child, breathe!' one of the Capitalists – a Sir Tweezers-Please or Bottomly-Rambunctious or other naff doppel-barrel – remarked, spluttering morsos of quacker at me. 'This is grub to be savoured, not shovelled down the gullet like gruel.'

'The chap holds his cutlery like a chimp!' a Colonel chipped in.

'And his pudding fork at that.'

'Do you know. How to use cutlery? Would you prefer. To use your grubby fingers?'

'Or perhaps his feet!'

'Aw haw hooey!'

Despite only a grumbler or duey of vino, the Christians and Colonics were 'squiffy' or 'squifferoony': lavs they used continually that juno to excuse their arroganki Coliseum-nostril behaviour.

'Shall we get him a coal shovel?!' Sir Noxious-Bottomfeeder again.

I glanced at the chinka feeli-palones, half expecting them to come to my rescue, but they were as tight-levered as ever. For una minuta I felt betrayed, but then I savvied the trust and love we'd built over the past few weeks was only in my revs. The sloppy embraces we shared, the tender lammers, the relentless probing of ambiguous sexual organs – the donnas had no real part in it.

'Then to finish off – pick the gristle out from his teeth with a chimbley sweep's brush!'

Though I was shaking a pogi bit, I put my efink and pudding fork down tranquil and asked the Lord and Lady with the utmost composure: 'May I please be excused to minge my dinner in my chamber, please?'

'Haw haw HAW HAW hoo!'

'My word, that was almost perfect Queen's from the lad! With one rather startling error, my boy!'

'Minge minge, minge munching! Aw phooey!' The Colonel again.

'You'll sit here with us and you'll enjoy your roast birdies,' the Lady hissed. 'And stop writhing around like you're infested.'

By the end of the ordeal I was somewhat in the mood to scream into a ditch or have my tet trampled underfoot by the beasties in the fields. To access the outside mond I had to use the SERVICE ENTRANCE down a frigid passageway leading off from the scullery. As I trolled huffily across the chequerboard tiles, I pondered what sort of coddy uptight upbringing the twonks back thataways must've endured to turn them into such meese humourless authority-flops. True enough, they'd been brought up to follow their own de-luxe Liberated Lavvy, but theirs was one based on arroganki privilege and entitlement, not a conscious glimmering rejection of oppressive uppity outside forces. Though they were just carnish and sludge like the rest of us, the bats seemed untouchable somehow. How bestest to penetrate these bastards' vain steely exteriors, I wondered? How best to exact revenge on the swines?

Before vagarying outways, I poked my tet into the scullery to shush some form of restorative toothsome petit-four – and found Kurt and Friedrich slumped by the marble countertop, sniggering at a full flute of this BUCK'S FIZZ fluid the toffs had been schlumphing. The slaves had collected all the slurped glasses and bevvy-botties from the munjarry-table and slopped them here – and Kurt and Friedrich seemed to find this hilarious. Nix doubt the twats were squifferoony too.

'The chimp returns!' one of them hooted.

I scanned the walls for efinks, rolling pins, a grandiose potato-masher ...

'Just the chappy we was after, me old chukka, haw-ee, s'il vous plaît!' the other squealed.

'Drinky-poos, Raymondo!'

Reering up again, the donkeys reached out and half cuddled each other with lallies jangling, like the hilarity was so much it showed up on the Richter Scale.

'We thought you might like a little quencher, brother. A cooling glass of orangensäft, mon petit chob-chob! Choo-choo! Haw!'

The taller one, Kunt or Friedrice, held out the flute of BUCK'S FIZZ they'd been so tickled by. Naturellement I was not fazed by this anglo pansy liquor in the slightest. 'Santé!' I bellowed, and necked it in one.

There was a foul glimmering sensation in my gargler as the bevvy went down. The feeli-omis snorted and scoffed, then regarded me with pogi distressed eeks as my own expression crumpled. True enough, twas a rancid beverage.

'Do you know what goes into a Buck's Fizz?' quizzed the right-hand donkey, nostrils twitchering.

Humouring them, I poked my piggy vonka into the flute and inhaled. Whatever it was, it was already taking effect. I tried not to let on, but then couldn't help reering skitterishly too as I felt the Golden Fairy attaching helium balloons to my brain.

'It's two parts orangensäft, two parts lovely bubbly champagne,' the left-hand donkey explained, 'and une petite thimbleful of this!'

The donkey held out a blank plastic botty with red lavs:

DOMESTOS KILLS ALL KNOWN GERMS DEAD!

My kishkas contracted, refilling my oyster with the cocktail plus my undigested festive din-dins. Nix doubt I looked maxi poked-up now, but the toffs' eeks were positively horrified as I vomited into the glass, then casually schlumphed the whole manky bitter-gator back down again. To doubly spite the fash bats, I reached for another botty marked COURVOISIER XO: some sophisticated froggy aqua I savvied should cleanse the poor old palate.

'Th— th-that's Mummy's ...'

'Bottoms up, chattes, chaps, twats,' I cooed, and glugged down a bona few gargleful s. I wasn't a hardened tippler by any stretch of the servo, but a proud, touchy omi then and now. Make nix mistake: I DETEST being slighted by any arroganki petty addle-plot. In fact, this may well be the cornerstone of my gloriosa aggro, the driving force behind my forthcoming fantabulosa crime. It's not that I can't take criticism – I REFUSE to take criticism!

Kurt and Friedrich's lappers and nostrils were still jiggling as I took a final lento glug-glug from the brandy botty and belched out a crack of lightning. They minced their lavs, trying to wriggle their way out of any responsibility, but I was in nix mood to chatter no more. My opals were like spinning-tops, my boomboomer thumping like a rapid tabla. An exquisite sickness came over – I clutched the marble unit with dribbly lappers and cackled hysterically at the kitchen utensils, then swung a soft schonk at the donkeys and minnied out on newborn lallies.

(At this point I propose a round of applause for my fantom-screever. Not only has she* been lally-shackled to yours truly for the past una-chenta nobba-daitcha-trey junos, but the lavs that follow are lucid and orderly only thanks to her patience and natty servo, and all in spite of my slippery memory and coddy temper ...)

As the alcool sank its fangs into my sang-cells, I vaguely remember the rush of greasy euphoria and a few smashed

---

* *She.*

fakements as I stumbled back into the hallway. I climbed the grand staircase with the gait of an omi being kicked down it. I believe there may have been writhings in my undercrackers. My platters heavy and opals struggling to focus. Boomboomer still clattering grotesquely. Wrong chamber. 'LIESL' above the mirror. Rumpled bedclobber. Naturellement I poked my vonka into her laundry sac. Plucked her dirty drawers from the mass of mumsy woollen monstrosities. Pictured her puckered pink levers, her tight asterisk dish. Tootering bugles! At some point I lost all my schmutta. Shimmied into her slippies, molto ill-fitting with my colin bursting soggy through the cotton. Von of feeli arva-organs. Sparkle-dazzle of exploding boy. I clambered under her sheets, sensuously drilling a hole into her fantom for una minuta before splurging molto atomic. Tugged off her sloppy scanties and attempted to jarry the evidence. Sultry retching rimbumbles. Naggy once more, I scrabbled like a grizzly mono through her rails of neatly pressed vetements. Wriggled into a naff frumpy drogle and abstractly screeved a squirt of maquiage across my eek: red clown-levers, green ogleshadow, rouge balloons. Reering up again, I redid Liesl's bedclobber with lazy lappers, then minnied back out onto the landing, hobbling and stumbling like the latty was now afloat on some violent seesawing sea.

I cannot rightly recall what was going through my tet as I slithered back down the staircase. It's fair to say this was all a gross improvisation. I nellied voches coming from the morning chamber, the pogi 'Haw-haw-phooey's reminding me of those meese insults I'd endured over din-dins. I clocked a flash of my own reflection in the conservatory fenêtres and cackled beastish. I may have ducked into the scullery for another snifter or duey of brandy. A final oysterful of roast flapper. Apparently I vomited in the fridge – I refute it.

After sniggering loony at the chequerboard tiles for una minuta or daitcha, I minnied my way into the morn chamber where the Christians, Colonics and munja-sluggish

Foster-Newmans were sitting stiff, taking herbata and fruit-cake. Some fungal double-act were jabbering away on the VadaVision, but they were nix competition for the gloriosa joggering-omi-palone that now appeared rev-like in Liesl's drogle before their very opals.

'O, good Heavens!' one of the Christians erupted.

'Je suis Les Divertissements!' I think I might've screamed before breaking into the chanting and walloping, and breaking duey Fabergé fakements in the process. The lavs of the song I was chanting are probably best described as scat – and anti-Capitalist scat at that, before I even identified myself as fully bolshy.

My audience was captivated as I frittied about the floorboards, trying to recreate Madame O's La Danse des Mannequins with Marta's nova pogo-stick and Toxic-Bottomfeeder's crutches as extra lallies. The guests were so entranced, they could barely bring themselves to clap along, despite all my encouragements. Liesl looked most spellbound of all, startled by my uncanny impersonation – herself a first-rate plastic donna, toff mannequin of the highest order!

With limbs over-lubricated, my dance soon degenerated to a deranged can-can as I lifted the drogle and kicked out my lallies molto rapido, forgetting I had nix knickers on underneath, my bijou cartso and quongs flappering like exotic berries in a windstorm.

Ogling backways, my privvy hope must've been to lure all five feeli-palones into this daisy-chain voodoo-walloping while outraging their elders, but nix amount of coaxing and screeching could wrench them from their seats.

As it fell out, twas the Lord who eventually joined me on the stompfloor. His Lordship – who up til now looked dowri stony and cosy in his vogueing-jacket and pantofels – was suddenly taken by the rhythms, lifting himself from his armchair and sashaying towards me with a pink eek, himself a pogi bit squiffy too. He tugged off his pantofels – I savvied so he could shimmy better on the polished floor – then gripped them both in one lapper and socked me hard across the jaw.

I don't believe I dropped – but certainly I stopped stompering. The rest of the revellers were politely tight-levered while I bawled French letters at the batatat, to which His Highness retorted: 'Shut your trap, you bloody fool! You're the Devil! The bloody effing DEVIL!'

The alert reader will nix doubt have clocked the Lord's lack of dialogue thus far. The grand toff was as clamp-oystered as they come – and so imagine my brooliment when the old addle-plot came at me with fists and more unreasonable lavs: 'You're disgusting! An effing poof! A pansy! Take that bloody ridiculous costume off now!'

Ô comrades. This was my intro to the idea of a right and wrong sexuality, and I still don't understand it well. What issue could any pop possibly have with an omi wearing a drogle? We live on a rock that revolves around a blistering sparkle. We schlumph down invisible gases to stay alive. We're surrounded by everyday absurdity: war, jazz, belching cabooshes, politicos, caged monos, asylums, dinarli, pointless travails. What difference does a petty morso of skimpy fabric make?

Nevertheless I reflex-ripped the drogle from my quivery bod and hurled it at the crackling glimmerplace. Pointing my shrivelled cartso in the Lord's direction, I attempted to squeeze out a petulant pissy arc, but could only manage a dribble of eggy blank froth: after-gunge from my molto forceful ejaculation earlier.

'You're DISGUSTING!' the Lord screamed. 'DISGUSTING! A bloody despicable POOVE!'

Dragging a thin silvery comet tail behind me, I darted rapid back up the staircase – and got the right chamber this time. Though I was sprightly compared to His Lordship – and beat him to the attic by a bona few secondas – my feeli bod wasn't yet strong enough to barricade the trapdoor against him. He frapped it open with trey schonks and, not having any nattier emags nor heavy artillery to barny with, I savvied I might as well cower in the corner, coiling myself up like a petty frozen prawn.

When he clocked the state of my libbage, His Lordship erupted yet again: 'O, good God ... O, for goodn– you insolent little nancy!'

Strangely, His Lordship wasn't impressed that I'd efinked most of the naff soft furnishings in the attic and turned them into fashionable schmutta. There was gildi lampshade fringing round my yee-haw Billy the Kid waistcoat, duey diamond-shaped holes in the Afghan rug and countless guttered cushions strewn about like decapitated bod-parts.

'And that was my father's christening gown!' the Lord squealed, spotting Le Bâtard joshed-up in his fetching blank doily-drogle. The doll gazed back at him coyly.

I covered my tet with my lappers, expecting another assault of slipper-sole but in the end His Lordship took his anger out on the ventriloquist's dummy. Le Bâtard seemed to writhe with convincingly humanoid death-throes as the Lord yanked the doily-drogle off and repeatedly batted the dolly's eek against the rosywood Chippendale dresser.

'Non! NON!' I screeched, that dummy being my only true comrade now.

'A growing lad shouldn't be playing with dolls and dresses!' the Lord howled.

'Twas only self-expression, m'lud,' I protested. 'I was only filling the empty ticktocks with a petty splash of creativity, a few new costumes for myself and my ragged darling brother ...'

'I'll make you a new costume, you horrible little sod. Striped pyjamas! You hear? Striped pyjamas with a great ugly PINK TRIANGLE attached!'*

---

* Tragically the climax of this chapter reminded Merritt of his relationship with his father. Stanley would always claim it was the rain that made him leave Paisley, but in truth it was Victor Merritt's jackboot parenting that propelled him south. Vic was a former policeman, an uncompromising Catholic authoritarian who saw sin in almost everything his son put his hand to. When he caught twelve-year-old Stan ogling a collection of smutty (frankly blurry) postcards, Vic attacked his son's eye sockets with a pair of locking pliers, leaving him

The Lord's opals had a frightening glaze now as he tossed Le Bâtard to the floor and continued stomping on the poor puppet's kishkas with his naggy heel. To the doll's credit, Le Bâtard stayed tranquil throughout, passive-aggro to the end. It was only when the Lord put his stamper through the doll's

---

with a sawtooth scar down his left cheek he now claims came from WWII. As he grew older, Stanley was made to feel like an Untermensch for preferring 'modernist filth' over Walter Scott or the Good Book and, as his schoolmates all married and moved away before the end of their teens, Victor mistook his son's studiousness and shyness for effeminacy. 'You're a fucking nancy, wasting away, rotting your mind with that fucking unreadable smut,' were just some of the pleasantries lavished on his only child. Stanley wanted to study art but, with war looming in Europe, Victor encouraged/forced his son to enrol at Glasgow School of Medicine – and in 1940 Stan found himself playing his part in the Mediterranean Theatre of War as sick-berth attendant on an all-thundering, all-annihilating destroyer. After returning to Paisley thoroughly fried and depressed, Stanley gradually tried to re-engage with the bohemian dream he'd left behind, but whenever his father saw the outlandish 'vulgar' fashions his son intended to wear in public (a double-breasted peacoat, silk shirts in shrimp, putty or gammon), Vic invariably sent him back to his room with a scream of 'Fucking poove!' – and all this coming from a man who wove women's shawls for a living. Still, in a roundabout way the insults worked: seeing no future in Renfrewshire (or Curfewshire, as he called it), Stanley moved down to London in the spring of 1946, and was married by the end of the year. Starting out in a small flat in Fitzrovia with just his vulgar schmutta and modernist filth for company, Stanley soon fell in with other like-minded 'sinners' – among them one Iris Reznik, an Eton-cropped, Chartreuse-drinking bobcat born to similarly contemptuous Russian-Jewish watchmaker parents. Once a Bright Young Thing of the 1920s (today sadly dulled, old and somewhat narrow-minded), Iris was almost fifteen years Stanley's senior. While her youthful recklessness had softened to a more maternal, considerate bohemianism, Iris had not lost her man-eating skills – and Stanley was willing prey. Also an avid devourer of modernism and erotica, Iris financed and co-founded the Glass Eye Press with Merritt and William Trefoil in 1959 and, a year later, gave Stanley a daughter. At the beginning of the 1960s, Merritt felt utterly content, but today he can barely remember what contentment feels like. Today his marriage and business are failing. Stanley and Iris rarely talk any more. He hasn't spoken to his father for twenty-three years, and he now leads a sad solitary existence in a small Fitzrovian flat not unlike the poky dungeon he started out in. And he's going to be fifty next year, which feels like a great arthritic freefall towards the grave. And his back aches, and his bowels ache, and his heart aches. And he perhaps didn't need to share all of this with you.

stomach, splitting him in two, that the dummy showed any sign of retaliation. His Lordship's cheeks lost their colour when he ogled what was inside the dummy's belly – and twas a surprise to me too.

As Le Bâtard lay static on the fatchared rug, the puppet's kishkas were still writhing. The hollow of his belly was filled with crawlies: worms, maggots, buggers, beetles, woodlice, pubic crabs, mechanised dandruff. For uno momento we regarded the doll in silence – then scarpered as more and more bijou beasties exploded from the cavity, filling the chamber like manky creeping concrete ...

Before vagarying downways, the Lord was clear enough in the tet (or so toffed-up it was reflex) to push the butler-bell by my bedside. 'SERVICE! SERVICE!' he screeched, clearly his answer to any crisis, gross or petty.

As the grotty insectoid lava oozed churningly from the attic hatch, I followed him cartwheeling down the staircase at a safe distance, trembling excitedly and trying my bestest not to reer, though my oyster was turned right up. Twitching critters plop-plopped atop our tets as we scarpered. A gross grumbling millipede slithered greasily down the banister.

'SERVICE! SERVICE!!'

I landed at the bottom step with a gay squeal, bruising my botty. I spat a stray cockroach from my gargler. This absurd mond, I ponced. This fantabulosa absurd mond!

Merry Christmas, everybody! Merry Fuckering Christmas!*

* It snowed heavily the night we received this chapter.

The Secondary Modernists*

JARRYING ALONE IN THE SKOL CANTEEN, NOVAK WEARS A BLANK CAMISHA, BURGUNDY TIE AND BLAZER, GREY TERYLENE LALLY-COVERS.

I turned up to my first school-juno on a penny-farthing, three-quarters of an hour behind my nova schoolmates, and about nine years behind them academically.

Under the pretence of making me more solo-reliant, the Foster-Newmans had banished me to an outhouse or glorified cowshed in the fields and, come term-time, I had to cycle the otta miles to this brootish secondary modern in Margate,† despite the quatra cabooshes in the garage. They forcibly removed my doppel-barrel surnom – I was now plain Novak for good. And the cooks gave me a distinctly bland packed-munja to jarry on my nibblebreaks. Nanti nine-birdy roasts nix more.

---

* Chapter received Monday, 8th December 1969 – 217 days to go.

† Once Iris, Merritt and Trefoil had founded the Glass Eye Press, they were always on the lookout for young radicals to join the vanguard. Strangely enough, Mark 'Davy' Noon was also educated at a Kent secondary modern before enrolling at art college and, if his tales are to be believed, he's our most nihilistic, far-out member of staff to date. Davy tried his utmost to get arrested at the Grosvenor Square riot in 1968, he's ingested every available mind-altering substance with apparently no adverse side effects, he believes he can bed any bird that sets slingback in his favourite Hypnogogo discotheque, and he claims he was 'heavily involved' in the violence against Rockers on Margate seafront over Whitsun Week-end 1964 – although it's difficult to find a Mod who doesn't claim the same. And we don't remember Davy turning up to work on a Lambretta with parka-toggles flapping until at least autumn 1965, once Mod had gone mainstream.

The only hint at my upper-class lavvy was the soldi-quartereen, or penny-farthing as the civvies would call it. I learned to ride the antique deathtrap more for my own amusement than anything else. I took a smouldering foto of Rab Butler MP to the barbers when their Lordships forced me to have my riah chopped. I joshed-up my burgundy blazer with a semi-erect bratwurst in my top posh.

On my first ride to the secondary mod I enjoyed the rowdy honks and hoots (some friendly, some less so) from my fellow commuters, but the reaction from my skol-comrades was almost entirely hostile. It wasn't just my ridiculous slap-tet politico-riah or the clammy wilting bratwurst. While I savvied only too well I was a meese teeni-omi, the way the chavvies went on it was like my eek demanded an X certificate. Then again, perhaps this is just the way norm chavvies are: ultra-discriminating, selfish, diabolical, militant, merciless petty critters ...

As it fell out, the teachers weren't overly enamoured with me neither. While I excelled at any lesson involving my lappers (plankwork, textiles), my servo was soon singled out as one of the worst in the institution. All the emphasis was on following THE RULES: grammar, numerals, decorum, servitude. Whereas in the Château Chanceux I was well versed in froggy poesies by the age of chinka (the Madame having sleeptalked Desnos, Rimbaud and Baudelaire into my nells), here we were forced to swallow musty anglo guff like 'Ye Canterbury Tales' or Billy Shaker. When I showed my Art Master my degenerate Surrealist expulsions (fantabulosa warped portraits of the fillies in my class, hazardous readymades, automatic splashback), the closest he could get to a compliment was: 'It's not right'!

Though I was only at the skol two terms, my nom appeared in the Punishment Liver more than duey-dozen times. The Headmaster's birch got so well acquainted with my corybungus, he might as well have shoved it up there for keeps.

I detested the whole codswallop charade, like I was cycling through wet cement every morn just to have my ignorance highlighted for me by all these fungal unfashionable plops in tweed with lank riah. Rapidly the teachers dismissed me as a lost cause - and yet all us secondary modernists were ultimately destined for the same dead-end future. As summer approached, none of us were encouraged to apply for university. The feeli-palones were taught naff subjects like Domestic Science so their delicate lappers were prepared for a full lavvy of housework, while the feeli-omis' lappers were toughened up ready for a full lavvy of hard travails. On our final juno I was almost expecting the teachers to pick noms out of a capella and have us paired up, married and parkered off to a prefab pronto, so as to eliminate any anxiety we might've had of not attaining this gildi eternal existence of drudgery and low dinarli.

When I returned to the Pile with an empty fistful of GCEs, I was in surprisingly gay spirits, savvying I still had an easier lavvy ahead compared to my skolmates, even if it was an animal's lavvy: incarcerated in the cowshed with nanti humanoid interaction other than the omi-servants filling my pig-trough twice each juno.

It'd been months since I'd vadared the Lord and Lady, and so it was a surprise when their twisted eeks appeared at the grate the noche my results came in. I was sweating and wibbering jitterishly in my sleep, revving I was a champion jockey in pink silks riding a gross white shark round and round an unsanitary municipal swimmering pool, when I nellied the polite tap-tot-tap on the doorframe.

'How did we get on today, Raymond?' the Lady asked. I could tell by their expressions they'd been expecting me to fail all along, and so I felt no need to embroider or sugarcoat my lavs.

'Mal. Very mally indeed. We tried our bestest, but business as usual I'm afraid. Qualifications still nil,' I replied, poncing the royal 'we' might help me swerve some of the blame, implicating the whole coddy skol-system in this naff meaningless disaster. 'You were right about secondary modern education, Ma'am. It wasn't worth the taxpayers' gent. We didn't take to it so well. Our servos weren't stimulated not a jot, Ma'am.'

The Lord and Lady regarded each other with a look I recognised: like I'd palavered out of turn or somehow soiled them without reefing.

'Well, Raymond,' the Lady began, all bullfrog now but with a princess's voche, 'the key is you mustn't give up. Do you remember what we suggested to you about employment? About finding a job if things didn't quite work out as you'd hoped?'

'A job? The Travails?'

'Yes. You remember.'

'We savvied it wasn't relevant to us, happy as we are with this jolly incarcerated Liberated Lavvy just like my past lavvy in the Château Chanceux. Our hopes were nil, Ma'am. So all hopes and revs achieved mightily well in our eyes. Business and pleasure as usual. And très très appreciative of it we are too. You keep out of our way, we'll keep out of yours.'

'Well.' The toff-palone's opals bulged. 'We're afraid this might come as somewhat of a shock to you, in that case. While we've done everything we can to look after you – and we've tolerated and enjoyed your company, we have, we have – we however feel it would be best for you, and for us, if you now left the Estate ... for good ... and found yourself some employment elsewhere. Virtue-through-labour, Raymond! We only want what's best for you, and in this case what's best is a salary, an occupation, freedom from our, ahem, silly old-fashioned ways. Ahem. We – O please, Raymond – O, we knew you might be like this but – O goodness, O, I – please understand – I, O Lord, O ... SERVICE! SERVICE!!'

As I turned the cowshed inside out, I clocked that the Lady wasn't using the majestic plural. She was palavering on behalf of the entire family – the fortuni feeli fillies, the omi-servants, the cooks, even the beasties out in the fields – and I savvied there was nix this royal 'we' could say to sway their toff addle-plot servos.

But I left my mark.

INTERMISSION*

'NE TRAVAILLEZ JAMAIS.'†

GUY DEBORD, SPECTACLED SITUATIONIST
ULTRA-FLANNER

* Poem received Friday, 12th December 1969 – 209 days to go.
† 'NEVER WORK.' Epigraph scratched out in blood.

Ye Jobseeker's Tale

When the Lady had thus her scolding told,
The swoote summer nightertale turn'd full cold.
Raymond wept, quoth 'QUEINTS!'* and smash'd his abode
But for one precious item: the sewing-machine he stowed.
A job now to find, Raymond had not in his corage
The will to go on this unholy pilgrimage,
But the Lady insisted – 'Or elles bend for the birch!' –
That longe folk to find good tough honeste wirch,†
And thus, saith she, from every shire's end
Of Engleland, to the Employment Bureau they wend;
This blissful virtue-through-labour they seek
For – on average – ten-and-one pounds per weeke!

Morning-song sprung in full brighte splendour,
Heralding the dawn of Raymond's forcéd surrender.
Fed, dressed and watered, in solace he masturbat'd;
Forthwith an invisible-horse-drawn carriage awaited
That toward Canterbury woulde ride
With Raymond in front and gangling chauffeur alongside.
Before setting out, the Lord saith 'Adieu'
And as though paternal respect were here anew,
Patted Raymond's presséd grey flannel breast,

---

* 'Cunts!' (Middle English)? Harry Howling sat back during this Intermission. Trefoil dusted off his dilapidated copy of Chaucer, squinted at his lazy schoolboy annotations and shakily took the reins. (Incidentally, does this poem not suggest Novak fared much better academically than he lets on?)

† Work, The Travails.

Flared his nose-thirls full likerous, and left.
'Mush-mush' quoth the engines; their carriage departed
With a fert of exhaust fume; Raymond's new life had started.

Naught saith the driver as the Cathedral approach'd;
The city unfamiliar, Raymond adrad was full choked.
'Why to this Canterbury?' the lad bethought,
'When Margate town centre must have good wirch to be sought?'
But then – reckoned he – 'P'rhaps this was all along planned:
To deprive the younge lad of cod and Dreamland.
Deposit thy not in fair Margate, for he conneth his way back;
Instead dump him in a city with no bearings, no map.'
And so it was thus, the carriage did halt
And unloaded was Raymond on ne'er-aforeseen asphalte.
'Fie! I wish not to return aniwei!' wept our eponymous hero
Though he did gaze with woe upon the solemn Job Bureau.

'Ye Youth Employment Office' quoth the insignia without:
A grete uglike cathedral for an agnostic devout.
Raymond felt for his birth-scroll and found something elles more:
Seven sterling pound-notes totalling – 'Good Lord!' – three score.
Back to his breast the notes disappeared
And now, taller and gay with a blush to the cheer,*
Cryeth he, 'Poppycock to this wirch!'
And townwards he lurched
With a mind to dwell rough and spend thrifty this fortune;
He hath surviv'd thus before: he could live on rats' portions.
But when nightertale eft fell a man o' law appeared
And to Raymond's sleeping buttocks were five lashes deliver'd!

* With a redness to the face.

Morning-song shoured, the Job Bureau eft beckoned;
Two houres he waited til 'Novak!' he did hearken.
Now behind a longe desk a clerke languidly perched;
Twas his proude role to blissen younge folk with wirch.
Alongside was a tray brimful with brighte index cards,
Upon each an occupation, from 'PHLEBOTOMIST' to 'COASTGUARD'.
Novak's sew-machine he espied, and proffer'd our school leaver
'Haberdasher, art college, tailor or weaver?'
But the lad listened not; no respect for his elder.
He thenched of his mother: 'Do what wouldst the Old Zelda?'
The soothsayer of Surrealism, the queen of happenstance!
'I know!' quoth plucky Raymond. 'I'll pick a card by chance!'

Now this clerke was a churl, found he the idea bad fay
But, with time ticking wayward, he proffer'd the tray.
Raymond's clumsy pale fingers by aventure y'fall*
Upon a card of green, full smoothe and quite small
On which was y'written in blue ink'd caps:
'MERCHANT NAVY'. His spirit collapsed.
'Please let me pick again squire, for to die I want not.
I cannot follow orders. In the Navy I'll be shot.'
'Calm yourself, boy, stint thy clap,' quoth this clerical man.
'Your fear for this job is sickerly mistaken,
For the Royal Navy has the guns, drums, lost limbs and torpedoes;
The Merchant Navy has rum, bum, fun and tuxedos ...'

* 'By chance fell ...'

PART III

SEAFOOD

'There is too much noise in the world as it is. Do not make matters worse ... There is no such being as a good noisy steward.'

PERSONAL APPEARANCE & BEHAVIOUR, SHIP STEWARD'S HANDBOOK*

---

* Epigraph copied out in a niffy pink substance that could well be Marie Rose sauce.

Tutti Frutti*

VOMITING BROOTISHLY, NOVAK WEARS STARCHED BLANK LALLY-COVERS, BLANK CAMISHA, BLANK JACKET, BLACK BOWTIE AND BLANK SLIP-ONS.

Aqua and electric don't usually mix but – HAIL, KING NEPTUNE! – I was soon floating on the Setta Seas aboard a gigantic sparkling pleasure-machine ...

When I hobbled aboard MS HIPPOCAMPUS, I'd expected to be working with omis in sou'westers, oilskins and bellbotties, but the first rating I ogled was joshed-up to the nobbas in lippy, a drogle and bolshy-red stilettos. I was wearing full-eek maquiage too, and I savvy now this might be why the Purser sent me to bed down in the Fruit Locker.

Gravesend Sea School was more punishing than the secondary mod – us lowly barkies being essentially forced to pumice-stone our past vulgar personalities and learn pernickety silvery-service skills in anticipation of a lavvy bending over for only slightly less lowly twats than ourselves – and yet there was nanti indication during my trey-month training that I'd be entering such a deliciously meshigena, molto absurdist, seesawing, gender-blending work environment. Had I known, I might've wriggled into something a little more gildi.

Given that I'd been hired sight-unseen as bellboy, I savvied it might be wise to smear on a pogi bit of slap to help soften my

---

* Chapter received Wednesday, 17th December 1969 – 208 days to go until Novak's fantabulosa crime.

frightening features before my maiden voyage. The omi-servants at the Pile were always immaculately turned out and, not being ultra convinced about my waitering skills, I didn't want to arrive with an eek the Purser might think was better suited behind the U-bends.

'Very presentable, Novak. This gladdens me! This gladdens me something rotten!' the Purser screamed at me as I came aboard.

I smiled through clamped oyster-levers, hiding my crowded shark-fangs. I'd grown my riah and Brilliantined it to cover my ratty-nells, and smoothed over my Vesuvian acne with a puppet-like layer of milky pancake. It should go without screeving I wasn't quite as bona-vadaring in a barky uniform as Anna Karina in UNE FEMME EST UNE FEMME, but I was certainly trying to act that way.

In case the Purser needed any more persuading, I bellowed: 'And I was born with the caul atop my tet, sir!'

'Pardon me?'

'The caul.' I tapped my gloopy scalp.

'I'll put you in Peak Number 33, Novak. Working corridors are below deck. Follow the signs, starboard side. If you see motorcars or burping engines and boilers, you've gone too far. Papers? Passport?'

My sang gurgled as he regarded my legal bimph.

'Sixteen years young! This pleases me. A young laddy embarking on a new life upon saltwater! This pleases me something rotten!' the Purser proclaimed, his servo all the way up there with Monsieur Gagarin. 'Well, bon voyage, precious polliwog.'

'Bon voyage,' I parroted, giving him a pathetic half-salute.

Yuri Gagarin was a sparkle up there somewhere as I shuffled gingerly across the gangway and down down down into the stewards' quarters. As tin-cans go, MS HIPPOCAMPUS was surely grander than Yuri's: a huge honeycomb hotel with trey swimming pools, setta decks, otta saloons, a cinema – and over nobba-chenta khazis ...

I tried not to dwell on the number of pissoirs as I trolled through the working corridors, sharpering for Peak 33. MS HIPPOCAMPUS was one of these nova motorised latties-on-water, and the décor was all luxury: pistachio-green paintwork, chrome fakements, natty Op Art carpets, and a strong von of de-luxe profumo coming from even the lowliest ratings' cabins.

When I burst into what I ponced should be the right peak, the three barkies in there squawked like I'd come to burglarise their groinage. Two of the omis were upright and dressed in the same blank schmutta as me, meaning they were also stewards, while the other was sprawled on the floor in smudged lippy, Japonaise shimada-shyka and stilettos. The maquiage looked like it'd been applied by an octopoid with the DTs, and I savvied from the chin-prickles and cave-groans coming from this chappy that she probably wasn't a bona fide palone.

'Pardon me, is this Peak Terty-Trois?' I asked, confident with my Queen's now but still not maxi certain about my numerals.

'The Widow's Peak it is today, ducky,' one of the omis in white replied.

'Poor Winnie split with her husband yester-noche,' the other explained, referring to the puddle of flesh on the floor.

'Is that some bona fresh trade I can vada up there?' Winnie squinted up from the swishering carpet.

'Pardon me?'

'O Lordy, give us a reef of that feeli-omi pronto!' the sea-queen honked. 'You're an easy-mort are you, ducky-egg? It's the only charvering hangover cure that'll save me. Felch me softly now, won't you, sweetness?'

'Nanti Polari?' the first omi in white asked me.

'Sorry?'

'Do you not speak Polari?'

'Um. Nein. No, that is.'

'Well, thank goodness for that. Make yourself comfortable, sunshine. We'll be molto molto gentle with you ...'

*

As you're aware, I rapidly picked it up. Polari was my adopted lingo by the time the anchor dropped on my aquatic travails three years later – and it wouldn't be the only aspect of the queer lavvystyle I picked up. But first, The Travails ...

Without doubt these latties-on-water were the most luxurious places I'd ever lavvy. While my libbage was cramped – quatra bunks to one berth below deck, with only a skimpy trade-curtain for privacy – above was all entertainment, rich munja, peacocking, slander and reering.

Twas MS HIPPOCAMPUS's mission to ferry mostly senile couples, dolled-up corpses, widowers and spinsters from King Georgie Five Dock to Malta via Gibraltar and back again and again and again. The solo fungal zeldas were most demanding, the munja or service never quite up to their plastic-toff standards, but I learned to humour the petty addle-plots soon enough. On my first noche in the hotel side of the ship, Winnie (the puddle of flesh, née William) taught me to 'Ferricadooz them with friendliness, my chovi'. By this point Winnie was back on her platters, shaved and looking more of an upstanding barky in her pressed blank tux. 'Then if they're still nanti happy, cough up a gross vonka-bomb in their apple-puffs and custard.'

For the most part the passengers seemed to enjoy being pampered by pooves, the homos being almost part lattywife, part joggering-pop, part fantasy bachelor – but they were less impressed by the daffy bellboy stumbling around in their shadow.

To be fair, I didn't take the travails at all seriously at first. I was wide-ogled at the ritzy atmosphere onboard and, savvying I deserved this gushing luxury as much as the leeches in straw boaters and ball gowns, I set out to follow a nova Liberated Lavvy, THE DUTY-FREE LAVVYSTYLE: to do minimum work, schlumph down as many free bovaries and finger-foods as I could shush, all the while blending into the blank wallpaper as we racked up the nautical miles.

From juno uno, the Purser told me it was my job to be invisible: 'If you catch the eye of the diners or staff, Novak, it usually means you're doing something wrong.'

Hé-hé-hé! I did not need telling twice, Ô comrades. Invisibility was my ideal job description. HOWEVER: we'd barely made it out of the Bay of Biscay when my coddy invisibility failed me. As the lowliest rating in the steward department, my solo mission was to clear away crockery and cutlers, but this particular thunderous noche the Purser pulled me up after clocking me jarrying leftovers on my way back to the galley. In my defence, these weren't your average leavings: my cheeks were positively bulging with turbot tets when the Purser let rip.

After catching me thrice more on consecutive noches (once with daitcha scrawny prawns' lallies hanging out of my oyster), I was deemed incapable of platter-gathering and sent to one of the steerage saloons, the Manatee Lodge, as their nova glass-collector. And yet this downgrading suited me immensely – the leftovers I shushed were all the more stimulating! By the time I ticktocked-off at 9 or 10 p.m., I was usually half-rats – sometimes illuminated to the extreme.

'Had a bona back-breaking day at the grindstone, Raymondo?' was the usual greeting when I staggered into the Pig & Whistle after my watch, oyster fully turned up and opals listing.

The Pig & Whistle was the crew bar, and the least gildi on the barka. In fact, it was just a hatch and a few drab benkels to park your aching corybungus. The staff were denied vino or spirits so all the queens would be sitting there ultra dolly and elegant with gross frothing butch pints of Allsopp's, cackling away.

When I wasn't being unanimously ignored, the sea-queens generally regarded me with envy, or randy malice:

'Vada the glistening levers on that petty pancaked chavvy.'

'Imagine them round your cartso. I'd fill that bambino up with so much seafoam she'd be spitting krill for junos ...'

'The brutality!'

Such lavs were as close as I got to compliments from my nova shipmates. To begin with I thought every member of the workforce was queer, but in truth the omi-palones had set up a kind of glittering commune in the starboard peaks 30–41, while the rest of the barkies were either straight or still in the water-closet.

Most noches the conversation was pure splatter. Given the stewards up topside had to politely butter up corpses for hours on end, twas perhaps no surprise they projectile-vomited all manner of daffy squalid stories and joyous slanderous jibber-jabber once they'd clocked off. Possiblement everything was an exaggeration – from the quong-shrivelling arva-tales to the servo-spinning shapeshiftering lingo – and I loved it. All at once the irregular seemed natty and spectacular, the frowned-upon now perfectly bona and norm ...

'A dolly choco-box cottage in Londres, was it?' a butch voche polled.

'Nix: the manky pogi brandy-latch in the Holloway Road. Khazi with the glory-hole. Anyway, so this manly-alice, this bearded-donna fucker, he sticks his cartso through and I'm going at it happily enough, schlop schlop schlop – when all this charvering grimy aqua starts pouring out the end of his cockle ...'

'Was it a lag?'

'Well, I had to enquire! I palavered: "Are you pissing, dear sir?" I might not've used the lav "sir". He promised me it was letch-water.'*

'Even so! Pouring, you say? Was the chappy in bona health?'

'If it's the golden-aquas you're after by the by: parker a feeli-omi a beyong† in Tangier,' the butch voche interjected. 'I had trey of the fortuni rascals hosing me down each morn last leave. Invigorating von! Bladders of profumo – like they schlumph down jasmine or rose petals specially ...'

---

* Howling relished enlightening us with this one: 'Letch-water? Yes: the transparent gunge that leaks from an enthusiastic penis prior to ejaculating, so I believe ...'

† 'Pay a young man a shilling.'

'GARDYLOO: Bellboy. Tumbler-shusher! Have you sampled the mighty catamites of Tangier yet?'

This last query was directed at me. I shook my tet and smiled dumbly at the swaying tabletop, a pogi bit poked-up having nanti experience in that area still.

'One isn't a virgin, is one, Raymondo?' polled Pamela (née Paul).

'She must be!' the butch belladonna Sharon (née Simon) chipped in. 'Vada the innocent eek on it!'

The sea-queens tended to swap 'he' and 'she', treating gender like a unisex swimming cozzy they could wriggle in and out of at will. They all had joggering-noms too. Strangely the omi-palones in Peak 33 (Winnie Repulse, Pamela Pola, Sharon von Scharnhorst) had shushed their surnoms from sunk battleships. I ponced there had to be some symbolism there – but didn't press them.

'Never fear, Raymondo, this Friday noche we'll make certain your dolly hairless dish is buggered once and for all!' Winnie hooted, herself none too dolly in just almond-rocks, corset and shoulders creepering with riah. 'Heck, I'd fuck it myself, only I consider you a sister now. Tis bad fay to split a sibling's arriss open, I find ...'

'The brutality!' Pamela splurted, munching a pork scratching.

I smiled back nervy.

Every Friday after The Travails it was tradition to have a gildi-drogle soirée in the Fruit Locker. We'd take our grotty work schmutta down to the dhobi-khazi, then transform ourselves from sober-omis to ultra-illuminated sparklets.

Fancy dress is different at sea. It's not like when norm civvies josh themselves up back home – comically, unconvincingly impersonating pops far more striking than themselves. When the sea-queens shed their blank uniforms and donned drogles, bombshell shykas and sparkling groinage, you felt they were becoming more themselves.

This particular Freitag the omi-palones had in mind an avian theme: a frenzy of ostrich fluff, beaks and painted talons. The feathers had been plundered during a recent trip to Sud Afrikkka, and I ogled wonderstruck as Sharon fed the quivering morsos rapidly into my croaky sewing-vacaya, dexterously conjuring up a bespoke cozzy for each of us. For a few minutas it felt as if a bomba had gone off at a battery farm but, as the feathers lento settled, there was nix doubt we'd be the mostest exotic birdies-of-paradise in the Pig & Whistle this noche.

'Et voilà!' Winnie cooed as we strapped on our final fakements: quatra maxi-phallic flamingo beaks and duey skytickling King-of-Saxony ogle-riders. 'Nellyarda: if you're not penetrated this dolly noche, Raymondo, we'll bat you overboard. Only a braindead coma-omi could refuse such juicy fresh fruit-de-mer!'

'SQUAWK!'

'Bona luck, sweet bambino,' Pamela added, slipping a tubette of KY Jelly into my vacant bra-pod. 'And remember: nanti pain, nix gain! If it doesn't make you parny, darling, you're not doing it right! True of romance, true of screwing, dear cherub.'

Little did they savvy – despite me arriving in conspicuous maquiage that first juno, plus my habit of wearing ladies' clobber thus far – I wasn't a poove. Or at least not a passive poove. I regard my dish as an exit, not an entrance.*

Of course, I wasn't averse to fucking an omi. In fact, being incarcerated on a giant latty-on-water with nanti palones under the age of fifty, I'd regularly wet-rev about penetrating one of the more feminine barkies. And so, with this privvy savagery in mind, I felt maxi enlivened as we minnied from the Fruit Locker down to the Pig, sashaying several leagues beneath the first-, second- and steerage-classes up thataways, but feeling like A-list Hollywood dames ...

---

* As is habit, Merritt first read this chapter in his personal WC, woefully constipated, his dish neither exit nor entrance. We'd often joke that Stan spent so much time in the lavatory, it was like a second office (in fact, he even had a private telephone line installed) – and yet still he refused to see a doctor about his bowel troubles. 'It's just where I go to do all my thinking,' was the usual excuse. Or: 'I am a bloody doctor.'

'SQUAWK! SQUAWK!' Winnie screamed as we entered the see-sawing bungery. The patrons' eeks – Dietrich eeks, seasick eeks, blank Pierrot-eeks, sooty stoker-eeks – ogled us first with mock horror, then outright grubby arva-hunger as we swished to the hatch, shedding feathers like pogi plumes of intoxicating smoke.

There were plenty of jolly fruits in drogles and kitty-heels, and pops joshed-up like Halloween beasties and Romanoid gladiators, but none of the cozzies were a match for our explosive ostrich fluff. This noche we were the alpha-queers. We strutted about like royalty, nonchalantly brushing off the barkies' greedy advances until, some hours later, the alcool had utterly obliterated any pogi morso of decorum we had left.

Ô, those salty noches! After a bona few Allsopp's-tops I would've happily inserted my tingly colin in any one of the meese prole botties perched around the bungery – but perhaps even more exhilarating was not my own randy jitterings, but the drooling glances I kept getting from barkies who up til now had barely even blinked at me.

By and large it was the manly-alices, the tattooed seadogs, the homos-in-heteros'-clothes ogling me with that manky lust that dripped off them once we'd been afloat a few junos. But was this genuine attraction, I pondered, or just hit-and-hope lechery like a squiffy toff firing blanks at a sky filled with dolly clay pigeons?

Just after last orders, the ship's carpenter sidled up to me, his opals like duey grotesque overripe plums.

'What are your plans for the rest of the noche, dearest?' the omi asked, his chubby nipplets clearly visible through his creamy vest.

I side-oystered: 'I have KY Jelly in my bra-pods, squire.'

'Well now,' he blurted, seemingly poked-up by my brazenness before the grotty sheen took over again. 'How old are you, my chovi?'

'Daitcha-und-heksa, so I believe. But fear not – I'm mightily well endowed. I'm fully capable of giving you a bona jolly rogering ...'

To this my nova comrade simply reered – his oyster a witchy mocking O, his lappers grasping at his thews – and just like that all arva-tingles and thundertwangs were instantly dissolved.

BOF.

While I'd eventually disembark the HIPPOCAMPUS knowing my colleagues nanti better rectally, the attention I got in ladies' slap and schmutta nevertheless made me feel desirable rather than disposable for the first time in my lavvy. Unaware quite how much stick they got ashore, I'd naively ponced omi-palones must be the master race, the superior sex: they seemed to have the quickest lingums, the thickest skins, and all the apparatus to charver and be charvered by any pop across the sexual spectrum. They were liberation personified, and yet bizarrely back home they could be slammed in gaol if caught with their colins in the wrong orifice.

I refused to bend over – and STILL REFUSE! – but this stubborness meant I only stuffed dishes in my dreams during my aquatic travails. The barkies and sea-queens didn't want a teeni-omi's tiny cartso up their overparticular sphincters. Bellboys were there only to take orders, to occasionally (sometimes forcibly) receive Cumberland cartsos up their tight dishes. But I never bent over.

Thankfully, I wasn't the youngest omi on the ship for long. Today I cannot stomach speaking or screeving the petty pop's real nom, but Herman Hermaphrodite (or Hermetically Sealed Herman, or Sub-Humanoid Herman ...) was a nova bellboy nix doubt drafted in now I'd been permanently demoted to tumbler-shusher.

Herman was a fortuni blond chavvy from the Provinces, with a natural milk-and-honey complexion and a slightly sharper servo than me. Being older than the bijou bambino (admittedly only duey months older), I saw him as my only potentially penetrable workmate, and so I pursued him unflaggingly between watches. It was love! But he was a slippery bat: always cackling and reering round the older seadogs, and yet he'd clam up whenever I tried to charm or pester him in the Pig.

The coyness was telltale – clear enough he had tinglings for me too, but he was poked-up screeching his feelings, fearful the top brass might not look molto kindly on their teeniest, tightest trainees pairing off like a couple of ultra-domesticated funguses. He was the consummate professional. He was a fuckering addleplot.

Noche upon noche I'd nelly Herman groaning and whimpering in the khazi – he'd refuse a helping lapper. I'd spike Herman's lemonade with shushed grumblers – he'd prudishly vomit overboard and then come back more sober than when we started. I'd follow Herman into the dhobi-chamber and strike maxi provocative postures in front of him – his opals never left the biddy-tiles.

By juno-lepta, I was ready to use force.

IT WAS LOVE.

Though Herman was stationed in a frigid peak far far away from the Fruit Locker, uno noche I accosted one of his bunkmates in the Manatee Lodge and, in nix uncertain terms, schonked screeched spat wept and battyfanged willety-nillety until the pleb kindly agreed to swap beds with me. When I revealed the bona news to Herman at breakfast, he near enough choked on his chilled pawpaw. 'You're to be my new bunkmate?' he stammered coquettishly. 'Oui, ducky.' Before vagarying to our separate action stations, I considered shushing a rapid kiss – but then savvied our lovemaking would be all the more rampant and luminous if we resisted reefing one another until lights-out that noche ...

HOWEVER: the sea is a fickle beastie. For some unfathomable reason, between frühstück and luncheon my darling Hermanoid's delicate thumper was thrown off course. He didn't show up at the Crew Mess for the celebratory fishcake I'd promised – and when finally I collared the chavvy lurking among the salted carnish and sundries down down down in the stores, I savvied some superior in white must've barnied with him on watch, or some old spinster or petty-bourgeoistard must've given him lip, because next thing I nellied, my Cupid wanted to jump ship!

We docked at Gibraltar duey junos later. Skittery fearful arrival like a lento-motion collision with a gigantic limeystone iceberg. The minuta the anchor dropped, I scarpered down the gangway and hopped ashore so I could vada which latties-on-water Herman had the option of signing onto next. We were able to swap ships whenever the mood struck, us being more or less eekless interchangeable robos in our blank tuxedos.

In the end I just followed Herman straight into the Personnel Bureau. I signed my nom after his on the legal bimph of a nova shipping line. And I offered to carry his valise aboard our nova home-sweet-home for the next duey months: SS UNMENTIONABLE. She was destined for Australia over the winter, meaning the bona-vadaring bastard couldn't jump ship for at least trey blissful claustrophobic weeks (first port of call: Cape Town!), and to begin with everything was relatively rosy – but in the end it was yours truly who wanted to jump ship after barely trey junos ...

Crossing the Line*

SCREECHING FOR MERCY, NOVAK WEARS NANTI SCHMUTTA EXCEPT INCONTINENCE KNICKERS AND A THICK LAYER OF SEVERAL BARKIES' BOD-FLUIDS.

36.1430°N

'Name, rank, article number, nationality, webbed feet? Speak speak speak speak speak!'

'Um. Raymond Novak. Bellboy. Well, tumbler-shusher. Glass-collector, I mean, sir. But a fine glass-collector.'

'What proportion chink are you? Speak!'

'Sorry, sir?'

'Yellow Peril, eh? Speak speak speak speak!'

'Pardon me?'

Chief Steward Sturgeon was an obscure omi, this unbearably handsome prick despite the blatant Roman-vonka, petite handlebar mouser and startling blue opals.

'I presume there must be some slope in you,' he polled.

'It's my ogles, sir. My eyes. Barely open, I admit, but I assure you I'm awake.'

'No, no, no, no, no. Glass-collector in the Merchant Navy. It's a gook's job. A dog's job. Speak!'

'I'm half-French, sir.'

---

* Chapter received Monday, 5th January 1970 – 189 days to go.

'Well then, you should be striving to serve up topside! Comprends pas? From today you'll be waiting tables like the rest of us whites. And I'll be shadowing you all the way. No – no! – don't speak, don't speak. Dismissed.'

I'm not sure if 'whites' was a reference to our bod-colour or our uniform, but twas a codswallop welcome all the same. I watched the Rock and the bona ship HIPPOCAMPUS shrink behind us, wondering what cateva travails I'd signed myself up for. My petty pistachio-green paradise swirly-whirlpooled down the plughole.

Ô, to be a first-class passenger on this ritzy spearmint barka (or even just a barnacle stuck to the bottom of the hull)! We'd only been afloat half an hour and the corpses were already setting up their deckchairs, cackling cut-glass lavs. I savvied pronto that the tourists on SS UNMENTIONABLE were a different calibre of toff compared to those on the HIPPO. These zots had the dinarli to chase the sol round the welt every winter and the gildi leathery eeks to prove it – but, as we'll see, my own lavvy just seemed to get worster and worster the closer we got to the Equator ...

35.7667°N

Love in the workplace! I don't recommend it.*

---

* We don't recommend it either.

We're not entirely sure what went on over the Christmas period but when we returned to work on the 5th, the tension between Audrey and Davy was horrendous.

Secretly most of us had hoped the pair's relationship would flourish – mainly so we wouldn't have to sack one of them if they couldn't work out their differences – but alas, it's upsetting how quickly love and warmth can turn to barbed wire and icicles.

At first we thought the frostiness in the office was just down to post-Yuletide blues but, as the morning progressed, it became clear Audrey's foul mood was focused entirely on Davy. Working her way sullenly through the backlog of complaints (mostly indignant/lonely males demanding their long-overdue Christmas erotica), she would periodically look up from her typewriter with a haunted glaze or grumble rebukes under her breath whenever Davy blurted a questionable opinion, whenever he laughed a little too loudly, whenever he touched himself under his trestle table.

When Herman uncleffed our nova peak, I was initially overjoyed to vada the Cunard chiefs had clearly clocked our blossoming romance and parkered us a privvy duey-omi cabin. Immediately I stripped down to my slippies and began improvising a slinky hypnotic courtship dance – however, I'd barely got the child pinned to the carpet when Chief Steward Sturgeon goosestepped inways and spray-gunned terrible lavs at us, the gist of which was: 'Work! Work! WORK! Work! WORK!!'

35.4161°N

Ugly travails.

To me, bona service meant moping around miserably doing as little as possible: the correct response to any nonsensical

---

Davy, to his credit (?), handled this latest tiff with maximum composure, ignoring Audrey's asides as if she were just a lunatic arguing with herself on the Tube. He diligently carried on with his work, blithely illustrating a ball-gagged woman in a valet's uniform for the cover of *The Moral Panic Motel*, until finally Audrey could take no more. With fingers like talons, she gathered the mass of complaints she had strewn across her desk, made as if to screw them all up into an enormous ugly snowball, then stopped herself, stood up gingerly – and stormed out in silence.

Merritt found her in tears half an hour later in her usual spot in Fitzroy Square, her face like a melting Camembert, her brown beehive more bedraggled than the tangled, withered bushes surrounding her.

'You don't have to tell me what's the matter,' Stanley whispered, sitting down next to her. 'I know how it is. Poor lamb …'

Audrey shook her head slightly, glaring at the paving slabs.

'One day – soon – you'll look back on all this and just laugh,' he went on, 'but for now, well, I need my staff to be fully committed, fully professional. You're very valuable to us, Audrey – *both* of you are very valuable.' He watched a cigarette packet spasming on the tarmac. 'It'd be a shame if we had to let one of you go just because of … you know … young love, young meaningless impulses …'

Audrey looked at him with a ghoulish expression.

'Don't give up on us, Audrey.'

She wiped her nose with her sleeve, still staring at him like he didn't understand her – or women – at all. 'I'm not giving up,' she snapped. She rose and started walking back towards the office, stopping just shy of the Post Office Tower to snarl over her shoulder: 'And it wasn't love.'

travails. However, it rapidly became clear that Sturgeon demanded unreasonably de-luxe pernickety toff-treatment for even the most meese and slack-jawed of his guests: help the invalids into their seats, serve with the right lapper, take away dirty troughs with the left, cutlers and crockery all lined up precise, nanti sneezing, coughing or vomiting within ogleshot, keep one's coddy opinions to oneself ...

35.1833°N

The lav 'gibberish' comes from Gibraltar. Apparently natives of the Rock speak this meshigena spic-rosbif lingo that makes Polari seem like the Queen's,* but – ALAS and ALACK – the daffy ex-pats in the Grand Columbia or Grand Cannibal Grill did not mince their lavs:

'This sandwich is structurally unsound!'

'The dumbwaiter is more engaging than this steward!'

'The child had its thumb in my compôte of prunes!'

33.5333°N

After the grotesque hellfire of my first breakfast-luncheon-dinner shift, I went out on deck to ogle the twinkly sunset and slurp up some much-needed sea-fizz.

We were in the dirty dishwaters someplace ajax to where the Med meets the Atlantic, the aqua flickering silver, peach and cheesemould-blue as the sol disappeared. The view was just about dolly and tranquil despite the floating freakshow tearing through. Roundabout me the tourists were playacting

---

* Merritt can vouch for the impenetrability of the Gibraltan 'Llanito' vernacular. He was posted at Gib during WWII, and at times the Barbary apes made more sense to him than the locals.

sophisticats: cackling away with dead opals, listlessly sucking caca-sized cigars, politely nodding along with their peers' breezy holiday bigotry, kishkas in tangles, obscene gluttony passed off as seasickness. For them this was relaxation: vagarying from port to port in a safe sterile container, sunning their repellent work-ravaged bods, grimacing at third-rate overworked monos, schlumphing extortionate bevvies, ogling the advertisements in the duty-free glossies. The cold boastful thrill of ejaculating dinarli into the Big Blue Deep.

The twistiness among these corpses was palpable. These trips were the highlight of their twilight years: seasick spinsters sharpering for love among a skeleton crew of mostly ineligible funguses and homosexual barkies, plastic toffs trying to inflate their status through their choice at the munjarry-table:

'Bouillon bourgeoise or Scotch broth, sir?'

'Bouillon bourgeoise!'

'Certainly, sir.'

And then the bastards look poked-up when a naff clear soup arrives.

I tried to spit into the waves as the last rays of sol snuffled out. The wind uncharitably slopped it straight back into my eek.

'Novak! What are we doing out here? Speak speak speak speak!'

I wiped my garglings away with my sleeve. 'Finished watch, sir. Just taking the healthy briny aero, then bed, sir.'

'Have we travelled through some special time zone I'm not aware of?'

'Pardon me, sir?'

'Speak!'

'Repeat the query please, sir?'

'The suppers! The passengers require their bloody suppers and nightcaps!'

Irritatingly my luppers were frittying now, but I managed to reply with the pogi morso of confidence I had left: 'I'm only sixteen, sir. By law I cannot work more than eight hours a ju— a day, sir. And a twelve-hour rest between each watch, isn't that right?' That was the solo legal morso I'd saved from Gravesend.

'You're in international waters now, Novak,' he snapped with his oyster turned right up, lappers flapping excitedly, musty feathers fizzing from his tropical tux-cuffs. 'Same laws don't apply. Smoothen your blouse, you prick, tighten your bloody bowtie, and fuckering –'

33.4962°N

Ugly travails indeed. To my horror SS UNMENTIONABLE rapidly felt like a petty floating sharpering-state, a slave-barka, a toxic spearmint oil spill. Cruelty and intimidation disguised as salty banter. Condescending boss-plops, pigheaded sea-lawyers. Sharks galore. Even worster (or at least saddest of all) were the lowly barkies reering along with the daffy abuse from the bats at the top: sycophantic footsoldiers happy to carry out ever more ridiculous orders so as not to incur their superiors' wrath. Soon they even start palavering the same fash batty lingo. These are the real slaves to The Travails, Ô comrades: the yé-omis, the inmates impersonating the turnkeys, the newts desperate to snatch frankly pitiful promotions and privileges at any cost, the rats trying to impress the ratcatcher ...

28.9625°N

Herman was one of those rats. He'd taken to The Travails well – too well, in my opinion. Had H.H. been brave enough to drag his knuckles and join me in the Duty-Free Lavvystyle, we could've spent the trip idly glass-collecting, dilly-dallying and lovemaking until the eagles forced us to minny the gangplank at Cape Town, but instead his brown-vonka and enthusiasm for drudgery revealed a chasm between us. His slavery-with-a-smile only highlighted my own indolence and ineptitude, and as a result I was targeted molto brootishly by the bigwigs for the rest of this horrendous voyage ...

What angered me mostest about the petty scab was his unflinching willingnesss to degrade himself for extra dinarli, to perform like a simpering mono for tips, like it was somehow a grandiose honour felching the trummuses of these detestable arroganki gillies and flatties for the odd manky medsa-caroon.* But then what did that make me? Slithering about on my bruised lappers and lally-caps, lathering the fo'c'sle for these f'ck'r'ng f'lthy f'sc'sts?

Owing to a pogi few mishaps the previous noche (scalding aqua in the diners' fingerbowls, vonka-bombas in the bouillon bourgeoise, sleep paralysis when interrogated), Chief Steward Sturgeon had downgraded me to galley-chavvy: a distinguished role, the highlights of which were scrubbing-out, peeling dirty terrapoms and mopping up vomitus on perhaps the most vomitus-inducing barka on the Setta Seas. Still, even though I had the mostest pathetic travails on the UNMENTIONABLE now, worster even than the ship's limping purrer, I at least still had my revs. I could just about blot out the pain and misery, picturing myself elsewhere: shimmying in a grass skirt on the tropical atomic shores of Bikini Atoll; splishing in a gigantic creamy bubbling Admirals' Pie with frolicking prawns and turquoise-sequinned mermen; commanding a bijou recreation of the Battle of Austerlitz, backed by a brigade of joshed-up Tricolore-flapping slugs and snails ...

These visuals helped me get through each dismal juno but – Ô, MAYDAY, MAYDAY! – little did I realise the toppermost officers had their own ultra-bizarre fantasies brewing in their batty servos, ready to unleash on us poor underlings in the heat of the bulging sol ...

---

* Your guess is as good as ours. Mysteriously, our authority on Polari went missing at this point.

13.4333°N

The posters appeared in the working corridors after a short stop in the Gambia to refuel and stare at the locals walloping in tribal schmutta. There were duey variations, printed on foolscap with official-looking lavs:

DOWN WITH THE WOGS!

DOWN WITH THE WOGS!

DOWN WITH THE WOGS!

and

SLIMY POLLIWOGS BEWARE!

Who was responsible for this cateva colonic claptrap? Had Chief Steward Sturgeon finally snapped? Or perhaps these were the pastings of a deranged tourist, some scatty parochial twat driven to bitter aggro after witnessing those delectable naggy-chested spade-omis walloping back thataways – or after receiving one exotic reheated meal too many?

Ô, if only there were a gross friendly iceberg in these toasty waters to put us all out of our meese cooped-up misery ...

8.4844°N

On the first juno of Decembre my fears were confirmed. There was a conspiracy afoot.

I was happily revving away – imagining the rebellious heiress Nancy Cunard herself liberating me from the galley, ravishing me and marrying me, allowing me access to her eagle-eek papapa's bottomless stinking glittering shipping fortune – when Sturgeon burst in with the following batty demands: 'WAKE UP! Look alive, ratings! The Equator is but days away! All trusty Shellbacks, please present your certificates!'

'Shellbacks?' I mumbled blankly.

As if savvying clear what the meshigena prat was palavering about, Herman reached for his valise and plucked some legal bimph out from under his pantofels. I vadared through crusty lids the lavs 'IMPERIUM NEPTUNI REGIS' and SOMETHING-SOMETHING 'OF THE RAGING MAIN'. Twas all just imperialistic jibber-jabber to me.

When Sturgeon handed back H.'s certificate, there was a sparkle of collusion between them, like they were enjoying some coddy joke at my expense.

'Novak! Your Shellback Certificate?' the Chief gurgled.

'Pardon me, sir?' I writhed helplessly in my cot like a maggot on hot asphalte. 'My passport, is it?'

'Passports are redundant at zero degrees! Present to me now your Shellback Certificate or else face THE FINAL SOLUTION!'

From this angle, the twonk's nostrils looked so cavernous he could've snuffled me up in one snort. I tried to humour the addle-plot: 'I'm afraid, sir, I don't yet possess this mostest scrumptious exclusive scroll ...'

'What are you?'

'Sorry, sir?'

'Speak speak speak speak!'

'Um. Bellboy. Well, galley-chavvy now, galley-boy, sir ...'

'Are you a wog?'

'I'm half-frog, sir, I've admitted that much. But a frog with full and pure British citizenship, sir.'

'Incorrect! You're a wog, Novak. A bloody slimy Polliwog!'

And with that, the baffling fash batatat stomped outways, unceremoniously clanging the bulkheads with his fists as he went.

Sturgeon had lost his tet, there was nix doubt about that now. I fancied he was suffering from some form of meshigena megalomania mixed with cabin fever. The zot wasn't the toppermost officer onboard, but he was acting like a supreme dicktittler, as if the latty-on-water was this de-luxe floating colony he wanted to ethnically dhobi before we hit Australia. But who were these so-called wogs he screeched about? And why was I counted among them?

I stretched myself out like a beached sparklefish, hopeful that the other officers would pull him up on it soon enough – or else straitjacket the supremacist cunt and slam him in the brig before some bloody uncivil war broke out in our cramped working corridors ...

8.3974°N

When I questioned Herman about the certificate, the limp prick was as evasive as ever. All he was willing to share was: 'Tis a ritual from quatra-chenta annos ago.'

I pointed out that he shouldn't encourage Sturgeon if the officer's servo was malfunctioning, and the Sub-Humanoid took it like I'd desecrated his dearest uncle's grave. 'Shut your screech, you charvering manky Polliwog!' he shrieked, claws bared and tongue hanging out like a demented griffin. 'The Chief's lavs are perfectly sane, bona and true!'

The fact that he was using Polari now confirmed he was a dish-licker, a pathetic petty catamite – and I savvied clear enough who'd been buggering him between watches. The chavvy was like a bijou version of Sturgeon. He'd even cultivated his own downy handlebar mouser, and I clocked the same coddy vonka-flaring glaze as he unleashed more grotty robo-lavs: 'Get on all-quatras, wog! Lick my sweaty, hard-working platters, why don't you!'

I was tempted to schonk him but didn't fancy spending the juno in the brig myself, especially if Sturgeon was likely to be slammed in there any minuta now. Instead, I got dressed tranquil, topped up my milky maquiage and said not another bona lav to the petty batatat for the rest of my lavvy.

Does it need to be stated that I wasn't attracted to the ingratiating slug now? If the chavvy was lucky, I conceded I might ply him with bitter-gators and drogas and drunkenly fuck him to death when we got to Australia – but nanti promises.

For now the natty option was to just keep my tet down, ignore the abuse, avoid the Pig, keep my oyster-levers clamped and ADVANCE AUSTRALIA FAIR!

The Chief Steward was probably all wind and piss anyhow – and yet, when I emerged above deck that morn, immaculately turned out and more or less ready to embrace another exhilarating juno of spirit-crushing head-scrubbing, I discovered with maxi brooliment that it wasn't just the servile impressionable Herman Sturgeon had servo-lathered.

The whole barka was baying for blood.

1.0027°N

The Dollydrums. I was sluggishly sweeping the aft-end of the Sun Deck when an announcement was made over the tannoy:

'Attention all Polliwogs, all slimy invaders! This vessel will soon be trespassing in the realm of Neptunus Rex, Emperor of the Unholy Aqua-Reich! Abandon all hope, ye who enter here!' I didn't recognise the voche. It sounded like a pop with a shuttlecock stuck in its gargler. 'The Royal Scribe, Mr Davy Jones, shall shortly come aboard to deliver writs and round up all wogs. The Final Solution is nigh. DOWN WITH THE WOGS!'

More disturbing than the announcement was the gay eeks of the passengers. I could just about vada them smirking and cackling as they frittied in their deckchairs, lapping at pastel-coloured gelato.

When I signed onto the UNMENTIONABLE, I wasn't aware I was waltzing aboard a floating fash kangaroo court. I'd managed to keep my tet down the past week as planned, but nellied meshigena rumours about preparations for this scatty Final Solution the Chief Steward was so enthused about. Apparently the toffs' sloppy sickbags had been stashed, the cooks had been putting rotting fish-tets and giblets aside, efinks had been sharpened.

When I tried to lell some information from the tourists, they just hid their vonkas in their cocktail glasses and mumbled unpleasantries. Fascists in the past at least had the courtesy to spell out what pops they found disagreeable. As far as I could tell, us tarred Polliwogs were a mixed bag of colours, creeds and classes. Surprisingly most of the slopes in the steerage galley had managed to get their lappers on a protective Shellback Certificate, while I'm sure I clocked our high-rank Aryan Petty Officer being branded a wog at high tea.

Still, there was some queer camaraderie to be found during all this baffling discrimination caca. When I caught wind of an apparent 'profusion of wogs' toiling in the boiler room, I scuttled down thataways to see what the sooty pops knew – and whether or not they were interested in mounting some form of resistance against these mysterious Shellback oppressors. Tiptoeing my way down the perilous steely ladder in full-eek maquiage and a skimpy camisole, I fancied I might appear to these butch lonesome proles as a fortuni avenging angel or vampish Théroigne de Méricourt character – and yet the lusty hoots and catcalls I received were perhaps not as chivalrous and comradely as I might've hoped.

'Welcome to Hell, princess!'

'Join us by the roaring fireside, you delicious tartlet!'

'FUCK ME SIDEYWAYS!'

'I'm not sharpering for arva, gentlemen – this is merely my sleeping attire,' I polled, trying to maintain a stiff battleaxe-eek as I clambered through the spiderwebs of metal pipettes and greasy whirligigs to the grupa of stokers standing by the telegraph slurping herbata. Naturellement I'd expected to find an army of shirtless sooty strongmen shovelling coal into a flaming monster oyster – however, these pops just looked bored as they manned their bewildering vacayas, pumping black sludge through the pipettes to the growling furnaces ajax.

'We're all wogs, are we not?' I opined, propping myself

against an almost unbearably warm railing. 'Are we aware of the meshigena punishments to be dished out any minuta by the dicktittlers up thataways?'

'Come again?' one of the stokers polled, a grinning goggled pop in a baker-boy capella. 'Dishes and dick-ticklers, you say?'

'Did you not nelly the announcement?' I persevered. 'We're straying into hostile aqua. Does anyone savvy who this stroppy Neptunus Rex chappy is? Some West Afrikkkan despot with a gross disliking for wogs? Some tyrannical prick in cahoots with the anglo Establishment?'

The stokers reered up, seemingly unbothered that we might all be sacrificed to this daffy tyrant before dawn: thrown overboard, or sold off like some naff perishable consumable.

'King Neptune doesn't frighten us,' the goggled pop giggled.

'She's a fucking pantomime dame, so she is.'

'It's a tinfoil trident, don't you know.'

I blinked back at them blankly. 'You've vadared the pop in the flesh? What, pray tell, does he want from us? And why is it we've been cruelly singled out as wogs?'

The stokers reered up again.

'It's something to do with the Equator, dear heart,' the goggled pop went on. 'Those barkies who have already intrepidly crossed this imaginary line are considered trusty Shellbacks. Those who haven't are slimy Polliwogs and must therefore prove their mettle to the topmost seadog, the supreme briny being. But don't panic your dolly little thumper – it's all just a daft bit of slap-and-tickle, a mere –'

Just then a nervy voche polled from behind the escape ladder: 'I've heard they'll force us to eat human faeces from a scallop shell.'

The stokers' eeks crumpled. A meese gloom descended. Black leeches of sweat slithered down our foretets. The goggled pop gazed glazed into the mass of humming wigglies and twitchering dials, before taking a long, brooding schlumph of herbata. 'Surely not,' he mumbled. 'Nay – balderdash. Surely not.'

In a desperate bid to lighten the mood, the other stokers attempted to flatter me once more:

'You're a natural beauty, aren't thee, sunshine? Look at it: twinkling in the blaze.'

'Not like those waxwork sea-queens up thataways.'

'What say you show us a tiny bit more carnish? Ay, come hither: the light from the furnaces is most becoming, dollface.'

'We're sex-starved petty elves down here, sweetness,' a pop with gross tonnage polled, topping up their teacups with a glug-glug of Vat 69.

'Ay-ay, we are that.'

'Come now – it's far too warm for that slinky maxi-flammable nightie ...'

Savvying my nova comrades were grossly overilluminated, I boldly made my excuses and tottered back the way I came, ostrich-lallying as ladylike as possible over the assault course of oily ducts and wigglies. And yet, all things considered, the zots' grubby advances were not entirely disagreeable to me. Given that I'd been roundly ignored (if not outright cod-oystered and traumatised) by every eligible barky and leather-eek up topside, twas a novelty to receive any daffy compliment at all – and in fact I allowed one stoker in particular (the owner of the pogi voche behind the escape ladder: a charming burn-scarred Transvaalian teen named Kenneth) to become maxi friendly with me as the voyage creepied onwards.

Naturellement I did not allow the poor deformed pop to charver me but, as we edged towards Zero-Juno, Kenneth made all sorts of slushy dorcas promises to me: he would take me out for coffee and milktarts when we got to Cape Town, he would parker me a nova drogle or duey, we could frolic in our swim-trunks and bikinis on Bondi Beach, he would love me forever ...

While it was a shame my solo sober admirer on the barka was a teen with an eek like a sackful of biltong, I appreciated the companionship during this ultra skitterish period. The noche before the UNMENTIONABLE was due to reach the Equator, the two of us were tucked up in our favourite hideyhole: a hammock strung betwixt duey ventilation pipettes in the darkest morso of the engine room.

'What nova gossip have you gathered as to tomorrow's proceedings, my love? Anything new at all?' Kenneth whispered in my nellyhole.

'Nantoise, I'm afraid. Just the same tight scornful oyster-levers.' I scritch-scratched the back of my tet. 'Though apparently the toffs had scallops for supper tonight at the Cabaret Ambergris.'

'O the brutes.'

'I know.' I squinted into the ultraschvartz, imagining all the jolly exotic fishies romping carefree around our rudder. 'This must surely be among the mostest ridiculous of all workplace punishments, is it not? Attacking staff solely down to the fact the mond has a wet centre ...'

'The bastards will punish anything, Raymond. Any excuse, they'll terrorise and demean you.'

'Is there anything we can do to stop them?' I murmured, half tempted to try scuttling the barka with my own naggy lappers. 'Could you not just stop piping the black sludge to the furnaces? Bring the barka to a halt just shy of the Equator?'

Through the inky munge I could just about vada Kenneth's opals flickering back and forth, like he was already rehearsing this gloriosa mutinous emag in his servo.

He clutched my lapper tightly. 'But what about Cape Town, Raymond? How else would we get to Cape Town? What about our milktarts? What about our future?'

0°

After almost a fortnight bulldozering the Atlantic at thirty knots, SS UNMENTIONABLE came to a halt at zero degrees.

I was struggling to liberate a pomegranate pip from betwixt the decking when a gross sea-beastie shadow creepied over me.

'Raymond Marianne Novak, loathsome wog, remain on your hands and knees!'

I squinted skywards and saw only a schvartz silhouette blotting out the sol before my opals adjusted. The monster had a peg-lally, plastic seaweed-riah, false beard, Jolly Roger capella, scaly trenchcoat, black famblers.

'The Royal Scribe hereby summons you to appear before His Loftiness Neptunus Rex and the High Court of the Unholy Aqua-Reich!' Davy Jones gurgled, prodding me with his peg-lally. 'All confirmed Polliwogs, Untermenschen, landlubbers, peg-lickers, imbeciles, mongrels, general twats and trespassers – THE END IS NIGH!'

After ordering me to strip to my incontinence knickers, the briny batatat snapped a doggy-leash round my neck and dragged me on my lappers and lally-caps down to the Fun Deck. At first I tried to barny, screeching the injustice, THE INJUSTICE – but Davy* wasn't here to give me a fair nellying. He called on some of his fash mermen colleagues – strapping Shellbacks in fish-scale drag – to help whiplash and boot me down the steps, which, this close up, I at least found to be relatively well swept.

When we got to the Fun Deck I was deposited with other vulnerable Polliwogs round a pogi paddling pool amidships, all of us naggy except for slippies and in meese servile poses, eeks flush to the floor. Among the twisted rabble I clocked Kenneth quivering in his apricot-coloured briefs, and I wondered if the zot had stopped parnying yet. The tears were down to my behaviour that morningtide and not these upcoming punishments, diabolical though they may be. When we met for herbata and buttered toast in the Crew Mess at 6 a.m., for

---

* Despite some probing, we're not entirely sure why our Royal Artiste Mark Noon answers to the name 'Davy'. We believe he only began using the nickname in 1967, so he may have appropriated it from Davy Jones of The Monkees – but more likely it's just another of the man's unfathomable affectations. (Incidentally, we discovered that the mythical peg-legged Davy Jones's forename comes from the Caribbean patois word 'Duffy' or 'Duppy', meaning 'Devil'.)

some reason the sentimental twonk felt this was the optimum momento to propose marriage to yours truly. Twas not a legally binding union the omi was suggesting – rather one of these flamboyant mock weddings that were all the rage those salty junos, to announce our love (and, moreover, our unavailability) to the barka once this daffy Crossing the Line ceremony was over. Ô comrades, the mess hall was positively teeming with jeering barkies even at that ungodly hour. We were goaded unsparingly from all sides as Kenneth dropped to uno lally-cap and unveiled the ring, which I believe was some form of nut or washer shushed from the boiler room. 'I'll protect you, darling – at zero degrees, and beyond ...' was the main thrust of the teen's gooey declaration. Unable to look the disfigured pop in the eye, I clocked an even less appealing eek across the chamber – the Sub-Humanoid himself, sneering at us with arroganki delight from his perch by one of the portholes – and, clinging to my scanty pride by my luppertips, I insensitively snapped at the feeli stoker: 'I can't, comrade. I just don't find thee attractive at all, I'm afraid.'

And then the parnyaqua erupted.

I lost sight of Kenneth as Davy Jones and his henchmen roughhoused us into single file, before taking their places on velvety cushions either side of duey ornate empty thrones. After much painful tootering of plastic bugles, King Neptune and Queen Salacia emerged from the bridge, joshed-up in revolting regal clobber: Neptune swishing imperiously with cascading seaweed-riah, a mogue beard and pearly caroon, Salacia full-spangling with lofty fyke-net pompadour bouffant, rainbow-trout ballgown, bristly lallies and flippers.

'The High Court hereby finds you insolent, slimy wogs guilty of trespassing without licence in my gildi waters!' King Neptune bellowed through a bullhorn, that same voche we'd nellied over the tannoy. 'I sentence you all to face the Final Solution! To be examined, mentally challenged, cleansed, dissolved and then resurrected as trusty Shellbacks!'

Flaring my nose-thirls derisively, I glanced around my ajax captives and clocked a few fellow slaves from the Grand Cannibal Grill, duey hungover stokers and our Petty Officer molto poked-up in his discoloured Y-fronts. Alas, I ponced, there would be nanti superheroic resistance from these dismal plops. Uno by uno we were wrenched to our platters and sent along the wretched assault course the Shellbacks had set up for us. With my foretet still stuck to the deck, waiting my turn, I could just about vada a long tarpaulin tunnel bulging with unpleasantness, a monstrous first-aid tent and some foreign caca floating in the pool-aqua. Grimacing from their balconies up above, the tourists were brootishly finishing off their greasy imperial breakfasts.

'Novak! What are you?' Davy Jones screeched at me when it was my turn to minny the gauntlet.

Learning from those who'd gone before, I savvied the answer he was looking for was: 'Slimy Polliwog, sir!'

'Exactly! Proceed!'

As I set off scarpering through the meshigena obstacle course, dodging schonks and whiplashes from pouting Shellbacks at every turn, twas nigh on impossible to distinguish what was mere coddy tomfoolery and what was all-out sadism. The whole scenario had the feel of a circus big-top landing like a daffy UFO at Dachau. Militant omi-palones in mermaid tails battyfanging naggy underlings with sharpering-batons and schvartz rubber phalluses. A glimmering red cross. The mostest unsanitary first-aid tent in all of Christinedom. Decapitated mannequin limbs littering the decking. Pools of blood, caca and parnyaqua. Dragged inways by duey nurses in jackboots and skimpy lime-green scrubs. Clamped in the stocks. Oyster wide-opened with a gross speculum. The doctor – this thoroughly unhealthy-looking fungus in a blank lab coat and jaundice maquiage – examined my flickering lingum before squirting a rapid syringeful of bin-jus or toff-vomit down my gargler. Futile screeches. More batons. 'What are you?' 'A wog! A nasty Polliwog!' 'Exactly! Proceed!' Next: locked in a vast gaol-like cot with an obese gurgling bambino. Twas my job to lell the tiny clef from the baby's navel without using my lappers. Eek forced into his stinking flab. Belly all greased up with bambino-oil, Tabasco, garlic, lemon jus, quong-sirop, et ceterarara. More screeches, more vomitus. More whiplashes. A tightrope strung across a pogi paddling pool filled with bloodthirsty crustaceans. Metal lobster claws attached to my nipplets, levers and oglelids. Smacked in the lally-caps. Strapped in a barbers' chair. Tet fatchared by a demonic riah-shusher. Clumps of my beloved Brilliantined bouffant flappering to the ground like shotgunned blackbirdies.

'What are you?'

'A wog!' I gasped through the parnyaqua. 'A wog, a wog!'

Worstest of all was the Final Solution. After crawling through the tarpaulin tunnel – an immense plastic lower intestine filled with rotting munja, dirty almond-rocks, luppernail clippings, green cheese, soiled sanitary napkins, fish-tets, dead rats and French letters – it should've been a relief to be cleansed in the cooling aqua, and yet this was more like the ordeal-by-water at a fuckering medieval witch trial.

The aqua in the swimming pool had been clean once but, after accommodating all the Polliwogs before me, was now filled with the Devil's backwash: the 'Final Solution'. Morsos of caca and raw onion floated by my oyster as I was dunked repeatedly by duey silent Shellbacks, held under the surface until my bod went limp, then hurled back outways over and over and over again. At one point, gasping for aero after my fourth or fifth dunking, I clocked Kenneth at the other end of the pool receiving the same treatment, firing chlorinated gunge from his vonka and parnying hysterically now. I tried to catch his opal, to offer some pogi morso of love and solidarity in this mostest appalling nightmare scenario, but, whether through bitterness or just blind distress, the teen stared right through me.

I was dunked once more – and almost blacked out.

When I resurfaced, King Neptune was casting his royal munge over me and, waggling his tinfoil trident aloft, declared through the bullhorn: 'And there you have it: another scaly slimy pleb, reborn! What are you, Novak?'

Still regathering my senses, I answered groggily: 'A wog, sir. A stinking, festering Polliwog ...'

Above us, the toffee corpses* all gasped into their baby-pink grapefruit jus and cackled, like I'd palavered out of turn.

'Incorrect!' Neptune bellowed. 'This lad is unsound in the brain, unfit to make his transformation! The cleansing took nix effect! Back to the doctor for a fresh examination!'

My boomboomer squelched as I savvied my mistake. I tried to reverse my answer, but mostly my lavs were just incoherent gurglings as the mermen grabbed me and dragged me back to the starting line. And so I had to scarper through the entire assault course again – jarrying the doctor's medicine, retrieving the bambino's clef, tiptoeing the tightrope, every last wisp of

---

* Novak's continual references to Nazism and corpses here irritated Merritt and Trefoil, given they both served aboard battleships during WWII: vessels that on occasion had to transport actual corpses around the Mediterranean and Middle East.

While Trefoil admittedly witnessed little bloodshed hunkered down in the ASDIC control room of HMS *Hostile*, Merritt was one of three sick-berth attendants aboard HMS *Legion* – and to this day he's still haunted by visions of his own ordeal-by-water: the dismembered limbs, the charred flesh, the rubbery death-stares ...

While undoubtedly unappetising and uncalled-for, it was frankly laughable that Novak refers to his Merchant Navy hazing as the 'mostest appalling nightmare scenario'. Night terrors were rife aboard HMS *Legion*, given that the ship was vulnerable to shadowy German U-boats and Italian frogmen as she valiantly escorted supply boats and aircraft carriers through the Strait of Gibraltar to our naval fortress at Valletta, Malta. The frogmen caused the most concern: these mysterious seaweed-capped silent assassins that targeted our ships in the Bay of Gibraltar, cutting through security nets and slithering through the water straddling motorised torpedoes, hellbent on strapping their ten-pound explosive cargo to our bilge keels. At night during these escort missions, Merritt regularly visualised his own body in pieces, strewn around the sick-berth floor – and yet his court martial in November 1941 (unfair and inhumane though it was) meant he was secure in a sanitarium in Hertfordshire when the destroyer was sunk four months later, beached and bombed sideways at Boiler Wharf after a Stuka attack off Malta.

riah fatchared, every inch of my bod smeared with sludge in the tarpaulin tunnel – before returning to the swimming pool for another dunking. Since I was now the last remaining wog to be converted, there were otta sadistic Shellbacks waiting for me in the aqua. I was parnying quite helplessly as I was dunked for the umpteenth time, feeling utterly untogether now, like I'd lost something of myself along the way. It wasn't just that my tet was full-baldy and my maquiage had dissolved – I felt like a bona fide Untermensch, like my whole identity had fizzled away in that murky aqua.

When I resurfaced, I schlumphed down gulp after gulp of warm prickly aero, bobbing inconsolably in the vat.

'We meet again, Novak!' King Neptune yelled. 'So what are you?'

I spat out a chunk of caca.

'Speak speak speak speak speak!'

'A Shellback, sir. A trusty Shellback.'

A half-arsed cheer sounded out around the Fun Deck.

'And a bloody ugly one at that,' Neptune added, to wild hoots of reering and lapperclaps from every pop – the corpses, the High Court, the nova converts and their captors, and not least Kenneth, cackling full-venomous from the sideylines – in ogleshot.

Mystery Levers*

NOVAK WEARS A BLACK VOGUEING-JACKET, SHINED BOOTIES, A FLEUR IN HIS BUTTONHOLE AND AN EXCITED COLIN TINGLING OUTSIDE HIS LALLY-COVERS.

As I grew out of my teens, I only seemed to get uglier. When finally my riah reappeared, it seemed wispier than before, my hairline grossly receded by stress – or was it just coddy genes? My adult fangs fell out, having never ogled a brush. My oink-vonka sprouted duey X-rated warts.

After escaping the fash black-fambler grip of the UNMENTION-ABLE, I decided to hop rapidly from barka to barka, trying to re-establish myself as a respectable, eligible sea-pup, but it seemed every queen in every Fruit Locker of every cruise-liner had caught wind I was meese – 'Nauseatingly meese!' – under the maquiage.

In the spring of 1964 I awoke one morn on my nova latty-on-water, RMS OPEN-MINDEDNESS, to a familiar he-she shriek coming from the peak nex-bor:

'Did you nanti nelly the Cosmonaut in the noche, duckies? Going at me full-blown. Like she was trying to shush secret intelligence direct through my cartso ...'

'That's twice in duey noches now! Did you not vada the fantom's eek?'

'Nix, he was going at it so aggressive, the sod's visor was all misted up. And frankly I wasn't going to pause to dhobi it with a chamois leather now ...'

---

* Chapter received Thursday, 15th January 1970 – 179 days to go.

The OPEN-MINDEDNESS had been afloat trey junos, but twas only now I clocked that the Duchess Winnie Repulse was nexbor. I'd been hiding hermit-like in my bunk, feeling my gruesome visage, irregular personality and lack of true acceptance were like some disease I'd never shake off – but at least Winnie was a bona fide comrade from voyages past.

Somewhere in the munge of the bunk beneath mine, a stirring voche groaned: 'Them fucking queens, the lucky bats. They get the Cosmonaut every noche; all we get is Wandering Norman's stinking almond-rocks and the Frog's sickening snoring ...'

With the Cold War showing nanti sign of thawing, it may seem unusual that this mystery midnoche guest known only as the Cosmonaut was so popular among the anglo barkies. Apparently every merchant liner had a fantom-gobbler onboard – a covert poof who creeps into omis' bunks after lights-out to suck them off incognito – but none were revered quite so highly as the Cosmonaut. Part of his appeal was his sheer audacity. The Cosmonaut mixed the slyness of a Soviet spy with the outlandish Futurist schmutta of Buck Rogers, preying on sleeping omis' cartsos wearing just a grandiose astro-helmet and silvery jumpsuit. Despite the conspicuous clobber, if roused, the Cosmonaut's lucky prey ogled nix more than a cherry-red bobbing 'CCCP' and duey slurp-slurping oyster-levers round their glistening cockle. According to those who'd encountered the Cosmonaut, any attempt to unmask the midnoche visitor resulted in the visor slamming shut and those silvery lallies scuttling off into the munge of the working corridors – never to be vadared again that voyage.

When I accosted Winnie later that morn in the Crew Mess, she was surprised the Cosmonaut hadn't paid me a visit:

'You're no anglo rose, Raymond, let's be frank,' she munched, hunched over a bowl of hot papaya, 'but, regarding you through a steamy visor in the munge, what could Captain Ga-Ga hold against you? You're nanti hung like a mealworm, are you, ducky?'

'Non!' I squawked. 'Heroically well endowed. Just woefully underused.'

'Bollocks! I nellied you were charvering a charming little burns victim aboard the UNMENTIONABLE.'

'Certainly not.'

'And what about that cherubic blond tinker? What's-his-eek? H***? Vadared you two eloping at Gib.'

'She turned out to be an unresponsive petty batatat. I believe she was being buggered by the Chief Steward, so nix chance of any –'

'O, don't give me that. We've all buggered that bijou chavvy. An easy-mort, an open-door policy in that little tinker's sphincter, was it not?'

Each oysterful of porridge felt molto difficult to swallow now, like I was shovelling spoons of hardening concrete down my gargler.

'You're nanti still a mary, are you?' she asked, moving on to a steaming pot of herbata.

I nodded bashful. 'Oui.'

'Good God, that's the mostest pathetic cheet I've ever nellied!' Winnie hooted. 'A virgin barky! Rarer even than the Virginal Maria herself. Can you definitely see out of those squinty opals, dear heart? You've vadared the smorgasbord of brothels in every port? The rent-chavvies and gillies-on-batter eagerly awaiting fresh salty cock as soon as the gangway touches land?'

I let my spoon sink into the congealed muck. 'I refuse to parker for trade, Win. It's against my principles. The Duty-Free Lavvystyle. I can barely stomach paying for cheets with a price tag in a bona fide bodega, let alone shelling out for something that's supposed to come gratis.'

'Free love, is it?' Winnie frowned at me, ruminating with her little lupper erect as she schlumphed down more tea. 'What sort of free trade are you looking for? Manly-alices, sea-queens, gimps? Fish?'

'No omi'll bend for me. And for all the success I had with that easy-mort on the UNMENTIONABLE, I'm probably bestest off chasing fish, palones, jolly fillies. Only there's very few fishies under the age of fifty in the shipping industry, isn't that right?'

'What about that Chinoise fish, works in the galley? Nellied about her?' Winnie's voche doddered to a whisper. 'The palone with the fancy-free flange-levers?'

'Nix.'

'She's a randy beggar. Goes by the nom Madame Ōgazumu. Loves cock in the noche. Barely speaks anglo – in fact, nanti polari whatsoever, she's a mute. Very shy fish. But she's been known to offer her clamshell after dark on the fo'c'sle. Former sing-song donna, showgirl, recovering Communist. She cares not for a handsome visage or bona conversation, nor even dinarli – so long as you can get that petty underused cartso hard ...'

'I can.'

'Well, fantabulosa!' Winnie hiccoughed, hunching over again to poll her next lavs in confidence. 'Parker me a few bovaries in the Pig this very noche and I'll put in a bona lav for you.'

'Should I wriggle into some gildi schmutta? Some fleurs perhaps?'

'Just make sure you can get that cartso hard, Raymond. All we need is that charvering cartso hard.'

Despite the advice, I savvied it was proper to josh myself up, dhobi well, and douse myself in profumo before my date with Madame Ōgazumu. Winnie hadn't specified if the Chinoise was feeli or fungal, fortuni or meese, but it mattered not a jot to me. Apparently she operated behind a gloryholed bulkhead: a mystery hortus employed by the shipping line to stop sex-starved sailors exploding during a voyage. Molto likely she was a bona fide harlot rather than a Bona Samaritan but, having spent the last decade or so revving fruitlessly about free trade, I didn't mind surrendering ten or fifteen shillings in the Pig for my first stab in the dark with a living, breathing palone!

By the time Winnie led me through the munge to the fo'c'sle, we were both a hefty bit daffy. I'd schlumphed down half a dozen Allsopp's Tops and, as we frittied in the efinky sea-whizz, I was beginning to doubt my ability to raise a colin after all.

'Madame? Madame Ōgazumu?' Winnie called out in a respectful voche, trying not to reer as she grasped my wrist and steered me round the slippery slalom of bollards and fairleads. The fo'c'sle was ultraschvartz at this hour: perfect for a midnoche tryst, but perhaps not the bestest spot for staying on your platters after a pogi few grumblers. Jupiter knows how Winnie was managing to stay upright in her bod-strangling kimono and quatra-inch getas.

Eventually we stopped behind the grand winches: the darkest morso of the OPEN-MINDEDNESS, despite being directly under the bridge and the Captain and Commander's vonkas. Still grippering my wrist, Winnie guided my lapper through the munge to a petty porthole drilled through one of the jackfrosty bulkheads. Winnie purred, 'Madame? Are you there, Madame? This is Raymond. This is Raymond's hand. And this ...' – Winnie turned to me as my luppers met wet flesh – '... is the Madame. I'll leave you to it, ducky-egg. Enjoy yourself – but keep hush-hush, ja?'

As Winnie retreated back into the shadows, I felt my boom-boomer rioting in my ribcage. Half out of politeness and half out of cluelessness, I left my lapper resting on the Madame's moist morso for una minuta or duey, not sure if it showed a complete lack of decency to just shove my cartso straight in there.

Winnie told me Madame Ō wasn't interested in bona conversation, but after a pogi bit more nervy probing and dithering, I felt obliged to doppel-check: 'Madame? Ahem. Are you ... ready for me?'

'Hai, hai. Shush shush shush,' spluttered a bijou voche ajax, followed by a rapid intake of aero I took to be a giggle or sniffle. Momentarily it prickled my servo whether the Madame was in full health or not, but even the savagery that she might be carrying some lavvy-threatening venereal disease didn't stop a pogi uprising in my undercrackers.

As I unzipped, I nellied her fidgeting behind the bulkhead but she didn't back away. Her flange-levers seemed to part slightly, like she was inviting me in. And she was wet. Mein Gott, she was slippery!

Jittering with sickly delight, I lined my cartso up with Madame Ō's soggy O, and practically welded myself to the bulkhead as I inserted. With my first few thrusts I clocked those same toilet sounds Madame Ovary made with her spiv lovers, but it didn't break my stride. My colin was holding up straight and true in spite of the bovaries, the windfreeze and the fact that I was essentially charvering a black hole.

My lovemaking probably had more in common with riveting than romance, but duey minutas in and I was enjoying myself immensely! The Chinoise was the consummate professional, remaining mute throughout – though I admit I couldn't resist the odd grunt or oink myself as I charvered her at high speed.

'Groin-groin! Groin! Groin-groin! Phoo, you manky petty sparklet, you!' I wheezed.

Madame Ō made a brootish erotic squelch in response. I took it to be an appreciative squelch. The dame was positively dripping with arva-sirop – so much so, in fact, at one point my slick cartso sprang clean out of the bonaroba's slit, glistening like a newborn bambino's lally. When I shoved it back in, I appeared to be probing a different, molto tighter hole. Madame Ōgazumu didn't protest so I carried on clanging away, lappers and eek pressed flush against the frigid bulkhead, dribbling and gyrating demonic!

Daitcha thrusts later, I was twitch-twitch-twitchering my way towards a maxi explosive petty-mort, my servo gaily sailing through space – when all at once the cargo lights sprang on, throwing a white blaze across the fo'c'sle, and throwing aqua on my love-frenzy. My guilty silhouette kenza feet long, splattered from bridge to bow.

Either her squelches or my screeches must've alerted the Captain or Commander, and my thumper thrashed painfully as I nellied the irate voche howling* above our tets: 'RATING! What in God's name are you doing?!'

At first the blaze was as blindingly blank as the ultraschvartz, but as my opals adjusted I let out another sickly oink, vadaring the palone through the gloryhole. It wasn't a Chinoise. In fact, it wasn't even humanoid. Drilled to the back of the bulkhead, with oyster grinning dopey and barbed tail flickering limply, I savvied my sexual partner was a one-eyed stingray. The fish's solo opal stared back at me with nanti passion. My cartso was shoved in its other ogle-socket.

---

* By the time we received this chapter, Howling had been missing almost a fortnight. Harry might not have been the model Sales, Marketing & Finance man, but he was usually capable of punctuality. Rumours and paranoia rumbled around the office. Trefoil phoned Harry's home daily, but the receiver was never picked up. Davy joked Howling might've been inspired by Novak to join the Merchant Navy after all these tales of bum and fun, but others wondered: was it a coincidence that, just as Novak introduces the mysterious, homoflexible H***** H************, our own H.H. goes AWOL?

Reversal Rehearsal*

NOVAK WEARS GEISHA MAQUIAGE, CHERRY-BLOSSOM KIMONO, SHIMADA-SHYKA AND GETAS.

During those salty junos I often wondered if an omi's object in life was to ridicule and belittle his brothers: that never-ending, backstabbing race up the social ladder to nowhere in particular.

By the time RMS NARROW-MINDEDNESS docked at Durban, I was in dire need of a stiff grumbler, and oblivion. I'd been avoiding the mocking-janes in the Pig & Whistle but, what with my conspicuous nova role – delivering NON-URGENT MEMOs round the steerage corridors – I'd often run into barky addle-plots who'd screech 'Stingrapist!' and other such hurtful lavs, and I couldn't battyfang a response. My new Chief Steward might not have been a megalomaniac fash tyrant, but he was most certainly keeping an eagle-eye on me.

Teetotal for almost a month, I was in a coddy uptight mood as the Captain announced Durban was looming. The sea-queens had planned to get dragged-up and hit the buggery-bungeries of the ritzy upside-down city and so, to spite Winnie, I'd brazenly shushed her favourite kimono and clogs from nex-bor and got joshed-up in them myself. I went full-slap with the geisha maquiage and wriggled into one of her schvartz shimada-shykas, and savvied I might as well shush daitcha shillings too while I was bent scrabbling through her fakements.

---

* Two chapters received Tuesday, 20th January 1970 – 174 days to go.

As I disembarked – hobbling ultra unladylike down the wobbling gangway before my platters hit hot concrete – I felt like an Oriental flicker-sparklet mincing onto the set of some cateva science-fiction splatter. While the city itself was fantabulosa – golden playas licked by turquoise aqua, the skyline erect with shuddering palm trees, puff-puffering industrial colins and de-luxe Futurist hotels – it seemed the natives weren't maxi enamoured with us seadogs coming ashore. At first I ponced they might be bitter about the old anglo rule, Sud Afrikkka having gone solo a few years before, but molto likely they just didn't take kindly to omis flouncing about their city in Oriental skimpies and full-eek maquiage. I fooled myself into thinking I could blend in like any other foreign palone, but when I got settled in a dolly prole pub teeming with strapping spades I immediately found myself the butt of vicious ridicule, daffy mogue flirtation and aggro on a par with some of the worstest torments I'd suffered at sea.

Bruised, deflated and not even a pogi bit illuminated by my spilled doppel-Pernod, after escaping the doomy shebeen I savvied my only safe haven in this schmutta was one of the dockward bugger-bungeries – and yet the idea of socialising with the rum twonks I'd been trying my bestest to avoid all voyage did not fill me with much sparkle.

The gildi gleaming parasols on the playa turned to poisonous mushrooms as noche crept over. There was a homo watering-hole in every port, and they were easy enough to finger. I can't remember the nom of the one I minced into in Durban (the Dolly Sailor? The Moustachioed Cephalopod? The Beef Screen? The Wincing Pillowbiter?), but they were mostly interchangeable. The tober-omis of these establishments rarely made any attempt at bona décor or olde worlde homeliness, and this one had the feel of a fuckering fish-filleting factory: corrugated steely walls, nix benkels and a frozen conveyor belt on one side loaded with botties of Black Label, which presumably was the bar.

The clientele in these pubs wasn't exclusively queer, but for the most part the tattooed barkies left the perfumed barkies to their own devices. When I trolled in, there were a fair few clusters of omi-palones in maquiage, everybody reering and over-oystering as they were wont to do on a first noche ashore. Usually I would minny straight for these queens and gaily leech off their gildi exuberance for an hour or duey, but this evening I simply wanted to slither into the munge and schlumph down my pogi earnings in peace. And yet – ALAS/ALACK – I was not dressed for a discreet entrance.

The momento my clogs crossed the threshold, the barkies reacted as if some mutant lotus-fleur or angelic kamikaze pilot had crashed through the fenêtre. I braced myself for yet more coddy ridicule, but then rapidly realised these were not condescending opals ogling me through the vogue-haze. These were flashbulb eeks. These were rapt, randy goggle-eeks.

Distantly a foghorn grumbled. And now occurs a scenario that, when crime scholars use my lavvy as a case study in years to come, may well be fingered as the catalyst, the dynamite-fuse of my devilry!

At the time I merely thought it mildly amusing.

As I wriggled my way to the bar, countless drunken eeks pearled at me and cackled:

'Winnie, my chovi!'

'Duchess!'

'What gives us this pleasure? You're not usually one for browsing the dockyard fish counter ...'

'The Pig still out of bounds, is it? O, the horror! Those poor twisted colons!'

'Put your dinarli away, Winnie, dear. Get this bubbly down your gargler.'

A mystery lapper passed me a frothing flute of what I presumed was champagne but turned out to be Black Label. 'Santé!' I cried, and schlumphed it down rapid before the rabble clocked I wasn't the omi-palone they thought I was. And yet, as the noche wore on, I savvied not one of these scatty bats had even the pogiest inkling there was an imposter in their midst.

As I loitered there gulping down glass after glass of gratis Black Label and grinning along with their privvy unguarded anecdotes and petty grievances, more and more sea-queens kept mincing past, sprinkling me with aero-lammers and the odd, 'Winnie, my darling!' or 'Goddess!'

Hé-hé-hé-hé-hé-hé-hé-HÉ! Ô, I'd never experienced love and respect like this in all my lavvy!

I was trying my bestest not to palaver much, wary that my cockney-froggy lingo might alert them to my true self – 'Sore gargler,' I croaked, clutching my neck, 'nanti polari' – but then almost immediately as I left the grupa to piss, some greasy addle-plot sidled up to me, grippering my pol and demanding we talk:

'Winifred,' he spat. 'This dinarli you owe us ...'

My bod stiffened.

Though he was dressed feeli in a black beatnik turtleneck and drainpipettes, the omi must've been well into his forties or fifties,* his eek-wrinkles badly filled in with crusty pancake or builders' putty. The omi gestured at a mob of glowering twonks: nobba plainclothes barkies passing duey pitiful botties of pop between them.

'Today's payday for the stewards, is it not?' the fungus went on, himself probably a stoker or chippy, judging by his thews. 'Time to empty out your purse, Duchess.'

I lifted my left lapper to my gargler. 'Cannot speak, dear. Nanti polari. Sore –'

'Nanti that!' one of his comrades screeched from the sidey-lines. 'We've nellied enough of your claptrap: the chronic abdabs,

---

* Howling would often lie about his age when trying to pick up men, but, as Trefoil pointed out, if Harry Howling and Herman Hermaphrodite were one and the same, the fact that the 'pubescent louse' was two months younger than Novak (see the anti-climax of 'Tutti Frutti') would make Herman/Harry twenty-five today. Rotund, moustachioed and fully silver up top, Howling looked about forty-five at best. And Merritt knew why he'd left anyway. He just wouldn't let on to the others yet.

the sick uncle back homewards, the stock exchange crash, the lame racehorsies, widows' weeds, the Cosmonaut shushing your fuckering piggybank in the noche ...'

'I –'

Given the ultragloom of these omis' opals, I savvied Winnie's debts must've been somewhat sizeable. Before vagarying from the barka that evening I'd stuffed my entire month's wages in my bra-pods along with Win's shushed ten bob – and it worried me now that these twats might feasibly battyfang me to a blood-ied pulp and take off with my hard-earned beyongs. What to do, Ô comrades?

Ogling backwards, perhaps the nattiest option might've been to admit I was not Ms Repulse, that I'd merely borrowed the crone's schmutta and persona for the noche – but I was enjoying the daffy masquerade too much to surrender that easily. Fluffing myself up like a gross mynah-birdy, I let rip with the bestest impersonation of Winnie I could muster: 'Look, dunnock-egg, I promise your dinarli will be with you pronto. My phynances are in bona nick – my only niggle is this: I've just this noche converted all my earnings to Sud Afrikkkan rand. Worthless bimph outside this topside-turvy territory, I fear. What say you wait til I've got the Queenie's tet back in my petty purse – then I'll parker you your fair dues? And in the meantime – let me offer you some bonus services of mine. Nix – not arva – but what say I dhobi all your grubby laundry over the week-end? You recall what peak I reside in? Numero 22, bottom bunk to the left. Deposit thy stinking slippies and rotten almond-rocks on my bed tonight, all your sweaty clobber, greasy overalls, et ceterarara. Twud be my pleasure to lather them pansy-fresh for Monday morn ...'

The omi ogled me curiously. 'You're happy to dhobi our underwear?'

'Oui, ducky. The lot.'

'After all the kishka troubles this week?'

'Kishka troubles?'

My interrogator seemed molto enthused as he enlightened me: 'Food poisoning. Been going round the Pig & Whistle all week. Nix doubt picked up on that last grisly layover in Namibia ...'

'Ô, is that so?' I too was tickled by this news but managed to keep a straight eek under the sing-song maquiage. 'Well, comrade, it's the least I can do, truly.'

'You weren't affected by the bacteriums yourself?' The sidey-line pops almost seemed sympathetic now, wrongfooted by my dorcas poppycock. 'Our knickers are in rather a mess. Watch you don't contaminate yourself, Duchess. We don't want that proud botty of yours in disarray ...'

'Nanti that,' I scoffed, discreetly shushing another Black Label from a passing prune. 'I haven't got a dish, don't you know? Nanti arsehole.'

'Come again?'

'Nix dish, darling.' I raised my voche, so all ajax pops could nelly my lavs. 'I was born without an arsehole, duckies!'

Horrified, my fungal comrade's voche was like a twisted chavvy's now: 'No, but ... still ... you must be ... How do you ... defecate?'

Grinning ghoulishly, I was ready to launch into some spiel about a Harley Strasse quack reversing my large intestine, enabling me to sick up my stools, when all at once my wig flew off and there was a brootish TILT-VLAM-SPLATCH! behind us. Spinning roundwards, I near enough screamed like a hysterical wolfy when I clocked the bona fide Winifred Repulse toppled on her corybungus, clutching the shushed shyka betwixt her painted claws. She looked like an upturned woodlouse in drag, albeit slightly less flamboyant drag than yours truly.

Savvying the wig had saved me from a painful scalping, I slurred something semi-triumphant, then scarpered for the portal before the louse righted itself. I am the epitome of James Bond in every respect except for a tendency to run away whenever my lavvy gets heated. I kicked off my clogs, missing

Winnie's tet by just an inch or duey, then vagaried naggy-plattered out onto the Esplanade, the palm trees all swishering revoltingly while the sea-whizz tried in vain to sober me up.

MERZ! The month of alcool-abstinence had not helped me in the slightest, Ô comrades. As I hurried away from the bungery, I felt so daffy I got motion sickness from the smooth paves. Vaguely aware that I might need the empty botty to smash across Winnie's skull in self-defence, I schlumphed the rest of the lager down rapid – and threw up three yards short of a bellydancing dustbin. When her venomous sequinned silhouette failed to appear, I hurled the botty PFFF! at a condescending lamppost instead.

Dithering through the hmmmming munge of the docks in search of our noble blue barka, I figured there'd be an almighty barny once Win got back to the Fruit Locker, but I wasn't ultra frightened. The sea-queen was older and molto heavily built than me, but the anaesthetic armour of the bovaries would see me through. I'd take my beating like a manly-alice: passive-aggro,* like those noble spade sitters of the southern states of Amerikkka (MULTILOVE AND SOLIDARITY, DEAR SOUL BROTHERS ...).

I crept aboard the barka and just about managed to slur my rating number at the chavvy on watch. I stumbled down the working corridors on alien lallies, the carpets even more hideous and swirly than I remembered. Sharpering for my starboard peak, I pondered if I should just hide in some other morso of the ship – down in the stores, or tucked up behind the bilge pump – but ultimately the lure of my fluffy eiderdown was too strong. The nattiest option for now was just to barricade myself in Peak 61 and play dead – and face the codswallop consequences in the morn.

I flopped through the door. Our cabin was ultraschvartz, but I could just about vada my bunkmates were still ashore, their bed-clobber flat-calm and tranquil. After a pogi bit of encouragement,

---

* We take it Novak has confused passive resistance with passive aggression here, but no need to flail our corrective Biros like police batons ...

my bedside cabinet eventually came free from the bulkhead. Squatting like a sumo bullfroggy, I brootishly shuffle-wrestled the cheet in front of the portal – then pronto collapsed. Ogling with hindsight, the bijou empty unit was never going to keep out raging invaders, but when I slumped onto my mattress I fell asleep surprisingly easy, the bevvies recklessly reassuring me I was as secure as a moth in a bulletproof cocoon, a pearl in a tight-levered oyster, a marble goddess in a concrete overcoat ...

Knacker's Yard

NOVAK WEARS HALF-EEK GEISHA MAQUIAGE, CHERRY-BLOSSOM KIMONO. NANTI SHYKA, NIX GETAS.

When I came to, the portholes were drippering with sol. At first I ponced I was hangover-free, but as I re-jumbled the memories of the previous noche and clocked the cabinet still blocking the portal, the throbs in my tet fired up ruthless. I wondered why Winnie hadn't blasted her way into the peak – or my fantom bunkmates for that matter.

Sharpering round the bulkheads for a ticktocker, rapidly I savvied I was in the wrong cabin. Judging by the direction of the sickly flowing glitter outside, I'd managed to find my way starboard, but the furniture and fakements were all wrong. The stiff Breton stripes on my bedclobber had contorted to jagged pentagrams. Pasted by my bunkside was a foto of a fattygayed palone with duey chavvies grimacing round a glimmering birthday caca.

I dragged the cabinet back to the bulkhead and ogled myself breathless in the mirror. I looked like I'd put my maquiage on with a lead pipe. There were nix valises or hanging schmutta in the peak, so I had nanti uniform nor civvies to change into. I straightened the skimpy kimono on my sweaty hunched bod, coughed up something greenish, then crept out into the working corridors, ultra poked-up and untogether.

'Excuse me there, pardon the schmutta,' I croaked at the first steward I came across. 'This is the OPEN-MINDEDNESS?'

'The what, sorry?' He regarded me like I was a blood-sucking lamprey.

'RMS OPEN-MINDEDNESS?' I repeated.

'Never heard of it.'

'The OPEN-MINDEDNESS, you say?' came a crackly voche from the peak ajax. 'Didn't it go to the knacker's yard?'

'Nix. No, no. I was on it just this last noche,' I shouted back. 'Just last night.'

'Decommissioned, I believe, matey,' the voche insisted. 'She was left to rot back at Georgie Five, was she not? The OPEN-MINDEDNESS? Knacker's yard, I'm sure of it.'

The first steward raised his ogle-riders.

'I'd best go see the Chief,' I conceded.

After a rapid dhobi I wriggled back into my clammy kimono, then reluctantly slithered upways to the officers' quarters. Huffering unhealthily, I at last found the Chief's bureau after umpteen wrong turns and let myself in without knocking. The boss was in the midst of fatcharing, his eek full-frothy save for a hovering petty mouser – plus he was naggy from the waist down.

'Sorry, sir,' I spluttered.

'Briefs! Pantaloons!'

'Excuse me, sir?'

With opals pasted shut with cream, the Chief gestured flappingly towards the Y-fronts and pressed lally-covers hanging by the dresser. Grudgingly I lifted the blank underpants by their elastic, savvying I'd best indulge the superior bat's whims, for the momento at least.

'Chop-chop, rating,' he snapped as I fumbled pulling them up round his thews. 'Who are you, sonny? Name, rank, article number, nationality?'

'Raymond Novak, sir. Bellboy. Zero-zero-two-zero-one. Half frog, sir, but full British passpo–'

'O, blood and guts – APPREHEND THIS HOPELESS STOWAWAY!' The lavs were so forceful, I lost control of the lally-covers, sending them skittering back down round his ankles.

'I'm sorry, sir. I savvy I might've made a mistake ...' I tugged them up again, and ZIP-ZIPped. 'Is this not RMS OPEN-MINDEDNESS?'

'You know what liner this is, rating. Listen to her sweet purring ...' Kenza startling pearls appeared under the Chief's mouser as he smiled rapt at the ceiling. I stuck out my bottom oyster-lever. All I could nelly was the same old seasick churn. He added, 'Well, perhaps this will jog your memory ...'

As the Chief carried on shaving, a familiar eek materialised through the fog of the fatcha-cream. Once rinsed, VLOP SPLATCH VLOP, the fash batatat flared his gross Coliseum-nostrils and declared: 'SS UNMENTIONABLE, rating. And she's carrying some very precious cargo this voyage! Who authorised you to board? Speak speak speak!'

My lallies buckled. 'Ô. I may have m-minced aboard by accident yester-noche, Mister Sturgeon, sir. A dark night, by all accounts. Alcool may have been a factor, I fear.'

The Chief Steward let out a sang-freezing scream: 'FUCKING INCOMPETENTS!'

'You're not pleased to see me?'

'Under present circumstances, rating: no, I'm not pleased to see you.' He grimaced, a pogi slug of shave-cream still clinging to his chin. 'If I remember rightly, you were a dish-monkey, a U-bend-botherer, and not a wholly competent one at that.'

I tried to stand straighter. 'After three years service, sir, I'm pleased to announce I was promoted to messenger aboard the OPEN-MINDEDNESS.'

'O, wunderbar – the OPEN-MINDEDNESS, you say? Well then, please kindly deliver this message to the noble crew of that glorified rubber dinghy: "Save our souls – stop – get this twat to fuck off back to wherever he came from – stop – and we hope never to lay eyes on the gruesome little shit ever again – stop."'

'I'll gladly rejoin the OPEN-MINDEDNESS, sir. Are you headed back towards Dar es Salaam, by chance? We were due to dock there in three junos, sir, then my hitch is over. Shore leave. Flight booked to London. FINITO. Puff-puff. Gone.'

'And now the runt speaks of air travel!' Chief Steward Sturgeon's opals glimmered pinkly. 'Well, I hate to spoil your stratospheric aspirations, rating – PLASTIC CUTLERS! PLASTIC DOLLYBIRDS! BLOODY REHEATED MUCK! TURBULENCE! ENGINE MALFUNCTIONING! DOWN DOWN DOWN! – but we're headed in the opposite direction.'

I edged towards the portal. 'Nanti worry, sir. Not to worry. I'm more or less happy to muck in here, once I get my tet straight. I'll take my leave when we next dock ...'

'O! Hearken this! O, you'll take your shore leave in the fucking Gambia, will you? You're holibobbling along with the wogs this year? We don't hit civilisation until Gibraltar, rating.'

'Give me some whites and I'll work. Or give me a jumbo beachtowel. I'll hide under it on the Sun Deck til Gib.'

Ô, what had I become, dear comrades? This natty shirker, this duty-free libertine now pleading the Chief for more ugly ugly travails!

Sturgeon's eek twisted, squeezing sang from the petty sores he'd hacked open with the fatcha-blade. After gazing off into the medsa-distance for some time, he polled: 'So, you're a frog who identifies himself as British, is that correct? Are you familiar with the British royal family at all?'

'I'm not on speaking terms, no ...'

'You recall me mentioning this precious cargo we currently have on board?'

'Vaguely, sir, yes.'

'Rating, nellyarda. You happen to have stumbled aboard a liner carrying de-luxe passengers: royalty, no less. No – not Liz herself, not Margaret and her swinging set of scoundrels. Minor royalty, but blue-bloods all the same. Some tedious goodwill crawl around the old colonies. Now – pay attention, imbecile – while it's tempting to just slam you in the brig or throw you overboard and be done with it, I admit we could use the extra hands. You understand where topside is on this ship? The first-class quarters?'

My opals brightened. 'Yes, sir!'

'Right, well, you're not to go anywhere near it!' Sturgeon

fastened his cufflinks. 'Stay well away from topside. Report back to me here in thirty minutes, Novak. There'll be whites waiting for you. And for Heaven's sake: dispose of that ghastly unpatriotic gook-clobber immediately. DISMISSED!'

Neptunus Rex*

THROWING UP ENTHUSIASTICALLY INTO A BUCKET OF ROTTING FISH-TETS, NOVAK WEARS A BAGGY BLANK CAMISHA, SKINTIGHT JACKET, SPLIT LALLY-COVERS, BROWN BOWTIE AND OFF-BLANK SLIP-ONS. STAINS PREVIOUS MODEL'S.

29.8831°S

As we headed north, I couldn't help wondering if these minor royals had their trusty Shellback Certificates ...

6.1333°S

For the first week or so I didn't vada the supreme toffs, unless they were mingling incognito among the plebs in mufti rather than mincing about like gildi hippos in their robes and caroons.

Sturgeon kept a close opal on me that first week. On the dolly OPEN-MINDEDNESS I'd been entrusted with only naff passenger-to-passenger memos like 'DORIS & MABEL AWAIT YOUR COMPANY IN THE SPINSTERS' LOUNGE' or 'MRS SIMON HONEYDEW ASKS MR SIMON HONEYDEW: PINK BISMUTH OR KAOLIN AND MORPHINE DARLING?' whereas on the molto formidable UNMENTIONABLE I was sometimes handed urgent

* Chapter received Monday, 2nd February 1970 – 161 days to go.

sang-sparkling telegrams like 'REBEL UPRISING ONGOING CONGO-LÉOPOLDVILLE, AVOID!'

While I appreciated not being instantly relegated back to head-latherer or oignon-chopper, by the time we crept past the explosive inlet of the Congo River, I was in a maxi rebellious mood myself. Boredom sets in rapidly on the Setta Seas, not least when you're grappling with the added savagery that you're supposed to be on your shore leave. Though Sturgeon had promised to parker me overtime dinarli for these impromptu travails, somehow this did not seem like adequate recompense. I weighed up my options – and savvied I had nix choice but to try to abuse my nova position, to take full advantage of my pogi nova powers, if I was to keep my waning morale up ...

A Latin phrase I saw screeved somewhere: 'SI VIS PACEM, PARA BELLUM!'*

3.7304°S

We were somewhere off the coast of Gabon when I sashayed into the Purser's bureau, Shellback Certificate poking proudly out of my breast posh. The Purser was higher ranked than Sturgeon but comparatively harmless and dorcas, with a fondness for cleanliness even the mostest rigorous obsessive-compulsive might've found excessive.

He seemed to be vacuuming the desktop with his vonka when I burst in. By now the Purser was used to me entering unannounced with news from below deck, so I pretended this latest query had come from the galley: 'A'noon, sir. Chef O'Hara asks: do we have any extra disgusting requests for this most royal

---

* Merritt and Trefoil doubted Novak had seen this phrase aboard a cruise liner. 'SI VIS PACEM, PARA BELLUM' ('If you want peace, prepare for war') is the motto of the Royal Navy, not the Merchant Navy.

Crossing the Line ceremony coming up? Fish-tets and sanitary hankies overboard or stored in a bucket now, sir? Vomitus? Stool samples for collection?'

The Purser's skeleton seemed to crumble at the savagery of it. 'Crossing the Line,' he mumbled. 'O, dear God. Of course, of course. Thank you for drawing my attention to it, rating.'

'A pleasure. I'm willing to be fully involved, sir.' I patted my certificate. 'Most conscientious trusty Shellback at your service. Poor hygiene guaranteed at zero degrees. An extra-specjalni ceremony is in store?'

'O, good Lord. Yes. Well. No. Absolutely. Special in that it'll have to be cancelled. Called off. Think of the royals! I'll make sure the Captain speeds straight through.'

'No, no, but –' I desperately scrabbled for a suitable mogue: 'Chief Steward Sturgeon's already given it the full go-ahead. A most specjalni ceremony to bring tears to the royals' opals. A stickler for tradition, so he is.'

'Hm.' The Purser sheepishly rubbed the dust from his left nose-thirl. 'The man's an animal. Not right in the head. Still shellshocked after Korea, I'd wager. Bloody Hell, what to do?'

'Tis an ancient tradition,' I asserted. 'And you know the royals are keen on their traditions. Twud be a shame to disappoint their majesties and mistresses and so on and so forth.'

'Quite. Quite.' The Purser nibbled his epaulettes for una minuta. 'Well ... bah, there's only one thing for it: we hold the ceremony, but only a very mild, very modest ceremony. No filth, none of the usual perverted malarkey. Just a quick slap on the arse and a dunk in the pool early in the morning, before the royals rise.'

MERDRE. My vivid revs of reddening His and Her Royal Botties with assorted unholy vacayas rapidly dissolved.

'You wish to be involved?' the Purser asked, noting my twisted eek.

'Yes, sir. Fully involved. Perhaps if I may even do the slapping of arses myself?' My luppers tingled hungrily.

'No, no. That won't do. I'll take care of the dirty work: a light pat on each of the laddies' buttocks. These are safe hands. You go round the officers' and ratings' quarters, Novak. Find out who's a Shellback and – careful now – who's a wog. Dear Lord, this was supposed to be a goodwill trip! Extending a neighbourly hand to our former subordinates. Imagine if the papers caught wind of all this talk of wogs and willy-nilly arse-thrashing. Be very discreet, rating!'

2.5819°S

For the next duey junos I did the rounds of the working corridors, sullenly snuffling out Shellbacks and pointlessly noting the noms of Polliwogs destined for this most addle-plot fairy punishment.

I left Chief Steward Sturgeon's bureau til last. I was tempted to avoid him altogether, savvying he was the mostest supreme Shellback of them all – and likely to be even stroppier than yours truly about this soft-lappered ceremony. When I explained the situation, he erupted accordingly: 'ARRGGGHH! What is this?! Battleship Potemkin? Mutiny on the Fuckering Bounty? What limp-flippered trout authorised this?! Fucking INCOMPETENTS! Speak speak speak speak!'

'Purser, sir.'

'That trollop down the corridor? SCHEISSE! What does she mean by a "mild, modest ceremony"? Speak!'

'A slap on the arse and a swift dunk, Purser said, sir.'

The Chief looked genuinely hurt. 'It's a blasted shame, rating. It's a blasted bloody shame.'

'I know, sir.'

'You hiked all the way up here to give me this hideous bulletin? Or was there something more? Something warmer, perhaps, to help soften the blow?'

I took up my clipboard and stylus. 'No further memo today, m'lud. Just the formalities. So if you'd be so kind as to present your Shellback Certificate, I'll tick you off, then gladly fuck off out of your way.'

Sturgeon's Roman-vonka flared slightly, and his oyster twitched downways. At first I ponced he was going to shriek at me for potty-oystering, but instead he merely let out a weak-levered: 'Dismissed, rating.'

'No, no, but ... the formalities, the formalities, sir. There are certain procedures, administrative necessities ...'

The Chief's opals bulged now, like he was a netted fishy about to be fed into the gutting-vacaya.

'You love the formalities,' I added with a smirk. In truth I cared not a jot for any formalities. But I'd sniffed a weakness.

'Rating, dismissed,' Sturgeon snarled, before polling his next lavs through the corner of his oyster: 'I misplaced my certificate along with my pantaloons in one of these blasted Bongo-Bongo ports.'

My cheeks inflated like puff-puffed bubblegum. 'Hé-hé! You're a slimy Polliwog, sir?'

'Of course not. I'm a Golden Shellback. I've circumnavigated the globe!'

'But nanti certificate to prove it?' I put on a mournful pantomime eek.

'I've crossed that fucking line once or twice a month for the last thirteen, fourteen years!'

'That may be so but I'm afraid you're a wog like the rest, sir, if no legal bimph can be presented.'

Sturgeon's handlebar mouser glittered sweatily as he tried to regain the reins of the scenario. Clomping heavy-plattered around the cabin, the desperate bat tried to threaten me with instant dismissal, disciplinary aggro, dismemberment, but then just as rapid a sort of calm came over and he murmured: 'It's a mild, modest ceremony, Purser said?'

'Yes. It's a blasted shame, like you say, sir.'

'A slap on the arse and a quick dunk, then fresh certificates issued out anew as if like lollipops at the fang-khazi? Speak!'

'Merely a pat on the botty, so I've nellied. Probably just a pogi sprinkling of aqua upon the foretet,' I confirmed, duey steps ahead of him.

'Scribble me down as Polliwog post-haste, rating! Better to take this minor punishment now than face another inquisitive clipboard-wielding prick like yourself further down the line, with proper punishment to swallow, eh?' Sturgeon's pearls were sparkling again.

'Ô yes, certainly, sir. Certainly,' I replied, struggling not to crackle as I jotted his batty nom down.

0.7167°S

As the Equator drew closer, I conscientiously offered to fetch King Neptune and Queen Salacia's cozzies but, after rummaging through the officers' dressing-up box for nigh on quatra-daitcha minutas, I was disheartened to discover the gildi clobber had vanished.

'Some rascal must've bloody shushed it, sir,' I explained to the Purser later that juno. 'Pinched, pilfered, gone. But fear not, sire – I can rustle you up a nova startling seaweed-shyka, caroon and toga pronto, if you wish?'

The Purser frittied uneasily. 'No, thank you, rating. Dismissed, please.'

The scolding glaze in his opals made me think the bat had hidden the cozzies himself but, be that as it may, I prodded and probed him nix longer. As we purred our way through the last few nautical miles, I savvied the Purser was ill at ease, wishing this invisible line could be avoided like a giant limbo pole barely twitching as our shimmying, belching, humiliating circus troupe passed under. Twas as if the twonk could see his (frankly scatty) hopes of a knighthood dissolving as we crept ever closer towards the Grand Zero – although in fairness I could scarcely relax neither, such was the anticipation of my daffy emags to come. Hé-hé!

I occupied myself with mono-travails in the top galley, posing as a terrapom-peeler in striped pyjamas, riah-net and a penny-black mouser, while the bona ship UNMENTIONABLE – Ô, formidable, meshigena barka! – lurched queasily towards her fate ...

0°

SS UNMENTIONABLE's mild, modest Crossing the Line ceremony commenced at 5 a.m. with a fantabulosa mishap.

The Purser hadn't accounted for the royals nellying his bimph-tube bullhorn from their quarters, so when he toot-tooted, 'Hear-ye! Hear-ye! Neptunus Rex and His Royal Party have joined the ship! Slimy wogs now bow before them, please,' their Toffee Highnesses naturally thought he was referring to themselves. Chinka minutas later they opened their curtains triumphantly and strutted out onto their grandiose balcony, offering a de-luxe view over the Fun Deck where the softly-softly botty-slapping was to take place. The Royal Omi even flapped an appreciative lapper, as if it were commonplace regarding his subjects in these meshigena poses: fash Shellbacks in merman schmutta with raised nightsticks, Polliwogs on all-quatras with their eeks pressed slavish to the deck. Chief Steward Sturgeon looked particularly poked-up, stripped to his ivory silk slippies, chuntering with his tet between his lally-caps.

When I vadared the royals, my oyster pricked. I was hiding behind the springboard, joshed-up to the nobbas in the King Neptune clobber I'd cobbled together regardless.

For una minuta the Purser lost his voche, uncertain how to proceed with the bejewelled grandees watching – and so I gladly lelled the baton. I plumped up my stinking cabbage-shyka, then merrily goosestepped onto the Fun Deck with my bijou tinfoil hammer-and-sickle aloft. My entrance was met with entranced opals and gaping oysters. I screamed into the Equatorial sol:

'WOGS! Slimy Polliwogs! ACHTUNG! You meese meshigena batatats have trespassed upon the Realm of the Unholy Aqua-Reich and thusly therefore must feel the full force of my scaly, dicktittly wrath!'

Above us, the royals were still all smiles, probably expecting some sort of skit or synchronised swish in the swimming pool. I ceremoniously wiggled my hammer-and-sickle in their direction, and the two of them waved back. I whispered to the Purser: 'May I do the patting of the arses, sir? Since I found the relevant clobber last minuta?'

'Um. Um. You ... may.'

I hadn't expected him to relinquish his powers so rapid – but clear enough the nervy mare wanted nanti further part in proceedings now, fearful to be seen to be hazing in front of his revered royal overlords. In fact, it seemed he wanted nanti further part in the ceremony whatsoever. The Purser made a petty warbling announcement – 'L-lowest rank P-Polliwogs first, um, visit King Neptune one by one. No pushing or shoving. Have fun – and, um ... keep it clean ...' – then retreated into the morning munge, palliass hunched.

As the sol ballooned, more blinking toff- and tourist-eeks appeared at the balconies and fenêtres. There was a dowri substantial crowd assembled by the time the first wogs came creepy-crawling towards me. As prescribed, I gave each pop a limp-lappered pat to the corybungus before directing them to the Final Solution. Instead of the usual meese onion, caca and parnyaqua, the pool had a pathetic smattering of fresh bananas and coconuts floating in it. The Polliwogs pretended to drown for uno momento before emerging rejuvenated and reborn as trusty Shellbacks, wriggling into fluffy towels held sportingly by their nova brothers.

When I blinked up at the Royal Box, the toffs' smiles had slipped a pogi bit, and rightly so. I savvied the entertainments for the ruling classes had been maxi sterilised over the last chenta or duey-chenta years. When their forefathers went to sea, their excursions must've been exceedingly gay affairs, sparkling with true violence, glistening sacrificial carnish, flaming tribal villages, raped peasant-palones, rolling tets – whereas these mod blue-sangs now had to settle for stage-managed saccharine sideshows, false smiles and finger-sandwiches.

When at last Chief Steward Sturgeon appeared at the head of the queue, ready for his petty botty-pat, I savvied now was my chance to liven things up for them. Twas to be the only noble cheet I would ever do in the nom of Queen and country, Ô comrades.

I tried my bestest to keep my eek straight as Sturgeon slithered forth, his overabundant pearls sneering brightly in the rising sol. I rested my right flipper on his shoulder and addressed the crowd: 'By royal decree, this omi is hereby sentenced to some bonus punishments, largely due to arse-crimes against bellboys, a grotty superiority complex and generally acting like a fash arroganki batatat!'

'Did he say "arse-crimes"?' some of the newly converted Shellbacks muttered among themselves as I grasped Sturgeon by the nells and dragged him across the deck.

To his credit, Sturgeon played along at first, causing nix fuss as I clamped his tet and lappers in the stocks and fish-wired his ankles. He was perhaps less enthused, however, when I introduced the bucket of rotting giblets, rats' tails, spoiled legumes, fuel oil and my fresh caca and quong-gravy to his tet. With a brootish rebel yell, I emptied the cheet VLOP! over his golden riah, shaking it up thorough, making sure the evil jus swirlied all round his fizzer and up his eagle-vonka.

I remember Sturgeon retching and gurgling, but mostly his protests were drowned out by my own manic reering and the tittles coming from the toffs and tourists up topside. Ô, how the upper-crusties loved a pogi bit of light-hearted persecution! In contrast, the Purser and other officers ogled in horror from the sideylines, not sure whether to step in and rock the barka in front of these delighted royals, or just leave me to it.

Savvying my jolly emags could be cut short any minuta, I hastily rummaged through my sequinned poshes and unfurled my next invigorating torture-vacaya: a juicy king prawn impaled upon the end of my tinfoil sickle. Holding the pink cheet aloft, I roared, 'Behold! All hail the Shrimp of Destiny!' or similar heroic lavs.

The rest of the ceremony is a blur. I recall yanking Sturgeon's slippies down, but the prawn's eek had barely made it quarterway up his sphincter when the top Shellbacks were all over me, wrestling me to the deck. I had plenty more planned for Sturgeon (namely a crayfish, crab, lobster ...), but, as the Shellbacks brootishly restrained me with my lappers twisted betwixt my pol-blades and jaw slammed against the bollards, I savvied I'd made my point well enough.

LONG LIVE THE SCATTY SALTY AQUA-REICH! et ceterarara. Hé-hé-hé-hé-hé!

By this point Sturgeon was screeching all kinds of ungrateful hateful lavs, his soiled eek peeking out of the stocks with brown parny rolling down. When they released him, I braced myself for a severe battyfanging, but with the royals still captivated overhead, the Purser and other mermen managed to hold him off.

Revving backwards, I like to think the royals were wonderstruck by my performance, showering the Fun Deck with glistening roses, demanding I join them at ze Captain's table for a nine-birdy roast that dolly noche. In reality,* the toffs

---

* Do you ever get the feeling when you're reading a piece of so-called non-fiction that the author is taking extreme liberties with reality? Perhaps because he's a former naval man (albeit the Navy of guns, drums, lost limbs and torpedoes), Merritt lost faith with *Mister Asterisk* during these 'Seafood' chapters. Up until now we'd tolerated Novak's Surrealistic embellishments, but this yarn involving the king prawn and the monarchy seemed a deviation too far. Bearing in mind Novak is a self-confessed fantasist, regularly 'losing himself' in his dreams (see 'Kinder, Küche, Kirsche', 'Pater Unfamiliar', 'Crossing the Line: 28.9625°N'), it would not be unreasonable to suspect that this entire novel is the flight of fancy of a dreaming lunatic. Some of us imagined Novak as a dull, washed-up old hack, desperate for attention. Others had faith he was a bona fide madman

were probably ushered back indoors immediately by their omi-servants, and placated with toasty squares and marmalade.

After another duey minutas of tussling and potty-oystering, I was hoisted back onto my platters and shooed along the officers' corridors to the Commander's quarters. Owing to the high rank of my victim – and my difficulty showing remorse (I was still reering hysterically) – the Grand Commander squawked a meese torrent of abuse at me, the gist of which was: INSTANT DISMISSAL.

'Strictly screeching, sarge, you can't discharge me,' I polled, straightening my eek. 'I'm not even meant to be on this barka. Regard the roll call, ask the Chief. I'm just a fantom, sir. A barnacle clinging privvily to the hull ...'

The arguing went on well into the Dollydrums, but it seemed nix amount of mogue parnyaqua or battyflappering could sway the Commander. My fizzer was a coddy mess of snot and glug-glugging sang when finally duey butch Shellbacks were summoned and I was dragged helplessly down down down to the brig. The carpets looked more hideous than ever as I vadared the working corridors for the final time, eek down, yanked by my ankles.

As fortune would have it, when we got to Deck X the brig

---

with genuine criminal intentions, a dangerous Walter Mitty with a very accommodating ghostwriter. As far as Merritt was concerned, he wished the stream of nonsense would stop now. Regardless of literary merit, after reading these latest swashbuckling chapters, he now feared the m/s might be libellous. If the royals really were involved in this mutiny on the *Unmentionable*, why didn't we hear about it back in 1964? New scandals break every day. If they couldn't keep the Profumo Affair covered up the previous year, how could they keep this far more public debacle under wraps? There was no mention of the aquatic farce when we scoured the newspaper archives at the British Library – but then again, could the nom de guerre of SS *'Unmentionable'* be a clue? Was there a gag order forced upon the crew and passengers? And if so, has Novak now breached it? The Glass Eye Press versus the British Monarchy's Public Relations Defence Force? O good Heavens, good Lord, what had we let ourselves in for? We had no white flag to wave. We could only sit and squirm while the stream of nonsense kept on coming ...

was already full, the petty cell crammed with twisted slopes nix doubt charged by Sturgeon with the solo misdemeanour of possessing non-Allied opals. Perking up, I savvied I might be turned loose after all, taken back to my peak to dorm in comfort until we reached Gibraltar – but, alas, when I suggested this to the Shellbacks, I was immediately schonked in the vonka by one of the gristly batatats. There was such venom in the strike, my lallies gave way like duey skittled milk-botties. Through the dizzying shooting pains, I squinted upways at my batty tormentor and clocked a familiar eek seething behind the elaborate merman màquiage. Whoever applied the slap had done a fabulosa job transforming the zot's chargrilled scar-carnish into dolly glittering fish-scales.

'Kenneth ...' I tut-tutted, wagging a scolding quivering index-lupper.

At first I felt only pity for the daffy Transvaalian – savvying these line-crossing ceremonies created not noble trusty seafarers at all but detestable hypocritters: lowly scabs weepingly enduring meshigena uncalled-for punishments only so they can join the other side and gleefully mete out the meshigena uncalled-for punishments themselves – but, when Kenneth socked me again, in the quongs this time, I savvied there was more to this than just arroganki chest-puffing thew-flexing. ALACK-O-JUNO, the twonk meant so little to me, I'd near enough forgotten how grievously I'd broken his lovestruck thumper in the Crew Mess.

'To the morgue,' Kenneth side-oystered ominously to his Shellback companion.

My tet felt like a pulverised garlic bulb as the batatats dragged me thunderingly onwards, through the deepest darkest kishkas of the latty-on-water to a portal marked with a discreet solo snowsparkle.

Ignoring my squealing protests, Kenneth and his comrade slammed me in the frigid cube: a cavernous antiseptic cell with full-metal décor and a mammoth freezer humummbling witchy curses and drippy gurgles in the corner. A hefty clef turned in the lock. As the Shellbacks' footstamps faded, I felt instantly icy in my skimpy King Neptune cozzy. I fancied I could nelly the stokers manning the furnaces through the bulkheads, but there was nix residual heat. I shuddered brootishly, ogling roundwards for somewhere to rest my clanging tet. Technically the morgue was big enough to sleep six pops, although the beds were just metal shelves on casters in the gross ultraschvartz freezebox. There was nanti khazi, nix munja-hatch, no pillows, no portholes. Only an array of unsettling science-fiction vacayas and frosty pipettes – and a full botty of ethanol that might not have been recommended schlumphing material for mortals, but it was fit enough for this king.

Dishonourable Discharge*

NOVAK WEARS ETHANOL PROFUMO, DISHDASHA, SANDALS AND A FEZ ATOP HIS BALDY TET.

Sunbathing dollybirds in djellabas! Humongous lemon sol. Hashish fogus-puffs. Sapphire seafoam lap-lapping up past the lally-caps. Mint herbata. Shark tagines! Loopers. Spies. Expats, stray cats. Magick carpets. Perverts and mugwumps. Just some of the splendid cheets I missed out on during my stay in Tangier.

---

* Chapter received Friday, 13th February 1970 – 150 days to go. An unsettling end to the week. Stanley was hunched in the water closet when Emily shouted there was a telephone call for him. The general rule was for staff not to disturb Stanley when he was struggling to pass a bowel movement, but Emily insisted it was urgent.

'How urgent?' Stanley groaned.

'The caller has a French-cockney accent, Mister Merritt. Shall I transfer him to your private line?'

'No – don't touch a thing, dear!'

Stanley scuttled post-haste to his secretary's switchboard. Upon picking up the receiver, he felt instantly light-headed as the caller bombarded him with braggadocio. The voice matched the description in 'Twenty-Four-Carat Yarn': 'at once effeminate, authoritative, anglo and froggy'. It was Lord Never-Never, sure enough.

Today we strive to record all incoming telephone calls, but, alas, Merritt was so flustered that afternoon he struggled to retain much of his and Novak's dialogue. There exists only a few quivery handwritten notes made during the call, fleshed out here:

SATISFT: Novak asked if Stanley was satisfied with the manuscript so far. Against his better judgement – and in spite of the incredulity of his previous footnote – all Stan could do was splutter how much he 'absolutely adored' the novel, firing all sorts of excessive, regrettable superlatives down the line.

150: Novak mentioned there were now just 150 days to go until his fantabulosa crime, and that he was more certain than ever of committing it.

The Blank City. The Queer City.

When I was finally released from the morgue, I felt appropriately mort-like, sick as a mallard and still terribly terribly drunk. The pristine royals were all smiles again as they waved their groiny luppers at the crowds of lickspittles gathered when we docked at Gibraltar. Having nanti mufti aboard the UNMENTIONABLE, I had to take the degrading Trot of Shame up to the Personnel Bureau in my Neptunus Rex schmutta, maquiage full-splattered and cabbage-shyka askew. The Scum King. The Hunchback King.*

As I entered the glistening bureau I savvied now was my chance to redeem myself, to inform the top Cunard pops of all the cateva draconian goings-on aboard Sturgeon's floating fash commune, but when the zots clocked me splatty-eeked in Romanoid monster-clobber (and babbling daffy to boot), my fate was screeved: INSTANT DISMISSAL.

Did I parny at this twisted news? BOF. Did I trout.

EFINK, FORK, PISTL, FERTILISER, DIESL, SCRS, TAR, FEATH, PEP-SPRAY, PICKL A, SCALPELS, CLOSH, NEEDL, THREAD: A charming list of items Novak claimed he'd already stockpiled in anticipation of the crime.

CLICKMTH: Merritt noticed the Emperor's mouth clicked while he spoke – possibly down to nerves, or medication? Knowing what we know now (see 'The Rag Trade', etc.), probably French Blues?

FUNERAL, BATH, SILK SLEEPS: As he'd pointed out in his initial letter to us, Novak seemed entirely convinced he would die committing his crime. Determined to be immortalised correctly, he gave directions for his funeral, which, if Merritt remembers rightly, involved being dropped into the Atlantic at the equator, in a shoe-shaped bathtub coffin, dressed in silk pyjamas.

BILLY S: Stanley remembers Novak's parting comments more or less verbatim:

> NOVAK. Ogling my gildi screeve, you'll have gathered by now I'm nanti much of a love god. But be patient, comrade. Since I cannot prove a lover, I am determined to prove a villain, and hate the idle pleasures of our junos!
>
> MERRITT. Sorry? Come again?
>
> NOVAK. Billy Shaker. Dicky Trey.
>
> MERRITT. Dick Tracy?
>
> NOVAK. Nein! You're a coddy detective, monsieur. Adieu!

The line went dead. Merritt rushed back to his WC, filling the bowl with his loosest stools for months.

* We realise now 'Dicky Trey' is Richard III, of course.

My solo worry now was to get off this coddy claustrophobic Rock, teeming as it was with these sycofrantic royalists, the royals themselves and my sneering crewmates. Ô Gibraltar. Trust the colonic anglos to shush a gloriosa dramatic morso of Andalusian soil and then just turn it into an eerie chip-shop Monte Carlo, a sunburnt maxi-nationalistic plastic de-luxe version of fuckering Grimsby or Ramsgate.

Every roaming barky had that jubilant hé-hé-hé shore-leave lustre about him, but I felt more vamp-like or insectoid as I staggered over to Barclays to fill my bra-pods with the pitiful petty dinarli I'd put away during my three years at sea. I threw a lapperful of notes at a palone in a BOAC camisha for a flight back to Blighty the following juno, then plopped myself by the twinkling Med at Europa Point, pondering my next move.

The ethanol, far from being a sterilising fluid, maxi ramped up my arva-drive as I ogled the tanned bods frolicking in the sparkly aqua, with the fuzzy rocks of Morocco behind. I ponced backwards to Winnie and the sea-queens' smutty palavering on the bona ship MS HIPPOCAMPUS, back where these twisted salty escapades all began:

'Have you sampled the mighty catamites of Tangier yet?'

'One isn't a virgin, is one, Raymondo?'

'She must be! Vada the innocent eek on it!'

From this vista, the distance between the nipplet of Gibraltar and the inlet of Tangier seemed almost ajax enough to hoppety-hop in one stomp.

Clinging to the savagery that even a quong-faced freak could 'parker a feeli-omi a beyong' in Tangier for all sorts of fantabulosa romantic debasement, I rapidly found myself aboard a bijou ferry to the Blank City, my cartso swelling as the port appeared like a grand Cubist pearly oyster grinning from the cliffside. Standing erect above deck, I clocked medsa-naggy chavvies playing on the playa. Nanti sharpering-pops nor lavvyguards in ogleshot. The Medina a cramped labyrinth of hush-hushy munge, sparkling secretive with doubtless countless souks-of-ill-fame.

Ô, I would lose my virginity in this city, that much was clear.

Once my naggy platters hit Nord Afrikkkan soil, I savvied I must change my clobber immediately. While the natives might not finger me as your typical exploitable Occidental pleasure-tripper, the plastic caroon, hammer-and-sickle, sequins and mogue willets were nevertheless not the mostest discreet attire to mince around a nova foreign territory in unchaperoned.

'I am but an incorruptible virgin,' I pow-wowed needlessly to the rag-merchant in the Medina, probably parkering him far too much anglo dinarli for the dishdasha and fez. I threw my gildi Neptune fakements at a glum beggar-zelda, retired to a rancid squat-khazi, and then gaily made my transformation ...

Ô, the Blank City. The Queer City. The City of Revs ...*

Plodding onwards along the crumbly strasses, I'd hoped my nova disguise would allow me to creep invisibly through the maze, but – ALACK-O-JUNO – I rapidly savvied very few locals josh themselves in this traditional frippery. Nonetheless, I felt distinctly free again for perhaps the first time since Madame O and I ruled our Surrealistic morso of Stepney. Trolling willety-nilly round the mudbrick labyrinth, I stumbled upon a few of the local landmarks (the souks, Café Baba, the Gross Mosque, the Grand and Petty Soccos), then, when I found a Bureau de Change, swapped chinka beyongs for dirham, and went eagerly sharpering for trade.

Tangier was built for trade, so it says in the guide-livers, and – ALL HAIL THE INTERZONE! – soon enough I was bartering heroically with an Arab ponce for access to one of his dishy chavvies.

'Kid? You like kid?' the Arab had side-oystered at me as I dithered for uno momento on the brootishly hootering Rue Siaghin.

'Oui, oui, possiblement, ducky,' I replied, savvying French was the Maroc-pops' second lingo thanks to some meese colonic

* Yes, it was the City of Revs all right (see Part VIII: 'My Grande Descente', Afterword, etc. – all in good time, of course ...).

stompering years ago. 'Quelle kind of kid? Nice kid? Nice bod? I don't want you parkering me off with some gross manky pock-marked chavvy, squire.'

'Oui, monsieur. Très agréable.'

'Fabulosa. Combien?'

'Cinq dirham.'

'I'll give you six.'

The sweat was rolling greasily off my bod as the Arab vagaried backways into some fleshpot latty just off the main alley. He was gone una minuta before pokering his tet back round the doorway.

'Argent,' he demanded, tugging me inwards.

After fumbling in my bra-pods, I handed over a lapperful of bizarre notes, quongs tingling like duey gross kiwi fruits going off in the sol. Then, with a straight eek, my Arab friend gave me in return not a dishy chavvy, but what can only be described as a petty lump of caca. The brown morso glistened gloomily in my lapper. It appeared to be animal caca – not ultra niffy, but caca all the same. Sheep- or donkey-dung, I ponced.

'What the fuck is this, squire?' I cried. 'Je ne comprends pas.'

'Keef.'

I squinted at the brown lump. 'Keith?'

'Keef.'

'Keith.'

'Kif.'

'Who is Keith?' I demanded. 'And what do I want with his droppings?'

'No, no. Kif, kif. You smoke. Fumer?'

'Nix. Nanti that. No vogue. I asked for a succulent kid, you imbecile.'

'Vous fumez. Ou vous pouvez manger ...'

'Eat this petty horrid plop? Jarry this manky morso of caca? You must be deranged, squire.'

'C'est très agréable.'

Before I could probe the omi further, all at once my Arab

friend became molto sheepish, ushering me back out of his knocking-shop, clicking the portal behind him tranquil but firm. Thwarted, I swayed dumbly on the cobbles, ogling the grim morso. I reasoned I might as well get it down my gargler regardless: uno bijou nugget of ballast before my planned grand afternoon of lovemaking.

Hoping for specjalni Morocco-choco, when I sunk my fangs in I was disheartened to find the amuse-bouche as tough as bark and more or less tasteless, like some naff manky tiffin left in the back of the pantry since Vicky times.

A queer city indeed – and, Ô comrades, it only got queerer as I continued my adventure, cruising the slither-channels full-blooded for rapid romance. Aware I had only a pogi few hours before the final ferry back Rockwards, I savvied I might settle for even a crippled chavvy (providing his dish was in bona nick), but as the ticktockers ran wayward the Maroc-pops seemed more alien to me than ever. Eeks sprouted bat-nells. Mousers crawling off top oyster-levers. Cluckers shrieking my nom from their cages. Bulging bushbaby opals. Floating niqab fantoms. A gigantic courgette patterned like the minaret of the Gross Mosque. Palm trees on wheels. Fountains spewing frosty champagne and hot steaming caca ...

Ô, Monsieur Keith, monster patissier! What in Jupiter's nom was in that bijou gateau?

The Queasy City.

Oui oui, ZUT and ZOUNDS, I felt utterly dicky as I stumbled through the pulsating alleyways, as if only now suffering some form of obscene culture shock. The feeling of being an unwanted foreigner intensified horrifically. At one point I believe I vomited into my fez. I half remember grabbing a feeli-omi round the trummus and being chased by huge salamanders in kaftans, but for the most part my remaining hours in the Interzone are a slippery mess. I believe I ogled the true meaning of existence in the buckle of a smart shoe – then instantly forgot it. I jarried vons and reefed rimbumbles. A momentary return to the womb (or was it a pogi glimpse into the Afterlavvy?): rankledankle flizz bammtankoo neeeeeeex, et ceterararara. Pirouetting eggy smoke, red-black slithering slime. Twisting tortoiseshell tails, rippling rainbow trails. Widespread dread.* Grotty sweats. Kishkas bagpiping.

'I've been poisoned!' I gasped at passing Arabs, or were they just stray purring-cheets? 'I am but an incorruptible virgin and I've been bloody poisoned! Poisoned by a ponce!'

Blank eeks. Bizarre scenery. Every cheet more foreign than the last. I reasoned: perhaps Morocco was not for me.

By the time noche dropped I was bent-doppel, desperately clutching the dinarli in my bra-pods with one lapper, my guts with the other. Vagarying on unfamiliar jelly-lallies. Mumbling mostly just vowels now. The Blank City a shifty maze, blind walls and black backstreets leading me like a blinkered goose round this queer old blankscape that just kept getting blanker and blanker and blanker – until I blanked out altogether ...

---

* The telephone call was a whipcrack, a 'gildi cattle-prod'. Given Novak's gung-ho insistence that he would go through with his crime, we realised we must now rapidly step up preparations for production, publication and promotion if we were to release this deranged tome in time for the bastard's Chosen Juno: Monday, 13th July 1970.

Finding a skilled yet unscrupulous printer was not a problem – our go-to firm, Roach & Reinhardt of Wakefield, West Yorkshire, would likely not read the proofs, let alone pass comment on their contents. More difficult was writing the jacket copy and designing a cover for a book that was still perhaps only half-finished, if that.

'*Dieu-du-Jour* – what does it mean exactly?' Davy asked, referring to the original title we were still yet to change. 'It's like "King for a Day", you said?'

'No, no, I believe it's a play on "Soupe-du-Jour", or *Belle de Jour* for that matter,' Trefoil responded. '"God-of-the-day", it translates as.'

'Mm.'

By the end of the day Davy's trestle table was covered with agonised doodles: half-baked images of dissolute sailors, disgruntled eagles and moustachioed frogs that soon degenerated to just anguished self-portraits distorted in a soup spoon. Why O why, Davy wondered, could the novel not have a more evocative, more straightforward title? Like last year's biggest seller, *The Woman with the Two Dozen Breasts* (223 copies sold to date! And only 2/6. The Glass Eye Press Ltd, 28 Newman Street, W1T 3ER. Discreet packaging).

Gibberish*

NAGGY, NOVAK SASHAYS THROUGH MULTIPLE GOSSAMER-LIGHT LAYERS OF PSYCHOTROPICAL HYPERCONSCIOUSNESS.

Difficult to savvy if I was in a molto sociable mood when finally I fell off the ferry at Gibraltar, reeking of vom and droggled-up to the ogleballs on this mysterious kif or Keith substance. Somehow I stumbled upon a specjalni soirée for the Cunard seadogs in a grand de-luxe latty halfway up the Rock. Perhaps I'd clocked the dazzling lights and voches from down below and staggered up there auto like some hideous exotic orchid shambling towards the sol. In any case, this morso of my story would've perished forever were it not for my bastard crewmates' arroganki pleasure recounting it to me the morning after.

QUELLE SURPRISE – my solo aim had been to avoid the bats of the UNMENTIONABLE and yet now there I was, joshed-up like a Maroc-pop with vomitus running like a manky chinstrap from my fez down to my bottom oyster-lever, swaying in the midst of almost una-chenta of the twats.

The moon whirled like an egg-custard unicycle. Twas a gildi party: dames with chiming groinage, gentlepops in disgusting colonic clobber, dry martini aero-lammers, a kidney-shaped swimming pool, first-class lupper-munja and plenty of high-rank seamen, judging by the stripes on their epaulettes (although my doppel-vision might've promoted a few lowly barkies to admirals).

---

* Chapter received Thursday, 19th February 1970 – 144 days to go.

'Bona noche, bonsoir!' I screamed as I set stamper on the prickly lawn. From the outset the atmosphere was frosty, hostile. My opals were swishering. I savvied I'd best get some alcool down my gargler pronto, to sober me up. I minnied over to the bevvy table, schlumphed down whatever I could grasp without smashing, then moved crab-like into the circle of dolly moony eeks and mingled. For una minuta or duey I reered along with the toffs' squiffy quips, gulped more throat-varnish, unsuccessfully ravished a few of the admirals' wives, then finally stumbled back to the bevvy table, where a petty hairy chap was standing apart from the crowd, blankly regarding the partygoers.

'Ô, they're all fash eagle-eek addle-plots, are they not, comrade?' I slurred at him, or similar bolshy lavs. 'Vada their vonkas!'*

'Rrummpff tillff too,' the chap replied, or lavs to that effect.

Gibberish. At first I ponced it was the booze disrupting my nellying, then savvied with some amusement I was palavering with a native of the Rock. This was the first time I'd experienced that meshigena Llanito lingo up close. 'You're nanti a barky then, squire?' I enquired. 'A landlubber? Tumbler-shusher, are you? Bung? Bartender? I'm no barky myself too, as of this juno. So pooh-pooh and fuck-off-thataways to all this lot and bona riddance, isn't that right, comrade?'

The petty hairy chap's oyster-levers twitched, then he practically hurled my next drink at me: a full botty of frothy Dom Perignon.

---

* Though Novak had explained in great detail the weapons he'd stockpiled in anticipation of his crime, there was still no indication who his intended victims would be. Initially Raymond's use of slurs like 'slope', 'spade', 'poove' and 'kosher-pop' made us fear he might be planning a Nova Kristallnacht or lynch-mob rampage, but after reading these past few chapters we felt (tentatively) more hopeful about his political beliefs and potential motives. Suppose, for instance, the Prole Dandy's plan was to hunt down fascist eagles on the Continent, picking off Nazi war criminals with efinks and explosives – who were we to stand in his way?

'Rrummpff tillff too, rattatata!' he added charitably.

'Well, I'm nanti connoisseur like yourself, sir,' I declared, turning the botty over in my lappers, 'but this is gildi plonk, is it not? You're parkering it to me gratis?'

'Rrummpff!'

'Oui or nein?'

'Rrummpff!'

This was flirtation, clear enough. I liked this omi. There was a sparkle of collusion between us, like it was our starry destiny to shake up this stiff seadog soirée ...

I side-oystered: 'I wonder how easily offended these eagles are, ducky? What say we push these cunts to their limits?'

'Rattatata rrummpff tillff too!' he agreed. I reered up heartily. THE UNIVERSAL LINGO OF HATRED! As I unpoppered the cork, my nova comrade now dropped his nonchalance act and leapt out molto lusty and loony from behind the table, hoofering drunkenly and cackling. By Jupiter! Was the zot as daffy as I? Taking another bona glug-glug from the botty, I realised with maxi wonderment the Gibraltan was naggy. The saucy bat! His excessive bod-riah meant I couldn't easily vada his cartso, but he was a fortuni specimen: muscular thews, athletic, exotic. My quongs tingled. More than his bod, the chap's spirit turned me on. Was he truly meshigena, or was this conscious madness? The gibberish lingo, the nudity, the whole Dadaist hoofering revolt against the stiffs – was this a natty act, or mere accidental lunacy? Whichever, it was beautiful.

'The Liberated Lavvy, my chovi!' I screeched. 'Is this a Giblet trait? Uncensored naggy anarchy? L'amour fou? Vada these pricks – they don't know how to live, do they?! Rrummpff! Oui, mein freund: RRUMMPFF TILLFF TOO! Lookee here – I've got nix shame neither, my cherry. I've got molto bod-riah too!'

I frittied rapidly out of my dishdasha, threw the vom-soaked fez into the circle of horrified dames, then joined my companion in his scatty tribal danse macabre, stomping frog-like with my clammy genitals flappering in the cooling sea-whoosh. I followed the chappy's movements, reering hysterically as we WIP-HUMPH!ed around the palms like toxic chavvies.

This was living!

'You're fantabulosa,' I cooed into his nell, savvying he might be an easy-mort too,* and gratis at that. I pressed my naggy bod into his, feeling his sticky thew-riahs cling to my quivering carnish. 'Sack these fash toffs anyway. What say me and thee shush more vino and vagary back to your libbage, squire? Do you live far from here?'

'Rrummpff tillff too!'

I ogled him glitterishly. 'Ô, wunderbar.'

I swung my lapper round the bung's pols, but as I tried to steer the dishy libertine downways back towards the town, duey admirals blocked our path.

'Unhand him!' the bulkier of the two quacked. 'You're a disgrace, rating! Bloody cover yourself up!'

'He was naggy first,' I snapped. 'He instigated this battiness – and quite rightly too ...'

'HUSH! You're frightening the guests, Novak.' The other admiral now. 'Don't you realise who's in attendance here? These are some of the finest faces of the shipping line!'

'I care not, toffs,' I said. 'You're all fash bats and you can fuck-off-thataways now for all I care. Isn't that right, comrade?' I pressed my raspberry oyster-levers to my friend's eek. 'I'm nanti a barky no more, so what does it even matter?'

The first admiral raised his lapper to schonk me, but quite possibly he didn't want to soil his blank fambler on my vomity mush. Instead he squawked: 'We'll sling you in gaol if you carry on like this, rating! A disgrace! I've never seen anything so obscene.'

'Why not chastise my companion too?' I spat, tightening my protective grip round my nova lover. 'Or can you not vada this petty hairy chap? Does he not exist to you? A landlubber, a lowly bung – all he's good for is throwing bevvies at you and keeping his

---

* Then again, suppose Novak is still a virginal mary? What if the Carnish Mincer is plotting a revolting gratuitous sex crime on home soil??

oyster shut, isn't that right? Another hairy native to exploit and look down upon. You're all the same, you fash twats: snootering around blinkered to the travails of the ones beneath you, the ones that prop you up! Why not chastise him too? Why are you picking on me? Why not scold the two of us? We come as a pair now ...'

'Well ...' The admirals shared a poked-up glance. 'First of all, it's YOU who's tanked up to the eyeballs on booze and Heaven knows what else. Secondly, your genitals are very clearly on show to some of the most treasured faces in the cruising industry. And thirdly, well, this may come as somewhat of a surprise to you, Novak, but this so-called petty hairy chap, as you put it, is a Barbary ape.'

I spluttered Dom Perignon down my front.

My crewmates claimed I was froggy-kissing the mono as this twisted news was delivered. I refute it. As far as I can remember, I roly-polyed down the Rock rapido, passed out in a red anglo phone-booth and woke the next juno with munge and sludge on the servo. Without savvying quite why, I had the convulsive urge to vagary back to Blighty pronto. The barkies goaded me in the BOAC lounge, filling me in on my daffy escapades, but they were all just fantoms to me now. I buried my vonka in the daily inkies – the screamlines screeching SAWDUST CAESARS, 'WILD ONES' INVADE SEASIDE, 97 ARRESTS, THE PERMISSIVE SOCIETY, et ceterarara – and when the tannoy finally squeaked the particulars of my flight homewards, the robotic voche was like a bugle from above.

Mincing through the gates, I fancied myself as Botty's Birth of Venus, trolling out of the salty aqua to a newly awakened mond of possibilities – but when I clocked myself in one of the mirrors, I looked like ultimate caca. Acne polka-dotted eek-carnish. Broken oink-vonka. Missing fangs. Gummy. Crusty, slitty mollusc-opals. Hunchback. Nix riah. Loose soldis rattling in my soiled bra-pods. Clear enough I was not a fashionable omi. I was not a bona-vadaring omi. I was not a happy omi. But this would soon change, I would make certain of it.

PART IV

THE CITY SWINGS

'O Venus was born out of seafoam,
O Venus was born out of brine,
But a goddess today if she is Grade A
Is assembled upon the assembly line.'

'THE GIRL WITH THE PREFABRICATED HEART',
JOHN LATOUCHE (1944)

Land Ho!*

NOVAK WEARS A SULLEN EEK, SAGGY DRESSING GOWN AND SLIPPERS, THIRTEEN O'CLOCK SHADOW.

Free love: Ô, that fantabulosa impenetrable fantom ...

I'd nellied there was some form of pop revolution going on back home, but the way the conservative inkies and chuntering fungal seafarers went on, I savvied it was probably an overreaction: a tame revolution compared to the line-crossing, cross-dressing, fantom-gobbling antics I'd left behind.

Despite how my opals appear, I'm nanti blind. However, to begin with it seemed like little had changed in Londres. I took the chugger back to Stepney and didn't vada anything particularly swinging en route: just omis wearing juno-suits in various shades of schvartz, palones in grizzly overcoats, NHS ogle-fakes, bruise-coloured cabooshes, sobbing pluplubashes, thick stockings, thick smog.

Trolling along Cable Strasse, I savvied slum clearance had come at last to my old stomping ground. There were still a fair few flattened bombsites hither and thither, but I could vada cranes pecking at the rubble in the distance, alongside bold nova Futurist skyticklers lording it over the petty sooty terraces ajax. For una minuta I stopped to ogle the omis working on a

---

* Chapter received Monday, 23rd February 1970 – 140 days to go. To cap off a terrible month that had as its highlights a frigid Valentine's dinner, countless nonsensical arguments and a final demand for unpaid taxes, Iris Merritt sued her husband for divorce this week.

vast cod-Corbusier lattyblock, fantasising about all the ritzy love affairs and Space Age lavvying that would soon play out in its concrete cubbyholes – and yet molto likely it would just wind up a naff container for boredom like everywhere else.

Tramping morosely onwards, I was harangued by huge but vague politico posters:

LABOUR WILL GET THINGS DONE
KEEP JOBS ON THE UP
VOTE CONSERVATIVE

After three years at sea I was drained, humiliated, fattygayed in both bod and servo. I savvied the State wanted me to sharper for nova work pronto, but nanti that. I felt I deserved the Vicky Cross and an instant hefty pension for all the sweat I'd splurted in service to the gloriosa codswallop Merch Navy. A chamber in a gildi mansion gratis. The leisurely lavvy. The Liberated Lavvy – at long last.

The closest I could get was signing on to the National Handbag. I found a six-by-nine-foot bed-sitter on Commercial Road for £2 a week, barricaded the front portal and played dead. My plan was to hibernate like a bona fide froglet, shut myself off from the brootish welt outside, rest and recuperate, vanish in revs, et ceterara. I blamed Capitalism for my malaise, and savvied there was nanti crocus out there who could cure it.

While Blighty enjoyed almost full employment, I was The Unemployable Omi. My aquatic travails had been an utter waste – three years of pathetic mono-travails culminating in the gildi reward: INSTANT DISMISSAL. I couldn't ask my salty superiors for a recommendation to springboard me to better travails on dry land. I refused to cruise the Job Bureaux, savvying my 'Pick a card by chance!' approach in Canterbury was perhaps my coddiest lavvy-choice to date.

I screeved UNTERMENSCH on my latty door in red lippy, and refused to open it save for the odd slippety-slip outside to shush more supplies, or the tet-thumpering occasion the mystery barky from RMS OPEN-MINDEDNESS appeared as if like a fantom from the deep.

He introduced himself as Arthur Winkler: a handsome spade with the tangy honk of summertime about him. I had the grey bedclobber pulled tight around me like a flabby cocoon. I'd been holed up so long I'd barely clocked the seasons changing outside.

'You look deadbeat, brother,' Arthur commented. 'Hayfever, is it? Summer cold?'

'The evils of Capitalism.'

'Well, chin up, old chap, I've come bearing gifts.' Ajax to the barky were duey tatty valises. He slid them inways with his stamper.

'A loaded shotgun? A noose? Plastic explosives, perchance?' I asked hopefully.

'Nix. Your sewing-vacaya, friend. And schmutta. And Shellback Certificate.' He wafted my uno solo worthless qualification. 'Apologies from the shipping line for it taking some months to return these particulars but we've been waiting to dock at Georgie Five. I was passing through. We found your forwarding address. Thought I'd deliver it first-lapper, so to speak.'

'That's very kind. And you sprekken Polari. Do I know you, squire?'

'Unlikely. Engine room, mostly. Greaser.'

'Would you care for some herbata? Some tea and biscuits?'

'Aye, I would gladly.'

Not being used to entertaining guests in the bed-sitter, my overriding savagery at this point was whether I could seduce the generous schvartza with charm alone or, failing that, BLOP him over the tet with a blunt instrument and feast greedily on his numb carnish.

'S-sit down, sit down,' I spluttered through randy levers.

'Been enjoying the spoils of the swinging city then, chum?' Arthur asked, himself carrying that gay shore-leave sheen.

'Nanti that. A bogstandard city awaits, I'm afraid. Just like all the rest. Post-war dollydrums. Inky propaganda.'

While the kettle blub-blubbed on the solo gas ring, I flopped open one of the valises and inspected my old seafaring schmutta: ridiculous drag I'd WIZZed up on the sewing-vacaya, offensive clobber dating back to a time I considered myself subversive, accepted and fortuni, but, alas, twas just an illusion.

'No free love then?' Arthur asked, puckering his dishy lips.

Through the fenêtre, there were just beige Brutalist blocks, drain-aqua skies, loitering plops with meese fangless eeks like direct descendents from Hogarth's grubby etchings. I pondered what it was about this smoggy city all the hacks found so swinging. Is a gasworks swinging? Are stumpy-lallied pigeons groovy? Is rubble with-it? Concrete? Hotpot? Parnyaqua? Limescale? Labour?

'Ô, mais oui,' I croaked, 'I've been getting it as much round here as I got bobbing along on the briny aqua. But you don't need clanging musica and a moptop to fish-hook fillies when you've got maxi charisma like myself.'

'Bollocks!' my guest trumpeted. 'I bet you're still a mary!'

Arthur paused for uno momento until the kettle whistled, then he lunged for the bubbling vacaya and flung it rapido at my startled eek. I stood frigid and helpless as the arc of fiery aqua sprayed across the chamber and sliced me ZIPP! down the side of my tet. MERZ! It felt like a scorpion was charvering my left oglesocket with its stinger. I must've been howling but through all the brootish dazzle and agony I recall Arthur screeching lavs to this effect: 'With your monstrous eek, Raymondo, you'd struggle charvering free trade through a fuckering gloryhole in a filthy brandy-latch, you twonk!'

'Who are you?!' I yelped, kicking and squawking now, holding the lardy bedclobber to my fizzer. 'Do I know you?!'

'Clear enough you don't recognise me without the blank skin, shyka and kimono,' Arthur snapped, his voche duey octaves higher now.

In all the excitement his schvartz maquiage had cracked. Utterly wrongfooted, I curled into an eggy shape as the Duchess Winifred Repulse now set upon me like a rabid goose, schonking me and battyfanging ungentlemanlike, slamming my baldy skull against the metal bedframe.

'Revenge, Raymondo!' she cried. 'Remember Durban?'

The agony was such, it took me a pogi few ticktocks to cotton on to what the meshigena sea-queen was palavering about. By the time I'd cobbled together a reasonably natty response, my oyster was bleeding, thin strings of red swinging from my levers.

'I apologise,' I gurgled. 'I take it back! Twas a mistake! I didn't mean to shush your clobber, nor insinuate you were lacking in the dish department ...'

'Un bijou accident, ey?' Winnie hooted, turning her palliass to sharper for an efink or other domestic cutlass.

'Surely we're even, are we not?' I squealed. 'Was your humiliation in Durban not just deserts for my poor cartso's humiliation in the oglesocket of that stinking stingray?!'

These lavs were spoken at speed, echoing willy-nilly as I scarpered down the spiral stairwell. As screeved previously: I am the epitome of your alpha-anglo Bond except for a tendency to run away whenever my lavvy gets heated. The model tenant would of course not surrender their lodgings so easily to a violent vengeful minstrel – but I cared little for that manky latty, nor my dinarli-jarrying tober-omi. I nellied the Duchess emit a twisted war-cry upstairs, then I was gone.

Aware I'd best escape East Londres for a bona few hours, I sprinted puffily to the Tube, slithering slug-like under the barriers and hoppety-hopping aboard the first available chugger, which happened to be headed for WEST RUISLIP – and ze WEST END.

Though I'd sailed the mond (ogling all sorts of foreign poplos, hoofering with naggy-chested negros, flirting with Giblet monos ...), strangely I'd never before set stamper in the central pleasure district of my own city. Was W1 always like this? Possiblement it was just the relief of escaping that blacked-up batatat back thataways, but my opals were near enough drooling out of their sockets as I regarded the unexpected goodies on show: palones in minijupes, omis in tight primary-colour pantaloons, beehive riah, go-go booties, feeli tinkers in fisherpop capellas. The warm sugary von of those subterranean passageways – then the gildi cymbal-crash of hurly-burly glitter-fakements as I emerged blinking above ground at the Dilly. The Dissolute Whirly-go-Round, the Wheel of Fortune. Drooling neon at noon: MAX FACTOR, MOTHER'S RUIN, LEMON HART, PAL INJECTO-MATIC RAZOR. Soho, square-mile bazaar of exotic carnish: pigstails in brine, chorizo nooses, frog-lallies, frilly tripe, garlic saucissons, dollies in scanties. ALL GIRL STRIP REVUE. Semi-erect brat-wursts. Quivering quongs!

Trolling past the kinky bodegas of Grand Windmill Strasse, I savvied that the apparently chaste shut-lallied anglos were in fact more like my spiritual brothers in Paris than I'd cared to imagine. While Stepney was still all murky council latties, gutter-urchins and fangless crones, W1 was all razzle, fruit and pricktease. True enough, the majority of civvies were still robos in juno-suits, but the solo switched-on mod-pops with arriss-length skimpies and peacock clobber were like fortuni priceless groinage shimmering in a junkyard.

THE PERMISSIVE SOCIETY!

My thirst was such, I had to calm myself in the next bungery I stumbled upon: THE NOVAK ARMS on El Rat-Bone Strasse.* I schlumphed down duey lukewarm Charringtons, then, by the third, I was mumbling obscene lavs at the tabletop. Through the petty fenêtres I ogled the teenyboppers minnying by. I pondered: is the minijupe the mostest stimulating invention in all of Christinedom? Nein. Of course not. Molto impressive is the H-bomba, naturellement. Then the sewing-vacaya, lav-hammer, snail tongs, speculum, crystal set, Kalashnikov ... but, bearing

* This must be the Newman Arms, Rathbone Street. After some research, we realise now 'Novak' means 'new man' or 'newcomer' in certain Eastern European lingos. From this point onwards we stopped drinking in our preferred local, the Burglars Rest, and patronised the Newman Arms instead, hoping to spy Signore Shapeshifter in the flesh at last ...

in mind I'd never set opals on a teeni-filly's thighs before (only fatchared barky thighs, or my Old Mare's thews with a spiv or bloodied brolly between), I had fuckering aggressive arva-shakes as I garglered down my last glug-glug of alcool.

Ultra illuminated now, I staggered back out onto El Rat-Bone and shimmied north. As I swished along the cobbles, all at once I felt as though I were being watched over by some dark sparkle, some evil presence just out of ogleshot. The aero prickled with electric. Lusty volts of sweat dribbled off my bod – or was it just the bovaries? Who to blame for this delicious beastly feeling? Surely it couldn't just be the nova fashions, these skimpy morsos of fabric making me come over full-fruity and queer?

It all became clear as I reached the end of the strasse. My boomboomer quickened as I clocked the gigantic metal totem pole rising from behind the lattytops, adorned with gildi electrical groinage: aerials, transmitters, satellite dishies, sparkly orbs and reflectors. A glittering bell-end of silver throbbering atop a smooth shaft of streamlined merman-green glaze. I dropped to my lally-caps and reered hysterically. Ô, how I reered! Those bloody anglos. The beautiful rosbif boffins had constructed a huge metallic cock in the centre of their stuffy capital city!

The robos in juno-suits and frumpy maxi-blouses scuttled past as if both the 600-foot-tall* erection and I were entirely invisible. After cackling, writhing and panting on the paves for a bona few minutas, eventually I got some explanation from a switched-on dollybird in polka-dots:

'Mademoiselle,' I asked from the ground, 'what in Jupiter's nom do they keep in that gloriosa filthy tower?'

The dolly blushed. 'O. The Post Office Tower?'

Clear enough she'd clocked my froggy voche. 'Yes.' I wink-twitched one of my ogle-slits. 'The Post Office, miss, ejaculating our bills and billy-doos across the sky. Hé-hé! I'm not a spy, dear. A bona fide anglo by birth. You don't have to parker me

---

* It's 581 feet actually – although chaps do tend to exaggerate these things.

the government's mogues. I'm with-it. I'm switched-on. The Post Office, of all cheets! I savvy it must be a phony front for all sorts of fabulosa revolting goodness going on behind that shiny exterieur ... pray tell, what really goes on in there?'

'Well, I don't know exactly ...' While she polled I pondered: did the Permissive Society permit one to plunge one's pearls into any delectable palone's ankles? 'I've heard they'll serve lobsters on the top floor once it opens. A revolving restaurant, that is, if that's the revolving goodness you mean ...'

'Revolving lobsters in that metallic colin's sparkly bell-end, ma'am?' I hooted. I'd nellied enough. When I wrenched myself back to my platters, I had half a throbbering colin myself. I vagaried rapidly in search of a gentlemen's WC to relieve myself immediately. This sordid Surrealistic city! Ô, how I loved Londres.

Lurching downways into the munge of the nearest pissoir, I felt compelled to ejaculate or vomit or both pronto – and yet, as the honking rimbumbles of the city faded to nantwar above my tet, I recalled Winnie's hurtful lavs earlier: 'With your monstrous eek, Raymondo, you'd struggle charvering free trade through a fuckering gloryhole in a filthy brandy-latch!'

I ponced: surely the gents ajax to this mostest grossest metallic totem to free love must be teeming with eager winky dishes? And surely my appearance wouldn't matter in the shade of this manky bunker? Still, when I regarded my reflection in the grimy mirror, I was startled by the Halloween beastie squinting back at me. I slammed myself in the first cubicle, locked, and set to work solo.

'Groin-groin! Groin-groin!' I panted, tugging with lusty aggro.

I was edging towards a grand orgasme of Trevi Fountain proportions when I clocked the bijou gloryhole drilled into the side of the khazi, and the lapper-screeved lavs: BONSOIR COLIN. I nellied rustling in the nex-bor cube. My greasy thumper galloped as I pictured a butch-omi poised with his fat oyster-levers or hairy dish puckered, oblivious that he'd soon be lovingly fucked by this most meese meshigena fangless mary! Ô, I almost exploded there and then – the scenario was foolproof. For all I knew my neighbour may well have been meese too, but I cared not. I was finally going to penetrate a living, breathing being! GARDYLOO, my sweet paramour! GARDYLOO! I slipped my stiff cartso through the grubby O and waited.

There was a pogi bit more frittying nex-bor, tense thumpering silence, then suddenly my own cubicle door SHEBAM!ed open and a sharpering-omi in uniform apprehended me with brutal lappers. 'MERDRRRE!' I screeched. For uno momento I believe my hideous visage fazed the orderly-daughter, freezing him like an ultraschvartz chess piece, but when I tried to scarper upways back to strasse-level, a whistle had been puffed and another copper came racing down the steps to stop me. I was manhandled in the most unromantic fashion: pinned to the mouldy tiles of the stairwell, roughed up, tet-twistered, lally-caps cracked by batons, stamped upon and finally ferricadoozed into a medsa-coma. Sang ran from most orifices. Pig-sirens howling* through the ultragloom. And when eventually I came

---

* On our second night together in the Newman Arms, we arrived around 5 p.m. and found Merritt sozzled and depressed in the corner, mumbling incoherently into a black Dictaphone. When we surrounded his table, our Director looked up at us as though we were hovering poltergeists and he stammered: 'It's, it's all gone wrong … it's all too much … it's over … it's over …'

At this point, none of us were aware of the divorce papers. When Stanley stumbled off to the toilet, he left his house keys and Dictaphone on the table, along with a beermat he'd been spitefully flaying for the past forty-five minutes. In spite of our almost unanimous protests, Audrey's curiosity got the better of her. She picked up the Dictaphone, rewound the tape a little and punched PLAY. Hoping for some insight into Merritt's troubled mind (all he'd given us thus far were grunts, sneers and muddled Paisley bile), our Head of Complaints held the device to her ear, but no sooner had she begun listening than Stanley returned gropingly from the lavatory.

'What did you hear? Anything?' McKinley asked Audrey later, accompanying her to the Tube.

'It just seemed like nonsense, drunken bluster. Something about a diving-bell, or diving-helmet. I'm not sure. Though one word was clear.'

'Go on.'

Audrey mimicked her boss's accent, put on a mournful clown face. 'Howlin'.'

to, I appeared to be incarcerated in a blank rabbit hutch in some monstrous sharpering-khazi or hospital or gaol, in some unfamiliar part of this now terribly terribly unfamiliar city ...

Offensive Tet*

VONKA FULL OF AMYL NITRATE, NOVAK WEARS A HOSPITAL GOWN, TIN CAN CAPELLA, ELECTRODES AND A PETTY RUBBER HORSEYSHOE BETWIXT HIS GUMS.

'The sexually immoral, Raymond!' the Shrinker shrieked at me, administering another electro-shock to my groin. 'The cowardly, the unbelieving, the vile, the murderers, the SEXUALLY IMMORAL, the sorcerers, the idolaters, the teenyboppers, and all liars – they will be consigned to the fiery lake of burning sulphur!'

The scatty whitecoat was reading from some specjalni tatty version of Gideons Bibble. By now (strapped as I was to the cot, tet viced and lallies akimbo) I savvied my protests were futile, but still I cried out through quivering oyster-levers: 'Fuck the Bibble, sir! What are you: an omi of science or religion? BANG! VLOP! ZIP! ZUT! I thought the two weren't usual bedfellows, isn't that r-right? MERZ!'

Another shock was administered.

How had it come to this: an innocent feeli-omi, a virginal ex-barky strapped to a cot with glimmering croc-clips attached to his poor underused cartso?

After much rough handling in the sharpering-khazi and weeks of tedious politico-babble in court, I was found unanimously guilty of sexual immorality, homosexuality, drunkenness, disorderliness, depravity. I was deemed to be the possessor

* Chapter received Friday, 27th February 1970 – 136 days to go.

of an exceedingly offensive tet and given a choice by the fungal wig-pop: kenza months in GAOL, or a mere trey weeks of PSYCHOLOGICAL REORIENTATION. Gaol seemed unbearably naff, grotty and limiting, and so I agreed to the molto dorcas prospect of servo-massages and Freud-waffle, unaware that the true aim of this second option was not to rehabilitate me as such but to simply fry me into an unfeeling vegetable with nanti memory, nix personality, no soul.

'FASH BATATATS!' I yelped continuously on the first juno, carted like some rotten lump of carnish to a frigid sanitarium somewhere in the dolly anglo countryside. The loony-bin was this meese concrete box with trembling pluplushes surrounding it, inside decorated with all the pomp and glitter of a sewage processing plant or abattoir. After they dragged me off to my cell and poked me with various medical vacayas, I was allowed the rest of the noche to relax in the ultraschvartz – although it should go without screeving that I was not feeling particularly refreshed when the Shrinker and his cronies appeared at 5 a.m. the next morn to wheel me off to the Lumière Suite.

For the first week they electrocuted my genitals. I was tethered to a cot and forced to ogle a slideshow of omis and palones in various states of undress, copulation, enslavement and venereal mal-health. Certain slides were accompanied by a gross shock to the groin. A fortuni butch-omi with a leather capella, mouser, hard colin and an index-lupper up his sphincter flashed on the silvery screen, and I was zapped. The pain was like taking a glimmer-fakement to the pelvis. Barbed wire dancing up my urethra. 'FASH BATATATATATS!' I screamed.

To begin with it seemed the crocuses were shocking me at random. The manky slides I expected to be chasered with electric (patriarchal caca: a business-omi charvering his frigid-eeked secretary atop a gigantic gold bullion, Genghis Khan civilising village-fillies with his gross bushy cartso, the Archbishop of Canterbury grinning beatific at his poked-up choirboys) flashed up with nanti painful consequences. Other, seemingly harmless slides (trey gentlepops enjoying a pot of herbata together in flowery surrounds, donnas with cropped riah lammering at a bus-stop, omis in women's schmutta, a bodbuilder holding aloft a grandiose concombre) resulted in me parnying and screeching, charvering the aero in agony.

Away from the Lumière Suite the quacks were mostly tight-levered, but I rapidly gleaned from the Shrinker's commentary during the slides that he wanted me to at least pretend to be interested in Christianity: 'Homosexuality is next to murder in the eyes of God, Raymond, is it not?'

These lavs were confusing, not least because I still considered myself beebee, gender-slippery, AC/DC, multipolysexual back then. I couldn't rightly recall where homosexuality lay on the arva-spectrum. When a slide flashed up with duey glistening omis in skimpies wrestling atop a heavily talcum-powdered canvas mat, I polled what I thought the Shrinker wanted to nell – 'Ugh, mally, disgusting! These plops should be shot!' – and received a doppel-dose of electric.

'These plops, as you call them, are males in the pink of condition. Fighting men. The epitome of masculinity!' was the quack's batty response.

Regularly the nurses plied me with gin and other quease-inducing* drogas to help reorient my servo – but now and

---

* Five days after receiving this chapter, a parcel arrived containing a gift-wrapped box with a handwritten label: DE-LUXE PÂTÉ-DU-JOUR. We presume it is Novak and not some other deranged Frenchman sending us these unsolicited *petits déjeuners* through the post. Prior to this latest offering, we'd gladly accepted a bottle of potent aniseed liqueur and a basket of cream éclairs from the mystery gourmand – however, this grey meat paste did not inspire quite the same greedy lip-smacking around the office.

Nevertheless, we tucked in. We sent Audrey out to buy a couple of fresh baguettes from a boulangerie in Soho, then shared out the rustic sludge among the five of us (Merritt was absent: possibly still in bed/at the pub/drowning in parnyaqua).

'In what way is this *de-luxe* pâté?' McKinley ruminated, chewing his morsel with a grim expression.

'It's making my eyes water.'

then they allowed me to ogle the slides sober, and twas on one such occasion I clocked something doubly sinister about these meshigena images. I remember the slide well: a sharpering-omi with a mogue beard and ogle-fakes terrorising a helpless gypsy in chains, her orifices stuffed with setta or otta gross black truncheons. Behind the beard the omi's sneering eek seemed familiar somehow. At first I pondered if this was one of the sharpering-pops that battyfanged me in Fitzrovia, but NEIN – NEIN NEIN NEIN! – as I squinted closer, I savvied with maxi disgust and horror that this was none other than the Shrinker himself, joshed-up in the leading role.

'I ... It's –' I spluttered, before another sickening jolt cut my whimpery lavs short.

Ô, mercy me.

While I savvied clear enough that the crocuses might've had difficulty sourcing these specjalni (supposedly therapeutic) pornographic fotos in the outside welt, twas ultra unsettling imagining the batatats acting out these obscene scenarios on a makeshift stage-set somewhere within the sanitarium. Above all it begged the question: weren't the deeds committed on kamera far worster than me innocently prodding my tingly colin through a hole in a privvy pissoir? Who was the more insane and depraved here?

Another slide glimmered on the silvery screen – the Shrinker naggy except for a Venetian plague-quacker's mask, penetrating a parnying, bleeding omi's botty with the mask's elongated vonka.

'It's ... it's you – ZIP! You fuckering – ZUT! You fuckering dirty batatat! ZOUNDS!' I stammered, spitting feathers as my

---

'I feel awful.'

All in all, 'It's ruddy garlicky' was about the most praise we could lavish on the dish. Davy claimed he enjoyed his share, but he was probably just trying to appear cultured and cosmopolitan. At around 12.30 p.m., after persevering with the muck all morning, Davy vomited violently into the nearest wastepaper basket, spattering Emily's nylons with specks of bile and undigested offal.

bod crumpled and contorted on the clammy cot with every stab of electric. 'It's you, it's you!'

The Shrinker ogled me coldly. 'Don't be absurd, Raymond.'

Another shock was administered.

'No, but –'

Another shock was administered.

'Ô, the coddy hypocrisy!' I screeched. 'MERZ! You say homosexuality is a sin, sir, but – VLOP! – but are you thusly therefore not the – AÎE! – not the mostest grossest sinner of us all here?'

A prolapsed rectum filled the screen – an image not dissimilar to my Old Mare's hortus following one of her grotty auto-abortions.* The quacks scrutinised my fizzer. I flickered not a jot. Another shock was administered.

'Look, we're getting nowhere,' the Shrinker grumbled, turning to his cronies. 'He's a peculiar case. Not susceptible to aversion therapy, it seems.' Though he was side-oystering, I nellied his lavs clear enough. 'There's nothing else for it. ECT. Twelve courses. Starting tomorrow.'

'ECT, sir?' I croaked as the crocuses unclipped the croc-clips from my cock.

---

* Abortions were not only rife in the kitchen-sink dramas of the late 1950s/early 1960s, but they also played a major part in the breakdown of Merritt's marriage. Between the years 1956–67 (before the Abortion Act was passed, decriminalising terminations), Stanley moonlighted as a backdoor abortionist, charging desperate women £40 for his 'kind, discreet service'. It was wretched work, but Stan made a lot more money disposing of foetuses than he did publishing dirty pocketbooks. Death vastly outsold sex. The terminations kept the Glass Eye Press alive. However, one of the many adverse effects of the job was that Stanley quickly found he could no longer please his wife in bed. Committing murder in strangers' wombs inevitably killed his libido. The self-styled Big Chief of British Erotica could not even raise an erection in his own marital bed.

Iris now lives out West with their ten-year-old daughter and refuses to see him. She moved out of their shared flat in Fitzrovia the same week she filed the divorce petition. The prying reader might wonder why Iris didn't leave him sooner. Why wait until 1970, three years after Stan hung up his abortionist's gloves? Was there something more that triggered the break-up?

The company logo now seemed so symbolic: a glass eyeball with the iris cracked.

'Electro-convulsive Therapy.'

My oyster pricked. To humour the twonk, I hooted: 'Beauty will be convulsive!'

'Quite.' The Shrink's eek was stiff. 'Quite.'

The following morning they electrocuted my servo. I was allowed a nourishing breakfast of duey measly aspirins before the crocs wheeled me back into the Lumière Suite, where there was a nova grosser shock machine leering by the cotside. Without too much aggro or parnying on my part, I was strapped to the libbage, a tin-can capella was roughly clamped atop my tet and duey jelly-sloppy electrodes pressed to my temples.

'Will this smart, squire?' I enquired as the Shrinker's cronies held me to the bed – quatra meese albinos in surgical capellas and goggles.

'Take some muscle relaxant,' the Shrink scoffed, thrusting a botty of coddy liqueur under my vonka. 'Amyl nitrate. You're a faggot, Raymond. You'll be well acquainted with it by now, I'm sure.'

'Sayest thou! You filthy ba–'

The stinking liqueur caused my eek to glimmer molto rosy and painful, like all my sang was now scuttling from every extremity direct to my tet. The Lumière Suite glowed ultra silvery and sickly. The curtains wibbling like vertical turquoise aqua. Twas almost like I'd been reefed by Keith again: the albino nurses suddenly quatra smirking, simpering barkies in stewards' whites, forked lingums flittying in and out while they concentrated on keeping me pinned flat to the cot.

'Bite down on this,' the Shrinker urged, cramming what felt like a rubbery horseshoe betwixt my gums. 'Now – welcome to the civilised world, Raymond ...'

The Shrinker dropped the TREAT switch: a molto misleading lav. There was a brootish crackle as the shockers went off. I felt a bijou H-bomba explode in my skull, then for una minuta or duey I was a twitchering wreck, thews like scrunched-up bimph and boomboomer coughing out thunder-sparkles. I tried to scream but could only manage a monotoned, 'Mnnnnnnnnrrrrr ...'

'There there, Raymond,' the Shrinker tutted once the spasms passed. 'We're only warming up, old boy. These are mere baby* steps on the grand staircase to normality!'

For possibly the first time in my lavvy, I was frightened, Ô comrades. Contempt for authority-flops had long been my default setting, but until now I'd never felt true fear towards the evil batatats. I spat out the rubber morso, and my solo remaining fang plopped out with it. My bod felt like I'd been SPLATCH!ed through a rusty mangle. My opals were spinning-tops, luppers trembling like tinsel.

'I'm n-not homosexual, sir,' I murmured groggily.

'Of course you're not, Raymond. An ex-Merchant Navy boy, caught with his excited prick thrust through the gloryhole in a gentlemen's public pissoir.'

'I'm a l-l-liberteen. I swing either way. In fact, I swing n-neither way, in truth.'

'I DESPISE this swinging society!' the Shrinker shrieked, puffing his chest out before drifting fattygayed into an ajax modernist armchair. 'Sinners, the lot of you. ECT is too good for scum like you! A stiff hot poker up the backside is what you need, Raymond. Lord have mercy.'

'I'm innocent. I swear,' I gurgled. 'Twas the gigantic m-metal colin that made me do it, so I believe. The filthy s-servo-lathering

---

* Authors often describe their novels as their babies. A heavy-handed editor can kill these babies.

Stanley's most difficult abortion was performed after-hours at the Glass Eye office, spring 1964. Emily, now relatively happily married to a bashful mechanic, was drugged and molested by a masked stranger one weeknight outside a Soho discotheque and came to Stanley after discovering the monster had made her pregnant. Merritt laid down a tarpaulin where we'd earlier been perusing Davy's way-out cover designs for *Sanctimonious Susan* (1964, 2/8), and for the first time in his sideline career he was aware of his hands shaking as he set to work between his secretary's legs. Merritt waived the fee, but ultimately the abortion cost Emily dearly. There must've been complications during the procedure. For five years now Emily and her husband have been trying for a baby, but the scar tissue in her uterus must've rendered her sterile.

Post Office Tower, sir, sending me mixed messages about this s-supposed nova arva revolution ...'

'There there,' the Shrink cooed, crunched up in the foetal posture in his chrome throne. 'Fear not, Raymond – we'll have these horrible, demented thoughts cast out of you soon enough, sonny, soon enough.'

I pondered blankly: what now? What next? The possibilities were maddening. I wept a pogi bit as they wheeled me back to Ward V, but for the most part my tet was numb, full-ultraschvartz.

As I quivered through the noche, I savvied clear enough that the aversion therapy was futile. I wasn't raised on these norm servo-shackling values of bona or cod, moral or immoral. I had no inbuilt guilt or God-fear. I didn't know right from wrong. Hadn't the zots savvied yet that I was an anomaly? A lone wolfy? Ô Jupiter, Ô Judith. What now? What next? What depths might these meshigena batatatatats sink to, to force an unbendable weirdy like me to conform?!

Elektrizität Macht Frei*

NOVAK WEARS UNFAMILIAR BANDAGES.

Chinka junos later I awoke from revolting slumbers to find morsos of me missing. My tet and groin ached. It felt as though I'd been droggled with heavy tranquil-pills, but still the pain cut through. I tried to cry out but could manage only a pogi high-pitched, 'Squeak-squeak!'

As far as I could remember, I'd been zapped with duey or maybe trey more courses of the TREAT switch. If the Shrinker's emag was to ferricadooz my libido in the mostest unerotic circumstances imaginable, the treatment had been an unequivocal success so far. Of course, I savvied that the true aim was to forcibly reverse what they thought to be a subversive homo-omi into a square hetero-omi. Like the old venereal Lord Foster-Newman, these fash crocs held the coddy notion of a right and wrong sexuality, but I'm nanti convinced sex preference is yin-yang, plus or minus. Are we all not a pogi bit queer now and then? Is it not more perverse to blockade your multilove impulses only for fear of embarrassment, sneering eaglets or being vadared as somehow outside norm society? ACHTUNG, my dear chovis: to be considered normal is perhaps the coddiest insult of all, is it not?!

I reached down to reef my genitalia, to ease some of the aggro. My cartso wasn't ultra tender now the crocs had stopped shocking my groin – however, there was something ajax smarting horrendously. As I prodded and poked round my undercarriage,

---

* Chapter received Friday, 6th March 1970 – 129 days to go.

I was puzzled to find only smooth fabric where my quongs should be. My boomboomer volcanoed as I glanced under the bedclobber. Sang-stained bandages covered my crotch. I reefed again, sharpering desperately for my petty egglets. Nix jewels. NANTI TESTICLES! Vomitus leapt up my gargler. Parnyaqua plop-plopped from my fattygayed ogle-slits. I cried out through my gums – 'Nein! Nein nein nein nein NEIN!' – and savvied my voche was an octave higher. 'Squeak-squeak!'

Fogged by panic, I blinked blankly up and down the cyanide-green corridor. Beyond the rows of other droggled servo-zapped comrades, I could just about nelly the crocuses clucking and chirruping in their staff-khazi. I opened my oyster to screech for help, and an unusual lav splurted out:

'Mama.' I rocked dumbly back and forth, weeping and drooling profusely, like I'd regressed back to some codswallop infantile state. 'Mama. Ô Mama. Mama Mama!'

Eventually one of the psychiatric eagles landed by my cotside in a swish of blood-flecked feathers. He or she palavered with worms or quong-strings dangling from its oyster: 'Problems, Raymond?'

Delirious, I blubbed: 'Wh-where am I? Wh-where is my mama?' Alas, my servo had been so thoroughly pulverised, I could not rightly recall my dear Old Mare's eek, let alone that she'd been dead half a decade.

The aquila-vonka regarded some legal-bimph on a clipper-board by my libbage. 'You have no next of kin, Raymond. We are here to look after you.'

Somewhere in the electric-numb mousehole of my skull, a twisted image flickered: the thunderthuds, le Château Chanceux collapsing, the clatter-shatter of bricks, the Madame mortified. A terrifying thought followed: clear enough this fiery ECT was intended not to awaken me from sin (as the shrinks insisted), but to anaesthetise me, to erase my past, to dissolve my memories,*

---

* O wonderful. We've promised to publish the memoirs of a madman who now admits he may have had swathes of his memories removed by force!

my revs, my libido, my sense of self – but I savvied defiantly: I still had a few threads to cling onto. I remembered my period of mourning, and went into mourning all over again, like the Mare had snuffed it there and then by my cotside.

'Mama ...'

Nix, nanti that – these batatats had no interest in reforming me. I was here only to be neutered, enslaved, then parkered off to some bland bed-sit half-lavvy with nanti tet-function, nix manhood, no objections. A brainless bod, a nonentity, a compliant sexless mannequin.

Were there nobba more courses of this to come? Daitcha? Uno cheet was clear: I had to vagary pronto. If the shrinks zapped my tet any more, I'd surely lose everything.

For the rest of the morn I considered my escape. The loonybin was positively teeming with vigilant vultures, but as I ogled the dizzying stream of billowing whitecoats scuttling by I savvied that their number – and naff uniformity – could well play to my advantage ...

'Norman, dearest,' I side-oystered to the dolly fungal fleur in the cot nex-bor. 'May I borrow a light?'

The poor tart was only capable of a slack-levered, 'Gnnnnrrr,' but I took it to be an affirmative 'Gnnnnrrr'. Astonishingly us inmates were not allowed soap nor fangpaste in the infirmary, but we could vogue all we liked. Helping myself to the Swan Vestas in Norman's top pyjama posh, I plucked out a lapperful of matches, then spent the next medsa-hour or so delicately whittling them down to bijou makeshift sew-needles with my luppernails.

Feigning loose kishkas (an all-too-common side effect of the TREAT switch), I made numerous trips to the khazi that juno and noche, shuffling molto cripplish with my eiderdown and blank bedsheet wrapped tight around my pols, before energetically whipping both off in the privvy cube and resuming my work on perhaps my mostest ingenious morso of clobber to date. Employing various scatty improvised techniques – unravelling the eiderdown for thread, rippering the bedsheet with my fangless gums and luppernails, patchworking the shreds back together with those infuriating petty matchstick pricks – I soon had a more-or-less passable quacker's lab coat in my gripple. The cheet would not cause a stir on the runways of Paris, true enough, but under the circumstances twas a gloriosa tour de force.

Retiring back to my cot around 7 p.m., I spent the rest of the noche discreetly tinkering with the garment under my frayed eiderdown, adding shushed buttons and duey contour darts for a molto shapely fit. I was determined to have the cheet ready by dawn, full-aware if I was dragged back to the Lumière Suite first thing in the morn, my third (fourth?) crack of electric could well make me forget I'd been working on the bona cozzy in the first place.

Once ultraschvartz descended on Ward V, I risked one last trip to the khazi to make a pogi few final adjustments – then I was done. Twirling in front of the cracked, spiderwebbed mirror, I conceded I would not personally trust the doctor ogling back at me, but as far as this meshigena institution was concerned, I'd fit in fantabulosa.

Staggering back to my bed, my plattershuffles felt a pogi bit lighter as I contemplated the nova freedoms and frippery waiting for me beyond the gaol walls. While it was tempting to make a dash for the exit there and then, I savvied it was nattier to wait until dawn, when the asylum filled up again with scuttling psycho-pops, so I had extra cover to move among them unnoticed. I plunged my tet into my breezeblock pillow, faking sleep though I was dowri fattygayed – until finally the gloriosa chubby sol-rise licked the fenêtres, and I clocked the crocs' clogs clomping back and forth across the swirly lino.

Ogling through squinty lids, I waited excruciatingly patiently for the quacks to slither off to the staff-khazi for their ritual herbata and drilling from the top brass – then I rocketed from my bedclobber. Boomboomer squelching, I wriggled into my nova lab coat, shushed poor Norman's dentures from the tumbler by his cotside, liberated Gregory's toupee, then trolled post-haste for the exit. Affecting insouciance, I minced outways down a long antiseptic corridor, nodding now and then at bleary-opaled quacks, before crossing an outrageously ritzy foyer to a sparkling set of doppel-doors.

'Morning,' I polled at the dollybird behind the desk, feeling Norman's fangs slipping slightly.

'Good morning, sir,' she monotoned, uncleffing the portals with a push-button ajax to her polari-pipe.

For uno momento I felt I recognised her as one of the poor molested actresses from the Shrinker's slideshow but – BOF and ADIEU, foul beasties – I did not ogle backways as I schonked the doppel-doors open and stepped out into the bracing rustic-whoosh. The Free Welt tasted divine, Ô comrades, and yet I almost let out a careless bambino-wail when I clocked there was yet another obstacle ahead: a gross locked iron gateway emblazoned with the gloomy lavs: ELEKTRIZITÄT MACHT FREI. Ducking into the munge, I snuck creepy-creepily round the prickly perimeter of the sanitarium until I found an unguarded morso, then – losing my dentures, shyka and lab coat in the process – flailingly cleared the lally-jangling electro-fence and sprinted. Ô, how I scarpered! My naggy platters swiftly turned to swollen bleeding piggy-trotters as I scrambled across the rocky rural caca – but I savvied I had to keep running. If these batatats had developed top-of-the-range secret servo-frazzling vacayas, they nix doubt had first-class security too: spy-planes, radar, guard-wolves, snipers ...

'Londres?' I squeaked at the traffic, once I'd scrambled through several acres of bristly twitchy pluplushes and snuffled out the main strasse. 'Londres?!'

Plenty of cabooshes kept on zoom-zooming past, ignoring my jiggly near-naggy gesticulations, until finally a grinning butch-omi in a tanker pulled up. Twas a relief to hop in next to a bona fide prole – the pop's vonka was more oinkish than eagle, just like my own, and the reading matter in his famblerbox suggested he wasn't at all ajax to those sanctimonious bats back thataways: KNAVE, MAYFAIR, MOUTHFUL OF LEATHER* ...

'You're in some state,' the prole commented as we set off. 'An all-nighter, was it?'

'Of sorts, squire. Been locked in that gross meshigena mansion there.' I waved a weak lupper behind us. 'It's a monstrous place, comrade. Severely aching in the tet and groin, yes. I suggest you put your foot down ...'

'Sex party, was it?'

'Nix. Not exactly.'

'Pah! I know what your sort get up to on these bloody retreats! Look at the clip of you, sunshine. No slacks! Lost in the heat of the moment, is it? You're not in the Cabinet, are you? You're not embroigling me in some new smutty scandal, are you, sonny? The Profumo Affair, is it? The bloody Permissive Society!?'

'It's mally, sir. Despicable.' Was this the TREAT switch palavering, or just friendly concurrence?

'Not at all! This Permissive Society I'm all for!' he bellowed. 'You've got eyes in there, have you? Birds in bikinis, sunning themselves in the parks. Bloody Hell, son! The Permissive Society I'm all for. It's these bloody two-faced politicians debauching themselves with the birds in bikinis I can't abide ...'

I raised an ogle-rider. 'Apologies, squire – I'm a pogi bit dazzleshipped to say the least – and I must admit I'm yet to vada exactly what makes this codswallop iron-fisted society so Permissive. In fact, I'm bearing the brunt of its brutality betwixt my lallies ...' I was about to divulge my meese punishments to the prole – but then savvied this alpha-omi might not take molto kindly to my fairy exploits in the public khazi, nor would he wish to ogle my fatchared perineum. 'Tell me about this Perfume Affair, mister,' I side-oystered instead. 'I've been at sea three years. A niffy business, was it?'

---

* One of our own releases! Our most popular pocketbook to date, racking up 791 sales since 1965, and still only 2/8! Discreet packaging, satisfaction guaranteed.

While I was bobbing along the ocean I'd spotted the odd screamline about this daffy Profumo carry-on – SOCIETY MORALS IN TURMOIL, DOG LEAD, J'AI MENTI!, THE GIRL WHO IS ROCKING THE GOVERNMENT – but until now never nellied the full details. As the tanker gobbled its way through the country asphalte, the butch-omi enlightened me. Twas an intriguing yarn. The Fairytale of Christine Keeler: a low-class teeni showgirl who, by gaily charvering a Tory baldy, Soviet spy, Harley Strasse back-quack and a pair of dolly pistolet-toting spades, effectively brought down the Establishment with her beauty and flange-levers!

For the most part the tale cheered me up – or at least distracted me from the butchery in my slippies – but I was left puzzled by some pogi details. The idea of monogamy, por example. I couldn't rightly comprehend why this Profumo chappy (or any pop for that matter) would choose to get married when clearly his natural arva-drive nagged him juno upon juno to keep chasering skirt. Yet again, the hypocrisy of the ruling classes was staggering – but still, what appealed to me most about the yarn was Christine's humble low-class sang. More so than those natty but ultimately untouchable bolshies like Red Rosa, Lenin, Trotters or Castro, Miss Keeler was a bona fide prole role model, giving hope to inferior plebs like you and me that we could shake up this codswallop welt – and look fuckering fortuni while doing it.

As we neared Londres, every other caboosh seemed to be carrying some foul eagle-eek in a bowler-capella. Despite flinching a petty bit whenever a sharpering-car screamed past, I felt safe ajax to this muscular trucker, but once coughed out at Hammersmith and chuggered lento back to Stepney, the twistiness came over me again.

On returning to my bed-sitter I discovered Winnie had destroyed almost every vacaya and morso of furniture in there, although charitably she'd at least left the door on the latch. I cleared myself a pogi space on the fattygayed mattress and crinkled into the foetal posture. I parnied for almost an hour or duey, then eventually summoned up the servo-strength to have another ogle between my lallies. I ripped the bandages from my weeping perineum and broke down all over again. There was just a congealed brown scab where my quongs used to hang.

FASH BATATATS. Ô Jupiter, Ô Christine. What next? What now?

As 1965 crawled onwards, I confined myself to my cave, slummocking in suspended animation, a meese sloth-omi with pogi-all to live for. 'Bed-sitter' basically summed up my entire lavvy at this point. Too frightened to vagary outside the latty and yet too fidgety to just vegetate indoors, I had nix clue what I was going to do with myself in the future. Ridiculously the Merch Navy appealed again, if only for the gratis lodgings and proximity to other sexually flexible outcasts, but I savvied the INSTANT DISMISSAL on my particulars was somewhat damaging to my chances of reemployment.

Ô, dearest comrades, this twisted period was marked by setback after setback. While I'd managed to cling by my luppertips to my memories, the electro-jolts had caused other cod changes to my servo. Whereas before in times of twistiness I'd been able to lose myself in my revs, I rapidly discovered the crocs' meddling had utterly ravaged my dreamworld. Some foul electric must've hit my rev-making lobe by mistake – unless it was just plain paranoia or post-traumatic abdabs causing the onslaught of wretched noche terrors. In place of my dreams, there were now just meese chronic nightmares. I no longer enjoyed sleeping – in fact, I slept rarely now. My nightly runway of delicious shapeshiftering beasties with milky willets and palavering flanges trolled into the void. Insomniac, clammy, glimmering with helpless rage, I shared my lib with just monsters now.

Ô, those feeli dreams! I miss them. I miss them.

Maxi fattygayed but too frightened to shut my opals, I pondered noche upon noche: what did the State want from us? Was this so-called Swinging City not only a marketing ploy to entice randy pops from abroad to boost the economy, but also a honeytrap to fish out subversives on home soil and promptly frazzle their dreaming freewheeling servos? Boffins suggest in the future we'll all be liberated once The Travails become fully automated, operated by robos – or maybe we'll be the robos: brainless cogs droggled and zapped into full compliance, grinding away just to keep the toppermost toffs' de-luxe dinarli-drenched dream lavvies intact.

I considered those lavs again: INSTANT DISMISSAL.

'Bon voyage, Raymondo,' I hush-hushed into my chest. 'Adieu ... adieu ...'

With nanti pleasant dreams to keep me occupied on the National Handbag and nix ambition to graft myself gradually, grudgingly to the grave, I made a bold, proud and ultra-liberteen decision to mortify myself pronto, on my own terms. According to my mogue birth-scroll, I turned twenty-one on 10th August 1965, and twas on this coddy juno I developed a taste for a nova illuminating liquor: methylated spirits. Only tuppence a botty from my local hardware-bodega, meths was the ideal poison. My ejector-seat, my nuclear button. My birthday bitter-gator.

Come, bitter conduct, come, ultra-unsavoury guide ...

As the fiery purple aqua went down, my boomboomer bucked and brayed in my chest. My tet felt as if it were being rapidly pumped full of sickly-sweet CS gas, my vision distorting the chintzy wallpaper into jagged snap-snappering flytrap patterns. I ponced drunkenly: will I sink tranquil into eternal sleep, or will this be a violent, vomiting, frittying, meese mortification? Thankfully, after the initial terrifying bod-shock, the meths had a calming (or dulling, deadening) effect, so I wasn't maxi nervy as I continued schlumphing my way to The Final Drop. As far as I can remember, I stripped full-naggy, writhed on my palliass like a blowdarted warthog, probably chanting some Dadaist voodoo gibberish. Death throes, nausea, vibration-white-lallies ...

Another half-botty later I blacked out, but as the alert reader will be well aware, I didn't die. My sacrifice to the mond comes later.

Jolted by a gruesome inkyboo involving my handcuffed lappers being fed through a spaghetti-vacaya, I awoke the next morn sick as a mallard and utterly utterly depressed. A meths hangover is ajax to having your skull scooped out by a gravedigger's shovelet and shat into by a skunk. After more dry-vomitus, I crawled back into my vonny cot and gazed slitty at the ceiling. Is there anything more pathetic than a failed suicide at the bitter end of years and years of gross and minor humiliations? I checked my poshes. I had a pogi few soldis left for another duey botties of meths. I conceded: if the bitter-gator didn't ferricadooz me this time I'd die of starvation anyway before my next welfare dinarli came through.

BOF.

VLOP.

The ferocity of the hangover delayed me scuttling pronto back to the hardware-bodega, then by the time I'd got myself semi-upright and enthusiastic again for death, there was a brootish SHEBAM-SHRACK! on the front portal. Ordinarily I would've ignored this intrusion, only I happened to be groaning like a bison just as the door was fisted.

'Mr Novak?' a clipped voche called out.

'Gnnnrrrrr ...' I grumbled in response.

I unclickered the latch and creaked the portal open. A loaded shotgun? A noose? The Shrinker and his cronies with a strait-jacket and electro-chair?

Alas – standing stiff in the corridor were duey reptiles in juno-suits. There was something familiar about these pops: the gleam of treacle, an aura of onion.

'O. Terribly sorry to bother you, old man,' one of the suits pow-wowed. 'Is there a Raymond Novak at this address?'

'I am Novak,' I stated, my shrill voche bouncing awkwardly about the corridor.

'Heavens, no. Is it really you?' Gramble exclaimed. 'Teenagers are growing up fast these days, but this is preposterous, is it not, yessum?'

'Were you not cleansed and rejuvenated, living out in the fields with the venerable Foster-Newmans?'

'What's happened to your teeth? Your hairline?'

'It's been a molto coddy dispiriting adult lavvy thus far,' I murmured, letting them in. 'I've lost not only my fangs, but my quongs, chaps. Regard the effects of Capitalism and Electricity on this poor zot. What can I say? What can I do? I'd love to tittle-tattle over some herbata but I'm afraid you've caught me at a busy moment, schlumphing myself into The Grand Void ...'

The legal-reps chuckled at first, before clocking the empty botty of meths upturned on the rug. Spinks snapped: 'Well, it's no wonder you've aged badly, Novak, imbibing that muck.'

'I've only been slurping it since yester-noche, as it happens. Money is a worster poison to omis' souls, isn't that right? Oui? Nein?'

The reps glanced at each other with some amusement.

'Well,' Gramble tittered, 'if that's your opinion, we come bearing bad news.'

My kishkas shrivelled. I pictured black-famblered bailiffs storming in, stripping myself and my latty utterly naggy, my schmutta sold off, my Shellback Certificate shredded, my sewing-vacaya scrapped.

I tried to cling to the positives. It would only be a passing humiliation. I would soon be dead.

'Pray, tell all,' I hiccoughed, slumping back down on my mattress and adopting the posture of a stamped-on locust.

'Remember this?' Mr Gramble removed a tatty chequeliver from his breast posh. 'Yessum? Or not at all? As of your twenty-first birthday, Raymond, you've become the sole beneficiary of a rather substantial sum.'

'Pardon me, sir?' I spluttered.

'Forty-two thousand guineas.'

The carpet seemed to swirl for uno momento.

'Hé-hé. Bona. Molto bona, darlings.' I ogled the legal-reps with maxi contempt. 'This is some coddy emag, is it? Some joke? Or a clerical error, I'm sure. Allez ... allez ... fuck-off-back-thataways to whatever gildi skytickler you've slithered from ...'

'It's no joke,' Spinks insisted. 'It's your entitlement. Forty-two thousand guineas, Raymond. All we need is for you to sign here, initial here, today's date here, sign here, countersign here, bank details here, and then the money is yours.'

'This is ridiculous,' I mumblered. Were these scatty pops just a figment of my nova inkyboos?

'You need not accept the money if you so wish, child...'

'No, no – I'll take it, I'll gladly take it. But may I ask where this jumbo dinarli's come from?' I side-oystered, rapidly inking the legal bimph. 'Or is the asking a pogi bit vulgar?' I pictured the Pile glimmering, struck by thunder-sparkles, the Lord, Lady and setta feeli Fosters roasted to crackling. 'The venereal Lord and Lady snuffed it, did they?'

'Not at all,' Gramble cackled. 'They're still thriving.'

'The dinarli, as you put it, was your mother's.' Spinks showed me the tatty chequeliver again, the froggy lavs, the foreign address.

'My Mare was penniless,' I squeaked.

'Not so, Raymond. Not so.'

'She was a shirker, a skinflint. We had nix, nothing. You're telling me she lived like a pauper by choice, not by necesses-sessity?'

'Heaven knows, Raymond. Your mother was to us just a decapitated head, albeit a very rich decapitated head.'

I ponced backwards to our time in the Château Chanceux, the Old Mare occasionally coming home with de-luxe goodies for the munjarry-table, her glittery groinage, the pompadour riah. Was she truly a well-off toff masquerading as a gutter-palone? At first I felt a petty pang of rage, savvying these filthy beyongs would've saved me from years of needless toil, pain and aggro, if only she'd let me get my lappers on them pronto after her mortification. Still, the daffy bat must've had her reasons. Possiblement she wanted me to struggle a while, to ogle the glaring tyrannical nature of this codswallop welt up-close before rewarding me with this mostest exceptional gildi ticket to the Liberated Lavvy Everlasting.

'Mama,' I murmured. 'Ô Mama!'

'The money should be in your account within three working days,' Mr Gramble explained. 'We suggest you celebrate* by drinking something a little more elegant than methylated spirits. No? Yessum? Or not at all?'

---

* Gone are the days when we'd celebrate our book launches with bottomless champagne and vol-au-vents. By the time we reached our 201st release, *The Nuremberg Nymphos* (Dennis Mesh, 2/8, published March 1970), we had to ask our guests to bring their own bottles. The launch was an utter disappointment. Only a tiny handful of the public attended, and most left promptly once they realised there were no complimentary refreshments (or once they heard the first paragraphs of Dennis's reading?). Not even our full staff attended. Audrey was absent, possibly still angry her likeness had been stolen for the molested Aryan bird on the book's cover. Still no sign of Howling. McKinley ill with flu. Dennis Mesh himself was barely there, soused and depressed in the corner like he too had been schlumphing methylated spirits, his face unappetisingly grey and greasy. By the end of the night the festivities had more the feel of a bland board meeting than a bohemian happening. Knocking back the dregs of strangers' abandoned bottles, we got to talking about Novak's m/s again. As scrupulous editors, we naturally saw many areas for improvement (for one, the current title *Dieu-du-Jour* was deplorable), but we wondered: could we get away with monkeying with the manuscript without hurting Novak's feelings? Was the author truly unhinged? Would he appreciate our supplementary footnotes – or would he disown the book if he felt we'd hijacked his life story, distorting it beyond recognition? That night we came to an agreement: if Novak survives his fantabulosa crime, we should keep the title and content exactly as delivered; if Novak dies, we can fiddle freely with the text and change the title. But change it to what exactly? Brainstorming into the small hours, we came up with all manner of dubious alternatives – *Une Petite Handlebar Mouser*, *Meese Meshigena-Omi*, *Man-Eating Typewriter*, *Beware the Eagle-Eeks!*, *The Milk of Liberty*, *Novak versus the Fash Batatats*, *Confessions of a Demented Frog* – before settling on a title that seemed to marry the Emperor's elusiveness with our own enthusiasm for annotation: *Mister Asterisk*.

The Emperor's Nova Schmutta*

NOVAK WEARS A FROG CROP, AMONG OTHER ACCOUTREMENTS.

Dinarli. That once ungraspable slime was now mine! Difficult at first to decide what to do with all that bimph. Almost ashamed to feel so gay about the baffling extra numerals in my account. Quite tempted to just blow it all on extravagant Surrealist sculptoids, make love to them for uno dazzling noche, then blow myself up with the collection, although that wouldn't be molto fair on the Surrealists (nor my ajax neighbours).

In the end the gruesome monster in the mirror screeched for attention. This was not the visage of a proud, prosperous omi. The meths and nova sleep-terrors had drained my eek to a purply smudge, my oglesockets like duey bloodshot craters on the wrong side of the moon. I was full-baldy now, a chinless humpback with scrawny thews, nix radiance, nanti pots in the pantry. Who in all of Christinedom could possibly love this freak-eeked weirdy?

LOVE was what I needed above all else. Prior to the Lumière Suite I gained dowri comfort frolicking with the fantom bombshells and frisky critters in my dreams – but I now felt utterly friendless at night, unsparingly harassed by all sorts of imaginary scoundrels: oinkers, eagles, periwigged sharpering-pops with googly ogles, tet-mirrored shrinks, flesh-jarrying rats, slugs, salamanders in kaftans, floating handlebar mousers, fountains spewing sang and steaming cacacacaca ...

---

* Chapter received Tuesday, 17th March 1970 – 118 days to go.

I needed some bona fide humanoid interaction pronto – but where to find a willing victim? Sadly by now I'd savvied most pops are too discriminating and uppity to truly love a meese beastie – but thankfully pops are also easily mogued and manipulated. With a few well-aimed splurts of dinarli, I could rejiggle my eek and bod, make myself over with the help of London's toppermost fash-gurus and plastic-crocuses. Then love would surely follow ...?

I ponced backwards to Durban, all the daffy sea-queens showering me with aero-lammers having mistaken me for their duchess Winnie. It all seemed so simple. Back then I'd commanded respect in just a shushed shyka and Oriental drogle – Jupiter knows what the professional eek-hacking quacks could achieve for me today!

BEAUTY WILL BE CONVULSIVE
BEAUTY WILL BE RECONSTRUCTIVE!

I picked up the polari-pipe immediately, clogging the switchboard with demands for a bona crocus, bolus, tailor, shyka-fencer, fang-mender ...

Just as Michelangelo must've started out carving Dave with gross swipes before delicately chippering the bijou details, I scarpered first to Harley Strasse to have my most glaringly grotesque imperfections seen to. Savvying Mademoiselle Monroe was also a chinless wonder before surgery and sparkledom, I found a plastic-croc who was willing and able to instal for me the Marilyn Chin, streamline my oink-vonka and pin my ratty nells back. Trey months later, once I'd fluttered free from the bandages, I had nova pearly dentures inserted. A back-quack fitted me up with a specjalni girdle to help fix my coddy posture. I tucked a juicy polystyrene mogue-basket down my drawers. Stocked up on Pond's acne-cleanser and Max Factor maquiage at the bolus. Breath-freshener. Fash glossies. Belmondo sol-goggles. Then I was set.

Once fully healed, my bod was like a pristine blank canvas, ready to be splattered with all the fabulosa fakements of high fashion. But what style and gildi individuality to parker? After all the turmoil of my sequin-squirting, feather-spitting aqua-travails, all I really wanted now was to fit in, to look natty and attract a lover without attracting the ogles or batons of sharpering-omis, wig-plops, tet-shrinkers – although of course it would not do to shroud myself in the naff drab uniform of The Norms ...

First off I needed a striking barnet. Whereas through the 1950s it seemed omis were allowed only one choice of buzzcut, today there was a multitude of riah-styles for the discerning dandy. In a shyka-bodega just off Charing X Road, my opals were instantly shushed by a short snappy style labelled 'FRENCH CROP/CAESAR CUT'.

'This Frog Crop, squire,' I pearled at the ruddy-eeked peacock behind the counter. 'The fringe is sold separately, is it?'

'No, no, this is the entire wig,' he replied, rushing out to manhandle me into the cheet. 'It suits you!'

I regarded the omi through semi-suspicious, semi-seductive slits. Were his lavs flirtation or just sales patter?

'I'm a frog myself,' I polled proudly, admiring myself in the mirror like a kinky budgerigar. 'What makes this a French wig, monsieur? I would've expected pompadour riah, pouf and powder, non? Daitcha-foot-tall barka-smuggling Marie-Antoinette riah? If you catch my drift?' I wink-twitched.

'Pardon me?' The peacock's beak was twisted now.

I felt my cheeks blaze. 'Nanti Polari?'

'Sorry? What?'

'Ô, forgive me, squire. I ponced you might be an omi-palone, all joshed-up as you are in that fine gildi fem clobber. Alack! Forget I ever croaked. You were telling me about this French wiglet. Proceed, proceed ...'

'Yes. Um. Well, this is how the teens wear their hair now, sir. It suits you. Mod cut. Sharp, snappy, not too flappy. Very chic. Like how they wear it on the Continent.'

'Formidable.'

I'd nellied not a lot about the Mods while bobbing along on my floating culture-vacuum: only that they were up for the odd barny on Bank Holidays, and horrified the crinkly generation with their taste for drogas, arva and camp clobber.

'Tell me more, camarade,' I urged as I counted out the dinarli for the shyka. 'What are the Mods' distinguishing morsos? As yet I've been unable to finger one in the wild ...'

As the peacock explained The Scene to me (fondamentalement prole dandies turning their palliass to working-class blandness, embracing musica, Pop Art, Sartre and pleasure-sharpering in Continental schmutta: dapper skinny suits, drainpipettes, turtlenecks, the odd froggy beret ...), I savvied this was the fad for me. It seemed to be the closest the anglos had yet got to la vie d'avant-garde: gender skewed, class smashed, colour bars gleefully limboed under, discotheques, Drinamyl, freeform jazz, freeflying bod-fluids, and all strictly above board in the ogles of The Law!

Before I trolled out with my nova riah glued to my tet, the peacock pointed me in the direction of a tailor who would fit me up with the right threads. I found Il Bozzolo not far from the glistening shaft of the Post Office Colin in the rag district of Fitzrovia: un bijou boutique that felt more like an end-of-pier pleasuredome than your norm bodega, the startling mannequins and tonic suits hanging from strings like daffy puppets alongside randy Roman statuettes with insect wings and floor-to-ceiling Op Art swirlies.

While the dapper eyetie sharpered round my contours with his tape, I was hoping for a pogi bit of sexual molestation round my inner lally, but true enough this appeared to be a professional establishment. I clocked the needle-pops backstage, and pondered what it was that made a certain cut stylish and another cut naff? Apparently Rome was the city-à-la-mode chinka years back – today it was Londres. Who decided on this caca? Who pulled the strings? United Nations? The Freemasons? Fellini?

Epstein? The alignment of the sparkles? A secret golden lapper-shake between the Pope and our Chancellor of the Exchequer?

'By Jupiter, you've huffed new life into this meese beastie!' I cackled several junos later, spinning round the boutique, admiring my nova cozzy: shimmery mohair bum-freezer manto, uncreasable drainpipettes, meths-purple merino camisha, ultra-schvartz winkle-pickers, pearls dazzling in the mirror, ecstatic sweat rolling down my tet ...

And now imagine me mincing out into the modern mond with an internal soundtrack of rapid jazz guitar, Hammond organ, fruity vibraphone and trompette!

As I minnied back through Fitzrovia, whenever I caught myself in the glaze of the bodega-fronts, my reflection felt at once alien and opal-spinningly fortuni. Hounds no longer bark-barked at me as I sauntered by, accepting me as master now and not just limping revolting carnish. Did the passing popsies feel the same, I pondered? I vogued up a Gauloise, ogling the donnas' tantalising lollipop bods from a shadowy doorway. How best to seduce these swinging fleurs? The way the conservative inkies and glossies went on, it seemed feeli-pops were still expected to fall in love and wed before any sloppy charvering went on. Meanwhile the mod teen rags were trumpeting the Arva Revolution: a bona fide Liberated Lavvystyle whereby pops can rut freely with nanti emotional wastage whatsoever. Without question twas dorcas LOVE and TOGETHERNESS I was sharpering for more than rapid rabid doggy-thrusts, BUT STILL: savvying I was only a pogi few stomps away from Soho, Ye Square Mile of Sin, I was intrigued to vada if I still possessed some morso of libido now my poor quongs had been shushed.

'Just make sure you can get that cartso hard, Raymond,' I mumblered at the handsome stranger in the fenêtres as noche dropped. 'All we need is that charvering cartso hard.'

Possiblement I should've tested my nova dashing visage and clobber on the high-class debs of the Savoy or the Ritz, but inevitably I found myself magnetised towards the grimy stinking knocking-shops and neon peepshows of the Dilly, in particular this garish duey-shilling revue in Grand Windmill Strasse, screeching glittery:

LE SPLEEN DE LONDRES
PALACE DE VERSATILES
FRENCH MAIDS
MARIE-ANTOINETTE
MARIONETTES
MONSIEUR & MADAME VETO
L'ANCIENT REGIME ON ITS KNEES
L'AMOUR FOU
LOSE YOUR HEAD!
FOR MADMEN ONLY

I parkered my beyongs to the chavvy on the door, then ducked inside, opals full-dilated and lappers all clammy like I was Howard Carter creepering through the gildi ultraschvartz en route to King Tut's tomb ...

Inside was a smoky dungeon-like stomping-khazi, decked out with papier mâché Rococo fakements and a fairy-light chandelier. The cartoon décor looked almost like it could collapse with one well-aimed sneeze. I plonked myself down carefully at the cardboard Louis 16 console in the corner and ordered a large Ricard.

'There are no Richards or Dicks available in this establishment, sir,' the slack-jawed bung humoured me. 'Large or otherwise.'

'Nanti that!' I snapped. 'Regard the botties behind you! Pastis, you lunatic! A large pastis!'

When the bevvy eventually arrived, otta beyongs seemed a pogi bit steep for what was essentially a provençal hick's poison, but my squeaky protests were soon cut short when the lights flushed and the arva-pops appeared. First onstage was an omi of about eighty, toffed-up in royal frog clobber (frock coat, silk stockings, high-heels, petticoat breeches, ermine furs, Louis 14 shyka), wrinkles filled in with concrete maquiage. The fungus hummed a few bars of 'Grand Dieu sauve le Roi'* before introducing the first looper-hoofers. He described these joggering-popsies as the warm-up act, but I was left notably frigid when atop the petty dais appeared what can only be described as duey miserable palones in slave-schmutta.

Was I turned on at all by the following spectacle? Possibly un petty purr at first. Sip-sipping my anis-sirop, I watched with terrible lust as the brunette and botty-blonde wheeled a bijou four-poster bed into the centre of the stage, jiggling out of step with the naff musica. Quite possibly this was what the rosbifs thought us frogs listened to on our crystal sets: piercing accordion and kishka-curdling garlic-stinkering oompahpahpahpah.

The fillies were joshed-up in tasteless chambermaid clobber: skimpy schvartz drogles with blank medsa-aprons, a feather duster and stilettos so brutally tall bona lattykeeping was surely impossible. At first I suspected the main thrust of this playlet would involve little more than naggy frantic frottage atop the bedspread – however, I was pleasantly surprised to discover these donnas had joggering talents and not just bona unblemished bendable carnish. Naturellement the Lord Chamberlain would not have approved, but the skit at least appeared to have a plot: duey rebellious au pairs unsupervised in their master's boudoir, turning their svelte palliasses to authority and abandoning all chores in favour of unbridled merrymaking and misbehaviour. 'Bravo, camarades!' I almost gurgled, beaming lovestruck. I watched with hammer-and-sickle sparkles in my opals as the donnas shushed the blank coverlet from the bed, then proceeded to monkey with the fabric, flappering it hither and thither like a fantom dancing partner. The brunette in particular was molto virtuoso when it came to manipulating the

* French anthem before the Revolution – same tune/lyrics as our national dirge.

sheet: una minuta she was a Romanoid goddess in a toga, the next a poked-up bunny with scrunched-up cottontail, a mermaid floundering in cascading seafoam, a polar bear, a poltergeist, Salomé and her setta hankies, the chinka statuettes of the Trevi Fountain spluttering arcs and jets of frothy thunder-nectar ...

As the dollies gradually disrobed, the blank sheet became a flimsy modesty screen, alternately concealing and leaking their gildi flesh under the searing leering lights. Bearing in mind the only naggy palone I'd ogled thus far was my own 'groin-groin'ing Mare, I was startled at how smooth and glossy these dolls' bods were. Striking elastic poses, the birds' nipplets and corybunguses pointed ceilingwards in quick succession, medsa-aprons frittied through the aero like jellyfish, their pink levers puckered, my cartso dutifully expanded – but then just as rapidly my arousal was punctured when the monsieur-of-ceremonies rejoined the maids onstage. Twas the same fungal twonk as before, only now dressed in anglo aristocratic plus-fours rather than the royal frog garb. He playacted horror, then pronto pounced upon the naggy popsies, triggering sickening strobe-lights and molto authentic squeals from his dorcas prey.

If there was any moral to the revolting plot-twist that followed, all I could grasp was: SURRENDER YOUR HOPELESS INFERIOR BOD AND SOUL TO THE BOSS MAN. While the innocent fillies were flogged, flattened, bound, garglered, gobbed on and diddled with their dusters, twas my gag reflex more than my cartso that was stimulated. How was this public humiliation legal? How was this not punishable by electro-jolts to the groin? How was this niche filth cheaper than the cheapest efinked seats at Stepney's coddy Troxy cinema?

Of course it wasn't like me to ponce in terms of morality. Had the Shrinker's servo-lathering worked after all? Was this repulsion a signal I was losing my Surrealistic feral beastie instincts? Jupiter forbid: was I maturing?

'Cartso hard, Raymond,' I murmured. 'All we need is that charvering cartso hard.'

Still, the dollies' eeks were so twisted it was impossible to gain even a grain of pleasure from this diabolical sketch. At one point I ponced tragically: couldn't the birds at least pretend to be enjoying themselves, so us punters didn't have to feel so poked-up and grotty? But even more tragically, the other punters (omis I hadn't clocked til now, frittying greedily in the foggy munge) didn't seem at all upset by the dismal spectacle. Possiblement they'd decided the dollies were just bona actresses, only IMITATING palones in pain, but the degradation was clear. Of course many professions require you to act, to adopt a nova ritzy or robo persona, but I pondered if there were any travails in the mond more depressing than a desperate feeli-palone having to pretend to be an even more desperate feeli-palone, expose her still-developing bod to strangers and endure onstage battyfanging over and over and over, all for the same pitiful petty dinarli of the skivvies they're imitating. Each noche the maids were reprimanded for not doing their job – and yet the naggy palones under the maid clobber WERE doing their job: obediently playacting disobedience and schlumphing the consequences uncomplainingly, all because the alternatives (dismissal, destitution, death?) were just a pogi bit worster than this subterranean half-lavvy, this codswallop funfair replica of oppression that seemed all too real to me.

By the end of the debacle these were not glamorous donnas. The grand finale involved the maids being clamped in a mogue doppel-guillotine, oysters quivering, otta cheeks blazing from all the whipcracks. Before the plastic blades dropped, I caught the opal of the brunette. She was a truly fortuni palone to begin with, but now her eek was midway between timid chavvy and deathbed zelda. Was there a sparkle between us as our peepers locked through the munge? I tried to give her a pogi blink of reassurance but possibly my eek was as twisted as hers. Molto likely she hadn't even registered me, considered me inhumanoid like all the rest, was ogling right through me.

The accordion blared. The razor dropped. The lights sputtered out.

By the time the headline act took to the stage (Marie-Antoinette pursued then gang-raped by pike-wielding serfs, her dish wide-opened with a speculum and choco gateau fired in/farted out), I was ogling in frigid disbelief. I felt maximumly grotty, complicit in the whole mally extravaganza for just sitting there and swallowing it all: THE APPALLING SILENCE OF THE BONA POPS.

Convinced the duey maids must've required rapid medical attention, I near enough fired pastis out through my nostrils daitcha minutas later when the brunette reappeared at my cardboard console, dressed in fresh slippies and suspenders, dollied full-eek again like nothing untoward had happened.

'Bonsoir, moy cherry,' she cooed with an accent that was anything but French. 'I saw you looking. Je sweeze Sabine. Pleased to meet you, monsieur. Nice threads. May I sit?'

'You don't consider me inhumanoid?' I asked glumly as she perched on the benkel, our lallies touching.

'Inhuman? Not at all. You're un homme très very handsomé.'

Again: was this flirtation or entrapment? The bung had begun hovering by us with an eek that suggested he'd sooner garrotte me than serve me up another delicious gargler-quencher. I regarded the menu and sent him away with a gross and complicated order, shushing more time to palaver privvily with the palone.

'Why do you work in this cateva dungeon, this horrible disco?' I whispered, schlumphing an oysterful of her profumo as I leaned in.

'I don't know. Why does anyone work anywhere? Pays the rent, I suppose.' Her voche was full-Londres now, her fizzer losing its robotic lusty shimmer. I pondered if these palones were programmed to act plastic, like they were bestest off behaving like consumer goods rather than bona fide warm-sang humanoids, so their ravenous consumers wouldn't get too attached, and so their innards (their true innards) were less vulnerable to desecration or destruction. I was flattered Sabine had allowed me a pogi peek behind the veneer – although clear enough her interior wasn't all buttercream and jazz-lappers.

I huff-puffed: 'Is this grotto even legal?'

'No idea,' she monotoned. 'I believe Monsieur Drench has a special relationship with the Dirty Squad. You're not the fuzz, are you?'

'Nanti that!' I blew a blue raspberry. 'But it doesn't take a sharpering-pop to see this chamber is jiggeringly depressing, Sabine. Why not just vagary, leave pronto?'

'I don't know what other skills I've got, mister ...'

'Come and stay with me.' I flashed my nova pearls. 'Allow me to liberate you from this manky oubliette, these terrible terrible mannequin-travails ...'

Her ogleslits narrowed. The mogue lusty shimmer returned. 'I don't go home with strange men, darling. Not for free anyway.'

'I'll give you duey-daitcha funts.'

'Sounds awfully kinky, mister. I charge extra for anything kinky.'

'Trey-daitcha funts then.' I took a wedge of dinarli from my inside posh and peeled off six fivers.

'Fantastique.' She tucked the notes surreptitiously into her garter. 'Well then, I'm all yours.'

Sabine's eek was like a mirrorball now as she lelled my lapper and led me out of the stinking dungeonette. The bung was still stirring our complex bitter-gators with a blank expression, Monsieur Drench slithering from table to table, entertaining his punters with all the charm of a valise full of lovesick maggots. Before we scarpered, he caught my pol and cackled in a presposterous cockney-froggy accent: 'Zirty quids! Flashy rascal! Bring her back in good condition, won't you now, garçon. Hé-hé-hé-hé-HÉ!'

Ô comrades, it took a great deal of servo-buffering to stop myself from schonking the zot there and then. I shushed a greatcoat from the rack by the SORTIE, swung it round Sabine's skimpy bod, then we scuttled upways like petty chavvies escaping a parny shower of cannonballs.

Outside, we were free. The crackly neon lights were like gildi fleurs winking at us as we scrambled up the skinny strasse. Clutching Sabine's left lapper, I felt molto protective and mumsy over her now, and not at all greased-up – while she seemed infinitely more confident and lively out in the lights, compared to her nervy jitterings under Drench's lizardy opals. Full-rosbif now, she demanded I take her for HOT SALT BEEF at the Nosh Bar,* bovaries at the Sparkle & Garter, then by the time we stumbled into a taxi and set off for Stepney, we were palavering like illuminated old comrades:

'Ô, I've had it with these piggy ponces, these filthy fash eagle-eeks,' I panted. 'Don't go back to Drench. It's revolting slavery.'

'It's slavery but at least it's paid slavery.' Sabine was fanging her luppertips. 'Isn't that just the point of all work anyway, Raymond?'

'NEVER WORK!' I honked. 'You take home a pogi few consolation pennies but at what REAL PRICE? You're parkering off your precious time and happiness to these bats at well below their rock-bottom value!'

'Yeah but it's all right for you to say that.' She puckered her oyster-levers. 'You nouveau-riche lot are all the same. It's easy playing down the importance of bread when you've got plenty. I've got nothing.'

'I've paid my dues.' I thought of my quongs. I pondered if the crocs had kept them for posterity, or just ground them down to fertiliser or mutt-munjarry. 'Fate and patience parkered me my riches. And molto well deserved they are too.'

'I hate the privileged.'

---

* Davy Noon also regularly stuffs himself at the Nosh Bar, claiming it's the salt beef as much as the purple hearts that give him the energy to dance and romance at his beloved Scene or Hypnogogo.

'I hate the privileged too! I detest all snobs! But this isn't privilege – it's fate. Accidental bona karma! And it's ultra fateful me and thee met this very noche, don't you see, Sabine? I savvy not the details this very momento, but I'll liberate you from that hellhole, trust me.'

The taxicab pulled up outside my prefab latty with a gasp. As I led Sabine up the stairwell the jolly filly refused to believe this was my bona fide home-sweet-home.

'Excuse the carnage,' I polled as I uncleffed the lock.

Worster than all the dirty cutlers, meshigena clobber and scatty fakements strewn around my latty, I was a pogi bit poked-up about the heavy gloop of fuzzymuzz on every surface.

'Tis my former self, not I,' I polled, running a lupper through the dust. 'Mally moulted carnish. A much lesser omi than moi. You didn't happen to bring along your feather diddler, did thee?'

'Nope.'

I licked my lupper, then vogued up a Gauloise and cleared a space on the mattress for Sabine to sit down.

'We'll need more room than this, Raymond,' she side-oystered, 'or do you get off on romping among all this filth and mess?'

'Excusez-moi?'

'If I'm giving you thirty quids' worth of intercourse, mister, we'll need more than a square-inch of mattress, put it that way.'

'Nein, nein – you don't understand.' I slithered down the slimy bedpost to sit by her platters. 'I refuse to parker for trade, dear. That money was a gift. In any case, it wouldn't be kosher ravaging your bod after ogling that horrific sketch at the stomping-khazi. I'm not even sure I could raise a colin.'

Sabine seemed to crumple nellying this, like yet again she was being forced to act humanoid and not plastic dolly. She snapped: 'So what is it you want me to do?'

'Do whatever you like! Be free!' I squawked. 'You said those ugly ugly travails pay the rent, but why not come and live here with me, rent-free? I'll find a new role for you, a new lavvy ...'

Sabine glanced about the gruesome boudoir. 'I'm not a maid, darling, I'm a whore. I don't know what other skills I've got.'

'Well, I could use the companionship.'

Sabine ran her luppers through my French Crop. 'You're sweet, Raymond,' she polled blankly. 'You probably feel like I've exposed myself pretty thorough tonight – but you don't know me at all. Why is it you want to keep me here? What do you want from me? You know where I work. You can come and see me whenever you like ...'

'I don't know why.' I ogled her with a milky expression. 'Just you deserve a molto better lavvy than that claptrap back at Drench's dungeonette ...'

Was I simpering? Was this rash dash for acceptance grotesque? Either way, my mission for the noche – to test my efinked libido – was irrelevant now. While I refuse to parker for trade, after ogling that degrading caca at Le Spleen de Londres I'd foolishly ponced I might be able to buy Sabine's love – and her freedom. I savvy now True Love cannot be packaged, marketed and parkered off at any price. You can't float love on the stock exchange. But how do you recognise it when it appears? Were Sabine's luppers in my fake riah the closest I'd yet got to truthful attraction – or was this still just part of the act, the Grand Masquerade? Possiblement she still just regarded me as plastic too, a walking wallet she'd rinse until it fell apart in her luppers. Encore une fois: sales patter? Entrapment?*

---

* Sales patter or entrapment indeed. Let us now be frank. Harry Howling was as incompetent a Sales, Marketing & Finance man as he was a one-night lover. And devastatingly costly on both counts.

For a self-styled heterosexual monogamist, Stanley Merritt has been to bed with a surprising abundance of men in recent years. Ironically it may have been his father's constant anti-queer screeching that stirred these feelings in him, awakening the urge to rebel, to live a freewheeling, sexually flexible life outside the dog-collar chokehold of raving Catholic morality. Was Iris aware of these impulses when they married? Certainly she was more or less present when herself, Stanley and Trefoil celebrated the publication of their first Glass Eye pocketbook (*Blimpziddung!* 1959, 2/8, SOLD OUT) with a clumsy ménage-à-trois at a rented pile in Surrey. At the time she felt Stan's enthusiasm for male flesh was brought about largely by the absinthe. The heady thrill of simultaneously breaking down the boundaries of good taste, 'normal' sexuality

'What did you really think of me when you first clocked me, Sabine?' I asked. 'Did you truly think I was un homme très very handsomé?'

She squinted at me. 'I thought you was a bit of a ticket, to be honest.'

---

and literary puritanism? (Or was it just that he wanted to punish Trefoil with sodomy after witnessing him penetrating his beloved wife?)

Less easy to excuse was the night of 12th December 1969. With funds so low, the Glass Eye Christmas party ended almost as soon as it began, after three bottles of imitation champagne were swiftly swallowed, and a fruitless tussle with our temperamental Dansette resulted in long swathes of silence that eventually drove everybody away. Once the last of the rabble had waltzed off to Hypnogogo or the Scotch of St James (or wherever the young ones currently enjoyed having their hearing destroyed), the office was empty and utterly dry save for Howling, Merritt and the emergency hip flask of whisky stowed under the loose laminate beside Merritt's sawn-off shotgun. Drunkenly or not (after all, there'd been barely a large glassful of fizz for each member of staff), Stan surprised Howling with a breathy exclamation: 'Sharda! It's only me and thee now, my chovi.'

Howling's ogle-riders pricked. 'Where'd you learn the term "sharda", Stan? I do believe our dear Novak hasn't used that one himself yet …'

'Well. Let's just say I picked up a thing or two in the Navy,' Stanley replied, at which point no more dialogue was necessary. To this day Merritt and Howling are unable (or refuse) to say who instigated what came next. Only one of the men was caught with his trousers down. The other had his colleague's hard penis in his mouth.

Whether intoxicated or not, the men were undoubtedly sobered by the unexpected arrival of a five-foot-two-inch elf in neon-green stockings and bell-ended slippers, brandishing two fresh bottles of imitation champagne. The elf had let itself in with its own key, and shrieked when it saw the unholy merrymaking going on in the Director's office.

'Iris! It's not how it seems!' Merritt protested, reflexively swatting his Sales, Marketing & Finance man across the jaw. 'Good God, man! This is bloody inappropriate, Howling! You're fired! FIRED!'

Regardless of the futile excuses that followed, Howling was indeed fired from the Glass Eye Press with immediate effect, Merritt fell headlong into depression – and within a couple of months Iris had sued for divorce.

If reality were indeed as straightforward as fiction, this footnote may have tied up once and for all the disappearance of our financial man. However, this regrettable denouement gave us no warning, nor explanation, why the very same day Stanley drafted this footnote (two days after receiving 'The Emperor's Nova Schmutta'), a decapitated head was found impaled on the railings at the bottom of Newman Street (*our* street!), resembling Harry.

'A ticket?'

'Riding on the back of the Mod craze. Look at your clobber. I bet you wasn't wearing suits like that five years ago. Now Mod's gone mainstream, every dull sod's wearing suits like that.'

'I'm not a ticket!' I erupted. All at once I felt ultra uncomfortable in my nova mohair armour, like the sly eyeties had duped me into joshing myself up like a Pop Art clown. 'I'm a bona fide Euro-pop. I've got Continental sang surging through my bod! It's Drench who's the ticket, riding on the back of your looks, your bod ...'

'Enough about Drench, Raymond. We're talking about you and your naff threads.' Sabine's oyster-levers were pricked. Quite possibly she'd savvied she'd prodded a weak spot.

'I cannot believe this,' I howled. 'A coddy servile maid who only an hour ago had a feather diddler stuffed up her dish now telling me what's clean and what's manky, what's in and what's not!'

'Good grief, Raymond – who's the snob now?'

'I am not a snob!' I squeaked. 'I am the epitome of Mod! I'm The Prole Dandy ...'

'You're a ticket! Look!'

Sabine leapt from the libbage and danced over to my scrappy rails of old seafaring schmutta: my stewards' whites, gildi-drogle morsos, sequined King Neptune gown. She plucked out a pair of silvery astro-trousers and CCCP helmet, and reered up: 'This is a lot more go-ahead and with-it, but you do realise André Courrèges done the Space Craze stuff last spring?'

'I've never nellied the zot's nom before in all my lavvy,' I hissed. 'I WIZZ!ed this garment up in '62, '63, while I was bobbing along in the Merch Navy. We didn't get the fash rags on the Setta Seas, sweetness.'

'You made these yourself? You're in the Rag Trade? Is that how's you're so rich?'

'There's nanti dinarli in schmutta, surely? Or not this schmutta anyway. I just clattered this caca up for fun. Ridiculous sea-queen drag.'

'Well, it's far-out if you predicted Courrèges's Couture Future. The sod must be a multi-millionaire now. What about this?' She lelled another garment from the rail: pistachio-green lurex lally-covers with a pointy packet inspired by the clipper bow of MS HIPPOCAMPUS. 'They're staggering!'

'Ô, hearken this!' I cackled, stomping round the lino like a daffy flamingo. 'Moi?! This freak-eeked ticket, this meese beastie now considered a top fash-guru, an omi of taste and finesse?!'

'Well, have you not never considered selling this gear? It's not for everyone, sure enough, but sling it on some skinny bint with no tits and the teenyboppers'd go wild for your threads. You'd be lonely no more, Raymond. You could be the new King of Carnaby Street, the High Commander of the Carnabetian Army ...'

The image startled me.

'Sabine.' I licked my levers. 'You understand what makes a certain cut stylish and another cut naff?'

'The more outrageous the better, I'd say.'

'Fantabulosa!' My luppers were twitching now. 'Well then, I may have clocked the perfect role for you, my chovi. From tomorrow you can work for me. Except it won't really be work – it'll be play!' I recalled her expertise manipulating that petty morso of blank bedclobber earlier, and my kishkas giggled. 'No more toiling for the Big Boss Man now, darling. No more slavery. From tomorrow we'll shake up this scatty batty fash industry! Together we'll gaily fatcha and rejiggle the very fabric of this coddy conformist consumerist society!'

Sabine blinked back at me blankly.

'Oui? Nein?'

She wrinkled her dolly vonka. 'What's my take-home pay?'

The Rag Trade[*]

NOVAK WEARS SILVERY ASTRO-PANTALOONS, EXPLOSIVE MARMALADE CHELSEA BOOTIES, OP ART MATELOT CAMISHA, KING NEPTUNE CAPELLO, FROG CROP SHYKA, JUMBO INSECTOID SOL-GOGGLES.

The warmest juno of 1965 so far and Sabine and I were on Hampstead Heath at high noon, huddled round a glimmering valise containing more than 40,000 guineas. I'd doused the valise in the dregs of meths left round my latty and it went up surprisingly rapidly, coughing out swirlies of smoke, burning beautiful as a Magritte tuba.

I unfurled the andouille sausage-wheel parkered from Roche's in Old Compton Strasse, impaled[†] it on a twiggy skewer and poked it into the fire. Sabine seemed a pogi bit wrongfooted by my nonchalance but fortunately not ultra ultra gloomy in the face of all that barbecued dinarli.

---

* Chapter received Thursday, 26th March 1970 – 109 days to go.

† How sure were we the impaled head was Harry's? Evidently the thing was badly decomposed, the eyeballs removed or rotted away, plus the scalp sliced open and brains scooped out. Though she wasn't first on Newman Street to discover the offensive tet, Audrey was there before the police cordon, passing by on her lunch break with a bag of egg custard tarts none of us subsequently could stomach. Her gut reaction was: this was Harry. The imperial moustache, the prominent nose, the arctic-white quiff (what was left of it). Her tears were infectious, whether we wanted to believe her or not. The rest of us were unable to verify the head's identity, squinting grimly through the office window once the cordon went up. It was too early to mourn in earnest, but a huge, hideous Harry-shaped shadow hung over our HQ as we struggled to keep ourselves busy that week, waiting for the coroner's report …

'It's a foul substance,' I upheld. 'Regard the cateva smoke it's giving off.'

Ô comrades, her reaction was everything. Aside from this being a flamboyant anti-Capitalist expulsion of the highest order, the major reasoning behind this bonfire of dinarli was to check Sabine wasn't interested in me solely for my money. If we were to enjoy the Liberated Lavvy together, we had to be equal – or at least appear equal. Of course I savvied dinarli helps streamline and sugarcoat this coddy welt's sharp corners, but, like my Old Mare, I'd sooner reject it and live lowly again than playact toff. I wanted my old lavvy back, the Duty-Free Lavvystyle: to squat, to shirk, to shush, to scrape by without having to bow before the Boss Man or suck listlessly on some plastic-toff embarrassment of riches I hadn't truly earned.

My kishkas gurgled. I lelled the skewer from the inferno and vadared the sausage-wheel had vanished, lost in the fire, frazzled to fuzzymuzz. 'Ô, bugger it.'

Sabine reered up, but I savvied I'd grown grander in her estimations this juno. Almost out of obligation she'd at first palavered how I must be meshigena to destroy all that manky lucre, but I clocked admiration there too, like she couldn't resist the profumo of risk and boldness I was now giving off.

'You've got balls, Raymond, I'll give you that much,' she polled.

'Au contraire, Sabine.' I plopped the twig back into the fire. 'We don't need the mogue security of that gruesome bimph, that garish straitjacket.'

'So what now?' she sniffled, dabbing her vonka with a mustard-coloured hanky. Predictably the poor mare had come down with a cold after being liberated from Le Spleen: the humanoid bod's cruel response to unexpected freedom, having been conditioned to and adrenalised by hard travails for so long. 'We're back in the g-gutter?' she sneezed. 'We're to live like paupers now?'

'Nanti that! We're all in the gutter but some of us are ogling the sparkles!' I squeaked. 'Fear not, dear heart. As you'll rapidly discover, it's maxi exhilarating lavvying on the edge of the abyss – but naturellement one should never trifle with The Void without first conjuring up a bona emag. A good plan, that is.'

Ô, mais oui: I had a fantabulosa plan. The coil of it involved misleading my dear Sabine (poor tart) from the start – but more on this later.

'First we need a majestic nova abode.' I squinted at the needles of the city tickling the aero to the south. 'The bed-sitter's a cateva khazi, you've said so yourself. Therefore I've terminated my tenancy bimph. We're technically homeless and penniless, oui, but allow me to introduce you to the fabulosa pursuit of gratis latty-sharpering ...'

'Come again?'

'Free shelter.'

It was to be our

NEW!

IMPROVED!

ALL-INCLUSIVE!

Liberated Lavvy. Whereas previously my Old Mare and I had shut ourselves away from society in the Château Chanceux, today I couldn't stand for that meese isolation again. I wanted to be surrounded by like-minded pops, to build an army of dolly companions like Sabine who would admire me not for my dinarli, but for my bona fide talents, my masterly seamstressing skills, my interior and exterior nattiness.

My grand plan was this: to shush a gross disused latty in the Rag District and build from scratch a bold nova fash empire, a glamorous bolshy commune, an ultra-inclusive boutique that would house not only gloriosa outlandish schmutta, but all the waifs and strays of the city like myself and dear Sabine. I pictured a utopian asylum, a dazzling sanctuary for 'les indésirables': loopers, duey-shilling showgirls, rent-boys, weirdies, roamers and reamers, droggle-gobblers, suburban losties. So long as they had The Look (and were willing to spread love and do the odd bit of needlework), they were in.

I never wanted to be alone again, and I ponced these beautiful lowly proles (hunched and dehumanised by humiliating baffling travails) would be an easy target: pops least likely to turn me down, pops most likely to abandon their restrictive cod norm lavvies and join me in this molto risqué, nonconformist, free-wheelering, freeloading, anti-authority-flop vie d'avant-garde.

'Where'll we find these empty digs though, Raymond?' Sabine bleated as I took her smooth lapper and led her down the herby willet. 'I've been done for breaking and entering before. Judge says if he sees me again, he'll bang me up.'

'Fear not. Molto likely the toff was only envious, dear heart. In any case, you're in safe lappers. I've got experience in this department.'

It took a fair bit of stomping to get to Fitzrovia, and by the time we started latty-sharpering in earnest the clouds were spewing parnyaqua. Sabine, bless her fluffy thumper, tried her bestest to finger suitable properties as we trolled through the puddles, but I was somewhat pickier than her.

Finally, after almost trey hours of exploration, I extended a handsome manicured index-lupper and exclaimed: 'Voilà.'

While the Château Chanceux had appeared to my Mare and I as if in a dream, mine and Sabine's nova abode appeared as if plucked from an estate agent's glossy: a stately trey-storey George-era terrace sandwiched betwixt a nursing-skol and derelict fang-khazi on a tranquil sideysnicket in the shadow of the Post Office Colin. The fenêtres were full-blank, blocked up by pasted pages from the inkies:

COUNTDOWN TO GAMBIAN INDEPENDENCE
BULLDOG PUPPIES THROWN ON RAIL LINE
CUNARD HEIRESS DIED PENNILESS

'Wait here, my chovi,' I polled, theatrically tossing her my brolly and ogling both-sideways. 'Allow me to do the breaking and entering.'

After gruellingly scaling the sooty wall ajax to the nursing-skol, I minnied casually down the cluttered rear snicket to the back portal of our chosen establishment. The security was impressive: the doors and fenêtres doppel-locked and barred with wrought-iron waffles. There was uno bijou unbarred fenêtre on the second floor but, rather than attempting to frap a cobble-stone through the glaze, I simply sharpered for an empty milk botty further down the alley and smashed that SHLACK! against the paves instead, for effect. Then, I took a bunch of glimmering clefs from my posh, gently unlocked the back grille and back portal, and minced inways, gay and unimpeded.

How did I acquire these clefs, I nelly thee screech? I admit it wasn't the mostest convulsive or risqué chance encounter of my Surrealist lavvy: I'd clocked the trey-storey latty in an estate agent's glossy chinka weeks earlier and parkered the property pronto in cash.

Before letting Sabine in, I tidied away all naff correspondence to RAYMOND M. NOVAK ESQ. from the doormat and checked the Other Valise was still safely stowed in the loft. Creeping through the munge like a dolled-up Nosferatu, I clambered gropingly over the spiderwebs of tripwires I'd set up until finally my lappers alighted on the antique suitcase. I unsnapped the locks and breathed out. The dinarli was still there: almost 15,000 guineas. I sniffed up the sweet meese stench of it all. Naturellement I hadn't burned my riches on the Heath – only a pogi few bona fide notes with bundles of fakes underneath. Tingling merrily, I gnashed the locks shut again, kicked the valise back into the ultraschvartz, then scrambled downways to greet Sabine with an affectedly startled eek.

'By chance I found the clefs hanging in the hallway, dear heart!' I cheered, jingling them. 'Bienvenue, my cherry. Welcome to UTOPIA!'

We set to work building our bold nova fash empire at once. I'd already settled on a natty nom for the venture, NEVER-NEVERLAND:* an apt nom given that the grand idea was to sell our revved-up clobber (and eternal youth?) on the never-never to hard-up punters at PAY-WHAT-YOU-CAN tariffs. The ground floor would be our boutique, the first floor our needle-chuggering

---

* Was it a foolhardy move, Davy and Trefoil searching out Novak's lair after work on 27th March? The evenings were lighter now and both men fancied themselves as sufficiently butch, but still they felt a chill penetrating the Scum King's territory without invitation. What did they even have to say to the lunatic? Naturally we were eager to find out what exactly Novak's fantabulosa crime would entail – although, if his plans proved unpalatable to us, was it not wiser to just remain ignorant innocents at this stage?

After the appearance of the severed head, workers and residents of Fitzrovia had been encouraged to keep off the streets at night. The papers quickly stank out newsstands with overblown comparisons to Jack the Ripper and the Manson murders, but was there really any call for the public at large to panic?

Our intrepid detectives set off just after 5 p.m. As they snaked through the blustery sidestreets, the men felt emboldened knowing Novak was effectively (for now at least) a colleague, a co-conspirator, a comrade-in-arms – and what invitation did they need anyway to drop in on the Prole Dandy's 'ultra-inclusive' boutique? These were public byways. There was even the possibility Novak *wanted* us to see his lair for ourselves, supplying us with just enough information to lure us in …

After scouring the area around the Post Office Tower in ever decreasing circles, a street sign appeared that grabbed Trefoil's attention: OGLE STREET. Sure enough there was a nursing school on the corner and a deserted dentist's two doors down, but in between no boutique, no NEVER-NEVERLAND. In between was just a shabby butcher's shop, closing down for the evening. The hooks and meat cleavers sparkled ominously – or was this just the men's imagination?

'Any froggy saucissons for sale, mister?' Davy asked the proprietor, a gruesome hulk with explosive black hair.

'Andouille sausage-wheels?' Trefoil chipped in.

'Sorry? What, boys? It's all B-British produce, this,' the butcher replied. 'You can g-get your frog's legs and sn-snails down Soho, lads.'

Davy and Trefoil lingered dumbly on the cobbles while the butcher padlocked his shutters. What more to say? The brute looked like Tiny Tim in a bloodied apron and he spluttered when he spoke, but just because he was a weirdy didn't mean he was embroiled in this whole sordid saga.

And plenty of boutiques in Swinging London close down within five years.

workshop and second floor communal unisex boudoir. I'd already screeved plentiful designs for schmutta that Sabine considered far-out and with-it: absinthe-botty paper dresses, International Klein Blue Napoleonic fusiliers' jackets, PVC barky cozzies, gross pompom capellas, go-go sabots. All that remained was to mass-produce these cheets, then hoodwink dolly impressionable teenyboppers into buying into our nova youthquake cult.

Wrongly poncing we were penniless, Sabine was molto eager to give everything for The Grand Cause. Our workshop was a sorry ogleful to begin with – just my solo sewing-vacaya and soggy brolly atop the battyfanged dissecting table – but soon enough we were churning out reams upon reams of retina-frazzling revolutionary schmutta ...

I left Sabine to the needlework while I sharpered for nova recruits. As I trolled round Soho for suitably degrading peep-khazis and horn-parlours, I ponced backways to my time at the secondary mod in Margate. The type of feelies I was sharpering for were those simultaneously bona-vadaring enough to be models and yet handy enough with their handies to cobble together maxi intricate invigorating clobber. I ponced (like yours truly) the dolly fillies in these filthy dives were not grammar-skol material. Surely they'd been subjected to the same naff subjects like Domestic Science that, while not a springboard to any liberated lavvy in norm society, would prove indispensable at my bold nova enterprise ...

Given that I was offering these poor exploited popsies free bed and board in exchange for just a pogi bit of modelling, needling and affection, I assumed I'd soon have a grand army of fortuni proles at my disposal. On my first noche prowling the square mile of sin I managed to snare a couple of jolly fillies (Priscilla from RED MILL, Veronica Rum Baba from FRANKENFRAÜLEIN: duey New Town escapees with eeks like Egyptian kitties), but many others surprised me with their wariness when I gushingly ladled out the guiding principles of our bijou utopian community:

'The State hates us,' was my usual opener. 'Let's not bend for nanti politicos, tober-omis nor boss-plops nix longer. Toiling under Capitalism is like being raped in your sleep, my chovis! Most civvies blindly accept conditions and ideas they should compulsively, convulsively and conclusively REFUSE, like degrading travails, like the mogues of the mass media, like the servo-lathering skol-system: the monotonous exhausting cutthroat whirly-go-round that plunges pops into a needy submissive stupor while the eagles gaily jarry our carnish and charver us blankly juno upon juno. Shake off the squares' shackles pronto! Escape drudgery. Embrace absurdity. Give your feeli lavvies to me for a gildi gratis re-fit! I am Pop. I am Dada! RISE! RISE AND SPARKLE, my cherries!'

Ô, it pained me that plenty of these poor bimbos preferred to stick to the twisted lavvies they already had rather than risk the wild unpredictable glimmer-fakements I was offering, all because their current lavvy (for all its faults) was at least familiar to them: a trickle of regular income and naff shelter, all watched over by some ponce of zero grace.

Occasionally I had to turn down hags who'd nellied about my enterprise and wanted to join the grupa (POR EXAMPLE: the scrubbers of Cable Strasse and Bayswater are eager, but rarely possess The Look), but for the most part I was squandering a hell of a lot of dinarli enticing delightful dames back to Fitzrovia who just could not be persuaded to stay. Possiblement they were frightened their pimp might find them and ferricadooz us all – but molto likely they recognised a dangerous beastie when they ogled one, having been subjected to these unscrupulous bats most of their adult lavvies. BOF and bona luck to them, those X-Ray Dollies ...

Nevertheless, as 1966 approached I had a modest battalion of beautiful naive seamstresses (plus duey beautiful rent-boys, Bruce and Lionel, abducted from a pissoir in Earl's Court) hard at work on my premier fash collection. I'd parkered duey nova electro sewing-vacayas from Woolies, installed a grandiose Art

Nouveau absinthe fountain, and swiped lapperfuls of exotic drogas from the bolus to help increase productivity as well as ward off my crocky nightmares. Ô, those hideous inkyboos! Since enduring the shock therapy, I was still yet to enjoy a solo bona night's sleep. Every time I shut my opals I was visited by the same gruesome fantoms: eagles with worms dangling from their oysters, bowler-hatted hippos, Ecuadorian shrunken tets, Genghis Khan, barkies wafting gross schvartz rubber phalluses. Barbiturates and Mogadon did little to ease the visions, only suspend me longer in the septic tank with the illusory bats. More successful was Drinamyl: speedy capsules with the majestic nom FRENCH BLUES that, rather than trying to soothe like Horlicks, eradicated sleep altogether, parkering me more time to oversee my empire, screeve more schmutta-patterns, screech more wisdom and spread more love ...

To this juno I often wonder where I'd be now had I unsympathetically stuck my colin in Sabine the noche I met her, rather than palavering with her civilised in the bed-sitter. True enough I was eager to reef, lammer and charver these delightful youths, but I savvied it was unfair to push them after only recently liberating them from tyrannical pricks and ponces. The nattiest option for now was to pamper them, to praise them, to earn their skittery trust – then surely uninhibited meaningful orgiastic merrymaking would soon follow ...

Feelings. Jawohl! I still had feelings in my slippies – and yet, after my enforced emasculation and brain-rape, even arthuring solo had its frightful drawbacks. While it was an honour being able to ogle these feeli-pops' glossy naggy bods as I fitted them for their outlandish cozzies, when it came to recalling the images privvily, my inky ghouls, goblins and vultures kept interfering with the smooth thews, biceps and willets I thought I'd memorised. Plus with nix quongs I was only ever capable of a disappointing dry ōgazumu: the arval equivalent of choking down a baguette without fromage, or some cruel plop interrupting a bona sneeze.

Still, it wasn't just my loss of quongs that had charvered my arva-drive. Drinamyl likewise strangulates your libido – but, even worster, my workerbees' incessant dredging up of past grievances and grudges never failed to crinkle my bulging thumper. To begin with – before I banned all dreary retrospection and egocentric palavering – my comrades polled often about their codswallop former lavvies. Veronica's twisted tale of how she came to work at Frankenfraülein seemed almost the industry standard: a suburban teen fleeing a stroppy step-papa, only to find herself at the mercy of an even more despotic ponce or madam. Meanwhile Priscilla's retelling of her ordeals (the lonesome chavvyhood, the joyless asphalte, Terror in Hemel Hempstead, tormented by skol-fillies, solo-esteem battyfanged to a quivery puddle, suicidal teen-plunges, the Disturbed Mama, the Hopeless Papa, possessed by a hypercritickal boyfriend, lured to Londres in pursuit of a non-existent dream, the barnying, the bailiffs, the eviction, the hazardous flattery of a notable letch outside a stomping-khazi in Soho ...) had the feel of a sprawling B-movie melodrama.

Some of my other recruits' histoires were altogether more meshigena. Bonnie, por example, was a palone in her thirties with the eek and bod of a petty chavvy, forced to josh herself as a gurgling bambino and sit in a glassy cube in a Clerkenwell cellar while shady pederasts splattered her fenêtres with quong-sirop. Bruce specialised in schvartzmarket fotos of omi-palones in balaclavas and hangman hoods before putting his own corybungus on the market, trolling round Earl's Court and the Dilly in a startling tangerine corduroy suit, whistling the swooping prelude to Hitchcock's VERTIGO. Rosa Winkel was a drag queen from Eastern Europa: a Cubist-eeked mare who claimed she thoroughly enjoyed being battyfanged by strangers, despite being hooked up to a lavvy-support-vacaya and jarrying her meals through a straw the noche I found her.

Oui – ALAS AND ALACK AND JOVE BLESS THEIR WRETCHED SOULS – I savvied it wouldn't take much to please these poor zots if these were the home comforts they'd been subjected to in the subterranean hideyholes of Londres – and yet, as our gildi utopia lento developed, I found we couldn't keep some of their past demons at bay forever ...

'Ran into one of the girls from the Spleen, Raymond,' Sabine huffed one noche after returning from bin-rifling. 'Monsieur Drench is looking for us. Turns out I might've been his favourite.'

'You're my favourite now, ducky,' I wheezed. 'You're nanti frightened of that jumped-up wrinkly, are you?'

'Dunno. He's got experience when it comes to menacing folks.'

'That fungal cunt?! Let him come! Let him tickle our necks with his daffy plastic guillotine!' I ogled round the libbage. The rest of the grupa were downstairs chuggering the sewing-vacayas, save for Bruce snoozing lazyboned by the blub-blubbing radiator. 'In fact, nanti that – we'll come to HIM! We could do with some action, an energy boost! And Jupiter knows we could do with the nova recruits too ...'

A date was set. The sol sparkled. Twas to be our first outing together as a family. A fabulosa morale-boost, a gross coming-out party for my merry band of tailor's misfits. A BONDAGE EXERCISE!

To Hell*

NOVAK WEARS A GROSS BLACK CAPE, BICORNE CAPELLA WITH BLOOD-RED OSTRICH FEATHER, TRICOLORE SASH, SABOTS, EXECUTIONER'S MASK.

First and foremost I forced Priscilla and Veronica to volunteer at Le Spleen de Londres as show-palones, which may seem meshigena seeing as I'd only recently liberated them from Red Mill and Frankenfraülein, but please bear with me.

Armed with the leftover barbiturates I'd given up on, the fillies set out for their first shift on a gloopy Tuesday afternoon, Novembre 1965. Of course it was tempting to disguise myself as a paying punter so I could ogle their supple gyrating bods while acting as their minder, but I savvied it was molto safer plonking myself in the Lion d'Or round the corner and waiting for the call to arms.

It must've taken the dollies longer than expected to spike the batatats – I was positively daffy by the time the polari-pipe went off and the bungery's tober-palone roared over the snotty tipplers: 'Mr Sanson? Is there a Mr Sanson?'

Sanson was my alias for the afterjuno. While I'd been a pogi bit nervy about this whole scenario when I awoke that morn, I was now in gay spirits, clad in Pernod-soaked armour, and practically danced my way across the tiles to the telephone.

'They're under,' was the breathy response.

'Fantabulosha.'

---

* Chapter received Monday, 6th April 1970 – ninety-eight days to go.

'But you'd better come quick.' Impossible to tell the dollies' voches apart but I ponced this was likelier Miss Rum Baba, her being the molto dominatricksy of the two. 'The old man's twitching and gurgling.'

'I'm on my way.'

I schlumphed down the rest of my Pernod, straightened my bicorne in the mirror, then staggered outways onto Dean Strasse on unruly Charleston-lallies. Ô, curse this wondrous aniseed jus! As I efinked through the French Quarter, I considered nipping into Roche's for a rapid saucisson to help sponge up some of the daffiness, but, savvying Priscilla and Veronica may well be in some danger, twas probably wiser to just keep scuttling.

Turning into Brewer Strasse, I gave myself a couple of soft schonks to the skull, desperately trying to recall the battleplan (NANTI VIOLENCE? NIX MORTIFICATION?):

Once the dolls had spiked the batatats' bovaries with barbiturates, the omis should've been under in a matter of minutas, at which point Veronica and Priscilla were to shackle Monsieur Drench and his bung in the mogue doppel-guillotine and pipe for me to come over. If the dosage were correct, by the time I reached Le Spleen the bats might have another half an hour or so of braindead snoozering before coming to, ultra groggy and pliable. From here, who knows? Certainly I intended to bombard them with hurtful lavs, but, with my servo now sloshing full of alcool, twas important not to get too carried away. I tried to keep telling myself: NANTI VIOLENCE, NIX MORTIFICATION! However appealing it might be to ferricadooz these tyrannical swines, the original plan was to strictly avoid stooping to their coddy draconian level. I am an omi of taste and bona grace, and I savvied clear enough passive-aggro was the superior revenge-du-jour: to get into these pops' tets rather than battyfanging heavy-lappered like an animal or sharpering-omi. These prats didn't deserve death in any case – I wanted them to live on with disturbed revs, like yours truly, forever in fear, forever watching their crumple-hunched palliasses ...

When I reached Le Spleen de Londres, I parkered the anaemic chavvy in the billet-booth my duey beyong entry fee, pondering for uno momento if this urchin was some sickly descendant of Drench. Stifling my sniggers, I descended the stairs into the stuffy dungeonette, lowered my executioner's mask, then brootishly elbowed my way through the faux-Rococo doppel-doors.

'COU-COU!' I squeaked, grimacing full-militant and jazz-lappering.

I'd expected to find the stomping-khazi in disarray, Drench stirring premature or even tangled in battle with my valiant vixens – and yet pleasingly the establishment was utterly tranquil. Veronica and Priscilla were both upright in their skimpies, doddering on the spot in kitty heels with twisted eeks. They'd done a fabulosa job, clamping the prats in the doppel-guillotine. The bung was slack-jawed, snoring boisterous like some gross industrial chimbley. Nex-bor, Monsieur Drench was perfectly placid: grey fizzer, opals open but vadaring nantwar.

Veronica blinked at me nervy. 'Feel his pulse.'

Important to screeve here that I have nix experience of quackery whatsoever, but when I placed my luppers against the old man's neck, I was able to give an assertive diagnosis: 'You've killed him! You've bloody mortified the cunt!'

I rapidly unshackled Drench from the chipboard guillotine and dragged his skeleton flat across the manky dais. Whether fuelled by adrenaline or bitter-gators, I was as surprised as any pop to find myself now giving my arch adversary oyster-to-oyster resuscitation, pumping his boomboomer while my dolls ogled in stunned silence.

'Veronica, you vicious sparklet, scarper upstairs pronto!' I screeched between schonks. 'Recall the grand plan? The billet-booth, the billet-booth! For Jupiter's sake, get rid of that petty chavvy. Keep all pops away, do not entice them in ...'

As Miss Rum Baba scuttled for the doorway, the faux-Rococo flaps frapped open and Sabine and Rosa Winkel now appeared, breathless after racing from a different bungery.

'Hihihihi! You have change of heart, Raymond?' Rosa scoffed, regarding me straddling Drench, lammering the fungus with passionate gulps.

'Bof. Bof off, you scatty zelda,' I snapped, more annoyed about her splurting my real nom than the coddy jibe. 'Turns out the old zot's got a skimpy tolerance for sleepers.'

Sweating soggy lightning bolts now, I pumped and lammered and pumped and lammered until finally there was some jittery response from the meese wrinkly. Monsieur Drench spluttered a pogi bit, gazing upwards with glassy opals.*

'ACHTUNG!' I hooted. 'Allez, ALLEZ! Help me clamp the bâtard back in the guillotine.'

As my dollies and I dragged Drench back into position, my nells prickled at some faint murmurings backstage. I clocked trey or quatra shadowy forms hovering in the wings: gross elongated Hammer Horror silhouettes clutching whips and pitchforks or tridents. Ô comrades, I was about to abandon the whole daffy escapade and scarper immediately for the exit, when a stray twirling spotlight socked one of the shadowy pops full-eek.

My lally-caps almost buckled at the shocking beauty of the eek.

'COU-COU!' I panted. 'Cou-cou, my chovis! Come out and play!'

The feeli show-palones emerged uno by uno from the munge.

---

* Monday morning the coroner made a statement about the severed head. It wasn't Harry's. Audrey's glassy opals must've been playing tricks on her, hysteria fooling her into seeing Howling's face where there were only the jumbled features of an anonymous deathmask, a Fitzrovian shrunken head. Apparently the flesh was so decomposed identification by sight alone was impossible. Perhaps she'd seen Harry simply because he was missing, simply because she was anxious about his safety – some terrible psychological jigsaw rejiggling?

Still, it was just as shocking to us when the coroner revealed the head's true identity. Dental records showed the dazzling pearls belonged to a certain Sebastian Sturgeon, known to police as a derelict around the Hampstead area. At first we didn't make the connection – until a police spokesperson announced that the Royal Navy would be paying for the funeral: a mark of respect to a Captain (!?) who'd given twenty-four years to Her Majesty's Naval Service.

Some of the donnas had the meese glaze of haunted Victorian dolls, while others – like Donatella, the spotlit sparklet – were almost agonisingly fortuni, joshed-up in ultramarine negligee with milky bods, cherry levers, opals like omi-jarrying fleurs. Twas beyond me how these fillies could end up grinding in such a grotesque dungeon as this, and not instead be gracing the glossystands up above like the Twig, the Shrimp, Miss Bardo, Jane Botkin ...

I tried to put the popsies at ease, shushing the role of maestro-of-ceremonies: 'Help yourselves to refreshments, my dearest darlings! Anything you'd like from behind the bar – anything at all. Work has now given way to leisure, to pleasure! And if you clock any peanuts while you're at it, please do hurl them thisaways. I'm afraid I'm ravenous. Pissed as a goose, my cherries ...'

Twas ultra thumper-melting the way the fills shyly helped themselves to a tumbler of soft-drinky each – although I savvied this surely meant they'd require a hefty bit of servo-malleting to bring them up to speed with the unruly rules of my Liberated Lavvy ...

'Rid yourself of your fairy humility, ladies!' I honked. 'Nellyarda: POLITENESS IS A COMPROMISE! EMBARRASSMENT IS A WEAKNESS! We're here to live unfettered, not slink around servile, prim and tight-levered. Spike your bovaries with any toxic liquor you desire! LUBRICATE REALITY WITH DREAMS!'

By this point the bung and Monsieur Drench were edging towards full-wakeyness. The old man's breathing was still a petty bit like a Hoover sucking up a bucketful of custard, but I fancied he was sentient enough now to appreciate the torture.

I brought my glistening levers an inch from the omis' foggy opals. 'Bonjour, gentlepops,' I polled. 'You'll see we've made a pogi few improvements round here while you've been under. First, I've liberated these fair maidens from your clutches – they're my maidens now. And second, well – ALL HAIL THE HUNGRY DOPPEL-HEADED RAZOR! – we've replaced your guillotine's naff plastic blades with duey nova sparkling steely efinks. Your necks are to provide the machine's first taste of sang! How wunderbar, ja?'

'Ô, mon Dieu, mon Dieu ...' Drench glug-glugged, cords of saliva dangling from his oyster.

'There's nix point whimpering to some revved-up invisible idol now, Drench,' I snapped. 'You're a hellish beastie, are you not? Getting off on these poor palones' misery and getting paid handsomely for it to boot!' I brought my eek back to the bung's. 'And you're just a grotty spectator, a tranquil collaborator! Drench does all the dirty work while you just dumbly schlumph it all down!'

'I don't know who you are,' the bung snapped, trying to assert himself, but by now he must've clocked that his forecast was bleak.

'I'm your favourite nightmare!' I hooted.

Drench's opals widened, losing their groggy fog for uno momento. 'Are you insane? Ze cash register is behind the bar. There's more money in the back. Just release us. I unlock, I unlock the safe ... please ... please spare us ...'

I reered up. 'Well, unfortunately for you I care not a jot for dinarli. Plus I've been drinking all afterjuno. I'm enjoying a certain looseness of compassion and composure, shall we say? In other lavs: fear the worstest.'

Sabine regarded me like she was puzzling over some nova Piero Manzoni sculpture. Was this fear or admiration? After all, I'd spent the morn babbling the virtues of passive-aggro like I was Gandhi or MLK. Certainly she wouldn't have expected this bloodthirsty palavering – and yet, when she opened her painted oyster to squeak, I was surprised by the frenzied lavs that fell out: 'Drop the blades! Slit their throats! Let's just kill the fucking cunts, then leave!'

'Now now,' I spluttered, clinging to my last morsos of sobriety by my luppertips. 'In the spirit of ze original froggy Revolutionary Tribunal, perhaps we should try to give these proceedings at least a pogi whiff of judicial kosherness before rolling tets willety-nillety. Ahem.' I blinked at Drench and the bung. 'Gentleplops: I shall give you each duey minutas to defend yourselves. Tell me plainly why you should be spared and the other condemned to mortification. The Natty Razor is molto eager to taste blood this juno – but what say we kill just one of you, whomsoever we deem most guilty of fash battery after nellying your heartfelt appeals? Let us be cleared of being tyrannous since we so openly proceed in justice, oui, nein?' I turned one of the standing spotlights on the quivering bung. 'You, squire. Tell us: why do you deserve to lavvy onwards and Drench perish pronto?'

'This is insanity!' the bung yowled. As the mogue Louis 15 grandpapa-ticktocker grunted away his duey minutas, the omi writhed helplessly in his bonds, babbling a skitterish defence: 'We've done nothing wrong! I merely serve beverages to thirsty punters, nothing more. And Mr Drench – well, he deserves none of this p-punishment neither. You lot clearly consider yourselves righteous, upstanding citizens, but Drench is no sinner. He's the only one who gave me a chance. I was a hard-up drunk when he met me. N-now I'm a well-off drunk – or at least debt-free anyway ...'

The bung's lavs petered out before his first minuta was up. Thoroughly irritated by this fairy performance, I sharpered roundways for some cheet to whipcrack more chatter out of him, then reered up when one of the popsies behind the bar uttered these unexpected lavs: 'Pickled onions?'

'Pardon me?'

'The sustenance you were after, sir. It's the only food we have on the premises.'

The jolly filly – was it Séverine, or Claire, or Solange? – held aloft a gigantic jar of silverskin oignons.

'Magnifique,' I polled.

Grinning ghoulishly, I strutted round the back of the doppelguillotine, crackled my knuckles, then viciously yanked down Drench's and the bung's lally-covers and slippies.

'ACHTUNG, gentlemen,' I croaked, 'if you refuse to talk, I shall poke these pickled nuggets up both your uncooperative colons!'

Lelling a lapperful of oignons, I found myself stomping excitedly round the stage chanting the 'Ça ira' and badly juggling the petty cheets, before settling down cross-lallied by our captives' clenched trembly botties.

'I have n-no more to say,' the bung blubbed, sharing a poked-up glance with Drench. 'We're innocent. We're innocent.'

'Bof,' I scoffed. 'Very well.'

Back on SS UNMENTIONABLE I'd found it relatively easy pokering a king prawn's eek up Sturgeon's* loose stinker, but

---

* Where did it all go wrong for Sturgeon? How did this authority figure – Chief Steward in the Merchant Navy, Golden Shellback, hobnobber to minor royalty, 'Captain of the Royal Navy' – end up derelict and landlocked in North London? While we had no reason to doubt the coroner's report, at first we tried to convince ourselves this wasn't *the* Chief Steward Sturgeon, Novak's Sturgeon, our Sturgeon. Why? Put simply: the truth disturbed us. Thus far the police seemed to have no leads whatsoever on the killer's identity – and yet for us the evidence was glaring. Just the fact that Novak flagrantly mentions Sturgeon in this latest chapter (not least that he impaled his festering head only a few blocks from our office) gave us no doubt as to the culprit.

But what to do with this terrible information? McKinley, ever in thrall to Lady Justice, urged us to share our knowledge with the police – but where would this leave us and Novak's half-finished glistening liver? Conceivably the Scum King could continue screeving his memoirs in gaol, but he wouldn't have his ghostwriter and, above all, he'd be denied the opportunity to carry out the climax of the whole story: his fantabulosa crime. An incomplete manuscript was worthless to us. If we were to survive as a company – thrive, even! – we needed Novak to see through his bloody destiny, and finish what he started.

So in effect he had our blessing to sever more heads? It seemed, with divorce proceedings in full motion now and self-esteem at an all-time low, Merritt had lost all sense of morality and civic duty. Rather than choosing to be the hero of this novel himself and put a stop to Novak's atrocities, Stanley secretly hoped for wholesale slaughter, a snaking trail of human entrails, a tidal wave of blood. With pound signs swirling in his opals – and less than 100 days to go! – Merritt could barely contain his excitement as he pondered what the Guru's climactic crime would be if this heinous debraining of Sturgeon were merely a dummy run, a limbering-up routine!

And yet again (as ever, as ever) there were innumerable dilemmas involved in keeping quiet. Of course we were at risk of being prosecuted for withholding information from the police, perverting the course of justice – but after some very-late-night deliberation we settled on a (hopefully) foolproof argument for

these were tight-dishy omis and nix mistake. The first couple of oignons simply splattered up the sides of their buttocks, rendered inedible whichever way you ogled it.

'What "judicial kosherness" is this?!' the bung squealed as duey plucky oignons finally found their way in. 'We've done nothing wrong! We don't even touch the girls! Drench – he's no –'

'Apologies, darling,' I hush-hushed, 'your duey minutas have long expired now, I'm afraid.'

I thumbed uno final silverskin up the omis' backsides, popped duey more in my oyster, then scuttled back round the guillotine to vada the chaps' disturbed weepy eeks.

When it was Drench's turn to speak, the bat took a somewhat different approach to the bung:

'Kill him, not me,' he snapped. 'Like he say, I am no sinner. You only think I am tyrant because I play ze role so convincingly in our petit théâtre. This is acting. I fight against fascism in ze Ninety-Forties. I move weapons for the Resistance. Mr Snell, this jean-foutre.' His opals flicked towards his neighbour. 'He is nothing. A drunk. He drink my business away. I should have sack him a long long ago. But my goodness prevent me ...'

By the end of Drench's tirade, the bung's eek was full-aghast, his bloodshot ogles bulging like duey maggot-infested nectarines.

'Well, that seems definitive enough,' I polled. 'I have made my decision.'

I plopped duey slops-buckets beneath the stage to catch the loser's rolling tet, then took up the ropes, one in each lapper.

---

keeping our mouths shut: surely Novak would include his hideous slaying of Sturgeon in a forthcoming chapter – a written confession without which the lunatic might never be convicted!

In the meantime we converted this and the previous footnote into code, hid them under the loose laminate in Merritt's WC and went about our business blithely, as if our hands were not completely caked in the blood of the madman's next victims ...

O, dear Lord, have mercy on our souls!

I announced to the crowd of twitchering donnas: 'Well, you'll be pleased to nelly: we have a victor – and we have a victim. Defendants: I recommend relaxing your neck-thews for a cleaner fatcha. On the count of trey I shall drop one of these hungry blades on ze loser of my choosing. BON VOYAGE, putrescent tet!' The bats writhed like landlocked fishies now as I began the brootish count: 'UN ...! DEUX ...! DEUX-ET-DEMI ...! TROIS!!'

I let go of the rope in my left lapper and Drench's blade dropped like a gross metal shark fang. The dollies all shrieked, scuttling backways, expecting a squirt of sang – but nothing came. Drench's tet remained attached to his bod. His opals were pink, parnyaqua still oozing from the sockets.

'Ooh la la,' I scoffed.

Of course I'd mogued about the nova steely blades. However tempting it was to dispose of these fash pricks, I wasn't daffy enough to roll tets hither-thither like some mod Robespierre.* Twas punishment enough just to see the slugs squirm. And squirm they did – for at least another minuta or duey – before relief took over and finally some faint sparkle returned to their fattygayed ogles.

'Alors,' I uttered, 'now let us vagary, my cherries ...'

As my dolls began to file out of the stomping-khazi, Sabine was frigid, seething, like she didn't want to leave without tasting sang herself.

'There's knives in the kitchen,' she snarled as I tried to coax her upways through the doppel-doors. 'Look at them – they were expecting to die! They both know they've done wrong. We should cut their bloody throats ...'

Sabine's fiery lavs unnerved me, and yet I felt brotherly pangs of twistiness too, savvying she must've felt particularly

---

* Where did it all go wrong for *Novak*? Here he acknowledges one must be daffy (drunk, daft?) to inflict such abhorrent violence on a fellow human, but, then again, in the first sentence of his first letter to us (dated 10th October 1969, four years after this scene at Le Spleen de Londres), did he not introduce himself as a 'meese meshigena-omi'? Time and time again we're forced to admit: we had fair warning.

dehumanised by these foul bats, like this pantomime revenge was just dorcas and fairy compared to her own meese past sufferings. I touched her pol and hush-hushed: 'We've left our mark, ducky. Let's not threaten our own grandiose liberteen lavvies by ferricadoozling theirs. Allez ... allez ...'

After shooing her up the stairwell, I returned to Drench for uno final slur in his nellyholes: 'Adieu, misters, monsters, monsieurs. Take this as a brootish warning, and not a dolly reprieve. I'll resuscitate these poor lifeless donnas of yours. At least do us the honour of leaving them to be revamped in peace, or else next time: nanti leniency! Au revoir, bonne nuit – et bona riddance ...'

I took Drench's clefs from his jacket posh, skipped up the stairway, deadlocked, then bolted. Catching up with my comrades on Grand Windmill Strasse, I nellied Veronica gurgling the virtues of Never-Neverland to our nova recruits, trey bijou meek teens with blazingly incongruous joggering-noms: Séverine Vivisection, Baroness von Fisty, Donatella Diptera. The way Miss Rum Baba was palavering, my boutique sounded like a bona fide pleasure-palace and not at all ajax to a Vicky sweatshop. And judging by the teenies' rosy-bonbon eeks, they weren't averse to surrendering their lavvies to this strange frog joshed in full executioner's clobber. Of course, I made a handsome headsman. My kishkas tingled. I felt gay, proud and poked-up all at once. Moi – a twisted, hideous, quongless orphan – now patriarch to an ultra-fortuni family that was expanding week upon week like gildi radioactive froggyspawn!

Once we'd safely traversed the brootish toot-tootering consumerist gangway of Oxford Strasse, Priscilla linked arms with me and polled with an expression like crème anglais: 'I'm a little confused, Raymond.'

'We live in a maxi bewildering mond, alas, dear heart.' I stroked her silky lapper. More than any of the fillies I'd recruited thus far, I felt a bona affinity with Priscilla, her having been criticised relentlessly for being meese in her chavvyhood before exploding as an exotic swan in adulthood.

'No, but this passive-aggro you said about,' she added. 'We can do whatever we like, so long as no one gets hurt, you said?'

I ladled it out for her again, how the aim was to disturb the revs of our enemies without resorting to animalistic aggro and lowering ourselves to their coddy level: an equaliser without getting one's lappers dirty, a thought-crime without leaving behind any lupperprints.

Priscilla fanged her camisha cuff. 'But do you not think they'll die in there anyway?'

My oyster twitched. 'Drench and the bung?'

'We didn't untie them, did we? Won't they starve?'

I pressed duey luppers to my levers in mogue consternation, although nix doubt she clocked me smirking. Secondas later I flung Drench's clefs into the back of a taxicab, schonked the roof and squawked, 'To Hell, driver! To Hell.'

We scarpered into the milky noche, reering loony ...

The Antichristines*

NOVAK WEARS LONG JOHNATHANS, INSULATED LALLY-COVERS, WOOLLY MAMMOTH MANTO, THEW-HIGH BOOTIES, HIKING ALMOND-ROCKS, NELL-MUFFS, PICCADILL RUFF AND FAMBLERS.

A gay period followed.

To celebrate the rapid expansion of my family,† I theatrically unplugged the chug-chuggering sewing-vacayas and declared a duey-week holiday. When I asked my dollybirds where they might like to vagary for this impromptu festival of fizkultura and frivolity, their responses were mostly codswallop:

'Canvey Island?'

'Forest of Dean?'

'Wanstead Flats?'

Then again, most of these poor zots had been trapped in subterranean strip-khazis for years – possiblement even

---

* Chapter received Thursday, 16th April 1970 – eighty-eight days to go.

† In contrast to Novak's swelling ranks, our own workforce was shrinking. Audrey disappeared this week. She'd been acting strangely recently – turning up to work late, chuntering sinister gibberish, her mind elsewhere – but there'd been no indication she was planning on abandoning us without a goodbye. No notice handed in, no doctor's note – although we presumed it must be trauma, emotional instability after seeing Sturgeon's severed head skewered on the railings. Her desk was left in a state of grim confusion: reams of complaints and half-written weary replies scattered around her battered typewriter, cigarette burns, torn fingernails, spilled gin…

O Howling, O Hulme. With these faces missing, the Glass Eye roll call now felt desperately thin: Merritt, Trefoil, McKinley, Noon, Ingram. And still so much work to be done, if Novak's published memoirs were to appear on time …

Fitzroy Square seemed like the Garden of Eden to them.

'Rummage a pogi bit deeper in your servos, darlings,' I demanded, pacing betwixt their vonny eiderdowns strewn across the boudoir floor. 'In fact, screech your revs at me! What say we let your privviest desires finger the way? Recount your dreams for me, my duckies. Whichever daffy rev appeals the mostest, we shall act on it immediately, relive it en plein air ...'

Since having my own revs pummelled to rustic pâté in the Lumière Suite, I'd developed a tingly interest in other pops' noche-flickers. Prior to my heinous brain-rape I cherished my dreams mostly because there were no rules behind my oglelids, nix obligations, nanti advertising, no mass-media mogues, nanti authority-flops, no coddy logic, nix ticktocks, no dinarli-exchange – but now I felt utterly untogether, cast adrift in this drab dinarli-driven welt with just a tet full of inkyboos to soothe me in my darkest hours. Partly through homesickness for my own Dreamland and partly through a nagging desire to dissect their feeli servos, I was eager to nelly what skitterish delights went on inside my followers after lights out. Privvily of course I hoped the palones were prone to ultra-elaborate erotic revs, having been raised in the skin trade – and yet, when they all began splurting forth their scatty fantasies, I was somewhat disappointed.

'There's a strange man in a brown trenchcoat,' Donatella Diptera polled, 'sanding down a small wooden pigeon until it's just sawdust in his hands.'

'I'm flying over the desert with a flock of bats,' Lionel monotoned. 'The bats keep shitting and shitting and shitting until there's just this huge load of stinking bat-dung. It looks like an Easter Island statue – except the face is Peter Lorre's, or just a big evil baby's.'

'I'm in a room like my childhood bedroom in Hemel Hempstead except it's not really my bedroom,' Priscilla polled. 'My family's been replaced by insects except they walk on their hind legs and they look just like humans. I'm tiny – I'm two years old except I look exactly like I look now, only many times smaller.

The clocks are all broken. In some rooms it's noon, in some rooms it's way past midnight ...'

Ô MERZ. I was resigned to the savagery that we might have to take the fuckering autobus to Canvey Island after all, when Baroness von Fisty murmured the following lavs:

'Um. I had a kinky dream the other night, Raymond.'

'Ô?' My kishkas twinkled.

'Um. It was outside the Houses of Parliament. Ahem.' The Baroness's joggering-nom might've led one to believe she was a domineering donna, an aristocratic crone with a brootish Teutonic tongue – but in fact our dorcas von Fisty was a meek teeni, an insecure chavvy with a sugary voche and soft manatee opals (her real nom was Peggy Fairweather!). 'We're in a circle, all dressed in white like we're brides, or white witches. Um. A white lacy finger points up at Big Ben. The clock tower's vibrating, throbbing, gyrating like a giant man's erection about to explode. Ahem. We start spinning in a circle, chanting, firing all these insults and curses up at the big golden member. I'm fearful the thing's going to erupt, rain down bombs or acid on our heads. But our spinning gets faster. We're going really rapid now, sort of speaking in tongues. The chanting gets louder, more forceful. Then all of a sudden the clock tower droops, it flops into the Thames like a pathetic, flaccid ... well ... you know. And the Houses of Parliament crumble to nothing.'

Despite the glaring logistical difficulties, the rest of my clan were ultra eager to recreate this scatty scenario. Perhaps unsurprisingly my palones had developed explosive anti-patriarchal abdabs after having to bend for all manner of male ponces and punters – but this unanimous fantastical demolition-lust was unexpected. I ogled my dollies hoofering round the boudoir like banshees, hellbent on vagarying pronto to Westminster and flopping Big Ben's gross gothic colin ŌM! SHLACK! VLOP! into the murky aqua.

'You don't recall any words of the curse?' Bonnie squeaked.

'Um. No. I'm afraid not.' The Baroness blinked down at the PVC floor.

'Fuck the words!' Veronica blurted. 'We'll just make it up as we go along. Cause a scene, get our mugshots in the inkies.' She struck a sparkly posture, a deranged runway model with a piranha's eek.

I admit I'd never considered the phallic architecture of Londres a gross problem before (in fact, as you're aware, I'm rather fond of the Post Office Colin) – but then we were all undergoing our politico awakening at this juncture, our political arousal. My only reservation was the choice of colin. Big Benjamin was undoubtedly the mostest heavily guarded architectural cartso in Britannia. If we were to mince down thataways and peform this flamboyant infertility ritual in the blazing junolight, we would surely be risking arrest, interrogation, electro-jolts to our flange-levers ...

'Achtung, my chovis – let us not peak too early,' I interjected. 'What say we practise our witchcraft first? Flop a pogi few less sturdy colins elsewhere before attempting to droop that most imperious of rosbif erections?'

'Where like?'

'Je ne sais pas – the Leaning Cartso of Pisa?' I suggested, before fingering a molto simpler, maxi prick-abundant destination: 'Oxford.'

Thankfully this seemed a natty enough back-up emag to the raving banshees. After taking the Tube outways to Uxbridge, we marched across duey sloppy overgrown fields to the A40, hoping to shush a spacious caboosh without attracting suspicion from other zoomzooming juno-trippers. While the rest of us hid in a ditch ajax to the asphalte, I nominated my most bona-vadaring popsies – Sabine, Priscilla and Donatella – to playact donnas-in-distress in the lay-by up thataways. From our shifty vista, lying flatfish among the pricklies, I could just about vada Sabine thumbing at lorry-omis while Priscilla tended to Miss Diptera, melodramatically suffering some form of broken lally, cateva ankle or ruptured spleen by the crash-barriers. Sure enough a blank Bedford van soon squelched to a halt.

An omi in a schvartz donkey-jacket hopped out and scuttled gallantly towards our vulnerable vixens, at which point the rest of us bullfroghopped from the undergrowth and ambushed the bruiser, dragging him back into the munge like a pack of snappy hyenas carrying away a startled antelope.

Once Rosa – our brazen Bondage-und-Disziplin mistress – had successfully hogtied, ballgagged and lipsticked the twonk, we casually minced back to his humbumbling caboosh, cramming ourselves in among his metal-detectors or Geiger-counters or whatever daffy vacayas he was transporting west.

Twas a mere quatra-daitcha miles to Oxford, but Bruce, our qualified chauffeur, was only capable of driving like a tranquilised fungus, so overloaded was the contraption with our lavishly bespangled bods. To keep my crushed comrades entertained, I suggested a pogi bit of storytime:

'Séverine Vivisection,' I cou-coued from the front passenger benkel. 'Dearest, would you please remind us how you happened to receive such an intriguing joggering-nom?'

'Well, it's not the most cheerful story,' came a tinny voche from the mass of jostled carnish back thataways. 'Before I got involved with Mr Drench, I was working at a nasty little cabaret in Stuttgart. Have any of you ever heard of – or worked for – Die Lederhand?'

The fillies in the back polled nantwar, swishing and vibrating like queasy seaweed as the caboosh juddered over a strip of chevrons.

'Well, rumour has it Die Lederhand was the name of someone in the organisation,' Séverine went on, 'the boss, the kingpin – though I never knowingly set eyes on him. Apparently it was also the name of a secret society operating in West Germany after the war, a sadistic shadowy boys' club, full of perverts in black gowns and gasmasks. Certainly it was the name given to the cabaret I worked at – though the building itself was unmarked.' In the rear-ogle mirror her eek looked like a slowly melting Reblochon cheese. 'I was offered a new job in Stuttgart by a man who claimed he was a Pomeranian duke, dancing for him one night in a velvet booth in Mayfair. I was only fifteen. The money was excellent – but lord, we performed some horrific acts for it. Apparently the organisation was funded by far-right West German politicians, or Swabian aristocracy – in any case, probably all paid for by the public's taxes.'

'What was your act?' the Baroness asked, her voche like a trampled trompette.

'Well, I was soon famed for my knife skills. "Das ist ein Live-Nerz!" I used to announce to the crowd. They gave me just one line of German to speak – the only German I knew at the time – and it was a lie, at that. "Das ist ein Live-Nerz, meine Damen und Herren. Das ist ein Live-Nerz!"'

'What does it mean?' Sabine polled.

'Ziss is a live mink,' Rosa answered for her, struggling to vogue up a soggy Gauloise.

'I had with me what the audience believed was a live mink,' Séverine continued. '"Das ist ein Live-Nerz!" After dancing round the stage a while, frolicking with the furry critter, I trapped the mink's head in a Mädchenfänger, a sort of one-ended Chinese finger-trap. We had a small bondage rig set up under a spotlight. Very carefully I had to tie the creature's legs apart – suspended spreadeagle position, if you can visualise it.' Séverine scratched her lopsided vonka. 'Then the music stopped. I took my knife – and, while the poor thing writhed and wriggled in its shackles, I had to skin the fur from its back. The sorry bastard had no tranquilisers, nothing. The men loved it. Their gasmasks all steaming up. Between each incision, I had to remove another item of my clothing. By the time the whole bloody hide came free, I was naked. They made me dance with the horrible pelt, swinging it round my shoulders like a luxury stole, rubbing it between my legs. Blood everywhere – all over my body, inside me. It was horrific.'

The caboosh let out an unhealthy gulp.

'But it was just a lie, you said? An illusion?' Bruce asked. 'It wasn't actually a live mink?'

'No, no.' Séverine's eek was stony. 'You can't tame minks. Too vicious. It was a ferret. They kept a ferret farm just outside Wolfshlugen.'

Whether or not this tale helped ease the pops' discomfort in the back of the van, there was silence until at last we clocked the dreaming spires molesting the clouds up ahead. After abandoning the caboosh in a sideysnicket ajax to the Shotover Arms, we trolled the final duey miles into town on foot, guzzling the fresh aero like grinning dolphins leaping from muddy aqua.

Compared to the smoggy splatter-frenzy of Londres, Oxford is dolly. Jolly dolly and full of fuckering embryonic Tories. As we sashayed through the cobbly strasses, sharpering for a suitable steeple to curse and jeer at, it seemed the place was entirely overrun by snooty skol-pops, fungal dons and frigid oiks. Possiblement I was guilty of tarring these pops with eagle feathers simply because I was intimidated by their overswollen servos – but still, I could not feel at home in their city. Everywhere we stomped, the antique latties and gothic portals were chiselled with Latin. I savvied nix doubt the toffs wished all roadsigns, bodega-fronts and munjarry-menus were screeved in Latin, to stop plebs minnying anywhere they weren't wanted.

Mingling ajax to these fusty provincial plops, myself and my dollies were like a gross Surrealist circus troupe, honking through the city centre bedecked in some of our mostest outrageous clobber to date: the Baroness and Séverine in PVC babydoll barky cozzies with fishy-scale maquiage; Bruce and Lionel joshed-up like Siamese-twin Jean Genet jailbirdies; Rosa Winkel a delectable shrimp in an astro-capello; A-line nuclear-fallout drogle-suits; ostrich-skin stockings ...

Naturellement my gloriosa designs were intended to startle civvies, but there was more to this than just daffy pantomime horror. Once my boutique opened its portals in the new year, I hoped my invigorating, servo-spinning schmutta might shock pops into questioning the immeasurably more ridiculous bland uniforms every twonk seems obliged to wear juno upon juno, inspiring them to josh themselves in increasingly risqué idiosyncratic cozzies (and ultimately FERRICADOOZ all humanoid conformity?!) – but ALAS and ALACK-O-JUNO, it seemed the zots of Oxfordshire were not yet ready to have the fabric of their naff strait-laced lavvies jostled nor fluffed not a jot. When my daitcha-strong army of beautiful weirdies halted for una minuta to chant unpleasantries at the jagged colin of Santa Maria, we were immediately frowned upon, tutted at and mumblingly harangued by countless twats in grey twill and anoraks. 'Tramps!' and 'Scrubbers!' side-oystered these pious batatats. Molto worster: later that juno I found myself holding hands with Lionel as we loitered at the gateway of the Bodleian Bibliotheque: a frankly innocuous occurrence that nevertheless inspired extreme spittle and malice from toffs and oiks alike. We were continually accused of abnormality – as if this were something to be poked-up about! – and when we attempted to peruse the local mock-Tudor WC for like-minded fruitmongers, we found our passage blocked by a blank-eeked attendant, and were told in some baffling rustic lingo either we or the khazi were 'out of order'!

Ô comrades. Savvying these prats were simply beyond help, we retreated east, to one of the dolly parks circling the city, clomping up up up to the prickly peak of a Christmas-firred willet that afforded a bona unimpeded oglefu1 of those bastard dreaming spires. By this juncture I was dubious our occult jabberings could have any effect other than us being promptly chased out of town by toffs with glimmering batons – but still, I didn't want to discourage my eager banshees.

'Vada these uppity brick pricks protruding from the tops of the universities!' I howled. Twas quite a vista: the pimply cateva-cartsos atop the Magdalen Tower, the chubby circumcised kosher-colin of the Radcliffe Kamera. As we blinked downways, a pogi snowfall started sprinkling the skyline like VadaVision interference. 'Ô, isn't it a travesty these eagle breeding-grounds exist?' I continued. 'Spoiled arroganki chavvies taught at opal-watering expense how to playact professional, diplomatic and cultured, then being squirted from these crooked antique colins direct into the toppermost jobs of our codswallop lopsided society. These plops will never understand dazzling untamed beasties like you or I. Here's to clumsiness, Ô comrades. Here's to unprofessionalism! Here's to accepting we're all just shambling wonderfully gracelessly through this baffling scattershot obstacle course of life!'*

'Oui, oui, oui,' my dollies responded, fangs chattering. Alas, their far-out schmutta might've looked glimmery against the blank snowy backdrop, but twas not the mostest frost-protective clobber, I admit.

'Allez!' I squawked. 'Join lappers, my cherries! Let us flop these stony cartsos pronto, parker a hex upon these snooty institutions – then we can fuck-off-back-thataways to Londres, back to our sweet, serene abnormality ...'

Even if the curses didn't work, I savvied some rapid pagan hoofering would at least keep hypothermia at bay. We began spinning in a rickety danse-macabre formation, hoofering anti-ticktockwise before breaking out into solo frantic whirly-dervishing and crab-lallying.

'DOWN DOWN DOWN! DOWN DOWN DOWN!' we chanted at the foggy spires. 'Lallyless Vietnamese napalm-schlumphers! Teenies on welfare! DOWN DOWN DOWN! DOWN DOWN DOWN! Supertax! Legalised buggery!'

I cannot remember the exact cheets we were screeching, but the general savagery was to shout out lavs that would likely cause a Tory's colin to droop during arva.

'Devaluation! Abortions on the NHS! DOWN DOWN DOWN! DOWN DOWN DOWN! Citywide guerrilla battyfangery! The Queen's tet on a spike! DOWN DOWN DOWN! DOWN DOWN

---

* For the record, there are no Oxbridge old boys on the books at the Glass Eye Press. In our time we may have been accused of obscenity, of moral bankruptcy, of anti-intellectualism, of abnormality, of redundancy – but pompous, privileged and nepotistic we are not. We wear our art-school rags and frayed secondary-modern ties proudly, like golden albatrosses round our necks.

DOWN! Monos in Harrods! Lenin's frigid corpse in your wifie's flowery nightie!'

Possiblement it was just delirium from all the spinning, but I'm certain the gross prick of Santa Maria was beginning to droop a pogi bit – when all at once we were disturbed by a dolled-up crone (Schnauzer, mouser, Elizabethan maquiage) screaming at us from an ajax thicket. 'At last, some youngsters talking sense!' she cackled. Her hound defecated simperingly by her side. 'I agree with you, darlings. Down with abortion! Down with homosexuality! Fan-tastic!'

By the time we'd stumbled back down the blustery willet, Oxford had more or less vanished, submerged under a dense blanket of snowfall and cloud-fuzz. We vagaried outways to the city limits, barely palavering now as we made snail-trails through the snow, like refugees shuffling listless and deranged from the epicentre of an atomic dustbowl.

'Yank your dolly oysters up, my lovelies – you mustn't be so twisted,' I polled encouragingly when finally we found the Bedford caboosh duey hours later, icicles hanging from our vonkas. 'Clear enough these heksa-hundred-year-old colins are firmer than we'd fancied. Possiblement your anti-eagle outpourings are not yet strong enough to dislodge solid bricklets. But fear not, you're only feeli pops, with feeli bods and servos. I shall train you up thoroughly and – jarry my lavs! – soon enough we'll gaily unravel the very threads of this stiff, dowdy, uptight society!'

My followers' eeks were emotionless, rigid with frost, but nix doubt they were glowing inwardly at this morale-boosting outburst. I gave each of them a bijou fruity squeeze as they crammed back into the auto, feeling for warmth under their glassy carnish – however, any bona spirits evaporated entirely when Bruce, cleffing the spluttering slit repeatedly, revealed: 'The van won't start, Raymond.'

I dashed roundways to check under the bonnet, but after glaring for una minuta at the mass confusion of metal spaghetti and oily wigglies, I casually plopped it shut again.

'Alas, I cannot cure the bugger,' I announced, joining my comrades in the back. The dolls ogled me desperately, each shuddering in their skimpy cozzies like humanoid hailstones. 'We shall have to stay put in this meese icebox over the noche, my cherries. We cannot risk booking our daffy bods into some backwards provincial guesthouse – and nix doubt the chug-chuggers have been halted in this despicable weather. However, I shall of course do my duty as alpha-omi-palone. Please allow me to provide a pogi bit of friction to each and every one of you ... allez ... allez ...'

Grinning beatifically, I pounced upon my huddled darlings, wrapping my lappers and lallies round their barely concealed carnish and rubbing vigorously. Given the horrific chill, twas surely not unreasonable of me to presume my devotees might wish to crank up the intensity a jot and indulge in a bout of sang-bubbling, thumper-thundering grupa-arva – however, when I attempted to snatch the remaining morsos of schmutta from their juddering goose-prickly bods, my reeferings were met not with appreciative groin-groins but skitterish squeals and skol-pop horror.

'No, NO, NO, Raymond!' they tittered, flailing about like stroppy bambinos before uno by uno theatrically collapsing upon the grotty floor of the van.

Despite the frost, sleep appeared to harpoon the zots almost instantaneously. ALAS, I ponced: perhaps the only drawback of unfettered merrymaking is humanoids' abject lack of energy reserves, the futile nightly tug-of-war between our lusty overilluminated servos and our ever-dwindling fattygayed bods. But still: weren't these supposed to be fresh-boomboomering athletic feelies? I myself had nix interest in sleeping that noche (fearing an onslaught of vengeful inky dons and oiks in the ultraschvartz), but nix amount of jostling, pleading or repeated prodding could wrench these pops from The Void once their opals clashed shut.

Ô, the frigid batatats.

The Free Love Formula, or: French Horn*

NOVAK WEARS MAINLY PINK POLYSTYRENE.

NELLY FRANÇOISE HARDY'S 'LE TEMPS DE L'AMOUR'.

The avid Novak devotees among you – my vast beautiful readership! – will be pleased to nelly I at last lost my virginity on 14th February 1966. How did it come to pass: moi, an inexperienced castrated mary, charvering otta eager flanges and duey eager dishes in a row, dressed as a gigantic contraceptive-droga dial-pack?

As you'll discover, I'm nanti much of a fan of foreplay, but I savvy a pogi bit of preamble here is inescapable ...

Cue the swooning violins.

While it was perfectly enjoyable harassing fungal ponces and phallic latties out thataways, I had to keep focused on the Grander Plan: to build our supercommunal, all-inclusive multi-loving fash empire in W1.

With a newly bolstered workforce, schmutta production was up umpteen per cent as we raced towards the unveiling of our bijou boutique. The increased stress (not to mention the lack of sleep, sol and arval satisfaction) was giving me frequent tetchy outbreaks, but I maintain my workerbees were never forced to grind in sweatshop conditions. I may have plied them with amphetamines to meet certain unconquerable deadlines, but the

* Chapter received Wednesday, 22nd April – eighty-two days to go.

aim was always to improve the lavvies of my sweet underlings. As I paced around the workshop barking gildi orders at my receptive bambinos, I felt like the puppetmaster of some classic rags-to-riches liver – Doc Coppélia, Vic Frankenstein, Stephen Ward, the Prof from PYGMALION – reinvigorating these lost, easily led prole pooves and popsies, injecting them with natty skills and a nova bona education they could use to better themselves in the outside mond ... not that the plan was for them to ever leave me.

Were the chavvies grateful? Regularly I'd test their loyalty by sending them out on specjalni missions – swiping discarded cloth from Hanson Strasse, conjuring bona munja from bins, flirting with those in charge of the local Gestetner, pasting up posters advertising our Grand Opening, 14th February 1966 (!) – but I savvied it was important to keep showing them I had merit too.

We shared everything in that latty (aside from my 14,000 guineas in the loft), and while the pops did their bestest to scrounge serviceable scraps from the streets, they were positively wonderstruck when I went on my own Fitzrovian forages, coming home with luxurious cheets (froggy fromage, Arne Jacobsen chaises, wax mannequins, Gaggia coffee-vacaya ...) I claimed to have shushed with just my wiliness and dextrous luppers. Nix doubt my dolls rapidly regarded me as some sort of bolshy superhero, performing miracles that simultaneously ramped up my loveableness and reduced the chance of any of these bona pops feeling the itch to escape. I loved them so much it was tempting to keep them all in lally-shackles or specimen jars, but I savvied there was nix risk of wobbly loyalty or all-out treachery – not while I was the ultimate hunter-shusher, not while I could provide for them this rich gratis glitz-lavvy compared to the drab scrabbly lavvies they'd left behind.

As a sanctuary for drop-outs, indésirables and the Easily Exploited, my boutique was unparalleled – but I didn't just want beautiful lepers and weirdies in my clan. Once we opened our portals to the general poplos, I hoped to snare impressionable fresh-eeked feelies from every corner of the city: pops free from naff arval hang-ups; pops untainted by grim travails in the skin trade; pops intrigued by the bod-quaking possibilities of the nova Sexual Revolution; pops hellbent on rebelling against perfectly bona mamas and papas; pops jaded by the Mod movement, eagerly sharpering for something more ecstatic, molto erotic, more extreme, maxi explosive ...

Education and aggressive marketing – PROPAGANDA, if you like – were key here. Despite being initially tarred as a ticket, I still respected Mods for spreading their peacock plague rapidly across the nation – embracing speed, narcissism, hedonism and multi aspects of my beloved froggy culture (Nouvelle Vague flickers, the French Crop, existentialisme, matelot camishas, du café, beatnik berets ...) – although I cannot comprehend why they all favoured meese rosbif noise like The Petty Eeks, The Gimps, The Bastards and The Swollen Quongs over wondrous froggy pop like Françoise Hardy, Annie Philippe, France Gall, Christine Pilzer ...* French

---

* For those of you who are curious to discover more about Novak's favourite French chanteuses, this list went on much longer (with manic annotations), regurgitated in part here:

> 'Françoise Hardy (la grande mademoiselle, taller than a trolleybuz, voche like a cannonball of Chantilly cream – possiblement her voche is in fact too gildi? But the queen nonetheless ... BOWN BOWN BOWN!), Annie Philippe (le mannequin, that bona froggy brat-voche I love so much, direct from the gargler of a sweet skol-filly blonde ... panther opals and vampy oyster, at times she looks like she'd rip out your brains and jarry them during arva ... not that I would protest), Monsieur Gainsbourg (jolie-laide king of the kosher-omis, multilayered lav-attack on the aunty nells, fashionable ashtray, one of the solo omis I forgive for his glaring aquila-vonka), France Gall (la poupée de son, the mostest delectable ventriloquist's dolly for Serge's subversive l'humour noir. Vive France! Gloriosa brat-voche, beauty-morso under her right opal like a permanent brown parnydrop, beautiful poky lateral incisors. Some pops ponce possiblement the poor tart was exploited, but those jolly peeking incisors screech to me: 'Non!' The doll savvied the mischief. LSD, Dady Dada, anus-flavoured lollipops? Ô France! 'Laisse tomber les filles,' you screech. Mais oui, my cherry, I would drop the other fillies in an instant to spend una noche with those incisors embedded in my clammy carnish ...), Stella (while we're palavering about mischief,

couture, culture and cuisine are superior to bland anglo fare in EVERY RESPECT!

OUI.

Before I got my claws into any fresh feelies, I took it upon myself to try to re-educate my existing followers, sending them out to shush French bagu**et**tes, French LPs, French livers, French inkies, French Blues. Soon we had a grand library of Lautréamont, Rimbaud, Baudelaire, Papa Breton, Lord Auch, de Sade, de Beauvoir, Debord, Jarry, Camus, Sartre et al, which I cackled into their nells while they clattered away at the sewing-vacayas. I parkered LE MONDE from the Librairie Parisienne in Soho each morn, often cutting up articles to twist their meaning and doctoring the masthead, tinkering with the 'L' and 'e's so it appeared to be a publication entittled:

Miss Vander is the ultimate 'non-non' donna – a sardonic froggy Polack who subverted the yé-yé scene with platter-tapperingly derisive singsongs, and maxi respect for a feeli chanteuse releasing un A-side entittled: 'Si vous connaissez quelque chose de pire qu'un vampire, parlez m'en toujours, ça pourra peut-être me faire sourire'! If I was a vamp, I would gaily slurp her sang but I fear she could ferricadooz me with uno sideyways ogle), Chantal Goya (bona fide Nouvelle Vague masc-fem dollybird, The Chanting Bob), Clothilde (only duey EPs but possiblement my favourite of all yé-yés ... another outré puppet, chanting Surrealistic lav-splatter at The Germ's mercy ... my darling disaffected Clothilde, twisted saintess of maxi hoofer-able trey-minuta H-bomba bonbons ... The Eek of Feeli Detachment: in her flickers she looks like she'd rather be lathering pissoirs than chanting to an audience), et cetera, et ceterarara ...'

After sampling some of these singers' hits, we agreed unanimously: we prefer the meese rosbif noise.

I cared not when the anglos won the Jules Rimmer in July.

As Charlie Baudelaire himself once proclaimed: worster even than drogas, daggers, rape or arson, capable of shattering and swallowing the mond in one yawn: 'C'est l'Ennui!'* Boredom, apathy – worster than rape, readers!

With this in mind, I savvied we must overload our boutique with all manner of meshigena dazzling fakements and diverting emags if we were to keep our nova punters entertained and coax them full-time into our commune. The lapper-billet advertising our Opening Noche was little more than a barrage of titillating promises and thundertwanging Pop Art vomitus:

NEVER-NEVERLAND
NOVA FASH BOUTIQUE
OGLE STRASSE, W1
THE GRAND OPENING!
25 PLUVIÔSE CLXXIV
(MON 14 FEB 1966)
SURREALIST ALL-NITE FREAKOUT
GILDI-DROGLE, WAY-OUT CLOBBER, SCHMUTTA-SWAP
LOVE-IN, LOBSTER-IN, FROMAGE-IN, FROTTAGE-IN
ENTERTAINMENTS: YÉ-YÉ GIRLS – MANNEQUINS – MASQUEERADE BALL
AUTO-SCRIBBLE – STRIP – FREE BEVVY – FREE CLOBBER – FREE LOVE – FRENCH BLUES
9 P.M. ONWARDS ...
FREE LAVVY MEMBERSHIP TO OUR NOVA BOLSHY FASH EMPIRE
ALL MOD-POPS WELCOME
(STRICTLY NIX EAGLE-EEKS OR ROBO-DRONES)
LUBRICATE REALITY WITH DREAMS!

---

* From 'Au Lecteur', *Les fleurs du mal* (1857).

While the overriding savagery of Never-Neverland hinged upon full equality – unisex clobber, unisex changing-chambers (in fact, nix changing-chambers at all), cut-price tariffs, equal pay for omis and palones (LOVE, MUNJA and SHELTER parkered in lieu of filthy dinarli) – I was rightly deemed leader and voche of our bijou utopia, and dictated all glittering particulars and peculiarities down to the pogiest detail.

Possiblement my most prized nova fakement was the papier-mâché effigy of yours truly protruding from the frontage of the shoppe. A week before our Grand Opening, I'd requested Sabine and Lionel rummage round the knackers' yards of the East End to sniffle out a figurehead as closely resembling Marianne – Madame Liberty herself – as possible, ideally with both gargantuan breasts exposed and holding aloft a glimmering torch or tyrant's decapitated tet. When the zots returned after nobba hours with a horrifying rotting woodworm-riddled sea-hag, I decided instead to revamp the figurine in my own image, replacing her weather-battered eek with a pristine plaster-cast of my steely smouldering visage, adding a PVC liberty bonnet and silver bobbin nipplets, and then installing the bold cheet above our front portal, to entice all floundering thirsty poplos like an intoxicating roguish androgynous siren ...

In a similar vein I transformed my daitcha seamstresses to statuettes on our Opening Noche. Partly inspired by the Surrealists' daffy fixation on mannequins (Bellmer's mutant poupées, Léger's Donna with the Prefabricated Thumper, Masson's gagged plastic dame with the birdcage tet) but mostly to punish the twonks for playacting possum in the Bedford caboosh, I turned my lovelies into static waxworks for the evening. Joshing them up with identical pancake maquiage, carnish-coloured stockings and baldy skullcaps, I posed my dolls alongside my dog-eared tailor's dummies on podiums and in the front fenêtre, urging them to keep as still and tight-levered as possible throughout the festivities. Before adorning them with my fantabulosa nova creations (porcupine camishas, astro-kaftans, doggy muzzles, blasphemous transparent vestments, squid-beak mogue-baskets ...), the poor tarts looked like naggy Pierrots or post-nuclear geishas: blank ashy eeks, opals like frozen fobwatches. I savvied the petty darlings weren't molto impressed they'd been denied their share of bovaries and merriment once the first punters arrived and started tucking into the drip-drippering fountain of absinthe, but nevertheless they twitched not a jot, noble stiffs that they were. Cooing drunkenly in their nells, I promised there would be revelry later. Ô, there would be revelry!

Meanwhile, I made my own transformation.

Always mindful of The Grand Aim (to be loved every which way!), I'd shushed a tonne of the contraceptive-droga for my followers in anticipation of what I hoped would be a noche of unbridled lawlessness and lovemaking – only to savvy I was of course The Walking Contraceptive. Ô Christine, Ô Cupid – I clocked that my castration was now less of a crutch, more a licence to charver irresponsibly. I could stick that lonesome colin in any ovulating orifice that would accept it, with nix risk of impregnation whatsoever! And so, to celebrate this thundertwangling savagery, I contructed for myself a gigantic pink polystyrene Ortho-Novin dial-pack cozzy, with ogle-sockets betwixt the toppermost revolving pills and a bijou dispensing flap at the bottom, behind which my cartso twitched and twinkled coquettishly.

When the first arrivals ogled me in my kinky clamshell clobber, the reaction was mostly poked-up reering or confusion mixed with mild dread. I welcomed each guest with a complimentary blank paper drogle and the same lucid screech: 'Welcome to Never-Neverland, my chovis! Welcome to utopia! Please, leave your inhibitions in the gutter. Leave your naff gender-shackles behind you. Strip off your square, fusty uniforms and wriggle into these blank paper blouses pronto! Allez, allez. STRIP! SMILE! SCHLUMPH my flavourful sirop!'

I admit I may have been a petty bit forceful when it came to serving up glugfuls of the absinthe, and in fact ended up spiking the fountain with a pound of French Blues when (after only duey-daitcha minutas) I felt the atmosphere was somewhat frigid. I'd expected the boutique to be swarming with inquisitive, invigorating, indecorous teenyboppers the momento we unclickered the clef, but in reality we must've promoted the noche badly, or else the cockneys just weren't as swinging and open-minded as they all made out. The pogi lapperful of guests that were milling around seemed vaguely daffy but on the whole just as waxy as my mannequins, frowning at my meshigena haute couture, sipping from green flutes awkwardly on the sideylines, sniggering at nantwar.

Naturellement the lack of changing-chambers was intended as a healthy rejection of Vickyish prudishness and twisted self-consciousness – and so I was molto disheartened when I vadared a grupa of jolly fillies shyly struggling into their paper drogles behind a barricade of winter-mantos held aloft by their comrades. How did humanoids develop this innate fairyness when it came to exhibitionism? What made the cave-pops become suddenly poked-up about their natural bona danglies?

I rejuvenated the punch with another duey fistfuls of French Blues, then, after some patience, my guests were full-moony-ogled and fang-grinding fabulosa like beasties.

Leaving my stony mannequins to guard the bodega, I flipped the portal sign to FERMÉ, then shooed my most liveliest customers upways to the communal boudoir, savvying any passing sharpering-omi would molto likely not take kindly to the lurid floor show I had planned next. Following the civvies up the stairway in my ungainly pink cozzy, I felt terribly overilluminated, tittering to myself as my booties shambled clattery up the crooked piano-fangs. When finally I squeezed my jumbo polystyrene bod HUMPH! through the portal of the libbage, I was pleased to clock my guests in full voche, cackling and reering or else mumblering dozy to themselves with ultra-droggled manhole-opals. Plenty were already flopped on our freshly dhobied eiderdowns, tets full of revs but wired to the sparkles. Grinning sharklike, I minnied direct to the Dansette, unsheathed Mademoiselle Hardy's 'Le temps de l'amour' and spinnered it, forty-five revs.

'Le temps de l'amour' moves like a beautiful purrer sniffling out a dead fishy in the loonlight. As the bass and twang-striller slinked out of the speakers, I announced to the grupa: 'Are we all nicely lubricated and loosened, my cherries? Any stiffs still among us? Well, perhaps we can get even looser. Let us now indulge in some Surrealist emags – some games, that is. Regard your blank paper dresses.' I parkered each lapper a colourful stylus. 'Now, while the musica tickles and titillates your nells, I'd like you to screeve any cheet you fancy upon your neighbour's blank schmutta. Draw anything you like! Ze wilder ze better! Run thine imagination ragged!'

Having grown up with Freud, Breton, Bataille et al. cackled into my nellyholes, I like to believe I've got a bona grasp (stranglehold, even) on the humanoid subconscious. I've played Surrealist emags like this molto times before (Cadavre Exquis, lav-association, scatty séances, inky cut-ups, auto-scribble) with sea-queens, officers and lowlies alike, and the outcome is often the same: sooner or later some clever plop screeves a mucky picture. Chavvies favour caca – adults reach for jugs, quongs, colins and flanges. The Puerile Spasm!

Standing erect betwixt the boomboomering speakers, I gazed googly as the punters uncapped their styluses and went about vandalising each other's schmutta. Typically, to begin with some pops were eager to show off their bona draughtsmanship – carefully screeved kitties, lotus-fleurs, politico caricatures – but sure enough, before long some grinning zot splattered a gross cartso across the front of one of the palones' pristine drogles. She reacted like a belching insectoid had landed on her privates. Plenty of her comrades cried out in protest too, like this cartso wasn't just coddy low humour but an image unfit to be ogled by any right-minded upstanding civvy in the twentieth century. Like they hadn't enjoyed – or even just once dreamed up – a gross throbbering colin between their lallies at some point in their lavvies! Hypocrisy! Raised ogle-riders! Wagging index-luppers! Outrage at the natural dribblings and impulses of humanoids! AÎE!

I rapidly reasserted The Grand Aim: 'Let us not shrink this cock with any hypocritterish snobbery, my chovis – let it RISE UP!' I lifted my right lapper in what might've regrettably appeared to be a fash salute. 'In so-called norm society, we're constantly having to quash or fly-swat our desires, our fruity impulses – but these bona filthy impulses are more norm, more natural than the phony petty-bourgeoistard primness and prudishness most pops have drilled into them from birth.' I vadared in horror as one chappy tried to metamorph the gross pencil cartso into a delicate flutterbutter. 'HALT! ACHTUNG, you swine! Were you twonks brought up by monks? If the subconscious urges you to screeve throbbering cartsos or frothing flanges, do it pronto! If the unconscious wants you to strip naggy and charver like animals, be my guest! Do not hold back! Screeve whatever your groin desires! Act out these privvy desires! The laws of norm society neuter us. The laws of norm society make us neurotic. Tonight, let us be free! Let us be gay! Let us be merry! Now – on with the emag ...'

Spurred on by my heroic lavs (or just robotically following the grupa), my punters now went about gaily decorating their paper smocks with all manner of gruesome/handsome coddily screeved cunts and cocks, rendering the clobber frankly unsuitable for resale but maxi gildi and exciting in the opals of this particular fashionista.

'Allez, allez!' I cheered. 'Those of you who, like moi, were expecting a pogi bit more in the free-love stakes shall not vagary empty-lappered! We have befouled and deflowered this clobber beautifully! Now let us strip ourselves of these lusty disguises and befoul each other! Swap schmutta, rip these flimsy cozzies apart at ze seams, throw your slippies to the floor, Ô comrades.

Get loose! Get naggy! Go Dada! Let the musica guide you. Come on. Please. Allez ... allez ...'

No matter how droggled these pops were, the bats still seemed unwilling to parker off the last of their inhibitions. I cranked the volume and spun all my favourite arva-dripping yé-yé chants like 'Ça va je t'aime', 'Il court les filles', 'Ne fais pas la tête', but at best these flippering frigids acted like they were under the headmaster's ogle in their stuffy skol changing-chambers.

The odd daffy filly swapped drogles with her neighbour and the odd omi ripped his smock or flung it off altogether, but for the most part these humourless twonks just sat tittering into their absinthe-flutes or hoofered floppily with jaws doing the Twist.

After spinning 'Le temps de l'amour' for the fifth time, it was clear the orgy I was hoping for wasn't going to happen. I'd tried burning peepholes in the palones' cozzies with my Gauloises, playfully smothering omis' eeks with meths-drenched pillows and even exposed my missing quongs ('Love me liberally! For I am The Walking Contraceptive!'), but alas, this foreplay was fruitless.

Desperate now, I snuck up uppity up to the loft for una minuta, then raced back down down down to the boutique, where my disorderly mannequins were sprawled in a circle, schlumphing the leftover absinthe greedily with green haloes.

'ACTION STATIONS!' I squealed. 'My dearest darlings, you're required upstairs to assist with this mostest magnificent meshigena merrymaking ...'

Having been deprived of the noche's amusements thus far, my dollies were only too keen to play their part:

'YES!'

'Finally!'

'What do these larks entail, Raymond?' polled Bruce, straightening his skullcap.

'Well, nellyarda,' I frothed. 'The filthy twonks are currently embroiled in un GRAND SEXUAL SPECTACLE. They've been lammering and charvering fancy-free up there, it's been truly meshigena, but these are insatiable fuckers. They've demanded

I showcase my prowess as Ze Walking Contraceptive. Will you please assist me? All I need is your bare botties for a few minutas, max. These are insatiable fuckers, and nix mistake ...'

These being former strip-pops, I savvied my mannequins were at least familiar with scatty kinky requests like this, but when I oystered brightly at them the majority didn't seem quite so eager to hop to it. I added: 'For the sake of the Liberated Lavvy, we must do it! Show them what la vie d'avant-garde is all about! If they can't handle it, we'll eject them, sweep them from our PVC laminate forever. If they join in, well, perhaps we can add them to our throbbering ranks. So how about it? Oui? Nein?'

Daitcha frosty eeks ogled back at me.

'I savvy it's extreme,' I babbled, 'us comrades charvering for the first time in front of strange opals, but we must EMBRACE THE EXTREME! Don't regard this as exploitation – nanti that. These filthmongers are under the daffy impression they're wilder, molto free than us! PFFF! We'll show them! In fact THEY'RE the ones being exploited here. Regard ça. Cou-cou!' Grudgingly I unfurled a plump lapperful of pound notes shushed from my bulging valise. 'I rifled through their pockets in the heat of the arva-pile. Bend over for me, my sweet cherries, and the dinarli is all yours.'

Naturellement I hadn't wanted to stoop to bribery, but lo and by Jove the dinarli acted as a gildi cattle-prod. Rapidly the light returned to my mannequins' glassy opals, as though awe and respect were here anew. Clearly here was a superior omi, they ponced: a man of bona taste and ingenuity, capable of penetrating and pickpocketing simultaneous. An appendage in every posh!

As we mounted the steps, I refused to entertain my dolls' naff whispers in the munge: 'What is it we're doing?'/'Where are we going?'/'Raymond, we're on our periods' ...

'I love you all,' I polled before we trolled into the communal boudoir. 'Let's really go cuckoo, get into these pops' tets. You'll clock they've defiled their clobber with X-rated imagery. These are complex twats, make nix mistake. Insatiable fuckers. They'll probably act ultra nonplussed when we start our bijou sideshow, but we'll soon vada who's with-it and who's nanti. If they can't handle it, they don't deserve to be here. If you don't enjoy it, you don't belong here neither. Vagary back to the gutter for all I care! Allez, allez. Follow my lead, my cherries. Do as I squeak and we'll truly blow some servos. La Danse Macabre! La Danse des Dix Orifices! La Danse des Mannequins!'

I admit I was full-droggled by now, jaw swinging so much I thought my plastic surgery might split apart at the seams. How many French Blues had I schlumphed up to this juncture? Chinka-daitcha? Heksa-daitcha? UNA-CHENTA?

When I pushed my dollies into the charvering-chamber, their bod-lingo was wooden and lavvyless – Ô, they played the mannequin act to perfection! I stumbled in after them, gave my gigantic glowing dial a triumphant spin and screeched at the dozy punters: 'Bonsoir! ENCORE! ENCORE! And now for the main event, my chovis! You've come for a FREE LOVE FREAK-OUT, and so you shall have it!'

I lined my dollies up by the far wall, efinked their dazzling clobber, then plinked the Dansette needle on Monsieur Delibes's 'Coppélia'. As the greasy antique strings swarmed out of the speakers, I manipulated the zots' lallies, twisting my naggy comrades into all kinds of robotic/exotic poses before finally bending them over, baldy tets pressed to the PVC.

'Voilà!' I honked at my guests' captivated opals. 'Now gape in wonder at the right-honourable Mincing Contraceptive doing what he diddles best! Feel free to join in if you've still got the stamina, although I must stress: my dish is exit only, comrades.'

I gave my plastic dial another gay spin, lining the dispensing slot up with my glistening colin, which popped out eventually in spite of all the drogas. Inside my polystyrene shell, my bod was sparkling with sweat. The sight of these feeli flanges and pert corybunguses had an electro effect on my boomboomer, making me shudder and stutter like an epileptic Elvis as I approached my first victim – excusez-moi! – my FIRST LOVER!

Poncing backwards, possiblement I should've lined the pops up specifically to lose my virginity to my favourite, Sabine – however, the charvering-by-chance approach appealed to me too when I savvied I'd queued them up willy-nilly and wasn't yet well acquainted enough to tell them apart by genitals alone. She was in there somewhere – that was enough. I tug-tugged at my clammy cartso for added strength, then inserted into the first hortus – bolshy with riah like Karl Marx with a pink orchid betwixt his levers – and let out a pogi 'Groin-groin'.*

Immediately as I started thrusting, the punters in the obscene paper schmutta seemed to be cheering me on: a brootish gay hubble-bubble of muddled lavs, like the screeches from a bullring as the plucky matador plunges yet another (and another and another) lance into his beastie's bucking botty. I was in such rapture, the whole boudoir felt like a swirling bacchanalian merry-go-round – and yet, once I'd been up and down the line

---

* An uncomfortable read, this. Admittedly most of our previous releases have featured much filthier, more far-fetched sex scenes than this, but those books belong in the FICTION department. They have no pretentions to NON-FICTION, unlike Novak's.

We've brought this up before (see footnotes to 'Neptunus Rex') and, yet again, we feel the author must be taking extreme liberties with reality here. We consider ourselves more swinging and open-minded than most (peruse our back catalogue! Buy our books!), but are we expected to believe this inexperienced monster was capable of ravishing ten youths at once using just his charm, a garish lump of polystyrene and his questionable rhetoric? Could this just be one of Novak's childish wet revs writ large to boost his ego, to overcompensate for his emasculation by the headshrinkers? The Puerile Spasm??

Even so, as Emily worryingly pointed out to us, girls in the 1960s often felt grossly under pressure to bend to the new 'laws' of the Permissive Society, to offer themselves up as free sex objects rather than face rejection as squares: to conform to nonconformity. The Sixties' mot-à-la-mode was 'YES!' – but as we'll see, it's a word that can be quickly stripped of all positive connotations, leaving behind just a desperate, pleading, I'll-do-anything husk …

trey or quatra times (producing all manner of jus: sweat, sang, caca, parnyaqua), I clocked that some of the cheers weren't quite so supportive:

'This is disgusting!'

'Unlock this door!'

'LET US GO!'

These humourless cunts were like many self-styled libertarians: they love the idea of total freedom in theory, but in practice they'd only parny and howl for MORE LAW & ORDER if they woke tomorrow to the sweet arva- and aggro-heavy anarchy of a truly Unshackled Mond. They like their lawlessness in livers. In life they want comfort and security and gaols far more than absolute freedom – they just don't care to admit it.

'Ô, hearken this! Nelly these frigid petty eaglets!' I squawked, flapping my lappers at the horrified onlookers. 'These aren't free poplos! They're as conservative as the fuzzymuzz down the back of Bloody Mary's* bedstead!' As I babbled, my colin drooped a pogi bit until finally I was merely slapping it sloppily against my comrades' tense buttocks. 'There's all this jibber-jabber about utopia and free love these junos, but these newts can't handle freedom. Regard their squinty little eeks. It burns too brightly for them! It scorches their opals!'

'We said nothing about utopia,' a voche called out from the twisted rabble. The omi's eek was like a dolly overgrown bambino's topped with ludicrous dandy-curls, the likes of which I'd only ogled before in paintings of doomed eighteenth-century froggy toffs and prats. 'As far as I'm aware,' he went on, 'we only came for the free clobber, mister. In fact, "free clobber" was about the only words legible on the poster.'

I glared at the twonk through grimy arva-frazzled opals. 'It's monsieur to you, ducky, not mister.'

'O, you're a frog, are you?' Some of his neighbours found this

---

* Bloody Mary, Queen of Scots? The Virginal Maria? Or Bloody Mary Whitehouse?

to be exquisite humour, hootering snottish. 'Only you sound more like a plastic cockney to me ...'

'I'm less a froggy, more of a snail, garçon,' I snarled. 'Are you aware snails can change gender at will? They're the mostest swinging of all molluscs, baby.'

'Well, you're certainly a slimy creature, mister.'

More hurtful reering from these ungrateful addle-**p**lots. Ô, the batatats! I'd laid on a fantabulosa noche of entertainments for them, free of charge, free from sneering sharpering-eeks – and this was their coddy reactionary reaction! Some even had the audacity to arrive in Che berets and bolshy red sparkles! Clear enough these plops were beyond help. Squares and robos, the lot of them. I'd filled them up with culture, a**l**cool, drogas and love – and yet still it seemed they preferred the servo-draining, responsible patter of this joshed-up pansy imposter, from here onwards unlovingly rechristened the Interrupter.

'Slimy? Moi?' I howled before turning back to my contorted mannequins. 'My chovis, you don't find me slimy, do you? I'm the bestest cheet that ever chattered to you, isn't that right?'

Fattygay**e**d but ever loyal, my charvered chavvies panted forth a resounding: 'YES!'

The 'YES!' was so forceful one of the fenêtres crackled. YES!! My dollies were bona pops, my dollies were faithful, but still I had to ponder: was this through LOVE or FEAR? It mattered not. By the end of the year, the two would be more or less indistin-guis**h**able. Interchangeable!

INTERMISSION*

'Si on se conduit comme ceux d'en face, on est ceux d'en face.
Au lieu de changer le monde, on ne réussira que le reflet de celui qu'on veut détruire.'

JEAN GENET, DREAMING JAILBIRDY

* Chapter received Thursday, 30th April 1970 – seventy-four days to go. Epigraph scribbled in silver ink: 'If we behave like those on the other side, then we are the other side. Instead of changing the world, all we'll achieve is a reflection of the one we want to destroy.'

Care Label: Instructions for Reverse-Servo-Lathering

NOVAK WEARS A DAZZLING LAB COAT, TET-MIRROR, PLASTIC FAMBLERS.

NELLY FRANCE GALL'S 'N'ÉCOUTE PAS LES IDOLES' ('... ÉCOUTE-MOI!')

Sartre savvied it clear: HELL IS OTHER POPLOS. After the civvies' codswallop complaints on our Opening Noche, I clocked it might not be quite as easy to summon up instant all-jarrying anarcho-supercommunism in a bijou bodega in W1 as I'd originally hoped. These happenings were supposed to convert norm pops to the delights of la vie d'avant-garde, not turn them off. Of course the problem was norm pops' slavish behave-yourself drilling from birth. Norm pops much prefer the safety of mass conformity to the seductive sang-sparkling danger of an off-the-leash lavvystyle. Most Western humanoids – despite having been forced to scramble through a meshigena obstacle course of strict/sluggish parenting, sneering skol-whippering, endless testing, desperate dinarli-chasing, ugly ugly travails – would claim they're in full control of their lavvies, they ponce for themselves, they're free oinks. This is preposterous. They have in fact been servo-lathered from birth to accept Capitalist battyfanging, to lavvy obediently and politely at the expense of their true desires and gay impulses, to fear God, to fear sharpering-omis, gaols, to step in line, to conform or else suffer ze consequences!

BANKRUPTCY! EMBARRASSMENT! LONELINESS! NEUROSES!*

The way these squares probably see it, they're secure in Capitalism's grip, even if it smarts a pogi bit. Offer them what they really desire (free arva, unlimited drogas, wish fulfilment, the infinite funfair lavvystyle ...) and they get all poked-up, too frightened to catapult themselves into the sparkles lest they lose themselves along the way – themselves being ultimately their jobs, their tedious decorous personalities, the precious petty pointless fakements and trinkets in their multilocked latties ...

These newts were no longer welcome in my boutique. True enough my devoted dollies had also been brought up to accept the brain-rape and soul-sucking of norm paternalistic society, but at least they had experience underground, and were eager to rebel. They were loyal to me, and together we clocked the system for what it was: a steely-luppered stranglehold on our happiness, our health, our liberty. Twas my duty to protect them, to cleanse them, to reprogram them. I felt certain there had to be a molto

---

* True enough, the majority of Londoners in the Sixties were a lot more conservative and square than rags like *Time* and *Queen* made out, but, as Novak fails to point out here, the switched-on libertarian swingers had their fair share of neuroses too. Back in 1964, while Stanley was carefully drowning Emily's foetus in saltwater squirt by squirt, he felt devastated that the so-called carefree joys of the Permissive Society had put her in such a miserable situation. And her nerves – and womb – have never recovered.

Emily claims she remembers little of the attack that made her pregnant, only that she blames herself for drinking so much and dancing with a number of strange men at Hypnogogo before passing out and waking the next morning in a grubby, unfamiliar hotel room with intense pain and a crusty snail-trail of semen down her thighs. She couldn't bring herself to tell the police. The shame was too much, but not only that; the only description she could've given of her attacker made him seem like a phantom, like she'd been molested by a disembodied pair of gloved human hands.

'Were you on drugs?' Merritt asked her, airing out the office once the foetus's dismal chop suey had been securely knotted in two binbags and stashed away in his briefcase.

'I don't know,' she blubbed, eyes bubbling with sticky lava. 'The features keep blurring. All I really remember is his right hand. A big black leather glove covering my mouth while he ... did what he did.'

gloriosa free alternative future still available to me and my beautiful comrades, and by Jupiter if it took ice-picks to the servo to access it, so be it.

I maintain to this juno: I never meant to hurt any pop.

The end justifies the meanies.

I quarantined my dollies soon after the monstrous Valenti**ne**'s debacle. As solo descendant of Madame O, founder of the original vie d'avant-garde, I was to be The Guru. I was the only pop in the latty (probably in the whole of Londres) to be brought up truly amoral, uncensored, untethered, out of the grip of the eagles' incessant oppressive servo-lathering.

I'd ogled the fash bats' devilish methods up close in the Merch Navy and in the lappers of the Shrinker and his cronies – I savvied clear enough the depths to which they could sink to get into pops' tets. Twas my duty to reverse this servo-lathering. Against my fan**t**omscreever's advice, I am including my methods here for all to ogle, in case you wish to start up your own fantabulo**s**a love-cult and spread my ultra-sane teachings hither-th**i**ther across your local community:

INSTRUCTIONS FOR REVERSING THE MOD MOND'S CODDY SERVO-LATHERING

1. As France Gall chants: 'N'écoute pas les idoles'. Beware of false prophets and false profiteers. Before one can embark on the ultimate Liberated Lavvy, one must gather up al**l** plastic idols and gross authority-flops – Jesus, Buddha, Stalin, Lennon, bosses, royals, sharpering-omis, politicos, headshrinkers, drones, robos – hurl them on the bon**f**ire and refocus one's nells and opals on the one and only guru on this coddy festering welt who seems to splurt any sense: myself.
2. Continually stress the disparity between US and THEM. WE are free humanoids, free lovedrunk feelies hellbent on enjoying our lavvies on this thoroughly meshigena,

punishing rock. THEY are cold cruel calculating fash eagle-eeks, determined to limit our enjoyments with their scatty fear-mongering and naff ultra-conservative rule-making.

3. BLAME BLAME BLAME. Pops love to have someone to blame for their own shortcomings,* therefore your delicate/defensive/desperate devotees will nix doubt be molto receptive to this aggressive US and THEM palavering. It must be drilled into them CONTINUALLY.
4. ISOLATE/INSULATE YOUR DOLLIES. The main problem with Capitalism and its eagle-eek enforcers is the beastie's masquerade as the one and only norm way of lavvying. Westernoid humanoids have been conditioned to accept this catastrophe of pollution, costly dinarli, thought-shackles, drudgery and humiliation. In fact, most civvies have been so thoroughly servo-lathered they tend to regard any pop who refuses to bend to these laws they gaily/grudgingly bend to daily as daffy, wrong, wastrels to be mocked and stamped out. How can you trust these robos? It is imperative therefore to prohibit any interaction between your beautiful followers and the eagles and drones outside.

---

* This paragraph reminded Trefoil of a dismal luncheon he once endured with his Director, during which Merritt drunkenly accused his staff (behind our backs) of being inept and wholly responsible for his failing business. He highlighted our 1967 release *Heart Massage Parlour* (one of many novels written pseudonymously by Merritt) as a case in point, citing its repellent cover, its lily-livered marketing campaign and Howling's three-week vacation in North Africa as reasons for its lack of success (completely ignoring the childishness of the prose, the cardboard cut-out characters, not least the ridiculous premise involving a heart surgeon reviving the inhabitants of a graveyard who all happen to be muscular homosexuals). While this conversation was never brought up again (and this footnote, too, was never intended to be published, buried in a neglected diary), Trefoil thinks of it often when the stress at work builds – like this Monday, for instance, finding himself caught in the crossfire of Merritt and Davy's creative differences, as the two debated the cover art for Novak's memoirs:

'It's an asterisk,' Davy protested. 'Simple. Sleek. Effective.'

'It's an outrage! It won't sell! It looks like a great puckered black arsehole, Mark!'

Exposure to these twonks can cause rapid relapse back to coddy robotic ways of lavvy**i**ng and poncing.

5. EXERCISE UNO (GRUPA PRESERVATION):
Without doubt the Western Welt is a CATEVA DYSTOPIA, and yet to begi**n** with many of your grupa will grumble if they're refused access to it. They may even regard you as a gaoler if you don't first use your initiative to pass the blame onto THEM out thataways. BLAME BLAME BLAME. Fortunately I already had control of the press. The only **i**nky allowed in our boutique was my daily doctored copy of RayMond and, with it being screeved in frog lingo, I was free to translate the screamlines however I pleased. The Gross Vietnam War was a regular fixture in the rag: possiblement the Ame**r**ikk**a**n eagles' most blatant tyrannical battyfangery to date. On the first juno of spring I drew my devotees' attention to a grisly foto of some arroganki napalm ejaculation in the jungle. 'The Johnson is sending more troopers in,' I polled, squinting twist**e**d at the lavs. 'Zut! Says here Harold's caved in – MERZ! – he's agreed to send anglo back-up. Lynda's promised to prop up the pound. I quote: "In spite of mass opposition to the barny among the public, rosbif armed forces will be deployed immediately, with Prime Minister Wilson set to reintroduce conscription as early as next week ..."' My dollies' fizzers were frigid with fright. 'Ô, mon Dieu!' I wept crocky parnyaqua. 'We'll perish if they parker us off to 'Nam! Imagine it – we're not cut out for warfare; we swerved our natty service, we've had nanti basic traini**n**g. They'll use weirdies, beatniks, passive-aggro-bats like us as cannon fodder! We'll be the kamikaze-pops: they'll send us into the jungle masquerading as lost minnying hippies, rucksacks full of napalm jelly triggered by Yankee satellites, suicide bomb-plops. Vada: says here there'll be mass surveillance on our strasses, undercover agents snuffling out draft dodgers and sending us direct to the front line! What to do, Ô comrades? Must we lay lowly, avoid all contact with

the pops outside – or else shall I lovingly injure you, disable you, render you thoroughly unfit for service?' By the end of my doomy pal**a**vering, my devotees were only too willing to stay indoors, lay low, shun the rotten welt out thataways.

6. Reprogramming can begin in earnest once your comrades are safely sheltered away from probing wrong-screeching eagle beaks. I closed the boutique indefinitely. Tugged down the shutters. Barred the fenêtres. Nanti radio, nada Vada-Vision. Unpluckered the polari-pipe. I vagaried from the latty only to stock up on essentials: tinned munja, drogas, the Daily RayMond. PREPARE AS IF PREPARING FOR A NUCLEAR BLAST. Minds will be blown.
7. Enforce strict rationing and routines. Sleep to be restric**t**ed to trey hours per noche, taken in rotating grupas of duey. Pops are more receptive to lavvy-changing slogans and manifestos when their servos are addled, their senses are shot. Amphetamines are a bona substitute for fresh munja, mortifying the appetite. Once full receptivity is achieved, cleansing can begi**n** ...
8. EXERCISE DUEY (BLANKWASH THE PAST):
   To establish maxi equality and emancipate my dolls from their guttery past lavvystrangles, twas imperative to full-dhobi the beautiful bastards' crippled interiors and exteriors and begin afresh. These former sex-grinders were used to stripper**i**ng naggy, and so I urged them to undertake UNO FINAL STRIP: to shed their daffy joggering-noms, efink all family tangles, wipe their memory banks, obliterate their egomaniacaca and be reborn free poplos!
   a. DEMOLISH THE ANGLO LINGO. Disgusting mongrel lingo! Teach your followers Polari at once – or invent your own specjalni privvy lingo. What better way to insulate yourself from the outside mond than by communicating with lavs the eagles are incapable of comprehending. The batatats might bug your latty, but they shall never shush your secrets!

b. FLUSH YOUR PAST LAVVY DOWN THE OUBLIETTE. Prohibit your followers from prattling about any exploits experienced prior to JUNO UNO: the Grand Wide-Opening of your nova bona utopia. Remove all remnants and reminders of this meese forbidden period: family fotos, birth-scrolls, religious fakements, tattoos, groinage, birth-noms, joggering-noms, dinarli ...
c. REVAMP YOUR DOLLIES. In the eighteenth century toffs wore excessive blank maquiage to illustrate that they lived a lavvy of leisure, they had not toiled under the sol's rays, they were pure unsullied poplos. Likewise: to ensure full equality and symmetry among your followers, fatcha every last wisp of their riah, slather with ultrablank pancake, streamline with bleached leotards and bodstockings. Adorn tets with matching shykas: brown beehives, French Crops, liberty bonnets, insectoid antennae – or just leave your beloved baldy zots au naturelle. Enliven bods with an ever-changing array of mond-shaking outré couture.

9. 'All you need is love,' I proclaimed in April 1966, beating The Bastards to this morso of wisdom by almost daitcha-chinka months. REWARD BONA BOLSHY BEHAVIOUR. Oversaturate your followers with love. There is too much hatred on this coddy welt. Be maxi creative: there are nobba hungry orifices upon every humanoid bod. Sharper for as-yet-unnamed erogenous nodules. Keep your followers entertained with a never-ending supply of fantabulosa no-holds-barred horseplay. This is not exploitation. We are not objects – nanti that. We are one beautiful multifaceted mass of like-minded angels. VISUALISE: daitcha glossy bods cuddled up like naggy mole rats round their noble throbbering generous queen.
10. Cleanliness has never been a gross issue for me, but I recommend compiling a handy Stool & Menstrual Chart your dollies must fill out daily, to ensure there is nanti manky

obstacle in either hole prior to intercourse. The bidet, also, is yet another froggy invention of unsurpassed ingenuity.

11. NEVER FORGET: you are THE SUN KING, you are THE SCUM KING. Squares and paranoiacs out thataways might ponder: why trust this particular cockney-froggy o**mi**-**p**alone above any other plastic-eeked idol? The answer is simple: establish yourself as solo heroic provider for the grupa and your dolls should never have any reason to vagary off elsewhere ever. Yet another rule of our otherwise entirely lawless utopia: I alone am allowed to vagary from the boutique. I alone am the dolls' hunter-shusher of munja and goodies. I am Pop. I am Dada. Make it clear: they will perish without you.
12. FINALLY: NOURISH THEM WITH PUNISHMENT (and by THEM, I of course mean US). While any bona utopia should be based on MULTILOVE, HARMONY and NON-VIOLENCE, it's important not to let your followers take the piss. Once you've drilled the laws of the Liberated Lavvy into your comrades (a lavvy of ABSOLUTE FREEDOM – free munja, free education, free entertainments, free bovaries, free clobber, free leisuretime, free love – albeit undertaken behind locked portals), if they can't handle the heady reality of this mostest gloriosa lavvystyle, they need to step in line rapid**l**y or else FUCK-OFF-THATAWAYS. I am not a dicktittler – I am simply a set of gleaming false pearls palavering sense. Disregard my teachings at your peril! I am not here to nelly criticism – either you accept my lavs and my love with an open boomboomer, or you are a drone and belong OUTSIDE, carrion for the eagle-eeks. WE are in this TOGETHER! But how – I hear thee screech – should one deal with petty infractions, mini misdemeanours among your jolly rabble? Under nix circumstances should your grand palace resemble the fuckering Bastille, but one certainly ought to retain a pogi space to isolate wrongdoers. Fortuitously Lionel was a relatively adept electro-fiddler, and so twas not difficult to convert the bijou storeroom ajax to our boudoir into the

de-luxe brig we now call THE BLANK CHAMBER. Decked out full-whitewashed and empty with duey opal-frying fluoro-strobes and continuously churnering white noise, the cubbyhole is a fine environment to quell any needless outbursts of self-centredness or dissent. Trey or quatra hours in the sickly flickering rimbumbling Blank Chamber and I find any pop comes out molto willing to rejoin the grupa with maxi commitment. A screeved apology and submission to some welcome-back servo-straightening arva and all is forgiven, the dissenter is cleansed, purged and can be loved again – and again and again and again and again ...

OUI: this was living. This was utopia.

By the summer of 1966 I had full control of my comrades. The Yé-Yé Dolls was an apt nom for the grupa given they now said 'YES!' to practically any daffy cheet I screeched. We spent our junos schlumphing down gloriosa froggy culture, conjuring nova outlandish clobber for ourselves and ourselves only, charvering freely, chanting, cod-oystering eagles, dabbling in Surrealist emags, punishing wrongprattling, slurping from the absinthe fountain, glugging French Blues ...

From my vantage point it was fantabulosa having these fortuni specimens all to myself. Our disastrous Opening Noche had proven beyond all doubt the anglo general poplos are hopeless complainers,* hypocritters, reactionary fuzzymuzz not to be mingled with. I did not want to share my toys.

---

* With Audrey missing, the pile of unanswered complaints on her desk quickly spilled onto the floor. Out of curiosity we opened a few, and regretted it.

It was always our hope that *The Nuremberg Nymphos* might surpass its predecessor, *Pink Baton*, but the only area in which this was instantly apparent was its almost unanimous unpopularity. *Pink Baton* was savaged by critics, true enough, but Dennis's nymphettes were subjected to such a frightening deluge of bile and hatred, if we were to compile the letters in a published volume, the book would be our most profanity-filled release to date, by some margin.

Huddled in a protective arc around the manila mania of Audrey's desk, we read out some of the more pleasant (or at least repeatable/publishable) responses:

However, ALAS and ALACKACACA, this bona period wasn't to last. As the pluplus**h**es stripped themselves naggy and summer crackled into autumn, we had some nova gripes to contend with. Duey twisted scenarios changed everything.

Despite me filling them with all I had - l'amour, l'anarchie, l'art et l'anxiété - my dollies near enough made my nells bleed uno Septembre noche when they palavered in unison: 'We're bored, Raymond. We're just utterly bored!'

And André Breton died. And And And And And André Breton died.

'Utterly disgraceful. The author deserves a sharpened swastika shoved up *his* anus, and twisted!'

'Please let me know when Mr Mesh will next perform his work to an audience as I would like to be present, with a chainsaw, to inflict the same damage on his body as he inflicted on my brain this afternoon.'

'Dennis Mesh is a cunt.' (This last notelet attached to a cocktail stick standing precariously in a Tupperware tub of liquid faeces.)

The most disturbing package, however, was not related at all to our most recent release. This was a brown cardboard box about the size of a loaf of bread, with a postmark dated 14th April 1970, Mount Pleasant. We carefully sliced open the Sellotape with spread-eagled scissors. Inside was another brown paper parcel tied up with string. By now we recognised Novak's (or his fantomscreever's?) loopy handwriting, and when we read POUSSIN AVEC EELS - GROSSES BISOUS! across the front, we presumed this was another of his unique Continental culinary offerings. The aroma certainly knocked us sideways as we unknotted the twine. This time it was decomposing flesh rather than tangy garlic that hit our nostrils. Difficult to recall if any of us audibly screamed or gagged when we saw inside, but certainly Trefoil, McKinley and Emily leapt for opposite corners of the office as if a dirty bomb had detonated. Merritt dropped the package. A small sausage rolled out across the parquet, with five tiny fingers attached.

PART V

THE MOOD SWINGS

'Of all the cants which are canted in this canting world – though the cant of hypocrites may be worst – the cant of criticism is the most tormenting!'

'Tâchez d'être vides et de remplir vos cellules cérébrales au petit bonheur.
Détruisez toujours ce que vous avez en vous.'

TRISTAN TZANDI*

* Tristan Tzara? Tristram Shandy? Epigraphs painstakingly copied out with elaborate squid ink calligraphy. (Translation: 'Try to be empty and fill your brain cells haphazardly. Always destroy what you have in you.')

Loose Threads*

IN MOURNING, NOVAK WEARS BLACK PAPAL REGALIA: VELVET VESTMENTS, TRIPLE-CAROON, SCREAMING BACON EEK.

NELLY STÉPHANE VARÈGUES' 'LE PAPE DU POP'.

The Pope was dead. No matter how vigorously I doctored that morning's RayMond (eventually fatcharing it to morsos with my fangs and luppernails, and sculpting it soggily into a papier-mâché bust of the bona pop), I couldn't bring Monsieur Breton back to life again.

Difficult to say what distressed me more: Breton's mortification,† or my dolls blurting out how bored they were by my bold

---

* Chapter received Tuesday, 5th May 1970 – sixty-nine days to go.

† Despite his best efforts, we were unmoved by Novak's grief here – in fact, we have removed a long, gushing eulogy for Breton from this chapter, to spite the bastard. How dare he claim to have respect for the dead in one parcel and send us a rotting, disfigured foetus in another!

One might imagine Merritt had been conditioned to cope with this horrific delivery better than the rest of us, but arguably he took it worst of all. Possibly this was down to the development of the baby: eighteen weeks, he estimated (twelve weeks had always been Merritt's cut-off point for terminations, and even then he was convinced the little beings could feel pain, panic, desperation). Or was it that Stan felt singled out, like Novak had sent this grisly gift as some sort of provocation or warning, a signal that he knew about Merritt's backstreet past? Why else would the evil swine send it? By his own admission Novak was a 'meese meshigena-omi', but this felt more like calculated cruelty than mindless lunacy. Was this some twisted form of blackmail? Had Novak researched his publishers' backstories, hoping to unearth past misdemeanours

nova regime. Breton was like a surrogate papapapa to me, the Mare having honked his lavs into my nells repeatedly through my feeli years, although of course he never reefed me direct. Meanwhile my dollies were my bambinos – not sang relatives either per se, but it hurt terribly nellying them complaining about the fantabulosa Shangri-La I'd sweated juno upon juno to set up for them.

Still, once my projectile parnyaqua finally let up, I savvied perhaps the petty zots had a point. I'd been so obsessed with keeping my devotees safe from the outside mond's meddling tentacles, I'd failed to clock that the utopia I'd created was just a bland, sterile utopia. A hermetically sealed toybox. MERZ!

'We just want to meet new people, Lord, ogle some nova eeks,' was the long and short of my dollies' argument.

The poor prats weren't content to fester in paradise – they wanted to mingle once more with the blundering mongrels out thataways. I thenched of my mother: 'What wouldst do the Old Zelda? What would André Breton do?'

I savvied clear enough: I had to wrench the magick baton from His Holiness's rigor-mortissed fist and waft it more fiercely than ever! Take la vie d'avant-garde back out onto the strasses. While I could not rightly see what benefit my dolls might gain from rubbing pols with the meese gurning Hogarthian plebs outside, it did occasionally nag my servo, knowing we were powerless to revamp and reinvent this dismal, sputtering, ultra-needy welt if we insisted on hiding behind barred fenêtres the rest of our petty utopian lavvies. Clear enough, some locks needed to be uncleffed. Some light needed to be let in. The mond was doomed without us.

---

he could use against us should we ever be tempted to report his felonies to the fuzz? Perhaps this was what attracted him to the Glass Eye Press more than any other publisher. In our own way, we were guilty of fantabulosa crimes too. Maybe sending us this POUSSIN AVEC EELS was a most abhorrent nod and a wink, a sick extension of Raymond's US and THEM palavering.

Perhaps he was saying: WE are all in this TOGETHER.

I immediately set to work on a nova range of schmutta: sandwich-board A-line minidrogles emblazoned with Papa Breton's mostest servo-tickling quotes:

IT IS NOT THE FEAR OF MADNESS THAT WILL OBLIGE US
TO LEAVE THE FLAG OF IMAGINATION FURLED
BEAUTY WILL BE CONVULSIVE!
THE MAN WHO CANNOT VISUALISE A HORSE GALLOPING
UPON A TOMATO IS AN IDIOT

Late one noche, twirling in front of the mirror in an enormous regal robe twinkling with the entire text of Breton's L'AMOUR FOU, I fantasised for uno momento that the heroic omi was in fact my bona fide father. It wasn't completely out of the realm of possibility: my Mare claimed she'd bedded countless Surrealists between the Roaring Twenties and the Sieg-Heiling Forties. I certainly felt I had delicious dege**n**erate sang surging through my bod. I too possessed a genius servo.

'Do I look like the bastard child of the Pope of Surrealism to you?' I asked Priscilla, clutching her under her eiderdown some hours later. Her lappers were like crayfish pincers: pink, gnarled and swollen after handstitching the vast text upon my gildi gown.

'Oui, Raymond. Oui, oui,' she polled through clenched pearls: by now the stock response to all my impossible queries.

'Bona dolly,' I purred, squeezing her tighter – until she squeaked.

I reopened the boutique on Monday, 3rd Octobre, duey junos after my papapa's funeral.* Unlike before, I refused to publicise our Grand Reopening, instead leaving it to pure unslurried CHANCE to coax snappy recept**i**ve customers through our portals. I envisioned a mob of beautiful hungry feelies marching like droggled ants across Londres, attracted by my queenly von or

---

* Though we presume the fool wasn't invited.

the grubby pulsations of the Post Office Colin – and yet, ALACK-O-JUNO, for the most part we just found ourselves playing host to dull mid-age blokes in macs. Twas not the opal-spinning schmutta or Surrealist slogans that enticed them, but the donnas in the fenêtres. Chaps often swung by the boutique after their travails to marvel at these fortuni specimens, these gildi pristine arva-objects that, for them, said more with uno naggy thew than all the inky lavs of Monsieur Breton put together!

'How much for that bootiful coatstand there?' one slimy omi enquired one noche, nodding at my dear Sabine postured like Madame Liberty in a chartreuse-green toga and flick-knife caroon. 'If I take her home and I'm not completely satisfied, can I get a full refund? Haw!'

'Ô monsieur, halt this coddy objectification pronto, please!' I howled, gripping his pol with a piranha-lapper.

'Objectification?' the omi objected. 'You're the one standing them up there like bleeding mannequins.'

'Bleeding mannequins? Regard the Menstrual Chart, squire. This particular model is not set to do any bleeding til Tuesday week at the earliest,' I may or may not have responded. 'Please ogle her as a work of art, not a platter of submissive carnish. Are you going to buy that cravat?'

And so on and so forth.

Did these petty momentos of drab flirtation from outsiders please my poor civvy-starved darlings? Did the illusion of interaction give them any satisfaction at all? Probably not. When they announced they wanted to meet nova poplos and ogle nova eeks, my ego was hurt somewhat, but then I savvied surely they weren't interested in cavorting with other omis, given they'd already been thoroughly charvered throughout their young lavvies and were now treated to the finest overflowing love gushes imaginable aboard this coddy hostile welt! I just had to remember: these were ultra-feeli pops I was dealing with. Most of them were barely out of their teens. The donnas were like bijou kitties: they still had the curiosity to explore our grand strasses-to-nowhere, our caca-riddled parks, our playgrounds. They splurted parnyaqua almost daily, made meshigena claims about feeling 'trapped' – hormones, nix doubt. They were not yet sick of the city concrete, like moi.

So what to do? Chance, as usual, led the way. I was sharpering for a nova bona mission to retest my dollies' loyalty and let them slurp a pogi bit of fresh aero into their bods, when this fabulosa baffling notelet appeared on our doormat:

DEAR SIR/MADAM,

WE DON'T KNOW WHAT SORT OF ESTABLISHMENT YOU ARE RUNNING HERE BUT CAN YOU PLEASE REFRAIN FROM DUMPING YOUR ROTTEN FISH IN OUR BACK PASSAGE FROM NOW ON.

YOURS,
NO. 49

Gloriosa correspondence! Ô, how we reered. We knew nantwar of any rotten fishies, nor the dumping thereof – but naturellement I reacted to this memo the way any sane pop should: by immediately acquiring kenza pounds of gurnard tets from Billingsgate and sending my dollies out in search of this molto presumptuous, mysterious 'No. 49'.

As it fell out, nix 49 existed on our strasse, and so my plucky puppets were ordered to search out every quarante-neuf within a mile radius and plop said fishy tets through each letterbox with a polari-bubble attached that shrieked 'BOF!' or 'BURP!' or 'OINK!'

My popsies positively delighted in this daffy Surrealist exercise – and so I conjured up more and more meshigena missions to keep them occupied as 1967 creaked open its petty petals. It seemed the more ludicrous and longwinded the mission, the happier my devotees were on their return. Mostly the emags were intended to nag the servos of selected squares, to ruffle the eagles' feathers by privvily disrupting their precious daily routines – or simply just to tire out my more stroppy, grumbling underlings. POR EXAMPLE: regularly I'd send Lionel out to stalk local fencers and corporate-omis, snap-snappering secret fotos of them as they trolled round Fitzrovia, which would then be efinked-and-pasted into marvellous Exquisite Corpse collages (intersplattered with dogs' bods, horsey pearls, cloven hooves, Hoovers, creamy cartso-tips and nipplets) and posted anon to their bosses with scatty anti-boss-man slogans attached. On specjalni occasions I'd send my lovelies out to the nova motorways, to shush and mesh* together a nobba-beastie roast using whatever roadkill they could safely scrape from the asphalte. I entered Bonnie, Veronica, Bruce and von Fisty in a race up the staircase of the Post Office Colin, joshed as trey-lallied, doppel-headed spermatozoomers. (Bonnie vomited at the twenty-ninth floor.)

As 1967 heated up, my dollies took over as chief hunter-shushers for our commune. I kept sending them out to sharper for ever more obscure cheets – giant snails, rare Yé-Yé LPs, Afrikkkan masks, quacks' prescription pads – in the hope that they'd be so distracted by the goosechase, they'd have nanti time nor inclination to mingle with prowling eagles or male predators out thataways. Mostly their forages were a success (since failure resulted in uno hour or duey in the Blank

---

* We were so preoccupied with the ghastly POUSSIN AVEC EELS, we almost forgot about Dennis. Diligent publishers that we were, once Merritt had disposed of the foetus (carrying it away in his briefcase, then dissolving it in a steaming bucket of lye in his bathroom), we carefully collected the reams of death threats aimed at Mr Mesh to pass on to the police. Perhaps we should've warned Dennis of the impact his newest novel was having on the general public, but writers are sensitive fleurs. If Dennis was soused and morose after our overindulgent platitudes at his own launch party, how would he react to this snarling cesspit of venom? Best to keep him in the dark, we felt. As far as Dennis was concerned, *The Nuremberg Nymphos* was just another overlooked masterpiece, a lost classic. He could take the lack of press interest as philistinism and continue typing up his next grotesque opus without the barbs of literary criticism prickling him, blissfully unaware that his minuscule readership despised him, blissfully unaware that we would never publish anything of his again.

Chamber) – however, occasionally my bambinos came home with some ultra-unwelcome alternatives.

Bruce and Lionel were struck down with a vile creative bug in the spring of '67. They'd shushed a Hindi-striller and bongos from some far-out temple and – entirely at odds with my ego-obliteration savagery – took to calling themselves Sage & Onion, a 'meditational psych-folk duo' or somesuch. PFFF! Ragas were all the rage round that time – all the anglo rock-sparkles were tuning out cross-lallied with sitars and dulcimers and tablas and the like: a kind of colonic arrogank that made me want to garrotte the cloying batatats with their marigold garlands. The rock-sparkles' schmutta had become maxi grotesque in recent months – floppy hats, wizards' gowns, grandmama's nighties, nosegays, flared lally-covers, Foolish drag – and it sent a quiver through my spinal jus imagining these twats mincing into the Hindi jungle, shushing the natives' strillers and showing the uncultured wogs how to score a hit single.

On an unseasonably sweaty Avril noche, Sage & Onion declared they were going to enlighten the rest of us with what they nell-grindingly referred to as a 'cosmic shindig'. Unsure at first how to sabotage this beastly jamboree without causing more parnyaqua and petulance, I snuck outways for the evening, lelling the last botty of Ricard and slamming the portal with enough venom to let the zots know I was nicht amused.

Seething, I stomped down Goodge Strasse and through the cool marble gargler of the Ministry of Truth, all the while pondering how bestest to upstage – and ultimately ferricadooz – Sage & Onion's daffy transcendental arrogank on my return. I savvied possiblement the prats had become a pogi bit too comfortable in their roles as my exclusive right-hand omi-palones – and so they needed some competition post-haste. An arva-rival. A butch bristly manly-alice to keep them on their toes, to keep them on their lally-caps ...

Swigging aggressively from the pastis botty, I felt what might prickle them worstest of all would be if I snared the most meese, overweight, oink-eeked rough trade I could find, and brought the pleb back to Never-Neverland to sodomise brootishly on the dancefloor while the zots played out their mystical ragas. Savvying N7 had a reputation for strapping labourers, impoverished Irish, squalor and khazis aplenty, I took the chugger direct to Holloway Road – the lav 'Holloway' itself tantalisingly accommodating a stiff cartso betwixt the 'H' and 'way'. And yet – ALAS/ALACK – when I peeked my eek into the pissoir ajax to the station, there was not a proletariat sausage nor overalled botty in ogleshot. Nor was there even a solo piddling winkle when I minnied down the strasse to the usually bustling brandy-latch by Madras Place and squinted inways. Ô, BOF and BUGGER ME SIDEYWAYS.

I decided not to linger in case the local omi-palones knew something I didn't and Holloway was privvily crawling with plainclothes sharpering-pops* this noche. Whisking my L'AMOUR FOU gown debonairly round my greasy bod, I plodded onwards, heading vaguely for the cottage in Highbury Fields – although

---

* Before Audrey's desk was completely cleared and disinfected, there was one last death threat to take care of. A death threat we would write.

While passing Dennis's mound of hatemail on to the fuzz relieved us of any blame (or at least guilt/shame/remorse) should he wind up having a sharpened swastika shoved up his anus and twisted, panic rose at the Glass Eye HQ when we realised the police might wish to search our premises again for other potentially hazardous material. Wary of the incriminating contents of Novak's novel (not to mention the growing stack of incriminating footnotes), Trefoil sent Emily a rapid memo on the morning of Wednesday, 6th May: 'N's m/s at risk of confiscation by s-pops? Pls facsimile/type duplicate at once!'

We were aware of course that the police would be on our backs anyway as soon as the expected chain of events (Novak's fantabulosa crime, immediately followed by our publication of the bat's confessional memoirs) led them straight to our doorstep. Dreading the worst-case ramifications of us having withheld this glaring, startling evidence from the authorities from the off, we felt it necessary to doctor a letter from the Emperor, a get-out-of-jail-free card as it were, to help vindicate us should Raymond's crime prove to be unspeakably, unforgivably horrific (and, given his recent gifts of a decapitated head and dismembered foetus, it was reasonable to assume, yes, there would be blood).

We typed:

by this juncture I was not holding out much hope of finding the flabby low-grade corybungus I was hankering for.

As I neared the Tube at Highbury Corner, I savvied I might just chugger back to ze West End and take my anger out on some dolly pin-cushion Dilly-chavvy for chinka beyongs or so – when all at once a mysterious portal caught my opal ajax to the autobus-stop, emblazoned with those magickal numerals: 49! A black leather fambler was nailed above the letterbox. A meese unidentif**i**able sludge was spattered across the lower half of the panel.

Naturellement I schonked the buzzer without delay.

The portal opened with a shuddery WHIN! SHTUCK! and I slipped inways. On first blink, twas not the mostest homeliest

---

Never-Neverland, W1
9th November 1969

Dear Sir/Madam,

Greetings and molto grateful salutations! My boomboomer inflated when I clocked your petite handlebar moustache in ye INTERNATIONAL TIMES, and thus, as promised, I hereby enclose the opening morsos of my most specjalni memoirs. Be brave. If at first you find my lavs cause you to parny, vomit or spontaneously glimmer while reading, I trust you will still find plenty to admire!

May I also take this opportunity to politely threaten you: if you screech my nom or show any morso of my glistening liver to the sharpering-pops (the police, that is), I will unleash a reign of terror on your bods and your families' bods that will leave you looking like regurgitated beef bourguignon pronto.

Kind regards,
Raymond Marianne Novak.

We felt we captured Novak's tone well – and yet there was one snag with this forged communication. While we'd managed to find a typewriter that closely matched Novak's omi-jarrying lav-hammer (Trefoil's old Imperial 'Good Companion'), when compared side by side with the original m/s, clearly our note did not come from the same machine. Under close scrutiny, we noticed some irregularities in Novak's lettering: the occasional emboldened character appearing unexpectedly mid-sentence, a partially clogged 'O' and, most distinctively, the lower-case 'i' seemed to have suffered damage to its tittle, causing the dots to look like tiny waning crescent moons.

establishment. Reefing my way down a long ultraschvartz corridor, I eventually came to a bijou foggy booth twinkling with petty blue lights, inside which a jackal-eeked omi with a pencil mouser sat vogueing listlessly.

'Are you a member?' he croaked.

How to respond? In scenarios such as this, I find it nattiest to just blurt the first snappy morso that enters your servo – and to screech it with gusto. Recalling the black fambler tacked to the portal, I honked: 'I am a close comrade of Die Lederhand.'

To my utter titillation and brooliment, the omi punched a button betwixt his thews, and a pair of privvy doppel-doors creaked open behind my palliass.

'Enjoy,' he grumbled as I scuttled into the void.

Quite possibly I could've squeaked any old daffy lav at the twonk and he would've granted me passage – but nevertheless I was feeling molto puffed-up and sparkly now as I minnied my way through the munge and into a deep, steeply raked auditorium. Immediately I clocked that this was not going to be Sunday Noche at the Londres Palladium. Framed by a grubby red proscenium arch, the stage was cluttered with chains, cages, bondage fakements, flogging-vacayas, torture-cheets. A variety of leather harnesses and nooses dangled from the rafters. Duey gross rabbit hutches stood upstage left, carpeted with gloopy sawdust. Bod-fluids gathered in pools hither-thither.

Taking a seat on the back row, I could just about vada the silhouettes of other punters in the munge: derby-hatted fantoms slouched with greatcoat collars upturned, in spite of the stuffy aero. The pops were dispersed solo around the auditorium, which suggested some pokiness or meese secrecy – however, when the first act hobbled upon the stage, the omis positively erupted, slapping their lappers together and howling giddy obscene encouragements.

As far as I could ogle, the main thrust of this opening sketch involved a miserable omi in a kilt and diving-helmet burying his wife and daughter alive in a petty jardin of carnish-jarrying fleurs. Twas difficult to finger any overarching moral or storyline to the noche's curious entertainments, but each skit was met with increasingly brootish hoots and gay yelps from the spectators. Sinking further and further into my vonny faux-velvet cushion, I ogled a jolly teen barky nailed to an Iron Cross and spinnered forty-five revs; an albino introduced as 'The Human Latrine', forced to kneel with his oyster agape while all manner of unsavoury corporate-omis appeared from backstage to use his facilities; a grupa of nuns smashing their Bibbles over a gutter-chavvy's bonce; naff Carnabetian popsies in polka-dots chasered then brutalised by sharpering-omis and black-clad gimps with seaweed riah ...

Possiblement I was by now full-desensitised to grotty floor-shows like this – and yet my overriding savagery as I ogled each sketch was: MOGUES MOGUES MOGUES. The aggro was so preposterous and uncalled-for, it had to be false. Twas just ultra-farcical Grand Guignol horror, I ponced, squinting suspicious at the pools of fake sang and caca as I shimmied down the stalls to sharper for the WC.

Ironically I'd forgotten to lag in one of the many pissoirs I'd patronised earlier – and so had to troll round this diabolical labyrinth in search of a serviceable khazi that ideally wouldn't instantly vomit up my piddlings as the Human Latrine was wont to do. Scuttling through the shady passageways underneath the auditorium, I ogled portals left and right, each labelled with the nom of a joggering-pop set in a jaunty silvery sparkle, like a meshigena Hollywood Inkybooulevard: THE OFFAL SISTERS, LORD & LADY CHAMBERPOT, THE WALKING TURKEY-WATTLE, STRAWBERRY BOY, THE MUSCULAR GUINEA-PIG, MISTER MYXOMATOSIS, THE AMAZING SOMERSAULTING KRIEGSKRÜPPELS, SAMANTHA THE GORILLA, EGGY RUPERT, KING ANEURYSM III, THE SORDID GOOSE CIVILISED ...

For nix particular reason – other than my bladder by now felt like a fuckering Montgolfier balloon – I schonked open this last portal and snuck my eek inways.

'BASTA! NO, BASTA!' a horrified voche hissed as I entered.

Twas a grubby petty cubette: more of a gaol-cell than a de-luxe sparklet's dressing-chamber, decked out with mouldy brickwork, a libbage with nix mattress and splintered slats, cracked crockery and a gross meese beastie of some description lurking in the corner, chained to the bedframe.

'BASTA!' the shadowy lump screeched. 'NO! PLE! MERCY! MARIA!'

'Fear not, ducky, I come in peace,' I polled, jiggling from platter to platter. 'If you'd kindly poke me in the right direction of the nearest pissoir, I'll gladly fuck off pronto.'

All at once the voche became less skitterish. 'Here. Pisciare qui,' the beastie murmured, flapping a fluffy lapper at the manky bedpan betwixt his lallies. As he kicked the cheet towards me, a pogi splish of greenish aqua sploshed outways.

Ô comrades. While instinct would usually restrict me from unsheathing my handsome cartso in such unsanitary conditions as these, I admit I was perilously ajax to exploding by now. As gracefully as I could, I took my bashful saucisson in both lappers and aimed through the munge at the gaping monstrous O of the chamberpot. While I lagged, I fancied it might be proper to avert my opals to some bland unstimulating morso of the chamber, but then couldn't resist privvily scrutinising my nova comrade's intriguing joggering-cozzy as my ogles lento adjusted to the gloom. Presumably the Goose was so-named because of the thick feathery fuzz covering his carnish, if not the daffy eek-disfigurement that gave his oyster-levers the appearance of a gross pink bullhorn or beak. The poor tart's tet had been fatchared, his platters crammed into duey bijou yellow flippers.

'Pray tell, squire,' I huff-puffed once my piddlings were finished, 'who produces the prosthetics here? I'm mightily impressed – and may have use for a lapperful of gruesome disguises myself ...'

'NO! NO!' the Goose blurted, lunging at me with frenzied talons and beak snap-snappering spittly. Had it not been for the neck restraint, the twonk might've battyfanged me to slurry within secondas. Twas a strangely exhilarating sensation, I admit, Ô readers. 'Not mask,' the beastie eventually mumbled, slumping back down on the libbage, then gingerly reefing his bulbous trompette-levers. 'Shrapnel. Granaatsplinters. Ferite da schegge. Bomb dam. War damage.'

'War damage?' I parroted.

'WWII,' I believe he polled next, though he pronounced it 'bur bmur der'.

'But the feathers? Presumably you weren't born with fluffy goose down, ducky.'

Once again the prat reacted as if my lavs were glimmering birdshot, this time clawing at his own temples and spitting venomous at the ceiling. 'Der Oberherr,' he screeched, flapping up thataways. 'The Overlord. He tar.' The Goose grasped a lapp**e**rful of the plumage covering his left thew. 'He feather.' As if the point needed illustrating further, the bat yank-yanked the feathers from his carnish, leaving a grotty red sore that, for the rest of this twisted chapter, would not stop fuckering bleeding.

As the sang mingled with his matted lally-fluff, this so-called Civilised Goose let out a petty whimper, halfway betwixt a pogi orgasm or fruity tottle-rattle. 'You,' he gurgled, proffering his thumpering breast, seemingly wishing me to pluck out a lapperful of feathers myself. 'You. You. Prego.'

'No, no, old chap, I –'

'Hurt me.' Drool swung from his bloated oyster.

'Pardon?'

'Help me.' As if woken from an i**n**ky trance, the Goose now flapped emphatically at the opposite wall of the chamber, where a pair of clefs hung from a bijou nail. 'Help me. Ple,' he polled, scritch-scratching at his chains.

Again: instinct would normally prevent me from unleashing a crazed caged half-humanoid/half-waterfowl into my immediate vicinity – however, it crossed my servo that this bizarre batatat could well be a bona addition to my family. His poplo-skills and repartee might be somewhat lacking – but his maxi-skitterish presence should at least ensure my dismal dollies would never be bored again ...

Ô, twas difficult not to reer there and then, imagining my grand re-entry into W1 with this nova horrifying plaything in tow. As I uncleffed his shackles, the Goose's opals were like gleaming pools of licorice. Thankfully the zot did not instantly tear my beautiful eek to morsos once released – although his excitement was such, the twonk unwittingly kicked the full chamberpot over my natty booties as he scarpered pronto for the portal. Instinctively I raised my lapper to schonk him, then, clocking his greedy masochistic fizzer, thought better of it and simply frogmarched him out of the cell, bundled in my billowing L'AMOUR FOU gown.

Patient reader, I shall spare you the account of our long-winded, agonising escape from this most twisted establishment – instead, please visualise duey plucky moles emerging triumphant and debonair from a battyfanged cellar-hatch some chinka-daitcha yards from where all this claptrap started. Twas a moonless noche but still I savvied it wise to shield the Goose's startling carnish with my gildi gown as I luppered at taxicabs, eventually slamming us safely in the back of a black caboosh skippered by an unquestioning Irish fungus.

'Dove stiamo andando? Where we go?' the Goose honked, frittying under the capello as the taxi set off southways.

'Fear not, dear heart,' I side-oystered, 'we are headed for a specjalni establishment of untrammelled recreation! No more chains, my chovi! No more slavery!'

The Civilised Goose seemingly belched through his vonka by way of accordance.

Though the pop was clearly not one of his Mutterland's grandest conversationalists, I pressed him for a pogi few extra details of his subterranean slave-lavvy as we grumbled through King's Cross. As far as I could glean, the poor zot had been imprisoned at No. 49 since the end of the war, kept as a permanent POW in that cateva dungeon, presumably struck off as MIA on his military bimph, subjected to freakshow reparations noche upon noche at the hands of this meese sadistic Allied Overlord and his cronies. I cannot screeve this with maxi certainty however – if indeed these were the lavs he polled, the drivelling bat pronounced 'POW' and 'MIA' much the same as he pronounced 'WWII': 'Bur bmur der. Bur bmur der.'

The Unknown Soldier – still entirely unknowable, alas.

BOF.

By the time the taxicab delivered me and my jibbering cargo to Never-Neverland, I was interested only in the future – our meshigena riah-raising funhouse future. I parkered the mick chinka funts on account of the Goose moulting feathers and leaking sang and caca in the footwell en route, then led the fluffy brute down Ogle Strasse, his yellow flippers making gay comedic slap-slaps on the flagstones as we trolled.

Tittering uncontrollably, I looked forward to vadaring my dollies' reactions when we made our glittering entrance. My feeli malcontents wished to ogle nova eeks – and so surely they'd be ultra elated with this dazzling addition to our ranks! And yet – BOLLOCKS and BOTHERATION – as we approached my smouldering papier-mâché figurehead, I was maxi aggrieved to nelly wafts of Hi**n**di-striller still whining and wubbering from the bodega. When I peeked my eek through the front fenêtre, I clocked Sage & Onion twangling cross-lallied and stony-fizzered while heksa or setta of my beloved donnas hoofered trance-like round the cleared parquet. Ô camarades, my innerbits shrivelled when I vadared how gay and luminous the dames looked – but worstest of all was their schmutta. Presumably to ramp up the naff colonic theme of the noche, the palones were all clobbered in gross unflattering mandala-camishas and tipi-drogles they must've shushed from a rival boutique. Hippy sacks. Biba caca.

Storming inways, I sent the Civilised Goose squawking and battyflappering frantic into the centre of the revved-up whirly-dervishing dolls – then for una minuta or duey simply ogled riveted from the sideylines as the inevitable carnage and brooliment played out. At first twas like a cross betwixt a pillow-fight and Kristallnacht: feathers frittying hither and thither as the Goose pounced upon my screeching devotees, clawing at their flouncy granny-garb, leaping from podiums, crashing into my clobber-rails and smashing the odd fakement. By the time my dollies had scattered, sharpering for refuge behind wibbling curtains or in privvy hideyholes under the staircase and betwixt livercases, the Goose was already maxi fattygayed, sprawled out on the parquet like a dicky spatchcocked vulture.

'ACHTUNG!' I howled. 'Where in Jupiter's nom did you lell these hideous rags?! Dispose of this detestable hippy schmutta at once, you daffy fleur-brained batatats!'

Ever obedient, my sisters silently wriggled out of their smocks, hurling them quivery-lappered one after another into the centre of the floor. Bruce and Lionel clutched their Hindi-strillers like timid chavvies clutching a comfort-rag or teddybear, horror-ogling the feathered lunatic splattered flappers akimbo in front of them.

To fill the poky silence, I began palavering how my cherished Yé-Yé Girls (Delphine, Jacqueline Taïeb, Clothilde ...) were allowed to use Indian strills because us noble frogs had nantwar to do with the arroganki 'civilising' battyfanging of the Rosbif Raj in the Vicky era – when all at once the front portal skreeeered open and Veronica and Donatella tumbled inways, followed by their own molto horrifying plaything.

'No no no, but the French weren't exactly averse to the evils of Imperialism now, were they, old cock?' the Interrupter cackled, joshed-up in a floppy hat, fringed waistcoat, flared lally-covers. 'Napoleon, 'Nam, bloody Algeria, waterboarding, Haiti – the list goes on, does it not?'

'Ooh la la,' I scoffed, for want of a snappier put-down.

Ô, MERDRE. The Interrupter was one of those tiresome know-all zots who seemed to start every sentence with 'No, but': the type of obstructive addle-plot who robotically regurgitates other twonks' bombastic right-on savagery while being completely devoid of any wisdom or common sense themselves. The sort of uncultured cunt who probably orders a pint of Watney's Red Barrel at ze VICTOR BERLEMONT.*

I ogled Veronica and Donatella. 'Where in Jupiter's nom have you been?' The pair were jittering like this floréal noche was somehow in the amidships of winter. 'I sent you out thataways chinka hours ago for a chainsaw and some nell-protection.'

'We got a pogi bit waylaid.'

'Bumped into these sweet sorts in Soho.' The Interrupter swung his lappers round the palones' pols. The sight of it made me want to pluck out my own opals and tennis-racket them in opposite directions. 'Took the skinny bints out for dinner. Thought they looked like they needed fattening up ...'

'My dollies have all the munjarry they need,' I snapped, wafting a limp lapper at the morsos of grub strewn about the grimy bodega.

'Shrivelled concombres and mouldy crumbs of crusty baguette, ey, old boy? O yes, this is quite the Romanesque bean-feast you've got here ...'

'Pray tell, what slap-up din-dins did you titillate my birds' tastebuds with? Wimpy? The Golden Egg? Hé-hé-hé-hé!'

My trumpety reering seemed to rouse the Goose, who up til now had barely twitched as he lay eek-down in the mound of shaggy schmutta strewn ajax. As he blink-blinked upways dowri dazzleshipped, I hoped the scatty bat might launch an impromptu assault on the Interrupter's snotty fizgog – however, the beastie seemed immeasurably more interested in the donnas cowering on the sideylines, given that the tarts were frittying in nantwar but their frilly skimpies now. I savvied the Goose

---

* The so-called French Pub – Victor Berlemont's York Minster – in Dean Street famously does not serve pints. Watney's Red Barrel is their only beer on tap.

had likely not ogled feeli femme carnish for nigh on trey-daitcha annos – the drool was positively cascading from his visible orifices.

'Excusez-moi uno momento,' I polled, rapidly steering the Goose up the staircase and into our empty boudoir. 'Upways now, comrade – time to rest and recuperate, oui, nein? There's plenty of time for spittle and lechery in the morningtide, isn't that right?'

I left him writhing dozily on the PVC, then scuttled back down down down, sporting a nova bruise or duey on my foretet and lally-caps. As I stepped back into the boutique, I hoped the Interrupter had kindly accepted defeat and buggered off back to whatever stinking hole he'd slithered from – but, alas, the bastard was still upright, simpering like a gross Toby juglet.

'Kettner's,' he polled.

'Come again?'

'Took these beauties out for some high-class nosh at Kettner's.' His levers crinkled spitefully. 'A little out of your price range, I expect. It can't pay well, sloth and slovenliness. In fact, I'd wager you've never worked an honest day's graft in your life, isn't that right?'

'What in all of Christinedom gives you that idea?'

The Interrupter wafted his lapper at the slogan splattered above the SORTIE, another choice cutlet from Papa Breton:

IF ONE IS TO FEEL TRULY ALIVE, ONE MUST NOT WORK

'Ô, I've grinded, don't you worry, my petty saucisson.' I too puckered my levers now. 'I've paid my dues, done my time bobbling unmerrily along the coddy ocean. Three years in the Merchant Navy, squire. Degrading travails. Bellboy, tumbler-shusher. Where have you toiled, you old bugger?'

'He's a fashion correspondent,' Donatella blurted. 'We reckoned he could screeve an article on the boutique, Raymond. Spread the word like how you wanted ...'

'PFFF!' I piffled. 'Are you completely daffy? Journalism is the mostest grubbiest, snottiest, selectively blinkered and contrived travails available to a plop! What gives this hypercritickal squid the right to scribble what's in and what's nanti? Vada the twonk: joshed-up in his daffy old grandmama's graverobbed clobber!' I thrust my vonka closer to the dolls' oysters. 'Come, now. What has he been feeding you? What mally polluting substance has he addled your servos with?'

The donnas struggled to keep their eeks tranquil as the sniggers frittied through their kishkas.

'Alors. Open up,' I demanded. 'Let me sniff your gases.'

Grudgingly the palones' oyster-levers creaked open. As suspected, the tarts were squifferoony. They honked of some meese rosbif alcool like gin or Dettol. LOOPERS! SHE-WOLVES! I was molto tempted to schonk them repeatedly like Bruce's glistening bongo, but instead managed – through immense willpower and dorcas sangfroid – to stick to the passive-aggro peace-be-with-you caca and I polled simply: 'Blank Chamber.'

The lavs were ominous enough to halt their titterings. The palones looked like twisted puppydogs now, strapped in for some doomed Soviet space mission.

'Excuse us una minuta,' I hissed, before leading the treacherous mares upways. As I clunked the portal behind us, the Interrupter looked like a chavvy deprived of his sweeties. THE INTOLERABLE PRAT. Whether or not he could nelly the birds' hysterical protests as I dragged them up the staircase, the twonk thankfully decided against chasering after us and playacting the hero.

'It's for your own good, my chovis,' was my usual justification as I frogmarched the palones to the toppermost floor, gripping their quivering wrists, then eventually yank-yanking their ankles once it became clear their platters were refusing to cooperate.

My devotees savvied better than to schonk or fang their master during tet-correctional sessions such as this, and so I fancied it must be the gin to blame for the onslaught of hurtful lavs as I carefully steered them towards the dazzling droning cube.

'Let go! Piss off!'

'Fuck off, you fuckering arsehole!'

The dolls' eeks were zebra-splattered with parnyaqua and mascara by the time I slammed them in the Blank Chamber: their nova abode for the next uno, duey hours or junos or so. On account of the birds screeching so much, I turned the blank noise up to maximum nell-frazzling volume and sped the fluoro-flickers up to kenza hertz – then cleffed the portal firm behind me, slithering both bolts shut.

Ô, the poor tarts. I loved them so much, it was I who suffered mostest from these meese disciplinary episodes. I dabbed my opals with a chiffon hanky, then drifted on downwards.

As I passed back through the boudoir, I savvied I must've been so preoccupied with shepherding my popsies towards The Light, I'd failed to clock the grim nova additions to the bedchamber's décor. The Goose had fatchared my followers' eiderdowns to morsos, reconstituting the scraps into a grand nest for himself, all bound together with what appeared to be spittle or sperm, and caca. Secondly, he'd scratched some form of loopy avant-garde poetry into the skirting ajax to his nest (SSSMMSMMMMSMSMMMSSSSSSSSSSSSSM was perhaps the most lucid stanza), and finally – in a feat of quite astonishing athleticism – he'd vomited in what can only be described as an ecstatic arc up the wall and halfway across the ceiling.

Given that I was not in the merriest of moods, it may come as a shock to nelly I responded to this ghastly splatter-frenzy with instant pearly laughter: 'Hé-hé-hé-hé-hé-hé-HÉ!' Irrespective of any hygiene concerns, the Goose's shameless free spirit was utterly fantabulosa. OUI! After suffering the Interrupter's dreary contrived efforts at one-upmanship earlier, twas almost a relief to vada this spontaneous unapologetic display of joyful unrestrained animalistic battyfangery. All at once I felt a rush of dribbly admiration and brotherliness – and yet I admit there was a pogi bit of envy there too. This zot had been imprisoned for nigh on trey-daitcha-chinka years and yet all this time he'd arguably been more free than I: spouting and splurting all his unconscious arva-desires and aggro-impulses with nanti care for the consequences, and nanti concept of bona etiquette whatsoever. Why Ô why, I pondered, after having been brought up an ultra-liberteen chavvy, was I not truly as wild and free as this daffy untamed Goose? Why was I still burdened with such pleasure-limiting feelings as shame, jealousy, guilt, remorse – feelings the Goose was clearly impervious to?

'Bravo, my cherry,' I chirruped, curtseying betwixt duey unfamiliar spillages. 'Good boy ... bona goosey ...'

The beast glared back at me from his nest, fluffed up like a gigantic monstrous mothball or thundertet.

'Ô, hark! Flower people!' I yelled next, craning my neck down the spiral staircase, still sniggering a petty bit. 'Mistress Fisty! Séverine! The Stuffing Brothers! Our nova pet has fallen ill, alas. Come and clean up this hideous slurry immediately!'

Diligent pops that they were, my devotees appeared una minuta later with detergents and dhobi-pompoms, although it cannot be said that they undertook their task with much relish. Some of their eeks looked downright horrified as they scrubbed away the ecstatic arc and, though the zots were tight-levered throughout, I fancy this may have had as much to do with the muffled screams coming from the Blank Chamber as the bod-fluids dribbling like brown parnyaqua down the blank plaster.

Je m'accuse ...![*]

NOVAK WEARS JODHPURS, JACKBOOTS, SHOCKING-PINK FLEUR-DE-LYS JOCKEY SILKS, HELMET AND GOGGLES, A RIDING CROP CLAMPED BETWIXT HIS GRINDING PEARLS.

NELLY CHRISTINE PILZER'S 'CAFÉ CRÈME'.

Fair readers, as you must be aware by now, I am a molto reluctant disciplinarian – however, as solo voche and Big Chief of our fragile wonderland, twas my unenviable duty to keep my beloved bastards continually in check.

To this juno I still ponder: how bestest to combine punishment and pleasure on the factory floor? How best to dis**g**uise stringent servo-manipulation as harmless frippery and frivolity?

After my followers' coddy lapse of self-control in recent weeks, I savvied it was imperative to give their servos another bona dhobi – and so I orga**ni**sed post-haste a soirée of invigorating tet-reform, une fête d'autocritique, a grand masquerade ball centred on that gloriosa theme: FULL EGO-OBLITERATION.

As I may have touched upon earlier, I detest all hypocritters, REFUSE to take criticism and do not enjoy criticising others not a jot – but I had nix objectio**n**s to my dollies lambasting one another, and in fact actively encouraged it on this specjalni noche in May. My natty masterplan was this: to josh my followers in ultrablank disguises, droggle them with truth serum (142-proof 'Elixir Vegetal' Chartreuse) and have them admit all

---

* Chapter received Thursday, 14th May 1970 – sixty days to go.

their faults and all their neighbours' faults while joining lappers in a rapturous spinnering circle. It was to be a jolly exorcism of sorts – a grandiose expulsion of all remaining unwanted personality traits and unrevolutionary claptrap. Once sufficiently nitpicked, roasted, humiliated and chastened, my broken dollies would be rewarded with a stirring rediscovery of the mostest titillating principles of la vie d'avant-garde – namely a de-luxe feast shushed from the finest dustbins of St James's, followed by an orgy shushed from the pages of L'HISTOIRE D'O – boldly steering my wayward wrongthinking wildebeesties back onto the royal road to UNADULTERATED ULTRALOVE, to ABSOLUTE RAYMONDOPHILIA.*

---

* We have been thinking about Novak's so-called 'vie d'avant-garde' a lot over the past seven months.

As London's premier avant-garde publisher, we at least stand together with the Guru in our longing for an uncensored, unhindered existence; a society uninhibited by pointless prudishness, political correctness or piousness; a culture industry not stifled or strangled by the sober tastes of the bourgeoisie. We're just not convinced Novak's reckless oversexed vie d'avant-garde is a realistic alternative to everyday life in the West – or at least Stanley keeps telling himself it's not possible.

Our director felt bluer than usual reading these latest chapters. Back in 1959 he, Iris and Trefoil launched the Glass Eye Press with the same subversive rhetoric and flamboyant audacity as the Prole Dandy, but when Iris became pregnant soon after, Merritt realised their money-guzzling folly must become profitable, for little Abigail's sake if not their own. All he's wanted since the baby was delivered pristine into this world is to protect her – but he's seen for a long time now that lurid pulp pocketbooks and the Avant-Garde Life are not the way to do it. He worries about her so much, his darling ten-year-old dolly, growing up in this so-called Permissive Society where maniacs like Novak are free to exploit young girls under the pretence of carefreeness and liberty. 1967 was a terrible year for exploitation. With all the jibber-jabber about free love, it seemed the media and arrogant misogynistic rock-sparkles gave young men a licence to be sex pests. Way-out underground discotheques soon became mass breeding grounds for perverts in paisley shirts, rabid dogs mistaking Women's Lib for a green light to sniffle round the female clientele's crotches without shame. Or perhaps Stanley just sees the world differently now his daughter is coming of age.

As if the divorce were not traumatic enough, Merritt was told this week that Iris will be taking full custody of Abigail. This pains him for innumerable

To ensure maxi anonymity during this soirée of unrestrained muckraking and character-mortification, I forced my dollies to wear matching expressionless blank masks, which, coupled with their freshly fatchared tets and bleached bodsuits, made the zots look more like mannequins than ever before. Twas impossible to tell the pops apart once we congregated in the munge of the shuttered boutique – save for the Sordid Goose who, despite also being clobbered full-blank, was somewhat conspicuous writhing like a melting snowman in the centre of the parquet. In any case the twonk was there for amusement only – I did not expect to nelly a great deal of incisive discourse from that particular gaping eek-hole.

To get things off to a lively start, I'd prepared a few scathing denunciations of my daitcha followers' behaviour over the past year or duey (some my own gripes, some overheard from the oysters of backbiting bambinos, some entirely falsified) – however, as I gingerly took to one of the lofty podiums to screech these constructive criticisms, I was nanti prepared for the effects of perhaps Ze Worst Café I Have Ever Schlumphed. As a proud frog, my kishkas can naturellement accommodate the most potent and snappy of espressos, but this slop was fuckering atrocious.

---

reasons, but there are a few grievances in particular that torment his scrambled brain more than the rest. Firstly, he's dubious about Iris's parenting skills. The old bohemian hag will no doubt see to it that Abigail is in make-up and a miniskirt before she enters her teens, permitted to have boyfriends, encouraged to prance around like a painted nymphette – putting her at risk of being abducted/violated/heartbroken beyond repair. (If it were not clear already: Stanley is not a true libertarian. He is seemingly one of those 'humourless cunts' who likes his liberty in livers only.) Secondly, the court's decision reinforces a fear he's had for some time now: that he's not Abigail's biological father, that he's actually infertile, that it was Trefoil who accidentally impregnated his wife at that rented pile in Surrey back in 1959. And finally – and this hurts worst of all – the old hag (now sole – SOLE! – custodian of the child!) *pleaded* for him to perform an abortion on her when she discovered she was pregnant in December of that year. If it wasn't for Stanley's resistance, there would have been no Abigail.

Merritt writes this on Sunday, 17th May 1970, in Fitzrovia, in bed, in tears.

I cannot rightly recall if I was daffy and in need of some cheet to sober me, or whether the manky liquor was thrust upon me by some overzealous prat. Vaguely I remember a rogue puppet-lapper emerging from the mass of ghostly b**l**ank bods, and lavs to this effect: 'Schlumph this down, your Lordship. An invigorating bitter-gator. Beans from Java. Should quicken the servo and sharpen the lingum mightily well, sir.'

Impossible to tell which of my **f**ollowers spoke these lavs, since I'd urged the zots to disguise their voches ready for the slanging match ahead. Upon downing the elixir, I admit I may have initially squeaked, 'Fantabulosa!' or some other gay superlative, but half an hour later my view on the beverage had sh**i**fted somewhat.

I screeve 'half an hour' cagily, since conveniently my timepiece went doolally almost immediately as the liquor took effect. Instead of the norm brisk tick-tick-**t**ick of the tocking-levers, the m**in**utas now seemed to drool molto lento round the clockface. A strange breeze entered the boutique, causing my rails of schmutta to bellydance and shimmer queasily as if possessed by invisible Javanese hoofers. My mannequins appeared carved from marble now: stone donnas snatched from the fountains of Versailles or a de-luxe Soviet cemetery. Kishkas cement-mixering pricklies. Glimmer-fakements in my oglesockets. Shrinking furniture. Rinky-dink organ-grinders tittering from the drain-pipettes.

MESHIGENA COFFEE BEANS.

Savvying my dollies were poised in readiness for my enlightening intro, I attempted to straighten myself atop the wobbling podium – but, ALAS and ALACACACACACA, my bold pre-planned spiel felt more like Arabic Scrabble in my tet. Holding the miniature bullhorn to my levers, I opened my oyster in the hope my denunciations might splurt out spontaneous, but in the end I was capable of only uno solo lav: 'Keith.'

The twisted truth is: there was nanti better way to describe what I was feeling. My subconscious held the clef to this peculiar servo-dissolving sensation and the clef was: Keith. Not since Tangier had I clocked the hoofering textiles, the bulbous bush-baby opals, the shifty shadows, the sniggering fixtures and fakements, the treacherous trompe l'œils. Why now? And why me again? Had Keith acquired a meshigena coffee plantation in Indonesia? Had some twonk plopped his droppings into my Gaggia vacaya? My skull was spilling over with all sorts of skit-terish savagery and paranoia, but, with those daitcha alabaster eeks ogling up at me expectantly, I savvied I'd best try to steer my voche back towards the invigorating constructive slander I had planned:

'I ... Bonsoir, ladles and gentlechilds ... um ... c'est grave ... I ... Ô mon Dieu ... Keith ... excusez-moi ... apologies, my chovis ... this is Keith speaking ...'

Baffled but ever loyal, my dollies clapped their lappers together and chanted beatific: 'Keith! Keith! KEITH!'

'Non, non,' I protested, but by now my lingum was in disarray, skittering about my oyster like an aggravated trout in a knotted binbag. 'It's not me, it's ... it's Keith ... I've been poisoned ... this is Keith palavering ...'

'Keith! Keith! O, holy Keith!'

Frosty sweat began to slither down my tet. The prickles in my kishkas turned to lashing hurdy-gurdy wobble-cramps. Vomitus burbling in my belly, metallic saliva gushing from my oyster-nipplets. I savvied, Ô comrades, I must abandon my perch immediately.

I scarpered from the podium like a rodent being chasered by a lattywife's broom, feeling about duey inches tall with the sneering eeks and cartoon fakements of the boutique all tower-some and unfamiliar around me. I just about managed to stumble through the mousehole leading upways, then practically crawled up the helter-skeltering staircase with buckling ectoplasm-lallies, and headed for the khazi. Some cruel plumber had shrunk the toilet bowl to the size of a medsa-caroon but miraculously I still managed to fire my bile into the pot without spilling a droplet.

I flushed, then clutched the sides of the bowl, breathing HUMPH-HUMPH-HUMPH while my bod continued jitterbugging shuddery. My tet felt horrendous, like some evil zot was pouring molten headache into my skull. I spat once or twice more into the pot, then rested my pounding foretet on the grotty plastic khazi-halo, parnyaqua seeping from every ogle-corner. A gay procession of ants goosestepped out from a crack betwixt duey ceramic tiles. A blank fantom shimmered shiftily behind the shuttered shower-curtain. My solo emag now was to sit tranquil in the biddychamber until the worst of these meese visions ceased, then I would retire to a de-luxe hotel to grind out the last of this toxic brooliment in peace.

I believe my clanging thumper was just about beginning to settle when the shower-curtain skreeeeeeeeered open and the blank fantom – a blond omi in an ill-fitting tropical tuxedo – leapt from the biddytub and slugged me full-eek with the loofah. Important to screeve here: the loofah must have been stuffed with concrete or some form of steely baton because just one schonk had me ultraschvartz and drooling, out cold.

Jupiter knows if I squealed on impact or how long I was unconscious, but when I awoke I found myself tethered to the khazi, wrists and ankles bound tight with fish-wire. The schonk on the tet, far from rousing me from my Javanese trance, only seemed to muddle my servo more than before as I blinked around the biddychamber. Time had stopped altogether, the room was a slippery Escher horrorscape, my assailant's eek a gross floating pearly grimace.

'Keith?' I enquired.

The pearls let forth a cackle: duey clattering jazz pianos. 'How'd you find those Javanese beans, my chovi? An invigorating bitter-gator, hm?'

Who was this diabolical batatat palavering at me in perfect queenly Polari? My opals may have been like full-moony fromage, but I savvied clear enough this wasn't a member of my dear family. 'You don't recognise me, Raymond?'

'Nanti that,' I honked. The twonk's visage kept melting and resculptering itself: for uno lento momento he was a barky, a cackling griffin, a giant concombre, a spinning disc of multi-whirly polka-droplets, Napoleon's deathmask, a platterful of sea urchins, a pink mushroom cloud in a blank vogueing jacket ...

Squinting with heavy dozy lids, I polled: 'You poisoned me, squire?'

My assailant reered up again. 'One omi's carnish is another pop's poison! Although one may have accidentally plop-plopped a glugful of LSD in your warming beverage, yes.'

'Why so, you evil batatat?' Impossible to ascertain the exact palavering here of course, but I like to think I was babbling back at him heroically and kept at least uno bijou morso of pride.

'Revenge,' the blond quacked. 'Remember the Setta Seas, Raymondo? The bona ship SS UNMENTIONABLE?' Pronto I clocked the tropical tux for what it was: an outgrown set of stewards' whites. 'MS HIPPOCAMPUS, oui, non? Certain actions of yours caused a certain lover of mine to lose his mind, become irreparably meshigena, and now derelict, down-and-out, kaputt. Love is no more.'

'Your lover?' I spat. 'I savvy not of any intentional boom-boomer-breaking I caused at sea. Pray tell, who are you? Please enlighten me or else do fuck-off-thataways back to whatever coddy mollusc shell you crawled out of.'

Once again I pondered: why me, why now? Between this vicious invader and that insufferable tart Winnie Repulse, there'd been rather a lot of unwanted seaweed washed up from my past aqua-travails the last quatra years ...

'Who do you think I am, Raymondo? I savvy all too clear who YOU are.' The blond smirked as he chewed his bottom oyster-lever. 'You gave yourself away the other juno, when I questioned your hard travails. I could not believe my dolly opals. You've changed a mighty great deal since you were just a humble tumbler-shusher. Though clearly I've changed a good deal too, given you still don't seem to recognise me ...'

'If you'd be so kind as to halt your grotty fizzer from decomposing, I'd be only too happy to finger you, ducky.'

The twat ogled me distastefully. 'I hear from your ladyfriends downstairs you refer to me as the Interrupter. It's not the first daffy nom you've given me ...'

'Herman?' I spluttered.

'I prefer * * * *,' the blond snapped, although as aforescreeved, I will NEVER NIX NANTWAR speak or scribble the petty bastard's real no**m**.

'So you're a swinging-plop now, ey?' I polled. 'How in all of bloody Christinedom did you find me, you swine?'

'Simply by chance!' Herman sneered.

I shook my tet. 'Nanti that. This isn't possible.'

'I'm a fashion correspondent, ducky. Tis my duty to sniff out the latest way-out freaky boutiques – although this hovel somewhat takes the biscuit.'

'Bof.' I let my tet droop downways and clocked that both my lappers and platters were fully pur**pl**e now. 'Who then, prithee, was this coddy lover of yours I so cruelly and heartlessly rendered meshigena? Not that supreme twonk Sturgeon?'

Herman seemed genuinely hurt now. 'He kept me as a catamite, and a molto willing and gay catamite I was too – until you vandalised his servo.'

'I vandalised his servo, did I? If I remember rightly I merely inserted uno juicy prawn up the chappy's guilty sphincter ...'

'His pride was hurt. There were royals present, don't forget. My dearest Sturgeon was demoted after the whole debacle. Lost his stripes, lost his mind. Poor angelfish. I'll admit the man had a fair amount of superiority complexity and arrogank that made the fall all the more fatal. He was an ambitious omi – in my opals one of the very best. Couldn't cope with the demotion. Signed off at Georgie Five. Last seen scrabbling for spare soldis in Hampstead. Derelict. A shadow-omi. I cannot bear to sharper for him. I prefer the poor old fruit in my memory: glittering pearls, starched whites –'

'ACHTUNG!' I howled. 'These are the most ridiculous lavs I've ever nellied! The bat was unhinged. Nix doubt his servo was ready to plop any minuta. It wasn't my humble insertions* that

---

* Our own humble insertions were about to get a lot humbler.

Regularly McKinley brought up the question: given the police would be on our backs the moment we announced publication of *Mister Asterisk*, how on earth were we expecting to make money from Novak's criminal screeve? We had no doubts the public would devour the book if Novak's crime was suitably gruesome, and hoist it to the top of the bestsellers lists – but would they allow us to reap the profits from this absymal crime once it emerged that we'd withheld information from the police? At best the Angry Mob might demand we give all proceeds to charity, to compensate the victims' families – at worst they'd fucking crucify us.

We were confident our doctored note from the Scum King worked well as a get-out-of-jail-free card, a watertight excuse why we hadn't shopped Novak to the authorities from the off – but how could we avoid the media and public at large turning on us?

The answer came to Merritt on the throne. The key here was our footnotes, our audacious incriminating footnotes. All we had to do was remove or rewrite those few foolish asides that suggested we were encouraging Novak, fully understood his murderous intentions and had already linked him to previous crimes (decapitation, abortion …), then certainly no jumped-up finger-pointer could accuse us of being aiders or abettors.

Of course there was nothing stopping us from removing *all* our footnotes from the final manuscript – nothing except our pride, alas. No: call us intrusive editors or desperate showmen, but we could not bring ourselves to completely erase our side of the story. The trick here was to simply feign ignorance and naivety. 'No, m'lud, we didn't see it coming – not all this bloodshed, not the severed heads, nothing.' If we could make the general public believe we were the victims here (shoulder to shoulder with Novak's true victims come Monday, 13th July 1970 – only sixty days to go!), hopefully the sweet, gullible masses would take pity on us and allow us to keep all proceeds from the Guru's grim, glistening liver.

We were the true gods here of course: Editor *and* Creator. We could rewrite our story however we liked. Look again at the footnotes of 'Womb Muzak', for instance. Back then many of us 'felt we were dealing with nothing more than a deluded egomaniac, a charlatan, a timewaster'. Who's to say we don't carry on that blissfully ignorant narrative, erase Novak's threatening phone call to us on 13th February 1970, remove all traces of Sturgeon's name and severed head from our footnotes, make as if the severity of Novak's fantabulosa crime will be a complete and utter shock to us! After all, as it stands (see 'French Horn', 'Care Label', 'Loose Threads', etc.) Novak and his passive-aggro followers don't seem particularly hellbent on violence. If forthcoming chapters take on a more vicious, bloodthirsty slant, we could always claim they'd been left unread on the

sent the fash bat doolally – the twonk was meshigena to begin with, surely!?'

'He loved me. This is full proof to me of his absolute sanity.'

'PFFF! Well then, you're both as batty as one another! Untie me pronto!' I squirmed in my nylon shackles. 'You mean to say this daffy revenge is all in aid of your coddy teeni colin shrinking when your inky bat pederast Boss Man turned out not to be ultra kosher in the tet?! PAH! Untie me, foul beastie!'

Snarling now, Herman rose stiffly from his perch on the edge of the biddytub, spat a vonka-slug in my general direction and cri**e**d: 'This daffy revenge, as you put it, is only the beginning, Raymondo. Only the beginning.'

The loon left me ogling sparkly pirhouetting retina-fakements, slamming the khazi portal SPLATCH! firm behind him.

'SERVICE! SERVICE!!' I **h**owled through the noche – but alas, my beloved bastards did not find me until many hours later.

---

slush pile until Novak's eventual crime pushed us to revisit – like wide-eyed fawns! – his discarded, disregarded novel.

But what then of The Truth? What then of *Mister Asterisk* – with all our illuminating/incriminating asides – as a factual document of a maniac, his innocent publishers and his innocent victims? Well, risky as it may be, we had no intention of completely destroying our original footnotes. The plan was now to have two versions of the manuscript: the uncensored original (currently in Merritt's grip in Morocco, autumn 1970) and a second, the version copied out by Emily, to be watered down accordingly.

While typing at speed, we urged Emily to alert us whenever she came across a passage that suggested our complicity or culpability, or any foresight as to what Novak's fantabulosa crime might entail (not that we knew at this point what the bastard had planned anyhow). Trefoil barked at her: 'Don't take any liberties, Em. Don't fuck with Raymond's text, just flag up anything in the footnotes you think might be problematic. Good girl.'

Emily followed her orders well, and in fact soon discovered something unusual about Novak's original m/s the rest of us had overlooked – however, it would take her some weeks to work out its significance and by then it was too late, too late …

(NB: This footnote – perhaps our most incrimating of all – was one of a dozen or so stored in five lubricated condoms stuffed up Merritt's backside when he returned to London by BOAC, November 1970.)

Nausea*

NOVAK WEARS BULLETPROOF FLAK-MANTO, CHAINMAIL LONG JOHNATHANS, ARMADILLO SHELL AND A COLANDER ATOP HIS TET.

NELLY STELLA'S 'TREMPE TES PIEDS DANS LE GANGE'.

For a pop who once enjoyed straddling dream and reality like a cowboy, I was not terribly enamoured of my first slurp of LSD. For the next few junos I was in a state of skitterish paranoia: ogling evil eeks in the most commonplace of household appliances, accusing every shadow of treachery and skulduggery, convinced Herman would strike any minuta with this bonus unwarranted revenge he'd promised.

Along with my nova bulletproof sleeping attire, I took other protective measures: chaining the Goose to the clobber-rail ajax to our front portal, appointing him as guard doggy – and bubbling up a batch of molto potent pepper-spray. I recommend any hypervi**g**ila**nt**† civvy should carry a botty of this damaging

* Two chapters received Wednesday, 20th May 1970 – 54 days to go.

† Perhaps you have already noticed what Emily noticed: the strange appearance of rogue bold characters in each chapter since 'The Free Love Formula, or: French Horn'. At first Emily felt these were just unintentional errors (an overexcited index finger stabbing the keys in the heat of Novak's stream of consciousness) and she corrected them accordingly in the new copy. However, by the time she reached 'Je m'accuse ...!' she felt a pattern was emerging: the overabundant **i**s and **n**s, the first bold character in each chapter always a **g**, the final capital always an **h**. What was the meaning of this?

elixir at all times! Londres is a dangerous metropolis positively teeming with psychopaths, but follow these simple instructions and you will rap**i**dly have at your disposal a fantabulosa opal-glimmering bitter-gator to disable any unsavouries:

1. Vagary to Notting Hill or another schvartz neighbourhood and parker a lapperful of Scotch bonnet chilli peppers.
2. Grind these into a paste with cayenne pepper, garlic, lemon jus, pastis, plenty of surgical spirit and a glug-glug of bambino-oil. (I believe bijou shards of broken glaze would work mightily well too, but in my unscientific experience I found they merely clog the **n**ozzle).
3. Allow cocktail to settle/marinate overnight.
4. Sieve through coffee-filter into a discr**e**et, durable spray-botty.
5. Enjoy.

After **t**esting the mixture on my own and my followers' opals, we all agreed the recipe worked wonderfully well. And so, I was as prepared as could be for Herman's next cameo appearance. I avoided coffee but grossly increased my Drinamyl intake, kept my palliass to the wall and carried the spray-botty with me everywhere I minnied. As the weeks slithered by, there was nix sign of the fa**s**h-lammering batatat, but I savvied he was probably biding his time like a panther-spider, waiting patiently in the wings for my guard to drop before pounc**i**ng. Ô, how I **l**ooked **f**orward to turning the cunt's condescending opals and uppity mush to toxic crackling! The omi would not upstage me nix longer.

While **i**t was **t**empting on fashion grounds alone to pepper-spray every floppy-hatted dandy who entered my boutique, I managed to refrain from this somewhat frowned-upon customer service throughout this tender period. **I**n any case the Goose's hissing presence by the front portal seemed to keep most punters away. Understandably the beastie did not appreciate being choke-chained to the clobber-rail after only recently regai**n**ing his liberty, and his **i**ncreased stroppiness now he was being fed only French Blues did not make him the **r**itziest, mostest welcoming doorman in Londres.

By the time spring turned to summer our weekly footfall was practically nil – and I was beginning to doubt this bonus revenge would ever materialise. Sweating under my col**a**nder, I quizzed my devotees one humstinking sleepless noche: 'Has anyone clocked that supreme addle-plot the Interrupter strutting around Fitzrovia since our ill-fated fête d'autocritique? Nanti suspicious civvies loitering outside the boutique? Nix peeking opals betwixt the fenêtre bars?'

My darlings shook their pretty tets.

'Was he even present at your Masquerade Ball, your Lordship?'

'We haven't ogled him since Sage & Onion's cosmic shindig, your Highness.'

'The Interrupter hasn't darkened our doormat in all of '67, we believe, mein vater.'

Curious lavs. Was my servo failing me? Had I hallucinated the whole episode? Sure enough I still had the fish-wire scars on my wrists and anklets to prove it – but, as the weather blazed ever more slimy and oppressive, I savvied it was probably safe to shed my stifling protective clobber (though naturell**e**ment I kept a bijou botty of pepper-spray tucked in my garter in case of emergencies).

Ô faithful, fertile reader, did you enjoy the fruits of the so-called Summer of Love? Did you charver more abundantly and more freely than previous summertides? I cannot say it i**n**spired any especially thunderish arva-twangs on my own part. Whether down to the Hippy Craze or just plain slovenliness, my devotees' appear**a**nce and personal hygiene took a rapid downturn during those vonny months. Soon the boutique felt more like a fuckering aadvark's den than a fleur-scented Elysium: grubby slippies strewn about the libbage, rats, ants, snot wiped across the walls, rotten munja stamped underfoot, puddles of pissy vinegary vino, grubby lupperprin**t**s all over the blank décor and blank paper drogles ...

QUELLE SURPRISE: this coddy lapse in cleanliness resulted in **n**ot only the (temporary) dwindling of my arva-hunger, but duey of my favourite followers falling seriously **i**ll within a week of each other in the height of Thermidor. Ô, the sickly bats – my mo**r**ning toilette was now disturbed by Sabine and **P**riscilla vomiting brootishly into their chamber pots, firing liquid caca about the biddy-chamber, groaning moronic, scratchering their bods as if infested with fantom parasites.

'ACHTUNG! Frightful ghoulies!' I howled when, trey weeks into this gruesome malady, the zots refused to **e**merge from under their eiderdowns. 'This is preposterous! What foul meshigena germ is capable of turnering such jolly lusty feelies to vegetables?! Allez! Allez!'

Sabine and Priscilla blinked at one another, their greenish eeks pressed together like duey rancid choufleurs. 'Perchance is the Goose to blame, your Lordship?' Sabine **m**umblered, drawing my attention to the crusted lightning-bolts of quong-sirop stretching in all directions from the beastie's nest. 'The boutique has not been the mostest sanitary latty since he was dragged inwards ...'

'Nanti that!' I roared. 'The Goose might not be the most refined gentlepop in W1 – but he deserves not a jot of the BLAME BLAME BLAME for your unruly leaky kishkas! The Goose savvies nantwar of bona etiquette and gildi lattykeeping, and all power to the prick! In fact his mess is an ULTRA-PRISTINE symbol of his pure liberty, his innocence, the beautiful ungovernable chaos of his batty servo. Your mess is just laziness, slovenliness!'

Sabine's oyster hung open dumbly for uno momento, before her lavs fell out in a jittery jumble: 'Well ... no, no, possiblement that's the point though ... maybe it's ... what if it's this whole Liberated Lavvy to blame? The hedonism, the bevvies, the Surrealistic emags, the grinding work schedule – we feel it might've taken its coddy toll on our health, our wellbeing ...'

'PFFF!' I trumpeted. 'I haven't clocked either of you so much as even sniffle a bitter-gator in the past few weeks!'

'We're just petty feeble feeli-palones, sire,' Priscilla bleated, before vomiting just aero into her ajax bedpan. 'We cannot take the pace. Perhaps it's high time we took our leave of the boutique. Possiblement a month or duey recuperating at a sanatorium might help us?'

'Bollocks and balderdash! It's just this slovenly lazybone-lavvying to blame, I'm sure of it. When was the last time your bods tasted soapy aqua?'

Sabine and Priscilla palavered not a jot now, clutching their lally-caps with quivery skeletal luppers.

'ACHTUNG! All you need is a bona dhobi, my chovis.' I scuttled to the biddychamber and clocked the tub was full-clogged with riah and a greyish-green foul-smelling sludge. 'Bof,' I side-oystered, before screeching back into the boudoir: 'Allez, allez! To the Turkish Baths we shall go! The steam will reinvigorate your bods and servos, I'm sure. Although I must advise you: tis omis only, my cherries ...'

After squawking at my remaining able-bodied dollies to make themselves useful and dhobi the boutique top-to-bottomly, I rapidly transformed Sabine and Priscilla from vomity palones to upstanding omis with a few cobbled-together fakements: pubic mousers glued above their top levers, furry chest wiglets and a jumbo knackwurst strapped betwixt their lallies. True enough these were not particularly handsome omis I found myself minnying along Queensway with quatra-dait-cha-chinka minutas later, but I felt sure the disguises would hold up in the vapour. Neither of us were propositioned by any roaming bonaroba or she-wolf as we efinked through Bayswater, but when I parkered our 10/6 fee over to the marble fungus at the entrance to the gildi sauna, nor was a sceptical ogle-rider raised.

'Where'd you get your dinarli from, Raymond?' Sabine enquired as we slop-slop-slopped down into the belly of the bathhouse. 'We haven't sold a drogle for months ...'

'Hush! Nanti polari! Your voches are duey octaves too high for this establishment, remember ...'

'You've nanti the manliest voche yourself, your Lordship ...'

'Merz! No more palavering! Regard the lavs.' I solemnly fingered the sign: SILENCE.

After stripping medsa-naggy, we shuffled in our togas to the steam-auditorium and sat tranquil in the blank fog, sweating out our manky toxins. As was habit in these establishments, I sprawled myself out like a sparklefish, hoping a butch fantom lapper might alight upon my pulsating carnish, but alas, at nix juncture was I cajoled nor harassed by a moist male sharpering for companionship. As the steam puff-pufffed thicker and thicker, a frightening inkyboo came over. Sabine and Priscilla's gossipy whispers faded to nantwar as the biddy-latty blanked out around me. I could barely vada my own luppers in the fog as I waggled them before my opals. I pondered: what if the cloud eventually lifted and I found myself entirely alone in this codswallop metropolis, all humanoids and beasties jarried up by the fog, young Raymondo Rex left to wander the city like a nomad, a lone lizard, a hermit crab with nanti shell ...?

'Sabine?' I called out in the inkyboo, aimlessly wandering the blank desert. 'Sabine? Sabine?'

I was rapidly awoken by a pogi CRICK-CRACKLE! ajax to my thews, and a womanly cry: 'Aîe!'

The blistering steam had cooked Sabine's and Priscilla's knackwursts, causing the skin to burst like some cateva cartso disorder. Sloppy crumbs of mogue penile tissue splattered hither and thither across the mosaic tiles. I savvied, Ô comrades, we must exit this suffocating netherworld pronto.

We minced back to the boutique through Hyde Park in what I imagined to be beatific silence. I ponced the lathery steampower should've left the donnas maxi rinsed and rejuvenated, and I looked forward to a nova era of gloriosa hygienic lovespreading – and yet the following juno the zots were back at their bedpans, bent-doppel, vomiting more violently than ever.

'What coddy unrevolutionary claptrap is this?!' I cried. 'What meshigena chronic affliction has caused your steely constitutions to dwindle so?'

'We savvy not, sire,' Sabine grumbled with worms of bile dangling from her vonka.

'Clear enough this isn't hedonism giving you the belly-wobbles,' I snapped. 'You've been purged and pampered, the boutique's been ultra-scrubbed – and yet still you're retching and rocketing this diabolical muck ...'

'Regard the Goose's leavings, your Lordship,' Priscilla sniffled.

The beastie blinked up at us, writhing and salivating in a smeary pool of his own caca, quong-gravy and feathers.

'We feel utterly mortlike,' Sabine added. 'Send us off to the sanitarium – we'll return molto revitalised and maxi revolutionary, we promise.'

'Nanti that!' I ogled them suspiciously. Was this all just an act? Had the palones been forcing their luppers down their garglers and forcing their din-dins from their kishkas as some sly getaway emag? 'You're going nowhere, my darlings. The quacks'll battyfang your servos out thataways. The eagles'll jarry your souls!'

Nevertheless, it worried me daffy my duey favourite dollybirds might keel over any minuta. They certainly looked convincingly dicky, their jolly eeks the colour of paving slabs, ogle-sockets like crusty volcanic craters.

Pacing around our tangy disinfected latty, I savvied I had nanti natty reason to keep the Sordid Goose captive as guard doggy now anyhow, given nix pop had ventured through our portal for months. For uno momento the beastie's eek was euphoric as I unclipped his choke-chain from the clobber-rail, then just as rapidly he flippered sour again as myself, Bruce and Rosa Winkel bundled him upstairs, dragging him by his riah, lappers and quack-platters to the flash-flash-hum-churnering Blank Chamber. After tethering the septic zot to the radiator and cleffing the portal SPLATCH! behind us, I gaily returned to my duey deathbed darlings and declared: 'Et voilà! The Goose is safely quarantined! And thus thence therefore there's nix bona reason why you shouldn't both be full-fettled and gleaming with health by the morrow. Oui? Nein?' I grinned sardonic.

'I don't know, sire,' Sabine blub-blubbed. 'What if it's not just the Goose's expulsions to blame? Possiblement we feel we've been poisoned. Perhaps hospital is the right choice after all – the nattiest precaution lest we've got something more sinister swimming in our sangstream?'

'Poisoned?' I polled. A familiar decomposing eek blazed before my opals. My ribcage jangled. 'Je te répète: has anyone clocked that supreme batatat the Interrupter mincing about here since our fête d'autocritique? Nanti suspicious civvies loitering outside? Nix leering opals betwixt the fenêtre bars?'

Sabine and Priscilla shared a nervy glance.

'MERDRRRE!' I squawked, savvying with lally-collapsing pangs that Herman had already struck again. Foolishly I'd ponced his bonus revenge would be aimed towards yours truly. Foolishly I'd failed to vada the swine might ferricadooz me where it hurt even worster: my beloved beautiful Yé-Yé Dollies.

'Spread yourselves flatly!' I commanded. 'You've been poisoned! Allow me to pump your kishkas pronto!'

Bizarrely my dolls did not seem ultra eager to be cured by this sane medical advice. I dragged them by their ankles from their grubby eiderdowns, growling through grimacing fangs: 'Allez! ALLEZ! We must purge your guts immediately, my cherries!'

'NO! NO NO, RAYMOND!' the donnas squealed, as if their servos had been so thoroughly addled by the poison, they felt their lavvies depended on keeping this foul muck on the inside.

After wrestling another few minutas and finally pinning my dollies down on the floor with my lally-caps, fists poised to pummel their bellies, the pair admitted: 'We've not been poisoned, Raymond. We're fine, we're fine. We're in perfectly bona nick.' The zots gave each other another pogi nervy glance, then polled in unison with the voches of petty microbes: 'We're pregnant.'

I collapsed - at first with momentary fatherly joy, before the coddy realisation hit: I was, of course, still The Walking Contraceptive, always The Walking Contraceptive. This was not my doing.

The Alienation of Labour

NOVAK WEARS CUCKOLD'S HORNS.

NELLY FRANCE GALL'S 'BABY POP'.

Trust me, dearest readers, I did everythin**g** I could to take care of those bijou bambinos. Almost immediately upon nellying Sabine and Priscilla's specjal**ni** **ne**ws[*] I vagaried outways to parker a pair of knitting needles, a quart of Coca-Cola and mustard-salz – but strangely the tarts did not seem molto eager to let me perform a backdoor abigail[†] betwixt their lallies.

When I pressed them to screech the nom of the father, the pair seemed genuinely flummoxed. They swore they had not been charvered by any pop but myself in the past duey years. The only sperma**t**ozoomers they had encountered, they polled

---

* Yes, there was a pattern. Emily counted thirty-one rogue bold letters in each chapter, always following this sequence: **g, n, i, n, e, t, s, i, l, f, i, t, i, n, i, r, a, e, n, a, t, n, i, r, p, e, m, p, l, e, h**. Aside from a few words standing out (**nine, nets, fit in, IRA, MP**), she was unsure what to make of this stream of nonsense.

Aware that it was her job to remove all incriminating asides – not add to them – Emily left what she felt was a subtle but striking memo for Merritt and Trefoil: 'Re: m/s at risk – bold characters? Meaning?? Em.' Then she shuffled back to her desk, ripped up her own hastily scribbled findings and carried on glumly copying out Novak's odious prose, wishing she felt more like one of the heroic female codebreakers at Bletchley Park in the 1940s, rather than a helpless, hapless collaborator with the other side ...

† Stanley wasn't aware of this slang term when he and Iris named their daughter Abigail, but knowing what we know now (O, what even *do* we know now?), was this a provocation from Novak, a spiteful christening by Iris or just more paranoia on our part?

with frigid crunched-up eeks, were the Goose's constant projectile outpourings. And yet, in spite of this utterly disturbing implication, the donnas still wished to keep the bambinos!

This is the problem with mothers. They become rapidly attached to the petty pink parasites invading their kishkas, confusing the lavvy-draining freedom-shushing monsters with bona fide morsos of themselves that they try their utmo**s**t to protect rather than STAMP OUT. I of course savvied clear as one-way glaze the detrimental effect those needy bâtards would have on our flawless utopia, but no matter how hard I tried laying traps for the bloated mares (trip hazards, scalding b**i**ddyaqua) or spiking their herbata with methylated spirits or Mogadon, come Fevrier 1968 the dolls were both spread-eagled at St Bart's, screechering brootish as they squeezed out the slimy critters. I was not present at either birth but I nellied later the bambinos howled immediately upon arrival, rightly c**l**ocking that they were in for a molto hellish lavvy if they were to stay put under my roof.

Parenthood: I cannot recommend it.

Ever **fait**hful to my Old Mare's gloriosa savagery, I'd urged Sabine and Priscilla not to register the births (partly so we could br**in**g the bébés up amoral, uncensored, under the radar, et ceterara – and partly so, should they happen to be accidentally murdered not long into the**ir** nova lavvies, nix sharpering-pops need find out), but squirting the batatats out in a bona fide hospital put paid to that. The duey mares returned to the boutique a week later with their squealing leeches wrapped in swaddling-bimph, and n**a**turellem**en**t our sweet, sumptuous Liberated Lavvy was never to be the same again.

To this juno I often ponder: had it been my own heroic sperm**at**ozoomers that produced these creatures, would I have showered them with reflex love and brought them up as bijou pri**n**ces or pr**i**ncesses? Certainly I could not blame (and did not punish) the Sordid Goose for this accidental frightful fertilisation. More than anything I just felt extra hateful and bitter towards our sick sha**rpe**ring-State and the Shrinker that shushed my quongs – and yet arguably the babes' perpetual parnyaqua, condescending bug-ogles and delusions of grandeur would've rapidly sent me sniffling for the rat poison either way.

So wise so young, they say do never lavvy long, ja?

BOF. This is all wind and piss now anyhow. I have thoroughly enlightened and entertained you with the intricate mille-feuille of my own feeli upbringing – I do not wish to waste any **m**ore precious pa**p**yrus on the codswallop upbringings of these two petty prats. I am sure you can imagine the effect the bambinos had on my bona egalitarian commune: the arrogank of youth, the bébés expressing nix but greed and dissatisfaction like a pair of mini fash dicktitt**le**rs, screeching for willet-milk, forcing my beloved dollies to slave over them all **h**ours of the juno. The combination of French Blues and parnying beasties at dawn meant I got nix rest whatsoever now. I became a medsa-omi, a munge-pop, a skeleton with all my flesh and vitality slopped in a heap round my ankles. Wakey inkyboos galore.

It should go without palavering: I was a somewhat touchy omi during this twisted period, and partial to bouts of skitterish behaviour. Trust me, comrades – TRUST ME! – when I screeve I had the beasties' bestest interests in mind when I filled the biddytub with rotting fish-tets, soiled sanitary napkins, bin jus, caca, sour milk, et cetera, and held the bambinos' eeks under the manky aqua. Naturellement their mamas screamed at me when finally they schonked open the locked portal (screaming seemed to be these palones' stock response to all major/minor quibbles in 1968), but I insisted it was for the bébés' benefit, it was character-forming, twas an ancient Romanoid ritual, twud strengthen the bats' immune systems, et ceterarararararar-ararara ...

The palones appeared in lurid fleur-riddled hippy clobber and near enough tore my plastic surgery from my skull – and to this juno I'm nanti certain what I found more vulgar and distasteful: their rancid hippy schmutta, or the fairy mumsy panic surrounding their daffy sprats' wellbeing. Either way, I savvied clear enough: my duey mostest prized dollies nix longer wished to obey the right honourable Lord Never-Never. My teachings had been ultra natty and my love was true – but some humanoids are just never satisfied. I fancy the puppet-strings were efinked the momento the umbilical cords were clipped. ACHTUNG! Fuck them. By the end of the year I would be left with just tangles.

Dandelion Fluff[*]

NOVAK WEARS SHIMMERY MOHAIR BUM-FREEZER MANTO, UNCREASABLE DRAINPIPETTES, METHS-PURPLE MERINO CAMISHA, ULTRASCHVARTZ WINKLE-PICKERS.

NELLY SERGE GAINSBOURG'S 'QUI EST "IN", QUI EST "OUT"'.

By springtide 1968 the anglo civvies seemed to have finally caught on to the anti-eagle savagery I'd been screeching my whole lavvy. The adorable bats had organised a grand protest against the Yankee/Viet Cong battyfanging in Trafalgar Plaza for 17th March and, poncing it might be an occasion of wunderbar merrymaking, I intended to drag my daitcha dour dollies down thataways to join in the revelry.

I fancied the united chanting under Nelson's Colin might help rekindle our heroic US and THEM savagery – although there was always the risk the square would be teeming with deplorable hippies and students hellbent on stealing away my darlin**gs**[†] with their own fluffy toffee peace and love caca. I was still only

---

* Chapter received Monday, 25th May 1970 – forty-nine days to go.

† Emily cracked the code over the week-end. The message spelled out backwards: **Help me print an ear in it if listening**. But what did the plea mean, who was responsible for it and who was it aimed at? Emily tried to arrange a meeting with Merritt and Trefoil to show them her findings, but given the more chilling discovery in just a few pages' time, they both seemed far too agitated and paranoid to pay their secretary much heed. (And we admit: we thought she might be manoeuvring for a payrise after taking on all this extra typing. Forgive us, Emily.)

twenty-three myself but felt more like a doddering fungus now, so out of touch I was with this crass nova youthquake cult of freeflowing riah, vegetarianism, mudlust and swamp musica. I could not stand these addle-plots! They put the hip in hypocrisy: claiming to be free spirits despite palvering about RIGHT and WRONG more often and molto tediously than a charvering cloth-pop, screeching the evils of Capitalism while Mummy and Daddy's dinarli probably plop-plop-plopped weekly into their Ye Olde Nova Barclays personal checking accounts, preaching free love despite not wanting to share their girls. Still, perhaps what I detested most of all about the Hippy Craze was the schmutta. These fleur-brained wastrels had nix concept of bona taste: they joshed themselves up like their grandmamas or the village idiot, nellied naff twiddly-diddly-dee medieval musica, all the while pi**ni**ng for some fantastical pre-industrial Arcadia populated by nymphs and goblins that definitely never existed. Liberty for these prats meant nanti hygiene, no carnish, nix backbone, nantwar well-fitting threads ...

To compensate for this nationwide lapse in sophistication, I forced my vegetating yé-yés out of their frumpy florid Victorian gowns and back into their old A-line paper minidrogles – and I too squeezed into my original Il Bozzolo mohair suit: the shimmery Mod cozzy from which all this beautiful Hell and shapeshiftering wonderment had spiralled. Ô, we would show these filthy hippies how to stage a gloriosa protest – and look fuckering fantabulosa while doing it ...

I was medsa-way through screeving a few rapid slogans across my followers' chests (CIVILISATION WILL KILL US ALL, UP THE GOOKS!) when the eek I detest more even than Uncle Sam's or Leering Timothy's appeared at our front fenêtre. Jolted by thu**n**derous adrenaline, I thrust my lapper down the front of my lally-covers, grasping frantically for the spray-botty so I could greet the bat with my own peppery napalm blast. And yet – Ô, MERCY ME – my charvering drainpipettes were so tight, as I tried to release the botty from my silky garter, the cheet went off unexpectedly, sneezing its fiery jus direct at my inner thew and naggy scarred perineum.

'****!' I howled, feeling the toxic sirop jarrying my nether-carnish like a glimmer-breathing piranha.

Writhing about the parquet, I ogled helplessly as Herman entered our abode, barely blinking at me as he strutted past, his riah all pouffed-up like a gildi tamarin mono.

'Appreh— hend this uns-sanitary bunt!' I dry-retched.

Naturellement I'd expected my darling protectors to immediately tackle the bastard to the ground and drag him back outwards, but when I clocked the greeting the arroganki prat received, for uno momento – in spite of my hellfiring nethers – I was rendered frigid.

Sabine and Priscilla were chanting some meese rosbif folk guff into their screeching lullaby-leeches' nells when Herman swept them up with a swish of his kaftan. There were bijou affectionate lammers and titterings, the bambinos molto gay now and tranquil, their mares all milky and oystery and kittenish.

'MERZ!' I squealed. 'When I polled, "APPREHEND THIS UNSANITARY BUNT!" I did not mean reef him like a fruity octopudding! What brings you to our sacred establishment, you insufferable blurt?'

'We invited him to watch over the bambinos,' Sabine answered. 'You said so yourself: you didn't want the babes joining us at this here jolly bile-extravaganza on the Plaza ...'

Priscilla ogled Herman with mogue reproach. 'Though he was meant to creep in through the back portal.'

'I'm not one for a discreet entrance, I admit,' Herman polled.

'He's molto bona with the babies,' added Sabine.

'Oui, oui, he's quite the humanoid chloroform,' I retorted, regarding the babes now slumbering dazed and hushy in their mares' lappers.

Sabine and Priscilla wrinkled a snotty blink-blink at me, but thankfully some of my other devotees had the bona grace to reer along with my natty quips and insults. Typically my most loyal followers were now those with the least symmetrical eeks (Rosa Winkel, Séverine Vivisection) and the least dazzling servos (Bruce, Bonnie) – those with nanti prospects outside the boutique, those with nix to gain and nowhere to go if coughed back out into the grotty welt pronto. They swallowed the US and THEM savagery like invalids schlumphing down medicine, like doggies rolling over and over again for their master – but still, with maximum regret and pokiness, I just did not wish to pamper and LOVE them as spectacularly as I did Sabine, Priscilla, Donatella Diptera: my mostest treasured fortuni dollybirds currently clutching that lion-riah invader like chavvies clawing at some cheap fairground trinket.

'This is utter lunacy!' I bleated. 'Clear enough you're nanti aware of the history betwixt myself and this idiotic blond blob. Clear enough you don't recognise him as the fash-lammering, poisonous, square, authority-felching, frigid, frightful eagle-eek he is!'

'O, they know me very well by now, Raymond, dear. We're much more well acquainted than you imagine,' Herman cackled.

'Nanti that!' I squeaked, rising gingerly from the parquet. 'I think you'll find I've drilled my dollies so wonderfully and thoroughly they'd never normally associate themselves with such a hateful newt as you. They must be under some coddy spell ... drogas ... Keith ... voodoo ...'

'Au contraire.' Herman sidled up to me like a venomous crab and side-oystered: 'In fact, to use your own vulgar lavs, I've also drilled them wonderfully and thoroughly.' He ogled the bambinos again with gay rosiness. 'And, unlike yourself, I don't fire blanks.'

My kishkas twisted. For uno momento I clocked the feeli bellboy eek of the young Herman in the features of the bambinos. Ô Jupiter, Ô Judas – it took a mighty amount of courage and composure not to vomit on them instantly, then scarper into the ultrablue morning. I ogled my quickest escape route, but then savvied I too had nanti other prospects outside the boutique, I too had nix to gain and nowhere to go if coughed back out into the grotty welt pronto. And so, I oystered my way into oblivion:

'ACHTUNG, my darlings: how could you let this fascist prat lay his lappers upon you?! He poisoned your noble leader – those filthy luppers forced some evil jus upon me, you recall? Nix doubt he's poisoned you all too. You must be delirious! Pray tell, what evil serum has he been feeding you?!'

Sabine blinked at me with smirking oglelids. 'Actually, Raymond, it was my lapper that handed you that revolting coffee, not his.'

Ô, MON DIEU. I clung to the countertop, concerned my lally-caps might buckle again any minuta.

'WE'RE all in this TOGETHER,' Priscilla snickered, hugging Herman and the other tart tightly.

'Ever pondered why we keep returning from your daffy Surrealist missions empty-lappered, or with the wrong requested cheet?' Sabine polled.

'Enlighten me,' I groaned.

'We've been seeing him on the sly.'

Ô, dear reader, twas as if the petty devils were unscrewing morsos of my bod with a gross fanging monkey-wrench. Outrageously the mares chorused: 'He's a bona lover.'

'NEIN!' I screeched. 'This fairy sea-queen is not who he seems! Do you not savvy this prat was a supreme dish-licker in the Merchant Navy, the lowliest of the low, a sycophantic nonentity? This is not the switched-on swinging-pop you imagine him to be! This addle-plot sucked up to authority, sucked off the Chief Steward even!'

The Sub-Humanoid merely reered up at these prickly lavs. 'The lowliest of the low? If I recall rightly, Raymondo, it was you lathering the heads and tumbler-shushing while I thrived as bellboy up topside ...'

'MERZ! Don't be ridiculous. Twas only my unyieldy aversion to bootlickering that forced me into those lowly postures. I may have been scrubbing caca from the khazis every morn, but at least I did so with my integrity intact! At least I did not EAGERLY BEND!'

'O yes, mighty dignified and unbent you looked, old cock, scrabbling about the deck on your lally-caps ...'

'Bof. I'm sure you looked terribly divine and unbent with Chief Steward Sturgeon's fash bushy cartso rammed up your pimpled corybungus ...'

'Doubtless more divine than you penetrating that rotting stingray, ey, no?'

Roundabout us my dollies' eeks kept shifting from bewilderment to twistiness to titillation. My mostest loyal followers hooted and clapped their lappers with each slur I splurted forth, while the traitors reered along with the Interrupter like idiot lattywives gurgling at the latest cod VadaVision comedian.

'Well, the past can fuck-off-thataways now for all I care,' I grunted. 'SS UNMENTIONABLE and MS HIPPOCAMPUS are but fantombarkas, ghost-ships in the old memory banks now. What concerns me more is your current status, squire, your coddy blossoming from pre-pubic dish-licker to full-fledged eagle-eek, sniffling around my personal property.' I regarded the treacherous mares again. 'This fash-felching slug was never destined to be a hip-pop – tis all a mally masquerade! He's an eagle-in-peasants'-clobber, a yes-omi, a tragic conformist. No wonder the zot doesn't take kindly to our bona bolshy utopia ...'

'This is utopia?!' Herman gestured around the chaotic chamber, littered with meese morsos (sloppy nappies, smeared munja, vomitus and caca) his own fuckering bambinos were responsible for, not I. 'If anyone's a fash bat, Raymondo, it's you: holding these youths here against their will, forcing them into all manner of ridiculous exploits, many certainly punishable under the Human Rights Act ...'

'Pah! These are free pops! This is our Liberated Lavvy! This is what freedom looks like! Oui, ducky, it's not the pristine, ultra-sterile PVC paradise the VadaVision makes us believe the future holds – freedom is dirty, freedom is meese, freedom is beautiful!'

'Nonsense. You're just a sloth – a manipulative slob forcing these so-called free pops to bend for you to compensate for all the bending you done in the Merch Navy. You just prey on the weak. YOU'RE the imposter, the authority-flop, not I.'

'P–'

'Nanti polari! Does it not worry you, Raymondo, that you've got to where you are today based on an elaborate illusion, a completely fictitious persona?'

'PFF! We're all actors, darling, and you more than most. I'm merely a sane-palavering, love-preaching frog trying to get by in this thoroughly square oppressive anglo metropolis ...'

Herman ogled my threads. 'You're nanti French – the ridiculous accent doesn't fool me! You're a ticket, you're plastic. A mogue Mod, a Futurist cunt, a Sawdust Caesar!'

'How dare you!'

'Regard your own cozzy. Eyetie tailoring, and not even particularly fine eyetie tailoring.'

'I'm a natty omi.'

'Natty as in Nationalist, as in Nazionalismo, as in Nazi.'

'Nanti that. I'm a bona fide frog. Je suis une Francophile!'

'A General Francisco Francophile.'

'I'm as French as they come. I pop forty French Blues a day. Imported from France. Vive la république!'

'Smith, Kline & French Blues, you'll find. Imported from the yee-haw Capitalist US of A.'

'I reek of garlic! I'm full of cheese! Regard my natural barnet: a French Crop, and nix mistake. Only the finest pedigree Gallic riah-genes could produce such a do ...'

'Haw-haw! No, no – this is not a French Crop. Your clumsy lappers must've picked up the wrong wig by mistake. Regard the brutally chopped fringe. This is the Caesar Cut. HAIL, CAESAR!' Herman hooted, casting his right lapper out in a sardonic Roman salute, then lunging for my bijou shyka and unsportingly ripping it from my scalp. 'Haw-haw! Now look at you! A boiled egg in a blackshirt, isn't that right? Il Duce, jawohl?'

My beloved bastard followers gazed at my baldy tet with a mixture of brooliment and queasiness. While this cruel unwigging did not drain away all my powers like the Philistines fatcharing Samson, I certainly felt molto nervy and weakly when I clocked the cateva mutinous eeks among my once-trusted devotees. Half my dollies seemed to turn on me, hooting and guffawing like it was I who was the meese circus freak, the lowly guttery bête noire – and not them. 'Hé-hé-hé-hé-hé-hé-hé!' they cackled.

Ô, as you savvy only too well by now, my faithful compassionate readership, I am nanti an omi who enjoys criticism much. In an ideal mond I would have installed in my jacket lining enough plastic explosives to completely erase the humiliation of scenarios such as this one. As it stood, I was given little choice but to respond like a rabid doggy and just hope for the best. Pouncing on the batatat with fangs and talons bared, I grabbed duey lapperfuls of his preposterous Beau Brummell bouffant and promptly dragged the bugger to the ground, screeching just Dadaist battle-fluff now. My rage was such, the details of this unprecedented physical aggro are blurry. I remember very little. My most loyal followers, sane pops that they are, undoubtedly provide the most reliable account: that I yanked Herman fully outways by his riah, dumped him on the cobblestones and pulverised him with the fabulosa cold efficiency of a caboosh-crushing vacaya or carnish-mincer. The treacherous mares would probably claim Herman vagaried of his own accord after pummelling me daffy, and that concussion is to blame for my sketchy memory. Either way, I was completely covered in some twat's blood when I staggered back inways. My return was met with molto triumphant tittering, cheering and jeering. I slurred at my dolls: 'D'accord. The parasite has shcarpered. Pray tell: have you all recovered your senses? Any lingering batty arrogank or mishplaced petulance among you? Alors. Let us abandon this tainted cube for the afterjuno. Trafalgar Plaza awaits – with fountains overflowing with bile! I fancy a gross expulshion of gaiety and hatred will bring our muddled servos and thumpers hurtling back into sweet alignment. Oui? Nein?'

'Nein,' Sabine snapped, a pink leech still hanging from one willet. 'We'll do as we please now. We're sick of following your meshigena orders – deplorable dicktittler that you are.'

I grabbed for my strewn wiglet and plopped it atop my tet back-to-front. 'Merz!' I croaked. 'How is it I deserve such ungrateful palavering?! Have I not liberated you from the ugliest of ugly travails? Have I not provided you with a de-luxe off-the-leash lavvystyle? Protected you from the gizzards of prowling eagle-eeks out thataways? And this is my reward: you've completely erased my ultra-sane teachings from your servos in one coddy swoop – and handed yourselves over willety-nilly to that most fash batty nonentity!'

'He's a bona omi, Raymond,' polled Priscilla. 'H*** reversed your reverse-servo-lathering simply by being nice to us – and listening to us. If he's the most fash batty nonentity you know of, I dare say we'll be absolutely fine rubbing pols with the lesser eagles out thataways – and thusly therefore that's why it's high time we took our leave. For good.'

'PFFF!' This lav was spoken horizontal to the parquet, yours truly having more or less passed out, so fattygayed I was after my heroic barnying with Herman. I mumblered softly: 'Help.'

'You're pathetic,' Sabine s**na**rled. 'You've got nanti sway over us now. We're sick of you stifling us, Raymond, telling us what to say, what to ponce, stopping us from doing what we really want ...'

'Ô, hearken this! Moi? Monsieur Astérisque,* censoring your

---

* Reader, were you as startled by this line of dialogue as us? Admittedly, on first reading, its chilling significance did not immediately strike us.

If you recall (see footnotes to Novak's title page, etc.), Raymond originally wanted to call his memoirs *Dieu-du-Jour*. *Mister Asterisk* was our title. When we initially read the above exchange, we'd become so used to our new title, Novak's Gallicised 'Monsieur Astérisque' registered not a jot – until Trefoil, combing through the manuscript later that night in the Novak Arms, was rendered instantly sober when the ominous asterisk went off like a big black firework on the page. Flustered in the office the following morning, we tried to recall: was

lavs and lavvies?!' I cackled from the floor. 'Pray tell, what is it you REALLY want to do?'

Sabine stiffened a bit straighter. 'We want to be free. Truly free. Free to learn for ourselves the highs and lowlies of the dolly welt out thataways. Free to make our own mistakes, free to make our own money, free to frolic with our own chosen comrades. We don't need insulation or isolation. You want us to indulge in all our animal impulses, but caged animals don't act the same as their brothers and sisters outside the zoo gates. You think you've liberated us by hiding us away from society! Pah! We're vagarying pronto, Raymond.'

'Nanti that!' I squawked, rising reinvigorated from the parquet. I ogled those twinkly-eeked dollies I believed were still loyal – Rosa Winkel, Bonnie, Bruce, Séverine, Veronica – and with taut levers I splurted: 'Clear enough these two treacherous tarts have lost their minds, have they not? Post-natal lunacy. Clear enough they need a gross dose of sparkle-therapy in the Blank Chamber, oui, nein?'

---

the appellation 'Mister Asterisk' inspired by Raymond's own words, or had we indeed made it up ourselves? We scoured the manuscript from the beginning, hoping to find evidence of the Scum King using it himself first, to no avail. Of course, if Novak's version of reality was to be trusted, he apparently blurted the above 'Monsieur Astérisque' long before approaching us to publish his memoirs: March 1968, more than eighteen months prior to his first communication with us. Was this all just a freakish/innocuous coincidence? Alas, it seemed unlikely. The term 'Mister Asterisk' was far too obscure – and we *insist* we came up with it first! After all, *Mister Asterisk* related not only to Novak's enigmatic elusiveness and the dirty bat's need for censorship, but above all it related to our *supplementary footnotes*, our meddling with his manuscript. Raymond was never supposed to be aware of our additions. Was this a sign he was all too aware? And if so: how? O, our disturbed brains could barely cope with all the unsettling possibilities! And yet we had to admit: if we indeed came up with the moniker first, it stood to reason Novak must have either bugged our HQ, has had access to our papers or – QUELLE HORREUR – the evil batatat was among us at the launch of *The Nuremberg Nymphos* (see footnotes to 'Elektrizität Macht Frei'), when we first brainstormed the alternate titles and uttered 'Mister Asterisk' out loud in public for the first (we believe the only?) time …

'O ... oui. O, mais OUI, your Lordship,' my loyal pops stuttered, quite possibly concerned they'd be slammed in there too if they answered otherwise.

'Hé-hé! This will give you a jolly taste of true incarceration, my cherries!' I squeaked as we yank-yanked the bitches and their leeches up the stairwell. 'This will make you vada what it REALLY means to have your freedom shushed from beneath your stampers, you daffy batatats!'

As I uncleffed and creepied open the portal to the Blank Chamber, a meese barnyard von socked the backs of our garglers. Peering inways, I clocked the usual diso**r**der: the **p**ools of congealed bod-fluids, the nest of pluckered feathers glooped together with spittle and caca, the open sores, the perma-screeching oyster. The Goose looked ultra-emaciated, having been fed only birdseed sprinkl**e**d through the hatch – and somewhat arva-starved too, stripped naggy and thrusting gruesomely on the end of his greasy leash.

'No! NO, NO!' the mares protested as we struggled to drag the**m** over the threshold. With manic opals, they appealed to their former sisters – but alas, this last-ditch balderdash was utterly futile. 'Can't you see we're all slaves here?!' Sabine screamed. 'HELP! STOP! AÏE! We're slaves and it's not even paid slavery! We were better off with Monsieur Drench! AÏE!!'

Hurtful lavs indeed. Difficult to recall exactly my response, though molto likely I let rip with **ple**nty more schonks, slaps and staccato insults – 'plastic bats ... papier-mâché mongrels ... cannot take the pace ... freedom burns too brightly for you ... dandelion fluff ... fuckering yokels ... suburban bints ... hangers-on ... frauds ... fakes ... unradical mares ...' – until finally they were safely slammed in the fluoro-flickering cell.

'L'INCARCERATION VOUS LIBÈRE!' I yowled at the doppel-bolted portal – though nix doubt the blank noise was so brootis**h**, this rousing slogan had nanti effect.

A Nightmare Sprang in Grosvenor Square*

NOVAK WEARS BRUTUS TRIMFIT CAMISHA, CREASED DRAINPIPETTES, A NOVA BONA FIDE FRENCH CROP ATOP HIS BALDY TET.

NELLY STELLA'S 'CAUCHEMAR AUTO-PROTESTATEUR'.

The first sign that this was going to be the fairiest, most sterile of protests was the sight of Nelson's Colin wrapped up in scaffolding like an overprotective rubber johnathan. My otta remaining dollies – Séverine, Donatella Diptera, Bruce, Lionel, Baroness von Fisty, Bonnie, Veronica, Rosa Winkel – seemed as gloomy as moi as we slithered into the crowds and nellied the bolshy softies' quibbles. These twonks had christened themselves the New Radical Left, but as far as I could vada, they were just plummy self-righteous squares with beards and duffel coats palavering abstractly about issues that depressed them rather than hot topics that ramped them up and made them ultra lively and luminous. True enough, on the face of it we were united by a glimmering hatred for eagle-eeks (the eagles-du-jour being Big Texas Lynda, Old Nix, Enoch, Wilson), but a nova radical mond overseen by these dour zots would be a maxi servo-numbing existence indeed. Each bijou grupa of chanters had their own banner – OSMOTHERLEY ANARCHISTS, ROYAL LEAMINGTON

* Chapter received Friday, 29th May 1970 – forty-five days to go.

SPA RADICAL SOCIALIST LEAGUE – which suggested a morso of manic merrymaking at the very least, but the whole scenario had more the feel of a gross garden party organised by fuckering teetotal vegetarians or Brownies.

'Ho Chi Minh! Ho Chi Minh! Ho Chi Minh!' was the ge**ne**ral gist of the grand lavvy-advice these plops had to offer.

'All these feeli like-minded pops,' I sighed, clutching Bruce and Séverine tightly, 'and they'd rather chant the nom of some distant Commie fungus instead of stripping naggy and indulging in some bona love-thy-neighbourly frottage in the fountains ...'

I pouted at myself in the reflective aqua, prodding suspiciously at the pogi cracks* and wrinkles forming around my opals and

---

* On our return to the office after a fraught pub luncheon on the 27th, we immediately began tearing open the walls with hammers and chisels. While most of us felt it was unlikely Novak had bugged our HQ, there were certain aspects of his memoirs that made us feel he knew more about us than could be gleaned from just our humble pocketbooks. For example: 'Monsieur Astérisque' aside, was it not too much of a coincidence that Novak telephoned our office just days after we'd stated our suspicions about the authenticity of his stories (see footnotes to 'Neptunus Rex' and 'Dishonourable Discharge')? Did Stanley not feel somewhat violated when the Emperor used his daughter's name as a slang term for abortion in 'The Alienation of Labour'? Was his repeated use of the term 'glassy opals' a sly indication that he was watching us?

'Balderdash!' was Merritt's response, looking on flustered and disgusted as we carved gaping holes in his smooth plasterwork. 'There's parallels certainly – but isn't that true of all decent literature? The author offers up random little truths and details the reader picks up on as and when they match his or her personal experiences ...' Merritt flicked through the copy of *Madame Bovary* he'd only recently purchased from E. Joseph in Charing Cross Road. 'Listen here – where is it? – "Motionless we traverse countries we fancy we see, and your thought, blending with the fiction, playing with the details" – mind the wires, mind where the fucking plug is! – "follows the outline of the adventures. It mingles with the characters, and it seems as if it were yourself palpitating beneath their costumes."'

We were incredulous towards this highfalutin guff. 'Our thoughts aren't *blending with the fiction*, Stanley. These are supposed to be Novak's factual memoirs! We're not *playing with the details* – he's playing with us! We're sure he knows certain things about us – and he keeps dropping hints, making these little threats in the prose, to keep us quiet maybe, to let us know he's got his eye on us ...'

'No, but we *are* playing with the details!' Merritt flapped his hand at our latest footnotes: scraps of scribbled shorthand stapled to Novak's dog-eared m/s.

levers. Was I still bona-vadaring? To spite that interruptering batatat back thataways, I'd parkered some nova threads from BRUTUS on our way down to the parade. I was arguably the snappiest dressed on the whole plaza, but still, judging by the bland cozzies on show, these New Left pops were more interested in taking fash advice from that faraway potato-in-a-grey-tunic Mao Tse-tung than peacocking for the fortuni dazzlers in their immediate vicinity. Ô, politics. Tis a most complicated subject at the bestest of times, is it not?

Thankfully we were soon distracted by what sounded like a far more promising orgy round the corner: a riot had apparently sparkled in Grosvenor Square! Scarpering eagerly thataways, I envisioned a splinter-grupa of bona fide anarchists shedding this dreary politico-palavering and shedding their corduroy strait-jackets, raucously transforming that prim, pruned and prudish lawn into an exotic, ultra-fruity Garden of Unearthly Delights - and naturellement I wanted in. And yet, ALAS ALAS ALAS ALAS, after greedily speeding through Mayfair, our glittery mood flopped when we reached Grosvenor Square and clocked the so-called riot. Twas a one-sided barny, to be sure. Apparently these Nova Radical pops regarded themselves as Blank Panthers, omis theoretically interested in physical aggro to spur social change, but these bearded thinkers were nix match for the

---

Needless to say, after turning all the walls to Swiss cheese, we couldn't find any rogue wires. Trefoil twice came close to electrocuting himself, snagging a snaking live wire as he probed around with his chisel, but other than a few grotty clumps of old horsehair, there was nothing untoward to be found hidden in the plaster.

Still, the paranoia was hard to shift. Without Merritt's blessing we raided petty cash and bought two transistor radios, setting them up in opposite corners of the office and tuning them to static, filling the room with piercing, protective white noise.

'Talk about blending with the fiction! You've recreated Raymond's bloody Blank Chamber!' was Merritt's response before locking himself in his own comparatively serene – if dismal, disordered and dank – office.

After an hour or so we barely noticed the squall, but perhaps subliminally it exacerbated our anxieties – and from June onwards the fear only escalated …

mounted plod charging the crowds like blundering Horse-omis of ze Apocalypse. Cowering behind a relatively large shrub, we watched with condescending opals as the sharpering-omis went after solo protesters like they were chasing streakers at a fuckering fussball match. For the most part the riot simply involved tweed-pops darting about aimlessly then falling over before being dragged off the grass by black-trenchcoated bully-boys. Twas a depressing spectacle, a twisted shitstorm that only seemed to cement the plod's superiority. Yippies yanked hither and thither by their matted riah. Puff-puff-puffs of tear-gas like cateva profumo from the trampled fleurs. Naff retaliation from the protesters: 'Ho Chi Minh! Ho Chi Minh!' Parnying donnas in Paddington Bear mantos. Mud and bluster. All watched over by the gross golden eagle* atop the embassy roof.

Later the inkies would praise the plod for coolly defusing the Angry Mob, but in truth this was typical uncalled-for aggro on the sharpering-plops' part and embarrassing to ogle. Admittedly there were pockets of bona fide troublemakers – like the sinister bald eagles on the sideylines with fatchared tets and checked camishas, chanting, 'Enoch! Enoch! Enoch!' – but for the most part all the Nova Lefties were guilty of was joining arms and grunting these tedious pro-gook lavs. The plucky twats who tried even just a pogi bit of violence were swiftly swatted like bluebotties and carried off in Black Marias. It all reiterated the savagery I'd been preaching throughout the Sixties: provoke the eagles and they will swoop down and swamp you full-militant, battyfanging and newtering you without mercy in the name of keeping the peace.

'Why have these twonks given up on passive-aggro?' I pondered, hunched behind the quivering shrub. 'The zots keep

---

* While Novak preposterously seems to tar anyone outside his inner circle as an eagle, Merritt nonetheless shares his distaste for this most fascistic symbol. The heraldic crest of HMS *Legion* – the destroyer Stanley served on during WWII – was a golden spreadeagle topped with a bejeweled crown: an emblem he would not hesitate to spit on should he see it again.

screeching about peace and harmony, but this is mere chaos, and one-sided chaos at that.'

Perhaps I was a petty bit naive to think I could reverse the damage and turn this hateful barny into a gloriosa love-in, but BOF and BALDERDASH to all that – I savvied these bolshy-pops needed help pronto. Unsurprisingly my following performance appears to have been erased from all newsreels and history livers (the Propaganda Machine keeps on churnering ...), but I believe, for uno momento at least, I was the star of the show. Leaving my dollies in the bushes, I scuttled like a frisky scorpion into the heaving mass of chuntering bods, then, finding a suitable spot to park my botty, sat down in the lotus posture and began blowing kisses indiscriminately at the scowling eeks passing by.

'What good is there in just joining arms and acting like a stroppy brick wall?' I pow-wowed, creating rather a lot of saliva. 'The plod will crumble you eventually! Why not join arva-glands instead – ALLEZ, ALLEZ – show the sharpering-zots what they're missing, what gloriosa glistening delights they have the audacity to deem WRONG WRONG WRONG but are of course perfectly natural and RIGHT?'

Sadly these so-called Nova Radicals proved themselves typical dreary reactionary fuzzymuzz. The general consensus among them was: 'Fuck off, you bloody imbecile! You fucking barstard! Honestly! O, fuck off!' et cetera.

'This isn't about exposing ourselves to the bloody pigs,' one voche snapped ajax to my nells. 'This is about the plight of the National Liberation Front, the plight of the Vietnamese peo-ple!'

'What coddy logic is this?' I screeched, feeling the crowd beginning to crush me from all sides. 'What about your own urgent Liberation? Why not protest about the servo-draining boredom and whipcracking shackles of our own drizzly dismal island – rather than some distant Commie-pops' bomba-scars, sad as they may be? Turn the mirror to your own dour eeks, you bloody bastards! You bloody frigid batatats!'

The grumbling mass of unwashed bods turned on me then, treating me not like the oracle as I'd hoped, but as some enemy worster even than the warmongers in the sexless embassy over thataways. Savvying now these zots were simply beyond help, I tried my bestest to wriggle free from their grotty hokey-cokey and return to my dollies, but these cunts seemed to ponce that the only natty response to this love-guru palavering sense was to rip the poor pop to morsos. ROMANOIDS! JUDIES! PHILISTINES! I remember a few schonks to my tet, but worst of all my nova shyka was swiped in all the hubbub, leaving me full-baldy again as I was pinball-flippered from fist to fist, then finally spat unceremoniously onto the prickly lawn, in the path of quatra oncoming rozzers.

'Nick that skinhead!' one eager sharpering-omi barked, mistaking my baldy tet and gingham camisha for the regalia of those nova-Nazis on the sideylines.

'MERZ! ACHTUNG! Nein nein nein!' I protested, carried off like a plucked chicken to one of the Black Marias ajax to the green. 'I'm innocent! Je detest those fash fatchared bats! Je detest the bloody longhairs too! Unhand me, kind-hearted bona-vadaring plod!'

In spite of my desperate dorcas pleas, Her Majesty's shock-troopers were stony-eeked as they slammed me in the back of the caboosh with chinka more of these sullen Nova Radical bunts. The bruised longhairs ogled me bitterly as we set off for whatever sharpering-khazi was to be our boudoir for the noche.

So addled was my tet from the brootish hippybattering, I initially thought nantwar of this bijou detour to the cells – however, as my servo lento cleared, a meese realisation struck. After escaping from the Lumière Suite back in 1964, in all likelihood I was a WANTED MAN. Would the inspectors finger me as this frightful froggy fugitive and lock me away forevermore? Ô, MERZ, MURDER and MERDRE! As the caboosh crept rumbly through Mayfair, I clung to the savagery that I'd undergone extensive plastic surgery since that twisted period. I prayed to Jupiter my nom and eek would go unnoticed among the multitude of feeli weirdy arrestees – and yet, as far as my Nova Radical neighbours were concerned, my humble visage was proof enough of my inexcusable guilt.

'Skinheads come down here for trouble, did you?' one of the omis polled, this snotty rhino with sideyburns like duey gross lumps of grandmama's tiffin superglued to his cheeks.

'I came preaching LOVE,' I slurred, oyster full of sang. 'Passive-aggro. Peace, man – and so on and so forth.'

'Bollocks! Saw your lot shouting, "Enoch! Enoch!" You don't like immigrants, is it?'

'I AM an immigrant, you lunatic,' I spat. 'A bona fide frog. Cut me and I bleed garlic, et cetera ...'

I savvy now the bobbies' nells must've pricked just then. Selective nellying: the cornerstone of any bona law-enforcement agency ...

'Let's cut him then!' another of the Lefties blurted, this hefty brute with the opals of a morose St Bernard. 'The pig wants us to cut him. Let's cut him.'

Nonchalantly I retorted: 'I'm nix piglet, comrades. In fact, I'm more bolshy than the lot of you put together. I'm a froggy libertarian, I'm a squatter, an anarchist, an arva-fiend. Je detest all authority! This unfortunate riahdo is no fash statement – only premature baldiness, repulsive as that may be.'

Yanked into the Interview Chamber some hours later, the grilling from the sharpering-pops followed a suspiciously familiar line: 'So you're a foreign national of no fixed abode, we hear?'

MERDRE. Fearful this could be curtains for yours truly – deportation, isolation, no more dollies, nix more MULTILOVE and ADORATION – I sat up a pogi bit straighter, fixed my eek, stiffened my upper lever and polled forth in perfect toff Queeny anglo: 'Apologies, chaps, I admit I've taken a few too many bashes about the head today – more from the bloody Lefties than from your boys, I might add.' I flared my nose-thirls. 'Must've been talking bunkum earlier. Foreigner, you say? Not in the slightest!

Raymond Foster-Newman's the name. Full British citizenship, British papers. Regard my particulars.'

'You don't recall referring to yourself as a "fuckering anarchist" at least thrice on your way to the station?' Inspector Silling enquired.

'Pah! I must've lost my senses. That bloody tear-gas. Rebellion in the air. Regurgitating nonsense. No, no, not at all – I'm a Capitalist, worry not. I run a little boutique. Top-class clientele. Exorbitant price tags. I pay my taxes, of course.'

'Of course.' The Inspector scratched his oink-vonka, duey gross pink shotgun barrels trained direct at my foretet. 'Address?'

'N-Neverland. N-Never-Neverland, that is. Ogle Street, W1. I could fix you up with some fantastic clobber. In fact, I couldn't help noticing when you entered: squire, Inspector, that is – and I say this with the utmost respect – are you aware your hungry backside is gobbling those chinos behind your back? Might I suggest a slightly roomier cut?'

'Hm.'

Ô Jupiter. As if it were not foolhardy enough bringing the Inspector's corybungus into this, why Ô why did I splutter the boutique's bona fide address?

'You don't occupy this property unlawfully?'

'Nein – no, no. Um. Check my particulars. Please.'

For a few minutas I was left alone in the blank cubette while the Inspector and his cronies rifled through their Filing Cabinet of Rogues or whatever data-gathering-vacaya they had out thataways nowadays. Under the bijou desk my lallies were jangling. All too aware these prats had my lupperprints on file after my twisted seizure in the public pissoir, I pondered what cateva punishment I could be in for if they clocked I was truly Novak and not this ingratiating Foster-Newman toff. Twenty years hard labour? Twenty more courses of the TREAT switch? Ô, if only I'd thought to have my lupperprints removed or replaced with gildi thimbles by the plastic surgeon!

I tried to stay calm. My prospects looked bleak, true enough, but I clung to the savagery that there must be hundreds more weirdies in the nick after this here barny on the green. Twud require the utmost care and superhumanoid scrutiny on the sharpering-pops' part to sniffle out every last past misdemeanour of this motley rabble – and what incriminating cheets could they uncover anyhow if they upturned my boutique in the meantime? I breathed a pogi bit easier for una minuta, savvying there was nothing more criminal than a few soiled nappies and unwashed platters at Never-Neverland – until I remembered the Blank Chamber, the treacherous mares, their screeching bambinos. Ô, encore une fois: MERZ, MURDER and MERDRE!

I was chewing ravenously at my muddy luppertips when Inspector Silling finally reappeared, self-consciously tugging at his arriss-hugging lally-covers.

'You know,' he polled, 'there are two dollybirds out there waiting for you.'

'Ô?' My kishkas twisted. 'Only two?'

Silling's oyster-levers pricked. 'Bonny birds, they are. Same funny mannerisms – one with a squint. Any relation?'

Tet still spinnering at all the sick brooliment of the past few hours, I was ready to panic-splutter: 'No, no, no, sire, they're no blood relation, no relation at all, take their bods, please examine them thorough, charver any orifice you desire, what's mine is yours,' et ceterarararara. I pictured myself forced into a nova servile role: grand ponce to the plod, bound by some grotty unscreeved legislature to provide popsies gratis to these meese snuffling piggies forevermore. Ô, twud be a codswallop existence, but preferable – endlessly preferable! – to being zapped to the consistency of a chargilled walnut again, or having my delicate undiddled dish drilled daily by some charmless brute behind bars ...

I started: 'No, no, no, sire, th–'

'Well, it's good to see the nobility breeding as rigorously as ever, that's all I can say,' Silling interjected, his servo elsewhere. 'Why did you not tell us right away your father sits in the House of Lords? Pride, was it? Ashamed of preferential treatment? Heavens!' He stroked his greasy riah behind his nells. 'Tell me: it was a closed-door affair of course, but do you know if your father voted for or against ...' – his oglelids twitched, seemingly conspiratorially – 'Operation Wet Nurse?'

A splurge of frost slithered through my bod. Ô Christine: how to respond? Did my liberty depend on this?

'Pray tell,' I polled delicately, 'remind me of the particulars of this operation ...'

Inspector Silling reered up brootishly. 'No!' he snapped. 'No, no. I apologise. You've been interrogated enough, my boy.' His voche was dorcas, but I could not help feeling he was ogling me somewhat distrustfully now. 'Inquisition over. You're free to go.'

'Freee,' I parroted with startled opals, already off my stool and squirming auto for the portal.

'You know ...' Inspector Silling held me back, grabbing me by the pol. My sang stuttered, icing over again. 'You know, I may well swing by your boutique, Master Foster-Newman. Take you up on that offer of some new slacks. If I can afford those exorbitant prices, that is.'

'Absolutely!' I panted, pearling erratically. 'Any time at all! I'll cut you a deal, naturally.'

The lavs sounded like meese kitty-weeps as they left my levers. I pondered what would become of my beloved boutique now: was it wiser to booby-trap the latty, ultra-sterilise it or just abandon it altogether? I held a cheery grimace, privvily sizing up the Inspector as his luppers dug under my collarbone. He had more or less the same bod-shape as mine – 30R, I'd wager.

'Well, cheerio, Master Foster-Newman,' Silling polled before turning me loose. 'No more "fuckering anarchy" now, you hear me? Haw-haw!'

I breathed out, wondering if there was even such a being as a comradely sharpering-pop.

Once outside, what felt like a terribly long long corridor of shame only hours earlier now felt a mere hop, squeak and a dotsie-doh as I minnied my way to the EXIT. For the most part I felt gay again, my boomboomer pumping sugary sirop round my bod immediately as I clocked my duey new favourite dollies waiting in the foyer, huddled on a benkel.

'Séverine! Veronica!' I gasped, embracing the beautiful beautiful bastards. They hugged and lammered me tenderly, with feeling. 'Where are the others?' I demanded, the dreary isolation making me lusty for multi-humanoid interaction again.

'They scarpered when they ogled you being nicked, your Lordship,' Séverine replied as we vagaried outways. 'The Baroness, Lionel, Donatella – Jupiter knows where they've toddled off to. Bruce, Bonnie and Rosa are round the corner. They've shushed a gildi caboosh, in case you needed some getaway wheels ...'

'Ô Heavens. Allez. In that case keep your bloody tets down, my darlings.'

Feeling maxi shifty now and as if all gaslamps and manhole-ogles were spying on me, I followed my dollies scuttly-lallied as they sharpered round the strasses and snickets for the hijacked caboosh.

'I'm afraid we must be ultra stealthy from now onwards, my cherries,' I polled. 'ALAS and ALACK-O-JUNO, the plod savvy where we reside! They forced me to splutter the address of our majestic headquarters. They positively tortured the information out of me!'

'O, Raymondo ...' The dolls clung to me molto dorcas, petting me like a purrer as we slithered through the shadows of whatever morso of Londres I'd been abducted to. When at last we fingered the shushed Volkswagen – after Bruce quite unsurreptitiously had to burp the horn several times from his position in the munge of a footbridge – I felt ready to collapse, so overcome I was with the skitterish abdabs and munjarry-pangs.

'Are we safe staying put in the boutique, Lord?' Veronica squinted at me nervily through her solo bona opal, the other having been lost to pepper-spray experimentation some tick-tocks ago.

'I believe so,' I polled, hiding my bloodied, gristly lupperprints under my thews as we chuggered off back towards W1, 'but any minuta some overenthusiastic sharpering-pop could come sniffling round our affairs. Therefore we must dispose of all incriminating cheets pronto, mostest of all the two birds in the Blank Chamber.'

'Dispose of?' Séverine honked.

'Not mortify, dear heart. Extract, I should've squeaked.'

My privvy hope was that Sabine and Priscilla would exit the Blank Chamber dowri refreshed and compliant again, ready to rejoin our ranks with fabulosa uninterrupted ultralove pokered fully my way and not Herman's. Twud be a wondrous bonus if the bambinos had accidentally perished in there of course, though nix doubt the five of them (lest we forget the Goose) had been subsisting well enough on the turncoats' willet-milk while I'd been away.

As the Post Office Colin stiffened before our fattygayed opals, a jolt of soppy homesickness came over me. Twas difficult to ascertain exactly how I planned to proceed lavvy-wise now I was firmly back on the plod's radar, but undoubtedly the nattiest emag was to project domestic bliss, perhaps conjure up some bogus mundane front for the boutique while continuing to indulge in everything wrongly deemed WRONG WRONG WRONG by the State behind locked portals.

Bruce dropped us off on one of the sideysnickets parallel to Ogle, before zooming along to some far-off clifftop or cave or swamp to dump the caboosh. Linking lappers with Séverine and Veronica, I felt a pogi splurge of contentment for the first time in a long while, savvying these chinka leftover dollies were bona fide comrades, Novak fanatics no less, well and truly devoted to just moi moi moi and our Grand Cause. They had their chance to vagary while I was in the sharpering-khazi – they did not take it. They were mine!

Gaily jangling my bunch of clefs, I was hopeful the other trey flighty twats might be waiting diligently outside Never-Neverland when we turned the corner, but alas the cobblestone strasse was empty save for what appeared to be a bulbous severed tet ogling skywards in the gutter. As we approached the grisly cheet, my paws began leaking terribly. 'Nein,' I mumblered. My own plastic visage gazed up at me from the paves. Some cruel vandal, aggressive gust or stray lightning-prickle had cleanly decapitated my debonair figurehead, the lifesize papier-mâché bust of yours truly that once jutted proudly from above the shoppe's insignia. 'Ô, nein nein nein,' I repeated, cradling the handsome cheet in my arms.

And yet there were worster discoveries to come.

'Your Lordship!' Bonnie hissed whispery.

The papier-mâché tet cracked in my lappers as I savvied that the front portal had been compromised: duey panes of glaze frapped through and the lock all jarried and mangled, crowbarred.

'Ô merz,' I honked.

Nellying closer, I was convinced there were pogi rimbumbles coming from inside the boutique. Ô Christ, Ô Christine. Were there sharpering-omis already inside, poised with batons and lapper-cuffs? Should I scarper pronto? Drop to my lally-caps? Pray weepingly to Jupiter?

'What to do? What to do?' I whimpered to no pop in particular.

Dithering like an anguished slug, ultimately I savvied I could not abandon the latty altogether. Not only was this khazi prime real estate, there was still around 10,000 guineas locked in my valise in the loft.

The quatra fillies ogled me owl-like, eager to see what super-heroic response I would splurge forth.

'Bof,' I grumbled, running my lappers down my eek.

There was nothing else for it. Puffing my chest out like a suicidal pigeon, I carefully creaked open the compromised portal and softly softly creepied inside. I whispered over my left pol: 'You four wait here. St-stay vigilant, beloved bambinos. If you nelly any police brutality coming from inside, don't just scarper. Help your dear favourite dicktittler to the end, won't you now?'

Feeling somewhat naggy with nanti shyka let alone any bod-armour or weapons to defend myself, I crept as quietly as possible across the disordered boutique, lunging like a daddy-long-lallies over the various strewn fakements and piles of splattered schmutta. Difficult at first to tell if we'd left the bodega in this frightful state, though I fancied the plod had turned the place over. There was a von of violence (or at least ultra disrespect) in the way clobber-rails had been overturned, posters torn down, livers disembowelled, slogans ripped to gibberish on the grubby parquet. I prayed their Stasi-sharpering had been fruitless, prayed the blank noise had just about drowned out any parnying or gurgling coming from the Blank Chamber, prayed they'd kept their crowbars away from my precious valise, prayed they'd buggered off with nix cause for concern ...

It wasn't to be.

'*******!' I hiccoughed as I reached the top of the staircase and clocked that the door to the Blank Chamber had also been compromised. I almost fell to my lally-caps right there and then and offered my naggy wrists, savvying it was futile trying to resist arrest at this late stage. I ponced, blue all over: these are my last coddy momentos of freedom, jittering like a cornered bunny, a pathetic baldy batatat who accidentally ratted on himself and now must twistily schlumph the consequences ...

Shuddering brootishly, I expected the plod to make the sting while I crouched there on the second-toppermost step, but clear enough the twats wanted me to emerge lappers-up from the munge and surrender like a bona diligent wrongdoer. I reached for a skimpy morso of broken clobber-rail and carefully squeaked the Blank Chamber portal wider. Inside, the Goose was curled up sideyways, fidgeting in a puddle of his own juices, neck still tethered to the radiator. There was nothing else. Just churnering white noise and uno stuttering strobelight flashing gibberish Morse code into the blank noche.

I flapped my left lapper at the Goose, trying to draw his crazed gaze. 'Are there sharpering-omis thataways?'

I mouthed, poking a lupper towards our libbage. 'Are the police still here?!'

The Goose's malformed oyster twitched for uno momento, but nix lavs emerged. BOF, I ponced. After reefing fruitlessly for a blank hanky, I lento rose from my gloomy hidey**h**ole, craned my tet round the Op Art wallpaper and blinked squinty into our communal boudoir.

Who knows how many pumped-up piggies will be dispatched when my fantabulosa crime is at last broadcast across the plod's polari-pipes, but even at this juncture (innocent omi that I was) I was braced for at least a couple of constables standing poised with batons aloft. Imagine, therefore, my utter brooliment when I clocked not piglets, not ravenous sharpering-omis but chinka wax mannequins, posed in V-formation in the centre of our otherwise stark naggy bedchamber. The mannequins glistened sickly in the drooping sol-rays, eeks blank as cement nymphettes, glassy opals locked accusingly on my quivery bod. Was this some foul trick conjured up by Inspector Silling? Was this just another waking inkyboo?

Shuffling closer, I savvied the perpetrator had left me a notelet: some bijou morso of bimph stuck to the foremost mannequin's left breast. A court summons possiblement, or some wretched blackmail caca. Grudgingly I leaned in to read the twisted lavs:

DEAREST RAYMONDO,

APOLOGIES FOR THE INTRUSION – OR SHOULD WE SCREEVE INTERRUPTION?

FUCK OFF YOU PLASTIC FROGGY AND FAREWELL – FOREVER.

H***, SABINE, PRISCILLA, DONATELLA, LIONEL, THE BARONESS & THE BAMBINOS

I crawled back through to the Blank Chamber and clutched the Goose vice-like, parnying hysterical.

PART VI

PARIS IN THE THE SPRING

'Au mois de mai, fais ce qu'il te plaît.'*

OLD FROGGY MOTTO

* 'In the month of May, do whatever you may.' Epigraph dashed off on soiled Brasserie Balzar letterhead.

Maydaytripper*

NOVAK WEARS A GROSS LIBERTY BONNET WITH TRICOLORE COCKADE, CANDY-STRIPE PANTALOONS, FRAYED NECKERCHIEF, ULTRAMARINE CARMAGNOLE MANTO AND SABOTS.

NELLY 'L'INTERNATIONALE'.

Pluplushes in full bloom – torn down across strasses! Overturned cabooshes. Exploding petrol tanks! Cobblestones with wings. Fluffy clouds of parny-gas! Glimmering garbage-willets. Citrus hankies. Students charvering in the institutions. Babyface Communists. Shuddering politicos. Beauty in the strasses. Sang and poetry splattered on scorched brickwork. Ferricadoozled gendarmes! Ahh OUI, none of the gay Parisien tourism-livers warned me of these meshigena delights ...

When finally I'd stopped parnying after discovering that the Interrupter had committed the Ultimate Interruption, I was tempted to just efink all ties to this mostest codswallop welt and blow up the boutique with me inside, but then a petty morso of hope twinkled in the back of my servo. The valise. Truly I expected the cheet to have been swiped, so thoroughly had the bastards ransacked my beloved cottage, but when I scuttled up the ladder and clocked that the case was still there, sparkling with bijou emeralds of mould and the lock still intact, Ô, twas as if a wrongful death sentence had been overturned at the last minuta.

* Chapter received Wednesday, 3rd June 1970 – forty days to go.

Praise be to Jupiter, this was uno morso of happiness to cling to as we brushed ourselves down and began reconstructering our nova Traitor-Free Lavvy. Full-aware the plod could still come sniffling round our upturned latty any momento, myself and my chinka loyal leftovers – Veronica, Séverine, Bruce, Bonnie, Rosa – dhobied the boutique top-to-bottomly once again, joshed it* up

---

* When at last Emily cornered Trefoil to discuss the secret message, the editor's immediate reaction was anger:

'Why did you not bring this up before?' he growled, spitting specks of custard éclair at her.

'You all seemed so tense, so wrapped up in everything else … Monsieur Astérisque, the wiretaps and everything …' Emily bleated, turning up the white noise on the nearest transistor radio. 'I left you that memo. I presumed you might be tackling it already …'

'A memo?'

'I left it on your desks. "Re: m/s at risk – bold characters? Meaning?" and so on. I tried to keep it subtle, in case it got into the wrong hands.'

'Yes.' Trefoil was unknowingly crushing the éclair in his left fist now. 'It was so bloody cryptic I just dismissed it.'

And yet Trefoil's anger only escalated as he tried to unscramble the secret message at his desk for the rest of the afternoon. **Help me print an ear in it if listening**. He presumed 'it' meant the manuscript, but why would Novak need any help printing an ear in it, and what was the relevance of the ear anyway? As tactfully as she could, Emily pointed out it was more likely one of Novak's long-suffering followers secretly pleading for help – his captive ghostwriter slyly hammering out a distress signal under the Scum King's vonka? – but still the eternal, infernal question remained: what was 'it'?

Blind rage is rarely the best approach to solving a problem, but had Trefoil not resorted to screaming 'IT! What the fuck is "IT"?!' in desperation just prior to our 3.30 p.m. biscuits, the mystery may well have gone unsolved.

'What's this now?' Davy asked, blinking languidly from his Pop Art-encrusted corner of our HQ.

After explaining the problem, Trefoil and Emily were left somewhat shamefaced when Davy (our foppish Art & Design man, for so long considered frankly illiterate and half-witted by the rest of us) solved the puzzle practically with his first brainwave. Smirking, Davy waved jazz hands at a newspaper lying on the dumping ground that had previously been Harry Howling's desk.

'What's that? Pick it up man,' Trefoil demanded. 'I can't see what you're flapping at.'

Davy's plucked eyebrows pricked as he picked up the paper. 'The Guru's asked us to print something in "it" before now, you remember?' He pointed to

to look like any other norm Capitalist bodega, then promptly skipped town. (The Goose I left tethered to the radiator, with enough birdyseed to feed the whole flappering population of Trafalgar Plaza.) Twas not any glimmering guilt on our part that inspired us to fuck-off-thataways through London's nearest exit-hole – rather, a bona honest craving for a peaceful, restorative Continental sojourn in the wake of all this fattygaying betrayal caca dished out for us by the anglos.

By now you may be aware that I am fond of France. However, it was not just the lure of froggy bonbons, popsies in berets or snappy avant-garde café-poncers that catapulted us across the Channel. I admit I was suffering a pogi bit of an identity crisis after losing so many of my sisters in one swipe, not least because the trey I loved mostest had gaily toddled off thataways with a meese nonentity who had the audacity to somehow accuse MOI of being the charlatan here, a non-frog! Why did the scatty batatat's lavs hurt so? Perhaps it was that, despite my ultra conviction that I was born on French soil, I had nix memories whatsoever of my grand fertile Fatherland. And not only that: ogling the detestable twonk with the bambinos and treacherous mares all lovestruck and cuddly around him only drove home the savagery that I had nanti bona fide relations of my own. More than ever I felt the runt of the welt, a naggy orphan, a lone wolfy with no parents and nix quongs to cultivate an army of my own: a litter of nova petty mond-shaking Raymondos. I was alone.

At this twisted juncture of my story I had very little knowledge of my Old Mare's feeli years in Paris, her Norm chavvyhood, her tadpole-lavvy – only a pogi few anecdotes she'd slurred at me greenly in le Château Chanceux. The Old Zelda felt more of a fantom to me than a full-formed Frenchwoman, but I savvied

---

the abbreviated logo of the latest *International Times*, the cartoonish initials glaringly obvious now, and Day-Glo to boot. 'I had to draw a little handlebar mouser, didn't I? Now it seems the psychos want an ear too.'

there must still be traces of her sparkling somewhere on her home turf, whether out on the blustery willets of Normandy, or down down down in the foggy vino-soaked caves of the Latin Quarter.

Oui. This trip was not intended to be just some jolly romp in la ville de l'amour, but a momentous journey of self-discovery, a chance to defibrillate my inherent Frenchness, hitherto suspended in animation like a hibernating froglet trapped in ice.

Admittedly I did feel a petty bit poked-up wafting my Grand Britannic passport at the border-pops at Calais, and they weren't molto enthused when I kept insisting, 'I'm a Frenchman of course,' twangling the tip of my liberty cap like a gross swollen nipplet.

'Says born in Kent, Raymondo,' Veronica cackled, squinting uno-opalled at my legal bimph.

'Nanti polari, you ridiculous tart.'

Crunched up in the back of a lorry carrying duey-daitcha tonnes of fertiliser pellets, I rapidly savvied my holiday attire had been pluckered in error as we crawlied across my beloved Mutterland. Just as in Tangier I'd wrongly ponced I might fit in joshed-up to the nobbas in a fez and dishdasha, so too I felt quite the conspicuous twat in my revolutionary sans-culottes attire once I'd clocked my first frogs in the wild.

Initial impressions of France were disappointing. Not only was the weather just as grimy as back rosbifwards, but when Paris eventually revealed itself can-can-like through the flickering flappering curtain-sider, I was sickened. Foolishly I'd imagined that every Euro metropolis must be a doodlebuggered Dada-collage of charmingly meshigena misshapen post-war architecture. When I first clocked the gildi pristine uniformity of the City of Light, it struck me as not so much testament to Baron Haussmann's genius, but more a codswallop reminder of how limply the frogs had bent to the Nazis. The French politicos effectively rolled out the red carpet for the Invaders, inviting them to move into their most de-luxe latties and jarry from their finest crockery in the hope that the Gross Obliterators would feel so at home they'd never think to caca on their own doorstep.

With this in mind, twas unusual then to nelly on the radio that a grupa of feeli froggies were lovingly vandalising and ferricadoozling the bona strasses of the Left Bank, only a cobblestone's throw from the jolly hôtel myself and my dollies were staying at. In our innocence, we'd tuned in to Radio Luxembourg to try to nelly the latest yé-yé hits not yet available across La Manche, but all the shoo-bee-dooing kept being interrupted by bulletins from what appeared to be a fuckering warzone just round the corner.

In the lead-up to our pleasuretrip I'd clocked the odd witterings of feeli discontent in LE MONDE, but after the gross anti-climax of Grosvenor Square, I'd dismissed these skol-pops' skirmishes as just overactive playtime, a hot squirt of pubescent angst that would simmer back down to teeni apathy just as rapidly as it detonated.

Joshing myself in a black turtleneck for the noche, I savvied these energetic tearaways would nix doubt be swiftly swept from the strasses by the gendarmerie, and so there was little risk of our plans being disrupted: to sip-sip-sip un bijou coffee in my spiritual home, Les Deux Magots, the gildi haunt of some of the most dazzling avant-garde poncers of the twentieth century (et ma mère, aussi?).

At the very worstest I fancied we might vada some unfortunate scholar being dragged about by its piggytails. HOWEVER: what awaited us as we traversed the BOOMBOOMering borderline between Montparnasse and Saint-Germain-des-Prés was altogether – how shall I screeve it? – ULTRA SERVO-WIDE-OPENINGLY ELECTRIFYING! (And there I was, poncing the froggies' cultural highlight of 1968 might be France Gall's nova LP.)

I should've given more credit to my bona revolting fellow country-pops! As we minced our way down the Boulevard Saint-Michel, thirsty for our warming espressos, what we were greeted with instead was a schvartz stinkcloud of glimmering cabooshbits and the thuk-thuk-thud chanting clattering rimbumbles of some mass barny just out of ogleshot. Naturellement I had nix intention of being blown up or arrested on my holidays – and yet, when we clocked on the next block a grupa of hysterical feeli-pops seemingly scarpering for safety down the Rue Gay-Lassac, hurrying alongside them in fact led us directly to the front line of the battyfanging. Pronto the youths lelled cobblestones from a pile yankety-yanked from the pavements and began hurling them at the riot-fuzz just about visible dueychenta yards away, beyond the smog.

Were these chavvies mentally ill? My gut feeling was to vagary immediately from this chaotic scenario and yet, clocking more barricades up ahead (not to mention hundreds of plod with batons and grenade-launchers), I savvied we may well have to put our plans for delicious coffee on hold uno momento.

Cowering in the munge of a smouldering caboosh some pop had kindly overturned for our protection, I enquired in skittish pidgin-froggy what all the aggro was in aid of. 'Les Viet Cong-peuples?' I spluttered at a snappy feeli-omi ajax.

Full-illuminated and panting brootishly, the omi explained: oui, there was a pogi thrust of anti-'Nam savagery behind the clashes – namely the meese realisation that our superheroic Allied leaders were as prone to scatty fascism as the evil zots they rallied against during WWII – but mostly these feeli-pops were protesting about lavvy-gripes on their own turf: the interminable mod BOREDOM, the conservative deep-freeze of Gaullisme, the naff rules and restrictions in stale skols and sexless universities, empty consumerism, wage slavery, the evils of banality, et ceterarara. I nellied the laddy's lavs enraptured, and not just because of his fortuni fat glistening oyster-levers.

'Still, you pops aren't planning on c-completely destroying the Latin Quarter, are you?' I polled, gripping my nova comrade's thews. 'See, I'm trying to uncover at least some evidence of my dear Old Mare's existence, only it seems everywhere she once minnied has a cruel habit of crumbling to morsos ...'

Before the omi could respond, there was a yowling whoosh-whoosh whoosh-whoosh as the fuzz grossly overreacted to our cobbles with a flurry of rockets. One grenade exploded just shy of our barricades, blurting splinters of broken strasse hither-thither and giving birth to a toxic thunderhead that rapidly mushroomed and bellydanced towards us.

'MERZ!' I squealed, rolling about the ground, nells ringing. 'I've been deafened! I'm dying! Je suis mort! I'm blind!'

'C'est le gaz CS,' my companion polled, holding a rag to his eek. 'Allez.'

Hyperventilating, I chased the retreating grupa down a sidey-snicket before the cloud of parny-gas jarried us completely. After a few more erratic zig-zags through the Latin Quarter, I savvied the rest of my beloved followers must've been left behind, or lost their way in the glimmering labyrinth. BOF. I did not ogle backwards, Ô comrades. The gay exhilaration of this bizarre barny was beginning to take hold – almost as if it wasn't parny-gas but giggle-gas the CRS was showering us with!

Plastered and painted all around Paris were these snappy sparkling slogans the students had revved up, or shushed from the Surrealists or Situationists:

SOYEZ RÉALISTES, DEMANDEZ L'IMPOSSIBLE
LA SOCIETE EST UNE FLEUR CARNIVORE
LA BEAUTÉ EST DANS LA RUE
L'IMAGINATION AU POUVOIR
SOYONS CRUELS!
ÉJACULE TES DÉSIRES*

Ô, oui oui OUI! These pops were lavvying in high-contrast the life

* Our *Harrap's French Dictionary* suggests: BE REALISTIC, DEMAND THE IMPOSSIBLE; SOCIETY IS A CARNIVOROUS FLOWER; BEAUTY IS IN THE STREET; ALL POWER TO THE IMAGINATION; LET'S BE CRUEL!; EJACULATE YOUR DESIRES.

I'd always wanted to see civvies lead – a shocking, eagle-baiting, anarchic, Surrealism-screeching, freewheeling, multiloving Liberated Lavvy – and perhaps mostest shocking of all: the beautiful meshigena bats were getting away with it EN PLEIN AIR, revelling right under the eagles' vonkas!

Why hadn't the armed fuzzers smashed the rebellion pronto like the dowri bumbling Metropolitan plod managed to the previous month? Palavering with more fashionable enragés at the next set of barricades, I gleaned the toppermost reason was: by and large the majority of Parisiens supported the students. Unlike Grosvenor Square, during which our general plopulation blithely tucked into their Sunday rosbif waiting patiently for the eagles to prevail and the unrest to blow over, media coverage of the Paris battyfanging only ramped up others to question their own tedious lavvies under de Gaulle and join in the barny. And it seemed the more these googly-goggled, trenchcoated, jackbooted gendarmes ploughed into the protesters, the more sympathy the feeli-pops got from norm civvies. It wasn't just teeni Commies on the front line – ogling roundwards, I was gradually made aware of the chavvies' teachers, striking factory-omis, secretaries, strasse-sweepers, and all manner of acronymed politico factions flappering banners, all lusting after a slurp of splattered eagle-sang. When pops on our side took a VLOP! to the tet or had a vomity reaction to the parny-gas, if the Croix-Rouge didn't get to them first, more often than not a local lattywife or gentlefungus lent a helping lapper, scooping them into their khazi to look after them.

'Ô, JAWOHL!' I screamed as another rocket detonated ajax. This – THIS THIS THIS THIS THIS – was living! The exhilaration of savvying that any momento your tet could be taken off by a gendarme's grenade, and yet never before in my lavvy had my tet teetered so close to both complete obliteration and complete enlightenment! We were superheroic tightrope-mincers, gaily running the gauntlet of instant mortification while in the meantime never feeling so alive!

Panting beastish, I pondered how many feeli-pops would charver passionately that week-end having only just clapped opals on one another, and how many bruised cops would lie sleepless next to their wooden wives, frustrated and frigid.

In the next break between missile-swapping, I added a few of my own slogans to the cackling brickwork:

LUBRICATE REALITY WITH DREAMS!
FUCK PASSIVE-AGGRO!
EMBRACE PERFECT SAVAGERY!
KILL KILL KILL
LOVE LOVE LOVE

The alert reader will have noticed a slight shift of my view on aggro during all this explosive merriment. Ô, MAIS OUI, comrades, I savvied it all clear now: the only natty response to a suffocating, insulting codswallop mond was to hit back harder – with brains, with brawn and with beauty!

I was trying to explain my epiphany to my neighbour ('Passive-aggro, mein camarade, I vada it plain now: no matter how well meaning your intentions, well, it's still utter submission to authority, is it not? Fairy masochism! The eagles aren't hurt not a jot if you just sit there and stubbornly take a heavy schonking in the nom of virtue and rightness. Bof. That caca does not ruffle them in the slightest ...') when the flics silenced me with another round of anti-free-speech rockets. A grenade whizzed over our tets like a startled swan moulting its feathers before crashing into the canopy of a polka-dot patisserie and exploding.

Our frontline pops responded perfectly reasonably: grabbing whatever heavy morsos they could find ajax and hurling them at the approaching fuzzymuzz. As far as travails went, clear enough these sharpering-pops had an utterly codswallop shift ahead – trying to subdue thousands of poplos glimmering with this superhumanoid lust for life no plodder had surely ever ogled before on the beat – but still, they continued following their orders from above with frosty unfeeling robo-eeks. In stark contrast, ours perhaps wasn't the style of warfare Napoleon would've been particularly enthused about, but twas maxi m**a**xi contagious. My whole bod was positively tingling as I plucked a cobble from the pile and lobbed it with all my clout at the fantoms in black. 'FUCK THE PIGLETS!' I screeched. The slab plopped only daitcha feet from my quivering platters – eliciting some frankly uncomradely lavs and sniggers from my neighbours – but all in all the feeling was heroic, the violence was fantabulosa.

The CRS responded with another brootish drive forward, creepering up the strasse like a gigantic leathery millipede, batting any feeli reb**e**llious tet that wobbled into view with its flailing black antennae. To hinder the beastie's progress, a couple of our pops set fire to the felled pluplush we'd been hiding behind – then we all promptly scarpered.

Whenever the order came to retreat, I did so with relish. This was a manoeuvre I excelled at of course. I still had a cobblestone gripped in my left lapper as I twirled then sprinted like a loose lab-rat back towards whatever morso of Paris we'd splurged from. Racing lightning-lallied across the swirling paves, I presumed the rest of the grupa were following eagerly behind – however, after only a pogi few twists and turnings in the labyrinth, I savvied I was utterly lost and alone. I stopped for uno momento by a shuttered TABAC, desperately slurp-slurping fresh aero back into my bod. Unhelpfully the stude**n**ts had blown out most of the gaslamps in this petty morso of the Latin Quarter, and so I was left minnying ditheringly in the munge, feeling maxi vulnerable now without the feeli mob by my side. Where had the buggers toddled off to? I tried to nelly sirens, explosions, chanting or barnying, with a mind to rejoin the aggro (or vagary in the opposite direction), but there was so much rimbumbling going on aj**a**x it was near enough impossible to finger the nattiest route to safety.

Loitering dumbly on a strasse with nanti nom, I was beginning to fear the next stop on my Paris itinerary might well be some unsanitary plod-cell, when I clocked a gay muffly whimper coming from down one of the sideysnickets. The alley was ultraschvartz, but I felt sure this whimpering was friendly: a privvy outpouring of pleasure rather than pain. My cartso tingled. There'd been much jibber-jabber in the froggy inkies of the spontaneous eruption of LOVE and ARVA among the feelies on the battlefield, and yet thus far I'd only ogled the odd couple lammering in doorways, skol-pops sprawled in each other's arms behind the barricades. Had I miraculously stumbled upon one of these fabled arva-fêtes? I pictured a pair of fortuni freedom-fighters cavorting covertly underneath the sparkles, an anarchist arthuring himself daffy, quatra virgins diddling themselves with unexploded Molotov-botties, a grand snaking daisy-chain of ecstatic queers buggering one another into this brave nova glittering future!

The Latin Quarter was a lawless zone now – why wouldn't pops use their hard-won strasses as gildi boudoirs, open-aero horn-parlours?

'Mmmmnr! Mmnnnnrrr!' the whimpers concurred.

'Cou-cou!' I whispered, slithering softly into the inky snicket. 'Comrades? Cou-cou?'

Tiptoeing towards the amorous rimbumbles, I rapidly found myself submerged in full-blackness, wafting my lappers out in front of me like a lecherous sleepwalker. Squinting did pogi-all to help navigate my way through the ultraschvartz, but soon enough my nells led me to where the groaning was most brootish. My boomboomer rattled like an ape in a cage. I was hoping for a couple of feeli fornicators at the very least, but as I knelt and gently reefed the outline of the whimpering lump, I wasn't all that poked-up to discover just a solo butch fantom splattered languidly in the gutter.

'Comrade?' I cooed.

It seemed the omi was unable to palaver, teetering somewhere betwixt slumbers and wakeyness, revs and reality. Not a problem per se, I ponced.

'Are you well, brother?' I polled. 'Ça ira? Do you need a friend? Jupiter knows I could use a comrade myself ... Vive la révolution, et cetera ...'

Twas impossible in the munge to ascertain whether this pop was drunk, wounded or both, but certain morsos of him were more alert than others. Reefing under his mackintosh for some sign of life, I gulped gaspish as my trembly lapper inadvertently closed around the chap's grandiose erect cartso.

'Achtung,' I gurgled. 'You're awake, monsieur?'

'Mmmmnr!' my nova comrade responded. 'Mnnnnnrr!'

Flirtation, nix doubt about it. Without any further ado, I dropped my cobblestone, dropped to my lally-caps, then took the pop's colin in both lappers and began droolingly gobbling him up with gusto. The squares among you may well ponder: wasn't this a pogi bit brazen, yours truly ravenously sucking upon the cartso of a comatose battyfanged stranger? But these were enlightened times, were they not? LA BEAUTÉ EST DANS LES SIDEYSNICKETS AUSSI! As I slurped greedily on the pop's rigid pipette, I soon became aware of more chanting and barnylingo rising in volume along the main strasse behind us, but savvied we were safe in the ultraschvartz, the plod surely being more concerned with flying cobbles out thataways than flying quong-sirop thisaways.

'Mmmmnnrr!' the omi reiterated. 'Mnnnnnrr!'

'Hush hush, nanti polari, darling,' I dribbled, tenderly flickering my lingum up and down his tense shaft.

'Mmmnnnrr! MMMMMNRGHH!!' he blurted as a grenade went off ajax to our hideyhole, illuminating us for uno momento.

'Merz!' I honked, clocking the omi's eek. There was a gross gouge above his right opal that was blub-blubbing sang all down his vacant fizzer – and yet it wasn't the blood that unsettled me. In that pogi flash of sparkle I was convinced my companion was a white omi with a gigantic negro cartso. I tugged at it again, and near enough thumper-malfunctioned when the rubbery cheet came free from his bod in my lapper.

When another wayward grenade lit up our hiding place, I savvied I was holding a drool-covered baton, a glistening nightstick. Ô MERZ. Ô MURDER. Ô MERDRE. A pair of googly-ogle goggles gazed back at me lovelessly from atop the cop's tet.

'Mmnnnnrghh! Mnnnnnrr!' was the pig's familiar repartee now as I clambered on top of him for my final gratification, pinning his pols down with my lally-caps. Reefing around frantically in the munge, my right lapper at last alighted on the bijou cobble I'd dropped. I raised the petty granite cube above my tet, then, as discreetly as possible in these scatty conditions, pummelled the twat's eek to pâté.

'MMNNNRGHH! MNNNNNRR!!'

'Hush, darling ...'

Dribbling like a wolfy, I forced the cobblestone into the wound above the omi's opal, schonking and twistering and grinding like I was pestling a gross mutant garlic bulb. Soon enough the plodder's protests fizzled to nantwar, but still I kept on pulverising his piggy eek until the gouge was so large I could've probably fitted my whole right lapper into it, if I was that way inclined.

Quite possibly I might've continued liquidising the twonk through the noche until he was just humanoid soup – but I froze when another brootish missile went off seemingly immediately ajax to where we were concealed. I tried not to move, though my kishkas shrivelled when I sniffled the CS gas. Bellydancing mist shimmied its way towards us, as if a dorcas heavenly cloud had come to carry the cop safely away – although this cunt of course was going to Hell.

As the blank fog swallowed us, an instant outsplurge of snot and parnyaqua oozed from my sockets. I unrolled my turtleneck up over my eek, desperately trying not to splutter, full-aware any slightest twitch of noise might alert the sharpering-omis on the other side of that meese blank thunderhead. I tried not to fritty. Tried not to vomit. Ô, mein Gott, twas ultra ultra painful, and yet I had to keep telling myself: this glimmering agony was mere rosy bonbons compared to what the fash robos would do if they discovered me hunched over the bod of their beloved pulverised colleague.

My lung-sacs felt as though they'd been replaced with sandpaper bagpipes. I was drowning, but with a super**h**eroic amount of servo-buffering I was just about able to stay tranquil. I recalled the feeling of cobblestone against carnish only momentos before, tried to focus on that gloriosa revolting sensation as the parny-gas jarried my ogleballs – and I wept. Ô comrades, I wept. I wept and I wept and I wept and wept and wept and wept wept wept wept wept – with privvy buttoned-up joy!

Nouvelle Vagueness,
or: Utopia Myopia*

NOVAK WEARS SANDALS, TUNIC, FULL BOD-ARMOUR AND A CENTURION CAPELLA WITH GROSS RED COCORICO ROOSTER COMB.

NELLY ALINE'S 'CENSURÉ'.

Is it not fantabulosa lavvying in a city in which you run the risk of being obliterated by random violence and gildi terrorism juno upon juno? Does it not make every day feel that pogi bit extra electric?

Not long after our first wondrous Noche of the Barricades, myself and my dollies gave up our plush hôtel boudoirs in favour of squatting gratis at the newly occupied Ôdeon Théâtre. Twas a grandiose antique playhouse and, having kicked out all the bourgeois thesps and fox-furred binocular-toffs, the feeli bolshies were now running it like some sort of meshigena politico cabaret. Any pop was free to palaver on the stage, constructive heckling was encouraged – meanwhile the rest of the latty had become a de-luxe dosshouse, all manner of switched-on feelies, dropouts, longhairs, aggro-fiends and tramps claiming their spot in the vast auditorium or down down down in the labyrinth of petty chambers backstage. Given that no pop wanted to partake in such slavish travails as housekeeping, after a few junos the

---

* Chapter received Wednesday, 10th June 1970 – thirty-three days to go.

hygiene in the place was abysmal, but I just kept telling myself: freedom is meese, freedom is ugly, freedom is beautiful!

And yet the question remained: was this niffy pit truly Heaven? At times the Ôdeon felt a pogi bit like being trapped in a month-long experimental existential am-dram production, while at other times twas a bona fide playpen of unshackled desires and shapeshifting merrymaking. Much to my delight, folks seemed to change personas at will down here – a molto natty tactic in lawless zonas and police states alike. Whenever the mood took, pops could wriggle into a nova disguise shushed from the cozzy department, reinvent themselves, shove their fusty past selves into the lost property box – hence I was joshed-up as a Romanoid centurion as I minced about the Latin Quarter at this most poignant juncture of my grand lavvy-story.

Jupiter only knows what the Interrupter might've screeched at me had he clocked me in this most imperial of fash clobber – however, I admit the armoured garb gave me a sense of gay invincibility and appropriate ridiculousness as I trolled about that ultra-Surrealistic square mile.

The Latin Quarter was still firmly in the grip of the feelies at the beginning of June, the plod visible hither and thither but temporarily newted until the politicos came up with some natty masterplan to politely force their future heirs to fuck off quietly.

I reered at the beautiful confusion of it all, zig-zagging through the charvered strasses and sideysnickets, wide-ogling the strange fruits of this tentative nova utopia: burnt-out cabooshes, uprooted pluplushes, strasses without paves, gross willets of rubbish honking on every corner (some glimmering), empty bodegas, smashed fenêtres, nanti public transport, nix petrol, cadavers in limbo.

Oui, OUI: this was what the first baby steps towards paradise looked like! Crucially the blue-collar workers of France had joined the barny, paralysing the country with a General Strike and adding their clout to the grand struggle that looked all set to topple de Gaulle's government, just as soon as the right pop squawked the order to march on the Élysée or Versailles or wherever the senile eagle was hiding. As far as the students and workers were concerned, revolution was well within their gripple. The workers brought the brawn, students and teachers provided the brains, and the beauty came from the gloriosa knee-jerk upsplurge of art, arva, poetry, free-palavering and togetherness.

Nevertheless: many mid-class general poplos seemed a pogi bit less enthused about revolution now their norm lavvies had been flippered by the Strike. Nanti strasse-sweepers meant the boulevards were stinking, nix deliveries meant bodegas were short of munja, no undertakers meant dead bods were piling high in the latties of mourners nix doubt mourning a pogi bit more than normal.

Ahh, the sweet stench of social upheaval! Sadly revolution is a meese nuisance for most westernised pops, and woe betide those who snuff it during a General Strike. With this in mind I took extra care as I snuck past the loitering fuzz on the Rue le Goff, always maxi tempted to splurt some sort of unpleasantry but full-aware twud be an ultra-undignified afterlavvy for me if they singled me out for a brootish ferricadoozling: rotting away in a plod-shop dungeon until some froggy bureaucrat finally deemed petrol stocks abundant enough to burn me or repatriate me to a country I don't even believe I'm from.

BOF.

As was habit most morns, I parkered a grumbler of pastis from Balzar, then waltzed over to the Sorbonne to see how those pops were getting on with their somewhat formidable task of sculptering a bold nova utopian civilisation. Just like in the Ôdeon, the feelies had set up an all-inclusive forum in the gross amphitheatre, with all the classrooms beyond transformed into bijou palavering-parlours, rumpus rooms, servo-clinics. And just like in the Ôdeon, no pop seemed to have cracked the Grand Problem yet: how to proceed with this superheroic toppling of the State and magickal reinvention of frigid froggy society.

Reform or revolution, that seemed to be the question – but nanti definitive answers had wobbled forth yet.

Not that I understood what most of these intellectual bolshies were babbling about half the time. Jupiter knows what meshigena form of Norman peasant lingo my Old Mare had taught me in the Château Chanceux, but whenever I stopped to nelly the voches at the Sorbonne I only ever seemed to grasp every other lav. (To be fair, every other lav seemed to be 'bourgeoisie', spat with such delightful ultradisgust the pops on the front row surely required brollies). Hundreds of so-called Action Committees had been set up to try to solve every petty imperfection of mod existence – but for the most part the only action I vadared was battyflappering squabbles betwixt rival red factions, surprisingly bashful love-fumblings among the teeni layabouts, or the left-right-left-right marching frenzy of pro- and anti-Gaullistes out thataways.

Perhaps, I ponced, twas high time for some clarity here, some straight-screeching debonair leader to slither to the fore ...

'May I palaver, polari, je parle?' I nudged one of the more official-looking omis at the front, possiblement a union-rep or Commie Party pop.

'Oui, asseyez-vous, camarade,' the omi snapped, ogling me like a scab, like I'd slurried him with pigswill for even slightly insinuating he might be running things in this gross freewheeling politico-go-round.

As I plopped myself down among the other anonymous froglets waiting patiently to palaver onstage, I savvied uno glaring downside of a completely egalitarian society is that I would nix longer be the solo centre of attention. Naturellement I had countless natty ideas to help rustle up ze ultimate Liberated Lavvy for my fellow countrypops and me – however, when at last my turn came to screech to the masses, I fear my daffy desperation to be the guiding sparkle here may have ramped up my garglings somewhat – or was it just that fuckering pastis?

'ACHTUNG! Who likes the taste of roast piggy? Oui? Nein? Crackling, ja?' I honked, clanking around the stage in my cumbersome centurion clobber. 'Speaking as un auteur, speaking as ze grand architect of an already thriving bijou utopian boutique back in Blighty, may I offer you all this morso of Perfect Savagery, a poke in the right direction, no? Alors. As we all savvy all too clear now, there is nanti better feeling than grinding uno cobblestone into a cop's slimy eek! The plod are scared stiff now, my cherries; the politicos savvy not a jot how to save their coddy careers, let alone their beloved conservative Mutterland. In fact, the top brass have scarpered, the fuzz are loitering dumbly like sitting quackers out thataways right this momento! Clear enough these twats have been given nix order to fire upon us with bona fide bullets – not yet at least, not yet, not yet. What say we arm ourselves pronto, beat them to it, make ze first move, march on the Élysée with glimmering batons, roll the tets of each and every toff or bureaucratic strangulator we clap opals on – and wipe these charvering eagles off the eek of this codswallop welt once and for all! The time is ripe, camarades! Button your sweet natty-palavering oyster-levers and let us RISE UP PRONTO with merciless vengeance, with grandiose ecstatic hatred!'

By this point I'd outstretched my arms, ready to soak up the gloriosa applause. When none was forthcoming, I rapidly added, 'Fin, finito, merci beaucoup, vive la révolution,' but still the frogs did not clap. Did they not understand my lingo, or was applause now seen as some hideously prim bourgeois behaviour to be stamped out?

'We should not instigate violence,' was my first heckler's coddy critique. Squinting into the crowd, I could just about vada the botty-blond agitator or irritator. 'We practise counter-violence only. We adopt the flics' tactics only when they provoke us.'

'It is the uniform we detest, not the man underneath,' another voche piped up.

Rapidly I felt myself melting under my hefty rusty armour.

'If we understand your monologue,' polled another, 'we agree passive resistance is futile now. But to act aggressively without provocation, violence for violence's sake, this is not acceptable.'

And so on and so forth.

Desperate to vagary now, I removed my helmet and mumbled feebly, 'I was ... only jokering.'

Confused, poked-up, aggravated and above all sagging horribly with sweat, I tried to march from the stage with as much dignity as possible for a gross pink blancmange in a centurion cozzy. Ogling backwards, I wish I had some snappy retort to leave these plops' tets reeling – something along the lines of 'Do the plod not provoke us by simply existing, by loitering spread-eagled out in the open, a symbol of all that oppresses us on this stinking hovering rock?' – but alas it was with maxi twistiness and pokery that I sloped out of the auditorium in ghastly silence.

After shedding my clanging armour and shaking off a bona medsa-gallon of brine, I slithered onwards through the lopsided corridors of the Sorbonne, sharpering for a dark chamber to rest my tet a while. I had nix great eagerness to return to the even sloppier, sweatier, meshigena confines of the Ôdeon just yet, and perhaps for the first time I clocked why my dolls had been complaining of homesickness lately. Though the beautiful bats seemed to genuinely relish the nova freedoms, the bottomless leisuretime and communal tomfoolery, the coddy lingo barrier and the frogs' innate haughtiness meant the poor twats never truly savvied what was going on all the time. Then again, perhaps this is just what happens when you gather pops together to try to organise anarchy.

Stumbling onwards, each portal seemed to open onto the same dull cross-lallied lecture about Mao or Trotters, until finally I gave Room 419 a poke and was greeted with heavenly ultraschvartz.

At first I ponced this was an empty cell, so total was the blackness. I felt about the void, ambitiously hoping for an

Omo-fresh eiderdown or queensize hammock, before my lappers alighted on what felt like a floating humanoid tet in the munge. All at once there were shufflings roundabout me, then a brootish CRICK-CRACKLE akin to a pistolet being cocked. I dropped to my lally-caps and rapidly swished my tet hither and thither, fearing I had stumbled upon a privvy gathering of gendarmes or other batty vengeful infiltrators.

As it fell out, the CRICK-CRACKLE was not a cocked pistolet but a flicker-projector shunting to life. As the screen illuminated, I clocked some duey-daitcha silhouetted tets dotted about the chamber, and their fungal professor sitting up front on a flimsy tabletop. I apologised hushily to the tet I'd inadvertently squeezed, then tried to discreetly shuffle back outways, savvying this was nix doubt more servo-numbing plotless vérité caca about the Soviet Onion or somesuch.

My soggy sandals were only duey or trey feet from the exit when I spotted the Art Deco title card wobbling on the screen:

LA LUNE PORTE UNE MOUSTACHE

Where had I nellied this nom before? As the opening sequence began – duey omis dressed as crabs slurping ratatouille from a sensible shoe, rapidly followed by a close-up of some plop's hideous feet – my boomboomer quickened. I recalled my Old Mare palavering about her daffy acting career in the 1930s, the smugness she splattered forth when retelling how these flickers were almost unanimously detested by all who ogled them ('a sign of true brilliance', she believed). Madame O claimed the fuzz had destroyed all prints of LA LUNE PORTE UNE MOUSTACHE and LE CON DU CHAT, hence I was more than a petty bit dumbstruck as I vadared the reel unrolling, revealing this most fortuitous flickershow of the Mare's feeli junos.

Through fear as well as skitterish eagerness, I couldn't help squeaking at the silent silhouetted tets: 'Hush-hush, everypop! HUSH! Ze Queen of 'Appenstance has struck again! The old bat is back! Hush now! My Mare ... My Mare appeared in this flicker, ma mère joue dans ce film!'

The prof caterpillared at me as if I'd shat into one of his flicker-canisters. 'Pardon,' I polled, crossing my lallies like every other plop and refocusing tranquil on the silvery screen.

In the womb-like munge I ogled the following meshigena montage:

Two stop-motion monochrome roses bursting into bloom, a skinned stag dragged through Pigalle, duey omis in bathing suits sawing through a chessboard, a platter of rotting carnish, a splatter of blood, the moon with a postage-stamp moustache, uno momento of wobbly ultraschvartz, another close-up of hideous feet, a clown juggling duey-dozen pamplemousses, more ultraschvartz, another close-up of feet, two stop-motion lobsters decomposing, the moon with a humanoid eek, more feet, different feet, seemingly endless horrendous feet, comparatively dolly snapshots of abattoirs and sewage processing plants, the omis dressed as crabs battyfanging a grupa of nuns with the sensible shoe, ultraschvartz, duey nipplets floating in the night sky, a tramp pissing through its pantaloons on the platform at Invalides Métro, more feet, dogs' feet, chimps' feet, endless endless feet, una medsa-minuta of wobbly ultraschvartz, howling doggies, a black leather fambler waggling on a washing line, a headless skeleton thrown into la Seine ... then 'FIN'.

Ô, this was not an enjoyable cinematic experience for yours truly. Yet again I felt as though the Château Chanceux had collapsed on my Mare, coating everything in a meese impenetrable off-white snow.

After duey more nonsense flickers (LES BÂTARDS ROYAUX and Antonin Artaud's LA COQUILLE ET LE CLERGYMAN), the lights went up, then the prof invited us to prattle our thoughts on what we'd just ogled. I remained tight-levered until all these horrifically conceited skollies had toddled off outways, then I slithered up to the fungus and cough-coughed: 'Pardon my intrusion, camarade. Pray tell: was that previous flicker truly

LA LUNE PORTE UNE MOUSTACHE? Is your crackly print not missing the grand debut of one of the mostest risqué joggering-palones this side of la Seine?'

The professor ogled me with contempt. 'There is no female role in LA LUNE PORTE UNE MOUSTACHE.'

'Ô, you're the grand authority, are thee?' I flared my nose-thirls. 'Only I've nellied from a maxi reliable source – the leading lady herself, nix less – that my Old Mare was the star of the show.'

'Trust me, garçon. I have over forty years experience of criticism in this field. There is no female role in LA LUNE PORTE UNE MOUSTACHE.'

'Well, I'd admit it seems that way, you daffy tart. Perhaps the zelda was mistaken, shellshocked after the Occupation, meshigena, skitterish to the extreme, losing her tet. Ever vadared the flicker LE CON DU CHAT?'

The prof practically scratched the sideyboards from his cheeks. 'Oui. An abysmal film. And I can assure you: there is no female role in LE CON DU CHAT either.'

My tet dipped. I pondered why my Mare would mogue about her scatty screen career – although of course many pops fluff the truth to compensate for hopelessly naff norm lavvies. Jupiter forbid: was my Old Mare a boring newt like all the rest? Worster still: was there any bijou trace of her whatsoever, anywhere on this coddy festering welt?

'Squire, do you perchance have a copy of LE CON DU CHAT we could ogle this afterjuno? Just to make certain?'

'There is no female role in LE CON DU CHAT.'

'You're sure of this beyond all doubt?' I cried. 'No holes in the old memory banks? Nanti splitseconda morso of a palone in there whatsoever?'

The prof ogled the ceiling now, where some agile pop had screeved: IL EST INTERDIT D'INTERDIRE!

'Camarade,' he polled softly, 'the film is mostly cat's anuses. Cat's anuses and amateurish camerawork. Tell me: are you truly interested in wasting forty minutes of your life watching a litter of kittens pissing and shitting onto a giant bushy out-of-focus vagina?'

I shrugged. 'Possiblement.'

Needless to say we were doing exactly this quatra hours later, sitting stiffly sidey-by-side in the fungus's loft somewhere in the suburbs to the south of the city. The prof finally agreed to project the flicker after savvying I would simply shadow and harass him until he relented or until one of us was driven to horrendous violence. With nanti public transport it took us hours to walk to his petty maisonette, and this was done almost entirely in clench-levered silence.

The prof's abode had its avant-garde embellishments (Afrikkkan masks, bizarre canvases, lewd sculptoids), but I ponced the disorder was mostly down to slovenly lavvying than any aesthetic savagery. Twas a thoroughly unhygienic morso of Paris – but not one that could be blamed on revolution or strike action. The omi was simply a slob.

To begin with, my viewing pleasure was disrupted not so much by the chinka-foot-tall kitty anuses on the silvery screen, but by the fungal twat brootishly jarrying a platterful of blue fromage, cold cuts and baguette directly ajax to my right nell. The twonk had offered me not a scrap of sustenance after our strenuous trek, and his eek was as smug as a beaver's as it became clear there was indeed no female role in LE CON DU CHAT. The gist of the flicker seemed to hinge upon the notion that exposure to purrers can cause pregnant palones to lose their bambinos, but even so the director evidently felt nanti female role necessary to make sense of this abstract claptrap. There were kitties' anuses aplenty, innumerable bloodied bedsheets, but nix sparkling palones, no Mare.

Not, at least, until the final secondas of the flicker. Following an extended parade of feline dishes winking and squeezing out petty slugs of caca, the film cut to a parting panning shot of a bourgeois Haussmann apartment littered with upturned Louis

15 furniture. I admit I missed the flash of a bobbed donna in the reflection of one of the gildi mirrors but clocked the fungus's brootish jarrying stop pronto.

'Merde,' he muttered.

'What is it?' I polled as the prof rewound the reel.

'Voilà,' he mumbled morosely, pokering a lupper at the fantom in the reflection. 'I must apologise. I remember – this is the star of LE CON DU CHAT and LA LUNE PORTE UNE MOUSTACHE.'

'That petty smudge there? The star of the show?'

'I'm afraid your mother was ... eradicated by the censors,' the prof explained with a gross morso of panam pouched in his left cheek. 'I recall the woman now. A forgettable actress, c'est vrai, but an intriguing hostess. We used to watch her dance – if you can call it dancing – at Le Spleen de Paris.' The prof was animated now, flapping his lappers and firing crumbettes of baguette from his elastic oyster. 'Difficult to say if it was the directors themselves or the Chief of Police who ultimately decided her scenes be deleted. I dare say the moments of blackout in LA LUNE PORTE UNE MOUSTACHE were a vast improvement on the woman's performance, or possibly it was the leading lady herself who demanded the cuts. Fear the Nazis would discover her degenerate side-project. She danced for the bastards in the Latin Quarter, do you know this?'

'Oui. When she was part of the Resistance.'

The fungus spat the half-chewed glob onto his floor. 'Well, she had a strange approach to resistance, if that's what you believe. The woman must've shown her vagina to over a hundred of the swines every night. Matinees also.'

'She was a Surrealist.'

The prof spat on his floor again – just spittle this time. 'Do not be ridiculous! She was a curiosity to them, nothing more! In fact, not even that – she was a nuisance. The way she spoke, her psychobabble, her demented dancing – this was all a ruse to make us believe she was a madwoman, the embodiment of the Surrealist ideal. The truth is her madness was nothing more than a masquerade, an act. She wanted notoriety, she wanted to be immortalised in the vaults of history like Augustine and her hysteria, like Nadja, like Jeanne d'Arc, even.' He spat on the floor again. 'But I'm afraid she was as conformist, dull and talentless as her brownshirted patrons.'

I blinked at the twonk incredulously. 'My memory of her is that of a meshigena palone, a bona fide absurdist, a black sheepy, a batty Queen presiding over our most unruly vie d'avant-garde ...'

'Pff! The woman was not mad. She was an attention-seeker, nothing more.'

With gross difficulty I just about managed to refrain from ferricadoozing the cunt there and then. 'Trust me, squire, she was a madwoman. I still bear the scars of it today. Proudly, I might add. The Mare brought me up entirely outside the gripple of norm civilised society: battyfanging every last morso of stiffness and straightness out of me. Possiblement one could argue her insanity was a sane, full-wakey, conscious rejection of bourgeoistard primness and properness – but then again, one would have to be at least a pogi bit truly doolally to parade one's flange in front of the Wehrmacht noche upon noche, do you not agree?'

'Non. When the Nazis moved in, she was miraculously cured of her lunatic tendencies. Self-preservation, certainly. Better to bend to the fascists' every whim and desire than risk expulsion to the concentration camps, although both of course are imprisonment. The fact that your mother chose the former proves not only her lack of true madness, but also her complete and utter lack of integrity. What became of her? Did she survive the war?'

'Comme-ci, comme-ça. The last upstanding latty on a bombsite in Londres collapsed on her tet.'

'What a pity,' the prof polled blankly.

I glanced at my Mare's feeli eek frozen on the screen. It seemed terribly twisted to think this was the same humanoid tet the plod would exhume from the rubble trey-daitcha years later.

This was a molto fresh, fortuni fizzer: flytrap opals, amused bouche, Louise Brooks' boxy bob. Ô, Mama. Mama Mama Mama.

'You barely have a bona lav to say about my Mare,' I grumbled after another minuta or duey of grotty silence. 'Did she perchance reject your advances?'

The prof reered up, spraying fromage. 'Now you're the absurdist.'

I chewed the tips of my luppers again. 'Well then, do you happen to recall my Mare taking a lover around 1943, 1944? She claims my papa was one of eight or nine possible omis.' I clocked the prof had a foto of André Breton nailed to one of the purlins, albeit the shot of him with the mocking thorny caroon and cadaverous eek. I lingered expectantly ajax to this doomy portrait, adopting the same expression. 'She bedded a pogi few Surrealists, did she not?'

The fungus shrugged. 'I expect not. Rumours were rife the woman was awash with venereal disease. I believe the only man who ever dared sleep with her regularly was her keeper, the proprieter of Le Spleen de Paris.'

'Ô? A razzle-dazzle omi of entertainments?'

'Pff! This is one way of looking at it.' The prof spat on his floor again. 'Like your mother, this man claimed to be part of the Resistance, but many suspected he was collaborating with the Gestapo. His cave was positively littered with swastikas during the Occupation – and after the Liberation, the swine promptly fled la Patrie.'

My gargler felt ultra dry now. I had a voche like a rusty seesaw as I asked next: 'Where did he flee, do you know?'

'Last I heard he'd set up a new nightclub across the Channel. Some awful little hovel, named after the last one. Le Spleen de Londres.'

PART VII*

PERFECT SAVAGERY

'La liberté est une garce qui aime à être couchée sur des matelas de cadavres.'†

COMTE DE MIRABEAU, THE GRAND POCKMARKED OYSTER-LEVERS OF 1789

---

* Two chapters received Thursday, 18th June 1970 – twenty-five days to go. Our advert appeared in the *International Times* that morning: another six-by-six-inch presentation of our latest titles (*The Nuremberg Nymphos*, *Milky Johanna*, *The Throne Room*, *Cannibal Cafeteria*) alongside a large, incongruous ear hastily illustrated by Davy. We were so anxious for our secret correspondent to see the ear, the drawing took up almost half the ad space, leaving no room even for our contact details or instructions on how or where to purchase the listed pocketbooks – but by now of course selling unprofitable penny dreadfuls concerned us very little.

† 'Liberty is a whore who likes to be bedded on a mattress of corpses.' Epigraph carved into the paper with a knife or razor?

Uno Sunny Juno

NOVAK AND HIS FOLLOWERS WEAR SICKBAG PAPER DRESSES.

NELLY DANI'S 'LA MACHINE'.

An**g**uish and disgust on the swishing salty aqua. We took the ferry back to Blighty o**n**ce we savvied the froggy revolution was all just wind and piss. After all the promise of the teen**i** revolt, come the end of Ju**ne** de Gaulle was miraculously back in power – partly down to the old prat threatening military aggro, but mainly down to the feelies being unable to rev up the ideal ideological replacement for the eagle regime, and norm civvies tiring of their lavvies being flippered by the General Strike, parnying for some bona old-fashioned LAW and ORDER once again.

Conservatism was deemed the lesser of duey evils (bester the devil you know, et ceterarara) and won ou**t**. Ô, BOF and BOLLOCKS to it all.

Further down the padded benkel, my chinka remaining dollies seemed molto excited to get back to Londres – I, however, was only too aware of the meese bear trap that awaited us, the Ring of Steel nix doubt set up by the anglo plod to recapture us after our snappy escape following the debacle at Grosvenor Square.

For the fourth time that journey, I excused myself to go and vomit brootishly in the seesawing khazi. Twas not fairy sea**si**ckness causing my kishkas to flipper – rather, the twisted savagery that I was returning to a hostile city that might crush me immediately upon rearrival (that is, if plain paranoia or exhaustion didn't ferricadooz me first). After flushing, I ogled myse**l**f in the streaky glaze – and let out a beastly groan. Ô comrades, twas as if the dreadful revelations of the past few weeks had aged me about trey decades. My eek was all out of joint: gross cracks around my oyster and oglelids (the worst being an enormous sawtooth scar slithering down my left cheek, like a petty mondshake had gone off just west of my vonka), blue levers, battleship-grey fangs, sagg**i**ng jowls and wilted choufleur nells. Was this truly an indica**tion** that I was decaying before my time – or was it just my coddy budget plastic surgery prematurely coming apart at the seams? Certainly my blue fangs and levers looked conspicuously mortlike – but then again I had been schlumphing a great deal of rough vin rouge en France.

'Ô, bof, balderdash and bollocks to it all,' I huff-puffed as I hunched over the khazi once more, vomiting just aero this time.

Upon returning to my followers, I felt a strange mixture of guilt and sloppiness, regard**i**ng their dolly glazed mannequin-eeks as the barka lento lurched and bobbled its way back to Britannia. Whether I survived to steer them b**ra**vely through the setta-daitchas or not, would the poor feelies ever vada a truly unrestricted, unsneering, ultraloving mond?

Wrapping my quivery tentacles around Séverine and Veronica, I let out a vinegary sigh, pondering what a bona fide international utopia might **en**tail ...

If one sunny juno I was made supreme dicktittler of this codswallop welt, I would first and foremost abolish all politics. There would be free shelter for all, free munja, free bevvies, free bonbons, free passage from zona to zona, free culture, free transport, nanti gaols, nix hierarchy, no bosses, no blobs on the beat. A Love District in every town: monogamy abolished, all desires c**a**tered for, all perversions purified, nanti arva-act or grot**t**y-thought a taboo nix longer! Everything dirty now considered clean! Think the unthinkable! Mention the unmentionable! A triumphant return to the gildi u**n**interrupted creative liberty of chavvyhood! STRENGTH THROUGH JOY!

'Ooh la la,' I nelly you squeak, 'but how on earth would this wunderbar utopia be funded, Raymondo?'

NELLYARDA: INCREASE MECHANISATION PRONTO. Gather the bestest scientists together and a grand compliant workforce to build robos and computoids capable of liberating all future humano**i**ds from degrading travails. Once these handsome slavish automatons are installed across the mond, we can sit back and enjoy our lavvies as they were intended to be lived: FULL LEISURE FOR ALL! At the very mostest pops will be required to take it in turns to work no more than uno hour a week, overseeing certain robos that require humanoid assistance or maintenance. In return the bots will keep this gloriosa not-fo**r**-**p**rofit welt ticking along, churning out all cheets necessary for a bona Liberated Lavvy: powering our free shelters, printing and delivering our weekly ration-billets and love-tokens, restocking and regurgitating all mann**e**r of de-luxe goodies and sundries from vending-vacayas, dhobying the strasses and pissoirs without co**m**plaint ...

Sce**p**tics and naysayers worry one day robos will become so advanced they'l**l** overpower us humanoids and keep us as mere pets – but I would squeak in response: 'So be it!' Regard the lavvy of a purrer or poodle. Is it not the most pampered free-wheelering lavvy imaginabl**e**? Couple this luxurious layabout lavvystyle with our grand added bonus of a consciousness to enjoy art, musica, love and poetry, and I say: 'What more could one wish for?!'

Oui. Ô, oui oui OUI OUI OUI! I had it all worked out. This was my nova improved grand plan to build a bona fide utopia upon this ridiculous rotten rock. But alas, I savvied it wouldn't come about, not in my lavvytime. So I chose to do somet**h**ing else.

Dearest Comrades! Join Us as We Crawl Wide-Ogled from the Oubliette!

NOVAK WEARS WELLINGTON BOOTIES, WWII GAS MASK, BLACK FAMBLERS, LATEX HAZMAT RADIATION SUIT.

NELLY CLOTHILDE'S 'LA VÉRITÉ, TOUTE LA VÉRITÉ'.

I'd not been ogling the fashion glossies quite as beady as I used to, but I felt certain (for us at least) Paris Green was to be THE colour this autumn/winter season. Paris Green is a truly remarkable hue. It sparkles like a sledgehammered emerald, like a dynamited absinthe distillery, like a sweet swirly seizure-inducing Van Gogh herbscape.

Paris Green was named not for its ubiquitousness in froggy haute couture, but because it was used as rat poison in the city's sewers during the Romantic period. The dye contains arsenic – hence myself and my dollies were joshed-up in full protective clobber as we rustled up perhaps my mostest dizzying lally-covers to date: 30R.

I was able to obtain a punnet of Paris Green powder from a connection I'd made at King **G**eorgie Five, the hue having historically been used to paint the hulls of barkas to mortify barnacles (and probably every other poor fishybit in the fleet's vicinity). We decked the workshop in a grandiose plastic drop-cloth, flung open the fenêtres, then set to work chopping and dunk-dunking Inspector Silling's unsolicited slacks into this gloriosa green slime.

'Regard my levers, my cherries: at some point a sharpering-omi will come sniffling round our boutique,' I honked through the gas mask. 'These are his lally-covers. Make sure he does not vagary without them.'

'Would it not be wiser, your Lordship, to offer up a more conservative shade of slacks?' Veronica ventured. 'Would a dull straight-and-narrow law-omi willingly accept a pair of luminous lally-covers?'

'Of course not,' I hooted. 'This glimmering green is for the lining only. As far as the Inspector's aware, he'll be parkering a pair of norm bland pantaloons.' I gestured at the roll of naff grey twill standing ajax to the spreading-table, which was to make up the outer layer of the garment.

'How long til the poison takes effect?' Séverine asked. 'What if the plodder keels over on our premises?'

'Fear not, my chovis,' I polled, carefully pegging the sopping toxic sheet to the line strung above the drop-cloth. 'The wondrous nature of arsenic poisoning is its symptoms are ajax to mortification by flu or munja-bug: vomitus, dish-squirts, feverish tremblings. Tis a gradual process, my lovelies. In fact, my grossest fear is that the dye might have nix effect whatsoever – hence these pogi few extra measures to help coax the ghastly goo into the bat's system ...'

Once the material had dried, I attached kenza bijou swatches of sandpaper to the lining, to itch and menace the Inspector's thews, hopefully encouraging the twonk to scritch-scratch his skin open and allow the venom into his bod molto freely. Once in his veins, I savvied it might take hours before the pop would start to sweat and tingle. Nix doubt he'd be back at Scotland Yard or even home with his wife by the time his kishkas flippered.

Uno bijou suggestion from my otherwise ultra dedicated/discerning dollies: was this creation of deadly lally-covers not a pogi bit of an overreaction, somewhat like the actions of a supreme paranoiac? 'POPPYCOCK!' I screeched. As my doctored copies of the Daily RayMond made only too clear now, the eagles were conspiring to wipe out all nonconformist weirdies like ourselves with renewed vigour. Shaken by the recent anti-establishment upsplurges in Paris, Prague, Londres, Chicago, et cetera, the Grand Illuminati had pooled together a crack team of crooked politicos, savage plodders and demented military-brutes to protect the existing coddy social order by any means necessary. With snifflers like Inspector Silling already on our tail, we could expect obliteration or gaol sharpish. Apparently Mr Wilson had already promised Lynda more anglo cannon fodder in the offal-dripping jungles of Dak To and Khe Sanh. Meanwhile nuclear warheads were being polished, the plan being: if the Russkis don't kindly drop the H-bomb on our rapidly multiplying welfare-dependent civvies, we may as well just do it ourselves – and blame the other side. Depopulate our groaning island with a motivational mushroom cloud or duey! Ease anti-eagle tension and disperse stubborn picket-lines in industrial maxi-flammable zonas like Glasgow, Sheffield or Manchester with incendiary bombas. Meanwhile the toppermost eagles can orbit the mond in a tin can brimming with champagne and freeze-dried tidbits, until radiation levels lower enough to allow a safe return to our molto gay, cleansed and compliant isle. And so on and so forth.

I of course did not truly believe all this meshigena claptrap (trust me, I am a sane, sane omi), but I needed maxi loyalty and full beautiful recklessness and sacrifice from my followers for the fiendish delights I had planned next. The bestest way to guarantee this was to make the poor zots believe their junos were strictly numbered.

'The eagles may well drop The Bomb upon our tets any juno now, my darlings,' I polled repeatedly. 'Alas, we cannot avoid the ultra-warming embrace of the mushroom cloud, but why surrender premature? Let us live out the rest of our petty doomed lavvies with maxi abandon, maxi luxury, maxi love, MAXI MISCHIEF!'

Once I'd WIZZed together the final morsos of toxic lally-cover, I locked the garment in an aerotight glass cabinet downstairs and attached a bijou tag:

SOLD, AWAITING COLLECTION

And yet: many months later the pantaloons were still hanging there unclaimed. The garment stood stiffly in the centre of our boutique, a tiny sliver of that dazzling green lining peeking coquettishly out from under uno lally-cuff.

Where was Inspector Silling? Possiblement the fungus might've forgotten about me, or found some alternative knock-off chinos elsewhere, or perhaps I'd overestimated the fuzz's interest in yours truly, although I savvied: if we weren't toppermost on the plod's Mostest Wanted list quite yet, we'd be there soon enough!

Since returning from Paris, something REVOLTING was bubbling in my servo. After ogling the fairy fizzling-out of the froggy revolt, nix longer was I interested in trying to build utopia upon this ridiculous rock – but all the same I wanted to leave my mark, to create some grandiose scandal or supreme all-jarrying aggro-extravaganza future pops would remember me by, to ensure that my poor twisted struggle through the Western Welt's codswallop cogs hadn't all been in vain.

This savagery struck me not long after vadaring LE CON DU CHAT. The flicker itself had nix philosophical value or answer to any gnawing existential quandaries – rather, it was the disappearance of my Mare's scenes that spurred me on to leave behind at least some petty legacy, some pogi sparkling morso to make certain that mostest majestic nom, RAYMOND MARIANNE NOVAK, would not be lost forever to the oubliette of history.

It saddened me that the only bijou trace of my beloved Mare on this entire planet was a solo splitseconda frame of some obscure Surrealist flicker even proud scholars of Surrealism consider frankly unwatchable. Other than that, there was nantwar: nix gravestone, no fotos, nanti latty, nix hand-me-down keepsakes.

Ô Jupiter, Ô Judith, it was overwhelming pondering how many billions of beautiful humanoid lavvies had been forgotten since the Neanderthals rose up from the sludge and made their first grunt. Alas, time jarries us. How then to counteract this cateva fizzling-out and cast ourselves in gildi marble, to be ogled and drooled over by generations of beautiful humanoids to come?

I pictured my smouldering fizzer on the front of every inky and glossy on every newsstand across the welt – and I savvied only one natty option remained for me to get there.

Crime

Do-gooders are rarely remembered. Spreading multiwhirly ULTRALOVE was out of the question now.

I envisioned a maxi explosive show-stopping crime – but what flavour carnage would it be, and against whom? Twas not enough to simply privvily poison a sharpering-pop through his pantaloons. The crime had to be as multicolourfluttery, flamboyant and conspicuous as a fuckering circus parade if I was to be held up in the same sickly-sweet blaze as Jack ze Ripper, Fantômas, Vlad the Impaler ...

Given the gravity and complexity of my monstrous emags, it would take almost a full twelvemonth before I had the whole operation full-plotted in my servo.* In the meantime I sent

* Of course, most of us felt genuine terror knowing Novak's monstrous emags were now full-plotted and only days away – and still, having endured more than 400 pages of the meese meshigena-omi's memoirs, we were no closer to uncovering what this 'maxi explosive show-stopping crime' would be. Stanley, seemingly growing more unhinged and irrational by the day, believed the more explosive and show-stopping the better – but he was in a minority of one. The rest of us were no longer enthusiastic about publishing Novak's toxic text, much less selling it to the general public. In fact, more than anything we were now determined to *save* the general public, to stop Novak unleashing whatever foul misguided act of terrorism he had planned. But what leads did we have to stop him? Truly it

was sickening that, despite the intense level of scrutiny we'd given the madman's life story thus far, we knew nothing concrete about his current whereabouts, his battle plan, his true identity. It was no surprise of course that no RAYMOND M. NOVAK could be found in the telephone directory. Whether or not he and his followers had genuinely occupied the three-storey Georgian latty on Ogle Street was irrelevant – no evidence of them was visible there now. And even if we wanted to involve the police at this late (O, how late!) stage, we could barely offer them a precise physical description of the Prole Dandy (Marilyn chin? Streamlined oink-vonka? Wilted choufleur-nells?), and who's to say he hadn't undergone yet more extensive plastic surgery since then, to further keep us and the plod off the scent?

All we had to go on was the knowledge that Novak (alias Raymond Foster-Newman?) had been booked by the police in the summer of 1964 and the spring of 1968 – and the chilling possibility that the bastard had been present at our launch for *The Nuremberg Nymphos* in February 1970 (see footnotes to 'Dandelion Fluff', 'Elektrizität Macht Frei', etc.). As ever, Stanley was grimly opposed to us informing the police, explaining with white horses galloping in the corners of his mouth: 'It's too late anyhow. They won't catch him. The man's sly, he's slippery – you know he'll just see this thing through no matter what, so why get involved? Why jeopardise the success of the novel, why jeopardise our safety? Suppose Novak has got us under surveillance somehow ...' He lowered his voice. 'He finds out we've gone to the police, he'll obliterate us all. He's intent on seeing this thing through – it stands to reason he'll stop at nothing to make it happen. So why put ourselves in the firing line?'

'He can't obliterate us,' was our response. 'He needs us to publish the novel.'

'Hardly. So long as the manuscript's intact, anyone could publish it. If Novak's crime's shocking enough, any publisher would jump at the chance to publish it. This.' He punched the grubby manuscript on Trefoil's desk. 'You might not like everything in it, but there's no denying it's got potential to be a beautiful fucking heinous masterpiece and our golden ticket to success, at long, long last. We need him more than he needs us. So let's not mess around, trying to intervene. Let the Guru do what he needs to do.'

Did our Director really know best? Was he drunk while delivering this speech? On the one hand Merritt's argument for keeping ourselves safe selfishly did make sense, and yet on the other we couldn't shake the feeling we were to be (partly, at least) responsible for the deaths of many innocent people, simply by staying quiet. True enough, we agreed it was too risky (or just futile) to involve the police now, but the majority of us knew we'd never get over the guilt if we didn't at least try to foil Novak's plans some other way.

Those of us in favour of stopping Novak began to meet every other night at different pubs across London. On the first night (Saturday, 27th June – sixteen days to go) we met at the Pillars of Hercules in Greek Street, and set about listing all those persons present at the *Nuremberg Nymphos* launch in February.

my dollies out to shush a Philips dicktittlerphone and chinka gleaming Impe**r**ial typewriters, replacing the sewing-vacayas in our workshop with these magickal machines that were to immortalise my heroic lavvy in ink.

Whatever my fant**a**bulosa crime might entail, I was full-aware twud molto likely lead to my instant mortification, the eagles having all the resources to flush out and ferricadooz those bold beauties that dare to question their all-flappering authority – and naturellem**en**t I could not rely on the media to tell my lavvy-story str**a**ight and true. Most hacks lack the inspiration or nattiness to describe perfectly sane terrorists like myself as anything other than brainless thugs, luna**t**ics, beasties, reptiles. Therefore I savvied I must tittle the tale myself, however inept I might be academically, however incoherent in the gargler, however biased my battyfa**n**ging storytelling.

And yet, ALAS and ALACK, as it rapidly became clear, the doll**i**es in my typing pool were even less literate than I. As I stomped around the workshop, emphatically squeaking my chavvyhood remembrances at them, I was not aware the zots were inte**rp**reting my lucid tales like so:

wwik unt f nover syhnta nor plstk srgyree
but mrs o fat need sm furm cmuflgyy to

Three of our quartet (Davy, Trefoil and Emily) were there, along with Merritt, Mesh and a very small handful of Glass Eye fans who we regrettably failed to engage in any conversation or eye-contact whatsoever. Howling had been missing a couple of months by this stage, Audrey and McKinley were ill, and Iris was keeping her distance, to put it mildly.

The details of the night were relatively blurry now, but we felt certain there'd been no one particularly suspicious lurking among us: no flagrant fashion iconoclasts, no waxwork dollies, no Goose. As the footnote to 'Elektrizität Macht Frei' made plain, most of the general public left promptly once they realised there were no complimentary refreshments. The way we remember it, there were only Glass Eye employees and two paralytic authors (Dennis Mesh and P.P. Flake) remaining by the time the event degenerated to a 'bland board meeting' and we began drunkenly discussing alternative titles for Novak's novel.

shdbi v need to vench t out in ct 9or shd the rbbbl
wilts funle clr and THE CUTY CMS TO US).

Not for the first time I pondered: were my immature darlings up to the task of assisting me in this maxi momentous murderous mayhem? Ogling roundways, the zots did not strike me as the mostest robust shocktroopers: Veronica squinting through her solo bona opal, Bonnie squeezed into a bambino's highchair with stubby lallies overhanging, Bruce snoozing slack-jawed and skeletal on a pillow of screwed-up bimph. If their twisted histoires were to be believed, some of my leftover donnas did have privvy skills I could put to bona use – Rosa Winkel's Bondage und Disziplin expertise, Séverine's mink-skinning efinkery – but above all I savvied it was my dolls' unquivering commitment to yours truly that was their grandest asset. These chinka feelies weren't here just because they had nowhere better to vagary. After quatra years of uncomplaining dedication, I savvied they must genuinely believe in my natty lavs, they must detest the eagles just as glimmery as I did, they must've actually meant it when they screeched YES to all my daffy demands and inflammatory claptrap. AND – dare I even screeve it? – they must truly LOVE me, without reservation.

Reader: I loved them too.

And so – what extravagant carnage could I conjure up to do myself and my beloved disciples justice?* Feeling somewhat

---

* Bolstered by gin, McKinley had a rash brainwave as he traipsed back to the Tube from Greek Street. After sweatily shaking hands farewell with Trefoil, Davy and Emily, he scurried to a phone booth and thumbed a scatterful of change into the machine.

'Hello, operator,' he monotoned, trying not to sound drunk or nervous though his heart was writhing like a seasick monkey in his chest. 'The Metropolitan Police, please. Chief Inspector's office.'

'Who is calling?'

'It's ... no one. Anonymous call, thank youpt!'

It aggravated McKinley that he wasn't able to conduct himself like the cool, collected characters of the pulp novels his company churned out, and perhaps as a result of this he was not put through to the Chief Inspector's office, but

uninspired in my waking hours, I took to leaving the dicktittlerphone running through the noche, hoping it might capture some unconscious ramblings that might help poke the way to our most fantabulosa criminal destiny. For a week or duey there was nantwar of value: just the blustery snores, parps and sighs of myself and my fattygayed angels. On noche nobba, however, the VU meter peaked just before dawn. An intriguing lav – my original lav! – was spluttered forth betwixt the inkyboos:

'Dada,' I gurgled through the hmmmmmmmmummmmering wow and flutter. 'Dada. Dada dada dada!'

---

instead palmed off to a dogsbody somewhere in the drab labyrinth of Scotland Yard. Looking back, was this brush-off decisive in the course of what followed? Undoubtedly it's a small comfort to believe the police were somehow to blame for the turmoil that came next.

Speaking in a gusty whisper now, McKinley asked the dogsbody if there was any record of a Raymond Novak or Raymond Foster-Newman in the Met's files. 'I have information about this man you might find useful.'

During the long silence that followed, McKinley was trembling, convinced a sniper's bullet could spiderweb the glass and shatter his skull any moment. He was about to hang up and flee into the night when the dogsbody reappeared on the line: 'Sir, we're not at liberty to release those details over the telephone. What information was it you wished to share?'

'What about … Silling? Inspector Silling? Can you get Inspector Silling on the line?'

Another long silence. More trembles.

'There is no Inspector Silling.'

'You don't have his extension?' McKinley snapped. 'His home number? It's S-I-L-L-I-N-G.'

'There is no Inspector Silling on the books, sir. Not that I can see.'

Queasily McKinley thought of the Paris Green pantaloons. 'Was there *ever* an Inspector Silling on the books?' he demanded. 'Did he retire? Or did he go missing? Who is his replacement?'

At that moment a pigeon or some other clumsy vermin landed with a VLOP! on top of the phone booth, causing McKinley to cry out and slam the receiver down. As he staggered away from the red box, he kept grumbling into his collar: 'Fucking incompetents … fucking foolish bastards …'

Still, was it not the Guru himself who screeved 'BLAME BLAME BLAME. Pops love to have someone to blame for their own shortcomings'?

Before McKinley entered the station at Leicester Square, he vomited colourfully down the side of the Palace Theatre.

Plume*

NOVAK WEARS CONCEALER, AMONG OTHER CHEETS.

NELLY FRANCE GALL'S 'DADY DA DA'.

Many times since 1965 I'd pondered: did we kill Monsieur Drench? How tightly were he and the bung shackled to the doppel-guillotine when we vagaried? How long can a fungus survive without aqua and munja? And of course since June 1968 I'd been constantly terrorised by the query: was this omi truly mein vater??

Plopping myself down at my joshing-table, I glumly pinched and prodded my meese creased eek in the mirror, stretching and crushing my features to form all sorts of horrific Halloween monsters. I pondered: were there glimmering similarities between myself and Drench? Certainly any trace of the fungus's eek must've been wiped out by my extensive plastic surgery, but twas intriguing – dare I splurt, even a pogi bit exhilarating? – to imagine my nova shiftering to crime had been aforescreeved in the sparkles, that I might've inherited the urge for devilry and aggro from the evil batatat. Ô, twas a delicious excuse at the very least.

Whether nature or nurture made me this way, I savvied it was vital to soften (if not blankwash altogether) this glaringly criminal eek before unleashing my superheroic, superhorrendous vengeance upon the mond. Naturellement I did not want

* Chapter received Wednesday, 1st July 1970 – twelve days to go.

the plodders to seize me pre**m**aturely on face-value alone – nor did I want to repulse teenyboppers and lattywives alike when at last my infamous fizzer is beamed across the Vadawaves. AU CONTRAIRE: I wanted all thumpers aflutter!

Gazing debonairly into the glaze, I lento filled out my wrinkles with thick concealer, then applied full-blank regal maquiage, hoping to conjure an air of rakish respectability, if not full god-like splendour. My beloved French Crop was now incapable of hiding my floppy choufleur nells and stubborn frown-lines, and so I wriggled into a voluminous curly schvartz perruque instead, fluffing it up to daffy Louis 14-size proportions. I applied duey flaming swirls of rouge, numerous beauty morsos, then – to cover the vast scar on my left cheek – attached a gross handlebar mouser, pricking the ends up with my anxious viscous saliva.

'Vagarying somewhere specjalni, your Lordship?' Séverine asked, slithering out from under her eiderdown, blinking misty.

'Oui – to Hell,' I cackled, repeating the lavs I polled back in '65 after slamming Drench's clefs in the back of ze taxicab.

YES: GARDYLOO and ACHTUNG, mes amis – I was crawling back to Daddy. I wasn't sure exactly what I was sharpering for from this cateva reunion – or if indeed my dear Dada was even still alive – but nevertheless I felt compelled to descend once again into that lowly dungeonette, like an injured mole blindly burrowing homewards, like a gay suicide leaping into The Void, like une petite madeleine dunked into a poisoned bitter-gator ...

Twas a meese swampy thunderous noche. To protect my nova pristine eek I reached for the hardiest rainclobber I could finger, which of all things turned out to be the CRS cozzy – trenchcoat, goggles, riot-capella, black famblers – I'd shushed as a memento mori after ferricadoozling the sharpering-omi in Paris.

Scuttling jackbootied through the gloopy strasses of Fitzrovia, it crossed my servo I could well be arrested for imitating a police officer, but once I'd made it under the swirly neon of

Soho I simply looked like any norm perv trolling in a dirty mac and mouser-fake.

Was I feeling skitterish and untogether as I approached Grand Windmill Strasse? Nein – not as far as I can remember. I'd requested Bruce and Bonnie linger in a caboosh by the solo phone booth in Brewer Strasse, but I didn't rightly feel I'd need to pipe for back-up this particular noche. Twas my intention to merely slip incognito into the duey-shilling revue, perhaps parker a French maid a funt to jiggle snake-like for me – and vada what had and hadn't survived since we ransacked the establishment back in '65. Truly I did not expect to find Monsieur Drench down there – unless the fungus was still strapped to the doppel-guillotine, a skeleton in a periwig – but, supposing the death-defying batatat had survived, I was undecided whether I'd like to shower the twonk with love or aggro now, or just ogle him quietly from the sideylines, scrutinising the meese beastie I might turn into when I got old ... if I got old ...

I had an array of uppers and downers – barbiturates, Mogadon, coco, French Blues – in my trenchcoat poshes, in case of an emergency. I had Largactil. I had arsenic.

And so: twas with a certain tranquil recklessness I slithered my way along Archer Strasse and turnered the corner onto Grand Windmill, only to discover the mighty Spleen de Londres was nantwar to be ogled. There were still plenty of duey-shilling revues and grot-parlours standing erect on the cobbly strasse, but my dear papapa's establishment had vanished. Yet again an unsettling image dribbled into my servo: a grand château collapsing, coating me in thick off-white snow. In place of Le Spleen de Londres was a nova garish discotheque brimful with brightly coloured prats. The swirly lavs above the door screeched in green reptilian neon: HYPNOGOGO.

At first I savvied the Old Bat must've snuffed it after all, and I lingered for uno momento, waiting for the obligatory ripple of twistiness to judder through me. As it turned out, nothing came. Clear enough by this stage of my lavvy I was not capable of shedding parnyaqua over any old codswallop cheet norm pops might frown about, like loss or p**a**tricide. I simply turned up my floppy collar and flared my nose-thirls derisively. I was more or less content to banish my Dada to the oubliette forever and toddle on homewards, when the sandwich board ajax to the portal of HYPNOGOGO shushed my opals:

TONITE!
FASCINUM PUBLICATIONS* PRESENTS ...
TOUCHED BY COLIN
THE NEW THRILLER BY MELODY AUTRUCHE
BOOK LAUNCH & SIGNING
ENTRY 10s (INCL. FIRST EDITION!)

Peeking inways, it did not appear to be the mostest swinging of parties, but the filthy nom of this glistening liver gave me hope there'd be easy-morts aplenty. I parkered my ten-bob to the trout at the entrance, received my hardback, then proceeded to the bar with pogi tingles in my slippies.

Thoroughly parched, I demanded the bung rustle me up a sopping wet martini (duey-daitcha parts Noilly Prat, uno part Londinium throat-varnish) then, as the twat bungled his way through the recipe, I cast my opals over the liver. The cover was meshige**n**a: a drab mid-age omi plunged up to his neck in a vat of what appeared to be rather unhealthy urine. Intrigued, I fingered inwards, sharpering for this gildi kinky scenario (to no avail) until finally my bevvy arrived.

---

* An awful publishing house. There was a time when we would receive a grovelling invite to each of their hopeless book launches – however, following a spat that blew up between Merritt, Howling and Fascinum's founder Dicky Berridge one night in the Salisbury pub in Theatreland, we were promptly (mercifully!) removed from their mailing list. We cannot remember exactly what the spat was in aid of – only that our 173rd release, *Charmless Phallus*, was a thinly veiled attack on Berridge and his staff, and sold far more copies than their own churlish effort, *The Evil Eye*, released six months later. AVOID THEIR BOOKS!

'Santé! And very merry pissings!' I bellowed to no pop in particular, and took a glug.

Ô, just as I'd feared, twas an utterly frigid soirée. The partygoers all looked as though they'd turned up to the wrong corporate jamboree but didn't have the kishkas to admit their mistake, violently upturn the tables and vagary pronto. Dead-eyed newts in juno-suits introducing other twonks in juno-suits to yet more blank-eeked zots in juno-suits. Pompous toffs with expense accounts: the type of omis who have the funds to get you thoroughly pissed, but make you feel molto sober the more time you spend with them. ENCORE UNE FOIS: the cold boastful thrill of ejaculating dinarli into the Big Boggy Deep ...

Twas easy enough to finger the leading lady in all this naff brooliment: one palone stood out, painted and peacocked like she'd spent as much time on maquiage and frippery as it takes to screeve a passable short story. I pondered whether she'd been dolled up at the publisher's insistence, and expense. She was a glossy zelda, nix mistake, but it excited me that she was wearing so much slap she could well have been hiding horrendous caboosh-crash scars under that pancake. Or perhaps there was nothing underneath. Just a couple of rub-a-dub-dubs with a gross turps-soaked cottonball and the palone might vanish altogether ...

I took another fortifying glug of martini, then strutted across the empty dancefloor to chivalrously liberate the palone from her conversation with two goats in pinstripes. 'Melody, darling,' I honked. 'You look ravishing!'

Clear enough the palone was incapable of smiling under all that warpaint, though her opals glistened appetisingly as I introduced myself: 'Raymond Marianne Novak. I'm un auteur myself. TOUCHED BY COLIN, hm?' I bit the liver, rolling my own googly ogles backways. 'I trust there are plentiful colins in this here titillating tome, are there? Colins galore?'

Ms Autruche let out a nervy titter. 'Only one Colin, I'm afraid.'

'But he plays a big part, oui, non? The leading laddy?'

'The leading role, yes.'

I bit my bottom oyster-lever now, almost drawing blood. 'Ô wunderbar. I'm currently in the midst of dicktittling my own deviant memoirs – I'd be maxi grateful for any squirt of advice from a grand dame in the dirty scriptures department like your dolly self ...'

Melody played the coquette now, glancing shiftily about the room. 'Well, I'm not sure "dirty scriptures" is the genre I'm working in. You've not read the novel?'

'Nein. Fill me in, ducky. What meshigena tomfoolery can be ogled within? At what point does our hero receive his gildi showerings?'

Ô, comrades – ALAS – my greedy arva-fever was not to last. As Melody robotically regurgitated the contents of her liver, I rapidly lost interest. 'The novel concerns a stockbroker, an everyman, Colin Golding, who wakes one morning to discover he has a special power: the Midas touch. Any human he touches turns to twenty-four-carat gold.' By this juncture I was only half-nellying, gazing glazy back towards the bar. 'Colin's hapless workmate Cameron is first to be infected by his golden fingers, then his best friend, his fiancée, then his entire extended family. Convinced there is nothing he can do to return them to life, well, Colin dishonourably pawns them. He makes more and more money trading his twenty-four-carat victims to pawn shops and antiques dealers, and is quickly addicted – only the market soon becomes so oversaturated with gold, the value of the metal plummets, until it is practically worthless. Colin falls into depression, he endeavours to find his family and friends again, to buy them all back from the pawnbrokers, to try to find some way, some miraculous way to bring them all back to life agai—'

'But they've all been melted down,' I interjected, 'in a gross fuck-off vat somewhere and turned into garish ear-fakes.'

'No. Well. I shan't give the ending away.'

I was feeling dowri sober and cheated now, and was in fact poised to hurl this most naff hardback across the dancefloor when Melody piped up with this gloriosa unexpected denouement: 'It's basically a great big fuck-you to the Establishment, an anti-Capitalist fable.'

Blood-red glimmer-fakements detonated in my servo. I clutched the glistening liver to my boomboomer. 'I'll treasure it.'

(And now for un bijou aside: I admit it has not been easy collaborating with my beloved fantomscreever on this chapter. Mademoiselle Autruche remembers certain pogi details differently to yours truly. POR EXAMPLE: I generously allowed the donna free rein to promote her daffy novel in that morso of dialogue up thataways, and yet the dorcas scribbler claims she would never use the term 'great big fuck-you' to describe any one of her lofty livers. It is worth noting, however, dear readers, that she was much more intoxicated than moi that noche. At the very least we agree on that much.)

Melody grabbed my lapper, then positively dragged me back to the bar to recharge our glasses. 'Two sopping-wet martinis, squire,' I yelped at the bung.

When our bevvies appeared, I bedazzled her with a stirring longwinded toast that ended with a brootish cry of: 'DEATH TO EMPTY CONSUMERISM!'

Melody snorted, enthused: 'Well, yes – only so long as it doesn't affect sales of my novel, of course!'

'Ô, mais oui! Naturellement. Hé-hé-hé-hé-hé-hé!' and so on and so forth.

BOFFLEPLOP.

'Tell me, duchess ...' I swung a lapper round her shoulders. 'Melody Autruche: tis an intriguing nom! Are you French, perchance? Any garlic running through your bod at all?'

'It's a nom de plume,' she replied, taking another sip-sip of martini. '"Autruche" is French for "ostrich", so I believe – but I'm from up Cheshire way myself.'

'Ah, bon – this all maketh perfect sense. The excessive maquiage, the daffy nom de guerre.* I too savvy ze importance

---

* Drinking on the night of Monday, 29th June at the Island Queen in Noel Road, it occurred to us: if we could somehow track down one of Novak's dissenting dollies – those five brave escapees from Never-Neverland – they might be able to help us locate the Scum King, if not foil his fantabulosa crime altogether. And yet, as we combed once again through the tatty manuscript, we found Novak had prudently kept all his closest comrades' identities firmly hidden behind their own daffy noms-de-guerre throughout.

All, that is, except one.

Scanning 'The Antichristines' with pink hayfever-jellified eyes, Trefoil made a sniffly hoot when he hit upon the following sentence: 'The Baroness's joggering-nom might've led one to believe she was a domineering donna, an aristocratic crone with a brootish Teutonic tongue – but in fact our dorcas von Fisty was a meek teeni, an insecure chavvy with a sugary voche and soft manatee opals (her real nom was Peggy Fairweather!).'

Mercifully, there were not too many Fairweathers in the telephone directory. The following morning we took it in turns to dial each entry from the phone booth in Cleveland Street, first enquiring if there was a Peggy Fairweather living at the residence and, if we got lucky, claiming we wished to interview her for a publication entitled *Fantabulosa Fashion Fillies* after spotting her at a Fitzrovian boutique or discotheque some moons ago.

By the middle of the afternoon our enquiries had uncovered three Peggy Fairweathers in Greater London, two of whom turned out to be octogenarians: a toffee-voiced dame in Upper Norwood who was nevertheless very willing to talk Emily through her bizarre sartorial history, and a less obliging crone from Belsize Park who seemed convinced Davy was trying to wheedle her out of her furs and jewellery.

Despite her father's refusal to put his daughter on the line, the third Peggy Fairweather seemed much more promising. Probed as tactfully as possible by Trefoil, Mr Fairweather revealed that his Peggy was twenty-one years old, she was still in bed at 2 p.m. on a Tuesday afternoon, seemingly in no fit state to speak to strangers – and yet, when Trefoil casually mentioned *Fantabulosa Fashion Fillies* and the fictitious sighting of his daughter at a discotheque in W1, Mr Fairweather became instantly frosty, insisting we must have the wrong number – and promptly rang off.

Knee-jerk detectives that we were, we presumed this must be our Peggy. Though more than two years had passed since she'd escaped Novak's clutches, it was conceivable she could still be recuperating after her ordeal, cooped up in her childhood bedroom while she gradually readjusted to normal life. Did the Polari lav 'Fantabulosa' sound an alarm in Mr Fairweather's mind? Would he notify the police about this telephone call? And was Peggy genuinely incapable of speaking to strangers, her brain still addled with anti-eagle rhetoric – or was her father the xenophobe now, stringently protecting his daughter from polluting outside forces just as Novak had before him?

The Fairweathers' address happened to be a mere ten-minute cab ride away in Somers Town. Not entirely sure what we hoped to find there – a fellow vigilante in Mr Fairweather, a straitjacketed, deprogrammed rebel banshee willing to spill her guts? – we set out for NW1 after a galvanising pie and pint in the Duke of York.

Armed only with a bottle of lukewarm imitation champagne and a practised apology, Trefoil and McKinley climbed the steps to the Fairweathers' poky laundry-perfumed council flat, sweat and trepidation turning their suits to wibbling seaweed on their backs.

'Good evening!' Trefoil croaked when Mr Fairweather answered the door, a scrawny foxy-bearded chap in a dressing gown. 'We must apologise for the intrusion – the two intrusions, I should say. It was I who telephoned earlier, requesting to speak to your daughter.' Trefoil held the champagne aloft. 'This is for Peggy – or yourself, if you'd like it. Um.'

Fairweather's face was like molten iron. 'What do you want with our Peg?'

'If she is who we believe she is,' McKinley droned his over-rehearsed lines, 'we feel certain she can help us with a slight conundrum we have.'

'We need help identifying a certain proprietor of a certain underground boutique in Fitzrovia,' Trefoil added, locking eyes with Fairweather, hopeful that some glint of understanding would bubble forth on his face.

'Well, she's not in.'

'Do you know where we might find her?' McKinley asked.

'You probably passed her just now.' Fairweather gestured at the two large women listlessly tramping around the children's playground three storeys below. 'There's Peggy there. Blue stripes.'

A sickly shudder went through us as we watched a middle-aged woman in a green anorak – presumably Mrs Fairweather – helping the girl in stripes onto the rusted roundabout. For half a minute Peggy was a blur of grinning, honking, squirming delight: a scene that might've been heartwarming to witness, had it not been for our spine-shrivelling shame and embarrassment. Peggy, the poor soul, plainly had some form of mental handicap: Down's syndrome possibly, or foetal alcohol syndrome or somesuch.

'O. We're sorry. We're terribly terribly sorry,' Trefoil mumbled, before drifting blunderingly back down the stairway without any further explanation or even a farewell.

Drinking heavily half an hour later in the Lord John Russell, Davy was either being wildly speculative or just outright facetious when he suggested: 'You can't deny her eyes were a bit like a manatee's though.' He took a loud swig of Red Triangle. 'And doesn't Novak describe his followers as a bunch of "beautiful weirdies and cripples" at one point? What if he was just exaggerating when he said he'd recruited stunning showgirls and sex workers for his group? Maybe they were all just invalids, poor vulnerable spastics?'

'Go back and interrogate her if you like,' Trefoil snarled, still cradling the bottle of cheap champagne, feeling all the more shoddy that he and McKinley had walked off with it and not handed it over as some paltry peace offering at least.

of adopting multiple personas, my cherry. I too have countless aliases. The ostrich pokes its tet in the sand, does it not? So you're comfortable operating untergrund, are thee? Not averse to minnying in criminal circles?'

'I don't know what you me—'

'Nonsense! Santé!'

On my command we drained our bitter-gators, then shimmied back onto the dancefloor. Thankfully during all that scatty palavering Melody had not clocked that her wet martini was somewhat mistier than mine. While we hoofered woodenly in the centre of the swirling linoleum, it did nag my servo that I may have slipped the palone arsenic rather than the intended lib-inducing Mogadon – but for the momento at least we were able to dance upright and carefree, like tribal pops spinning round a gay bonfire of glimmering livers.

The musica was typical anglo twaddle: longwinded fuzz-tone odysseys chanted by morose wizards, repetitive cosmic caca that may well have sent the donna to sleep anyway had the drogas not got to her first. As we spun each other daffy, she rapidly began to complain of a heavy tet and jelly-lallies, to which I retorted, 'Come and gulp some aero with me, dear heart.'

Before the palone was entirely a blancmange in my lappers, I casually steered her outways into the munge of a sideysnicket just off Ham Yard. We were able to troll like upstanding comrades at first, but when we reached the petty nook where the bins and empty barrels were stationed, Melody was experiencing the full rugby-tackle of the revvy drogas. She kept slamming her palliass against the wall, tittering, fading, and groaning, 'Og. Og. I feel ... og ...'

'Nanti polari. Stint thy clap, dear,' I urged, trying to hold her upright but her lally-caps kept dissolving. 'Can you walk straight, ducky? Can you make it to Brewer Strasse? Come and sleep in my car, dearest. Time for bed, oui, nein?'

'My party ...' Melody gurgled.

Ô, the insufferable bunt. The palone had been socked with a gross tranquillising baton and yet still she wanted to carry on mingling with the pseuds and dish-lickers nex-bor.

I hissed at her: 'Come with me, you daffy prat. Walk to my car. I have a grand business proposal for you, ducky. An una-in-a-lavvytime opportunity, nix less. The chance to screeve my gildi memoirs, to join me in ze publishing sensation of the century! Forget those twonks back thataways ...'

'No!' she shrieked, leaving me nix other option but to sharper for the Largactil. As aforescreeved I'm no qualified quack, but I ponced un bijou squirt-squirt of anti-psychotic jus should calm the donna down grandly, hopefully without mortifying her altogether.

Though I undoubtedly possess some of the mostest dextrous luppers in all of Londres, I admit I had some difficulty at first pokering the syringe in the petty glass botty and extracting a bona glugful of sickly-sweet sirop without Melody clocking what I was up to. When the palone vadared the needle, the poor queint needlessly panicked, screeching and battyfanging the aero. This was molto uncomradely behaviour – not the reaction I was expecting from a friend I'd just offered a fabulosa business opportunity.

'Hush! Hush-hush!' I snapped, frapping my black-famblered lapper across her oyster, cla**m**ping her jaw shut. 'Compose yourself, Ms Autruche! This is merely an initiation test ... just a pogi bit of administrative horseplay ...'

Still the donna would not calm down. Melody was not the largest palone and yet she was barnying like a cave-omi now, grumbling incoherently and schonking me willety-windmilly about the eek. Ô, this was ridiculous. Savvying it was bestest for both our careers, I booted her between the lallies, slamming her repeatedly against the wall with my full bod. My famblers had smudged her maquiage to such an extent she looked like a guttered herring, parnyaqua fanning her mascara out into duey startled black asterisks.

As I continued grinding her tet against the brickwork, I savvied this was perhaps not the mostest elegant recruitment drive I had undertaken lately – but I promise (promise promise promise) I was doing this through LOVE and RESPECT, as well as desperation.

In any case we are now the bestest of friends, Melody et moi, no matter how much dazzleshipped hatred was in her opals that grotty noche. Sweet Melody!

Having schonked all the venom out of her now, I calmly pulled the syringe from the botty and clocked the chamber was full of jus, the tiplet glistening, ready. Still clamping my lapper over her whimpering oyster, I rapidly hiked up her drogle and stabbed her deep in the corybungus. She let out a murky 'Mmmnnnrrghh' as I squeezed the plunger. Then within una squirmering minuta she was out cold.*

---

* This scene was horrifying to us all, but most horrifying was the effect it had on Emily. As our secretary's eyes flicked from left to right, she almost seemed to have an allergic reaction to the prose: her fingers trembling like rats' tails before giving way to full body shakes, her face a waggling jellyfish of snot and tears.

'Emily … dearest …' was the best we could come up with to try to console her. 'Emily … what is it, girl? What's wrong?'

Struggling to breathe, it took Emily almost a minute to respond, and only then was she capable of two honked syllables: 'Stan-ley.'

She gestured flailingly for our Director to take her into his office, her legs almost buckling as she slammed the reinforced door behind them, leaving the rest of us shuddering dumbly in our swivel-chairs.

Quivering by the bricked-up window, Emily bombarded Stanley with staccato gasps and gurgles: 'Do you not … can you not see it? Do you not remember what I told you … back when you …'

'Remind me?' Merritt responded foggily.

'On the tarpaulin.'

'The tarpaulin?'

'What I told you. Do you not remember the details? Do you not recognise the details?!' The poor girl barely looked like herself any more, her face all puffed up and leaking. 'It's all come back to me … reading that … my God … the … I don't even want to, I can't even …'

'What?'

'The … rape … the abortion …'

Alas, Stanley had aborted so many foetuses and tried to reassure so many

Possiblement it was shock more than the drogas to blame for her passing out, but either way we were both pleased to have some peace and tranquillity at last. Ogling roundwards, there wasn't a great deal of humanoid activity in the main strasse out thataways, but I savvied it was far too risky to try to drag the deadweight zelda through the glimmering neon of Soho to the getaway caboosh. For uno momento I considered stashing her in a dustbin and rolling her, but in the end I simply gagged Ms

---

desperate women, he could no longer remember what dismal account of abuse or misadventure matched which patient.

'O, Emily … darling …' was all he could offer right now. 'Start from the beginning.'

Agonisingly Emily managed to compose herself long enough to explain: 'The way he describes that scene – it's almost exactly what happened to me. The same nightclub. The same figure … that face … I told you I'd seen a face in my dreams, my nightmares. The goggles, the black wig, the policeman's uniform. It's like his doll. Le Bâtard. But now it's him as well. The same uniform. The same nightclub. It's him … it must've been him …'

Merritt hunched forward and said nothing for a few moments. At first Emily wasn't sure if he was crying too, until finally he uttered: 'You're sure it matches? You're sure it's not just a horrible coincidence?'

'No!' She burst into tears again. 'I always thought I must've been drugged. I remember my vision going from side to side, the sickness, in and out of consciousness … and it all matches – or almost everything. Some details are back to front. There was no syringe, I don't believe – but … he penetrated me. He hurt me. It matches, Stanley. It must've been him. It must be.'

'O, Emily … dear …'

'It matches! Remember I told you: before now all I really remembered was his hand, a big black leather glove across my mouth while he … did what he did. Black famblers, Stanley. Novak specifically mentions black famblers.'

Merritt's head flopped between his knees. All at once he felt cold and dizzy, like his office had shrunk to the size of a refrigerator around them. He wanted to hold Emily, he wanted to upturn all the furniture, he wanted to scream into his fists as the realisation hit: perhaps Novak was not the noble vicious freedom-fighter he'd hoped for. With only twelve days to go until his wretched fantabulosa crime, it was clear Novak was no Robin Hood, no Che Guevara, no Ned Kelly. The despicable madman now seemed no more than a sadistic sex offender, a subordinate Ripper, a fiend, a fraud.

After giving in to a couple of silent sobs, Merritt lifted his face from his lap and said with as much assurance as he could muster: 'We'll stop him. O, Emily, we *must* stop him now …'

Autruche with a tricolore sash and hid her floppy bod under a handy splattering of aqualogged cardboard ajax to the dustbins. The donna was spasming a pogi bit as I slithered back into the razzle-dazzle of Grand Windmill Strasse, but I fancied she was fit and feeli enough not to sputter out completely.

By this point the thunder-parny had let up, and yet still I found myself sopping wet with sweat as I scarpered the chin-ka-daitcha yards or so to Brewer Strasse. I scuttled zig-zagging from pave to pave until finally I fingered our nova getaway auto nestled between duey abandoned bicyclettes.

'A limey-green Beetle,' I scoffed as I clambered inside. 'Molto discreet.'

'Is discretion required, Lord?' Bruce asked, starting the engine. 'Did you ferricadooz Monsieur Drench?'

'Drench? Good grief, no. I've found us a nova plaything, my chovis. A Heaven-sent collaborator to help bring my lavvy-story, my gloriosa natty teachings, to the masses!'

Nervy drool cascaded from my oyster as we blundered our way through the sluggish one-way system, taking nigh on dait-cha minutas to cover the same distance I'd scarpered in duey on foot. When at last we reached Ham Yard, thankfully the petty scribe was still snoozing spasmodic under her soggy bedclobber. Difficult to say whether the self-absorbed twonks in Hypnogogo had even noticed Melody had vanished* – peeking through a gap

---

* We wondered: at what point did those self-absorbed twonks raise the alarm and, more importantly, why was Melody's disappearance not mentioned in the publishing industry periodicals, let alone the national press? Had we missed the newsflash? Ms Autruche might not be famous enough to warrant a national outcry, but given that she must've been missing more than a year now, was it not strange that none of us had heard of her, either in her capacity as a published writer or as a hostage?

It seems 'Melody Autruche' was indeed a nom de plume. When we investigated at the British Library, there were no publications credited to her. There was no *Touched by Colin*. And when McKinley again plucked up the courage to call Scotland Yard (this time from a phone box by Hammersmith Bridge, miles from our office and his home), his insistence that he knew who was responsible

in the back portal, I clocked the same old blank washed-out eeks and haughty rabbitting pinball-garglers.

Taking care not to rouse her or inadvertently maim the poor lamb, we carefully fished Melody out of the gutter and had her stuffed in the vonny footwell before any alarm was raised. Chuggering away from the scene, I felt as though I had some priceless Pompeian plaster-pop or mollusc fossil betwixt my lallies, ogling the palone crunched up in the foetal posture, her spanglies twinkling as we crawlied through the gaslit noche. At one point Melody appeared to be struggling for aero so we loosened her gag and swished it round her opals instead. Plunged into the munge, the scribe would have nix idea where her nova home-sweet-home for the next lepta months would be – but then again, as me and my beloved stormtroopers ZOOM-ZOOMed into the glit**t**ery* beyond, into our strange savage ultraschvartz/ultra-sparkly future, arguably we too were wearing blindfolds ...

---

for the kidnapping of Melody Autruche was met with the eerie response: 'There is no Melody Autruche reported missing, sir. Who is Melody Autruche?'

* What with all the tears and turmoil surrounding this latest chapter, we almost failed to notice a new message had appeared in the manuscript: **The name is an anagram.**

The Banality of Evil*

JOSHED-UP AS A NATTY TURNKEY, NOVAK WEARS JACKBOOTS, GREY PANTALOONS, GREY TUNIC, RED ARMBAND WITH 'NN' NEVER-NEVERLAND INSIGNIA, SCHVARTZ TRENCHCOAT, PEAKED GREY CAPELLA WITH SKULL AND BEAKY SPREADEAGLE FAKEMENTS.

NELLY DELPHINE'S 'LES PRISONS DE SA MAJESTÉ'.

Naturellement the cynical squares among you may feel Melod**y**'s abduction was somehow ultra unpleasant for her, but do not forget: I was letting the palone lavvy rent-free in gildi accommodation in the centre of Londres, I was offering her the mostest sensational liver-commission of her career, I would make the dame a household name† without her having to get her lappers

---

* Chapter received Tuesday, 7th July 1970 – six days to go. We presumed this would be the final chapter sent by Novak before committing his crime, unless he intended a last-minute flurry of confessional bile before Doom-Juno. Many loose threads still remained. Would Novak cram his activities of the past (his potentionally final) eighteen months into this slim chapter? Would he let slip any damaging details to help us foil his fiendish plot? Would he at least give us some clue as to the fantabulosa heinous misdeeds he had planned? Who – and where – was Melody Autruche? Who was sending us secret messages in the m/s? And what of their latest disclosure: **The name is an anagram?**

We prepared ourselves for the worst. Prepare yourself for many footnotes …

† First: the anagram. With nothing more concrete to go on to help us foil the madman's crime, the five of us dedicated all of Thursday, 2nd July, to solving this puzzle. THE NAME IS AN ANAGRAM. What name? Eager to earn our spurs in this ghastly game of cat-and-mouse, we all claimed to be talented anagram-untanglers, and we split the work accordingly. Though Emily was still

markedly distressed after the revelations of 'Plume', she was more determined than ever to unmask the monster that had attacked her, and so we gave her the two most notable names in the book – RAYMOND MARIANNE NOVAK and MADAME OVARY – to crack. Trefoil was entrusted with MELODY AUTRUCHE and HERMAN HERMAPHRODITE. Stanley tackled CHIEF STEWARD STURGEON and MONSIEUR DRENCH. McKinley toyed with WINIFRED REPULSE and her fellow sea-queens – PAMELA POLA, SHARON VON SCHARNHORST – while Davy was left with some lesser likely suspects: THE SORDID GOOSE CIVILISED, THE SHRINKER, INSPECTOR SILLING.

As we wrestled with the scattered letters, exam-room silence quickly gave way to waves of primitive grunts, agonised screeches and curses. Various first names (STUART, HERCULE, TRACEY, SERGE ...) rose from the alphabet soup, but always left far too many clashing letters to form a recognisable surname. While grappling with RAYMOND MARIANNE NOVAK, Emily was alarmed to see RONNIE KRAY materialise from the circle of letters she'd jotted down. Still, though Ronnie was a murderous bisexual paranoiac like our own Prole Dandy, we agreed it seemed unlikely he'd been bombarding us with a fake delusional autobiography from his cell at HMP Durham. RONNIE KRAY MADONNA or NOVA MADMAN RONNIE KRAY was the most sense Emily could conjure from the remaining letters, before dismissing that thread altogether.

Hours went by, each of us seemingly taking it in turns to denounce the exercise as hopeless before regaining our enthusiasm in fits and bursts usually prompted by coffee, cigarettes or just sheer fear. We were like deranged explorers trying to decipher hieroglyphics in some dark bat-dung-infested tomb. Groping through the ultraschvartz, Merritt found UNFETTERED HOG WAR in CHIEF STEWARD STURGEON. McKinley extracted FRIED PENIS from WINIFRED REPULSE. Davy's sheet was just a bloodied rag of red Biro scribbles and scrubbings-out.

Exasperated, we were close to abandoning the task altogether and heading out to the pub when Trefoil looked up sharply from his notepad, face tinged with pink. 'My God,' he said. 'Look here.'

We gathered around his desk, and squinted at his workings:

MELODY AUTRUCHE
= ~~HEARTY CLOUD EMU~~
= EMU CLOUDYHEART
= CAMELOT ~~DURY HUE~~
= DRACULE YÉ-MOUTH
= ~~UR~~ MOULDY CHEATER
= TRACEY HOLME ~~TUD~~
= ~~RAYMO~~
= AUDREY HULME ~~OCT~~

dirty whatsoever (unless she wished to spill a pogi bit of sang in the nom of research, or revolution). Ô, we were to make g**r**and immortal art together, Melody et moi ...

The palone was parnying a petty bit when I emptied her from the VW into our boutique, but I took this to be gay parnyaqua. My faithful dollies distr**a**cted her with cuddles and more soothing drogas while I prepared her libbage upstairs. For the next lepta months Melody was to reside in the Blank Chamber. To ensure these lodgings were molto comfortable for my nova treasured guest, I first of course had to evict the Sordid Goose. I entered his lair casually, oystering jovially before strongholding and strangulating him with fish-wire until he was the consistency of a gro**ss** spoiled kiwi fruit. His pitiful pleading gasp-gasp-gasps petered out rapidly. I untethered the Goose from the radiator and dragged his stiff feath**e**ry bod to the workshop, to be fatchared and disposed of later.

Once my followers had finished dhobying the bat's lair, I laid down a makeshift red carpet and dragged Melody's equally stiff bod up up up up up the stairway and into her nova boudoir. For her own safety we attached lally-sha**c**kles, tethering her to a bijou cruiseliner screeving-desk we'd shushed from the knacker's yard and bolted to the floorboards. While Ms Autruche slept off her Largactil hangover, we installed a few final fakem**en**ts: inkwell, papyrus, Imperial 66 lav-hammer, kitty litter.

Once awakened, Ms Autruche was at first not entirely eager to begin tapping out my gildi memoirs,[*] but I put this down to

---

* Was Audrey truly Novak's fantomscreever? Sure enough our Head of Complaints had disappeared under mysterious circumstances (see footnotes to 'The Antichristines'), but of all the people operating in the underground publishing industry, why would Novak choose our humble provincial clerical assistant to ghostwrite his memoirs?

As Davy pointed out, she did have literary aspirations. If one casts one's mind back to the footnotes of 'Womb Muzak', Audrey once burdened Davy with a few sheets of poetry he dismissed simply as 'wrong'.

'In what way was her writing "wrong"?' Merritt challenged him now. '"Wrong" as in depraved? The type of "wrong" that might appeal to Novak?'

Davy's head wobbled from side to side. 'I just thought badly written, but ... I'm no expert.'

droggle withdrawal, or disillusionment a**f**ter that most dreary book launch duey noches previous. In the interim I lento chopped the Goose down to petty manageable morsos, while my dollies took it in turns teaching our nova guest the basics of Polari. To prepare her for the ultra-illum**i**nating savag**e**ry that lay ahead, I began playing Melody my most lucid anti-eagle rants through the dicktittlerphone long into the noche – although for the most part she nellied the tapes with a blank eek and baggy ogles, molto unreceptive to my natty tittlings. Amusingly, it was not until she clocked the Goose's brains being scooped from his skull – in my opinion, only a very minor episode in my grand majestic lavvy – that she felt inspired to s**c**reeve again.

We set to work on DIEU-DU-JOUR in earnest in the summe**r** of 1969. While Melody sat poised at the lav-hammer,* I marched

---

'O, Audrey ... poor Audrey ...' Emily muttered, dabbing at her mascara with Stanley's hanky.

'But how do you suppose he knew she was a writer,' McKinley chipped in, 'if we barely knew ourselves?'

'Maybe she replied to a letter of his ... a complaint or something ...' Davy ventured.

'Or he might've found her at Hypnogogo,' Emily sniffed. 'She used to go there a lot. Book launches, all-nighters. Maybe he got talking to her, drugged her, hurt her ...'

'Or maybe she came to him,' Merritt suggested. 'She knew his plans. She seemed thoroughly out of sorts just before she disappeared. Mumbling sinister gibberish, turning up to work late, detached and bedraggled. Maybe his depravity appealed to her?'

'No, but –'

One glaring inconsistency stood out. As Trefoil pointed out, according to Novak's timeline he abducted Ms Autruche from Hypnogogo in the spring of 1969. Audrey was still working for us in October 1969 ('~~OCT~~'??) when Novak first contacted us, clearly stating he'd already enlisted the services of an 'esteemed scholar' as his ghostwriter. Audrey disappeared in April 1970.

* Still, even if the dates and details didn't exactly match, we had to assume it was Novak's ghostwriter (whether Audrey or not) leaving us these secret messages. Captive by the typewriter, this was the poor scribe's only possible contact with the world outside, slipping these tiny cries for help into the text under Novak's vonka: **Help me, print an ear in it if listening. The name is an anagram.**

Or was this just Novak playing with us, wafting red herrings? If he indeed had us under surveillance, the Scum King would know we were now hellbent on foiling his fantabulosa crime. He would know Audrey went AWOL in April – feasibly he could've invented the name Melody Autruche to tally with our missing colleague's, to send us on a wasteful goosechase in the final days before his explosive denouement.

O, this twisted yarn.

With no other firm leads or inklings as to Novak's next move, our priority now was to find Audrey, whether she was being held hostage, or just being used by the Emperor as a decoy while she blithely went on with her life back in Stepney or the Industrial Provinces.

The men of the office split into pairs: Trefoil and McKinley set out to find Miss Hulme, or at least find some evidence of her wellbeing from friends or family, while Stanley and Davy brazenly set out to hunt down Monsieur Astérisque, to reinvestigate his former haunts and – if it came to it – try to save Audrey from his clutches. Emily, still regarded as too delicate to join in these perilous expeditions, was left alone to look after the office.

The telephone number we had on file for Audrey – STEPNEY GREEN 5027 – was engaged throughout the day and, when Trefoil and McKinley made it to her address just before 5 p.m., they found a grim, unoccupied bed-sitter. The neighbour who allowed them access to the building said she hadn't seen Miss Hulme for months, possibly not since winter. Peering through the letterbox, Trefoil saw no sign of life, only a light snowfall of unopened mail and a poster on the far wall advertising Gitanes cigarettes. The neighbour had no idea where Audrey might've gone, or if she was coming back, and likewise Trefoil and McKinley were at a loss when they tried to recall the specific town Miss Hulme was from and might've returned to. They wished they'd paid more attention to her bland stories of the Industrial Provinces. There would be far too many Hulmes in the phone books of the North. Cold-calling seemed futile.

Meanwhile, Merritt and Davy focused their search on Hypnogogo. The nightclub was closed to the public until Wednesday 8th (the day after we received this latest chapter, which we promise we'll let you read eventually), but Stan managed to get in touch with the proprietor over the phone on the 4th. When Merritt suggested to Mr Legrand that a serial rapist had been operating on his premises over the past couple of years, the proprietor became somewhat defensive to say the least. He insisted Hypnogogo was a high-class establishment. He claimed his clientele were not interested in animalistic pleasures – rather, they were switched-on, cultured citizens who patronised his nightclub only to engage in stimulating mixed-media happenings and 'to savour the newest, most way-out cocktails from Europe's top mixologists such as Esteban and Doctor Whimsy'.

'You mean to say,' Stanley interjected, 'you've not once seen a chap manhandle a lady in your nightclub?'

round and round the bijou chamber in lopsided circles, bombarding the palone with my wunderbar reminiscences and wishes for ze future. The boutique was no longer **o**pen to the public and so for the most part we could plough on with our work undisturbed, save for the odd occasion when Melody **f**ainted from lack of munja or just her mid-class squeamishness.

Perhaps b**e**cause we'd replaced the NEVER-NEVERLAND insignia out thataways with the more innocuous façade OSTRICH COPYWRITERS LTD, there had been not a sniff of Inspector Silling round our parts – but by this juncture we were more intere**s**ted in grander aggro and devilry of course. We barely batted an ogle-rider in July when the Yankees thrust an omi upon the moon, instead focusing our servos full-blooded on our far greater leap for mankind, our molto symbolic shock therapy for all Western humanoids: my fantab**u**losa crime.

When I wasn't conjuring up this bona screeve with Ms Autruche, I probably had my vonka in some fuzzymuzzy ballistics liver, jotting far-out designs for my own lavvy-shaking glimmer-fak**em**ents. Or you may have clocked me ogling the behaviour of birdies-of-prey at Londres Zoo, or practising slapdash taxidermy, or furiously fatcharing scribbled bod-parts into grandiose exquisite corpses even the Surrealists might've

---

'Not on my watch, no. There are establishments for all that on Great Windmill Street, as I'm sure you're aware. But you won't find it at ours.'

There was nothing else for it. On the evening of Wednesday 8th Merritt and Davy planned to don disguises and prop up the bar at Hypnogogo, keeping a lookout for male predators matching Novak's (admittedly slippery) description. We knew his techniques – the sopping-wet martini, the drugs, the police uniform, the alleyway, the violence – but of course there was no guarantee he would strike again, this night of all nights. Many many months had passed since he had assaulted Emily and Melody/Audrey, if it was indeed him. Novak was probably in hiding miles away from Soho by now, poised zen-like, ready to see through his hideous endgame. But then again, given the Walking Contraceptive clearly had a weakness for abducting young dollybirds from this particular establishment, there was always the chance he might return for one final fling, one last ego-boosting, bloodsucking abduction and violation before his fantabulosa destiny came calling for him …

considered a pogi bit degenerate. It would not be until Octobre '69 when finally I finalised the full details of my fantastic crime, but in the meantime I thoroughly enjoyed imagining all the abstract squirting sang, charred carnish, lost lallies and bamboozled **po**li**t**icos. The printing presses of the mond panickingly spitting my eek and screeve hither-thither! My creepering into the inkyboos of chavvies and adults in every corner of Chri**s**tinedom. Meanwhile: an Alpine-fresh hideaway on the glittering peaks of Europa?!

Hé-hé!

Starting that summer, I enforced a nova fitness routine on my dollies, toughening them up with gruelling gymnastics, barked orders and red carnish. As aforescre**e**ved, my chinka remaining devotees were fawningly, unflinchingly committed to MOI MOI MOI – and so naturellement I expected them to act as my fearless bodyguards on Our Chosen Juno, if not outright cannon fodder. I did not screech this kamikaze caca explicitly of course, but it was maximu**m**ly implied. BE PREPARED TO DIE FOR THE GRAND CAUSE was the gildi galvanising thrust of my palavering that humstinking Thermidor. WE are in this TOGETHER!!

As far as I could nelly, the only petty outburst of dissent from my dollies came early in the nova regime, when I served up some unusual munja for luncheon. My shocktroopers had become accustomed to just a pogi lump of sloppy steak tartare avec terrapoms at midjuno – however, after hammering the final full-stop in perhaps my mostest appetising chapter to date, 'Kinder, Küche, Kirsche', I felt inspired to treat my family to a **pl**atterful of maxi decadent froggy offal.

'This is peculiar grub, Lord,' was one of the more lenient reviews. 'What rotten carnish* is this?'

---

* Merritt and Davy of course passed through Ogle Street on their way to Stan's flat to don their disguises, but, as before, there was just a miserable shuttered butcher's shop where Never-Neverland should be. Merritt even felt the urge to

'It's prime foie gras,' I replied. 'This is what all bona urban guerrillas jarry, my chovis. The Romanoids guzzled it up with gusto. Tis molto bona for the servo, molto bona for the thews ...'

Selfless dicktittler that I was, I did not gobble a solo* morso

---

duck into the Catholic church opposite, searching for some last-ditch salvation or message from above – but felt nothing. O, dearest understanding reader, trust us when we say we did all that we could!

* Emily hated being left alone in the office, not just because she felt fearful and powerless, but because she had very little to occupy herself with while she waited for news from outside. The duplicate manuscript was now all typed up and there was no correspondence to attend to, business having all but dried up aside from our shaky ongoing dealings with Monsieur Astérisque.

On the afternoon of Wednesday 8th, with everyone but her out of the office, Emily barricaded the door, pulled down the blinds and tuned the transistor radio nearest her desk to Radio Caroline. She wondered not for the first time: what was she even doing here? The madness of the past weeks was visible all around the room: the scraps of paper covered with anagrams and scrambled hunches, the ashtrays overflowing with cigarette ends and stinking cheese rinds, the spilled gin and pill-bottles, the gaping chiselled holes in the walls ogling her like giant tarantulas' eyes.

After the horrific revelations of 'Plume', Emily felt utterly violated and humiliated, like Novak's novel was a sprawling sick joke at her expense – and she wasn't convinced her bumbling colleagues could hunt its author down like a band of cartoon private dicks. The Scum King was too slippery, too stealthy. Throughout this horrible saga, Novak had twisted reality and good sense to such an extent, it was near enough impossible to tell what details of his life story and persona were true or not. But likewise: what could the police do now anyhow?

Brewing a fresh pot of tea, Emily grudgingly began tidying the debris strewn around the office. As she sifted through the scattered scraps of paper on her desk, one smudged sheet of foolscap caught her eye. It had been her job to try to crack the RAYMOND MARIANNE NOVAK anagram, and yet she didn't recognise this ragged handwriting:

RAYMOND NOVAK
ARYAN DOOM
ROMAN VONKA
KOON V-MARY
RANDY MONK
DARK NAVY MOON

As her eyes passed over those final three words, a name leapt out at her like a burst of toxic squid ink to the face. The kettle screamed. Her arms and legs felt like jellified electric as she scrambled for the telephone and frantically inputted the number for Hypnogogo.

'Hello?' a male answered.

'Hello. Can you help me please? Is there a Stanley Merritt at the bar? Tell him it's Emily. Quickly! Please!'

'Club's empty,' the man monotoned. 'Don't open til 9 p.m.'

Emily returned the receiver to its cradle, then paced anxiously around the office in erratic patterns resembling hexagrams, question marks, asterisks. She checked the scribbled sheet again, checked she wasn't mistaken, rechecked the manuscript, then dragged her hands down her face and whined despairingly for a minute or so.

Tacked between two of the larger gouges in the plaster were the contact details of the Glass Eye staff. Emily spun the number for Stanley's home into the Bakelite phone with pulsating fingers. After five rings, her boss picked up.

'Hello? Merritt speaking.'

'Stanley!' She tried to stay calm, but she couldn't help barking her words at him. 'It's Emily! Are you – where are you? Can you talk? Are you with Davy?'

'Yes. What is it? What's happened?'

'It's …' She had tunnel vision now, tears writhing in the corners of her eyes. 'There's another anagram.'

'What?'

'RAYMOND NOVAK,' she panted. 'It's another anagram – and it's him!' She glanced again at the chaotic, unfamiliar handwriting. 'Rearrange RAYMOND NOVAK and it spells out MARK "DAVY" NOON.'

There was a grim period of silence as Merritt ran through the anagram in his head. By the time the dancing letters had settled in his mind, Merritt was already searching around the room for a weapon. Stanley had been grilling waffles in the kitchen while Davy lounged in front of the TV next door. Softly Merritt pushed the door shut, tucked a large cheese knife up his sleeve and continued in a whisper: 'He's in the other room! What does this … what do you think this means?'

'It's him, Stanley … you've got to stop him. You've got to stop him!'

'Yes, but –'

'He *wants* to be stopped!' she cried. 'Did you not see the new message in the manuscript? There's another message. It says, it says: HELP ME, STOP ME, USE FORCE IF NECESSARY!'

Merritt's brain felt like a tangled, knotted mass of fishing wire by the time he put the phone down. Were these secret messages to be trusted? Was our Art & Design man truly behind this whole meese meshigena chicanery? Was the Guru – servo-latherer, tet-chopper, strangler – really sitting in Stanley's leather armchair next door, giggling at *Watch with Mother?*

O, there was barely any time to weigh up all the sick possibilities, to separate the facts from the riddles. In a moment of what seemed to him like lucidity, Merritt recalled an episode from earlier in the manuscript, a sentence or two that leapt out at him now – but was this upsurge from his subconscious a guidelight to follow, or just another red herring, a fault in the circuitboard?

He pictured the young Novak on the Fun Deck of SS *Unmentionable*, a dog-leash fastened around his neck, paraded in front of his superiors by a malevolent, badly dressed pirate. If Stanley wasn't mistaken, in the lead-up to his first Crossing the Line ceremony, Raymond was accosted by one Davy Jones, 'the Royal Scribe'. And to quote our complimentary footnotes (see 'Crossing the Line: 0°'): 'Incidentally, we discovered that the mythical peg-legged Davy Jones's forename comes from the Caribbean patois word "Duffy" or "Duppy", meaning "Devil".'

All at once Merritt's nostrils were flooded with the acrid tang of burning. It was almost as if a portal to Hell had opened up in the adjoining room, flames and sulphur rising from beneath Davy's leather throne. Trying to compose himself, Stanley shakily turned off the grill, threw the blackened waffles into the bin, then, after checking the cheese knife was still securely secreted up his sleeve, he thought twice and removed the knife altogether, placing it back in the drawer. He ran his fingers through what remained of his hair, nodded to himself encouragingly once or twice, then stepped assertively into what was after all his own front room. Davy was sitting cross-legged in the armchair, picking at a callus on his left foot.

'You know, my chovi, I think I've had a change of heart,' Stanley said, standing in the doorway. 'I think I want Novak to go through with his crime after all. This was the plan all along, was it not? Novak commits the crime, we get the financial rewards, he gets his immortality. Oui? Nein?'

Davy seemed amused as he looked up from the armchair. 'What's brought this on?'

'You look after me, I'll look after you, Raymondo. It is you, isn't it? Hiding behind that daffy nom de guerre?'

'Come again?'

'Don't be coy. We've cracked the other anagram, your Lordship.'

Merritt's trepidation was quickly turning to queasy admiration as he regarded Davy sitting there, the Prole Dandy, unruffled in his ruffles. Was this the magnetism of evil? Or had he always found Davy vampirishly attractive under that faddish camouflage?

'Well, you're a master of disguise and nix mistake,' Stanley added. 'Operating under our vonkas all this time ...'

'Have you gone mad?' Davy snapped, grabbing the armrests as if to make a lunge for Stanley.

'I wouldn't recommend aggro, comrade,' Stan urged. 'You need us as much as we need you, remember. WE are in this TOGETHER, are we not? In fact, if there's anything I can do to help your fantabulosa destiny run smoothly, you let me know. All I'd really like to know is: what's happened to Audrey? Where is she? Is the girl safe?'

For a moment Davy remained frozen, halfway in and out of the armchair. With a smirk that could've been nerves, exasperation or even outright coquetry, he asked: 'Why do you think I'm Novak?'

'The anagram.'

'AUDREY HULME with OCT crossed out? What is OCT?'

'No. The other anagram. RAYMOND NOVAK. MARK "DAVY" NOON.'

Davy slumped exhausted back into the padded leather. His criminal allure faded fast as a look of genuine consternation took over – or was this another smokescreen, Signore Shapeshifter's subterfuge hard at work again?

'I don't understand,' Davy mumbled feebly. 'Why would he use my name? You don't really think I'm him? You don't truly think I'm behind all this?'

'Well …' Stanley rubbed the back of his neck, thoroughly unsure of himself now too. 'It would seem whoever is leaving us these secret messages – and it could well be Audrey, trapped somewhere, forced to type out the Guru's maddening screeve – well, whoever it is, it seems they're trying to warn us Novak is you or, I don't know, otherwise someone's trying to stitch you up, implicate you …'

'I'm being set up,' Davy said assertively, though his face had taken on a sickly grey-green hue. 'But … why?'

Merritt regarded his Art & Design man shifting uneasily, the leather armchair seemingly gripping him like a gigantic black fambler. 'O good Lord,' Stanley groaned, dragging his hands down his face, 'I just don't know what to believe any more. Supposing you *were* Novak, what reason would you have to deny it? I've already told you, you have my blessing, I want you to commit the crime, whatever it is. So why hide the truth?'

'I'm not Novak! What else can I do? What else can I say?'

Merritt shook his head, gazing blankly at the carpet tiles.

'Does this prove anything?' In a moment of blind panic or flagrant exhibitionism, Davy hurriedly unbuttoned his velvet pantaloons and, after some rummaging, squeezed his plump bollocks out through the fly. 'I'm not castrated, at any rate …'

Stanley spluttered a burst of laughter, wrongfooted by these unexpected guests in his living room. He tried to think of a cutting retort but ended up simply smiling inanely until Davy tucked himself away again. Merritt waddled over to the window and perched on the sill with his back to the city. 'I don't know, my friend – we have no proof Novak is truly without quongs,' he said, still smirking. 'And let's face it: you can't deny there's a few glaring similarities between you and the Prole Dandy.'

'Such as?'

'Well …' Stanley tried to visualise the manuscript as police evidence strewn across a detective's desk. 'The women's schmutta, the constant costume changes. You frequent Hypnogogo. You were involved with Audrey for some time, were you not? You've not got her locked up somewhere?'

Davy shook his head, staring into space now. 'It was a mutual break-up,' he murmured.

Had Merritt had the manuscript to hand he could've found many more connections between Mr Noon and Mr Novak – their formative years in the Kent countryside, their apparent involvement in the Grosvenor Square riot (see 'The Secondary Modernists'), not to mention the countless sketched ideas for

of the nourishing fatty liver myself. In the final months of the heksa-daitchas I subsisted mainly on petites madeleines, pastis and French Blues, feverishly plotting my future and palavering my past at Melody while my soldiers boldly bulked themselves up for the carnage to come. By the end of the decade my chinka-strong army were in fabulosa condition. (The foie gras, alas, played nanti part in it, however: immediately after schlumphing down this de-luxe carnish, my ungrateful legionnaires vomited pell-mell.)

---

the cover of *Dieu-du-Jour* featuring Davy's very own self-portrait distorted in a soup spoon (see 'Dishonourable Discharge') – but this is all just wind and piss now anyhow.

'I don't understand this at all,' Davy went on, viciously picking at the callus on his foot again. 'Why would he use my name? Why would he want to set me up like this?'

'Do you have any enemies?'

'No! All I can think of is: maybe he's seen me at Hypnogogo, entertaining some woman he likes. Maybe it's jealousy. When did Novak first get in touch with us? Before Christmastime?'

'October last year.'

'Me and Audrey were courting around that time. That could explain him using our names – maybe he saw us together at the club. Maybe he probed around, found out we both worked for this publisher. Maybe that's why he singled out the Glass Eye Press. Maybe he wanted to get close to Audrey – and now he's kidnapped her ...' Davy's eyes were fluttering frenzied in their sockets. 'I just don't know what else to think. Maybe we're miles off ...'

Merritt made a gesture of mutual bewilderment. He shuffled across the carpet tiles and touched his employee affectionately on the shoulder. As the sun went down over Fitzrovia, the rooftops opposite blazed peach-pink: a shade, Merritt noted, not unlike the colour of Davy's tense, chubby testicles.

Novak's Hit Parade*

CLUTCHING A GROSS TINFOIL SICKLE, NOVAK WEARS SCHVARTZ ROBES, SANDALS, SCHVARTZ FAMBLERS AND SKULLY-EEK MAQUIAGE.

NELLY GILLIAN HILLS'S 'TUT, TUT, TUT, TUT'.

I can finger the exact juno the plot for my fantabulosa crime finally penetrated my servo. On Saturday, 4th Octobre 1969, I minnied as usual into Soho to pluck my daily copy of LE MONDE from the Librairie Parisienne. By this juncture in my lavvy I nix

---

* Chapter received Monday, 13th July 1970.

On the morning of Thursday 9th (the day after she solved the second anagram), Emily was appalled to find that Davy was not only still a free man but sitting langorously at his desk when she arrived at the Glass Eye office. She could barely look at him as tears turned her mascara to black lightning bolts. 'Stanley!' she sobbed. 'Stan-ley!'

'Don't panic, my girl,' Merritt cooed, rushing in from his private WC. 'We thought you might react like this, but ... well, we've been through the evidence.'

'The evidence!' Emily wept.

'We believe he's innocent, he's been set up.'

As far as Emily was concerned, the evidence indisputably pointed towards Davy's guilt: the anagram, Hypnogogo, the misogyny, the falseness, the chameleon-like chicanery. Of course she'd rather not believe that, all this time, her attacker had been going about his business right before her eyes, that they'd been sharing the same workspace, the same coffee cups, the same toilet seat – but for her there was no doubt.

Faced with the cold, embarrassed expressions of her superiors, Emily didn't feel strong enough to accuse Davy outright and so she just sat there sobbing incoherently, waggling demonic fingers in Davy's general direction, waiting for the bastard to confess. But it didn't come.

longer spent the morning doctoring the screamlines – however, as I thumbed the inky over my traditional breakfast of petites madeleines and pastis at Roche's, one article leapt from the page like a grotesque papier-mâché cobra, horrifying me more than any of the daffy sensationalist claptrap I'd cut-and-pasted myself in the past.

Under the innocuous screamline LE QUATRIÈME CHANT, some fungal frog named Jean Schuster – apparently toppermost doggy in the Surrealist grupa after André Breton's mortification – declared in nix uncertain terms: SURREALISM IS DEAD.

I care not to go into the exact details of how and why Monsieur Schuster ponced this mostest **g**randest everlasting movement was somehow now old hat, banished to the oubliette for good – after all, I do not accept the tart's scatty lavs. All in all it struck me as a cowardly retreat back into the munge for some old zot who clearly just could not be arrissed to continue the Pope's bona noble adventure: tunnelling to ze centre of the servo and smashing all fash daffy hypocritterish social norms and niceties ...

As I sip-sipped my invigorating aniseed sirop, I pondered how bestest to respond to this twaddle from across the Channel. After fatch**a**ring the article to morsos and schlumphing down

---

By this point (around 9.30 a.m. on the 9th) the rest of us were aware of the second anagram, but whether down to Merritt's persuasiveness or just a gut feeling that Davy wasn't capable of any monstrous criminal activity, we felt Noon and Novak could not be the same man. In any case, the latest secret message in the manuscript – **Help me, stop me, use force if necessary** – suggested Novak was now speaking, and was begging us to apprehend him before he carried out what he may now have felt was horribly out of his control. If Noon was indeed Novak, why didn't he just own up here and now, and put a stop to this whole miserable charade once and for all?

Given her distress, Stanley gave Emily the rest of the day off – not that we had any real work to do anyway. Our business now solely concerned tracking down Audrey and the Bona Fide Novak, fumbling with the riddles and inconsistencies that still remained, and – if we couldn't stop him in time – readying ourselves for the Scum King's crime and the release into the wild of the meshigena bat's memoirs ... neither of which we were particularly looking forward to ...

the shreds (to be sardonically shat outwards later), I scuttled rapidly back to the boutique, back to my books.

Initially there was the temptation to return to Paris, to hunt down this Schuster chappy and ferricadooz him in the most diabolical ritualistic fashion – but then this aggro too seemed a pogi bit cowardly, preying on an antique froglet who was clearly losing all his faculties already anyway.

I savvied it was my duty now to solo-handedly resuscitate the exquisite corpse of Surrealism, to spread its gloriosa disease hither-thither, throttling awake all sceptics, heretics, newts and unbelievers – but how to put this abstract savagery into actual tangible action?

With my beloved Madame Ovary and Papa Breton now snuffed out, I had only my old froggy livers for guidance. When I got back to Ostrich Copywriters Ltd, I lelled together a selection of suitable texts to snuffle through for inspiration: LES CHANTS DE MALDOROR, LES FLEURS DU MAL, THE UNA-CHENTA DUEY-DAITCHA JUNOS OF SODOM, NADJA, LE CON D'IRÈNE, MORT AUX VACHES, LA RÉVOLUTION SURRÉALISTE ...

I had a petty inkling of what I was sharpering for but could not rightly recall in which tome these particular lavs lavvied. Fingering the livers, I clocked all sorts of bona advice,* everything from astronomical aggro:

---

* O, how we could've done with some bona advice ourselves at this point! Once Stanley had seen Emily safely onto the 134 bus home, he, McKinley, Trefoil and Noon took advantage of the early opening hours of the Nag's Head in Covent Garden to try to untangle the latest strands of this hideous mystery …

'First and foremost, we agree Davy is not Novak,' McKinley stated, prompting an emphatic doe-eyed nod from our Art & Design man, 'in which case "Raymond Novak" must be a pseudonym picked by the author of the manuscript to implicate Davy. If that's the case, I'm afraid someone must have a personal vendetta against you, old boy, someone who was probably present at *The Nuremberg Nymphos* launch, or has had access to our papers – unless this has all just been set up to cause confusion among us: a smokescreen to slow our progress in stopping the madman's crime …'

'How about Howling?' Trefoil put forward. 'He was a mischievous bat at the best of times. And he knows Polari.'

'Or Dennis Mesh?' McKinley suggested, supping the froth off the top of a fresh pint of Mac's Brown.

'What about one of our many detractors?' Davy chipped in. 'Who was it who sent a human stool to Audrey that time?'

'It wasn't to her specifically,' said Trefoil.

'Even so,' Davy went on, 'we've had plenty of hate mail. What if Audrey sent some snide response back to one of them, and now they've got revenge. Kidnapped her. Maybe they thought me and her were together. That'd explain them trying to pin all this on me. A crime of passion. We've got all the hate mail still, haven't we? In the cabinet? I dare say we could go through it, find a letter that matches up with Novak's handwriting, or his typewriter. What was it – the dot of the "i" is chipped? Looks like a half-moon?'

Judging by their expressions, the other men were not particularly eager to spend the rest of the day rummaging around that filing cabinet of hatred.

'But how then would they know about Monsieur Astérisque?' McKinley put forward, mercifully. 'How would some distant suburban reader know we changed the title of his book to *Mister Asterisk*?'

'Dennis Mesh, then.' Davy crumpled back into the damaged leather. 'Or Howling.'

Merritt, who had been staring gloomily into his pint until now, thumped the tabletop and hissed, 'It's not Howling. He'd already disappeared before the *Nymphos* launch. And in any case, he'd be hard pressed to commit any heinous crimes against humanity next week. The poor sod's been hospitalised. Colitis. Ulcers in his sphincter. He's not even in London, in fact – Leicester Royal Infirmary, so I believe.' He took a glug of ale as we all contemplated this grim news. 'Dennis Mesh, on the other hand ... well, I suppose the old dog has motive ...'

As Merritt explained his reasoning, Mesh wobbled into focus as a certain contender. Not only could Dennis write, he knew everybody at the Glass Eye Press relatively intimately, was present when we uttered 'Mister Asterisk' at his launch and, above all, Dennis's dire lack of recognition – not to mention all the hate mail and death threats directed at him – was surely ample fodder to push him over the edge and inspire him to carry out some diabolical crime against society ...

'But is he definitely aware of all the hate mail and death threats?' McKinley asked. 'Did we not agree to shield him from it all?'

'There can't be too many Meshes around,' Trefoil commented. 'Folks could find his address in the phone book and bombard him direct.'

Davy shrugged. 'And you've got to admit he looks like a scoundrel. He's a weirdy all right.'

'And there's another link I've thought of,' Trefoil piped up, leaning across the table with a white beery moustache. '*The Nuremberg Nymphos*. Never-Neverland.

Is Raymond not wearing a Nazi uniform with "NN" insignia in that last chapter he sent?'

Merritt thumped the greasy wood again. 'Good God, man. Yes. And consider the subject matter of *Pink Baton* and the *Nymphos:* policemen and fascists, sharpering-pops and fash bats. Well, I'll be damned ...'

'So the old drunkard wants putting out of his misery?' Davy wondered, taking a sip of his third pink gin. 'Dennis wants us to stop him?'

'It would seem so,' Trefoil agreed, 'judging by that last secret message: "Help me, stop me, use force if necessary".'

'It could just be a cry for help,' McKinley suggested. 'The chap could be suicidal ...'

'Maybe we can talk him out of it – the crime, or otherwise,' Merritt said, striding to the telephone by the side of the bar.

After struggling with the operator to locate a Dennis Mesh 'somewhere south of here, the Home Counties, I can't bloody remember', Merritt led the rest of us back to the office to scour the files for Dennis's particulars. When at last we found his number, another operator told us the line wouldn't connect. We checked Dennis's address, and our hearts sagged. The remoteness of the residence – Organt Farm, Herstmonceaux, Sussex – meant we had to drive, however drunk we might be, out of the city.

The journey was horrendous. Merritt's driving was erratic at the best of times, but that afternoon his clutch control and cornering quickly turned our stomachs to rancid cocktail shakers.

'Imagine if by some incredible stroke of luck we happened to mow down Novak,' Trefoil commented, trying to lighten the mood after a horrifying near-miss with a lady pushing a pram on Commercial Road. 'This is his old stomping ground, is it not?'

Merritt snarled at the asphalt: 'I don't know – it'd be a bloody horrible role reversal. I'd go to gaol and the bastard would die scot-free ...'

Still, these thoughts of gaol did not improve Merritt's driving – and in fact by the time we entered Sussex, he was kicking himself for not bringing along the sawn-off shotgun. As the car lurched into Herstmonceaux, our faces were the colour of paving slabs, our guts more twisted than the diabolical roads that got us there. The four of us pissed vigorously into a hedgerow, then staggered into the village, scaring off the wildlife with our startling metropolitan modernity – or perhaps just our monstrous inebriated shadows.

The sun and moon shared the same sky, watching us like the unmatching eyes of some malevolent teddybear while we tried to locate Mesh's lair. The building was not the quaint chocolate-box we'd expected. Obscured at the roadside by a mushroom cloud of gnarled vegetation, Organt Farm eventually revealed itself as a small corrugated metal shack – a converted pigpen or abattoir perhaps, with no driveway, no WELCOME mat, no lights on, and no Dennis.

We rapped hard on the front and back doors, but it was like knocking on an empty coffin.

'I told you he was a weirdy, man,' Davy said, clambering onto two upturned milk crates so he could peer into the tiny slitted vents just beneath the corrugated roof.

'What can you see?' McKinley shouted, though by this point he was already shuffling backwards, away from the scene.

'It's dark,' Davy answered, 'and bloody cluttered. Papers and books everywhere. Kitchen looks like it's been burnt out.'

'Novak did say he's had his "vonka in ballistics livers" in that last chapter ...' Trefoil remarked. 'An experiment could've backfired.'

'What say we just break in?' Davy blurted. 'Have a little rummage around?'

'No, Davy ...' McKinley moaned, still clinging to his beloved Law & Order even at this late, late stage.

'No, but if we find that incriminating typewriter, we've got him!'

Trefoil joined McKinley, the two of them disappearing into the foliage like nervy badgers. 'Who are the criminals here?' McKinley lamented. 'We can't go around breaking into our authors' homes! We don't even know if Dennis is guilty – or if he even still lives here ...'

'He won't know it's us. What say we – I don't know – we can make it look like some wild beast, some angry goat butted the door down ...'

'Some angry goat?'

'I don't know!' Davy squinted through the slits again. 'We're here now – we may as well make the most of it. And if we find that typewriter – Hell, we might even find Audrey in there ...'

Davy looked to Merritt for the final decision. More or less sober now, Stanley threw his cigarette into the moss and huffed, 'Come on, Davy – get down. Even if Dennis *is* Novak, I doubt he'll have left his typewriter behind. That last chapter he sent – we all thought it would be the final piece of the puzzle, the climax to the story, but Novak's memoirs still feel distinctly unfinished, some way off being all tied up, do they not? I dare say wherever Novak's gone, his typewriter's gone with him ...'

Reluctantly Davy hopped down from the milk crates, spattering mud up his flared pantaloons. 'There could be other evidence: the ballistics livers, all the French books he mentions ...'

'We'll leave a message,' Stan said, taking a crumpled shred of notepaper from his jacket. Guarding it from the wind in a cupped hand, the words came out unnecessarily quivery:

DEAREST DENNIS. YOU ARE OUR MOSTEST TREASURED AUTEUR. NEED TO TALK. MONDAY 9 A.M.? GLASS EYE HQ.

Once the slip had gone through the letterbox, a sense of relief came over us and we found we could converse relatively carefree again as we walked back to the car – although inside we probably felt just as powerless as before, knowing the note would surely go unread, knowing there was little else we could do to find

> 'O! if, instead of being a Hell, the universe had only been an immense celestial anus, look at the motion I am making with my loins: yes, I would have thrust my verge into its bleeding sphincter, shattering, with my jerking movements, the very walls of its pelvis!' (LES CHANTS DE MALDOROR)

to twisty resignation:

> 'Everything, alas, is an abyss* – actions, desires, dreams, words!' (LE GOUFFRE, Baudelaire)

until finally I vad**ar**ed what I was sharpering for. Duey pages into Papa Breton's Second Surrealist Manifesto, my carnish tingled as I ogled these delicious, vicious sentences:

Dennis/Novak, and knowing above all that we were wholly unprepared for the publication of the Scum King's memoirs, let alone the fatal repercussions now it seemed almost certain his fantabulosa crime would go ahead …

* Oui, we faced the abyss.

Though we spent the whole of Friday 10th frantically preparing for the quickfire release of the meshigena-omi's memoirs, it struck us not for the first time that, should the Guru be killed in action, we could always burn all evidence of *Mister Asterisk*, liquidate the Glass Eye Press and walk away from this more or less guilt-free. And yet, for Merritt at least – though he swore his priority was to stop Novak – there was still the tantalising hope that the bastard's crime might surpass all crimes that had gone before, and propel our humble little floundering publishing house to notoriety, to solvency, to greatness at last.

Looking around our offices on the 10th, Merritt's main worry was whether or not his skeleton staff was up to the task of steering the book into the bestsellers lists. McKinley was undoubtedly vital for the legal assault course that would spring up after Doom-Juno – but as Senior Editor and Artist respectively, Trefoil's and Davy's work was more or less finished now. Annoyingly our absent members of staff – Harry Howling (Sales, Marketing & Finance), Audrey Hulme (Head of Complaints), Emily Ingram (Publicity, Marketing & Secretarial) – held those roles needed most to ensure the book had the best chance of success in the wild.

After a couple of neat Scotches, Stanley made a call to the Ingram household in Muswell Hill. There was some stony passive-aggressiveness from Emily's husband until finally he agreed to put his wife on the line.

'Emily, dear heart,' Merritt spoke softly, 'how are you feeling? Well rested?'

'I've barely slept.'

'The simplest Surrealist act would be to dash down into the street, revolver in hand, and fire randomly, as fast as you can pull the trigger, into the crowd. Anyone who, at least once in his life, has not dreamed of thus putting an end to the petty system of debasement and cretinisation arguably deserves a place in that crowd, with his belly at barrel level.'

'O, I'm sorry to hear that.' Merritt scratched at his wispy pate. 'Look, you get all the rest you can this week-end – but, then, well, would it be at all possible for you to come into work on Monday? We're now convinced Dennis Mesh is responsible for the manuscript. We've tried to locate him, to no avail. And so, well, there's not much more we can do – it looks likely the crime is going to go ahead. We'll need all hands on deck when the news breaks ...'

'Where's Davy?'

'Davy? He's here.'

'I'm not coming in if he's there.'

'No, but ...' Merritt clamped the receiver between his jaw and collarbone while he wiped the sweat from his hands. 'We need all the staff we can get. And he's innocent, Emily. He's innocent.'

'How can you say that? The evidence is there in the manuscript!'

'Wait until you see the evidence in the footnotes!' Merritt pleaded. 'The new evidence in our new footnotes!'

As Stanley explained the previous day's expedition to Herstmonceaux, Emily gazed gloomily at the windowsill of her peppermint kitchen. She had the telephone cable practically coiled around her neck – and when finally Merritt paused his prattle, she simply repeated: 'I'm not coming in if Davy's there.'

'Well ...' Stanley glanced at his Art & Design man, chain-smoking at his cluttered trestle table. 'If Davy *is* responsible for all this, doesn't it make more sense to keep him where we can see him on the day of the crime?'

'No, but –'

'Hell, we could even tie him up if it'd put you more at ease?'

'It'd put me at ease,' Davy piped up, smirking between puffs. 'Hell, if I'm getting paid to just sit on my hind all day, that suits me fine. You said I'll barely be needed. Tie me up.'

'Um. Does that sound at all reasonable?' Merritt appealed down the line.

'I don't know, Stanley ...'

'There'll be a rather large payrise in it for you if everything goes to plan,' Stanley added. 'But either you're in on Monday or you're out forever. I need full loyalty – no unbelievers, no part-timers, no half measures ...'

'You're all insane,' Emily grumbled – but nonetheless, come Monday morning she arrived for work at 9 a.m. sharp.

Ô OUI. Ô OUI OUI! This was perfect savagery. These were the lavs of wisdom and bloodlusty encouragement I needed – the razor-edged clef to my fantabul**o**sa crime!

Thumpering deliriously, I waddled to the fenêtre and blinked down at the proles dithering hither and thither on this mo**l**to sloppy fuzzy-rainbow juno. Clocking their grizzly expressions, I savvied I could not carry out Papa Breton's instructions exactly – not here. If I was to scar**p**er into the strasse this very momento and splurge bullets willety-nilly, I would surely massacre mostly the unemploy**ed**, dolly solo palones and bambinos. This would not do. What I needed instead was TARGETED RANDOMNESS. OUI!

Savvying I could not get close to the toppermost eagles (Queen Liz, Mr Wilson, Old Nix ...), nor did I have the bona ma**r**ksmanship for any Harvey Oswaldesque long-distance servo-splattering, I would instead have to target sitting-quackers, pops least expecting a joyful explosion of terrorism on their doorstep. It seemed to me the most obv**i**ous choice would be to randomly chop down conformist eagles at their workplaces: civvies sleepwalking through travails they detested, slavish twats who would never have the kishkas to screech fuck-off-thataways to the B**o**ss Man – and so needed putting out of their misery pronto.

After pondering what professions might be most guilty of blinkered fash-battery and therefore bestest to target – sharp-ering-omis, prosecuting lawyers, pawnbrokers, stockbrokers, AdMass-pops – I vadared I could honour Papa Breton's lavs at least a pogi bit and pluck a business at random from the pipe-directory. I'd nellied the eagles, in their eagerness to fan the mally flames of Capitalism, had just this year brought out a specjalni nova phone-tome entittled the YELLOW PAGES, brimful of commercial khazis and fencers, with nix unemployed pops' or lattywives' particulars in sight.

After sending my glum-opalled dollies out to parker a copy of this monstrous yellow liver, I pondered what gloriosa date I should carry out this de-luxe aggro. While it was tempting to unleash a gay burst of dismemberment immediately, I needed time not only to amass the relevant weaponry, but also to finish my wunderbar memoirs.

As before – as ever, as ever – CHANCE seemed to be the bestest approach. Like Dicky Trey before me, I had set my life upon a cast, and I would stand ze hazard of the die! Scrambling through our chaotic haberdashery cabinets, I lelled a bijou fold-out calendar of the forthcoming year and spread it haphazardly across the counter. With a sewing-needle pinched betwixt thumb and index-lupper, I squeezed my ogles shut and then – SHTUCK! – violently pricked a date: M 13 JULY 1970.

Fantabulosa.

I left the needle sticking uppity at a jaunty angle in Our Chosen Juno while I waited for my dollies to reappear, wondering with only a pogi bit of morbidity if I had just fingered the date of my death. Naturellement of course I would like to survive this first wave of aggro, perhaps even lavvy long enough to pick another trey, quatra or duey-daitcha naff establishments to attack, spreading healthy fear and vital workshyness among the anglos before scarpering into The Void ...

In the olden junos, cheap erotic froggy novelettes were distinguishable by their yellow jackets – however, when my fillies returned wielding the anglos' grandiose YELLOW PAGES, it was clearly not the mostest sensual volume, and yet still it gave me tinglies. I took the cheet from Séverine and examined it with an amused eek, before SPLATCH!ing it open ceremoniously atop the counter.

My faithful dollies twitched skitterish on the sideylines as I readied myself to prick the unlucky establishment. I plucked the sewing-needle from M 13 JULY 1970, then, squeezing my ogles shut once more, rapidly flick-flap-flickered through the yellow liver, fanning its flimsy pages this way and that, before lashing out like a Zulu ...

The needle penetrated. I let out a pogi orgasmic wheeze.

When I reopened my opals, I clocked I'd jabbed with so much venom I'd near enough stabbed through quatra-dozen pages. I had to squint to vada the Doomed Establishment. The needle's point of entry was neatly inside the loop of a lower-case 'a'. I ogled the letters either side and let out another pogi wheeze. The lavs screeched:

THE GLASS EYE PRESS LTD,
28 Newman St, W1T 3ER (MUS 2794)*

---

* Trefoil had just finished reading this chapter, his face locked with shock, when Novak appeared at our doorway with the weapons.

DURINGWORD

I was hunched constipated in the water closet when I heard my colleagues exploding. More than the screams, I can still recall the rotten-egg stench of spent gunpowder creeping under the toilet door. Between the blasts, somebody was screeching in an anglo-froggy accent: 'You filthy fash bats, money-grubbing dish-lickers! Tinkering with my bona screeve! I've been ogling your footnotes! I'll crucify you all! I'll fuckering crucify you all!' Or am I just putting words in the madman's mouth?

Once the initial paralysing shock had subsided, I kicked aside the carnivorous plant and ripped up the loose laminate, only to find an empty cavity where my sawn-off shotgun should be. My heart clashed frantically in my ribcage. Despairingly I hoped Trefoil, my fellow war veteran, had the shotgun in his grasp and was fighting back valiantly against the Scum King – however, when finally I summoned the guts to inch open the lavatory door, the gunfight looked decidedly one-sided. The office was full of ammonia-scented fog, sour clouds hanging solemnly over the splattered entrails, scattered limbs and shattered skulls of my staff. My beautiful, hopelessly devoted staff.

Molto sang guaranteed, just like the bastard promised.

Peering through the slit, I was just about able to glimpse Novak while he reloaded for one last volley. The madman wore a handlebar moustache and a ragged naval uniform, the white tunic and cap sullied with smeary beige filth. By his side, he had his ammunition stored in a large black perambulator. I watched the bastard reach into it for another couple of rounds, cock the shotgun, then fire cackling into the fog with the evil abandon of a chavvy wielding a water pistol.

In spite of all the direct hits, I got the impression Novak had not handled a shotgun much before now. He had a scattershot approach to shooting, the recoil sending him reeling backwards jelly-legged each time he pulled the trigger. I ducked back into the WC as the final shots thundered through the building. I believe Novak may have blurted more bolshy gibberish before fleeing, but it was impossible to make it out clearly what with my ears ringing so much. When I again nudged the lavatory door ajar, there was just pirouetting sulphurous smoke where the madman had been.

Judging by the distant crackles, Novak continued shooting as he escaped down Newman Street, but in our office there was just eerie silence now as I gingerly emerged from my hiding place. Creeping out breathlessly from my untainted WC, I felt sick as the smoke gradually cleared. The volume of blood was horrendous: three distinct pools of red-black slime slowly slithering together to form a gruesome lagoon underfoot. Trefoil was face-down in one of these pools, limbs splayed out like a gigantic crushed spider, Novak's latest (last?) chapter fanned out around him. McKinley was still sitting upright at his desk, his suit and tie in perfect order, his head an action painting of skull and brain matter splattered in an arc across the wall behind him. I couldn't bear to inspect Davy's or Emily's bodies closely. It was far too upsetting, knowing I had positively forced Emily to come to work that morning and, given that Davy was tied to his chair, I expected he'd received the worst of the Blitzkrieg.

Even more so than the shock and sorrow, it was guilt and shame that plagued me as I stood shuddering among the bodies, almost as if it was me who had pulled the trigger. I felt like a monster for encouraging Novak, for selfishly wishing this atrocity to occur, and for not realising exactly what the bastard had planned, despite scrutinising his inner workings all this time.

When Novak first got in touch with us, it was Emily who wanted to immediately phone WHITEHALL 1212. Now, nine months later, I would finally make that call – too late, too late …

And I held it off for another couple of minutes. Heart still rampaging in my chest, I lunged on tiptoes between the red-black pools, circling my colleagues' desks. Sensibly or senselessly, I snatched the original manuscript and Emily's sanitised duplicate, carefully plucked the bloodstained chapter from what remained of Trefoil's left hand, then hastily hid the wad of papers under the laminate in my WC.

Fogged with panic, I felt like an imbecile as I now frantically Dettoled my bloody footprints leading to the manuscript's hiding place. I even considered disposing of Novak's spent twelve-gauge slug and buckshot cartridges strewn around the office, horribly aware that they may well have been fired from my stolen sawn-off shotgun – but in the end I just left them where they were, flushed the bloodied rags down the toilet, then finally dialled through to Scotland Yard, desperately trying to communicate grief, shock and unquestionable innocence to the operator on the other end.

It seemed to me almost an hour had passed before the fuzz and ambulancemen arrived, although our clock claimed it was just a matter of minutes. While I waited, I struggled to settle on an appropriate pose: head in hands, upstanding steeliness, wildcat back-and-forth pacing, foetal position, kneeling slavish with wrists bared ready for cuffs?

No sooner had I assumed a stony Rodin's *Thinker* stance behind Howling's vacant desk, than one of the corpses startled me with a guttural greeting.

'Ggghhhllrghh … fuck … fuck …' Davy uttered, eyes still closed but his head swinging in a loose, dozy figure-eight above his tethered body.

'Davy!' I croaked. 'Good boy, good man … good man! Hang on in there, my friend.'

'Whghhh …' he murmured. 'Was … where's Emily? I'm innsn …. you see I'm innocent …'

I now glanced at Emily, and instantly regretted it. Blood leaked from her eyes and mouth in ugly glugging pulsations, her body twisted and punctured by an unspeakable amount of buckshot.

One of her arms was no longer in its socket, splayed fingers pointing accusingly towards the back door of the building.

Instinctively I wanted to take Davy in my arms – partly to console him, partly to shield him from all the horror. As I gingerly dipped my foot back into the congealing blood, a whirlpool of sirens spilled through the air outside. I jumped back into Howling's swivel armchair, and just about managed to give Davy a barked command – 'Don't tell them why you're tied up – don't tell them anything!' – before our quiet, freeze-frame Hell was awash with noise and movement.

Yes: ignorance seemed to be the wisest option once the police and paramedics stormed the building. The rest of the morning was a blur. I sat in half-sincere, half-simulated stupefaction as the authorities went about their business: stretchering Davy and Trefoil into ambulances (miraculously Trefoil also had a pulse, albeit a pulse the strength of a dormouse's), photographing the scene, dusting for fingerprints, making solemn calls to Scotland Yard loaded with acronyms and codewords.

Listening attentively with a glassy expression, I gradually became aware that there were more dead bodies. As suspected, Novak had continued firing as he fled our HQ. Two elderly gentlemen had been killed, one from buckshot wounds, the other from shock; a passing baker had his loaves, and his brains, blown across a parked taxicab's windscreen; a middle-aged man died from two slugs to the belly and groin; a dogwalker's Labrador was found in Newman Passage dumbly licking at its master's wounds.

Initially the police believed these were indiscriminate killings, a tragic case of wrong place/wrong time for the victims – until the identity of one of those fallen came to light. The man who received shots to the belly and groin was a writer from Sussex, a man police were already aware of, having investigated a number of death threats made against him in the past.

My heart and guts lurched again when I heard that Dennis Mesh had been gunned down. Our dear friend must've seen our message and rushed to London first thing Monday morning to see us, pressurised by the urgency in the note, which of course was all my doing, my handwriting, my fault.

While the police continued gathering evidence around the office, I was allowed to go home to mourn in peace, although being in the flat now felt like living in the stinking, throbbing interior of a great white shark. I'd agreed to be questioned by detectives the following morning, and my brain ached as I tried to weigh up the pros and cons of telling the truth about Novak and his diabolical plot, or throwing the DIs off the scent while I decided what exactly to do about the bastard's precious memoirs, his terrible legacy.

I turned on the television hoping for some light relief, only to find a devastating blonde on the nine o'clock news telling me there were yet more casualties. Almost simultaneously as my colleagues were being butchered in Newman Street, timed bombs had gone off in five Victor Value supermarkets across London. The fatalities currently numbered twenty-nine, although apparently there was upwards of a hundred more victims receiving treatment in hospitals across the capital. The bombs had been built to cause as much damage to stock and flesh as possible: screws, scalpel blades, broken glass and glovers' needles were found in one casing that failed to detonate; tar had been added to create choking smoke; there was enough powdered explosive in each device to turn each establishment into a giant flaming human stew.

Despite the timing of these atrocities, the authorities felt the blasts were not connected to the murders in Fitzrovia. I switched the TV set off and stared at the skirting boards for an unhealthy amount of time. In my peripheral vision the décor of my flat flickered blood-red as I thought over and over again: we could have stopped him, this all could have been avoided …

And yet: despite the knowledge that Novak was still at large and may well strike again (see that bloodstained chapter 'Novak's Hit Parade'), when detectives arrived at my door the next morning and proceeded to bombard me with their vague questioning and flawed findings, I did nothing to steer them towards the truth.

Owing to Dennis's demise and the countless death threats aimed at the poor man since *Pink Baton* was released in 1966, the fuzz were convinced this was a pre-meditated attack on Mr Mesh and those responsible for publishing his work. I suggested the detectives might wish to inspect our vast filing cabinet of hate mail for potential suspects, fully aware that this overcrowded fishtank of red herrings would keep them busy for days while I firmed up my own game plan, or battle plan, or business plan – whichever it would be.

'We're very grateful for your cooperation, Mr Merritt,' Detective Roland said as I accompanied them to the Glass Eye office later that morning, to point out the cabinet in question.

'It's the least I can do, really,' I replied. 'I just want to see Dennis's killer brought to justice,' and so on and so forth.

While they boxed up the masses of hateful correspondence, I wondered whose job it was to clean up the blood. Naively I'd expected some hardboiled Mary Poppins might've already hosed down our office – but it seemed it was probably down to me to find someone willing to disinfect my colleagues' entrails.

Lingering in the only unspoiled corner of the room, the detectives wanted me to recount once more what I'd seen the previous morning. They had precious few leads on the identity of the gunman (other than an abandoned Rolls-Royce discovered near St Giles, rented under the name Keith Caesar) and so, as chief witness, they were eager for me to dredge up any other details I could muster, 'provided it's not too distressing for you of course, sir'.

'It is rather,' I replied, gazing glazed at the grotesque parquet.

As before, ignorance seemed the best policy here. In terms of the killer's appearance, I simply regurgitated what many eyewitnesses had said already: a scrawny chap, white suit, black pram, brown moustache.

Though the police found only twelve-gauge cartridges littered around the office, the great gaping holes in our walls led them to believe the gunman had been firing a more heavy-duty weapon along with the sawn-off shotgun. I admitted I was no ballistics expert but 'certainly the blasts were deafening, yes, it sounded very heavy-duty'. Of course I was not going to tell them my colleagues had chiselled the holes themselves, to search for bugs. We had to seem like the innocent party here – not raving paranoiacs eagerly counting down the days to the bastard's crime.

By the time the detectives and I left the building, I was convinced they did not suspect any foul play on my part. As far as they were concerned, I was just a slightly unsavoury publisher who had miraculously avoided being slaughtered by some delusional, self-righteous pulp fiction fanatic. However guilty I felt about the bloodbath, I had to keep telling myself I was the victim here too. I was the victim here too. I was the victim here too.

I took a long detour round the rump of Regent's Park on my way back to the flat. As I trudged between the quivering green fields, my thoughts again turned to the manuscripts stashed in my private WC. I wondered if, after all this, there was still a chance I could make my fortune from Novak's despicable memoirs. Previously I'd been wary we wouldn't be able to profit from *Mister Asterisk* if it seemed we were at all complicit in his foul activities (see footnotes to 'Je m'accuse ...!', for instance) – but who could argue we were the predators here, when clearly we were just the poor helpless prey?

My insides tingled queasily as I pictured the folks in the park – the young couples, the war veterans, the suits and secretaries, the bohemians and beggars – all transfixed by the same 2/8 pocket-book emblazoned with his name. I had no doubt Novak's crime was horrendous and mysterious enough for the public at large to take notice. The only potential pitfall was me having to explain my apparent ignorance when questioned by the Met detectives, why I'd somehow failed to mention I had a 400-plus-page confession from the murderer on our premises. Then again, I could always blame shock, trauma, amnesia. Or better still, I could pretend I was completely unaware of the manuscript's existence, unearthing it only while deep-cleaning the office after the massacre. 'My fallen comrades must've hidden it from me,' I could say. 'They must've been aware – and quite rightly too – I would've reported it immediately to the authorities, had I known of its terrible contents,' et ceterarara.

As I wandered trancelike round the dripping red rose garden, I soon hit upon a much nobler, more heroic excuse for my silence: I didn't want to share my intelligence with the police because I wanted to capture Novak *myself.*

Yes. The more I thought about it, the more excited I became. I couldn't publish *Mister Asterisk* with the ending it had currently anyhow: not with Novak being the victor. As it stood, the bastard would seem like a criminal mastermind, having thoroughly butchered and outfoxed us, vanishing in a puff of egg-scented smoke.

I would find the frog myself. I would destroy him. I too had a typewriter – I could screeve a happier ending to this horrific saga. I could be the victor, the vengeful vigilante.

I could be the hero.

Novak may well have finished TAP-TAP-DING!ing his meshigena memoirs, but as far as I was concerned, this novel was not finished yet.

Stanley Merritt (Director), The Glass Eye Press
From the interior of the great white shark,
Whitfield Street, Fitzrovia
19th July 1970

PART VIII

MY GRANDE DESCENTE

'Est-ce un délire de ma raison malade, est-ce un instinct secret qui ne dépend pas de mes raisonnements, pareil à celui de l'aigle déchirant sa proie, qui mà poussé à commettre ce crime?'

COMTE DE LAUTRÉAMONT

'Nous marchions gaiement sur un tapis de fleurs qui nous cachait un abîme.'*

COMTE DE SÉGUR

* 'Is it a delirium of my deranged mind, is it a secret instinct independent of all reasoning, such as that of the eagle tearing apart its prey, which impelled me to commit this crime?'/'We stepped out gaily on a carpet of flowers, little imagining the abyss beneath.' Epigraphs clipped and pasted from foxed paperbacks.

Distribution of the Eagles[*]

NOVAK WEARS A BUTCHER'S APRON. BLOODSTAINS NOT MODEL'S OWN.

NELLY CHRISTIE LAUME'S 'ROUGE-ROUGE'.[†]

COU-COU! Hé-hé-hé-hé-hé-hé-hé-HÉ!

Ô, isn't chance such a wondrous hazardous substance!?

Given that I was already medsa-way through screeving my gildi memoirs with Ms Autruche, I was ultra delighted when my needle pricked this petty publishing house of ill repute! I savvied with almost hysterical glee: I could parker the liverish pops this molto illicit, unsolicited manuscript ahead of my fantabulosa crime, enabling the sharpering-omis to find my

---

* Two chapters received Tuesday, 4th August 1970. No, this novel was not finished yet. Iris and I were loading books into boxes when the aerogramme landed in our viciously disinfected foyer.

One tiny consolatory side effect of Novak's atrocity was the renewed interest my ex-wife now showed in me. Iris had spearheaded the cleaning and redecoration of the office, she cooked for me, she let me sleep in her bed whenever I complained of terrible nightmares (which was all too often) – and it was Iris who that morning pointed out the obscure postmarks on the wafer-thin tricolour envelope.

'Par avion,' she said, which at first sounded to me like witchy gibberish. 'Royaume du Maroc.'

† Clearly Novak was just toying with us now. The chorus of this song concerns a teenybopper turning red from embarrassment – but if Novak is trying to suggest he's feeling bashful about his appalling crime, we're sure they're just crocodile tears. More likely the 'rouge-rouge' of the title represents the gallons of blood Iris and Stan had to scrub from the floors, walls, furniture, ceiling …

startling confession while rummaging round the dismembered bods and shrapnel for clues. They would be able to ogle these very paragraphs (COU-COU!) and savvy I will kill again and again and again and again* until they take me down with their batons, or until I scarper superheroic back into the wilderness ...

After a week of bloodlustful carousing and plotting, myself and Melody settled down at the lav-hammer to draft the following notelet to the doomed publishers:

Never-Neverland, Londres W1
10th October 1969

Dear Sir/Madam,

I am an ugly man, a meese meshigena-omi, but a fashionable omi. And soon to be a molto famous omi. Lell my lapper.

Esteemed publishers of glistening livers, myself and my devotees cordially invite you to join with us in this forthcoming fame. We hereby offer you an una-in-a-lavvytime lucrative share in the high-flying, hallucinating, espresso-schlumphing, pâté-nibbling, jibbering, both-way-swinging, reprogramming, reverse-servo-lathering, Polarising, paranoid, cobblestoned, mono-bothering, line-crossing, cross-dressing, omi-jarrying, lav-hammering Raymond Novak Experience!

In duey-chenta setta-daitcha-heksa junos (276 days, for those without the lingo), myself and my devotees will commit

---

* I apologise. As you may have noticed, I cannot decide whether to write these footnotes in first person plural or first person singular now most of my colleagues have died. On 21st July 1970 the death-toll reached forty-one when doctors decided to switch off Trefoil's life-support ventilator.

Drunk at Trefoil's wake, I told Iris and Davy my plan to hunt down and destroy the Scum King. Miraculously Davy had made a full recovery, save for a slight limp caused by shards of shattered typewriter in his left leg. That night, also emboldened by drink, Davy insisted he would do whatever he could to help me in my pursuit and seizure of the bastard – but, as far as the following footnotes are concerned, the illiterate child was no help at all.

a fantastic crime, a fantabulosa crime that will revolt the mond. My nom will be on the oyster-levers of every daffy jittery civvy as news breaks of this dazzling atrocity. My eek splattered across the cover of every inky and glossy on the newsstand.* The Establishment brought to its lally-caps. The system left thoroughly smashed and charvered!

In anticipation of my untimely (and yet molto likely) demise on this date (batons, bombas, pistolets and molto sang guaranteed – or else all costs reparkered to you in full!), I am screeving my memoirs. What I propose is: if you are interested, I will send you morso-by-morso each chapter as it is tap-tap-DING!ed out upon the lav-hammer.

I am your man. But I am a meese omi, and a coddy auteur to boot. My achievements in education have not been up to dick to say the least, but do not fear: I have enlisted the help of a devoted comrade – an award-winning scholar and author – to fantomscreeve (ghostwrite, if you will) my autobiography.

I want nanti dinarli for my liver, nanti advance, nix royalties, no money for this venture. Only immortality, the lavvy-everlasting. The chance to screech my story to the masses in the event of my (ultra inevitable?) death come next summertide. And you, in turn, have this una-in-a-lavvytime opportunity to publish my truthful screeve immediately as news breaks of this mostest fantabulosa crime. It will be a real humdinger, a bona dinarli-spinner, I assure you. REVOLTING!

Esteemed publisher, if you are interested, give me a sign. Post a petite handlebar moustache in the 'Small Ads' section

---

* While Novak's crime had indeed proven to be a cause célèbre, almost a month after the massacre there was still no mention of Raymond's name in the press – only the same old laughable photofit of a man in a false moustache reproduced millionfold to no avail. After turning down police protection – a Met bodyguard shadowing us day and night! – we seldom interacted with the authorities, but anyone could see the inspectors were struggling to crack the case. We'd promised to let them know of any unusual correspondence we received at the Glass Eye HQ, but, of course, when the aerogramme from Morocco appeared, it immediately went missing under the loose laminate in my WC.

of the INTERNATIONAL TIMES, and in return I shall send you, chapter-upon-chapter as they are bashed out, these most specjalni sensational memoirs.

Bona lavs,

Raymond Marianne Novak (alias Lord Never-Never, alias The Guru, alias The Emperor, alias Raymond the Bastard, alias Raymond the Ponce, alias Signore Shapeshifter, alias Les Divertissements, alias The Walking Contraceptive, alias Ray le Roy, alias Ray la Purée, alias Neptunus Rex, alias Mr Sanson, alias Keith Caesar, alias Raymond the Poissonnier, alias Raymond the Poisoner, alias The Prole Dandy, alias The Scum King, alias The Carnish Mincer, alias Le Dieu-de-les-Indésirables, alias Le Dieu-du-Jour ...)

Of course I did not truly intend to let this random firm publish my gloriosa screeve – after all, the plan was complete and utter destruction of every pop involved in the business. In fact, the only cheet stopping me from bombing the latty to ultra-rubble was I needed the plod to find my glistening liver intact among the cadavers, so it could be parkered over to a more reputable, much higher-flying publisher (COU-COU!) to do the honours instead.*

The reputation of this meshigena GLASS EYE PRESS LTD mattered not a jot to me. If they did not take the bait, if they did not squirt une petite handlebar mouser in the INTERNATIONAL TIMES, I would simply pluck another publisher at random from the YELLOW PAGES, until I had my captive audience!

As it fell out, nanti additional pluckery was necessary. My boomboomer clanged with monstrous joy when I clocked the petty morso of facial furniture the doomed bats had inserted alongside a vulgar ad for their gloomy livers on page kenza of that radically naff toffee-beatnik hippy inky. For my own amusement I purchased the chinka pocketbooks on offer, filling out

---

* O, but we *will* publish this grubby book, you despicable bat!

the ajax order form with a mogue nom and clippety-clipping a bad cheque. When the novelettes arrived (I had them delivered to a Post Office box in Howland Strasse), uno cursory ogle told me all I needed to know: this was a truly codswallop enterprise, utterly worthy of my unsparing wrath!

On Monday, 10th Novembre, I plopped the first chapters of my memoirs into the postbox directly ajax to the Post Office Colin. I let out yet another pogi orgasmic wheeze as the parcel penetrated, then minnied onwards to Novak Strasse, to vada the very latty I would ferricadooz some otta months later. The city enthralled me as I trolled along the grimy byways. I had strange vibrations in my bod and servo now I savvied I would splatter these strasses with sang in the summertide. Only a month before I had blinked through my bedchamber fenêtre and shuddered at the prospect of gunning down innocent weekday wanderers – unemployed pops, solo mamas, bambinos – however, this after-juno it seemed to me every civvy that passed by me possessed a hideously glaring eagle-eek. How had I not clocked it before? Lattywives toddled past with grotesque aquila-vonkas, talons clenched round bulging bodega-bags. Plague-quackers' beaks protruding from beneath bulbous bowler-cappelas. The cold inky opals of the lollipop-palone ajax to the All Souls primary skol. Tufty plumage moulting from starched cuffs and collars. Squawking chavvies hovering outside Middlesex hôpital. Hook-vonkas tearing at flesh in the fenêtres of carnish-kens. Bald eagles, harpy eagles, gildi eagles, guttery eagles, toff eagles, tramp eagles, carooned eagles, kosher eagles, bolshy eagles, jackboot eagles, bombshell eagles, bonaroba eagles, Blitzkrieg eagles. The horrific noise of the city just one gross piercing sustained SQUAWK!

NEIN. I could abide it nix longer. I would feel nanti twistiness whatsoever when I rained birdshot upon this sordid corner of W1. These thousand-yard-stare conformists needed some bona terrorism to wake them from their stupors, make nix mistake. Twas open season for eagle obliteration, jawohl, mein camarades ...

When I reached Numero 28 Newman Strasse, I was pleasantly surprised by the dolly bijou bureau. The latty itself was quatra storeys tall, but, judging by the lavs on the buzzer, the Doomed Glass Eye Press Ltd occupied only the ground floor: wunderbar for a rapid getaway, I ponced.

Initially I imagined I'd need my full army of dollies to assist in attacking Our Chosen Establishment, but this cottage was almost embarrassingly petite. A splurge of queasy bliss juddered through my kishkas as I savvied I could ferricadooz this latty solo, and therefore pluck yet more dismal businesses from the YELLOW LIVER for my followers to Blitz simultaneous.

For my own amusement I pressed my eek up to the fenêtre, hoping to ogle a pogi few of my future victims and/or goose-pimple them with my ominous fantom-like silhouette – but all I clocked was my own daffy jittering reflection splattered across the glaze.

BOF.

I would become maxi well acquainted with them all soon enough.

Your Local Friendly Warmonger

NOVAK WEARS HERRINGBONE TWEED, FLAT-CAPELLA, PLUS-FOURS, WAX JACKET AND WELLIES.

NELLY FRANCE GALL'S 'BOOM BOOM'.

After much tet-scratchering deliberation, it was decided my dollies would ferricadooz a lapperful of Victor Value supermercados on Doom-Juno: that codswallop bodega where I first ogled the mod horror of Capitalism as a tender innocent chavvy. I recalled with some internal titterings the slogan plastered all over that particular shoppe:

SAVE MORE
AT
VICTOR VALUE

Hé-hé!

In preparation for my dollies' glimmering visit to the grocery-bodega, I screeved a specjalni shopping list:

DUEY-GALLON SUNFLEUR-OIL DRUMS
AMMONIUM NITRATE FERTILISER
DIESEL
ALUMINIUM POUDRE
SCREWS
SCALPELS
BROKEN GLAZE

GROSS NEEDLES
TAR
BATTERIES
TICKTOCKER
WIGGLIES
INSULATING STICKY
FUSE
DETONATOR

I discovered how to cobble together a bona bomba using mostly fertiliser and diesel oil from a naff innocuous pamphlet entittled ARTIFICIAL DUCK POND EXCAVATION I snuffled out at the Natty Central Library in Store Strasse. Pleasingly the components were readily available to any budding pyromaniac, many shushable from one's local high street or skip. Even a seemingly niche item like aluminium poudre could be easily rustled up by whizzing my gildi tinfoil hammer-and-sickle to dust in our electro coffee-grinder.

The only ingredient we struggled to locate in Londres was the fertiliser – however, our trusty YELLOW LIVER coughed up plenty of bona farm suppliers just outside the city limits. Hoping to cajole some gullible bumpkin into parkering me duey tonnes of the muck gratis, I joshed myself up as a lofty rural toff, and sent Bruce and Veronica outways to hijack a natty Land Rover or Austin Countryman or somesuch. They returned with what looked like a fuckering ice cream van painted fern green. While the daffy caboosh idled outside, I savvied I'd best lell some back-up dinarli from the valise, lest the soil-pops fingered me as an imposter before we even reached their vonny gateway.

Frugal devil that I was, I had not dipped into my Mare's riches much at all the past kenza months. Aside from feeding the gas meter, I'd whittled our overheads down to almost nil, so determined was I to save every solo stinking soldi for the high-stakes carnage to come. Every pogi extravagance had been eliminated from our lavvies – por example, my followers now subsisted on whatever dismal carnish we could extract from strasses and dustbins; Melody received uno bijou morso of panam for every daitcha side of screeve produced; my fangs had turned black from schlumphing only rough vin rouge for nourishment.

As I creepily clambered through the spiderwebs of tripwires in the attic, I pondered whether my Old Mare would've been proud to vada her dinarli splurged into such a cheerless cause as all-out eagle mortification? It tickled me somewhat that, had the legal-reps allowed me access to her fortune when I was still just a naive teen chavvy, I might've splashed the lot on toys and bonbons rather than arva-slaves and wholesale slaughter. Hé-hé-hé-hé-hé! Ô how I snickered as I scrambled and shimmied my way through the ultraschvartz – and yet my daffy titillation was not to last.

As I unclippered the clasps of my battered valise, I let out a twisted hoot. My opals had not yet adjusted to the gloom, but reefing through the innards of the box, I could find only a pogi pitiful lapperful of notes. My luppers trembled as I gingerly totted up the gent.

'Ô merz,' I whispered. 'Ô merz, murder and merdre.'

How had my Mare's 42,000 guineas fizzled to just duey-daitcha measly funts in five years? Did my beloved bastard followers know the dinarli was up here? Had some dastardly civil service eagle pecked its way through the roof and swiped the lot to make up for unpaid taxes? Worstest of all: was the success of my fantabulosa crime now under threat??

Squinting through the munge, Queen Liz's beaky oyster seemed to be turned up full-sardonic on each chinka-funt note. I screwed up the remaining bimph, stuffed it under my flat-capella, then minnied back downways, trying my bestest to maintain a ritzy aero though I felt like a pathetic pauper under my tweed camouflage, like the guttery rubble-urchin I'd started out as, before I even savvied what dinarli – that meese, baffling, despicable slime! – was for ...

Deserters*

NOVAK WEARS PIGSKIN.

NELLY ELSA'S 'AILLEURS'.

As reckless as it may seem, blowing my last remaining funts on coddy fertiliser pellets, the purchase would give me immeasurable pleasure in the long run, I was certain of it.

Once we'd cobbled together what I felt was a bona prototype bomba, I cabooshed my beloved femmes brûlées out to Dungeness, to test the magickal cheet. Savvying the Yankees tested their A-bombs in the Nevada desert duey decades earlier, I picked Dungeness for our experiment after nellying some rum fungus in the Blue Posts refer to the place as 'Britannia's only desert'. BOF. When we reached the coast, I was nicht impressed. This meese blot was not a desert – twas merely a gross baldy

---

* Chapter received Monday, 10th August 1970. Myself and Davy weren't entirely sure what we expected to find in Morocco, but as we boarded the BOAC flight to Gibraltar, we both agreed it felt better to be actively hunting the bastard, rather than sitting back passively with glass eyes, waiting for him to resurface and attack some other vulnerable prey.

Iris agreed to forward any more correspondence from the Scum King to us in North Africa, and cover for us if the police came sniffing around our HQ again. This chapter arrived the morning we were due to fly – again, an aerogramme stamped ROYAUME DU MAROC. I added it to the pile of reading material I intended to scour for clues during our stay: the Surrealist manifestos, *Madame Bovary*, *Richard III*, *Les Chants de Maldoror*, etc., as well as the original copy of Novak's manuscript, leaving Emily's sanitised duplicate under the loose laminate. Before we departed I noticed the carnivorous plant had died: an ill omen as we steeled ourselves for this perilous – needless/heedless? – trip into the unknown?

pebbly beach. The only advantage was the dribbly weather: on this meese Decembre juno there were nanti sunbathers nor fisherfolk in ogleshot – and so we blasted the vacaya regardless.

HAIL, JUPITER! I admit, in my naivety, I'd expected uno ounce of ANFO to explode like a toddler's rattle. Au contraire: standing duey-daitcha feet away from the cheet, the brootish blast almost shushed my powdered wig and ogle-riders. Stamping the smoking shyka underfoot, myself and my dollies reered like demonic chavvies – cuddling one another, crazed, drooling, lappers on lally-caps, oysters like glittering bear traps – before scarpering back to the caboosh. As we zoomered away from the coast, a bijou skully mushroom cloud lingered in our reverse-vada mirror. I could not stop sniggering, imagining the gross smouldering rubble on Our Chosen Juno, the aeroborn lallies and dismembered tets, the sang-soaked consumer goods, the BEAUTIFUL TERROR that would incite pops to abandon their gruesome travails altogether, to turn their palliasses to pointless pain and drudgery, and to RISE UP with PERFECT SAVAGERY against the lavvy-strangling eagles once and for all!* And if this

* Novak may have correctly predicted his crime would be a national sensation, but his wild fantasies of civilians instantly dropping tools and taking up arms against the powers that be were way off the mark. Rather than paving the way for a bold new utopian future, Novak's 'BEAUTIFUL TERROR' in fact had the opposite effect: increased police presence on the streets, increased hostility towards young people (especially groups of young women), mass seizure of 'hazardous literature' by the Dirty Squad, freedom of speech strangled, all weirdies now eyed with maximum suspicion …

The harassment of women was down to eyewitness accounts of the so-called 'beehived witches' that planted the bombs at Victor Value on the morning of 13th July. Tabloids were quick to blame women's lib and a fictitious rise in 'undomesticated feminist guerrillas' for a crime they did not realise was masterminded by a cross-dressing Frenchman. Clueless journalists suggested the perpetrators were young, disaffected housewives rebelling against their daily chores by targeting that embodiment of modern consumerism: the supermarket.

Ultimately, the 'stiff, dowdy, uptight society' Novak wished to overturn seemed more uptight – and more secure – than ever in the wake of his atrocious crime. Why couldn't the insufferable bat see this would happen all along? Today, thanks to Raymond, we live in a slightly more restrictive, paranoid, overpoliced

was the ultrashock from just uno ounce of the slop, Ô mon Dieu, I barely dared imagine what half a ton could do! Hé-hé-hé-hé-hé-hé-hé-hé-hé-HÉ-HÉ!

Ooh la la, I must apologise: I am hyperventilating somewhat.

It was of course a pogi bit early to start rejoicing willety-nilly. Much as I detested that foul substance dinarli, I savvied we needed more pronto if we were to survive the winter, let alone survive to ogle the wondrous sparkling fallout of my fantabulosa crime.

While myself and my dollies continued experimenting with bomba recipes and target practice, I pondered how bestest to raise some rapid funds. It seemed maxi foolhardy holding up a bank – risking arrest for a naff namby-pamby crime that would certainly delay (if not ferricadooz entirely) my future grand plans. I savvied my only asset on this coddy welt was our hallowed Ostrich Copywriters Ltd – but as far as my followers were aware, we'd been squatting there gratis all this time. Naturellement the nattiest option was to sell the latty, pocket the dinarli and sharper for a bona fide squat elsewhere – but how could I persuade my starving darlings to vagary our jolly home-sweet-home without admitting I'd been a rich omi all along?

Though I'd been continually jabbering about eagles trolling the strasses and circling the skies of Fitzrovia, after months of more or less undisturbed tranquillity my yé-yé fillies seemed unconvinced we were under surveillance by the sharpering-pops – but then lo and by Jove an orderly-daughter appeared at our shoppe one Tuesday morn in Janvier. Twas yours truly in a mogue piggy uniform.

I entered nostrils first. When my dollies on duty, Séverine and Bonnie, clocked the plod clobber, they became immediately prickly, frittying skitterish.

Great Britain – just as the eagles like it. It's not so much that the top brass rubbed their hands together on hearing of Novak's murderous extremism – but any excuse to instal or reinforce a police state in the name of public safety and security, and the Establishment will lunge at it like vultures to carrion.

Bravo, Raymondo. Bravo.

'Good day,' I announced in toffee tones.

'Good day,' the palones batted back. 'Can we help?'

'Possibly. I must say I was enticed by this STRANGE PERFUME emanating from your establishment.' I trolled about the bodega, flaring my nose-thirls, snuffling for some rogue von no other pop could sniffle.

'Strange perfume, sir?'

'Yes.' I poked my vonka to the slit of the portal leading upways to our bomb-making workshop. 'Not an entirely unpleasant odour, I might add, but certainly a ...' I ogled the ceiling with suspicion.

'Strange perfume?' Séverine mumbled.

'Strange! Yes.' I slithered back towards the chirruping exit. 'A strange perfume indeed.'

Judging by my fillies' frigid fantom-eeks, I savvied I'd done enough to splurge the shivers up them. I was content to minny back into the fog, leaving them to mull over the implications of this molto irregular visitation, when Bonnie spluttered forth an alarming suggestion: 'Perhaps it's these lally-covers, sir? These trousers giving off that exotic whiff?'

She wafted a lapper at the natty twill pantaloons still hanging in their protective glassy cube. 'We've been expecting you. We're a swinging boutique nix longer, but all outstanding orders shall be fulfilled. These are the perfumed slacks you requested, are they not, sir?'

Possiblement my eek flushed under the brute maquiage. 'Ô, no, no, not I ...'

'Vada: they're your size,' Séverine chipped in. 'We WIZZ!ed them up bespoke for you, don't you recall? Paris Green lining – 3OR. Molto chic.'

'No, no.' I felt my girdle chinois-burning my innards as I tried to straighten myself grander. 'You must be mistaken. I'm no fash connossieur. I'm utterly tasteless, in fact. I came merely to inspect that suspicious perfume. Now if you'll –'

'Suspicious, you say?'

Before I could poll another lav, I was schonked in the eek by a monstrous noxious glimmerball. MERZ! Whether it was Séverine or Bonnie who administered the pepper-spray, I couldn't possibly squeak. All I remember is my opals turning to crêpes Suzettes while the witches* tackled me to the parquet and yankety-yanked down my sharpering-pantaloons and slippies. Did the daffy bats nanti recognise my handsome lonesome cartso, my castration scars? Of course it was tempting to honk my true identity, but I savvied this gross emag, this whole natty charade would crumble if I did so. Flailing helplessly, I nellied one of the dolls frap the glassy cube open – VLAM! SHLACK! CRINKLE-CRANKLE – then all I was capable of was futile animal hoots as the toxic pantaloons were hoisted up my trembling lallies. By this stage Bruce and Rosa had rushed from the workshop to help pin me to the parquet. I believe the batatats blasted me with another trey or quatra poof-poofs of the pepper-spray. I felt the sandpaper swatches in the lally-covers nibble at my thews as the chinos were unlovingly tugged upways, and then I savvied with bona fide tears mingling with the pepper-parny: the bastards had shushed my immortality. The fuckering bitches had thwarted my fantabulosa crime in one codswallop swoop. Whether it took secondas, minutas, hours or junos, once the arsenic slithered into my bod I was done for.

My boomboomer clashed and clattered horribly – was it the poison, or just the screeching abdabs? Blinded by fiery throbbering opal-fakements, I frantically scrambled for the exit, luppernailing myself across the floor while keeping my lallies as straight and still as possible.

Thankfully my dollies didn't give chase as I slithered my way out onto the cooling cobblestones. Cowering betwixt duey parked

---

* This reference to witches raised the question: was Novak aware of the tabloids' bile and vitriol following his crime, their tarring of his pyromaniac devotees as 'beehived witches'? Davy and Merritt agreed there couldn't be a great abundance of outlets in Tangier selling British rags. Possibly these specialist newsstands would be a good place to start, to stake out, to track down the bastard?

cabooshes, I carefully unpeeled the poisonous lally-covers, tossed them with uno lupper into the opposite gutter, then vagaried ditherishly away from the boutique.

Savvying I needed to dhobi my lallies immediately, I flapped furiously at taxicabs once my platters hit the main strasse. Any reluctance my chauffeur might've had picking up an omi with nix slacks or slippies was rapidly quashed when the fungus clocked my piggy trinket. I ducked into the cab and squealed: 'Allez, ALLEZ! Go! Aqua! Wasser! WATER!'

'Water?'

'The Thames! Trafalgar Plaza! The fountains, the fountains!' I squealed, before savvying my mistake. 'No, no – too many ogles. The fuckering ... slithering ... Serpentine? The Ladies' Pond?'

'Come again, mister?'

'MERZ!' My naggy thews were horrifically itchy from the sandpaper aggro, but with superhumanoid servo-strength I managed to refrain from scritch-scratching myself to death as we dawdled round the daffy one-way system. 'Somewhere molto discreet, squire,' I demanded. 'Where are the nearest baths, comrade? Rapido! For the love of Christine: RAPIDO!'

My chauffeur suggested an establishment in Jermyn Strasse – the Savoy or Saveloy Baths – perfect for a bona going-over and ultra discreet, he insisted.

'Fantabulosa,' I honked, panting like a St Bernard. 'MUSH-MUSH!'

As the taxicab shunted agonisingly lento past the toffee clubs of St James's, I pondered twistily if it was all too late anyhow. My veins felt like jibbering electro-eels, nix doubt flooded with arsenic by now. I tried to convince myself I'd had a gloriosa lavvy, that I'd enjoyed my petty time aboard this rotten terrestrial apricot – but I savvied my bona achievements thus far amounted to nix, nantwar. If I couldn't commit my fantabulosa crime, I would be instantly forgotten like all the other insignificant lice upturned atop the Earth's baldy scalp.

When finally we pulled up outside the Saveloy Baths with a whiplashering WIP-SHTUCK! I parkered the fungus all the shrapnel I had left jangling in my inside posh, then hurled myself outways onto the dolly Georgian strasse with a pained eek and a terribly shrunken cartso.

Savvying the steamy omi-palones within might not take molto kindly to a sharpering-pop dashing unannounced into their hot soggy sanctuary, I unbuttoned my schvartz trenchcoat, turnered it inside-out and lashed it round my waist before entering.

'Good day, sir,' the gentle-omi in the foyer monotoned. 'Entry is ten-and-six. Do you require a private cubicle?'

'Nein. Nein nein nein!' I polled despairingly, savvying I had not uno solo soldi to my nom now. 'How can your aqua-vapour be so extortionate, squire? I only have these to give.' I panickingly ripped the gildi buttons from my flapping trenchcoat. 'They're solid silver,' I mogued. 'Plucked by the mostest nimblest dolly Bolivian, so I believe. They're worth a full week of steam each at least.'

'Entry is ten-and-six.' The omi took back the towel he'd flopped down. 'It entitles you to stay all night, sir.'

'That's what I'm afraid of! I hope to mince out of here rejuvenated pronto, not linger unfound in the fog, a cadaver in a sweaty morgue. Comprenez-vous?'

'Come again?'

'I have exceedingly filthy lallies, comrade!' I splashed the silvery buttons atop the marble counter. 'These are all the riches I have left on this coddy monstrous welt. Please, squire. I only intend to use the baths for fifteen minutas max ...'

The twonk was not convinced by my woeful lavs, but miraculously a dorcas voche came to my aid. Standing stampers-akimbo in naught but a skimpy towelette, a bushy-eeked brute called out from the changing-chambers: 'I'll pay the lad's fee.'

Jubilation fizzled to yet more agony as my saviour struggled to find the right change in his privvy ditty box, and then, once the debt was straightened and the two of us were toddling towelled together into the grand elaborate steam-palace, it seemed the omi would not let me vagary onwards solo.

'There's tea and biscuits here,' he polled, as if these were exquisite lavs of seduction. 'Are you down on your luck, lad? I've got my own private cubicle. And cards for gin rummy.'

I flashed the chappy a meese grin. 'Nellyarda: I shall rip your eek off, squire, schlumph down your brains and piss you out faster than a Scotch douche if you don't refrain from ogling or palavering at me right this very momento!' I scuttled away as rapidly as I dared on the slick surface, adding over my palliass: 'Piss off, thank you and good day to you, sir.'

And now, at long last – medsa-naggy, utterly penniless, ultra peeved and ajax to mortification – I was able to plunge myself into the purifying aqua. Savvying the hothouse Tepidarium and Caldarium would gape open my pores, possiblement guzzling more toxic residue into my bod, I headed direct for the Frigidarium – and near enough suffered a thump-attack when I SPLATCH!ed into the frosty broth.

'MERZ! FUCKERING MERDRE!' I hooted, bobbing in and out of the pool like a flapper terrorised by transparent crocodiles. I dhobied my lallies together rapidly, shrieking and shuddering and spasming until finally I could take nix more. I hefted myself out onto the sloppy walkway, the marble soft as lard now under my juddery bod. Opals like stamped-upon clamshells. Servo like shredded crabmeat. Blue levers. Boomboomer jack-in-a-boxing. But I was breathing.

Once I'd towelled myself back to some form of norm vitality, I tentatively ogled my lallies. My knowledge of bod-absorption was not up to dick whatsoever, but I savvied it was a bona outcome my thews were not bleeding, only a pogi bit chafed and full-goosepimpled. Content there was nanti morso of poison left upon my bod, I hobbled my way to the ajax sauna, clambering up to the toppermost benkel and sweating out manky snail-trails of brine until I was little more than a humanoid damp patch on the oriental tiles. Twas tempting to vagary to Harley Strasse and cajole some quack into giving me a full sang-transfusion, but then I recalled parkering the taxi-fungus my last remaining bottytops – and pronto felt poked-up all over again.

Savvying it unwise to wriggle back into my tainted plod cozzy, I shushed duey extra towelettes from naggy snoozers and fashioned a makeshift toga for my troll back to Fitzrovia. Twas not ideal clobber for that witchybreezy Janvier juno, and as I shambled through the Dilly I was aware of yet more passing eagles ogling me scornful in the neon blaze. Traffic tootering like plebs jeering some twisted out-of-favour emperor re-entering Rome. My platters bleeding from pave-friction. Maxi dehydrated. And when at last I stumbled through the portal of Ostrich Copywriters Ltd, I was alarmed to vada nanti dolly on duty. Coddy vibrations ribbitted through my bod as I recalled my historic grand betrayal at the lappers of the Interrupter. Had my dollies bolted?

Sharpering frantically around the frigid silent latty, I pondered with parnyaqua bubbling in my ogle-corners: was I mistaken about my comrades' everlasting dedication to yours truly? Had they been conspiring against me all this time, to try to jeopardise my fantabulosa crime? Had they shushed my Mare's riches from the valise? Ô Keith: had they been droggling me privvily with LSD, causing me to vada inky eagles everywhere I blinked? Did the foul batatats savvy only too well it was moi in that mogue piggy uniform and – JUPITER FORBID – had they knowingly poisoned their master, hoping to mortify me completely??

I was full-sodden with parnyaqua and huffing like a heartbroken warthog when I nellied a pogi scritch-scratch coming from the gross mound of grubby eiderdowns ajax to the Blank Chamber. Peeling back the covers uno-by-uno, I half expected a venomous viper to lash out at me, but then all twistiness and aggro-pangs swiftly evaporated when I clocked a dolly humanoid lapper poking out from the muddled bedclobber. I hurled the rest of the eiderdowns this way and thataways, and found my chinka beloved devotees cowering in a huddle like orphan naggy mole rats, missing their queen.*

---

* Our search for our missing queen began in earnest on Wednesday, 12th August 1970, after crossing the Mediterranean in what can only be described as a floating greenhouse filled with miserable Arabs and grotesque salmon leatherette. As we watched the port of Tangier gradually appear through cloudy plexiglass, Davy and Merritt sipped Cruzcampos and discussed yet again whether or not we would kill Novak when/if we found him. In a perfect world we would carry out a swift heroic citizens' arrest and, with the manuscript (sans footnotes) as evidence, Interpol would intervene and bring the bastard to justice – but realistically we realised the authorities were unlikely to accept this peculiar novel as conclusive proof of the Guru's guilt. If we wanted closure, we would probably have to dispose of the maniac ourselves.

Inspired by Novak's toxic lally-covers, while in Gibraltar Merritt searched out an old ally from his Navy days, a morally elastic seadog named Duffy who now lived with two maids and two bloodhounds in a prefab on the sandy east side of the Rock. After sinking a dozen Double Diamonds in Casemates Square, Merritt casually enquired about the availability of Paris Green paint at the docks: the hue apparently used to cover ships' hulls in the Victorian era (according to Novak anyway: see 'Dearest Comrades …').

'What are you looking to do? Kill barnacles?' Duffy asked, his face rigid and sun-soiled like stale fudge.

'Something a little larger than a barnacle.'

'How much do you know about poisons? Anything?'

'Almost nothing.' Merritt's eyes twitched behind his sunglasses. 'It's a precaution, that's all. Nothing sinister.'

'How much effort are you willing to put in?' Duffy took another gulp of ale, then fired snot from one nostril onto the pavement, just missing his Birkenstocks. 'You could go foraging for mushrooms, you could try extracting cyanide from fucking hundreds of apple pips, or there's a dirt-cheap poison you can buy over the counter, and it'll make your Mickey Finns taste extra sweet: antifreeze. Slug down enough of that, Stan, and it basically crystallises your kidneys. Turns them into a pair of fucking razor-sharp useless brown rubies.'

'Fabulous,' Stanley said, for want of a better word.

And yet: where does one find antifreeze in Africa in the height of summer? By the time we disembarked at Tangier, Davy and Merritt were resigned to the fact that we may have to use muscle rather than medication after all. Were we up to this bloody task? Clear enough we were risking our lives confronting the mass-murderer head-on, but, the way Merritt saw it, we should have been dead already. This awareness gave us not so much a reckless kamikaze deathwish, rather a sense that we were superhuman, protected by Lady Fortune, Fate,

'Your Lordship!' they whisper-screeched. 'ACHTUNG! GARDY-LOO!' et ceterarara.

Séverine blink-blinked at me nervy. 'A dirty piggy came snuffling round the latty,' she explained in gasping chavvylike blurts. 'We parkered him the toxic lally-covers. Hopefully he's mortified now – but you were right, Raymond. They're ogling us. Eagle-eeks at the fenêtres. The batatat could sniff our bombas. We're not safe. We must vagary pronto pronto pronto ...'

Utterly exhausted, with bloodshot fattygayed opals and barely any clout to my gargler, I responded: 'Bon.' Then promptly collapsed.

Chance, Happenstance: those 'wondrous, hazardous substances' Novak valued so much. We were relying heavily on good fortune to find the Emperor – but we had no purpose in life now except this. We would not give up until we had the madman in our grasp. We would butcher the bastard, we would steal his immortality, we would overshadow his fantabulosa crime with our far more fantabulosa revenge!

If the authorities caught up with us, could we convince them our premeditated murder was just a spontaneous act of self-defence? Then again: wasn't the Interzone lawless anyhow??

After checking in at the Hotel Continental, we set out into the Medina to get our bearings in the White City, the Blank City, the Alien City. To our immense dismay we quickly discovered the centre of Tangier is a shadowy anthill of narrow passageways, blind alleys, erratic zig-zags, dog-legs, dead ends. A maze of crumbling mudbrick and stucco corridors-to-nowhere. We had – literally and figuratively – set up camp on the edge of the monster's Labyrinth.

My Nuclear Family*

NOVAK WEARS A GROSS SCHVARTZ ARP WARDEN'S HELMET, FIRE MASK, PULLOVER AND PENCIL-DROGLE.

NELLY CHANTAL GOYA'S 'LAISSE-MOI'.†

Ahhhh, the Atomic Age!

---

* Chapter received Tuesday, 1st September 1970. As feared, our search for Novak proved fruitless while we acclimatised to the heat and chaos of the City of Revs. Given the number of expats, there were far too many newsstands selling international rags for us to keep under surveillance and, likewise, innumerable French bistros where the frog might partake in his morning petites madeleines and pastis.

With no fixed physical description of Novak to work with, Merritt and Davy traipsed around the labyrinth aimlessly in dark glasses, hoping Lady Fortune might furnish us with some clue, some compelling lead to follow. Conversations with Continental rakes in the cafés of the Petit Socco served up little more than bland tales of stomach troubles, recommendations for bordellos, dubious politics, casual racism. Even more so than London, this was a city in which an unconventional weirdy like Novak could creep around anonymously: another faceless escapee from the uptight West, another shadow among shadows. At times we wondered: was he really here? This latest chapter again came stamped with Moroccan postmarks, but of course it wasn't outside the realm of possibility the Guru could've fabricated the rubber stamp himself and hand-delivered each aerogramme. Be that as it may, the Metropolitan Police were still no closer to pinning down the Newman Street gunman nor the 'beehived witches' in London. Were we one step ahead of the plod, or just listing round and round in circles, miles off course?

† Our favourite waiter at the Café Centrale told us 'laisse-moi' means 'leave me be' or 'leave me alone'. Most likely Novak picked this song to illustrate his and his followers' self-imposed exile in this chapter, but it crossed our minds: could this be directly addressed to Merritt and Noon? Had Novak or his devotees spotted us creeping around Tangier, were we being followed, did the Emperor have a network of spies working for him in this Alien City? Was this a threat?

In keeping with my doomy savagery that the eagles were readying to drop the A-bomba atop our weirdy tets any minuta, I set out to find us a nova squat in Hampstead as I'd nellied the Nordic Line is at its deepest here: a bona subterranean hideyhole to survive ze inevitable nuclear holocaust.

There were plenty more reasons to pluck NW3 as our nova stomping ground: the Heath must be the mostest gloriosa picturesque cruising site in all of Christinedom, the place was renowned for its liberal intellectual exiles like yours truly, plus I had vague droggled memories of that detestable plop Herman Hermaphrodite uttering the lav 'Hampstead' at me while I was tethered to the khazi back in '68 – and I wished to taste more sang before Doom-Juno.

While on the lookout for a suitable squat, I undertook a pogi bit of reconnaissance on the Heath – and pronto found myself the leading sparkle in an orgy of shadowy, shifty woodland omi-palones. Delicate manicured lappers swamped my bod like dolly pink tarantulas, creepering under my rainclobber, pinching my tits and tugging at my cartso like I was some de-luxe hamper of carnish. Almost on a par with the arva-tingles, I was ultra stimulated by the savagery this lush jardin of fleshy pleasures could one juno be turnered to radioactive ash, us pooves flash-fried to pocket-size morsos of coal, ten dozen raving beautiful queens frazzled in the heat of ten thousand glimmering suns! Clinging to his glossy bod, I imagined the omi I was charvering instantly dissolving to dust in my lappers, and I ejaculated molto forceful than I ever have before ...

Alas, when I re-emerged muddy-luppered from the Heath, I vadared the rest of the community was not quite so go-ahead and frisky. Hobbling betwixt the lofty mansions and slimy churchyards, everywhere I blinked the civvies had the same beaky vonkas and talons as the bourgeoistards down in Fitzrovia. There were nanti exploitable gutter-chavvies, nix extremist show-palones, no provocative neon, nantwar subterranean shebeens – but still, I savvied we were safer in NW3 than back thataways.

Apparently Hampstead Tube is as deep as Nelson's Colin is long. If the nuclear holocaust came first, we could hide down there like bijou spermatozoomers, breeding a nova utopian colony of bona humanoids until we felt safe enough to re-emerge upways among all the rubble. Alternatively: if the eagles could keep their luppers off the nuclear button long enough for me to see through my fantabulosa crime, I felt strongly that we should flee the Western welt altogether once the deed was done: away from the eagles, away from the codswallop shackles of the Capitalist carnish-mincer, away from the A-bombers' crosshairs, away from all backward-ogling addle-plots and authority-flops forever ...*

---

* … and, so it seemed, away from the prying glassy eyes of his predators.

After weeks of futile prodding and probing around the Blank City, we soon lost our enthusiasm for round-the-clock detective work. Possibly it was the heat, or just sheer helplessness, but we convinced ourselves we were better off conserving our energy and allowing fate to run its course – waiting for the Scum King to come to us, rather than chasing his shadow in a labyrinth that was, by all accounts, just one big impenetrable shadow.

As best we could, we remained vigilant throughout September. The pleasures of the City of Dreams only ever distracted us for short periods – but, O, what pleasures. While Davy chased bored debs in the five-star antiseptic surrounds of the Hotel El Minzah, Merritt looked for love in the gutter. An eager 'bottom', ideally Stanley wished to be buggered by hirsute Arab brutes, but there was a disheartening lack of rough trade whenever he sleepwalked into one of the many garish bordellos. The rent-boys in Tangier were all of the doe-eyed variety: lean, submissive, pouty little devils. Not his type in the slightest.

And yet: aware that Novak was a committed 'top', an insatiable penetrator of vulnerable youths, Merritt felt it not unreasonable to follow his example, to sodomise a few of the local boys in the name of investigative psychology, if nothing else.

Stanley's French had improved since arriving in Morocco, but conveniently he refused to understand simple numerals when the boys told him how old they were. He just nodded with cold eyes and buggered them anyway.

Merritt's morals dissolved in this murky uncritical underworld. Soon his days and nights became a kif-colourised carousel of lithe brown limbs, parted damask curtains, parted buttocks, sucked pipes, broken French, moaning Os, glossy white spiderwebs splurted across tanned adolescent flesh …

Depending on his mood, after sex Merritt told himself he was doing this to get closer to Novak, to escape the horror of 13th July, to just try to feel some momentary meaningful sensation again, to feel something akin to living once

I blinked up at the glimmering speckles hanging in the aero hundreds of millions of miles away from our doomed meshigena rock. I pondered: wouldn't it be delightful to begin our lavvies afresh atop one of those untarnished sparkles, free from all travails, politicos, dinarli and naff 'civilised' savagery? How much ANFO to skyrocket us to Jupiter, por example? Apparently there was ice, fresh aqua on one of its bijou moons, Europa. A frigid morso, nix doubt about it, but at this very momento lavvying on a frosty alien rock seemed far more appealing than carrying on with this deranged sphere the eagles had thoroughly charvered after only a pogi few thousand daffy years of 'progress'.

BOF. For the time being at least, we had to make do with soggy Londres. Trolling around Hampstead, ideally we would've liked to squat in one of the district's molto notorious addresses – Freud's mansion, the Grand Isokon, Goldfinger's mod-block or Lee Miller's dolly cottage – but alas, breaking-and-entering into these abodes did not seem wise, given that we'd binoculared uppity families still lavvying within. Eventually, after otta gloomy hours trudging through the parny, we happened upon a domicile nanti estate agent could declare particularly homely, but for us it was perfect.

We found it in the overgrown foothills of the Heath: a meese isolated lock-up with rats rutting and shitting ajax, mould jarrying the bricklets, nanti neighbours in ogleshot and, molto importantly, only chinka minutas from Hampstead Tube.

Pleasingly the shutters were so manky and decrepit, we were able to gain entry with only a pair of rusty bolt-cutters and a pogi heave-ho of a spade shushed from an ajax shed. After installing our modest personal fakements – the lav-hammer, our bomba-making vacayas, some clobber – and starting a fire in one of our gross sunfleur-oil cans, the empty latty felt more or less

---

more. And yet he moved like a phantom, like a soulless estranged ghoul as he penetrated deeper, ever deeper into the sick, stinking kishkas of the crumbling citadel …

hospitable. True enough it was a lair fit only for wild beasties, but as you'll have clocked by now, I considered myself barely ajax to the rest of humankind at this juncture in my grand but skitterish lavvy.

And so: we laid lowly as winter crisped and fogged the cobbly strasses around our nova hideyhole. Once we'd perfected our bombas and emags for Our Chosen Juno, there was little else to do but lurk indoors while Melody and I tried valiantly to finish my memoirs in time for ze Grand Exposé. Fuelled by French Blues and rough vin rouge, we tap-tap-DING!ed long into each noche, knitting together my scintillating yarns of LIBERTÉ, INÉGALITÉ, INDIVIDUALITÉ, the clatter-shattering of bricks, the scaly legal-reps, 'SERVICE! SERVICE!' The Punishment Liver, Ye Youth Employment Office,* the Fruit Locker, the petty scab, DOWN WITH THE WOGS! Madame Ōgazumu, an upturned woodlouse in drag, the Shrimp of Destiny, the ultraschvartz freezebox, the humiliation, the horror, et cetera et ceterararararara ...

By and large Ms Autruche remained tight-levered while I dicktittled my stories at her – however, early in the screeving of that mostest salty morso of my memoirs, 'SEAFOOD', the palone divulged an intriguing nugget of information about one of my future victims. Whether down to the French Blues loosening her lingum, or a bona fide desire to help our natty cause, Melody's

---

* As he became less and less occupied with hunting down Novak, Merritt would often pay his favourite boys double or triple their asking price (still only around sixpence) to stay with him the rest of the evening, tucked up in some badly decorated, badly ventilated fleshpot boudoir. He enjoyed cuddling the boys' soft fuzzy flesh, clinging to them like a lovedrunk sloth, imagining the bed levitating high above all the sickness and pain of the city he'd left behind.

The boys' English was practically non-existent save for bartering vocabulary and 'I love you' – but occasionally Stanley picked up on the odd French phrase that made his heart gallop.

In a tiny hall of mirrors above a knocking-shop in the Rue Almansour, one boy mumbled: 'En hiver il neige dans les montagnes du rif.'

And just like that, in spite of the slimy heat of the room, Merritt felt savage icicles stand up all over his naked body.

Il neige. Il neige ...

luppers froze mid-sentence (I believe it was the sentence 'Twas MS HIPPOCAMPUS's mission to ferry mostly senile couples, dolled-up corpses, widowers and spinsters from King Georgie Five Dock to Malta via Gibraltar and back again and again and again ...') and she polled: 'I imagine this part'll appeal to Stanley a great deal ...'

'Pardon me?' I hissed, a pogi bit peeved to be halted mid-splurt. 'Who or what is this Stanley character?'

'Stanley Merritt. The director of the Glass Eye Press.'

I ogled the dame blankly. 'Since whence have you been on first-nom terms with ze Boss Man?'

'I –' Melody seemed poked-up for uno momento, before recomposing. 'Well, let's say he's a notorious figure in the publishing industry – and not in a good way.'

'Ô?' My ogle-riders pricked. 'Pray, tell me more. He has a fondness for salty shirt-liftering sea-queens, does he?'

'He's not homosexual, no. He's a married man.' Melody chewed the tip of her index-lupper. 'You're not aware of his history, Raymondo?'

'Nein. I've not ogled the omi's eek nor particulars nantwar, ducky.'

'Well, let's say he's had a chequered past. Dismissed from the Navy on the grounds of madness, so they say.'

'Ô wunderbar. A scatty cunt, is he? And this delectable morso is common knowledge, is it?'

'Not entirely. Just rumours. Some say he was court-martialled during the war – some horrific moment of recklessness on the Mediterranean ...'*

---

* For the record: I am perfectly sane of course.

The incident Novak's fantomscreever refers to occurred on the very waters I am looking out across as I write this footnote, soberly sipping tea on the sun terrace of the Hotel Continental.

Though I was encouraged by my lawyer to plead insanity at the court martial, I can assure you I was of sound mind when I was caught cavorting with Sub-Lieutenant Griffin in the sick bay of HMS *Legion*, September 1941.

By and large officers of the Royal Navy turned a blind eye to homosexuality during WWII. Officially gay men were not allowed in the armed forces – and

I clapped my lappers together like a sea lion. 'Ô Jupiter! These rumours please me! These rumours please me something daffy, Melody! Anything more to divulge?'

'Well ...' Melody's eek blazed again. 'He's famous in publishing circles not for the books he's put out, let's put it that way.'

---

still faced imprisonment back home if caught acting 'indecently' – but there was such need for extra manpower in the fight against that other band of queer-hating, death-dealing imperialists, the sexual orientation of new conscripts was not called into question, and in fact it was quite common to see chorus lines of fruity 'Squaddies in Skimpies' keeping up morale in the camps overseas.

Why then, after all the unpunished middle-watch mano-a-mano masturbation and fantom-gobbling that went on aboard our noble L-class destroyer, was my innocent dalliance with the Sub-Lieutenant punished so harshly? Why was I not merely chided and wrist-slapped like the rest of my lady-starved comrades? Why the dishonourable discharge, the humiliating court martial, the brutal (and futile) corrective therapy?

The Sub-Lieutenant squealed rape.

I do not deny that, when the two of us were apprehended by the officer on watch, Griffin had blood running from his mouth – but is blood not commonplace in the sick bay of a destroyer? The Sub-Lieutenant had sought out my assistance after cutting himself badly while shaving and, while I maintain I did all I could to treat his wounds, the bugger just would not stop bleeding when we later indulged in what by now had become our nightly tossing and rolling.

It was love, so I believed.

The Sub-Lieutenant and I were both twenty years old, unmarried, and wholly unrepentant when it came to breaking the Catholic moral chokehold forced upon us by our fathers. Hugh Griffin exuded an alluring tart-tongued Continental loucheness despite hailing from Splott, South Wales – and to this day I believe he was the most delicious, bewitching trade I ever had the pleasure of manhandling.

The Sub-Lieutenant claimed he enjoyed sex most after (even during) a particularly vicious firefight with the Axis. He routinely ordered me to use my forceps on his nipples, moustache and scrotum, and, though I may have occasionally loved him a little heavy-handedly, I insist I did not rape the seaman. I am a devout 'bottom' after all, am I not?

I can only surmise the bastard betrayed me just to save face and avoid the wrath of our despotic superiors on the bridge. I was utterly inconsolable when I was shipped back to Gibraltar to face the court martial, and yet my dishonourable discharge at least meant I was not aboard the *Legion* when she was sunk on 26th March 1942 – and, though they weren't killed in the wreckage, I have it on good authority the Sub-Lieutenant and the Captain who recommended me for corrective therapy are dead now anyhow.

'Ô?'

'For a time he was the go-to abortionist for women in the industry.' Her opals dipped momentarily. 'A sad character, really. At functions we'd pretend never to have heard of him or his ghastly little publishing house – but in truth many of us were very well acquainted with him.'

I reered up. 'Ô, this is FANTABULOSA! You mean to say the deplorable twat not only releases dreadful lies – fictional muck! – into the wild, but he's been dismembering bambinos on the side?'

'I'm afraid so.'

'Hé-hé-hé-hé-hé-HÉ!'

ALL HAIL MONSIEUR MERRITT! As if any further incentive were needed to obliterate Numero 28 Newman Strasse, this savagery made my kishkas positively jazz-lapper with excitement! This lowlife twonk, this meshigena Stanley chappy, sounded like an even worster reprobate than yours truly. What ultra fateful prickery from the silvery sewing-needle!

For my own amusement I polari-piped the bastard on Friday, 13th February 1970: 150 junos until the poor oblivious bats' annihilation. After uno fortifying Ricard at the Holly Bush, I snuck into a misty phone booth in Frognal Rise and dialled up MUS 2794. A jolly bureau-filly answered, her voche like a bijou spoonful of crème-caramel squirted down the line. It gave me indecent throbberings, imagining this feeli creature's eek uno momento before I unloaded my hailstorm of buckshot upon the lot of them.

'Monsieur Stanley Merritt, please,' I polled molto politely. 'A dolly comrade-in-arms calling, merci.'

When Merritt picked up, I found it maxi difficult not to reer hysterically while we prattled like chummy fuckering business partners. From the off the Boss Man made it clear he simply adored my scribblings thus far, causing me to emit a honking guffaw I rapidly disguised as a sneeze. Oyster full-pricked, I took gross pleasure in assuring the doomed prat I was molto certain than ever of committing my fantabulosa crime, that its particulars would be unthinkably gruesome – even going so far as to list the various mortifying-vacayas I would use on him and his staff on that ultra-climactic juno!

Did I feel any sympathy at all for this lonesome Scotch voche, quivering on the aerowaves? Nanti that – did I trout. By the end of our palavering, the bat had exposed himself as not only a sycophantic pleb, but also maxi dimwitted in the classic anglo literature department ...

I recall regurgitating this apt quotation, expecting a natty response: 'You'll have gathered by now I'm nanti much of a love god. But be patient, comrade. Since I cannot prove a lover I am determined to prove a villain, and hate the idle pleasures of our junos!'

'Sorry? Come again?' the ignorant fungus polled.

'Billy Shaker. Dicky Trey.'

'Dick Tracy?'

'Nein!' I shrieked, schonking the receiver against the glaze. 'You're a coddy detective, monsieur. Adieu!'

Ô, THESE INSUFFERABLE PSEUDS AND DILETTANTES! Come 13th July I would make the deplorable twat wish he'd been able to stick his eek betwixt my Old Mare's grubby lallies and abort me back in the quatra-daitchas!

Hé-hé-HÉ-hé-hé-hé-HÉ-HÉ-hé-hé-HÉ!

COU-COU!

Cou-cou, Monsieur Merritt!!

I'M STILL HERE.

L'autruche et l'autrichienne*

JOSHED-UP LIKE A FREAKSHOW MARIE-ANTOINETTE, NOVAK WEARS BLANK POWDER, RED CLOWN-SWIRLS, INNUMERABLE MEESE BEAUTY MORSOS, PEACH ROCOCO FROCK WITH H-BOMBA DERRIÈRE, BROKEN GLAZE DIAMOND SLIPPERS, TREY-FOOT-TALL STEEL-WOOL RIAH POUFFED UP LIKE A BIJOU POST OFFICE COLIN WITH ELECTRO-WIGGLIES AND SATELLITE DISH FAKEMENTS ATTACHED.

NELLY LAURA ULMER'S 'AMOUREUX D'UNE AFFICHE'.

Aside from the ongoing everyday threat of total nuclear annihilation, in the lead-up to my fantabulosa crime our mostest niggling enemy was boredom.

While Melody and I were content chiselling away at what I now consider to be ze mostest important liver ever screeved in the (not-quite-) anglo lingo, I savvied once our chinka bombas were perfected my dollies had pogi-all to keep them occupied as the junos crept towards our beautiful explosive destiny. And so: to keep their eager feeli bods and servos in bona nick, I concocted a number of petty warm-up crimes for the sparklets to splurt at their leisure.

The first involved disposing of a local doggy whose incessant bark-barkering was grossly impinging on my gildi creativity.

Another involved discreetly eradicating all consumerist visual pollution in NW3. I detest mod advertising so much that

* Chapter received Thursday, 17th September 1970.

the only way I felt we could overcome this vulgar virus was to put into production a hefty print-run of my own dazzling lavvy-affirming savagery and paste it in place of all existing money-grubbing marketing littering our dorcas district.

'Consider it subliminal servo-lathering for when my glistening liver finally crashlands in the book-bodegas, my chovis!' I exclaimed, filling their lappers wih reams of Day-Glo posters screeching some of my nattiest quotations to date:

LUBRICATE REALITY WITH DREAMS
INDIVIDUALITY FOR SALE!
POLITENESS IS A COMPROMISE
EMBARRASSMENT IS A WEAKNESS
THINK THE UNTHINKABLE!
SPEAK THE UNSPEAKABLE!
MENTION THE UNMENTIONABLE!
BLEED THE PRESENT DRY
OBLITERATE ALL EAGLES
LET THEM EAT CACA
LONG LIVE THE SCUM KING
VIVE LE DIEU-DU-JOUR™
COMING SOON TO A DOOMED WORKPLACE NEAR YOU ...

To punish any eagle who might try to remove our polite notices, we secreted bijou fatcha-blades under the stickies and mixed arsenic in with the wheatpaste gloop. This was agitprop at its finest, was it not? An acidic apéritif, a pogi burst of political pesticide before the Grand Purification ...

Occasionally I joined my darlings on their flyposting sojourns, but for the most part when I wasn't feverishly dick-tittling my electrifying memoirs at Melody, I tended to unwind on the Heath, halfway up a stranger's sphincter.* Depending

---

* After years of ineffectual experimentation with herbal, chemical and even yogic remedies, Merritt's constipation promptly disappeared during his stay in

on my mood, I'd either josh myself as rough trade (escaped jailbirdy, eelmonger, Père Duchesne) or toff trade (The Fugitive Viscount, The Deranged Sultan, The Chief Secretary to the Treasury), sharpering for willing victims to maul or mollycoddle accordingly.

One icy-grip February noche I trolled into the woods dolled in full-Rococo Marie-Antoinette garb, hoping for a swarm of shadowy serfs to paw, claw and drool over me ultra-beastish. Possiblement my daffy arrogank was ballooning brootishly at this juncture and so I was sharpering for some lowly ruffian to bring me back down to earth – or perhaps it was just outright megalomania. Either way, I felt like a gross Christmas bauble as I swished my way through the pluplushes, pouting imperious – only to discover that the woods were utterly deserted. Not one solo plebeian eek was illuminated by my almighty regal radiance

---

North Africa. Shortly before receiving this chapter, Stanley was struck down by violent dysentery, passing a seemingly never-ending stream of explosive red diarrhoea through the decrepit plumbing of the Hotel Continental.

Since contracting the illness Merritt had swapped his de-luxe diet of mint tea, imported wine, eels and baby shark for just bottled mineral water and unleavened bread. He cursed the bug-riddled tapwater of the Hotel Incontinence, but he knew it could just as likely be down to all the street children he'd been rimming lately. Or was it just nerves? After seeing his name appear in the previous chapter, Merritt felt more vulnerable than ever in this wholly unpredictable, abnormal city. Was Novak watching us? Was he readying himself to strike? Or was he just toying with us, tap-tap-DING!ing these final taunting chapters from the safety of some secluded spot in the Moroccan outback?

For the time being at least, perhaps it was an advantage to be incapacitated behind the locked door of Room 220. Stanley strove to make good use of the lull, reading through the stack of literature he'd brought, and beginning work on what would become the Foreword of this most twisted, glistening liver.

Stan was spread-legged on the lavatory when he scribbled these opening sentences: 'Raymond's reign of terror started with a paper cut to a girl in a paper dress. Later there would be wooden caskets. But first: pulp.' As he filled his notebook with defiant, strident prose, Merritt became more convinced than ever that this story was now all about Him versus the Scum King. Two renegade writers, two mavericks, two so-called 'deplorable twats' fighting it out to become the true leading sparkle in this monumental meshigena yarn, the victor of the battle royal, the last natty omi-palone standing at the grand masquerade ball …

as I swanned by the shrubs and ticklies. The fog thickened as noche dropped. All peripheral twinkles and rimbumbles faded to nantwar. I was alone, Ô comrades. I was The Exiled Queen, lost in a maxi overgrown jardin maze.

'Ô, bof, ça ira, ça ira, ça ira ...' I grumbled feebly, picking at my excessive beauty morsos like some meese malignant melanoma.

As I trotted glumly back homewards, I would never have believed this codswallop non-event would feature prominently in my gildi memoirs, and yet – HAIL, NEPTUNE! – the noche was immediately lifted by a molto peculiar encounter on the corner of Willow and Willoughby.

At first I barely clocked the figure, given the chappy was lurking almost horizontal in the munge. Twas the pogi few glittering soldis in his capella that initially shushed my opals, and only then once I'd tripped over the fuckering cheet and scattered them with my diamond slippers.

'Apologies, squire,' I polled, retrieving the dinarli from the pave-cracks. As I plop-plopped them back into the pop's capella, I vadared the rest of his blank clobber: the tropical tux smeared with gutter-gunge, the stripes on his epaulettes twisted to gildi barbed wire. 'You're a war veteran?' I enquired. 'An ex-barky? I was a barky too, once upon a ticktock ...'

'Eh?'

Ogling closer, the tramp looked like he could've been bona-vadaring once, though the pangs in my boomboomer were not down to arva-hunger nix longer. Despite my grand plan to obliterate swathes of innocent civvies from the meese eek of Londres, I would like it known I am still capable of sympathy for my fellow citizen. War veterans especially make my thumper droop and drool, given that they are perhaps the ultimate homegrown victims of the eagle regime: the feeli beasties servo-lathered into robotically carrying out the meshigena demands of the toppermost authority-flops, barnying heroically/idiotically for an imaginary cause that more often than not leaves them with missing lallies or shrapnel-servos, if not mortifies them altogether.

Savvying this down-and-out barky might have some bona warfare secrets and stratagems he'd be willing to squeal, I added: 'You've been let down by the toppermost eagles, old boy? Kicked to the kerb by our codswallop Establishment? What say me and thee retire to a cosy bungery, a homely freehouse, for a pogi few pints and a warming supper? Oui? Nein?'

And yet, alas, it seemed the veteran was soused enough already. His jaw creaked open like the drawbridge of a haunted château and he shrieked up my nostrils: 'TRAITOR! TREACHEROUS COW! BEND! BEND FOR QUEEN AND COUNTRY!'

'Pardon me?'

'The Hippy Craze, eh? You consider yourself anti-establishment, do you?' The barky ogled me with horror-opals.

'I ...' I fumbled round my servo, still a dowri bit woolly after my fruitless tramping round the Heath. 'I ... well, I've never been so insulted, you scatty bat. Je detest the hippies, squire. This is regal garb – molto Rococo.'

'The Western world's no good for you, is it?' He scritch-scratched his unruly Kaiser Bill moustache. 'You'd prefer to be gambolling in the muck like some bloody braindead hippo in Bongo-Bongo Land, is that it?'

'I –'

'Speak!'

My opals widened. My thumper drooled no more.

'Speak speak speak speak speak!'

Ô comrades, I palavered nix longer. Oyster pricked, I tucked my luppers into my bra-pods, fished out uno grubby soldi and flick-flicked it into the barky's blank capella. As I trolled off tranquil into the noche, I felt gloriosa savage trompettes tootering in my tet. And I savvied: here was a fabulosa warm-up crime I could commit all on my bona lonesome ...

Officers' Mess, or: From the Captain's Log of the Coddy Ship SS *Forgettable**

NOVAK WEARS A MOGUE BEARD, SCRAPS, RAGS, HAND-ME-DOWN PYJAMAS.

NELLY CORINNE MARCHAND'S 'SANS TOI'.

And now for uno bijou aside to those cynical vultures among you who might be pondering the plausibility of yours truly mincing (as if by hazard!) upon my old Chief Steward in the gutterways of Hampstead. AU CONTRAIRE, my lovelies: this chance encounter was by nix means puppeteered by chance. I may have been droggled up to the ogles on meshigena coffee beans when the gossip was spluttered, but I recalled full-wakey Herman referring to his 'poor angelfish' Sturgeon as 'derelict', 'last seen scrabbling for spare soldis in Hampstead' while I was unsportingly strapped to the khazi.

GARDYLOO!

The anglos endure fuckering horrific weather all year round, but I waited patiently for an especially spirit-crushing parny-hammering gloom-juno before accosting the fash tramp again. Joshed-up in skimpy rags, I was drenched by

* Chapter received Monday, 5th October 1970.

the time I located my unsuspecting prey,* huddled like a manky sea-sponge in a doorway ajax to the Flask.

---

* There had been some abhorrent news in the Moroccan rags on 23rd September. Though we were by now fully embroiled in the City of Dreams, occasionally the thorns of reality woke us violently from the trance. Merritt's bowels had been settled for almost a week when he saw the teenager peering from the papers lined up at breakfast on the morning of the 23rd. He took a copy of *Libération* and *Le Journal de Tanger* back to his room and, nervously referring back and forth from the columns to our trusty *Harrap's French Dictionary*, his intestines felt terrible once again.

Two nights before, a thirteen-year-old boy had been found strangled in a bordello in the Rue Nasiria. It wasn't so much that Stanley frequented a number of fleshpots on this very street, nor that he felt he recognised the child's face (after all, he'd used so many Arab boys by this point, their faces all seemed the same, as if joined to one giant gyrating pubescent Hydra), but he felt sick as he gradually deciphered the statements from the police. After piecing together eyewitness accounts that included a neighbour, a waiter from Les Deux Rêveurs and, presumably, the Madame or ponce of the bordello, detectives were looking for a man matching the following description: 'culottes d'équitation, bottes à l'écuyère, chemise en soie rose, casque, lunettes de protection, cravache'. (See 'Je m'accuse …!' Flick-flick back to that chapter at once, dear reader.)

Quite reasonably the Moroccan authorities felt the perpetrator must be a foreigner. Why Novak chose to commit this latest murder in such conspicuous fancy dress bothered Merritt and Davy when we met for luncheon later that day. Was Signore Shapeshifter sending out yet another threat, aware that we alone would recognise his disguise? Was he laughing at us, goading us for not capturing him yet, despite him flagrantly mincing around in ludicrous pink jockeys' silks in broad daylight? Alternatively: was the child's death an accident, some perverse sex game gone wrong? Or was Novak just entirely deranged by now, oblivious of our presence in the Alien City and oblivious of all moral values, incapable of staunching the flow of blood since gunning down our beloved colleagues?

At first it was encouraging knowing the Moroccan authorities were now on the lookout for the bastard, but then of course it wouldn't do if they captured him before us. If the Sûreté Nationale got him first, they'd lock the madman away for the comparatively minor crime of strangling a gutter-child, unaware of his far more horrific roll call of murders outside their jurisdiction.

While Merritt got the impression Davy was losing his nerve now and wished to return to London, our Director felt re-energised by this latest gruesome development, utterly hellbent on personally meting out the punishment the Ponce deserved. Wisely or not, Stanley began visiting the bordellos of the Rue Nasiria more frequently, determined to catch the bastard with his lally-covers down. He considered it mixing business with pleasure: as he fucked his way through a seemingly endless supply of faceless youths, Stan sometimes wondered if he was penetrating the same warm territory, the same tight rectums as Novak's lonesome cartso only weeks, days, even hours before? Or was he just fantomfucking, sleepwalking lecherously into the Guru's carefully laid trap?

'Piffling bottletops today, eh, my mate?' I polled, gargling up a cod Northern voche.

Sturgeon ogled me grizzly, peering from a petty slit in his aqualogged bedclobber. 'What?'

I plopped myself down next to the dismal wretch. 'The weather and so on and so forth. Shite, is it not? No streetlife, no grubby pennies flick-flicked our way ...'

'Bah.' Clear enough the bat was in nix mood for bona conversation. He gazed stony into the medsa-distance, as if still clinging to his mally superiority complexity, refusing to consider us comrades-in-rags.

'Too malnourished to talk?' I persevered. 'Or have you already toddled along to the Sisters of Mercy, God bless their heavenly souls? Seafood supper this aft, so I heard ...'

Sturgeon's ogle-riders wobbled. 'What?'

'You're not acquainted with the Merciful Sisters?' I aeroluppered an upside-down cross ajax to my boomboomer.

'Tarts of the cloth, I presume? No, I'm not intimate with the crones.'

'Well, God bless their fluttery souls, they run a de-luxe soup kitchen by the Heath over yonder. Come with, my friend. I was headed over that way myself. Come and get some lovely seafood inside you.'

Had Sturgeon still not been molto enthused by the offer, naturellement I would've tranquillised and dragged the bugger – but lo and by Jove his vacant gurgling kishkas splurted the decision for him.

'Seafood supper, you say?' he parroted as we trolled up the cobbly willet to this fantom soup kitchenette. 'I'm a man of the sea myself.'

'You don't say.' I blinked at his grubby tropical cozzy. Was it a fiddling of my imagination, or had the fash bat attached a gross spreadeagle to the front of his peaked capella since I'd last ogled him? 'What's with the uniform, dear heart? Still wistful for the jolly old days listing atop the swishering brine?'

'Hush, rating!' the meshigena-omi blurted, halting abruptly

and grabbing my pol. His eek was like a quivering jib sail. 'What are our coordinates?'

'Our coordinates, sir?'

It was at that momento I clocked the extent of Sturgeon's nova madness. After insisting he could nelly enemy U-boats humbumbling under the manhole covers of Well Walk, Sturgeon took a blank morso of bimph from his posh and pointed out a petty crease to me. 'Look! I knew it. I knew it. The bastards! Radar's picked them up. Drop a depth charge, gunner! Let's blast these bloody eyeties out of the soupy deeps!'

'I –'

'Depth charge, gunner! Hedgehog! Squid! DEPTH CHARGE!'

Struggling not to reer, I gently steered the twonk away from the glug-glugging stormdrains. 'Panic not, Chief, twas just a drill,' I polled delicately, 'plus I'm only the humble galley boy, Cap'n. Come now, they're waiting for you in the Officers' Mess. Seafood supper, you recall? Something tells me you haven't eaten for some time, yes? Warfare is hungry business, is it not?'

'Yes ... yes ...'

With flimsy lallies and frosty opals, forgetting the threat under our platters for uno momento, Sturgeon greedily followed me onwards.

We were both fully sodden by the time we reached my privvy lair. Thankfully the rapid pasting of giant lavs 'SOUP KITCHEN' above our mangled shutter hadn't attracted any other batty itinerants sharpering for grub. I uncleffed the padlock, then lured Sturgeon inways with more scrumptious palavering: 'How do you feel about French cuisine, comrade? The Sisters have a certain penchant for bouillabaisse, fruits-de-mer, cornichons, homemade pâté, et cetera et ceterarara ...'

Sturgeon's eek took on a haunted deepfreeze again. He clutched my scrappy sleeve and barked apprehensively: 'Who are we at war with?'

'Not the frogs, Cap'n. They're allies as it stands.'

'Marvellous. Yes. Dish it up, gunner.'

After yanking the shutter down behind us, I led Sturgeon through a pair of grubby plastic curtains to our bijou kitchenette, where my dollies were oystering demurely, joshed-up in black scapulars and habits. No sooner had I introduced Sturgeon to the Sisters, the dorcas nuns introduced their botties of pepper-spray to the twat's ogleballs. Sturgeon screamed as the hissy mist hit him like a cayenne flamethrower. His lallies buckled, but before he flopped to the concrete my dollies and I swamped him, man-handling the squealing twonk into a makeshift gynaecologist's chair, strapping his lappers and stampers akimbo.

While my devotees stripped and shackled our prey, I flung a gross blank fishmonger's apron on over my rags.

'ACHTUNG! COU-COU!' I yapped once Sturgeon's weeping red bubblegum-ogles had creaked open again. I took from the refrigerator a silvery slithery platter of seafood – jumbo prawn, crayfish, mud crab, lobster, swordfish – and spittled into his eek: 'Recall the Shrimp of Destiny, you swine?'

I plucked the juicy king prawn from the platter and raised it aloft. Sturgeon shook his tet groggily. 'What is this, gunner? What are you doing?'

I reered up. 'This is revenge, dear heart. Or unfinished aggro, at least.'

'Who are you? What is this? Speak! Speak!!'

'Hé-hé! Clear enough you don't recognise me with my nova doctored eek – but perhaps this will rejiggle your memory banks ...'

With nanti foreplay nor lubrication, I jammed the jumbo prawn up Sturgeon's backside, fighting my way through his matted dish-riah before finally the pink cheet disappeared upways. The fash batatat howled hellfire, swishing hither and thither in his leather shackles, parny gushing from his ogle-sockets.

'Now you recall who I am? Oui, nein?' I scoffed. 'ALL HAIL KING NEPTUNE! Yessum? Or not at all?'

'I don't understand ...'

'You don't recall yours truly dishing out bonus punishments at zero degrees? Punishments, if I remember rightly, largely due to your arse-crimes against bellboys, a grotty superiority complex and generally acting like a fash arroganki batatat?! Comprenez-vous, ja?'

'I have no idea what you mean ... I've got no idea who you are ... what mission, what operation was this?'

'MERZ!' I plucked the still-wriggling crayfish from the platter and viciously corkscrewed it up the twonk's corybungus. 'Well: you may have blocked the meshigena scenario from – don't scream now – from your memory banks, but I'm here to rejiggle your batty servo and finish ze job I started back in soixante-quatra! NANTI FASH BATATAT SHALL ESCAPE MY SCALY WRATH! Et ceterarararararararara ...'

Grinning frenzied, I schonked the live mud crab with a mallet, then spitefully shoved each serrated shard up the Chief's stinker. Sang dribbled from his petty porthole like rotten Marie Rose jus. Horrific von of Billingsgate sewers. Riah-frizzling screeches.

'LONG LIVE THE THOUSAND-YEAR AQUA-REICH!' I screamed. 'Oui? Nein?'

'I swear, I swear I've got no idea what you mean ...' Sturgeon ogled the lobster's enormous claws twitchering on the platter. 'Please ... you've got the wrong man ... you've got the wrong captain. Speak! Please speak! Explain yourself!'

'You truly are a blinkered old bat, aren't thee?' I huff-puffed. 'Of course, I admit our escapades may be a pogi bit fresher in my servo, given I've been screeving this particular morso of our history in my gildi fantastical memoirs only uno month or so ago ...'

'Good God – what is this? Who are you? Please: speak! Speak!'

I brought my cracked eek closer to Sturgeon's. 'I'm Raymond Novak, sir,' I polled, pouting like a dorcas teen barky. 'Bellboy. Well, tumbler-shusher. Glass-collector I mean, sir. But a fine glass-collector. The Grand Cannibal Lodge. SS UNMENTIONABLE. Alles klar now, ja? You remember me at last? Or have you wiped all lowly dissenters from your servo completely?'

'I've never heard of you! Or your ship. I was captain of a destroyer ... HMS LEGION ...'*

This was unbearable. Was the bat so addled he'd genuinely misplaced all memories of his Merch Navy junos – or was this just his blind egotisticaca arrogank (or just plain madness) all over again? Gritting my fangs, I grabbed the rest of the gross critters from the platter and rammed them uno-by-uno up the bastard's crowded, ransacked rectum. The swordfish refused to go any deeper than its gills, but still I reered up, imagining the rest of the petty sea-beasties now impaled on its snout like a cateva shish kebab.

For the next minuta or duey I vadared the broken omi blankly, until my own whimpering kishkas efinked the silence.

'Well now, you're a greedy houseguest, aren't thee?' I grumbled. 'What are myself and my Sisters supposed to jarry now you've gobbled up all our fresh sea-munja?'

'I ... I ...' Sturgeon's lavs came out in just wisps now.

'MERDRE!' I screeched with a fully upturned oyster. 'We've provided a bona feast for you – it's only courteous you should provide a tasty meal for us. What have you to give, squire?'

'I ...'

'This is most unbecoming of you, you swine! Well, fear not, I'm sure we can find something at least a pogi bit palatable about your person.' I vadared my dollies. 'Darlings, bring me a suitable instrument for stripping riah from carnish, s'il vous plaît. Who here is for homemade pâté and cornichons?'

'Yé!' my dolls squeaked. 'Yé-yé! Yé-yé!'

'I simply adore froggy cuisine,' I purred wistfully, before lunging at him with the butcher's efink. While my Sisters held his screeching tet still, I grasped Sturgeon's greasy riah in one lapper, and scalped the bugger. I admit my coiffeuring skills are not maxi up to dick, but, painstakingly hacking and sawing away at the bastard's tet, I managed to remove a wide thatch

* ??!

of arctic-white quiff intact from his riahline down to his nape. I flopped the bloody wiglet aside, then ogled the twonk blinking up at me with soggy horror-opals, his raw pate glistening like the surface of Mars or some gross mutant rosebud.

'Clear enough your brains are defective squire, but they may make bona eating yet,' I polled, bringing the hammer down on his skull. Quite possibly Sturgeon was out cold after the first schonk but there were a pogi few indecorous grumblings and gurglings while I continued pummelling the cunt, chiselling my way into his dense caroon.

Once the bat's brains were safely liberated from their manky hideyhole and chop-choppered into manageable morsos, nix more ludicrous amnesiac palaverings spouted forth from the barky's gaping oyster. In an ideal mond I believe all fash bats' servos should be removed and turned into harmless fromage-de-tête before the tinkers reach voting age – and yet, after nibbling a bijou tidbit, I savvied (perhaps not surprisingly) the Fascist Brain is not the mostest flavoursome of organs. I realised – with some dismay and some delight – I would have to rummage around his bod for something more appetising, more piquant to add to the pot.

While my dollies fired up a grand saucepan of froggy butter, I snip-snipped my way into Sturgeon's lower palliass, sharpering for his liver and kidneys. When finally I extracted the gruesome cheets with efink and tongs – after fishing fruitlessly for daitcha minutas through the batatat's cascading blutwurst intestines – I clocked they were in somewhat coddy condition: tough as hardbacks and mottled with scars and grey-green blotches, nix doubt alcool-related. Still, the lavvylong marination might well give them a bona punch, I ponced.

Once the butter was gaily chirruping and foaming, we added to the pot: Sturgeon's servo, liver and kidneys, oignon, garlic, doppel-cream, beaten eggs, thyme, blank pepper, plenty of salt. As the mixture cooked, twas my followers' noble task to retrieve rogue shards of skull and skim the scum from the blub-blubbing surface. Quatra or daitcha minutas later, I chucked the cooked carnish into a nova saucepan, and deglazed the first with brandy and absinthe. Once mixered with this daffy reduction, I vigorously schonked and whisked everything to a pungent grey gloop. To ensure maxi smoothness, I demanded my dollies wriggle from their stockings, to sieve the gunge through the sheer denier.

Et voilà.

Finally: disinfect floor and worktops, dhobi stockings. Squirt pâté into petite ramekins, cover with clarified butter, refrigerate – and enjoy.

My dollies' eeks were translucent with hunger by the time I served up the muck with crusty bâtards and cornichons. Though we gobbled clean trey ramekins, it was ultimately agreed the Chief's carnish did not make for a bona pâté. The aniseed HUMPF! from the absinthe and the charming creaminess from the stockings could nantwar detract from the fact that we had just ingested a fungal tramp's meese diseased innerbits.

'What should we do with the last portion, your Lordship?' Séverine asked foggily, poking a limp lupper at the lonesome ramekin. 'Plop it outways for the dogs?'

'NEIN!' I belched. 'We don't want to attract more vermin thisaways. Allez – summon me up some postal packaging pronto: a bijou boxlet and brown papier. I have a better idea ...'

After a rapid toddle downways to Hampstead High Street, my Sisters returned with some suitable gift-wrap. While Sturgeon's stiff bod drip-dripped sang and the odd sea-beastie into the red-black oil slick betwixt his lallies, I carefully bow-tied the solo ramekin with a dolly ribbon, and screeved on the box in spidery lavs: DE-LUXE PÂTÉ-DU-JOUR™ – GROSSES BISOUS! Then, after doppel-wrapping with brown bimph, I scrawled: THE GLASS EYE PRESS LTD, 28 NEWMAN STREET, LONDON W1T 3ER.*

Carrying this meese cadeau to the Post Office the following juno, I cackled jibberingly into my grand mandarin collar, imagining the sycophantic twonks at the Glassy Opal tucking into my

---

* O God. No. No no no no no (see footnotes to 'Offensive Tet') ...

homemade munja with relish. 'Wizard tuck!' et ceterara. 'We simply adore your novel!' Hé-hé-hé! And yet, ajax to my amusements, I was unable to shift a cateva nagging gloom in the pit of my kishkas. The gloom was not entirely down to the afterquease of that ghastly pâté – rather, it grossly aggravated me that Sturgeon had not remembered me. Even as I was indiscreetly ramraiding his anus with an enormous lobster, spouting lavs from my ultra-lucid memoirs, the fash bat still could not bring himself to recall the feeli rating he had revelled in tormenting for months aboard the cod ship SS UNMENTIONABLE.

Was my personality not forceful enough to make even a pogi impression on the arroganki zot? Had I played a mere forgettable* bit-part in the history of that grand meshigena shipping

---

* The origin of the name of our favourite café in Tangier, L'Oubliette, comes from the verb 'oublier': to forget. By the beginning of October Davy and Merritt met up rarely after dark, but we still kept up our daily routine of sipping tea and gobbling omelettes at 4 p.m. at the eaterie on the Rue Siaghin.

Apparently in the 1920s the café was a poky unhygienic dungeon, but today L'Oubliette is anything but: the white marble interior decked out with erect orchids, statues of headless Roman gods, and Rif-fresh air conditioning; the exterior an appetising crush of chequerboard tables, loose-lipped expats and impossibly young waiters shuffling under a canopy of rippling red chevrons.

Perhaps one day, when Merritt is recognised as the true hero of this grotesque yarn, youths will make pilgrimages to the Café Oubliette, to sit in our usual spot by the decapitated boy-god Mercury and enjoy whiskey berber, kif and omelettes aux jambon, just as we did.

Depending on our nerves (or the weather, or our love lives)', some days Davy's pessimism would rub off on Merritt and the two of us would deliberate why we still risked being turned to pâté-du-jour in this strange, claustrophobic city. Other days Stanley's gung-ho bloodlust made Davy wish he could get his hands on Novak before his boss, so he could do the throttling and maiming himself …

Months had slithered by and yet still there was no breakthrough, no foul scent to follow, no sighting of the Scum King or his Yé-Yé Dolls. In the beginning Merritt used to appreciate these daily tête-à-têtes with Davy, swapping hunches and Blank City anecdotes at L'Oubliette – but the dandy's nonsensical prattle just irritated him now. Stanley had little interest in the women of Tangier, but it seemed lately all Davy was capable of talking about was the females of the labyrinth – the faceless debutantes, the faceless chambermaids, the faceless Moslems …

'See, your instinct is to think these religious birds are all surly and haggard under their veils,' Davy jabbered between slurps of tea, 'but I bet the more extreme the veil, the more beautiful the bird is underneath. Their husbands – or their fathers, brothers, whichever – they're only too aware other blokes would hassle their stunning wives or daughters, so they demand they get covered up head to toe. Not a sliver of flesh on show. It's oppressive, man. But it's also bloody tantalising! They're inviting your imagination to splurt the girl of your dreams under those black sheets …'

Not entirely convinced, Stanley nevertheless found himself drawn to the scarved women as they wandered up and down the cockeyed alley. Just as Novak noted in 'Dishonourable Discharge', very few locals joshed themselves in the traditional dress of dishdashas and fezzes, but, for the most part, Moroccan women kept their heads and chests covered, adhering to codes of modesty that seemed utterly alien to us as we recharged ourselves after yet another night of hallucinatory debauching.

Stanley took a long, gulping toke of kif, watching the stream of inscrutable disembodied faces float by. Occasionally Merritt felt we should try to befriend some of these natives rather than just prattling inanities to overly polite waiters and coy catamites, in the hope that some insider information might lead us to Novak – but, then again, the Arabs all seemed largely oblivious (if not downright hostile) to the brash, grubby world of us expats. The Moroccans probably preferred to pretend we didn't exist – and likewise it was more convenient for us to imagine this was just a blank harmonious nationless playground and not a disaster zone we were all making much worse with our presence.

Tapping his pipe out over his half-finished omelette, Stanley watched a young woman in a white headscarf struggling to exit the nearby Poste Maroc with a large white pram.

'This one almost looks Western,' he commented, gesturing into the crowd.

As the mother drew closer to L'Oubliette, her eyes gazed just past us for a moment, as if locked on the headless stump of Mercury. Merritt's heart thundered like a kettledrum. Considering how stoned we both were, Davy was alarmed at how fast his boss leapt out of his chair. Merritt launched himself across the café terrace, only to find his route to the street blocked by numerous overflowing plant pots, stacked stools and impassive expats. After scrambling over a monstrous cactus bursting with neon flowers, his left foot snagged on two crossed chair legs, bringing him floundering into the path of one of the young waiters.

'L'addition, monsieur?' the boy asked, squinting with dark shark-like opals.

'No … non, non …' Merritt snapped, staring off down the street, but by now the phantom was long gone.

Sheepishly Stanley clambered back to our table, where Davy was still seated, knife and fork frozen between his fingers.

'What was it?' he asked. 'It wasn't … not the man himself?'

'No, no. You didn't see her?' Merritt flopped exhausted back into his chair.

'No. Who? What was it?'

'That Western woman in the white headscarf.' Stanley's hands trembled as he grasped the chair arms like the safety rail of a rollercoaster or ghost train. 'I swear – she looked just like Audrey Hulme.'

line? Jupiter forbid: had I been drifting invisibly through life all this time like a daffy fantom?

BOF, I ponced. I would not be doomed to obscurity, Ô comrades. As I waited restless in the queue at the Post Bureau, squashed ajax to all manner of bland coddily clobbered civvies, I indulged myself in a delicious vision: the parcel suddenly exploding in my lappers, flooding the bodega with humanoid pâté, the hapless civvies all floundering, submerged up to their opals in this meese rising tide of puréed entrails, screechering my nom, howling for mercy, drowning, drowning – while I floated debonairly atop the gory aqua, riding a gigantic neon-green inflatable cornichon, joshed in a robe and caroon, foil trident pricked upways to the sparkles!

Bobbing merrily along the putrid pink waves, I clocked the flip-flopping ticktocker behind the counter. TUES 3 MAR, it squeaked.

ONLY QUATRA MONTHS TO GO UNTIL DOOM-JUNO, IMPATIENT BLOODTHIRSTY READERS ...

ONLY QUATRA PETTY FULL MOONS UNTIL MY GILDI UNFORGETTABLE FORCED ENTRY INTO THE GLITTERING SANG-DRIPPING ANNALS OF HISTORY!

The Eagle Has Crashlanded*

NOVAK WEARS A HANDLEBAR MOUSER, ARCTIC-WHITE WIGLET, GRUBBY TROPICAL TUX, PEAKED CAPELLA WITH SPREADEAGLE TRINKET.

NELLY DANI'S 'SANS ASTÉRISQUE'.

In my quest for immortality, I would like a nova term entered into the rosbif dictionary:

---

* Chapter received Tuesday, 27th October 1970. When Merritt collected this latest sliver of airmail from the concierge at the Continental, it crossed his mind he'd probably witnessed Audrey posting the damn thing on the Rue Siaghin almost a month before. In the time it took for the letter to rebound from London back to Tangier, Merritt and Davy had vacillated between all sorts of explanations for Miss Hulme's sudden reappearance, none of which were particularly convincing, or comforting.

Discounting the frankly unfeasible possibility that she was here purely by chance (and had converted to Islam?), the version that appealed to us most was this: Audrey was indeed 'Melody Autruche', kidnapped by Novak in 1969 to ghostwrite his memoirs. After the massacre in July, Novak had forced her to join him and his followers in Tangier, to finish the manuscript. Audrey – Heaven help her – had meanwhile won the bastard's trust to the extent that she was no longer held prisoner, her lallies no longer shackled to the table-lallies. She was deemed reliable enough to post the remaining chapters to London unescorted – but was this dependability down to her being brainwashed, or was it a cunning ruse, a false display to eventually help engineer her escape? Could Audrey assist us in bringing the Emperor to a grisly end – or was she still on his side, a devout devotee, dedicated to spreading his evil lavs hither-thither and, most worryingly of all, perfectly blasé in the aftermath of all that spilled blood?

Whichever way we looked at it, so many factors refused to add up. Most glaringly, as Trefoil pointed out just prior to the massacre (see footnotes to 'Plume'), Audrey was still working for us in April 1970, almost a year on from Novak's alleged kidnapping of Ms Autruche from Hypnogogo. Was Audrey therefore not a hostage but a willing collaborator, moonlighting for Novak while still answering the mountain of complaints at 28 Newman Street in the daytime? Had she been aware our office was to be the target of Novak's fantabulosa crime from the very start, or did the bastard enlighten her only days before the attack, when he dictated 'Novak's Hit Parade' to her? What was she doing now, wandering the streets of Tangier unaccompanied in a white veil? Was she on the run from the Scum King? Or was she bait to lure us to him?

'You know what would make this all a lot simpler?' Davy remarked, spooning another sugarcube into his tea.

'Dropping the H-bomb on this stinking city, taking us and him with it?' Merritt was barely blinking behind his dark glasses.

'Well, the version I like best is: you were mistaken. It wasn't Audrey at all. You need an eye-test. Novak's still out there, but Audrey's far far away. Safely home in the old Industrial Provinces.'

'Bah.' Merritt rubbed away some cottonmouth and took another deep toke of kif. 'I know what I saw.'

Just like every other afternoon since the sighting, we were staked out at a bar further down from L'Oubliette: Cabaret Vertigo, a miserable little nicotine-stained rat-trap whose only redeeming feature was its location almost directly opposite the yellow door of the Poste Maroc.

At times, bolstered by drink, we felt suave in our fedoras and sunglasses, but mostly we just felt like bogus private eyes, very public dicks, like we were the leading actors in some godawful film noir, some incomprehensible French-Moroccan arthouse flicker with no plot, no beginning, no end …

Time and time again we pondered: had Audrey spotted us sitting by the headless Mercury before she dissolved into the crowd? Merritt was convinced their eyes didn't meet – but even so, there was no guarantee she would visit this post office again anyhow. In fact, once we'd read this latest chapter (which we promise we'll allow you to do too, soon), it troubled us that Novak's novel could feasibly be considered finished now and, if this were the case, there might be no need for Audrey to set foot in a Poste Maroc – or walk these streets – again. For all intents and purposes, she – and the Scum King – could disappear into the shadows for good, their odious work done.

Still, we waited. Through the grim blustery autumn we waited, hopelessly addicted to these last few loose threads like leeches hanging from the chest of a dilapidated tailor's dummy. While most expats treated their teabreaks as a serene respite from the city's chaos, we treated ours as a mission of grave importance and supreme endurance: the earlier we could get seated at the Cabaret Vertigo

THE SCREECHING NOVAKS, pl.n. the feeling of maxi rage, pain and dehumanising humiliation whenever the powers that be stifle even just a pogi bit your grandiose free beautiful lavvy.

Dearest comrades, the momento is nigh. Lell my lapper. Join me as we dance beyond the pain barrier ...

Ever fearful of premature mortification or seizure by sharpering-pops, in those final quatra months before Our Chosen Juno myself and my dollies continued to lay lowly, scuttling outways only to shush more bin-munja and penetrate the swollen post-box on Willow Road with my electrifying weekly communiqués. ISOLATION and INSULATION were the key once more. And yet:

(sometimes Merritt would be here before the place opened at 7 a.m.) and the later we could leave (shutters went down at 11 p.m.) became an obsession, a Herculean test of our stamina, our sanity, our spines. We mastered the art of making a pot of tea or teenth of kif last for hours, taking it in turns to keep lookout while the other read, or snoozed, or retired to the bathroom to piss or scream silently at our own reflections.

Finally – after what we estimated was more than 200 hours of fruitless surveillance – we saw the phantom again. We had been paying particular attention to every white-clad woman who entered our field of vision, and yet this time Audrey appeared all in black: black headscarf, black robe, black pram.

'Achtung,' Merritt whispered, nudging Davy awake.

Our bloodshot eyes bulged behind our dark glasses.

'Let's grab her while she's in the queue,' Davy hissed as we watched her enter the post office. 'While she's trapped in there.'

'No, no – let's not startle her just yet. Not in front of the locals.' Merritt unfurled a couple of 100-dirham notes from his wallet and slid them under his saucer. 'She could be in a fragile state.'

'*I'm* in a fragile state,' Davy grumbled, but nevertheless we remained seated until the black phantom re-emerged from the yellow doorway, again struggling to manoeuvre her pram down the tiled steps.

Davy and Merritt's table allowed immediate access to the Rue Siaghin between a pair of potted oriental poppies – however, we let Audrey gain a good forty-yard advantage before we rose and made after her. Our hearts were clanging in our ears as we padded down the street, though we tried to look casual, matching her slow, ungainly shuffle as she pushed the black pram onwards through the centre of the labyrinth ...

I could not resist mincing back to W1 for uno or duey bijou bonus agitations before the grand finale ...

After bubbling up the rest of Sturgeon's bod in a vast vat of fash-bat-bourguignon, I took his decomposing tet on the Nordic Line in my battered valise, to let him ogle the bright lights of Londres one last time. Earlier that week I had endured the dubious pleasure of attending a Glass Eye liver-launch: a servo-numbing soirée celebrating one of their molto unforgivable expulsions entitled THE NUREMBERG NYMPHOS. Joshed-up as a fungal rat-de-bibliothèque, after schlumphing a guzzle-load of lukewarm mogue champagne, I nellied the bastards on the staff palavering about a mysterious tome they had in their possession: an apparently dangerous liver concerning a debonair froggy-cockney reprobate that naturellement could only be MOI MOI MOI. I shuffled closer to nellyarda – however, it seemed the daffy bats barely had a bona lav to screech about the cheet. So much for the fickle fiends simply adoring my novel! The impression I gleaned, loitering almost within reefing-distance of the doomed cretins,* was they doubted the authenticity of my gildi stories! They doubted my criminal credentials! They doubted the liver would sell!

And so, savvying the philistines had just recently ogled my scribblings concerning Sturgeon and the cod ship SS UNMENTIONABLE, I ponced not without a pogi bit of amusement: what better way to illustrate my credibility, my cruelty, my creativity, than to impale the fash barky's rotten tet upon a railing just chinka-daitcha yards from the bookish bastards' very own front portal?!

De-luxe pâté-du-jour, a decomposing tet, my genius screeve: was there nix end to my gifts to this pathetic petty publishing house?

BOF.

My grossest gift was still to come.

---

* We do not recall a fungal rat loitering within reefing-distance, but as we and now Novak have made perfectly clear, we were all exceedingly drunk that night.

On the noche before Doom-Juno, myself and my dollies were in a rattly mood – not ultra nervy but certainly prone to skitterish outbursts as we pondered each step of our grand emags to come. To calm our wobblings we passed a botty of radioactive-green absinthe back and forth, sitting cross-lallied ajax to our deadly vacayas: the chinka duey-gallon sunfleur-oil drums packed with explosives, the shotgun, the caboosh-rental clefs, the disguises, the periscope, the ammunition-perambulator,* the synchronised ticktockers. To pass the time I suggested we might indulge in uno final Romanesque orgy – a sloppy climactic celebration of comradeship, arva, munja, liberty, love, buggery and the Lavvy Everlasting – but perhaps my choice of lavs was not altogether natty.

'So you believe this is our final noche together, your Lordship?' Veronica asked, grimly glugging another grumblerful of absinthe. 'You mean to say you don't expect we'll still be alive this time tomorrow?'

'Nanti that!' I cried. 'Who savvies for certain what will happen tomorrow? All we need to worry ourselves with is this: if the bombas detonate, if enough sang is spilled, we will have our fame either way ...'

---

* As we followed Audrey through the Medina, it dawned on us the pram she was pushing could well be the same contraption Novak had with him on the day of the massacre. Were there explosives hidden under that shadowy canopy? Merritt's sawn-off shotgun? Edging closer while Audrey waited for a convoy of belching motorcycles to pass, Stanley glimpsed the wispy head of a baby wrapped snug under its blankets, and his anxiety lifted slightly. Clear enough the Walking Contraceptive couldn't have impregnated Audrey – had she therefore been knocked up by some beautiful interruptering Arab and been ousted from the group like the other 'treacherous mares' (see 'Dandelion Fluff')?

Clinging to the scanty hope that she was now a dissenter/deserter and not a devotee of the Guru, Merritt called out to her as she reached a crooked door on the Rue Tétouan, rummaging for her keys in a small black leather purse.

'Audrey. Audrey!' he shouted, as affectionately as he could muster. 'Audrey, dear!'

The phantom gave us a look that was half sugar, half cyanide. Her eyes widened in what at first appeared to be horror, before her lips gently pricked, and she said with relief, or just exhaustion: 'You're alive.'

'Yes, but ...' Séverine took the botty. I regretted opening the cheet now – the dolls were becoming unreasonably oystery. She took a lento sip-sip and blurted: 'Remind us of the contingency emag again. Remind us what the plan is if we all happen to survive ...'

'MERZ!' I shrieked, slapping the botty out of her lapper. 'What's all this palavering about fairy self-preservation all of a sudden?! Tomorrow we will be immortals, dead or alive! Do you truly think I wish to be ferricadoozled by the pigs? Do you truly think I want to die spreadeagled in my own juices betwixt some authority-flop's jackbooted lallies?!'

'No, your Lordship, but we'd be molto appreciative if you'd at least screech clearly what the plan is if we all make it out alive.'

'Well ...' As I opened my levers I felt an unexpected rush of gloopy drunkenness. The lavs spilled out like cateva bunny-rabbits: 'Well, we've all got our synchronised ticktockers, have we not? If we're still free pops after this hellish carnage – this noble heroic hellish carnage, I might add – meet me at Dover at high noon. I shall be in disguise but keep an opal out for my battered valise. Ahem. Hooey! From there we vagary to Calais, to Spain, to Gibraltar. Europa Point.' My dollies blink-blinked dozily in the hazy munge. 'I have connections on the Rock – and not just the apes. Top-brass connections. Toppermost seadogs. Astro-omis. The natty old Gibraltans will look after us from there, I promise you that.'

Bruce flared his nose-thirls. 'What if you die but we survive?'

I ogled him stony. 'Would life be worth lavvying without me?'

My dollies swapped poked-up glances.

'MERDRE!' I screamed. 'WE are in this TOGETHER, are we not?!'

'Naturellement,' Veronica polled. 'We disagreed not a jot, sire – but should we not take down the particulars of these toppermost contacts you have on the Continent? Should we not be parkered a bona lapperful of dinarli, to see us right should the worstest happen?'

'Are we expected to hitch-hike to Dover?' Bonnie chipped in.

'My passport's gone astray,' Bruce lamented.

'Mine too,' polled Rosa Winkel.

'This is unbearable!' I howled. Possessed by the Green Fury, I launched myself across the chamber and pronto doppel-padlocked the shutter and back portal. I unbuttoned my camisha, pressed the bunch of clefs to my boomboomer and Sellotaped them firm to my thumpery chest.

'ACHTUNG!' I shrieked, ripping up a manky pallet with my naggy lappers and hammering the morsos SHTUCK! SHEBAM! SHRACK! across the petty fenêtre ajax. 'Nellyarda, my chovis: if you give me ANY REASON WHATSOEVER to doubt your ultra dedication to our fantabulosa cause, I will creep-creep out of my bedclobber in the middle of the noche and detonate the fuckering bombas right here, right where we sleep! Alles klar, ja? Do I make myself clear?'

As the final plank went up, my dollies' eeks vanished in the ultraschvartz, but their voches – squeaky now, drained of all drunken arrogank – tinkled through the munge: 'Yes, your Lordship. Of course, your Lordship.'

'Trust me: the eagles will not prevail,' I spittled. 'Destiny, bravery and our bona Lady Fortune will see us through! This time tomorrow we shall still be alive – Ô, more alive than ever! – safely, gaily en route to our gloriosa nova home, somewhere just a pogi tin-can's-throw from the sun-kissed nipplet of Gibraltar. Hé-hé-hé-hé-hé-HÉ!'

Another pogi rib-tickling anecdote in the lead-up to our fantastic destiny:

When I hired the duey Rolls-Royces on Saturday the 11th – joshed-up as a toff in tweed and plus-fours, with Bruce alongside in chauffeur's clobber – my dear Brucey did not savvy the passport I used to secure the cabooshes (under a nova alias: the debonair Keith Caesar) was his very own identity-liver doctored by yours truly.

The prune at the desk probed us only a petty bit before handing over the clefs. 'What's the occasion, sir?' he asked before we minnied back into the peach-fuzz Sloane morning. 'A wedding?'

'No, no, a funeral,' I barked impulsively, and almost tittered when I clocked the implication. 'A very grandiose funeral.'

'O, I'm very sorry to hear that, sir.'

'No, don't be. I admit by now I'm rather untroubled when it comes to death. We'll be striving to make this occasion more of a celebration than some stiff sombre doom-juno. Ahem. And so on and so forth. Adieu!'

When finally – at long last! – M 13 JULY 1970 arrived, myself and my followers awoke before dawn in relatively tranquil spirits, jarrying a petit déjeuner of glimmering crêpes in battle-focused silence.

Before wriggling into their matching brown beehive shykas, my dollies looked like a bijou army of Joans-of-Arc: their tets freshly fatchared, their eeks like polished concrete, opals shimmering with bold angelic parnyaqua. I'd shaved the zots to help blankwash their identities should some loose-levered civvy clock them planting the bombas and, vadaring them now in the munge of our medieval-cell-like lock-up, twas almost tempting to send them out thataways au naturelle, full-baldy. Joan was a fantabulosa role model for my Exterminating Angels – a cross-dressing palone-omi, a bona heretic in sparkly armour, maxi dedicated to a higher being, hellbent on ferricadoozing the anglos, and with an exquisitely high tolerance for pain and suffering – but when I mentioned the similarity to my devotees, the dolls just smiled thinly and tugged on their pouffed-up beehives regardless ...

As we struggled to cram ourselves and our cumbersome weapons into the duey Silver Shadows, I savvied hiring a VW campervan would've been a molto simpler and cheaper option – but of course it would not have lent the vital aero of pomp and luxury to this mostest sensational heinous occasion. We were so tightly packed in the cabooshes (duey-gallon bombas on laps, shotgun clenched betwixt my inner thews), we risked premature mortification every time we turned a sharp corner, and yet at the same time we felt protected, full-aware we were far less likely to be pulled over in toff convoy than if we were belching along in some meese chubby hippy-wagon. We were like deranged royalty, cackling and ogling dreamily through the silvery fenêtres as we cruised the early-morn strasses of our grand, beloved, doomed capital city ...

Chinka branches of Victor Value had been pluckered at random from ze YELLOW PAGES and, as I dropped each dolly and their explosive cargo at each stop – from Neasden in the nord-west to Nova-Cross south of the river – I felt squelchy electro-sparkles tingling the tips of my luppers, vadaring this drab snoozing metropolis would soon be transformed beyond all recognition. And so would we.

When at last my darling devotees were scattered across town, I carefully steered the caboosh back across Waterloo Bridge and dumped it in a shadowy snicket ajax to St Giles-in-the-Fields. Joshed-up in Sturgeon's naval cozzy (complete with original riah and beaky aquila-capella), I stashed my shotgun and periscope along with plentiful slugs and buckshot cartridges in the black perambulator,* pulled down the frilly canopy, then marched onwards – to my gildi destiny!

The levers of my ticktocker had already scritch-scratched past 8.45 a.m. by the time I reached Novak Strasse. The steely bell-end of the Post Office Colin looked fit to burst, sparkling blood-red in the morning sol. Twas gloriosa weather for a bona act of terrorism, I ponced, feeling the tropical tux clinging sticky to my tingly bod.

---

* 'May we come inside?' Merritt asked as we lingered on the cracked paving slabs outside 41 Rue Tétouan.

'What are you doing here?' Audrey demanded: a question we had struggled with a lot over the past three months – and the answers we gave now were new to us.

'The Hippy Trail,' Davy blurted.

'Fact-checking,' Merritt interjected. 'Adding some local colour to a story we're rewriting. What's your excuse, Audrey?'

She eyeballed Davy for a moment or two. 'Trying to escape, I suppose.'

There was something unsettling about Audrey's mannerisms – her cold, fish-like eyes, twitching lips, fingers repeatedly opening and closing like talons – that made us think she must've suffered some severe trauma or breakdown since we last saw her, although, as Merritt recalled, there were already signs of her instability in the final weeks of her tenure at the Glass Eye Press. He remembered her 'acting strangely … turning up to work late, chuntering sinister gibberish, her mind elsewhere' (see footnotes to 'The Antichristines') after discovering Sturgeon's decapitated head on the railings at Newman Street and, as he scrutinised her now in the brash flashbulb sunlight, he wondered if she'd escaped to Morocco simply to release herself from that solitary, chance moment of horror.

'We've been worried about you,' Stanley continued, treading gently. 'You vanished without a goodbye. We were nervous you'd done something … foolish.'

'No. Only this.' She tapped the canopy of the black perambulator.

It occurred to Merritt she must've been pregnant while still working for us, which begged the question: 'Do we know the father?'

'Yes,' she murmured. 'We do.'

Just then a gutter-child in sports attire sidled up to our group, flapping his eyelashes at Stanley and cooing: 'Monsieur Astérisque, bonjour, Monsieur Astérisque …'

Merritt's blood curdled. He glared at his penny loafers, pretending not to recognise the beautiful urchin who was now tugging coquettishly at his linen pantaloons.

Brazenly or brainlessly, Merritt had begun using the alias 'Monsieur Astérisque' during his visits to the bordellos. If Audrey was unsettled by her former boss's apparent popularity among the teens of Tangier, her face registered not a trace of emotion as she snapped a few French slurs at the catamite, who promptly fled, his bottom lip puckered.

'Pests,' Merritt grumbled halfheartedly, rubbing the back of his neck. 'Look, there's no privacy on the street. Who lives here with you, Audrey? May we come in for just a minute? Or can we take you out for luncheon?'

'Baby's sleeping,' Audrey monotoned. 'I should be sleeping too.'

'Well then, we'll wait out here for you.' Stanley gestured at the bar across the street. 'We've got stamina, believe me.'

Audrey let out a long breath. 'You're going to shadow me until I give in, aren't you?'

'I'm afraid so.'

Audrey waved us inside with a limp hand, wheeling the pram backwards down a dark, soapy-scented corridor to a grey door marked VI. As she undid the lock, she said over her shoulder: 'I can't promise good conversation. I've barely spoken English for weeks. Cut all my ties. It's just been me and the baby.'

There was certainly something robotic about Audrey's way of speaking now, but once Merritt and Davy saw inside the small apartment, we were comforted by how ordinary it all seemed. Audrey may well have been suffering some form of mental instability – but she still managed to keep a good house. It was as if she'd transplanted Middle English suburbia to this ramshackle rihad: heavy floral curtains kept the front room in shade, the adjoining kitchenette was all bleached Bakelite and bone china, a small embroidery hung above the Dansette with the unexpected message: 'JOY TO THE WORLD!'

Most comforting of all, there was no trace of the Scum King's presence: no pepper-spray, no pastis, no sewing-vacayas, no lally-shackles, no planks across the fenêtres. If indeed there had been a connection between Miss Hulme and Monsieur Novak, we felt hopeful the relationship had by now been roundly terminated.

'O, isn't chance such a wondrous hazardous substance, Audrey!' Merritt hooted brightly while he continued scanning the room for irregularities. 'So, what have you been doing here all this time?'

'It's just been me and the baby,' she repeated. 'London was getting … too heavy.'

'But why Tangier?' Merritt fumbled with something inside his jacket, then let his hands hang limp by his sides. 'You might not be aware of this, but we believe Novak is at large in this very city …'

'I thought he'd killed you all.' Her expression was like wallpaper paste. 'It's strange seeing you here now.'

Was she bluffing? Had she not in fact just handed over a despicably thorough blow-by-blow account of the Newman Street massacre to a postal clerk in the Rue Siaghin? Or was it something entirely innocuous: a postcard to her parents, a visa renewal?

'You haven't been reading the reports in the papers?' Merritt raised a thick eyebrow. 'You didn't realise we survived?'

'I've just been trying to block everything out from back home,' Audrey said, pulling the pram into the kitchenette, 'and start afresh, I suppose.'

Merritt scratched his lower lip. 'Well then, I can imagine us turning up here out of the blue doesn't help matters much. We're sorry to thrust the old world on you again so suddenly …'

Audrey gave us a crooked smile. 'It's OK.'

'How old's the baby?' Davy barked, struggling to keep his composure in the slimy heat of the apartment.

'A couple of months.'

'So born in the Interzone?' Merritt assumed. 'What are the hospitals like in this queer city? Sanitary?'

'It was Royal London Hospital actually. We're still relatively new in town. Four weeks.'

Merritt and Davy shared an awkward glance. As Audrey filled up the kettle next door, Davy called out to her: 'We've been here three months nearly. We're practically part of the street furniture. We could recommend some cafés …'

'That might be nice,' Audrey monotoned.

As the kettle began to squeal on the stove, Davy caught his colleague's eye again and nodded towards the door. He mouthed: 'We should leave.'

Merritt held up a finger, shaking his head. Discreetly he pointed down at a battered green valise stowed between Audrey's books and LPs. Davy's brow furrowed. He whispered: 'Novak's money?'

Stanley shook his head again. 'Her typewriter.' Carefully he slid the case off the shelf and unclipped the clasps. 'Keep her talking.'

While Davy woodenly jabbered the names of drab bars and cafés at Audrey next door, Merritt fed a scrap of paper into the machine and played a swift crunching melody on the keys: VLOP-CLIP! CRAP! HUMPF! VLOP-SHLACK! CRACK! SMACK! CRAP! CLIP! SHEBAM! VLOP-SHLACK!

Audrey and Davy reappeared with the silver tea set just as Merritt was unwinding the printed scrap from the roller. His face was the colour of gunmetal. He held the sheet out so they could read it. 'We know who you are, Melody,' he said coldly. 'You've been here longer than you say, haven't you?'

The sheet read:

O Jupiter!

'I don't understand,' Audrey croaked. Davy's face too was crumpled with confusion.

'The "i".' Merritt flapped the paper. 'Your typewriter's got the same fault as Novak's. Regard the petty morso missing from the dot of the "i".'

Audrey's face remained blank, like the Sphinx in a bedraggled brown beehive. She deposited the jittering tea set on the dining table, then swayed awkwardly on the spot, saying nothing.

'We're here to help you, Audrey – if you'll help us,' Merritt said, still treading carefully – though he regretted not cooking up his own vial of pepper-spray now. 'We know who you are. We cracked the code: THE NAME IS AN ANAGRAM. MELODY AUTRUCHE. AUDREY HULME. Are you still ghostwriting the bastard's memoirs? Where is he, Audrey? We'll take care of him now …'

Audrey let out a slight snort. 'He's not here.'

'Where is he? You don't have to cover for him any more. Where's he been keeping you? Where is he now?'

'He's not here,' she repeated. 'He's not anywhere.'

'He's dead?'

Ignoring the question, Audrey held Davy's gaze and she snarled: 'Why did you all disregard the other anagram? RAYMOND NOVAK. MARK 'DAVY' NOON. Why isn't this bastard locked up? Why isn't *he* dead?'

As she glared venomously at our Art & Design man, Merritt recalled the tang of burning he'd experienced in his kitchen at Whitfield Street in the early days of

July (see footnotes to 'The Banality of Evil'). Momentarily he saw eagle feathers moulting from Davy's polka-dot cuffs, his nose sharpening to a serrated beak ...

'This is the pig you should've disposed of by now,' Audrey went on. 'He's the masked man, he's the serial rapist. He assaulted me and Emily and however many others at Hypnogogo ...'

'No ...' Davy protested weakly. 'No, no ...'

'He drugs young girls at the nightclub. Drags them out dressed as a policeman. Rapes them – then discards them.'

'This is ... no ... this is ridiculous,' Davy warbled, his face reddening.

Audrey flapped a hand back towards the kitchenette. 'It's your baby, Davy. I considered abortion – but then I didn't want to suffer like Emily, I didn't want to risk never being able to conceive with someone who'd actually care about me one day ...'

'We slept together,' Davy murmured. 'We had sex – it wasn't ... rape.'

'You think I wasn't conscious. You think I'm still dreaming.' Chillingly Audrey's mask-like maquiage cracked as her mouth widened to a clownish grin. 'You drugged me, I blacked out, but you don't realise I was in and out of consciousness while you did what you did. I pretended I was asleep – with my eyes wide open! I saw the mask slip. It was you, it was you ... the goggles, the wig, your black famblers across my mouth ...'

'You're deranged!' Davy snapped. 'It didn't happen that way. It's not me! Stanley – you know it's not me. I'm innocent ... she's delusional ...'

All at sea, Merritt wasn't sure whether to restrain Audrey or his Art & Design man, or just escape back into the relative calm of the chaotic street outside. He ventured cagily: 'But where does Novak come into all this?'

Audrey huffed a gust of air through her nose. 'He doesn't exist. He's a figment of my – *our* – imagination.'

'No...' Merritt's features trembled now. 'No, he does exist! I saw him. I watched the bastard gun down our colleagues, our friends ...'

'Regard-ça, my chovis.' Audrey pulled open her wardrobe and fished out a frayed black polythene bag from what looked like a mound of old fancy dress costumes. She tore the bag open with her talons, and a grubby white tuxedo tumbled out. 'Et voilà,' she snapped. From the jacket's inside pocket she removed a tiny handlebar moustache, spat on the adhesive and stuck it above her top lip. 'Hé-hé-hé-hé!'

Horrified, Davy and Merritt could only stare and quiver now as the Bastard materialised before our eyes. We wanted to run, we wanted to tear her to pieces – but the shock rendered us useless.

'No ... God, no no no ...' Merritt croaked, tears now skidding down his cheeks. 'You ... O God, no. Why, Audrey? Why?'

'The same reason you're here now: revenge!' As Audrey ladled out her scatty logic, the moustache gradually unpeeled itself from her top lip and drifted to the ground. 'You humiliated me.' She pointed a crooked finger at Davy. 'It all started innocuously enough. We went on a couple of dates. I showed him some poetry I'd written and he just dismissed it as rubbish.'

'I said, "It's wrong"!' Davy intervened, before appealing to his Director. 'Stanley, this is ludicrous! Hell, I'm not to blame if she couldn't take the criticism ...'

'Nanti that!' Audrey howled. 'The criticism spurred me on! I wondered: how can I get back at him? Bearing in mind Davy couldn't resist badmouthing my work to a few of you at the office, well, I thought: maybe I could ridicule the bastard in a novel, a little hoax novel I'd send in, unsolicited. It was just meant to be a joke to start with, a caricature, a grotesque parody. The Novak character, he was meant to be an overblown, fairy version of Davy: pretentious, false, ridiculously attired, a terrible lover, hideously ugly under the camouflage. At first I wanted you to solve the anagram simply to turn everyone against him, to mock him, to question his behaviour, his sexuality, et ceterarara – because I know how precious he is about his rotten masculinity. At most I thought you might report him to the police – maybe he'd spend a night or two behind bars. I never intended there to be any bloodshed – but then this pig raped me. He raped me in December. The book was already under way. The police wouldn't listen. And you were all glassy-eyed – you thought it was just a lovers' tiff! And I watched as you started meddling with my writing, adding footnotes, changing things around – turning the book into something it was never meant to be. You were all violators, vultures, desperate for Novak to commit some horrific atrocity just so you could make some money from other people's pain and misery! So I thought: I'll get you all. I'll get you all, you bastards ...'

'You're out of your mind,' Davy blurted.

'Now now – let's, um ...' Merritt interrupted feebly, horribly aware there could be a shotgun or two-gallon drum of ANFO scereted somewhere within Audrey's reach. 'Let's not just hurl insults ... um ...'

'She's completely deranged. She's killed all these people just based on some outrageous fantasy!'

'I'm not dreaming,' she scowled, eyeballing us both now.

Desperately trying to steer the conversation away from some potentially fatal flashpoint, Merritt babbled: 'What I don't understand, Audrey, is: if the whole novel started out as a joke, a ploy just to ridicule our Art & Design man and exaggerate all his flaws ... well, all this time I couldn't help feeling it was *me* in Novak's crosshairs, that it was *my* life he was ridiculing: my time in the Navy, the sea-queens, Gibraltar, shock therapy, frogmen, my sexuality, my infertility, the abortions ...'

Offhandishly Audrey responded: 'It might've slipped in unconsciously.'

'No, but –'

'We're all in there somewhere,' she added. 'We all contributed. We're all culpable.'

'Nonsense,' Davy grunted, his fists clenched, knuckles like icebergs.

'But why set off the bombs, Audrey? Why target civilians in the supermarkets? It doesn't make any sense.' Merritt could barely see now, so clogged were his eyelids with tears. 'And what about Sturgeon? You don't mean to say you cut off his head yourself? Where does the Captain come into all this?'

'You triggered those bombs, Stanley. It's what you wanted, wasn't it? A heinous massacre. A bona dinarli-spinner ...'

'No, but –'

'Nellyarda: I was made to feel like nothing – like a naff mechanical vacaya, an object. Answering complaints all day – and yet no one was there to hear my complaints, let alone respond to them. And so this was my recompense! For una minuta there I felt truly alive. I felt like somebody. But now you can shush my caroon. You've got it all now, Stanley. You've got your unspeakable atrocity. You've unmasked the culprit. You can publish the novel now. You're the hero. Just let me vanish with my baby. We won't bother you any longer ...'

Merritt rubbed the back of his neck once more. 'You know as well as I do: I can only be vindicated, I can only be the hero of this story, if I get you locked up.'

'Well boo-hoo-hoo and fuck-off-thataways – you don't have my confession in writing,' Audrey scorned us. 'You can try all you want to replicate – and twist – what I've just babbled at you in your feeble footnotes, but it won't stand up in court! How are the legal-reps meant to separate fact from fiction when you've been meddling all this time with the threads of the story? All in all this might just seem like a grand twisted fantasy conjured up from your servo, Stanley, your stylo, your lav-hammer. Oui? Nein?'

'Au contraire,' Merritt retorted, removing a small black device from his inside pocket. 'I've had the dicktittlerphone running all this time.'

Audrey's face seemed to bloat like a poisonous mushroom. After a few moments of grisly silence, she mumbled: 'Bravo.' She glanced around the room as if looking for weapons or a hidden trapdoor, before admitting defeat: 'Well, in that case, let me retrieve my last rites, gentlemen. I've screeved one final chapter, to be bellowed aloud in the event of a dismal climax such as this cateva entrapment. Let your meshigena dicktittlerphone nelly this, if you'll excuse me uno momento to retrieve the miserable bimph ...'

As Audrey made for the door Merritt snapped: 'You're going nowhere. Tell me where it is – I'll fish it out.'

'It's in the bathroom. Nailed under the floorboards. You'll not find it.'

'I'll escort you then.'

Audrey's face was like rock again. 'Look, I'm exhausted. I don't want to run any more. But if you must know, I really need to change my serviette hygiénique, my sanitary pad ... then I'm yours. I'll tell all.' She wiped her nose with her sleeve. 'I'll be only a minute. I'm not going to escape. Not without my baby.'

In spite of all the disturbing disclosures and despair coming from the three of us, Audrey's baby was still sleeping soundly next door. Merritt mutely nodded his consent. Moving like a shadow, Audrey slithered through the flimsy lavatory door, and locked it behind her.

While the Dictaphone hungrily gobbled up the silence, Davy and Merritt glanced at each other like worn-out Marines.

'That poor child,' Merritt muttered, returning the device to his jacket.

'I know: the doomed bat,' Davy said. 'The bastard child of me and that murderer.'

Stanley looked alarmed. 'No, well, I mean: what'll happen to it now? The poor little soul'll be an orphan once Audrey's locked away.'

Davy flashed his boss a sickly smile. 'Well, I don't know – there's two parents, don't forget. Maybe I'll feel some connection to the kid. Maybe I could take care of it. I could be the hero of this story too, Stan.'

Merritt felt queasy as he watched his Art & Design man limp into the kitchenette, to introduce himself to the child. 'Hello there, sunshine,' Davy sing-songed, peering into the black perambulator. As he peeled back the child's covers, he let out a sound like a rusty bicycle and instantly recoiled, as if confronted by some hideous creature.

'What is it? What's wrong?' Merritt demanded, rushing in to see for himself.

'O fuck … O fucking Hell …' Davy spluttered, dry-heaving into the sink.

As Merritt leaned in, he saw the thing in the black pram was not human. Lying prostrate with lallies akimbo, the doll gazed back at Merritt with a dozy expression. It was a ventriloquist's dummy, joshed-up as a sharpering-omi, with dead opals, chattering fangs, googly spectacles, black periwig. The doll's splintered mouth flopped open, emitting a single soundless squawk.

Heart thundering, Merritt yanked open the kitchen drawers, scrabbling through all manner of strange debris (pornography, melted keys, tangled typewriter ribbons, sex-aids, snail tongs, leather restraints …) until he found a sharp knife – then he launched himself ape-like at the bathroom door, kicking it open after three or four attempts. Unwittingly he let out a piercing shriek as he entered the tiled cubicle, seeing five, six or seven assailants with knives awaiting him before realising it was just his own reflection, multiplied in the many hanging mirrors.

A soiled blank tuxedo lay crumpled in the centre of the floor. The tiny shuttered window swung gently open then closed, seemingly too small to fit an adult female – but this was her only escape route.

Merritt broke down, curling into a ball on the floor with the stinking tux between his legs. As he dropped, a series of buried images reignited in his mind: a brown package, a small sausage rolling out with five tiny fingers attached. POUSSIN AVEC EELS. And he realised – like waking from a terrible dream only to find oneself in an even more nightmarish reality – she must've aborted, and posted, the foetus herself.

Settling myself down in the munge of the Brutalist Futurist office block opposite, I upturned my capella on the paves, posing as a vonny vagrant while I waited jitteringly for the post-omi to appear. As I basked horizontal, twas exhilarating to vada the staff of the Doomed Glass Eye Press – a meese catfish-eeked omi in pinstripes, a pasty feeli donna in an apricot maxi-drogle – scuttling through the portal of Numero 28 uno by uno, nix doubt full-aware this juno was THE JUNO, but utterly oblivious to the specjalni part they would play in my fantabulosa climax!

'Can you spare a soldi, sir?' I polled as the supreme dicktittler himself, Stanley Merritt, marched past – though clear enough I was invisible to the scatty bat in my naff vagabond clobber.

BOF. My presence would be felt soon enough.

When finally the postal-omi materialised, minnying round the corner of Eastcastle Strasse at 9.49 a.m., I let out a pogi euphoric gulp. This – THIS! – was living, my cherries. My bod was positively jangling with electric as I vadared the omi flip-flop each and every letterbox in the lead-up to Numero 28. When at last he inserted his lapper in Our Chosen Slit, I let out another pogi orgasmic whimper, clocking the chartreuse-green envelope I'd pluckered especially for the occasion.

Grabbing my periscope from the perambulator, I remained rooted to the grubby paves as I ogled the solo fenêtre of the Glass Eye Press. Inside, the pasty donna was fanging her painted luppernails. A portly rhino-omi sat behind his desk, chuntering mono-lavs into his polari-pipe. The pop in pinstripes paced back and forth, struggling with his cuff-buttons. Ô, twas a dismal ogleful, a twisted mise-en-scène littered with the empty gestures of servo-numbing, time-shushing robo-travails – but fear not, dear reader: I would improve the vista pronto ...

Once the omi was satisfied with his camisha-cuffs, he padded through to the petty foyer to retrieve the postie's droppings. My boomboomer was pounding so rapid now I felt like I was squinting through a strobing kaleidoscope as I ogled him carry the pile back through to his desk. Clear enough the omi had clocked the handwriting – he immediately efinked the seal of the chartreuse-green sheath, and flopped into his seat to read my latest greatest chapter, entittled 'Novak's Hit Parade'.

Ideally I'd hoped the chapter would be bellowed aloud to the rest of the staff, but the chappy's oyster was clamped shut as his opals swished from side to side. I savvied it should take between setta and daitcha minutas to read the entire screeve. After heksa minutas I rose from the concrete, plopped the spreadeagle-capella atop my crusty quiffed tet, and lento wheeled my omi-jarrying perambulator across the strasse. My dollies had reered that morn when I packed a blunt butter-efink alongside my shotgun – but with only a pogi few flick-flicks of the cheet betwixt the door and the strike-plate, I gained access to the doomed latty. Alone in the foyer, I pressed a bijou handlebar mouser above my top oyster-lever, swapped the efink for the shotgun, then ogled my ticktocker with a frosty expression, sang thumping in my nells like a voodoo death-march drum-rimbumble ...

After daitcha minutas, I schonked the inner portal open with my stamper – then, cackling and oystering like a meshigena clown, gaily made my entrance ...

AFTERWORD

Now I can put an end to the first person plural, this royal 'we' or otherwise.

After spending another tense week or two in the City of Dreams, I eventually returned to London to find another two chapters waiting at 28 Newman Street – but it seems inappropriate to share them with you now. Given Audrey's admission that the novel was just a hoax, just a figment of her *(our!?)* imagination, the prose seemed almost offensively farfetched as I skim-read the sheets in the sickly silence of our empty, tainted HQ. To give the curious reader a very brief outline of her nonsensical climax: the chapters followed Novak's grand plan to skyrocket his most trusted followers to Europa, the smallest moon of Jupiter, to build a 'bona nova snowy utopia' from scratch atop its frozen surface. After convincing the poor sods they would be blasted into space from Europa Point (the southernmost tip of Gibraltar), the Guru instead drugged his devotees, crammed them in a van stolen in Spain and ferried them across the water to Morocco. Three weeks and 3,000mg of Mogadon later, having dozed across North Africa under the sweltering sun with virtually no aqua or munja (and having lost Bonnie to heatstroke/'decompression sickness'), Novak finally resuscitated his remaining dollies on the Saharan side of the snow-capped Atlas Mountains, claiming: 'This, my chovis, is paradise! Bienvenue, achtung – and fuck-off-thataways to Westernoid civilisation! Welcome to The Void, to Deep Space, to our whitewashed wonderland, to EUROPA!'

As early as February 1970 I'd aired my reservations about the plausibility of Novak's/Audrey's version of reality (see footnote to 'Neptunus Rex'). A slick marketing man might've suggested these memoirs are not so much lies but the perfectly accurate outpourings of a person driven mad by modern society – but BOF and POPPYCOCK to all that. This tome is not intended to be a clinical study of lunacy, some quack justification for wholesale slaughter. I myself am perfectly sane – and it is my duty now to deliver THE TRUTH to the general public, however hideously slippery it may at first appear ...

Reading back my footnotes to 'The Eagle Has Crashlanded', I wonder if readers will be satisfied with the denouement at Audrey's apartment? The chance sighting of the white/black phantom, the gushing confession, my secret Dictaphone, her eventual escape through an implausibly small window, the mirrors, those frightful fuckering mirrors ...

I thought the accusation of rape seemed a feasible enough motive – but have I written the scene convincingly, to prove beyond reasonable doubt this was all not just some daffy kif-spiked dream?

'What's your verdict? Can you make out anything at all?' I asked Davy on our last afternoon together at the Café Oubliette, holding the Dictaphone to his ear.

His face was like vacuum-packed luncheon-meat as he strained to hear the recording over the din of the Rue Siaghin. 'Nope. Still zero,' he replied. 'It's just interference. Like putting your ear to a shell ...'

'It's useless,' I agreed, flopping my forehead towards the chequered tabletop.

Agonisingly the Dictaphone had failed to pick up a word of Audrey's confession through the fabric of my suit jacket. At times my own voice is just about coherent – '... cut off the head yourself?' for instance, 'No, but –', 'No, but –' – but alas, just as she predicted, I have had to approximate the Scum Queen's dialogue in the previous (anti-?) climactic footnote.

Yes: boo-hoo-hoo and fuck-off-thataways – we do not have her confession in writing.

I ejected the microcassette as our food arrived. I had barely been smoking that day, and yet for a moment I felt sure the waiter had served me up a dismembered foetus with a side salad, until slowly, slitheringly the dish began to resemble the omelette au jambon I'd ordered.

It should go without saying I did not eat my last meal in Tangier with much relish. I listlessly pricked and prodded the eggy slime before finally pushing my plate aside, and I grumbled through gritted fangs: 'O, I'm tired of this place now. Thoroughly tired. It'll be a relief to see the back of this twisted city, isn't that right?'

'Even with the bastard still at large?' Davy had scoffed his omelette at breakneck speed and was now trying to hail the waiter with his final gruesome forkful aloft. 'Two more teas, garçon! *Deux thé!*'

'She said she doesn't want to run any more,' I stated with a voice like frozen dishwater, 'but I don't think I've got the energy to catch up with her – not again. We've got our confession, more or less. The world'll just have to take my word for it. She might not end up behind bars, but we've done our bit – capturing the mad bastard in prose, if not in police handcuffs.' I paused for a moment while the pockmarked garçon took our plates. 'Yes, the momento is nigh, my friend. At long last, it's time to share this meshigena yarn with the public. Whether they'll hold me up as a hero or not, who knows? But I'm sure these final footnotes prove I'm beyond recrimination at least. I may have wanted blood – but I'm not to blame for any of this. My conscience is clear.'

'Mine too,' Davy yapped, almost making me spit whiskey berber across the tabletop.

'There's just the Afterword to write,' I continued, maintaining my composure. 'I've got no idea what it'll entail exactly, though there are certainly still some inconsistencies that might need clearing up ...'

Not for the first time that afternoon I shifted my penny loafers, checking the typewriter case was still securely wedged between my calves. While it might seem reckless of me to take possession of Audrey's incriminating Imperial 66, I couldn't allow the witch the opportunity to return to her apartment and destroy the only blasted piece of concrete evidence we had against her. And so, the deadly contraption was coming back to London with me.

Taking another sip-sip of tea, Davy seemed unusually gay all of a sudden. He peered at me coquettishly over the top of his dark glasses and asked: 'So, do you really think we'll make our millions from the book, Stan?'

Again: I almost spat my beverage at the twonk.

'Us? We?' I snapped. 'Davy, let's be frank. Your input has been minimal.'

'Minimal?'

'Yes. You're practically illiterate for a start.' I tried to remain calm as I straightened up in my seat. 'As Director of this cursed little publishing house, I'm the one who's taken care of all the footnotes. I'm the one who'll stump up the money for printing and publicity. I'm the one whose balls are on the line. And so I'm the one – the only one – whose name will appear on the royalty statements. And it'll be my name alone on the frontispiece: "Executed by Stanley Merritt".' Davy looked injured. 'I've suffered abysmally for this book, Davy!' I hooted. 'It's only right I should get my due recognition! Monetary and otherwise.'

'I've suffered too!' Davy's knuckles were like icebergs again. 'We're the last men standing, Stan. It's only fair we split the proceeds, fifty-fifty.'

'Pah!' I let my head roll back, mouth agape like an amused wolf. 'Look, I regret you were caught up in the bloodshed, I really do – but just accept your frankly miraculous survival as adequate recompense for your ordeal. So many others weren't so lucky.' As I lit up a Gitane, I was annoyed to catch my fingers trembling slightly. 'I've enjoyed your company throughout all this, old boy, I really have – but your contribution to the finished product has been, quite frankly, almost nil.'

'Bollocks!' Davy screeched. 'I started all this! Without me, there would be no Novak, no bloodshed, no book …'

'Pardon me?'

'I'm not proud of it, Stanley, but you can't deny I started all this, by sleeping with that bloody freak. I triggered this whole terrible chain reaction. With no MARK 'DAVY' NOON there could be no RAYMOND NOVAK, remember. I'm integral to this story – however much it sickens me. I'm more of a victim than you. I should at least be compensated adequately, fifty-fifty.'

Ay, there's the rub, I thought. Since our stand-off with Audrey my mind had been overrun with her abhorrent logic and motives, and yet Davy's role in all this demanded some careful probing too. If indeed our Art & Design man raped Miss Hulme (and how many others?), triggering her madness and ultimately her grim vengeance against society, the dandified bat had thus far got off lightly. Was he just playing the victim? Were more women still at risk? Or was Audrey using him as a scapegoat, sparing his life only so she could keep on twisting the knife in his back, adhering to that BLAME BLAME BLAME rhetoric like a poisonous toadstool clinging to a cowpat?

'I can't give you fifty per cent, old cock,' I said.

'Forty per cent then,' Davy hissed.

'No.'

While the streetlife of the Rue Siaghin shimmered queasily in my peripheral vision, Davy stared me down with a cold, demonic expression. Thankfully I was still wearing my dark glasses – otherwise I fear he would've seen my eyeballs nervily dancing the jitterbug.

'This is as much my story as yours,' he grumbled.

'Au contraire,' I sneered. 'I'm the Director, the Editor. I'm the one pulling the strings. Ultimately I'm the one who decides how much airtime you get, how much dialogue, how sympathetic your character comes across on the page. As far as I'm concerned, yours has been merely a mildly intriguing bit-part up to now, squire.'

Davy breathed out deeply through his gross Roman-vonka. 'Well, in that case, let's go about this a different way.' He leaned across the table, covering his mouth with a filthy cupped hand. 'I'll take a one-off fee. Ten thousand pounds. But there's one condition: that you remove all references to me in the final manuscript.'

I smirked, raising a scornful eyebrow. 'Why? What have you got to hide, you dirty bat? You admit you assaulted the girls?'

'My conscience is clear, Stanley,' he monotoned.

'Well, unfortunately it's not possible to edit you out of existence – sorry, old chap. This conversation, for one, is fast beginning to feel like prime material for my Afterword.' I rubbed my hands together clownishly.

'Come on. You're the puppetmaster, as you say. You're the Editor – you're used to butchering manuscripts. Emily managed to remove all incriminating footnotes from her copy without disrupting the overall story. Clearly you don't want me to be a hero in all this – so just wipe me out. Pretend I never existed …'

'No can do, my friend. The whole story'd unravel.'

'Ah, so you agree I'm integral!' Davy's face was like a child's now, albeit with teeth like gravestones. 'Come on, Stan, split the profits. Fifty-fifty. Sixty-forty?'

I blew out a gust of smoke, feeling faint from hunger now. 'No, Davy.'

Noon responded by viciously plunging his fork into my right kneecap and lunging under the table for the typewriter case. The bastard wasn't after the machine itself – foolishly I'd told him I'd secreted the original manuscript in the valise's interior pocket once we cleared out our rooms at the Continental.

We grappled with one another like clumsy praying mantises, until a stray floral elbow caught me flush in the chin, and the repellent dandy prevailed. He pulled the Imperial 66 to his chest and snapped: 'I'll hurl it off the docks.'

What else could I do, dear comrades? Clutching my weeping knee, I scowled at the twonk and said through grinding pearls: 'Look – don't be so melodramatic, you old queen. I'll give you your blasted ten grand. I'll edit you out. It's of little consequence really. You won't be missed. In fact, your absence will only make me seem all the more important, all the more the leading sparkle.' I extended my hand out to him. 'The lav-hammer, please.'

'I want it down in writing first.' Davy took a serviette from the dispenser. 'Garçon! Un stylo, s'il vous plait.'

I watched with hooded eyes as Davy hastily scribbled the terms of the agreement:

I PROMISE TO PAY THE BEARER OF THIS NAPKIN THE SUM OF £10,000 STERLING, et ceterarara …

The bugger went into such detail about demanding final approval of the manuscript, how the money should be delivered and so on and so forth, there was barely any space left on the rag to fit my signature.

'O, isn't this adorable?' I scoffed. 'The rapist worrying itself over minor legal trivialities, when only moments ago she was pleading for an equal share of the proceeds of one of the most horrific crimes this century!'

Nevertheless, I initialled the scrappy document – and felt better once the battered valise was back between my calves.

'You pay the bill,' Davy grunted, rising from his seat. 'I need to piss.'

I pouted petulantly, watching the parasite sashaying between tables, smugly tucking his precious napkin into his kaftan pocket.

'The detestable addle-plot,' I mumbled, although already a feeling of jittery joy had overridden the annoyance – because I too had something precious in my jacket.

Glancing roundabout me, in one smooth casual motion I took the vial of antifreeze from my inside pocket and swiftly emptied it into Davy's tea. Next to mine, his drink now looked unusually electric-green, glowing and dimming like a tube of uranium or Kryptonite as the sun went in and out behind clouds. Shifting his glass into the shade behind the serviette dispenser, I felt hopeful the twonk wouldn't notice the difference through his dark glasses, nor would his unrefined palate raise alarm when he knocked back the bittersweet bitter-gator …

While I waited for the bastard to return from the lavatory, some strange fantasies ensued. I pictured Davy staggering through the Medina, his intestines rapidly turning to barbed wire; his freshly fatchared carnish served up in a gigantic omelette au jambon; me mincing around the French Riviera wearing his crystallised kidneys as gildi earrings …

When finally Davy reemerged, I was so eager to get the bugger to drink up, I feared I might've blown my cover by bellowing a squeaky, 'Santé! Here's to disappearing, my chovi!' and downing the rest of my tea in one ceremonious gulp. Davy paused for a moment to fight off a tick that was harassing him before finally, luxuriously, schlumphing down his emerald poison.

'Right then, squire,' I chirruped, emptying a clatter of coins into the centre of the table. 'I have one last pogi bit of business to attend to. A bordello and a beautiful backside on the Rue de Commerce I'll be quite sorry to part with …'

Davy's face crumpled: was it the onset of stomach cramps, or just plain revulsion? 'You're a disgusting dog, Stanley,' he grumbled.

'I'm afraid so.' I lifted the typewriter case from between my legs, hoisting it under my right arm. 'Well, I'll see you at the ferry, you old swine – 8 p.m. sharp. Don't be late. Adieu, adieu.'

Strangely enough, Davy did not make the crossing with me. As the ferry hmmmed and chuntered across the Strait of Gibraltar, I watched the brownish lights of Tangier slowly shrink to the size of a petrified kidney on the horizon.

Did I feel at all guilty, leaving him to die painfully in a foreign city? BOF. Did I trout. If the bastard's conscience was truly clear, there was no reason for him to request cuts to this glistening, pristine liver. The ponce admitted his guilt and sealed his fate when he made those ridiculous demands at the Oubliette. Oui, boo-hoo-hoo and fuck-off-thataways, Mr Noon – all I had done was selflessly remove yet another eagle, a vulture, a violator from the crust of this coddy welt.

At least, this is how I prefer to remember him.

Adieu, Davy. Adieu.

When I returned to London on 12th November, the city felt like a concrete netherworld, like it had been vomited scattershot from a gigantic cement mixer with no consideration for symmetry, aesthetics or joy whatsoever. A new Tory regime had taken over the Houses of Parliament, and all around me the faces of citizens seemed unbearably dour, haggard, weather-beaten. Or possiblement I was just missing my dolly-boys already.

I admit I felt terribly nervous walking through customs at Heathrow with the Imperial 66 (not to mention the knowledge that I'd just that afternoon increased Novak's death-toll to forty-two) – but of course the authorities had nothing on me (yet). No sharpering-omi had seen a solo morso of the Scum King's memoirs thus far, let alone fingered the fault in the 'i's. But this would soon change. The momento was nigh.

OUI: at long last, after a year of manic creativity, anxiety, molto molto sang and heinous contagious skulduggery, I was ready to unleash these mond-shaking memoirs upon the public. Of course Novak's original wish was for us to release his gruesome screeve immediately as news broke of his fantabulosa crime – but, given the authorities are still (!) no closer to unmasking the mystery madman, I feel the delay has surely only intensified the public's hunger to discover what type of monster was responsible for these utterly appalling acts …

Halfway between Hounslow East and Osterley I realised I'd been so eager to stash the manuscript and typewriter safely out of reach of the authorities, I must've left my valise of clothes and other accoutrements revolving round and round the baggage carousel. For a few prickly, panicked seconds I tried to recall whether there was anything damaging in the suitcase but then came to the conclusion I was safe – I could leave it a day or two to collect it from Lost Property. I wasn't going to face the guillotine just yet.

I slithered off the train at Piccadilly Circus, then practically goosestepped my way through the sideysnickets of Soho as I sought to rid myself of the flying cramps. The sickly retina-singeing neon – PEEP SHOW, NON-STOP STRIPTEASE, HYPNOGOGO, LE MACABRE – seemed awfully vulgar when compared to the blank mudbrick mystique of the bordellos of Tangier, but for once sex and violence were not at the forefront of my mind as I hurried back towards Fitzrovia.

Repainted copper-green and stripped of its bookcases and desks, the Glass Eye office felt eerily unfamiliar as I stepped inside for the first time in three months. I kicked through the scattering of post – which contained, among the many condolences and prying hacks' business cards, Novak's final chapters – then headed straight for my private WC, which, as requested, Iris had refrained from redecorating.

After painfully excreting the five condoms filled with folded-up footnotes (see 'Je m'accuse …!'), I removed Emily's sanitised version of the m/s from under the loose laminate and replaced it with the Imperial 66, the excreted scraps and the rest of the original manuscript, at that point all finished save for this Afterword.

At dawn the next day, as I watched Emily's painstaking but pointless handiwork burn in a fire pit in my ex-wife's back garden, I wondered if this whole sordid saga was truly finished now. Would Novak's meshigena memoirs (and our illuminating footnotes) be taken seriously as the authoritative account of the bloodiest massacre on British soil since WWII? Was the ending adequately conclusive? And – most crucially – would my arrogance come back to haunt me, given that I could quite easily rewrite this Afterword to frame Audrey for Davy's death but, after all is said and done, I too want my fame …? (History will absolve me??)

Certainly, however, there are still some nagging inconsistencies in the story. For one: where did Audrey learn Polari? How did she go about amassing a vast vocabulary of these privvy lavs, some so obscure even Howling and myself (two dedicated speakers of the queens') were entirely flummoxed as to their meaning? Why did she target five branches of Victor Value? And, encore une fois: why did the coroner have Sebastian Sturgeon down as a former captain of the Royal Navy, and not Chief Steward of the Merchant Navy?

Alas, none of these supporting characters are still around to explain themselves.

A fortnight after burning the duplicate manuscript, I was alarmed to read in our morning paper that a woman's decomposed body – identified by her dental records as one Audrey Hulme – had been found at an abandoned quarry in the Industrial Provinces. Her cause of death was not revealed, but I like to think perhaps the guilt had caught up with her at last, her destructive nature turned inwards, forcing her to return to where she came from – and to finish herself off there.

Audrey's demise might've been a neat, fitting end to this long, twisted yarn (a tiny morso of justice perhaps, or closure) had there not been yet another glaring inconsistency brought to light in the newspapers' accounts.

You may have already read quotes from the coroner's report, in which Dr Cubitt claimed Miss Hulme's body had been decomposing for seven months before it was found – but this is preposterous, is it not? Does he mean to say she was killed – or killed herself – in April 1970, more than six months before we confronted her in Tangier? Heavens, no.

Looking back over the manuscript today, it amuses me that Novak's original rationale for writing his memoirs was to counter the inevitable MOGUES MOGUES MOGUES the press would spread about him after his fantabulosa crime, and yet what we have ended up with is nothing more than a sprawling cock and bull story, a psychotic megalomaniac's fantasy – albeit a fantasy that has resulted in real carnage: forty-two innocent civvies losing their lives for nothing (forty-three if you include Audrey).

Before banishing them to the fire pit, I sifted through the final two chapters received from the meese meshigena-omi, to see if there were any clues to suggest the author of these ludicrous pages was considering suicide. As with 'The Eagle Has Crashlanded' and everything else before, there was no self-doubt, nix guilt, nanti repentance, nantwar last-minuta apology. The only morso of note, perhaps, is a scene that comes towards the very end of the final chapter, concerning Novak and his followers' passage across North Africa:

Chuggering delirious and dehydrated through the moony desert, the place names were just extra-terrestrial gibberish now anyhow: Tisseldeï, Tigzaouine, Izerki. I believe we were somewhere betwixt Skoura and Lbour when I made the illuminated decision to leave the daffy highway for good, veering squealingly from craggy asphalte to sand at a bona seventy miles per hour or so.

'Je repars à zero,' I chanted defiantly as I propelled myself and my slumbering stormtroopers headlong towards the empty glittering horizon – away from all prying Arabs, Western eagles, weirdy-seeking bombas and Interpolluters forever. The Void would keep us from harm, I ponced. The Void would hold us tight.

By the time the solo strasse back thataways vanished in our reverse-vada fenêtre, the drooping sol had turned the dunes ahead to just wibbling pink. I urged the caboosh onwards, following what I believed were camel tracks or gay sideywinder swirls to some privvy bountiful oasis just out of ogleshot – only to find the coddy contraption sinking miserably into the gildi dust just minutas later. ACHTUNG and GARDYLOO-BOO-HOO-HOO, et ceterarara. Was I maxi fearful of the ramifications of this rapid halt to our heroic journey? Nanti that. I savvied clear enough: once my followers were awake there should be more than enough golden aqua in their bladders to keep me hydrated for at least a few junos – and, given Bonnie had kindly perished at high altitude, we had plentiful humanoid biltong in the boot to see us through. The oasis was right here, my darling chovis. The Void would embrace us, love us, nourish us ...

For my own titillation I kept my stamper to the accelerator as the munge crept over, running the tank empty while running the caboosh ever deeper into the sand. I reered as the tyres kicked up sparkles, like I was ogling the stars rushing past the fenêtres, like we truly were skittering across some meshigena frigid moonscape, myself and a wagon of silent wax mannequins, a glimmer-powered tincan of beautiful skeletons commandeered by some superheroic frog-god – like Napoleon crossing the Alps, like Marat martyred in his biddytub, like the fortuni Mademoiselle Marianne herself leading the fattygayed proles with a smoking musket and floppy Phrygian capella, squirting the milk of liberty hither and thither from my grand voluptuous naggy breasts!

Yes, perhaps the most unsettling aspect of the bastard's life work is that he actually seemed to believe in all this rot. It is one thing to lubricate reality with dreams, after all – it is something else entirely to reject reality outright and carry out your private violent fantasies in public: butchering and raping reality with your preposterous paranoiac persecution nightmares.

And yet I too am plagued with persecution nightmares as I write this. While it is high time I shared THE TRUTH with the world, again and again I am haunted by the predicament: was I utterly foolish admitting my less-than-virtuous role in the original footnotes and this murderous Afterword (not least this very sentence)? McKinley had brought this up many months ago (again, see footnotes to 'Je m'accuse …!'): how could I expect to make money from Novak's hideous screeve if the police would be on my back the moment I released *Mister Asterisk*, with all its incriminating asides? I could no longer plead ignorance – not if I wanted the general public to appreciate my startling, sparkling role in all this.

O comrades, I am maxi paranoid the authorities could seize the m/s at any moment and take me with it, but perhaps there is still time to redraft, to twist the text some more, to make everything tally up and avoid fingers wagging in my direction upon publication? OR: could I sell the book pseudonymously to one of the godawful Establishment publishers in Bloomsbury, demanding they pay upfront in cash for this mostest sensational revelatory volume? OR: if it is fame more than money I am worried about, should I just fall on my sword pronto, leaving the manuscript as an exceedingly elaborate suicide note?

Alas, how do you ever know if you are doing the right thing in a world that seems unrelentingly wrong? More and more it feels as though it is myself at the wheel of that sinking caboosh, kicking up sparkles, seeing stars – and going nowhere. For my own titillation I may well just keep my stamper to the accelerator, until the inevitable happens.

I screeve these lavs on Audrey's Imperial 66, Novak's omi-jarrying lav-hammer, my man-eating typewriter – sweating incognito under a blank bedsheet, sawn-off shotgun at the ready.

Stanley Merritt (Supreme Dicktittler), The Glass Eye Press
28 Novak Strasse, Fitzrovia
3rd December 1970

THANK YOU

Matt Abbott, Paul Baker*, Lee Brackstone, Peter Cleak, Faber & Faber, Ellie Freedman, friends & family, Alice Graham, everyone at Heavenly Recordings & the Social, Nina Hervé/Rough Trade Books, Paolo Hewitt, David Keenan, Holly Kyte, Danny Lowe, Paul McGee, Jim & Chris McGuinness, the Milwards, Frances Rooney, Gavin Smith, Society of Authors/Authors' Foundation, Glenys Stevens, Clarissa Sutherland, Becky Thomas/Lewinsohn Literary Agency, Ellen Turner and everyone at White Rabbit/Orion

Special thanks and ultralove to Beth, always

Not forgetting John-Paul Conley, Kate Downey, Mervyn Mendus and Bill Stevens

---

* Novak's Polari is unorthodox to say the least, filled out with bastardised French, German and other Euro lingos. For a precise account of Merchant Navy and Theatreland Polari, Paul Baker has written a number of fabulosa books – and they were indispensable for the writing of this one.